First Edition: 2011

Remastered Edition: 2025

Cover Design: Solomon Woytowich

Published in Canada by Ground Zero Publishing

ISBN: 978-0-9866209-9-7

For more information on this book and the series:

Follow on Facebook™ @solomonwoytowich

Contact the Author at: solomonwoytowich@gmail.com

Ground Zero Publishing is a Canadian Indie Author Publishing Company

based out of Edmonton, Alberta.

www.groundzeropublishing.ca

TO MY WONDERFUL WIFE AND DAUGHTER

Thank you for all the love, energy, and creativity you give me.
You inspire me in ways I never thought possible.

PIERCING THE VEIL
BOOK I
TEARS OF OMEGA SERIES

I hope this story gives you hope in your darkest times like it did for me

CHAPTER 1
ORIGIN

Our story begins on
the 108th Day,
of the 122nd Year,
of the 7th Age,

in the village of Daunt

The day began as any other, though this day was the last day remembered of an Age, for this day humankind would strive too far. Kindness had failed, and anger was released over the world. The Last Age of Humanity drew to a close, after fifty ages of the sins that they had committed: conquest, war, murder, hate, greed, and defiance of a creator god. The oldest were judged first, as they were responsible for failing to correct their children's attitudes and offenses. The sky darkened, a great stage was being set in motion. Fire burst from the sky, barreling down towards the city streets. Children ran towards their parents, screaming in terror, when men and women burst into flame. None were judged innocent.

The ground tore open, ripped open; the earth screamed in pain. Cities were reduced to rubble as the world gave up its life. Fire issued forth from the depths, and oceans gave way to dust. Even the sky retreated as the cold empire of open space conquered the last breath of life. In the breath of one day, the world had been reduced to a dark ball of ash, cursed for humanity's sins. The coldness of space embraced the dead world as it was flung off into the depths of the universe.

"Was this a mistake?" Mr. Yad looked around at the students in his classroom. "Could no atonement have been made for mankind? Zeph, what do you think?" Zeph jerked up in his seat. He looked around with a blurry-eyed expression on his face. The words his teacher had been previously stating were nothing more than a faded dream in his dazed consciousness. He tried to redeem his composure and searched his mind for a suitable answer. "If you are going to sleep in my class, Zeph, I would suggest coming back when the suns sets," said Mr. Yad as he glared over the rims of his small, round glasses.

Mr. Yad was a nice old man. Zeph had to admit that the old teacher did give him a lot of leeway. Yad had been teaching since he was a little older than Zeph, but now he was somewhat absentminded and frail. The old teacher would not likely continue at the school for much longer. "I'm sorry, Mr. Yad; I'll try not to let it happen again."

Mr. Yad grunted his disapproval in Zeph's direction. "Well, next time, you may find a sphere of water floating above your head. Now, since you are with us once again, why don't you continue where I left off?" Zeph began to frantically scan the pages of his textbook. After hearing the story so many times, it should have been easy for him to locate the correct page.

"Pssst!" came a subtle voice from the desk behind him. "Page 65, second paragraph." Zeph silently thanked his lifelong friend, Marcus, whom he knew was sitting right behind him. After a quick flip of the pages, Zeph found the spot and began to read aloud to the class:

And so the world was abandoned and adrift in the vast emptiness of the universe for untold ages. In the depths of space, the god Omega found the world. Remembering the world, as it had been the only world to be struck down by its God, he looked upon the lifeless ball and was filled with sorrow. Omega wondered if this world would always be remembered for the sins that brought forth its destruction. He held the forgotten world in his hands,... and made the choice.

Mr. Yad motioned for Zeph to pause. "What is it, Marcus?"

"Well, don't you ever think it's degrading to say we are the second try of a screwed-up world?" It was not uncommon for Marcus to speak his mind on a daily basis. If not for the constant teaching instrument for the rest of the class, Mr. Yad may have stopped it years ago. Marcus was by no means an imbecile; in fact, it was quite the opposite, as he had a grasp of looking at the world as few do. In his defense, it was more of his antagonistic nature that would cause the most disruptions.

Mr. Yad removed his glasses and looked up. Even before he spoke, he already had a feeling of where the conversation with Marcus would go.

"Everyone has the option to change, to become better, Marcus. Choice is what separates us from the Last Life of our world. We don't know what this world was once called, but we know that Omega named it Arkhay."

"Yeah, I know, which means 'a beginning'. That doesn't mean that we won't screw up like the last time." Marcus stated with a hint of self-righteousness in his voice.

"The peak of their existence only lasted for fifty Ages. We have already been through seven Ages since this world was reborn, and we have grown so very fast. Perhaps we will fall once again. Perhaps we will once again bring about our destruction. Our world was blessed with gifts from Omega; you have the abilities of Fire, one of the seven great powers used to remake this world. We must not abandon them as some have. We must not look towards our own creativity to bring us to the future, but to hold onto the things that make us."

Mr. Yad raised his fist in triumph as he spoke. His mannerisms made it clear that this was not a new conversation. "There is a place for everything, and everyone has unique abilities. These mystical elemental powers given to us will save us, not the inventions we build."

"Everyone always says technology will bring us down, but I think tha..." Marcus trailed off as Mr. Yad motioned that he would speak no more of this in class today. He then turned to the rest of the class.

"Although today's class is only a review, I expect you all to listen. You are all here for a reason; you were born with abilities that allow you to do amazing things." He noticed that at least half the class shot a glance in Zeph's direction. "Some of you will take longer to discover your full potential than others. This doesn't mean that you cannot do amazing things. I believe some of you will become something I could never hope to reach." He shot a look at Zeph. "This world needs you; keep it safe."

Just then, the chime rang out, and the students began to pack up their things. "This is all for today. Please re-read the chapters on Origin, Fallen, and study the chapter about your specific Element. I will have an extra page on the final for each of you on your own element and ability traits. Have a good day, everyone."

Zeph and Marcus stood from their seats, and Marcus turned his attention to Zeph. "Well, that was fun. Don't you just love being the class reader?" Zeph looked up at Marcus as he stretched.

"I actually don't mind doing it. Mr. Yad is actually quite helpful, plus he's been helping me with my research," Zeph replied as he finished packing his books into the brown sack on his desk.

"So, how is the research going anyway?" Marcus asked as he finished gathering his belongings and threw a similar brown sack over his shoulder. Both boys walked to the front of the class; Zeph turned towards Marcus.

"It could be better, but that's nothing new. When you're born with the rarest Element in the world, not a whole lot can be told to you about it. It would be different if someone on this side of Appagon had been born with it within the last Half-Age."

Mr. Yad lifted his eyes from his paperwork to observe the two boys standing before his desk. They seemed to not take notice that he was a busy old man. He was very familiar with the nature of their conversation since Zeph had been seeking his guidance for quite some time now. He shook his head and returned to the papers on his desk.

Marcus began to walk towards the door, "Well, we live on a fairly small continent; I'm sure there are more books elsewhere in the world. Anyway, let's go."

Zeph stopped just short of the door. "You go on ahead; I want to talk to Mr. Yad a bit." Marcus turned back. "Alrighty, you talk with Yad; I'll meet you at your place later."

Marcus was just about to leave when Zeph remembered something. "Oh, could you find Iggy and just make sure he's heading home? You know how mischievous a little brother he is." A grin came over Marcus' face, and he laughed. "No more than me or you. Yeah, that's okay. I'll go find him. See you at your place in a bit."

With that, Marcus left, and silence seemed to fill the schoolroom. The ragged book bag in Zeph's right hand just brushed across the old, worn wooden floor. He looked down at his boots; they too were dirty and worn. His pants were not the best for wear either; the dark brown had faded to a mocha tone in many places. The navy shirt he wore was undoubtedly his best decision that morning. It was well-kept. The sleeves were extra long, long enough to cover his hands when they were at his sides. That was the way he liked it. It had been one of his father's shirts.

He turned to face one of the classroom windows. Gentle rays of light passed through the window into the now-empty room. A section of hair hung in front of his left eye, blocking the light from view. Lifting his hand, he brushed away the white strands. His hair color had begun to change from light brown to white when he was a toddler. His father had always said with a smile, 'It's a sign of wisdom. He will be destined for great things.'

He was in his eleventh year of school now, and only a handful of people other than those closest to him knew that he was eighteen. He would have started attending school at age five with all the other children his age, but his parents felt that because of his abilities, he should wait.

What abilities!! He thought in disgust. Eleven years had passed, and he was still no closer to understanding what or who he was. The name Omega held no meaning for him other than a symbol on his forehead. He walked over to Mr. Yad's desk.

The old teacher continued to mark the papers on his desk. Without looking up, he said, "I had a feeling you would be staying after class." A grin came across his face as he lifted his head to look at the young man. "So what can I do for you, Zeph?"

"You said that on the final, there would be a page on each of our elements, but I..." his voice trailed off. A wave of discouragement washed over his face; he stepped back and sat at one of the desks. Mr. Yad stood from his desk and pulled a chair next to Zeph. The teacher's kind eyes almost sparkled as he ran his hand down over his white beard.

"You want to know how you are supposed to study something you know nothing about. I know how hard it must be for you sometimes, not knowing who you really are." The words flowed out quite easily as Mr. Yad looked across at Zeph's face. They had spoken of it many times, but something about Zeph's body language on this particular day made Yad pause momentarily.

Zeph pulled the sleeves of his shirt down, which he often did when he was frustrated or emotionally distraught. "I don't want this," he whispered softly out into the room. After the words had been spoken, a silence remained suspended in the air. They seemed to surround Zeph in a chilled blanket of sadness.

Mr. Yad was known for having a soft, welcoming face, yet somehow, his face became even softer upon hearing Zeph's words. He moved closer and put a hand on Zeph's shoulder. "We don't get to choose what Element God gives us. But you should feel proud to share the same name as Him. Omega was the last of the seven elements given to us; it was given after he remade this world. The scrolls say He gave up part of himself in the final act to remake this world. You have part of the God Omega in you, a part of him greater than any of the other six elements."

Zeph listened with his head hung low, then looked up, "I just want to know what it means to have the Omega ability." He stood up from the desk and walked around the room. "I've grown up with Marcus since before we started school here. I watched his Fire abilities get stronger with every year, and I watched him discover new ways to use them. I have nothing to show for myself." The frustration was evident in his voice and on his face.

"Yes, that Marcus," said Mr. Yad with an annoyed grunt, "but that aside, I may have something for you." The old teacher got up, walked over to his bookshelf, and searched for a moment. He then removed a large book. From where Zeph was sitting, the book looked familiar. "That's just our world history book," Zeph said with a puzzled look.

Mr. Yad placed the book on his teaching desk and took the appropriate seat behind it. "Oh, is it now?" he said with a somewhat disappointed look. Turning the book to face Zeph, he motioned for the boy to sit in front of the desk. Zeph grabbed the closest chair and pulled it up to the front of Mr. Yad's desk.

"No, wait," said Zeph as he ran his hands over the old book cover. "It does look similar to ours, but this is about twice as thick and looks much older. Why is that?" he asked with a tone of curiosity.

Mr. Yad flipped open the book. "You see, there was a time when these sorts of books were written only by Mages. It was thought that only once you reached that level of mystical ability, you were wise enough to pass the knowledge to the next generation. Along with the previous knowledge from the past edition, the mage was to add any of their additional knowledge to the new edition." He paused for a moment to let his words sink in.

"How old is it?"

It was the first thought that came to Zeph's mind, as he did speak his mind a lot.

"It is believed to be eight generations old. So it could have been written as long ago as five hundred years, the middle of the Sixth Age," Mr. Yad explained. "The difference between this book and the books students are currently using is that your books are mere copies. Your textbook was made when I was a young man in school; it includes our world history but much less elemental history by comparison."

Zeph began to flip through the book as Yad continued, "Our town council felt that it wasn't needed since this book was not used until a student's last year of school, and by that point, the student would already know a great deal about their abilities. So it was revised with only the sections on world history and basic elemental traits."

As Yad finished speaking, he picked up the book and handed it to Zeph. He began flipping through it, trying to find the sections on elemental history. "Now, hold up here; I want you to take this home, read up on it, and get back to me. And, before you even get into the elemental sections, I want you to finish reading the world history section we started today. That part is still the same in this old addition. You'll need to know it for the final."

The two of them stood from their seats. Zeph placed the book in his school bag beside the regular History book. "Thanks a lot, Mr. Yad. You're an excellent teacher."

"And you're an excellent student. It's funny how those things come hand in hand," the old man said with a smile. "What about Marcus?" Zeph asked with a grin.

"I must admit that he is a good student, besides his outbursts in class. But you should be off. I'll see you tomorrow, lad; say hello to your mother for me." They exchanged handshakes, and Zeph headed off.

IGGY SAT IN HIS SEAT and listened intensely to his teacher. Even though he enjoyed Mr. Edge's teaching, he was looking forward to studying under Mr. Yad next year, when he would graduate to Upper-Class. Today's topic was of particular interest to Iggy, though. They had been studying Talents over the last month. He learned that Talents were mental abilities that anyone could acquire. Of course, some Talents were more effortless for certain people to learn than others based on their Element.

Mr. Edge addressed the class, "All right, everyone. I want to see some practical use for what we've discussed today. I see most of you have tried to master some sort of projection field talent. I do hope some of you will try some other talents."

When the class first heard about Projection Fields, many students jumped at the opportunity to learn more about them. Fields were the process of projecting one's elemental abilities through mental concentration onto an object or person. This differed from regular elemental use, which usually required the user to cast their Element, completely disconnecting it from themselves.

Since Iggy had Light Abilities, he was familiar with the concept. Whenever he used his elemental abilities to heal someone, he used the same principle as Projection Fields, projecting his Light Element onto a wound. Of all the fields he had learned about, including Destruction and Illumination, he found Protection most interesting.

A Protection field created a wall of protection around the person you were concentrating on. This process could be accomplished no matter what Element you were born with. Iggy felt it was the best option for his first field to try and learn. Just then, a hand tapped Iggy from behind. It was Pierce.

"Hey, can you help me out, Iggy?" the young, timid boy asked.

Since they were in open class time, they were allowed to converse with each other and lend a helping hand if needed. Pierce was two years younger than Iggy at twelve. He had a shy, timid quality that Iggy had always connected with.

"What can I do to help?" Iggy asked in the eternally optimistic tone he often used when speaking to Pierce.

"I've tried a handful of different Talents, but I can't seem to make any of them work," Pierce answered with a disappointed look. Iggy thought about it for a moment. He and Pierce shared the same Light Element, so it made sense that he was asking Iggy for help. There were certain aspects of their Element that Iggy had grasped quite quickly when they were younger, but Pierce was still trying to find ways to channel his Element.

"Alright, here's what I want you to do. I want you to concentrate on my mind, okay. Just picture that you're me; close your eyes." Pierce did as he was told. A moment passed as Iggy focused his mind so that it would be receptive to Pierce.

'Can you hear me, Pierce?' Iggy thought in his mind.

"Of course I can," Pierce answered aloud.

Iggy smiled, but he was careful to hide his thoughts for the moment. He continued, 'Good, now why do you think nothing is working for you?' It wasn't as though Iggy was forcing his thoughts into Pierce's mind, which was indeed possible. He was trying to get Pierce to focus on nothing else but him and, by doing so, would allow his thoughts to be heard clearly.

"I guess because I'm concentrating too hard. I keep trying to focus my mind so hard that I think it's not working."

'I want you to keep concentrating on me, but now I want you to open your eyes,' Iggy thought.

Pierce opened his eyes. "What?" he asked, puzzled.

'Can you hear me?' Iggy thought.

Pierce's eyes widened as he heard Iggy's voice echo inside his head. Iggy smiled and patted Pierce on the shoulder. "See, you've got a lot more potential than you think. I bet you're only one of a few students in the class who has learned some of the Telepathic Talent."

Pierce smiled. It was nice to see; most of the time, his expression was blank.

'Well done, Pierce!'

Pierce looked around. That didn't sound like Iggy this time. Confused, he searched his classmates' faces, but no one seemed to be looking at him. Disappointment began to wash over him, and then he looked to the front of the classroom. Mr. Edge was looking directly at him with a smile on his face. After observing the interaction between Pierce and Iggy, he felt it would not be intrusive to speak directly into Pierce's mind.

'That's quite an accomplishment, lad; you should be very proud of yourself. Learn to control it and always use it wisely, and you will go far in life,' Mr. Edge thought. Iggy wasn't sure who Pierce was connecting with, but he saw the biggest grin ever appear on Pierce's face, and he knew that his friend had found a part of himself that day.

Iggy now turned his attention back to his task at hand. He had been playing with the protection field for a while and wanted to try something new. Raising his hand, he asked, "Mr. Edge, could I please have a candle?"

Mr. Edge soon brought one over to Iggy's desk. Rather than lighting it with a match, he asked one of the nearby students with Fire abilities to do it for him. Mr. Edge encouraged his students to use their abilities whenever possible. The candle was now lit. Mr. Edge walked back to his desk and watched. Iggy was one of his brightest and most creative students, and he was intrigued by what Iggy would do with the candle.

Iggy placed his hands on either side of the candle and began to concentrate. If you looked closely, you could see the protection field start to form around the candle. It was nothing more than a slight shimmering field that perfectly encased the flame and moved with its motions.

'Now for the test,' Iggy thought to himself. He poked the flame on top of the candle and squished it between his thumb and index finger.

The flame squished like a soap bubble but remained intact. Iggy felt no heat from the flame as it danced on the candle's wick.

'It works!' he exclaimed inside.

Mr. Edge walked over to Iggy's desk. Puzzled, he looked down at the flame. Reaching down, he touched it in the same manner Iggy had.

"This shouldn't be possible, or at least I've never heard of it. What kind of field were you trying to create?"

"It's sort of like a protection field, sir. I know that it's usually meant for people, but I thought, why not try it on something that's still technically alive?" Iggy replied as he made an air quote gesture. Mr. Edge stood there and thought about it for a moment. It was true that a protection field was usually used on a person or other living beings. When channeled around someone, it would create a thin barrier that would provide brief protection from things like falls or impacts.

"That's brilliant; I'll have to record this in the school archives."

Just then, the chime rang out in the school. Iggy began to gather his things together. He hoped that Zeph and Marcus would come and get him today. As he gathered his things, he fully expected to see them walk through the doorway at any moment.

Marcus headed down the hall from his classroom. The school consisted of three main rooms and a small assembly hall for all the students to be addressed together. Of course, a student body address only happened once in a while. Marcus headed to the next room down the hall, which he knew Iggy would be coming out of any moment, if not already. The room he had just come from was for students in their last two years of schooling, the next was the four years of middle school, and the previous was for those attending any of their first five years. Overall, the three rooms covered the eleven years of schooling that any student would go through.

Stopping at the doorway of Iggy's classroom, Marcus peered in. The students seemed to be packing their belongings, just as he and Zeph had done moments before in their classroom. Suddenly, Iggy flew through the door, nearly knocking Marcus off his feet.

"Whoa there, little man. Where are you going in such a hurry?" Marcus asked as he leaned against the wall and regained his balance.

"Hey, sorry, Marcus, I was on my way to find Zeph. I have something new to show him about my powers," Iggy replied as he stopped and stood with Marcus.

The height was unmistakable between the two of them. Iggy was a good full head shorter than Marcus. Even though he was fourteen, he had a look about him that made him look closer to ten years old. It was a trait that was frustrating for him as he got older. But in many ways, it also caused him to hold onto his innocence, if even for just a while longer.

"Powers, eh?" Marcus asked in a somewhat sarcastic tone. Iggy glared at him. At this, Marcus let out a chuckle. "Alright, well, your bro is hanging back with Yad. However, he asked me to grab you and head back to the house. So what do you say we head over there?" Iggy nodded, and they headed for the large archway leading out of the school.

The suns were still high in the sky when they left the school. Dust flew up from the ground as he and Iggy ran down the old dirt path from the school. Marcus had always enjoyed hanging out with Zeph's little brother. It was always so easy to get away with more when Zeph wasn't around, and Iggy was just as mischievous as Marcus had been when he was fourteen.

Iggy ran alongside, keeping up with Marcus. Although he wasn't as fit as the young brown man, he could still match him. His eyes darted over as they ran through town; Marcus always seemed to have a smile on his face. This, in turn, made him smile too. He had always looked up to Marcus just as he did to Zeph. There were two years between him and Marcus, and four between himself and Zeph. This had always made him thankful that they would include him in their adventures.

Within a few minutes, they ran past the shopkeeper section of town and began to move towards the houses. Zeph's house was one of the last in town, on the north side. This caused a bit of travel on a daily basis, going from the north end of town all the way to the school near the beach at the south end of town.

The two continued as they made their way through the village until they passed the last several houses, including Marcus' house. Zeph's house was only a little farther down the road. Usually, it would take the boys no more than a few minutes to run from home to school, or around ten if they walked.

They ran up the pathway leading to the house. Both boys stopped and sat on the front steps to catch their breath. The sweat had beaded on Marcus' brown skin and, in turn, on Iggy's pale skin. They both looked over at each other and let out a laugh.

SOMEHOW, THE AIR FELT better, and the suns shone brighter today. Zeph was a blissful young man. He paused momentarily at the top of the hill and looked out on his village, which looked tranquil and content.

The day began like any other day in the small coastal town of Daunt. People awoke and went to work, children ran to school, and mothers tended to the young. Life was simple. The sea breeze filled the town that morning as the gentle sea washed against the shore. Life in Daunt was simple, but this was not the life for most. Even though it was not the largest village on the continent of Appagon, Daunt was the only town or village to have a Temple. Zeph turned to look at the Temple. Although it was across the village, it was also on a hill, just like the school. The town was pleasant, and from this perspective, it looked like it was wrapped in a soft green blanket of hills.

Since Daunt had a Temple, many people came to their village during certain times of the year. It was uncommon for a town as small as Daunt, only several thousand, to have a Temple. The rolling hills to the north of the village always had a pleasurable view, always fresh and green, with a tree atop every small hill. On many evenings, you could see the townsfolk sitting under each tree: lovers, children, and parents, as the suns set. It was said this was the best place in the world to watch the suns set.

Two brightly blazing balls of light could be seen shining down on the world from the sky above. The blue sun, giving a brilliant purple hue to the sky, was the first to set, and soon after, the orange sun. Of course, that all depends on which solar cycle you are in. Zeph was told that he had seen a Solar-Alignment Sunset before, but since the last one was almost eighteen years ago, just after he was born, he was looking forward to the event again. There were just less than four more months to go now.

This event brought people from all over Appagon and other parts of the world to Daunt. The colors of this sunset were said to only exist here at the edge of the Eastern shore. When the orange sun crossed the threshold and passed in front of the blue sun, a flare of energy was released and washed over the world. The next solar alignment would see this phenomenon happen again exactly at sunset; it was said that the colors from the energy wave could only be seen by those watching in Daunt. To sit at this place was perfection; with the village below you and the ocean forward, one could easily lose oneself here forever.

West of the village were open fields for hours, a vast forest, and the Appagon Mountains in the distance. The white peaks dotting them could be seen from Daunt. Zeph had always wanted to go and see them, to reach the top and see the world on every side of him. Someday, he and Marcus would do it.

Marcus! He pulled out his pocket watch; it was almost seven. It actually wasn't that late. The school had only been dismissed an hour early. Still, Zeph knew his mother would be frustrated if she were left alone with Marcus for too long. His stories and jokes could become very tiresome at times. It felt odd sometimes starting school at noon and getting off at six. As the positions of the suns changed throughout the solar alignments, making the suns rise earlier or set later, it would dictate the school hours. Zeph liked this time in the solar alignment; it had been nine years since the last time the sky had given the appearance of only having one sun. Since it took eighteen years for both sun cycles to occur, you had those short times in the middle of each cycle when Pythus would either pass in front of or behind Cronus.

Zeph looked up at Cronus, their great blue sun. A slight aura of orange light could be seen on the edge of Cronus as Pythus passed in front of it. He remembered nine years earlier when the last alignment had happened. Yes, it would be only a few more months till they aligned.

He had always wondered if the alignment had somehow made him special. Solar-Alignments only happened every nine years on precisely the same day each time. Somehow, it seemed like an odd coincidence, but his mother had always said it was just that and nothing more. She used to say, "Think of all the other babies around the world that were born on the same day as you." He used to say right back, "Yea, well, how many of them have this damn mark on their forehead."

Once again, he was jolted out of his thoughts. Home! Marcus! Mom! He quickly ran down the path away from the school and into town. As he hurried through town, Zeph suddenly felt his body connect hard with someone else, and before he knew it, he was flipping through the air. Landing with a thud, thoughts of pain went through his head as he picked himself up. Turning, he found his reason for colliding and rushed to help pick Breeze up.

"You okay, Breeze?" he asked with a worried expression. He and Breeze had first met five years earlier in his grade six year, when she and her father, Gus, had moved to town. Gus was a lot of fun to interact with, if not a little eccentric at times. Having an inventor for a father always seemed so fascinating to Zeph.

There was a time when Gus had owned a shop in town until the Town Council asked him to close it down. He seemed to be 'crossing over,' as they called it. He started to go past practical inventions and straight into technological inventions. Like many towns and villages that resided in one of the purely Mystical Realms, there was a stigma about reliance on inventions and technology.

Zeph never really cared about that sort of thing; if something made your life easier, why was that such a bad thing? The pocket watch he carried had been a gift from Gus when he had started his Upper-Class years at school. 'A man should be able to take time with him,' Gus had told him that day.

Now, Gus and Breeze lived just out of town, where Gus could still work on his inventions away from the townspeople. It's not as though people didn't like Gus or shunned him; it's just that people did what the Council said was best. Despite not having a shop in town, many people would still come to Gus for small items here and there.

Breeze stood up quickly and brushed the dirt off her clothes. "I'm just fine, no thanks to you!!" she hurled the words with a somewhat angry look. "Why the heck don't you watch where you're going?"

Zeph felt his cheeks flush as embarrassment washed over his face. "Sorry, I was running to get home; Marcus has been there for over an hour, and-"

"Oh, well, that's a different story," she quickly interrupted. I feel sorry for your mom, just her, Marcus, and Iggy." Zeph reached down and picked up his book bag, which had also gone flying when he did. "Um, yeah, that's why I'm in a hurry."

"Well, that's okay. Say, do you and Marcus want to stop by later? I know Daddy would like to see you boys. You haven't been over for weeks. Why is that?" No sooner had the words left her lips than she began to blush slightly and turned her face away.

Zeph smiled as he saw her blush. They had always had some chemistry between them, but neither had made a move to pursue anything other than their years of friendship. "I've been doing some research, and it's sort of been taking up all my time. I'll get into it later, okay, but I need to go." Before Breeze could say anything to the contrary, Zeph took off running up the street. He knew Breeze would understand, or he would be getting the yelling of his life later. Either way, he wanted to deal with it later in the day.

Reaching the end of the road through town, he rounded the corner and ran up the slope to his house. No screaming or crashing of furniture could be heard; that was always a good sign. Bursting into the front door, he was shocked to find that everything seemed normal. He looked to his right into the small living room; nothing seemed out of place; the cat was sleeping softly on the far couch. Dropping his book bag, he headed straight ahead to the kitchen. He found his mother working over a large pot on the stove there. Upon entering, his mother looked up, "Hello, dear, how was school today?"

"Uh, it was pretty good. Say, where's Iggy?" Zeph asked, slightly puzzled by the lack of confusion in the house.

His mother continued to stir the large pot on the stove. "Oh, he and Marcus have been upstairs since they got home from school."

Zeph's eyes seemed to bug out of his head for a split second. "And the house is still in one piece? Are you sure it was your youngest son and my best friend?"

His mother turned around, hands on her hips, and looked extremely serious. "Be funny, if you will."

"Oh, it has nothing to do with funny; those two are like fire and oil." As hard as he tried, he couldn't keep his grin inside as he spoke.

His mother glared over at him, her hands still on her hips. "And where were you if Marcus was the one who brought Iggy home?"

"I stayed after school to ask Mr. Yad a few things about next week's final."

"Oh, what kind of things?" his mother stopped what she was doing and sat down on the stool. This made Zeph kind of nervous.

"Just stuff, Mom, it doesn't matter." He felt as though he was shrinking inside his already oversized blue shirt. His mother caught the expression on his face. "It's about your abilities, isn't it?" He nodded slowly, "I just need to know, Mom." She stood up from the stool and walked over to her son. "I know, dear," she replied softly.

"You do? Normally, you are against me trying to find information on the Omega Element," he said with an odd look.

For some reason, it was always a mother's disposition to disagree with her children, so his mother's statement did seem rather odd to Zeph. "Yes, but I also didn't think you would go this long without some sign of your abilities coming through. If they aren't going to find you, then you should seek them out." She turned and picked up some vegetables from a nearby basket.

He watched as she held her hands over the carrots. After several back-and-forth motions, the carrots had grown to almost three times their average size. "There. See, even that," he said, pointing at the carrot in her hands.

"What?" she asked, puzzled, "the carrot?"

Walking into the kitchen, he took one of the carrots from her. "One of the littlest things Earth abilities can do, and it's right there. You most likely learned that when you were younger than Iggy. I just want to do something!" Zeph instantly realized how loud he had just gotten. The same frustration that had filled his voice at school was now evident in his voice as it filled the kitchen.

A silence fell over the kitchen for several minutes. The sound of the pot boiling and a slight breeze coming in through the window filled the room. Zeph looked at the ground; he felt as though he had gone too far. He didn't mean to get mad at his mom over his frustrations.

She walked over and lifted his chin. "Yes, you are right. I learned how to use parts of my Earth abilities at a young age. However, being able to use this ability, any ability, is not the most important thing in the world." She hugged him; he felt as though he needed it.

"Now, I want you to go upstairs and see what those two are doing. This house has been far too quiet since they got home." He nodded, forced a smile, and walked out of the kitchen. Just then, he remembered the book Mr. Yad had given him and walked over to his book bag. He grabbed the book out of it and walked back into the kitchen.

"Hey, take a look at this book Mr. Yad gave me," said Zeph excitedly as he handed it to his mom.

She studied the book for a moment. "This looks very similar to the history book you use in class. What's so special about this version?" she asked.

"This was handwritten by a Mage and includes a lot of information that was excluded from our current books," he explained. "Mr. Yad said it is most likely hundreds of years old. The books we use at school are simply duplicate copies that were transcribed within the last hundred years, and much of the information was either shortened or removed altogether."

"So what do you hope to find in this book?" she asked as she flipped through it.

"Well, I haven't had time to read through it yet, but I'm pretty sure it will have some information on people born with the Omega Element," Zeph excitedly answered. She looked over at him and smiled; returning the book, she turned her attention once again to the meal cooking on the stove.

Zeph now had a smile on his face. He had always found that one of his mom's best qualities was her ability to make others smile. Maybe the simple ability to make others smile was considered mystical to some. Ever since he was a small child, she had always been there for him. Even after

Iggy was born, her attention was divided between the two of them, and in Zeph's eyes, she was still the best mom ever.

Their father had disappeared when Zeph was nine, and his mother had remained strong. It was said that the voyage that took his father was the only one to have been "lost" in the last hundred years of Daunt's history. It made sense for his father to be a fisherman, having been born with the Water Element. Zeph remembered that when he was in the bathtub as a child, his father would bend the water and make shapes for him to play with. He remembered how talented his father was at controlling and manipulating water.

This is why he never really believed that his father was lost. He would never let the sea take him, even if he had to walk on the vast ocean back from Sire to Appagon. His father used to tell him stories about Sire, the continent across the Eastern Sea from Appagon. When his ship reached the shores, they docked at the port of Thai. He used to say it was a wondrous place, and at night, the city would be illuminated with lights that weren't oil lamps or candles. He said it was like a dream, something that only the mind could create.

Zeph grabbed the railing of the staircase; he missed those days. His mother glanced from the kitchen and saw him standing there. Somehow, she knew what he was thinking. He grabbed his book bag and walked upstairs. Stopping at the top of the stairs, a puzzled look came across his face. His mother was right. It was far too quiet. Walking slowly, he proceeded to the left down the hallway towards Iggy's room. Pressing his ear to the door, he could hear muffled conversation coming from the other side. Now, the decision came as to whether he should knock or simply enter.

After thinking it through for a moment, Zeph burst into the room, flinging the door wide open and making his presence known. Marcus jumped out of his seat as the small fireball in his hand went flying across the bedroom. Zeph dove for the floor, just as did Iggy. He shot a glance over at his little brother. Iggy had a guilty look, similar to a puppy when it knows it's in trouble with its master.

The ball of Fire began bouncing around the room. Zeph's eyes followed its every move; finally, he slowly stood up. The ball wasn't igniting any of the surfaces it was coming into contact with. Marcus lay laughing on the bed. Zeph's eyes continued to track the ball; he quickly reached out and grabbed the hot ball of flames from the air. However, to Zeph's surprise, it was not hot in the slightest. Zeph studied the ball briefly as it rested in the middle of his palm. He looked over at Iggy, "How did you do this?"

Iggy slowly poked his head up from the other side of his bed, Marcus still rolling around giggling. Zeph glared down and slapped Marcus upside the head. "Dude, snap out of it, and you," said Zeph as he turned his attention back to Iggy, "how did you do this?"

Iggy peered over the side of the bed. "It's a protection field," he replied as he stood and walked over to Zeph.

Now, Zeph knew little about fireballs or protection fields. "I thought you couldn't place a protection field on inanimate objects?" he questioned as he continued to study the glowing ball in his hand.

"Well, yeah, normally you can't. But a ball of Fire isn't a true inanimate object. It doesn't have a constant physical form, but it still has energy, just like people. I've wanted to try something like this since we started our latest section on how different fields manifest. We've been studying energy fields in my Light Ability class." Zeph remembered that class in grade nine, or at least the option for it. No surprise that no one taught a class on Omega Abilities. The teachers had allowed him to attend the class on Shadow Ability as an alternative.

Zeph held out the glowing ball of Fire. The ball looked as though it was encased in glass, yet he could squeeze and squish it in his hand. The Fire swirled inside the sphere form, giving it a calming, hypnotic quality. Marcus jumped off the bed and grabbed it from Zeph's hand. "Pretty neat stuff, huh? Your kid bro has some really unique ideas in that head of his." Zeph's eyes shot over to Iggy sitting by the bed. "How long will this field last?" Zeph knew that most types of energy fields formed by elemental abilities required active concentration by the caster.

"Well, the flames inside the field are trying to consume my energy field," replied Iggy. "But like this, if I were to keep concentrating, I'm sure I could hold the field around it for quite some time. As soon as I stop concentrating, though, it should dissipate within seconds."

Marcus stood there tossing the ball up and down. "Oh, here it goes!" exclaimed Marcus. Zeph and Iggy glanced at the ball of Fire as it floated up into the air. With a small burst of light over the surface, the glass-like energy field covering the ball disappeared. Marcus extended his hand, and the flame swirled into strands that flew into his palm.

"You know, my mom always told me not to play with my fire as a kid," Marcus said with a chuckle as the flame effortlessly passed through the skin of his palm and into his body. "Anyway, we were going to head over to Gus' later and show him this. Are you in?" asked Marcus as he turned to Zeph.

"Absolutely! In fact, I ran into Breeze earlier, literally. She was wondering if we wanted to stop by. I think Gus has something new to show us." Marcus' eyes began to glimmer at Zeph's words. "Slow down," Zeph said with a chuckle. "I need to do some reading before we head out; plus, Mom is almost done with supper by the smell of it."

"What are you reading right now?" The words seemed to come out of nowhere. Zeph quickly glanced over at Iggy. A look of embarrassment seemed to wash over his little brother's face. "What? I was just wondering."

"I need to finish a section we were working on in class, Iggy."

"Can I listen?" questioned Iggy.

"What makes you think I will read it out loud?" Zeph said with a somewhat superior look.

"Oh, come on, dude. Just read the section for him. You have to read it anyway. Plus, it's not like I'll review it without you around anyway," Marcus said with a glimmer in his eye. Zeph glared at Marcus and watched as he put on his 'puppy-dog' face.

"That doesn't work on me, but okay, whatever. Iggy sit there, and Marcus cut that out and sit down." Zeph couldn't help but grin and shake his head. Marcus was the best for that. Zeph looked around the room and grabbed a chair. He opened up the new book Mr. Yad had given him and began to read aloud:

Omega wondered if this world would always be remembered for the sins that brought forth its destruction. He held the forgotten world in his hands, and made the choice. In that single moment, His heart broke, and He cried.

The first tear fell like a blazing comet; it struck with a force to destroy or to reforge. It fell into the center of this dead world and burst, renewing the core of our world. The second tear, full of life and deadly strength, fell like a mighty stone. It broke and crumbled across the face of the world, covering the surface and sealing the flames deep within. The third tear, with the power to reveal or conceal, fell like a great cloud. It burst upon the world like a mighty storm, and swept the ash and dust away. Now, a great tear fell like a rushing flood; it washed our world clean and filled the oceans. This was the fourth tear.

For a moment, Omega stopped and looked down on the newly forming world in his hands. This was a world that had once been destroyed for its own undoing. At the peak of its existence, it was consumed by evil, greed, and destruction. At that moment, Omega cried a great tear of darkness to hide the world from the universe. It fled to every corner and covered the world in Shadow.

Omega looked down on our now darkened world; in the dark depths, he saw all the possibilities for good and what it could become. He knew that he could not leave the world to drift in darkness. And so He cried a sixth tear, a tear of pure Light; it shone like a thousand suns. The rays of light broke from the tear and spread across our world to balance the darkness.

As He now looked down upon this new world, He cried a seventh tear, full of Himself, so that this world may have Hope to become not what it was before. It fell to the world and was scattered to only a few places. It created seven great beacons of light to guard our world, beacons for only the few to find.

"And I might as well stop there," said Zeph, closing the book, "since that's the end of the first chapter in the Origin section."

"Okay, seriously," Marcus said with a somewhat dazed look. "I need to start listening in class more; I don't even remember what you just read from the first time we went over it."

"Why are there some blank pages at the end of that chapter?" Iggy asked. Zeph raised an eyebrow and opened the book again. It was true; there were several blank pages separating the chapter from the next one. Flipping through the pages, Zeph had no explanation for his brother. "Hmmm, well, I guess it could be because this version was handwritten,"

Zeph suggested. "It may be to leave room for extra notes or something like that." Just then, a voice echoed up the stairs, "Boys, come for dinner."

"I guess we should go for dinner," said Iggy.

"You two go. I'll be there in a minute," Zeph replied as he motioned for them to proceed. He walked down the hall to his room. Did he ever need to do some cleaning? He thought as he tried to find the path to his bed. He opened his book to where he had left off and looked at the blank pages. At the end of every chapter, it seemed there were several blank pages. The standard textbooks weren't like that. He tried to focus on the page, but nothing appeared. Maybe he was just having a long day, but he could have sworn he had seen illuminated writing coming off the page while reading moments before. He finally dropped the book on his bed and headed downstairs.

The book lay open on Zeph's bed to the last page of the chapter. '*It fell to the world and was scattered to only a few places. It created seven great beacons of light to guard our world, beacons for only a few to find.*'

The blank pages began to glow softly, and glowing words slowly appeared. '*The few, the chosen, one will come from every Age. The one chosen in the Seventh Age will bring forth the destiny of this world. They will be the last chosen and the last chance of hope for the world.*' The words stopped, and three glowing symbols appeared above the text, causing the phrase to vanish. The symbols grew brighter, light shone in the room, and then the pages turned blank once again.

DAY 1

> Everything written in the past was written to teach us so that through endurance and the encouragement of the Word, we might have Hope. For it was from Omega's Tears that our world found new salvation.

~ The Book of Ta'Hor

CHAPTER 2

NIGHTS OF SHADOW, DAYS OF FIRE

The evening quickly grew into the night. Dusk was falling as the suns set, and the dim glow of hanging oil lamps lit the dusty roads throughout the village. A faint glow was still visible on the horizon, and a peace fell over Daunt. People were up on the hills north of town, as was the typical pastime among many of the townsfolk. With the solar alignment only a few months away, life seemed to have a tranquil quality to it.

Zeph stared out the living room window at the evening sky. He remembered the last alignment; it was the Pythus-Solar Alignment. He was nine then and remembered his mother telling him all about it. She had explained that even though he couldn't see it, their orange sun, Pythus, was exactly behind their large blue sun, Cronus. She said that the alignment meant the start of the Pythus half of the Solar Cycle, when Pythus would start to follow Cronus, and over the coming years, they would start to see two suns in the sky again. Almost nine years later, the suns were nearly aligned with Pythus centering itself in front of Cronus.

There was something about these times of the solar alignments that Zeph always found fascinating. He didn't remember much from when he was four years old. But he did remember clearly seeing two suns in the sky. By the time he reached age nine, the suns had aligned again, giving the appearance of one sun. As the years went by, he watched them go through the same cycle of separating and joining again.

As Zephhe gazed out the window, his eyes drifted toward the sky. The moons were bright and full that night. As a child, he always loved to lie on his favorite hill and watch the moons. In children's stories, the moons were portrayed as the guardians Pia and Cia, the great guardians of Arkhay. Pia, the larger moon, hung low in the sky above Zeph's head, almost as if it were reaching out to him. He turned to lie on his back and looked up at it. The surface of the moon was rough and covered in many deep craters. The smaller moon, Cia, was out of sight as he scanned the sky for it. Zeph knew it would be visible in the next few days when it came out from behind Pia.

When Zeph was a child, Zeph's father told him children's stories about how the moons had once been brothers who had wanted to fly up to the world's edge. As Zeph got older, he remembered telling the same stories to Iggy. In school, Zeph learned that the stories were tall tales and their origins were very different. It is said that Cia had once been some sort of celestial body that had threatened to come crashing down to their world back in the Third Age, but as it passed close to Pia, the moon grabbed it from the sky and made it its own.

Something soft and fuzzy brushed against Zeph's ear, causing him to jump. He looked over to see his cat Teak. Scooping her up in his arms, he cuddled her close. The day they got her had been one of the best of his life. Zeph had always wanted a cat like her, but her breed was rare. Most people love getting kittens, but they grow into full-sized cats too soon. Unlike other breeds, Teak's breed remained in a kitten-like state for most of their lives. Teak was perfect. She was gray with a few black stripes and eyes that glowed pale green in the dark. You could always find her, even when she was trying to hide.

Marcus walked to the edge of the living room archway and watched Zeph and Teak for a few minutes. The room was dark, and the dim glow from the lamps in the kitchen cast a distorted shadow across the room. He walked into the room and plopped down on the oversized chair next to the couch Zeph was on.

"So, are you ready to head out? I finally convinced your mom to let Iggy come with us." Zeph looked over at Marcus.

"What are we doing here, Marcus?"

"Uh, well...we are going over to see Gus," Marcus replied, searching Zeph's face in the dark, trying to see if his response was what was expected.

"That's not what I mean. I mean, what are 'we' doing here? In Daunt, in Appagon, on Arkhay. I just wish I knew," his voice trailed off as he turned his eyes away from Marcus and moved them back to the window and the sky above.

"I know a lot's been going on with you lately, Zeph, and I don't hope to understand it. But I've been with you since we were kids, back when we didn't think about the mystical, or elements, or abilities. Back when it was just you and me and that massive sandbox on the edge of town."

Zeph smiled, "Thanks, man, I needed that." He put Teak softly on the couch and got up. "So I guess we should get going since it's already dark. Let's grab Iggy and give my mom the heads up." They walked out of the living room and into the kitchen. "Alright, brat, let's get going," Zeph announced as he entered the room. Iggy jumped off of his chair and headed towards Zeph.

"So, how long do you boys plan to be out tonight?" his mom asked. "Don't forget you still have school tomorrow."

"Don't worry, Mom, we won't be too long; just popping in for a quick hello and to show Gus a few things," Zeph replied as he knelt by the front door and tied up his boots. He stood up, looked at Marcus, looked at Iggy, then just shook his head and smiled. The trio left the house and began walking down the path towards the Main Road in town.

The night was oddly cool for the time of year, although it was still during the Growing Season when the nights were more relaxed. The three of them chatted as they walked down Main Road. The glimmer of candle and lamp light danced across their path as light flowed out from the windows of the houses they passed. A large oil lamp stood on every corner, lighting the night.

Just then, Zeph stopped, "Wait a second, why exactly were you two going to see Gus? I don't think you ever explained that to me yet."

"Well, both Iggy and I want to show Gus the awesome fireball thingy. If I know Gus, he will have some awesome ideas for making it even better. And I think you're coming 'cause you tragically ran Breeze over after school, and she will kill you if you don't come," Marcus replied with a somewhat boastful look on his face.

"Uh huh," Zeph said with a raised eyebrow, "Well, alrighty, I guess that all makes sense."

They began walking again, continued to the Main Road of Daunt, and headed south from Zeph's house. Marcus and Iggy talked back and forth while Zeph walked several paces ahead. Zeph looked in the windows of the shops and houses they passed. Everything seemed to be just as it should be. Zeph's heart felt heavy as he walked down the road; his thoughts began to turn inwards to his own life.

Iggy slowly came up behind him and placed a hand on his big brother's shoulder. "Are you okay, Zeph?" Zeph stopped and hung his head. Marcus motioned to Iggy,

"He's just got a lot on his plate, little man; he'll be okay. There are just a lot of things he's really trying to figure out in his life right now."

All three turned to continue but stopped abruptly in their paths. At the same time, they all seemed to spot a man walking up the road toward them. Each shot a glance at the other; this man was notably a stranger to Daunt. Also, he was walking from the south end of town, which meant he must have come from the docks.

As the man drew closer, none of them knew how they should react; they just felt that it should be different from how they were reacting at that moment. The man was large, at least a head taller than any of them. He wore a pair of dark goggles over his eyes, and a long black cloak flowed down to his large boots. An armored vest was evident beneath his cloak; several large buckles ran down the front. The end of two curved blades strapped to the man's back could be seen at the bottom of the cloak.

The boys shifted their path towards the right side of the street, making their way towards the turnoff that would take them out of town. The stranger also matched their direction and pace.

By this point, it was clear that the man's destination was the three boys, but for what purpose, none of them knew. Zeph scanned the man's face, trying to find something familiar in its features. The light from the street lamp fell across the man's face, and Zeph froze. On his forehead was the Shadow Elemental symbol. Zeph now recognized the man's attire; this man was a Shadow Mage of *The Order*.

"We have to go!!" Zeph whispered urgently in Marcus' ear as he turned away.

The man stopped. All three of them quickly turned their heads.

"*Fire Guardian*, *Light Emitter*, I have no questions for you!" the man's voice was bold and forceful. "I only wish to speak with the *Chosen One*." Marcus and Iggy immediately looked at Zeph. His face had faded to a shade of white that almost matched the white of his hair.

"Who... who are you?" the words came out broken and twisted from Zeph's lips.

"My name is Xa'an; I belong to the *Seeing Order of the Shadow Mages*. Please come closer, young sir. My intention is not to harm you. If that was the case, all three of you would be dead already." The three boys all took a step forward. Xa'an raised his hand. "I wish to speak only to the *Chosen One*." Zeph looked at Iggy, then Marcus.

"These two are my protectors; they travel with me at all times," Zeph had no idea where that thought had come from. Xa'an looked back and forth between Marcus and Iggy. They could feel him reaching out with his mind.

"A life friend and a brother, place your faith in them well, and they will become your true protectors." His words startled them; they had no idea the stranger knew so much about them. "Come now, I must speak with you."

They followed him slightly farther down the road towards the Rolling Hills Inn. "Who the heck is this guy, Zeph?" Marcus asked with anxiousness in his voice. "I've never seen him before in my life," Zeph blurted, looking over cautiously.

"Yeah, and what's with that name?" Iggy piped up. Both boys shot a glare at Iggy.

"If my name confuses you, young master Iggy, you may call me Xa." Eyes wide, the three swung their heads again towards Xa'an.

The night seemed to grow darker. Zeph looked up and saw the moonlight extinguished by a coming storm. The lights from the inn were ahead, the dimly lit windows of the first floor softening the darkness. Zeph's gaze drifted to the windows of the second floor, all dark except for one window with a single candle burning.

They reached the door of the inn.

"Okay, just to clarify, does it matter if we whisper or just think something? Can you still hear it?" Marcus asked as he looked Xa'an up and down. Xa'an leaned in close. Marcus could see his reflection in the goggles across the man's eyes.

"You think quite loudly, Marcus. I am surprised that these two cannot hear your every thought." Zeph snickered, "Most of the time we can." And with that, the four of them entered the inn.

The inn was quiet. No other patrons seemed to be in the pub, which seemed strange to Zeph. They walked upstairs with Xa'an leading the group. Zeph looked around the second floor, realizing he had never been on the inn's second floor. He had lived his whole life in Daunt, which gave him no reason to stay at the town inn.

They walked down the hall and stopped at the last room. Xa'an gestured for the three boys to enter the room. The room had a small oil lamp burning on the table in the middle of the space and a candle by the window. The boys walked over to the table and took a seat. Xa'an locked the door and walked over to claim the remaining seat. The light stood still on the table now, the flame an unmoving pillar of light as it burned.

Xa'an turned his head, eyeing each of the boys, and then stopped on Iggy.

"You have a question for me, young sir?" A flush of embarrassment came to Iggy's face,

"I was just wondering if I could see your eyes." Zeph and Marcus quickly looked at each other, then at Iggy, and then back at Xa'an. A small smile came across Xa'an's face as he reached for his goggles.

"You are quite a bright young boy, Iggy," said Xa'an as he removed his goggles to reveal glowing orange eyes, "you knew that if I am truly a Seeier my eyes would glow."

"It is not unlike the blue glow that a *Seeier of the Light Mages* would have," Iggy replied while studying the man's eyes. Xa'an replaced the goggles on his face and turned towards Zeph.

A clap of thunder rumbled in the distance. The gentle pitter-patter of the rain fell gently against the window. A half-hour had passed since the trio had left Zeph's house. The events of the evening had taken a different direction than their original plans. Xa'an scanned Zeph's face.

"You have many questions, *Chosen One*; I can see them clearly on your face."

"My first question would be, why do you keep calling me 'chosen one'?"

Xa'an raised his hands and leaned back, "Perhaps I should start from the beginning. I journeyed here from an island called Tarn, which lies south, a day's journey across the sea. Tarn is nothing more than a small island compared to Appagon; however, I have noticed that many people believe Appagon is much larger than it actually is. I belong to the Shadow Order; I am a Shadow Mage blessed with the gift of Seeing. *The Order* has been in existence since the Second Age. So you can see that we have been around for quite some time."

He paused, seeing Marcus' raised hand.

"I have a quick question. If you're a Mage, why are you armed so heavily?" Xa'an reached behind his back and pulled one of his blades from the sheaths concealed beneath his cloak. He then placed it on the table. The blade had many engravings on it, along with some mystical symbols Marcus had never seen before.

"I chose my own path, as you will someday, Marcus. Within *The Order*, there are many roles. I was once a deadly assassin, but now I am a protector. This blade alone spilled more blood than you could ever comprehend. Please pick it up." Marcus did as instructed; the blade was unnaturally light and fit his hand perfectly. "Now, I want you to strike me." Marcus' eyes widened at the request. There was a slight hesitation, but Xa'an simply nodded to Marcus. He brought the sword up and swung it down with a clash upon Xa'an's shoulder.

Marcus opened his eyes, feeling slightly disorientated. He now lay sprawled on the floor, although he wasn't sure how he had gotten there. He grabbed the blade off the floor and stood up.

"What happened?" he asked while holding his head.

"The force of your blow was brought back upon you," Xa'an explained. "All my weapons have many enchantments, one being that they cannot harm me. Zeph, take the blade." Zeph took the sword from

Marcus. "Run your finger across the edge of the blade." As Zeph did, he found that the blade was quite dull and had no sharpness at all.

"How can you fight with a blade like this?" he asked, perplexed. Xa'an took the sword back. He removed a silver coin from his pocket and balanced it on its edge in a groove in the table. Centering the blade over the coin, he pushed the blade down. Each half of the coin fell to the side like two pieces of sliced bread. The boys' eyes grew wide, and their jaws dropped. Xa'an handed half to Marcus and the other to Iggy. "When my swords are in my hands, they become incredibly sharp, but only while in my hands. Remember, young protectors, things are not always what they appear to be." The boys placed the coin slices in their pockets.

Once again, a clap of thunder rumbled loudly, closer this time than before. The rain was still steadily falling on the window. The lamp remained motionless on the table. Xa'an replaced the sword back into its sheath.

"This is not why I have come. I have come because of you, Zeph; you are the *Chosen One*." Zeph waved his hands in a frustrated motion as if to say, 'Which means?' "At *The Order*, we are keepers of ancient texts and scrolls. Our oldest collections date back to the Second Age. These scrolls speak of *Chosen Ones*, one from every Age. They will be able to see things unseen by others. You have seen something like this, haven't you, Zeph?" As soon as Xa'an asked the question, Zeph began to awkwardly look around,

"It's never made any sense before; I even thought I saw something in my history book earlier."

Marcus looked oddly at him, "What are you talking about?"

"I've seen things, words, symbols, but they aren't actually there," Zeph replied.

"In many of the old texts written within the last several hundred years, there have been a handful of accounts where individuals have seen words or messages within the pages of ancient books or on objects," Xa'an explained.

Xa'an stood up from his chair and removed a satchel bag from around his body. He placed it on the table. "I have brought something for you, but first, I must explain more. *The Order* has been studying the accounts of the 'chosen ones' since we first found the texts.

A thousand years ago, around the beginning of the Sixth Age, the Shadow Order brought forth a young girl. She was an exceptionally brilliant student, rising through the Magical ranks faster than anyone in *The Order* had thought possible. She reached the rank of Master even before she finished her training." The boys seemed impressed, and each nodded with amazement. "But then something happened," Xa'an began to explain.

"*The Order* found a metal scroll case that no one on the council could open. As you may not be familiar, scroll cases can be enchanted so that only specific people or elemental types may open them. After several years of research, we discovered that the scroll was somehow connected to the *Chosen Ones*. With several years left in her schooling and already at the rank of Master, the girl asked if she could see the scroll. *The Order* granted her request only once. The scroll reacted to her and was immediately confiscated and placed in the Sacred Archives for safekeeping. The leaders of *The Order* were afraid that if she could find a way to open the scroll, the power held within it would make her more powerful than they could control."

The boys began to lean forward, taking in every word as Xa'an continued, "Shortly after this, she claimed to see things: messages coming to her in the night, words appearing out of shadows. She also saw messages in books and on parchment that no one else could see."

Zeph breathed in deep. Marcus and Iggy looked over at him. Xa'an motioned for the boys to hold their questions for the moment as he continued.

"*The Order* didn't know what to make of this. She demanded entrance into the Sacred Archives, where forbidden and unknown texts are kept. She kept claiming she had been chosen, that the scroll was calling to her. The council would not permit the request," he paused as though his heart was heavy. The boys looked cautiously at each other. Xa'an continued, "She unleashed herself upon those within *The Order*; she fought her way into the archives, killing anyone who stood in her way.

She brought herself before *The Order*, claiming to be the *Shadow Chosen One*. *The Order* tried to explain to her that it wasn't possible, seeing as the time of the *Shadow Chosen One* had happened the Age before. Oddly, she agreed with them but still claimed to be chosen. No one understood what she meant or what the scroll did to her. But she did take the scroll with her, a scroll just like this one," said Xa'an as he reached into his satchel. He pulled out a metal scroll case engraved with ancient markings. "This scroll has never been opened due to the fact that none in *The Order* know how to do so. The Shadow Scroll we once had was identical to this in every way."

Xa'an reached across and handed the scroll to Zeph. He took it and looked it over. He recognized some of the markings, but many of them were foreign to him. Xa'an sat back and studied Zeph as he turned the scroll over and over again. Zeph flipped the scroll horizontally and stopped at what he decided was the front. There was no obvious latch to allow the scroll case to open from either the middle or the ends.

He looked up at Xa'an. "May I try something?" he asked. Xa'an gestured to go ahead. Holding the scroll out horizontally, he looked at each of the ends. It seemed odd that neither end had any engravings or markings. Just as he was thinking this, a symbol began to appear on the end he was looking at. He immediately looked at the other end, and the same symbol was also there.

"What is it, Zeph? What do you see?" Xa'an leaned in towards him.

"I see the Omega symbol on each end of the scroll." Marcus and Iggy could see the ends of the scrolls from their point of view.

"I don't see anything," they said in unison.

"Do you see anything else?" Xa'an inquired. Zeph held the scroll up, holding the ends on either side with his fingertips. He pulled the ends closer until they pressed into his palms.

Zeph's arms stiffened, his gaze focused on the scroll. The deep blue of his eyes began to glow as strands of energy started to form in their depths. He tried desperately to speak but clinched his jaw shut hard. Xa'an burst up from his seat and motioned for Marcus and Iggy to move. Zeph's arms began to shake as he lowered his head; pale blue light traveled up the veins on his arms and made their way into his chest.

Zeph's body was thrown back in the chair, and the Omega symbol on his forehead burst with light. Marcus reached out in an attempt to knock the scroll from Zeph's hand, but a force hit him like a massing punch, sending Marcus flying across the room where he lay unconscious. Confusion and fear were mixed with a growing sensation of pain; it was evident on Zeph's face as he continued to clinch his teeth tightly. He desperately wanted to scream; he could feel it swelling inside, but he was unable to utter a noise. Xa'an stood near the room door, weapons now drawn and raised.

Iggy was kneeling on the floor with his arms outstretched, trying with all his might to place a protection field around his brother. Zeph's head shot back, and his gaze looked straight up towards the ceiling as his body arched, his arms fully outstretched in front of him, still gripping the scroll firmly. Tears began to flow down Zeph's face as his body began to slowly levitate into the air. The Omega symbol suddenly appeared on the tops of his hands, branded in place with burning bright light.

Iggy looked frantically at Xa'an and screamed, "I don't know what to do!"

Just then, Zeph began a deep guttural scream with a voice that was not his own, a sound like nothing Xa'an had ever heard before. It was as though Omega himself was crying out from within the depths of Zeph. His arms shook violently, and Zeph let loose a final blood-curdling scream as he let go of the scroll. Zeph's body suddenly dropped from where it had been suspended, the chair breaking beneath him as he collapsed on top of it. Zeph lay on his back, gasping for air. Xa'an replaced his weapons and extended his hand toward Zeph. He tried to stagger to his feet but could barely find the strength to lift his arm. Iggy sat against the wall, crying. Zeph turned towards his little brother.

Through the tears streaming down Iggy's face, he whimpered, "I'm sorry I couldn't save you, big brother."

Zeph turned to see Marcus unconscious in the corner by the window.

"Please go help him," he whispered to Xa'an in a raspy voice. The Shadow Mage walked over and picked up the boy, placing him on one of the beds in the room.

A flash of lightning filled the room, and a loud clap of thunder followed. The rain poured down the window. Zeph lay on the floor next to Iggy while Xa'an watched over Marcus.

"Is he okay?" Zeph asked while staring at the ceiling.

"He appears to have obtained no permanent injuries from the blast," Xa'an said while looking down at Marcus. Zeph looked at his hands, which now had burnt palms. The same symbol, the Omega symbol, which had appeared on his forehead at his Christening, now appeared on the top of each of his hands.

He tried to roll over, but his body ached. Iggy sat motionless in the corner, eyes wide. Zeph held his hands out towards him,

"Do you think you could do anything about these burns?"

Iggy slowly crawled towards him; he took Zeph's hands and began to concentrate. The burns started to heal, and within a moment, Zeph's hands were healed. Zeph rubbed his hands.

"Thanks, little bro, that's a great trick, I sure wish I had that." Iggy smiled a little bit, then stood up. He helped Zeph up and onto the nearby bed. "Can you do anything for Marcus?" Zeph asked, noticing his best friend was still lying unconscious on the bed.

"Yeah, maybe." Iggy walked over to Marcus, placed one hand on his forehead, and took one of his hands in his. Zeph lay on the bed holding his head. Xa'an stood up, leaving Iggy to tend to Marcus. He walked over to Zeph and pulled up a chair.

"How are you feeling, young sir?" Zeph glanced over, wondering if he looked as bad as he felt. Xa'an smiled, "Not quite, but pretty close." Remembering Xa'an's ability to read his thoughts, Zeph smiled.

"Can you tell me what happened to me?" Zeph asked.

Xa'an's eyes widened behind his goggles, "I was able to read you for just a moment as you gripped the scroll, but after that, I dared not read you while you were in such a state. There was a massive amount of energy flowing into your mind. I was unsure of what was going on."

Zeph held his head; it felt like the ocean had been pumped into his brain.

"I remember something, something I heard." His eyes darted back and forth as he searched his mind. "A voice from inside the scroll said something to me. It said, 'The journey of The Last begins within. Seek the Six and stop the Sin.'"

Xa'an stood up and strolled around the room. "So you are the last then."

Zeph looked up, "What?! You know what that means?" he asked heatedly.

"Master Desiree, the girl I spoke of earlier, claimed the scroll spoke to her and called her to be 'chosen.' It said, 'Learn Within to Find the Last.'" Xa'an explained.

"I don't understand what that means," Zeph said.

"What if the scroll was some kind of mythical storage device used by the *Chosen Ones* to pass their essence and knowledge on from Age to Age? This would explain the knowledge Desiree obtained after opening the Shadow Scroll."

Zeph looked over at him and pondered it for a moment. "But why was she the only one able to open it out of your whole *Order*?" Zeph asked.

"Perhaps to ensure the knowledge would only go to someone worthy, there were certain conditions within the scroll," Xa'an suggested, "There was never a clear account as to why she was the only one able to open the scroll."

Zeph lay on the bed, taking it all in. He looked over at Marcus; he still lay unconscious on the bed across from him. Xa'an stood up, walked over to the table, then turned and faced Zeph. "I can only conclude that whatever this 'journey' you spoke of, you must find the other six scrolls. I suggest that you first seek out what happened to Desiree.

"Why her first?" Zeph asked with a puzzled look as he gently rubbed his temples.

"It's my guess that, unlike the other scrolls, wherever they may be on Arkhay, the Shadow scroll will not be kept in a temple or sacred place. Unless it was once again found after Desiree's death."

Zeph walked over to the table and picked up the scroll. The metal was warm. "The scroll tried to unlock itself, but I wasn't ready since I had no knowledge of the Omega Element." He looked down at his hands. "What do you make of these marks?" he asked Xa'an.

"All I know about those is that Desiree also received Shadow marks on her hands after her encounter with the Shadow Scroll."

Marcus began to stir on the bed.

"I think he's coming around," said Iggy. Xa'an and Zeph walked over to the bed. So many thoughts were going through Zeph's mind; it felt like his head had been hit with a forging hammer full of knowledge he didn't understand. The feeling in his head would only get worse, he feared. As the days passed, he knew his thoughts would return to the scroll with every spare moment. Kneeling beside the bed, he took hold of Marcus and helped him sit up.

"Dang! That scroll sure has some kick to it. How long was I out?" Marcus asked, holding his head in both hands. Everyone looked at each other, then at Zeph.

"About about twenty minutes," Zeph replied.

"Well, what happened? Because it's clear that something happened while I was off in dreamland." The three of them helped Marcus over to the table, where Zeph recounted the events while he was unconscious. Zeph showed Marcus the tops of his hands, where he now had the Omega symbol. Marcus sat there, trying to process everything. After a short while, he finally spoke up.

"This is all a little heavy for me, guys. I know we've been best friends forever, Zeph, but this is all a little crazy to believe." Zeph felt the disappointment flood his stomach, but he couldn't blame Marcus.

Xa'an stood up from the table, and the boys followed suit.

"I must be going, young sirs. Please follow me to the shore." With that, the four of them left the room and proceeded downstairs. The innkeeper gave Xa'an an evil eye as he approached the desk.

"My pardons for the noise; I hope we have not disturbed your other guests," Xa'an said as he reached into his waist bag.

The innkeeper grunted, "What guests? You're my only guest this week. I have no real need for the place except for passing merchants, the occasional festival, and, of course, during Alignments." Xa'an placed three gold kessas on the counter. The innkeeper's eyes widened. "The room only cost ya one silver kessa for the night."

"Then consider it a gift from *The Order* of Shadow Mages; may you always welcome us in your inn." He smiled and nodded his thanks toward Xa'an.

The night air had cooled with the passing storm. Mud squished around their boots as the four of them continued southward through town. The sky had cleared, giving the night light from the moons and stars above. They continued down the road, past the last buildings, and stood atop the slope by the shore. A gentle breeze from the ocean brushed across their faces as the four of them stood and breathed in.

Xa'an turned slightly towards Zeph and extended his hand; Zeph shook it. He then reached into his cloak and extended the Omega Scroll to Zeph. Some hesitation fell over Zeph, and he was unsure if he should take it.

"I understand why you don't wish to have this. Not a day ago, you were struggling to find your place in this world, and now you fear that place is too much for you to fill." Zeph fought to control the tears that wanted so badly to break from his eyes at hearing Xa'an's words. The pain began to swell inside as he knelt on the ground. Iggy and Marcus watched but knew it was not their place to speak. Xa'an knelt as well and placed his hand on Zeph's shoulder.

"To release emotions, whether it be from despair or gladness, is what truly binds this world together. Even the great god Omega cried when he made this world Zeph. Do not be afraid; you will find your place. Once you are ready for your journey, I will return to you. But take this scroll; it has now called to you, and only you can answer that call."

Slowly, Zeph reached up and took the scroll from Xa'an. He watched as Xa'an walked down the slope toward the shore. Even in the dim night, the light of the moons showed a small boat of some kind just out past the shore. The other two boys knelt beside Zeph as Xa'an disappeared into the night.

Marcus turned Zeph to face him. "I'm sorry, bro; I didn't know how hard things had been for you lately." He nodded his thanks to Marcus, then turned his attention to the object in his lap. The scroll now lay in his hands. How was he going to even start explaining everything to his mother?

THE FURY OF THE NIGHT had died. Water pooled in the road, creating a field of mirrors for the night sky. A gentle breeze brushed through the trees, disturbing the silence of the night. The severity of the earlier storm had inflicted minor damage to the town but would still make for a rude awakening the next morning. But that would have to wait. The orange glow of the fire reflected softly on the glass window. If you were to stand outside the house on that particular night, you might see a silhouette of a young girl dancing across this window pane.

Breeze sat on the bench beneath the windowsill with her hands held together inside the sizeable flowing blanket she had wrapped around herself. The night sky filled her eyes as she continually scanned the road leading up to her and her father's house. The fire popped, grabbing her attention for a moment. She turned to look at it. The fire had been roaring hours ago when she had expected the boys; now, only mostly hot coals remained.

She looked around the room. The soft light danced across the paintings lining the walls of the den. Her eyes moved slowly until they fell on the image of her mother. 'What would you do, Mother?' she asked herself. When her mother had become sick many years ago, an artist in their town had offered to paint the family as a gift to ease her suffering. Her father did not want him or Breeze to be painted alongside her. He said he wanted to cherish her like this. But now, as the years had passed, she wished that the painting had included everyone. She had no image in her mind of her and her mother together.

Gus walked to the archway of the den and stopped. Even in the faint light of the dying fire, he knew his daughter was staring at his passed wife's face. He hung his head for a moment, then stepped into the room. Breeze turned and looked at her father as he walked over.

"What are you still doing up, sweetie?"

Her eyes turned back towards the night sky. "The boys didn't come tonight. I hope nothing happened to them."

Gus pushed his daughter forward and sat behind her so she could lean on him. "With a storm like that tonight, I don't think anyone left their houses. I'm sure you'll see them at school tomorrow." Breeze fell farther back into her father's arms. "I know you care about them a lot, dear, a great deal more about one in particular, I think." She sat up with a start and turned to face him. He grinned, "Oh, you've found out I'm not just a crazy old inventor and that perhaps I do pay attention to my daughter's love interests."

"Daddy, Zeph and I are just friends."

Gus tilted his head and gave her a soft, fatherly grin, "Somehow, I don't think you would have waited into the night if it was simply Marcus and Iggy coming over." She opened her mouth to reply, then closed it. Her father was right, of course, but she would not draw him into a conversation that would allow him to win.

Both of them stood up. Gus approached the fire and lit a small oil lamp on the mantle. He then put out the fire and walked over to Breeze as she waited by the archway. He handed her the lamp. She looked up at him.

"Will you be able to find your room okay without it?"

"I'll do fine, sweetheart. I always do. You get some sleep now; worry about future loves on a later night. I'm going to work on my glass project a little longer," Gus said as he kissed her forehead goodnight. With that, he walked down to the house's main hall and off towards his lab, which also held his bedroom.

Breeze turned and walked up the stairs to the loft. Every stair creaked along the way, but the second from the bottom was always the loudest. She walked over to her bed and sat on the edge. Staring at the lamp somehow gave her peace. The flame flowing back and forth was somehow hypnotic. She crawled under the covers and blew it out. Tomorrow would be another day, and hopefully, she would find out what had happened to the boys in the morning.

Gus stood just under the loft, waiting for his daughter to fall asleep. He heard her bed creak and knew she had finally crawled into it for the night. Ever since his wife died, he had kept close watch over his daughter. When Breeze was born, it was the happiest day of his life. He had become even prouder when he found out she was also blessed with the Wind Element, just as he was. Even after the death of his beloved wife, the thought of anything happening to Breeze filled him with far more grief.

He stepped down the stairs from the house's main hall and entered his lab. His sleeping arrangements were similar to his daughter's, with a sleeping loft area hanging above a section of the lab.

Running his hands through his rather messed old gray hair, he sat at one of his workstations. He picked up a small stack of his notes. The words' Glass Project' were on the top of the first page. He had been working for some time now on creating a type of unbreakable glass. After months of experimenting with different kinds of sand and temperatures, he had finally made a breakthrough.

Parts of the coast near Daunt had an odd sparkle to the sand. Gus had created several different sifting machines to separate the sand and, in doing so, discovered the 'sparkly' part of the sand was, in fact, a specific form of crystal. This crystal could easily be crushed or ground into powder, but when heated to a molten temperature and allowed to cool, it became indestructible to both physical force and temperature. This crystal was most likely mixed with traditional sand used when making glass, which is why no one ever realized its unique properties.

Gus stood from his seat and walked over to the machine in the corner of the room. He was going to make practical use of his discovery by allowing this machine to heat the crystal powder and, once hot enough, spray a thin, thread-like stream of it out the bottom. Now, all he had to do was create molds of different objects to cover with the glass. Windows would be the easiest to make, having already made a standard window-sized flat metal mold several weeks earlier.

The night was getting late, though, and he knew that he should also get some sleep. Climbing the ladder in the corner, he retreated to his own loft. He also hoped the boys would be coming over in the morning; showing them his new inventions gave him such pride. The house grew quiet as both father and daughter fell asleep. The gentle light from the moons fell softly across the house. Tomorrow would be another day, and each new day always brings something new.

"HEY, SLEEPYHEAD, ARE you going to wake up anytime soon?" The words filled Breeze's ears so softly. She turned her head to see Zeph's face looking down at her. Was this a dream? It had to be. She had never had such a pleasant dream before, though. Zeph's hand reached down and brushed her face; it felt warm and gentle. Her eyes opened wider as she realized that this wasn't a dream. She sat up with a sudden jolt.

Zeph awkwardly jumped off the bed, startled by Breeze's sudden movement.

"Whoa there, are you trying to freak me out?" Zeph said, holding his chest. She looked around, trying to grasp hold of her conscious mind. "Good morning to you, too," Zeph said as he regained his composure. "You know most people speak when they first get up." She looked around for a moment, then looked at him.

"What time is it?" she asked as she squinted through the messy strands of long black hair that adorned her head.

"Oh, it's about one in the afternoon, so about lunchtime," Zeph replied, pulling out his pocket watch.

"Wow, I guess I'm late for school, huh?" she asked while climbing out of bed and walking over to the mirror, her long white nightgown flowing with every step.

"Well, you would be if there was any school today."

"What do you mean? Why is there no school?" she asked while brushing her hair.

"Well, during the storm last night, a few large branches from that tree we usually hang out under by the school fell on the school pretty badly. They'll be fixing the roof today and repairing the tree."

She walked over to him and hugged him. "It's good to know you're alright. You had me very worried last night. I guess no one left their homes last night, huh?"

"Uh, actually, you should get dressed; I have a lot to tell you about last night if Marcus and Iggy haven't already started telling Gus." She shot him an odd look, which, in turn, he deflected a sarcastic one back. Pushing him away, she grinned and told him she would be down in a minute.

Zeph chuckled as he walked down the stairs. Stopping at the mid-level, he walked into the den, where he found Marcus, Iggy, and Gus sitting. They all turned their heads in unison and looked at him, which made Zeph bug his eyes out and comically turn to look behind himself.

"Okay, where's this guy we're all giving the weird looks to?" Zeph asked in the most serious tone he could muster. Turning his head back, he saw that nobody was smiling, "Okay, tough crowd this morning I see."

Marcus jumped from the couch, "You can't simply ignore what happened last night." Zeph sat down in one of the oversized chairs opposite Marcus.

"I'm not trying to. It's just a lot to take in. You expect me to handle something like that? I have absolutely no idea where to even start?" Gus raised his hand, which caused Zeph and Marcus' bantering to stop momentarily.

"Alright, you two, I would love to get in on this as well, so why don't you fill me in on what exactly happened last night?" Just then, Breeze entered the den and took a seat on the smaller couch next to her father. "And now that we're all here," Gus continued, "This would be a perfect time to fill us in."

Zeph stood in the middle of the room like a professor would stand before an anticipating class of students. He explained how they had met Xa'an in the middle of town. He started explaining the inn's events slowly, not wanting to simultaneously dump too much information on them. As soon as he mentioned the scroll, though, everyone began to lean forward. A look of excitement came across Gus' face as Zeph started to explain what happened when he held the scroll. This, in turn, caused a look of horror on Breeze's face.

Zeph paused for a moment and rubbed the tops of his hands. Everyone's gaze quickly shifted down from Zeph's face to his hands. Both Gus and Breeze immediately noticed the Omega symbol on the tops of his hands.

"Did the scroll do that?" Gus asked as he walked over. Zeph held out the tops of his hands for everyone to see.

"I'm not really sure what this means," Zeph said with a note of concernment in his voice, "but it's just like the mark we get on our foreheads after Christening," said Zeph as he reached up and touched the Omega symbol on his forehead. Gus sat back down as Zeph continued to recall the night's events.

After Xa'an had departed, they returned to Zeph's house. His mother had already gone to bed. He found it odd to find his mother sleeping. Then he remembered that she had expected him to go to Breeze's and knew nothing of what had transpired. Since Gus had a rather large house for just him and Breeze, it wasn't uncommon for Zeph and Marcus to spend the night there occasionally if they stayed late.

Iggy headed up to his room, and Zeph and Marcus settled in the living room for the night since Zeph's room was a little too messy in its current state for the two of them to sleep in. It was also not uncommon for Zeph or Marcus to stay the night at each other's houses. It was a familiar ritual that had started many years ago when they were just children. They awoke in the morning to a Town Council messenger knocking on the door. She had informed them that the school would be closed for the day.

After rousing Iggy, they decided to head to Breeze's place. Zeph spent a good deal of the morning trying to hide the marks on his hands from his mother. Of course, they made up a convenient story for where they had been, which did have some truth to it. They said they had been caught in the storm and stayed at the inn until it passed. After some quick morning chores, the three boys left the house and headed for Gus'.

"I guess this brings us back to now, doesn't it?" Zeph asked as he sat down next to Marcus. Everyone else in the room exchanged glances for a moment, and then Gus began to chuckle. "Well, boy, you sure don't do anything the normal way, do ya?" He asked, looking down at Zeph. A wave of embarrassment washed over Zeph's face. "I don't mean to embarrass you, Zeph, but you're a very unique lad."

Gus stood, and with him, everyone else in the room. They walked down the stairs into the main hall of the house. The tall ceilings complemented the stained wood walls of the house. The house had always felt like a place where one would go for a vacation, not a place for everyday living. Light bathed the room from the skylights above. There were four in the main hall and two in the other rooms. It was a huge house, and you would expect many events or parties to be held there, but that was not the case. Most of the house consisted of Gus' lab towards the back and the main hall in the front.

Zeph looked around the room. It was large and gave off a very gentle yet exciting atmosphere. He remembered the first time he had entered the house after it was built. Entering the main hall, he stopped and gazed up at the ceilings. No building in Daunt has ceilings this high. The ceilings reached at least the height of four grown men.

Everyone was now in the main hall. Marcus was the first to speak up,

"We did have something we wanted to show you, Gus," he said, motioning to Iggy and himself. Gus turned towards the boys,

"Well, let's have it then."

Marcus stepped forward, and Iggy walked to the opposite side.

"Now, this will involve some fire, just to let you know." Gus raised an eyebrow, but he was an inventor, after all. He motioned for the boys to continue. With that, a grin spread across Marcus' face. Placing both hands in front of him, he began to form a small ball of fire in his hands. He allowed the ball to grow until it was about the size of a man's fist. Then he aimed his hands forward, and the ball drifted out to the middle of the group. Iggy now followed suit and placed his hands out in a similar manner. He concentrated very hard, and the small fireball took on a perfectly spherical shape within moments.

Everyone was staring at the ball now. Iggy walked over and grabbed it out of the air. Such a symbol of power in the hand of the small boy could have been frightening if they did not know him. Astonished, Gus walked over. Iggy held the ball out for him to see. Taking it in his hand, Gus was surprised he felt no heat.

"This is fabulous, boys!" he exclaimed. "You must explain to me how this works."

"Well, first, I create a fireball," said Marcus.

"Then I create a protection field around it," Iggy said, jumping in.

Gus studied the ball for several minutes. Then he asked the question the boys knew was coming sooner or later.

"How long will it last?" Now, neither of the boys knew what to say. They had only tried it once before, and even then, it had only lasted a few minutes.

"Well, uh, that's a good question. I think most of that is up to Iggy. Being that he's the one that creates the field," Marcus said, looking over at Iggy.

"Just to be clear, it's not exactly a protection field. We tried that, which we initially thought seemed to make sense, but the fire ate right through it. After a while, Marcus and I figured it was a lost cause. Then, one day, I tried a 'shell' field. I had just recently learned in class about creating different elemental fields to protect a person from physical or elemental attacks. For some reason, it worked on the fire; the field held, not for long, mind you. It all depends on my concentration because this field is lasting much longer than my previous attempts." Iggy finally stopped talking. A slightly stunned look was on everyone's face. No one could remember the last time, if ever, Iggy had talked so much.

Gus pulled up his pants, walked over to Iggy, and said,

"Alright, boys, I think it's time I showed you a little something, and with what you just showed me here, we may have a great invention about to happen." Whenever Gus got an idea, he pulled up his pants, which was a warning for those who knew him well. He led everyone into his lab. There in the corner was his new machine.

"There in the corner is my new machine," he exclaimed. Gus sometimes had a horrible knack for stating the obvious. Everyone chuckled a little as they approached the machine. Gus picked up a nearby flat mold, the kind he would use to make a window. Placing the mold underneath the nozzle part of the machine, he motioned for Marcus to join him.

"I have a few questions for you. First, can you help heat this machine to the temperature I need? Second, how long can you keep a fireball floating in precisely the same spot?" Gus asked as he started up a pressure boiler on the side of the machine.

Marcus looked at the machine; he quickly found where to focus his Fire ability. He then turned to Gus,

"Well, I've never really tried to keep a ball completely motionless, but I'll definitely give it a try."

Everyone else took a step back as Marcus and Gus went to work. Marcus began to heat up the pressure boiler, which, in turn, pushed large blasts of heat into the main chamber where the crystal power was loaded. Gus looked at the gauge on the side of the chamber and motioned to Marcus that the temperature was where it needed to be. Iggy walked over. To those watching, this could have been some freak experiment concocted by three crazed inventors. The truth wasn't that far off.

"You boys ready to go?" Gus yelled over the rumbling sound of the pressure in the machine. The boys nodded. Gus pointed over to the wall where several pairs of goggles hung. The boys knew what to do. Putting their goggles on, they took their positions next to the machine. Marcus began to form the ball in his hands as Iggy started to concentrate. The ball floated underneath the nozzle. A momentary flash across the surface told Gus that Iggy had placed the shell field around the ball. Gus pulled the handle, and a thin spray of molten glass began to coat the surface. He motioned to Marcus to spin the ball. The surface was starting to glow much brighter than the ball as the thin layer of molten glass covered the whole ball.

After several minutes of coating, Gus released the handle, stopping the spray of molten glass. Gus pulled the depressurization handle down hard. A loud boom was heard above the house as the pressure was vented. Everyone began moving their jaws in an attempt to regain their hearing. Looking over at the machine, the illuminated ball was still floating in the same spot.

"Um, Gus?" Iggy asked with great nervousness in his voice. "Exactly how long does this take to cool and harden?" Gus looked over at the young boy and saw how much of a struggle he was having. Outstretching his hand, Gus sent a blast of wind toward the ball. It wrapped and swirled around the ball and began to cool it. Just then, Iggy's field gave out. The surface of the ball started to get brighter. Gus looked over at Marcus.

"Let it go, Marcus; it won't cool like this." Marcus did as he was told, and the ball of fire began to morph and change shape. The bits of molten glass levitating in the air quickly fell into the mold as the fireball completely disappeared into Marcus' palm.

"Well, if anyone needs a small window, I'll have one for you shortly," Gus said with a smile, looking down as the molten glass oozed and spread into the mold.

Zeph was the first to walk over to them. The room had become quite hot during the experiment, at least double what it had been before. Sweat ran down his face. He could feel it dripping off his chin and clinging to his clothes. Breeze stood beside him in a similar state. They looked at each other and smiled for a moment. Turning his attention back towards Gus, Zeph asked,

"So, what went wrong?"

"I should have seen this before we started. I didn't consider the cooling process when I ran through the experiment in my head. It's not Iggy's fault; I could not expect him to maintain a new Talent for hours, at least not until he's mastered it more."

Zeph face twitched at hearing the term 'Talent' from Gus. It was the term his father used to say whenever Zeph failed an attempt at his Ability. He would say, 'Just because you don't know your main Abilities doesn't mean you don't have Talents.' Most people associate a handful of abilities with an individual's Elemental. For example, if you were born with the Fire Element, you could create and control fire with your fundamental skills. However, since no one knew how far a person's abilities stretch, those outside the norm are referred to as Talents.

Gus and the two boys walked over to Zeph and Breeze. Everyone had a brief chuckle at the sweatiness of everyone else. Gus walked towards the kitchen and returned shortly with a handful of hand towels. As everyone whipped themselves off, Gus spoke up,

"Well, I do think that this experiment has great potential. We just need to work out a few kinks."

Zeph looked up, "Just so I'm clear, what are we attempting to make with this?" Gus looked at Marcus, and in turn, Marcus turned to face Zeph. Holding out his hand, Marcus made a small fireball.

"Take a good look at this. This is at least five times brighter than a candle or oil lamp. What if we could place this in a glass ball where it would never dim and never burn out?"

"You want to market this?" Zeph asked, raising an eyebrow.

"This could be one of the greatest inventions of our generation."

"But it doesn't work yet." Zeph pointed out.

"It will, though. With your help, I'm sure we could do it."

Zeph sighed. What could he do? He held out his hands, and his eyes caught the symbols on them. Then again, many strange things had happened over the last day, maybe Marcus was right.

The large clock chimed in the main hall, which caused everyone to realize how much of the day had already passed. Zeph stood up and waved to Iggy to do the same.

"Well, this was a fun, crazy afternoon, but we should be getting home. Are you coming with us, Marcus, or are you going to stick around here?"

Marcus looked up, "I think I'm going to try brain-storming with Gus and Breeze." Breeze shot Marcus an odd look. "Okay, fine then, just with Gus."

ZEPH AND IGGY LEFT Gus' house as the day drew close. It was strange to think that Zeph's world had seemed so normal only a day earlier, and now, it was being thrown in every direction. Somehow, though, Zeph wasn't worried like he had been the previous night. The one worry that did still remain in his mind was his mother. She knew nothing of what had happened over the last day, and so much had transpired. He hoped that things would slow down.

The two of them began their walk back to town. Zeph glanced down at his little brother. He was growing up, and it felt odd to Zeph. Iggy's size made him seem so much younger than he was. In just two more years, Iggy would be graduating just like Zeph. Maybe as early as one year, the way he was going. He was impressed at the brilliance of his younger brother.

Zeph stopped as they stepped onto the main road in town. Iggy kept walking for a moment, then turned around.

"What is it?" he asked.

"Before we go home, let's go see Siah," Zeph replied as he began to jog down towards the docks.

Siah was the Trade Master in Daunt; he ran the docks, the Trade Post, and the local pub in town. He had his hands in a good number of businesses in Daunt. Zeph knew they would have to talk to him once they worked out the issues with the glass fireballs.

They bounded down the slope towards the docks. Siah was down at the end of one of the piers helping some merchants. It wasn't uncommon for ships to dock at Daunt. However, most merchants would sail to one of the larger towns on Appagon. Even Zeph's father worked mainly in fishing, aside from his trips to Sire. Thai was the only city on Sire that his father had ever been to, but he was sure that there were many more coastal cities on Sire.

Siah noticed the boys heading down the pier towards him. He was a big man, a huge man at that. In his youth, he was an awkwardly tall boy who stood almost seven feet tall. But after many years of working as a fisherman and merchant, he had transformed into a hulk of a man. Zeph's father had been best friends with Siah. They had gone on many voyages together. Oddly enough, though, he had not accompanied Zeph's father on the voyage in which he had disappeared.

"What can I do for you boys?" Siah asked with a smile as Zeph and Iggy approached.

"I have a couple of questions for you," Zeph answered.

"Go for it, lad."

"If we had an item to sell, let's just say for now we're selling a new kind of oil lamp. What kind of demand is there among the merchants for that sort of thing right now?"

Siah gave Zeph an odd look, then glanced over at Iggy. Iggy just smiled and shook his head. Turning back to Zeph, he replied,

"Well, lamps are something that everyone needs. Daunt, however, is not known for supplying them, so sales are not normal for them."

Zeph thought to himself for a moment. Should he or shouldn't he let Siah in on their little invention? Failed invention, he reminded himself for the moment. He decided to only mention some minor details.

"Let's say someone could make a lamp that never ran out. How would sales do then?" Zeph asked in response to Siah's statement. Again, Siah gave Zeph an odd look. The merchant ship's captain had been eavesdropping and approached the boys.

"Now, I don't know what you boys are concocting over here, but if someone could make a lamp that never ran out... well, I tell ya, I would give you boys two silver kessa for each one you could sell me."

Zeph and Iggy's eyes lit up upon hearing the captain's words. Zeph had just found his place in their whole scheme. He would be in charge of marketing.

"How long will you be in Daunt, good captain?" Zeph asked.

"Oh, a day or two. Why, you have a proposition for me?"

"Not yet, but give me a day or two,'" Zeph said with a smile.

With that, he grabbed Iggy and ran back toward town. Siah raised his hands and shouted something about leaving him in the dark. The boys laughed as they ran through town. They stopped for a moment and looked up towards the school. All the damage seemed to be repaired. It looked like tomorrow would be another day of school.

It didn't take long for them to arrive home. Zeph stopped Iggy as they were about to enter the house. He reminded him that their mother still didn't know about anything that had transpired. Like most mothers, they were never really sure how she would react to any given situation, but Zeph had a feeling that this was one of those times when things should remain a secret for as long as possible.

They entered the house and found their mother working in the kitchen, as she did almost daily. She developed a love for cooking over the years of using her Earth abilities. It was her pastime; when she wasn't cooking for herself and the boys, she was cooking for others.

"Hello, boys. How'd the afternoon go over at Gus'?" she asked, entering the front hall. They looked at each other for a moment.

"It was fun," they said in unison. She raised an inquisitive eyebrow. They smiled and retreated upstairs. The room was dark, and the heavy curtains still hung in front of the window from the day before. The only light came from the hallway and several cracks around the edge of the curtains. Iggy walked over and opened the curtains, letting in the evening light. In another hour, the suns would set.

Even though there were three distinct points to the suns' alignments, the town only rotated its time system at the peak of each alignment. The suns would be their farthest apart in four and a half years again. Sunset would be the same, but since Pythus would be rising before Cronus, it would make the sunrise happen several hours earlier. Of course, four and a half years earlier, Pythus was following Cronus, which made sunset happen several hours later. It was discovered long ago that Cronus always stayed where it was in the sky, and it was, in fact, Pythus that revolved around Cronus.

Screwy system, Zeph thought. Why not adjust the time system leading up to each alignment so that classes started at eight and ended at three? Well, once the next alignment hit, he would be done with school and wouldn't have to worry about class starting at six in the morning.

His room was a mess, but that was nothing new. Zeph looked around his room. The only actual free space left was on his bed. Sitting down on his bed, he picked up the open history book, which he had dropped there the previous evening. Holding the book in one hand, Zeph fell back onto his bed. A look of disbelief and confusion came over his face as he was shocked to see three symbols burnt into the wood of his ceiling.

"What the heck is this?!" Zeph blurted out with disbelief.

"Language boy!" his mother shouted up from the kitchen. Zeph quickly clasped both hands over his mouth. He had to watch his mouth around his mother unless he wanted it full of soap.

Zeph and Iggy stood in the middle of the bedroom, their heads craned up, looking at the ceiling. Zeph tried to walk around while still fixing his eyes on the ceiling. He soon found this impossible after tripping over his many belongings on the floor.

Iggy was the first to say something about the ceiling,

"You think mom will notice?" Zeph stopped for a moment. That thought had yet to enter his mind.

"Oh, crap!!" Zeph blurted out.

"Don't make me come up there, boy!" his mother shouted up the stairs. Again, Zeph clasped both hands over his mouth.

"Yeah, maybe you just shouldn't talk for a bit," Iggy suggested.

Zeph placed a hand on his chest and tried to calm himself down. This day was very quickly turning into a possible nightmare. He looked back at the three symbols on his ceiling. Whispering this time, he leaned over to Iggy,

"How do you think those got there?"

"Your guess is as good as mine. They look burnt right into the wood," Iggy replied as he jumped onto Zeph's bed. Even though he was short, he could still reach out and touch the marks. Nothing felt odd; the marks seemed to just be a discoloration. Iggy's gaze shifted from the marks down to Zeph.

"You don't think Marcus, you, and I had anything to do with this, do you?" The question seemed a little strange, but Zeph was willing to listen.

"What makes you think that?"

"Well, if you haven't noticed, the three symbols are the Fire, Light, and Omega symbols."

Zeph looked up at the symbols and walked around the room. Once again, he fell, tripping over the clutter on his floor. Falling against the side of his mattress the history book bounced off the bed, falling in front of his face on the floor. The cover lay open. The first several blank pages were the only thing exposed.

"Whoa, this is crazy," Zeph whispered as he touched the page.

"What is it?" Iggy asked, jumping off the bed.

"Don't you see it?"

Iggy looked down at the page Zeph was touching but saw nothing.

"Well, let's just roll with this for a moment. What do you see, Zeph?"

"It's the Omega symbol. It looks like it's floating just off the page," he replied, running his hand over it. "When I run my hand on the page, my hand blocks the glow from the symbol, but it looks like I should be able to run my hand underneath it."

Zeph closed the book and looked down at the front. It had a thick leather cover. The title was stamped into the leather along with various symbols Zeph had never seen.

"What do you think these symbols mean?" Zeph asked his little brother as he scanned the cover. Iggy leaned over,

"Your guess is as good as mine. We haven't covered any sections on Symbology or Glyphs."

"Yeah, we haven't either; it's one of the last things we learn. I think we start it next week once we finish this unit," Zeph said.

"I know this is the last thought in your head, but maybe we should tell Mom about everything that's been going on." The words filled Zeph's ears, and he shot his little brother a crazy look.

"Are you insane?! Mom would kill me!" Zeph gasped out.

"I'm pretty sure she could handle this. Plus, she's going to find out sooner or later. Don't you think she can handle it better now rather than later when it's more complicated?"

Something in Iggy's words rang out the truth about the situation. He was right, of course; that was his thing. Pointing out the obvious was what he was best at. Zeph picked up the old history book. Unlocking the small chest on his desk, Zeph removed the Omega scroll. He took a deep breath and looked at his little brother. Iggy assured him that things would be okay, and they walked downstairs together.

The next several hours were some of the longest that either of the boys could remember. Zeph took his mother into the den and began recounting the last day and a half. He began to realize more and more as he spoke that the last day had been the most monumental day of his life. He watched the expressions on his mother's face change to cover a wide array of emotions as the story unfolded.

Hours later, Zeph finally stopped talking. The room was quiet. Iggy stood by the fireplace, tending to the dying fire. The Omega scroll rested in their mother's hands. She reached across and handed it back to Zeph. Tears began to form in her eyes. Zeph immediately stood up and walked over to her.

"What's wrong?" he asked, sitting beside her.

"You're just like your father," She replied. "He was reckless and always strived for so much more in life."

"Oh, Mom, I can assure you I did not strive for this. I have no idea what I'm doing." After several minutes of regaining her composure, she stood up. Waving both her boys towards her, she hugged them.

"You're growing up too fast, both of you. I just don't know how to take it."

Zeph sighed, "We're not going anywhere, Mom. Things will be okay, you'll see."

She looked at him sternly and said, "No, Zeph, things won't be okay. Not on the path you're going down. If you truly are destined for greatness, only danger can lie ahead."

He had never heard his mother speak that way to him before. Not knowing how to take her words, he simply sat down. She said goodnight to the boys and walked over to her room. Iggy sat down next to his brother.

"So, what happens now?" Iggy asked.

Zeph looked over at him. He had no idea what to do now. Come to think of it, telling their mom had been all Iggy's idea. If anything, he should be the one deciding what should happen next.

"Well, hopefully, when I get a chance to talk to Marcus tomorrow, he'll tell me that they figured out some way to perfect the glass balls," Zeph replied with a look of confidence.

"So till tomorrow then?" Iggy asked.

"Till tomorrow, little brother," Zeph replied.

With that, the boys went off to their separate rooms. Tomorrow would be another day.

DAY 2

Like a light shining in the darkest place until the day dawns, so we are called into the Light so that we may bring it into the darkness for the entire world to see. No one is chosen by mere prophecy; it is the Will of Omega

~ The Book of Ta'Hor

CHAPTER 3
ENCASING THE FLAME

Light shone through the windows of the classroom. Soon, the desks would be full of students ready to learn, although a few would be sure to fool around or daydream. It was just a matter of which students you were referring to. The damage from the night before was almost unnoticeable. When all the townsfolk pulled together, nearly anything was possible in a short amount of time. One of the town's oldest trees had partially fallen on the school. This was devastating not only for the school but also for the tree. Several people in town with Earth abilities had spent much of the day returning the tree to perfect health.

Mr. Yad looked up from his desk to see Zeph standing in the doorway. Both of them took out their pocket watches in unison. A grin formed on the old teacher's face. He glanced over his glasses at Zeph. In turn, Zeph smiled and shrugged his shoulders as if to say, 'What can you do.' You see, Zeph was not known for his punctuality, something Mr. Yad had tried to instill in him for several years.

He walked over to his teacher, pulled a nearby chair towards the desk, and sat down. Even though it had been two days since he had been in this classroom, Zeph's appearance seemed not to have changed. Most of Zeph's clothes were the same style and color. Not many people could afford a full-scale wardrobe. At least not the minimalist kind of people found in Daunt.

Zeph's white hair hung in front of his face. He hadn't had it cut in some time, and it was at an awkward length where it wasn't quite long enough to hang, so it stuck up in patches. Zeph turned his face towards the window. The midday suns poured through it. The suns caught the blueness of his eyes, causing them to give off a radiant, glowing appearance. Zeph never really liked his white hair, but he loved his eyes. They were a brilliant, almost crystal blue in the middle and faded to a deep, rich blue at the edges, not unlike the shoreline of the ocean. The color stood out so much against the whites of his eyes.

Mr. Yad removed his glasses and leaned back in his chair. He was wearing his brown three-piece suit today. Although the jacket hung on the back of the chair, he wore the vest. His long white beard accompanied his attire perfectly.

Zeph looked down at his attire. He was wearing one of his long-sleeved navy shirts and faded beige pants, just as he had the last day he was in class. The only real difference anyone could make was the Omega symbol on the top of his hands. Of course, he kept his hands inside his sleeves.

He placed a hand on his chest. Why did his heart feel so heavy? Could it be that everything was finally catching up with him? He didn't want to think about it. So many other thoughts filled his head. A limitless number of questions waited at the edge of his mouth. Mr. Yad was the first to speak up between the two of them.

"Well, Zeph, I do believe that this is the first time you have ever arrived an hour before class. What's the occasion?" asked Mr. Yad with a gentle grin.

"You know, I think you would be the only one to one-hundred percent believe the last day of my life the first time you heard it," Zeph said with a sigh.

Mr. Yad raised an eyebrow, "What's been going on, lad?"

Once again, Zeph told his story. At this point, he felt he should simply write it down and hand it out to people to save time. However, he did not include the experiment at Gus' house. He only recalled what was relevant about the scroll and the history book Mr. Yad had given him.

Zeph finished his account of the events of the last several days by placing the Omega scroll on the desk, revealing the marks on his hands as well. Mr. Yad took it in his hands. A twinkle filled the old man's eyes, like a child's eyes when they gazed upon fireworks for the first time.

"Never in my life have I seen such a scroll as this," Mr. Yad said in awe. "It seems to have no latch or lock on it, yet it feels as though it should indeed open. You are still unable to open it, I assume?" The question came as a slight puzzle to Zeph. He realized that since the night everything had transpired with the scroll, he had yet to try opening it again. Perhaps he was still afraid of it. Or maybe he was afraid of himself and what the scroll might do if the powers contained within were unlocked.

"No, I haven't been able to yet. Based on what happened before, it seems as though I should be able to open it. From what Xa'an told me about what happened with Master Desiree and the Shadow scroll, she had the same reaction to it before it fully opened for her." Upon hearing his own words, the idea of opening the scroll didn't seem so scary anymore.

Mr. Yad handed the scroll back. Zeph returned it to his bag and pulled out the old history book. The old teacher seemed insulted by Zeph's gesture. "Oh no, Mr. Yad, I'm not trying to return it to you. I just have a few questions about it."

"Good, because it was a gift for you, and I don't accept gifts back," Mr. Yad said with a chuckle.

"I was wondering, in all the time that you owned the book, did you ever see anything strange?"

"Well, most books don't usually come with strange things attached. What sorts of things do you mean?"

Zeph flipped open the cover of the book. The first blank page was still showing the floating illuminated Omega symbol. "Well, for starters, do you see anything on this page?"

Mr. Yad was a wise old man. He would soon reach one hundred years old, or so his students joked. Scanning the page momentarily, he turned the book back to Zeph. "Well, I don't know what to say to you, lad, I'm afraid I don't see anything, nothing other than a blank page. But from the look on your face, I know there must be something you're seeing."

Zeph nodded, "It's the Omega symbol. It's glowing and looks like it's floating just off the paper's surface. But I guess no one else can see it." He sighed, taking the book back. Just then, an idea came to Zeph. "Mr. Yad, is there some way someone could write a message or symbols in a book so that no one but themselves could read it?"

The teacher thought about it for a moment. "Well, yes, there is. But not so much in the way you're talking. Glyphs can be created so that only certain individuals can see them. For example, you could mark your house to let people know someone with the Omega ability lived there. All you would need to do is write the Omega symbol on your door with some of The Tears of God. Anyone with the talent to read Glyphs would see the illuminated symbol on the door."

How could anyone get enough of The Tears of God to use it for writing? The Temple had only one vial, no larger than a wine bottle. It had been used for the Christening ceremonies in Daunt for generations. Only a few drops were needed on a baby's forehead.

"So let me get this straight. The Tears of God can be used in Glyph writing?" The confusion Zeph felt was evident on his face.

"I can understand your confusion. I think you will be very interested in our next unit, *Symbology & Glyphs*. Daunt has had very little interaction with people that use symbols or glyphs. That's one reason I don't teach it until the end of the last year of school."

Just then, some more students began to file into the room. Both teacher and student once again pulled out their pocket watches. It was already time for class. Zeph replaced the chair he was sitting on and found his usual seat. Wow! He thought. There was so much he didn't know. Why did it seem like all the questions were coming at once?

Marcus came walking through the door. His new shirt was unmistakable. It was bright orange and made in the same fashion as the one Zeph was wearing. Their mothers enjoyed sewing together. The black pants he wore enhanced the overall brightness of the shirt. Somehow, the fire orange shirt with black pants seemed to add to Marcus' personality.

Marcus was your typical Alpha male. His highly energetic personality, combined with his dashing good looks, made him stand out, especially with the girls at their school. It was his eyes that caught most people's attention. Because of his brown complexion, you would expect dark brown eyes, but this wasn't the case with Marcus. Zeph figured it had something to do with his Fire element. Whatever the reason was,

Marcus had bright amber eyes that faded to a deep orange on the edges. If the light caught them just right, they looked like glowing embers.

Taking his seat behind Zeph, the boys clasped hands. "So, a new shirt, I see," Zeph said with a smile.

"Heck yeah, I love this shirt!" Marcus exclaimed. Zeph just rolled his eyes.

"Anyways, how did the brain-storming go yesterday after I left Gus'?" questioned Zeph.

"Well, it could have gone better. We have two options at this point; we either have to figure out a way for Iggy to maintain his field longer or a faster way to cool the balls down."

Zeph pondered the options for a moment. Just then, Breeze entered the classroom and walked over to her seat. Since the class hadn't started yet, the boys both turned in their seats to face her. She looked fantastic today. Of course, in Zeph's mind, she looked amazing every day.

Slap! For a moment, Zeph was unsure where the hand had come from. He reached up and rubbed the back of his head. Then he glared over at Marcus. "You can daydream later, man, but for the moment, let's chat."

The three of them began to chat about the glass balls and how they could solve the problem. Zeph suggested trying wind instead of water. The idea had already occurred to Gus and Breeze. Gus was working on a way to funnel a large amount of wind into a jet system that could cool the balls. Since both he and Breeze had Wind abilities, creating the blasts of wind wouldn't be a problem. Based on what Gus had told him, Marcus explained that unlike ordinary molten glass, which would crack and shatter if cooled too quickly, this glass needed the opposite. The glass balls needed to be cooled rapidly so the fire held within wouldn't disrupt the indestructible nature of the glass.

Zeph began thinking about the merchant captain. Was now the right time to tell the others about it or not? They only had two more days until the captain left. Maybe telling them would be an excellent way to motivate their progress.

"Hey, I have news to tell you both," Zeph said, interrupting the open dialogue. "I don't know if this will help our motivation or not, but I have a buyer for the balls if we can perfect them. He says he'll give me two silver kessas for each ball and buy as many as we can give him."

Both Breeze and Marcus' jaws dropped. They looked at each other, then at Zeph. "When did this come up?" asked Marcus.

"Yesterday after Iggy and I left, we stopped by the docks. I ended up talking to a merchant captain. We have to hurry, though. He's only here for two more days."

Marcus was about to open his mouth again when Mr. Yad rang the bell. The classroom bell was hooked to a cord connected to the classroom door. When Mr. Yad pulled the cord from his desk, it rang the bell and closed the door simultaneously.

Mr. Yad stood up from his desk and walked to the front of the class. Every seat was filled today. The room's layout consisted of six rows with eight seats in each. The two rows against the window side of the room only had seven seats. Two seats had been removed from the back of each row to accommodate the large bookshelves in the corner.

Zeph looked around. He sat in the middle of the row closest to the windows. Marcus sat one seat behind him, and Breeze sat one row over and one seat behind Marcus. In the class of forty-six students, they were lucky to still be sitting near each other. Their class was one of the largest in years. A handful of families with children in their Middle-class years had moved to Daunt within the last few years. This caused Mr. Yad's class to fill up once they moved to the Upper-class level.

This was only half the class. Since Upper-class was two years long, second-year and first-year classes were intermixed throughout each day and throughout the week.

Mr. Yad looked out over the class. Many of the students had lived in Daunt for their whole lives. Even though they hadn't entered his class until this third segment of their education, Mr. Yad felt a connection with each one of his students.

He cleared his throat and began to address the class, "Good to see everyone here today. I trust you enjoyed your day off yesterday. I hope you also took the time to read over the chapters on Origin, Fallen, and your Elements as I asked you to." Groans echoed from student to student. Mr. Yad shook his head and continued. "I thought not, but I always try to give you the benefit of the doubt. Since we covered most of the Origin section in review at the beginning of the week, we will proceed with the Fallen section review."

Mr. Yad picked up a piece of chalk and began writing on the large blackboard behind his desk. When he turned around, the words 'The Uriel and their connection to Mankind' were written on the board. "Let's start this easy. Who are The Uriel?" he asked the class. A girl on the far side of the class raised her hand.

"They're the first humans Omega created," she replied.

"Not bad. Can I hear a more descriptive answer?"

Marcus raised his hand, "The first humans created and only recorded beings to Ascend without dying."

"Good, thank you, Marcus." 'Wow! The boy remembered something', Mr. Yad thought.

"As you should know by now, The Uriel are the first humans Omega created. He created them with complete knowledge of their Elements and their abilities. Which, in turn, allowed them to become powerful enough to rid themselves of their physical bodies, existing in whatever form they chose with the power of their minds and Abilities. We refer to this state as Ascended." Mr. Yad stopped speaking and wrote some more on the board.

"Fallen," He said pointing at the word on the board. "Why are The Uriel most commonly referred to as the 'Fallen'?"

Skye, who sat in the front row, raised his hand. "Because Omega did not intend for them to ascend with the knowledge he gave them."

"Correct! Now, we don't know how old they were when they Ascended or how long they lived on the world. We do know, however, that once Ascended, they no longer aged," he paused for a moment.

Continuing, he wrote several more lines on the board. 'How many and Where?' was the following line on the board. "To the best of our historical knowledge, we know that at least five humans made up The Uriel. Although, referring to them as humans may be a little impractical. Can anyone tell me how they were divided?"

Breeze was the first to raise her hand. Mr. Yad nodded in her direction. "There were three men and two women. Many historians suspect that there were more than the five history records."

"Well done, Breeze," Mr. Yad congratulated. "Although we don't know everything about them, we do know the names of three. Everyone take out a piece of paper and a lead piece from your desks."

After several minutes of rummaging, everyone had one piece of paper and a small piece of lead. Mr. Yad then asked each student to write their name at the top.

"Write down the three known names and what they mean. I'll give you an extra five percent for each name towards the 'Fallen' section on the upcoming final exam," Mr. Yad said, sitting back behind his desk.

Zeph thought about it for a short while. He could only remember one of the known Uriel. His father told him the stories of Iyr when he was little. Iyr's name meant 'watcher and guardian.' After the first people ascended, Omega gave them names based on their lives while on Arkhay. It was, in fact, the subsequent creation of mankind that had called them The Uriel. The name meant 'Flame of God.'

Minutes had passed and Zeph could still not remember the other two names. He wrote down Iyr's name and meaning. Zeph looked around the room. It seemed most people were done or had given up. By the expressions on several students' faces, that was the case.

"Time's up class," Mr. Yad announced. "If you would, please pass your sheets forward to the first student in your row." Mr. Yad walked over to the front of the rows and collected the sheets. "Alright class, since the next period will also be review, I'm going to let you break for lunch a little early today. Remember, even though today's third period is a first-year class, I still expect all you second-year students to return for the last period."

With that, Mr. Yad sent the students off. It was nice to have a whole extra period of free time. There would, of course, be students who would study, but most would go off and have fun.

A standard school day consisted of four periods. Each period was an hour long, with a twenty-minute break between the first and second, and third and fourth periods. Lunch was also an hour. Classes were held six out of the seven days a week. You didn't always go to all four periods every single day, though. The first and second-year Upper-class students still attend the same number of weekly classes.

Zeph, Marcus, and Breeze walked out into the afternoon light. They had three hours to do whatever they wanted. Zeph looked over at Breeze. She was wearing a dark green ensemble today. Her sense of fashion was always spot-on when putting her outfits together. She wore a short-sleeved white shirt with a green vest that buckled up the front, a matching green skirt that came to just above her knees, and a pair of black leather knee-high boots that her father had gotten her several years earlier. Her long black hair fluttered in the breeze.

"However much fun it is to see Zeph drool all over you, Breeze. Don't you guys think we should go do something?" Marcus asked, breaking Zeph's train of thought. This caused both Breeze and Zeph to blush.

"Well, what do you propose we do, Marcus?" Zeph asked sarcastically.

"We have almost three hours to kill, so why don't we go to my place and see what my dad has done so far today?" Breeze suggested.

"Sounds good, I'm in. What about you Zeph?"

Like he had a choice? Zeph agreed, and they headed toward town. They walked down the dusty road through town chatting along the way. Zeph glanced up at one of the street lamps. It would be fantastic if they could make their glass balls large enough to be used as street lamps. He thought for sure the town Elders would buy them; after all, it would be an unlimited light source.

They began to walk up the path leading out of town toward Gus' house. Even from here, they could see smoke rising in the distance. Gus must have had his machinery up and running already. Perhaps he'd figured out a way around the cooling problem? Rounding the bend just before the house it was clear that Gus had powered up the machines. Large amounts of white and grey smoke rose from the large smoke stack at the back of the house. Breeze also noticed something that hadn't been there before.

"Hey, look on the roof! There's another smoke stack on top of the lab. Dad must have created another venting system," she observed.

Entering the house, the temperature had climbed to staggering heat like the day before.

The three of them quickly headed to Gus' lab. He was working on some sort of smaller machine near the pressure chamber. Breeze called out her father's name, grabbing his attention. He tried to reply, but the noise from the pressure chamber made it impossible. They walked out into the main hall of the house.

"Good to see you, kids," he yelled, "I may have solved our little temperature problem. I was just about to test it out; come follow me." He motioned for them to follow him back into the lab.

Gus placed a metal mold underneath the machine's nozzle. The mold resembled a large wooden bowl Zeph saw at most meals. Gus took hold of the machine's controls and began to coat the inside of the bowl with a thin layer of molten glass. After several coats, he stopped and turned off the machine. A loud bang followed as he vented the excess pressure.

Removing large wooden tongs off the wall, he picked up the mold and walked several meters over to the new machine. He asked Zeph to open the door on the front. Gus then placed the mold on the rack inside and closed the door. The so-called machine looked like a converted wood stove, which it most likely was. It was big, black, round, and had a pipe running out of the top. It also had two pipes running straight out on either side of the door on the front. They were about the size of your palm at the opening but shrank to the width of a finger once they connected to the central section of the contraption.

"So, care to explain, Dad?" Breeze asked.

"Glad you asked," He said with a grin, "You see, both you and I are going to power this machine. It isn't really a machine at all. Here's what you do." He motioned for her to stand in front of one of the pipes pointing out from the machine, as he took the opposing spot.

Breeze could feel the heat emanating up the pipe. The glass bowl inside was still molten but solid enough to hold its shape. Gus instructed her to close her hands over the end of the pipe and send a blast of wind down the pipe. On the count of three both father and daughter sent a continuous blast of wind into the pipes from the center of their palms. Loud noises began to fill the machine as the rushing wind swirled inside. They continued for several more minutes until Breeze motioned that she couldn't go on.

Exhausted she began to slump over. Zeph quickly ran over to steady her. Gus opened the cover on the door. The bowl no longer glowed. This, however, did not mean that its surface had cooled entirely. Gus picked up the metal mold using the protective gloves he had made. He quickly set the mold down as he felt, through the gloves, that it was still quite hot.

The west side of Gus' lab had large doors. Opening them Gus revealed a blacksmith section of the lab just outside the house. For some reason, Zeph couldn't remember Gus having a blacksmith section of the lab. Turning the mold upside down, Gus made several heavy hits with one of his metalwork hammers. Upon hearing the glass separate he placed the mold aside and picked up the glass bowl. There was a large metal basin of water outside which he proceeded to drop the bowl into.

Smoke and steam mixed, clouding the house. One could easily assume it would rain any minute with the amount of cloud cover they had created from the machines. Steam sprang up from the basin as the glass submerged. Everyone was surprised the glass bowl didn't simply shatter when dropped into the cold water. After a minute or so Gus reached into the water. It felt relatively warm. He knew that only a moment earlier, the water would have felt ice cold from sitting in the shade all day.

Zeph, Breeze, and Marcus looked over as Gus pulled his hand out of the water revealing a perfectly smooth glass bowl. They were sure their shouting and yelling could be heard back in town.

"YES!!" Marcus exclaimed.

"Right on!" Zeph burst out. "But why didn't the bowl simply shatter when it landed in the water?"

"Oh, that's nothing; look at this," Gus said, placing the bowl on the metalwork table. Raising a giant sledgehammer, he brought it down on the bowl. Everyone except Gus had raised their arms in front of their faces, expecting to have glass fly everywhere. They opened their eyes and looked over at the bowl. Not even a scratch was on the surface. "It has to do with the crystals I make the glass from," Gus explained. "It has to be rapidly cooled like this for the indestructible properties to form."

"This is the most amazing thing I have ever seen!" Marcus exclaimed. "When you said it was unbreakable I figured you meant dropping it on the ground. But when you said this glass is unbreakable you meant it."

"Have you ever thought about making a line of dinner wear, Dad?" Breeze asked in a joking manner as she walked over to her father. Gus stopped for a moment and pondered it. "I'm only joking," she said with a shove.

"What's to joke about? People need plates and bowls that aren't made out of cheap tin or wood. But first things first, we need to complete at least one glass ball before I start any other projects."

Zeph walked over and picked up the bowl. It was truly astonishing. The glass felt so smooth. Which, he had to admit, was because of Gus' craftsmanship of the metal mold. He carried the bowl into the house's grand room, where everyone was sitting. Breeze was exhausted. She wasn't used to pushing her abilities at that magnitude. On the other hand, Gus made it a point to practice his Wind techniques several times a day, every day.

Gus and Marcus began walking around the house, opening up any windows that could be opened. Zeph sat next to Breeze on one of the couches. Both were covered in sweat. She looked as though she had just run a marathon. Her long black hair was sticking to her face, shoulders, and back. She looked over at him and smiled.

"This is all a little crazy, isn't it?" she asked, leaning over. Zeph wasn't sure how to respond. Everything was a little crazy lately. If only things could just go back to the way they were. He looked down. In his hands, he held the newly made glass bowl. It symbolized everything new, and he realized that no matter how much he wanted to, he couldn't go back.

Gus and Marcus returned to the main room. Rather than sitting around talking about the experiment, Gus suggested that they take the afternoon to relax. Everyone agreed. Zeph couldn't remember the last time they had all just hung out with each other.

As the hours passed the house cooled, and so did the feelings in Zeph's heart. He felt his anxieties fade away as he talked with the others.

Though his anticipations did remain for the knowledge that awaited him, he felt content to wait. The end of the week could not come soon enough. He yearned to learn more about symbols and glyphs. For the first time in his life, Zeph felt as though he was starting to connect to his element, if only in a small way.

The large wooden clock in the corner of the room let out one resounding ring. The clock was an engineering masterpiece. Gus had spent a large portion of his life trying to learn how to craft machinery. His clock was his finest work. Although he had made many more complex machines in his time, none could stand up to the clock's beauty. Gus had spent a great deal of time crafting or ordering the many components and brass needed for the internal parts and housing.

Everyone's attention was directed toward the hands on the clock. It was four-thirty. The next class would start in half an hour. The three teenagers stood up and began to collect their belongings. Gus walked them to the door. He stood in the doorway and watched them walk away from the house. They were good kids, he thought to himself. Better than good, they were truly amazing kids.

Gus closed the door and walked back to his lab. It was time to clean up. Grabbing a broom he began to sweep the floor. The dirt quickly built up on the floor of the lab. He swept everything into the open section of the lab. It was better than sweeping it under a rug he thought. Carefully, he swept around the pressure machine. Even though it was not powered up it was still hot. He had to keep a flame burning inside the base of the machine. There was no way he would let all the molten crystal go to waste by something as careless as letting it cool and harden. Besides, oil was much easier to obtain than the lengthy process he went through of sifting the crystal from the sand.

The place looked much better now, all nice and clean. Looking around, Gus felt a little out of place. There was nothing he could really experiment with. Their latest experiment had been a success; all he had to do now was wait for Iggy to see if the ball would also be a success. Gus was sure the kids would be back this way in several hours. After all, things had been perfect with the glass earlier. Who wouldn't want to try a crack at it again?

Leaving the house, he walked up a path opposite the main path towards town. Several minutes later, he reached the top of the hill, a short distance from his house. This was his training area. A large circle measuring nearly fifteen feet across was drawn out by an arrangement of small logs. The ground had been covered with a thick layer of soft sand. Stepping into the circle Gus removed his shirt, boots, and socks. He was in excellent physical condition for a man of almost sixty, and it showed. The sand felt warm from the day as he sat down in the middle of the circle.

Gus arranged several small stones on the ground around himself. He never used to train in this manner, but he was trying to expand his abilities and several of his talents. When he was a child, one morning at breakfast he sneezed and caused everything on the table to end up on the kitchen wall. Gus couldn't remember for sure, but on that day, he told himself he would always strive to control and master his Wind abilities.

Placing his arms out in front of him, he closed his eyes. He had placed ten stones in an evenly spaced circle around himself. Slowly he moved his hands behind his back until they touched. Concentrating he began to slowly extend his arms forward. The stones began to lift off the sand as his hands passed over them. As his hand passed over each stone, it would rise softly up to the level of his hand and then float back down once his hand moved away.

Gus opened his eyes. Even though his eyes had remained closed, he was still aware of what he had done. The Talent of Levitation was more common among people born with Wind abilities than anyone else. However, it was not commonly researched or practiced by Wind Elementals. Many with Wind abilities would simply use the wind to propel themselves or objects into the air. Levitation was different, however. It required a highly concentrated mind.

Gus picked up two stones and placed them in the center of his palms. This was a conditioning exercise that he found most difficult, but necessary in his mental practices. Opening his left palm he used his Wind abilities to make the stone float. The stone spun slightly as the wind from Gus' palm wrapped around it, making it rise several inches into the air. Gus opened his right palm. He tried to let his body continue with the stone in his left hand as he concentrated on the stone in his right hand. The stone began to rise. He felt his mental restraint struggle as he fought to keep each stone in the air, using different parts of his mental concentration, but he pressed on.

An hour had now passed since the youth trio returned to school. Gus still sat in the circle. He had failed his particular conditioning test once again. Perhaps his mind was not strong enough to be used in two different, yet very similar, ways at once.

Picking up the stones he placed them back in the leather bag at his waist. Stopping for a moment he took one of the stones back out. Looking towards the direction of town he threw the stone as hard as he could. He didn't even use his wind abilities to propel the stone farther. The stone went sailing into the air. Gus reached his hand out and concentrated on the stone. A moment later the stone came rushing back into his hand. A smile came across his face as he looked down at the stone. Even if he hadn't mastered using his abilities and talents simultaneously, at least his Levitation talent had grown stronger through his constant practice.

Gus returned to the house and immediately went to the bathroom to clean up. The house did not have the luxury of water fixtures controlled by the pressure of a reservoir like Daunt. Gus pumped the handle next to the sink, and the water splashed out. The water drops ran off his face, mixing with the dirt and oil draining down the sink. He ran his hands through his grey hair. He didn't feel old, but he was sure starting to look the part. Perhaps, at some point, he would dye his hair back to the dark brown it had once been.

Gus walked out into the main room of his house. Strolling over to the kitchen he proceeded to make himself something to eat. He hadn't realized how hungry he was until that moment. The house clock rang out with six chimes. The rest of the group would leave school shortly and most likely return to the house.

Taking his food he sat down in the den. The painting of his departed wife gazed down at him from the wall. He missed her. Breeze was the near-perfect image of her, which could be why he loved his daughter so much. Soon she would be gone too. He didn't know for sure, of course, but he suspected that in a few months when she graduated, she would leave Daunt. Why shouldn't she? The world was a wondrous place. A place that Gus had spent a great deal of his life searching out, and he knew he had only scratched the surface.

He finished his food and proceeded back to the lab. If the group was coming soon he would have to start preparing again. Gus started up the machine and added more water and wood to it. He closed the venting hatch and watched as the pressure valve began to rise. Then, he simply took a seat and waited.

ZEPH, MARCUS, AND BREEZE rushed into the classroom just in the nick of time. Mr. Yad scolded them as he closed the door and gestured for them to take their seats. Marcus seemed to be the only one not out of breath. Then again, he was a nature runner and got around Daunt primarily by running from place to place.

Mr. Yad stood before the class and asked for a volunteer to uncover and light the oil lamps mounted on the walls throughout the classroom. Several students stood from their seats and completed the task. He then asked Zeph and Marcus to shut the curtains since they were closest to the windows. As the heavy drapes met together, sealing off the light from the world, the room was now dim. Only the light from no more than half a dozen oil lamps cast flickering light throughout.

Mr. Yad once again reclaimed his position behind his desk. The room fell silent; it was as if the light was the only thing filling the room. After several minutes of silence, the students began to look around at each other. No one knew what was going on. Several of the students started to whisper questions amongst each other.

"Silence!!" Mr. Yad's voice boomed in the room.

Many students grabbed their desks to avoid jumping out of their seats. Zeph felt his heart race, and he knew Marcus and Breeze must be feeling the same. Everyone's eyes were fixed forward. The old teacher walked to the front of his desk. In the soft lamplight of the room, they could see that he was forming a sphere of water between his outstretched hands.

"This class is not about literature or history. Nor is it about knowledge or abilities. All your knowledge will not save you from conflict. All your abilities will not save you from struggle. What you have learned here in my class is nothing compared," he stressed the word 'nothing' as he spoke, "to the world that will lie before you."

A brilliant aura of light burst from the ball of water creating an almost blinding shimmering light that filled the classroom. Many students raised their hands to shield their eyes. Zeph didn't, though. He gazed straight into the light, as if somehow the meaning of his life would be waiting for him on the other side. Marcus, Breeze, and a handful of other students did the same. Mr. Yad searched every student's face and kept a mental note of those who continued to gaze forward unabated.

Lowering the sphere of water, the students were shocked to see that nothing more than a pin-sized point of light in the center of his palm had caused the display. It was clear to the students that he must have used the sphere of water to refract the small beam of light. Even though he was a Water Elemental, Mr. Yad had practiced channeling his elemental abilities into a small beam of focused glowing energy. However, it was nothing compared to the light displays that those with Light abilities could produce.

The floating sphere of water slowly flowed smoothly back into the palm of their teacher's hand. Returning once again to his desk, Mr. Yad asked Zeph to open the drapes. The bright light from the day was nothing compared to the light the students had just seen.

"Marcus, would you take care of the lamps, please?" Mr. Yad asked.

With a simple raise of his hand, the flames jumped from the lamps and into the palm of Marcus' raised hand.

"I know that most of you were not expecting anything like this, as this period is usually not an elemental-related class. That was a mere test. Some of you passed, and some of you failed. Do not be discouraged or proud of either outcome." The students exchanged confused glances with each other. The thought of failing something when you had no idea there was a test disconcerting to the students.

Mr. Yad now addressed the topic of the period. Just as in the day's first class, this class also ended a section and continued to the next. Not all of the classes in a day revolved around elemental education. Otherwise, many adults would have mastered their abilities but lacked the basic knowledge to read and write.

Not to be confused with a person's signature mark at the bottom of a letter, written language was called Initial. Even though everyone on Arkhay spoke the same language, many different dialects existed within the various Realms. People from different Realms would pronounce words slightly differently, sometimes making the words sound like a completely different language. Symbols and Glyphs represented two other forms of written languages. Initial consisted of several dozen letters, so words could be spelled out, rather than having a symbol representing a word or meaning.

"As you may know by now, our next units in both your elemental and social classes will be merged. Symbols and Glyphs are both part of written language and greatly connected to the Elemental powers of this world. This also means I will expect twice as much effort from you." Several groans were heard amongst the students.

"Of course, all of you, I'm sure, are ready for your finals at the end of the week. You will have your Elemental Final in the morning and the Social Final at the end of the day. Most of the Social final will include Trade, Marketing, Literary Representation, and an Essay. You will be able to choose your own topic for the essay. I will be looking for evidence of the literary rules of Initial that we covered in this unit."

Most of the students were taking notes while Mr. Yad was speaking. He never gave out notes, even if they were requested. Whatever you needed to know, he would mention. It was up to the students to write them down themselves.

Zeph glanced over his shoulder at Marcus. He was actually taking notes. Marcus was starting to grow up, at least a little bit. Zeph caught Breeze's eye as he turned his head back. She gave him a quick wink, and he shot back a smile.

The class continued at a smooth pace. Social class covered all of the standard knowledge of life and the physical world. Zeph had always enjoyed the Social classes more than the Elemental classes. It made sense since he was not able to grasp hold of his elemental abilities. He enjoyed reading and writing. When most kids were out playing with their abilities, he was writing in his room. He had kept a journal after his father had been lost at sea. Reading it always made him feel better when he doubted his father was still alive. No matter what anyone told him, he refused to believe his father had died at sea.

Zeph looked down at his hands. He hadn't looked down at the Omega symbols since that morning. Surprise, surprise, they were still there on the tops of his hands. He wondered if they would ever go away. Everyone else he knew had a symbol on their forehead. What was the big deal if he had an extra one on each hand?

He finished writing up his notes as the chime rang out. Quickly gathering his books, he walked to the front of the class. Marcus and Breeze followed. Mr. Yad motioned for the three to come to his desk. They stood off in the corner while the other students left. When the last students had left the classroom Mr. Yad turned to them.

"I did not need a test to know that the three of you are destined for great things. But out of all my students, you three never batted an eye earlier. Not even a flutter of an eyelid. Why do you suppose that is?" he asked.

They looked at each other unsure of how to answer. Zeph was the first to speak.

"For me, I guess it's cause I'm always trying to understand everything I can about the world around me."

"Very true; what about you two?" Mr. Yad asked glancing at Marcus and Breeze.

They were not as quick as Zeph, but they ran over their answers in their minds.

"I enjoy exploring new possibilities and new ideas. I was intrigued by what you showed us and felt compelled to watch," replied Marcus.

"I guess for me, it's simple. It looked beautiful, and I didn't want to look away," Breeze said, jumping in.

"Excellent answers from all of you. Your answers show who you are inside, the kind of person you are, and long to be."

Just then Iggy walked into the room. Mr. Yad turned his attention toward the young man. "How are you, Iggy? Are you paying attention in your classes?" Mr. Yad asked with a grin.

"Yes, sir," He answered.

Mr. Edge has told me great things about you. Are you looking forward to my class next year?"

"I sure am!" he answered enthusiastically.

"I have a strange feeling that you are meant for more than my class. But time will tell for sure."

Everyone became puzzled at that statement, but Mr. Yad shooed them off before they could ask. The four of them walked out of the school. It had been a good day, of both school and fun. Of course, there was still more fun to come.

"What do you think Mr. Yad meant by what he said to Iggy?" asked Zeph as he stopped momentarily.

"Yeah, I was going to say something about that too," Breeze said with a confused look.

They continued to talk about it as they walked down the path to town. Approaching the Rolling Hills Inn, Zeph had an idea. He told everyone to follow him and led them into the inn.

A sole musician was playing off to the side, but all in all, it was just as empty as it had been the other night. Zeph walked up to the counter. The innkeeper walked over; he was a grubby man. He looked as though his clothes hadn't been washed in weeks. Looks aside, he was a kind man, but he did speak with a slur. Obviously, he drank too much while on the job.

"Aren't you the boys that were in here the other night with that Shadow Mage fellow?" asked the innkeeper.

"Yes, we are, sir," Zeph replied.

"Well, you tell that fellow to come back again. I enjoy his overpaying."

"Oh, I will, Mr...." Zeph trailed off. It just occurred to Zeph that this man had been the innkeeper here for several years and he never learned the man's name.

"Oh, I'm no 'Mr.' I ain't no fancy teacher or leader or nothing. People call me Gibbs."

"Well Gibbs, I'm looking for someone. He's a merchant captain on one of the ships in town. He told me he's staying here for the duration of his stay."

Gibbs pulled out a clipboard from under the counter. Holding it relatively close to his face he squeezed his eyes together. The rest exchanged grins as they watched the innkeeper read the check-in list.

"What you'd say his name was?" he asked looking at Zeph over the clipboard.

"Uh, I actually don't know it."

"Well, when did he check in then?"

"I'm not sure of that either. Within the last few days, I think." Zeph was slightly embarrassed by his lack of knowledge of a man he was supposed to be in business dealings with.

"I believe you're looking for me," said the stranger behind them.

They turned to see the merchant captain Zeph had talked to the day before. The man wasn't as scruffy as he had looked the previous day. Perhaps he had cleaned himself up since landing at the docks.

The man's dark hair had been neatly combed back and was tied in a ponytail. He wore a plain white shirt and a black sailor's coat, usually reserved for the captain. His massive belt buckle was unmistakable, and his grey pants flowed into his large leather boots. The most noticeable difference was his clean-shaven face.

Zeph looked up at the man's face. The man had a kind look in his eyes. He extended his hand to Zeph, to which Zeph shook it firmly. The man went around the circle shaking all of their hands.

"Where are my manners? My name is Victor, Captain of the Merchant ship *Nephesh*."

"Breathing Creature?" Iggy asked. Everyone shot a glance at Iggy. Victor smiled.

"Well done, few people know the meaning of my ship's name. The ancient names must not fade away as time passes. Only by remembering the past can we hope to brave the future."

They walked over to the sitting area of the pub. Victor motioned for the four of them to have a seat. "So, a lamp that never burns out? I have to say it sounded pretty farfetched when I heard you speaking with the Trade Master. But I'm not one to pass up an amazing opportunity. Care to explain it more to me?" he asked Zeph.

Without going into specific detail, Zeph explained how they planned to trap elemental fire inside impenetrable glass. Victor remained skeptical despite Zeph's explanation. Zeph then told him about the bowl they had made earlier and how it truly was unbreakable.

"Well, as I told you yesterday, Zeph, I'll give you two silver kessas for each one you can supply me with. Now I do have an odd question. If these flames are encased in glass, how will you package them? You can't simply hand someone a glowing ball that can never be put out."

Zeph hadn't thought of that. He glanced at everyone as if to say 'I'm open to suggestions.' Marcus spoke up, "Well, what about those thick, tiny black bags that most shops sell to carry crystals or coins?"

"I doubt there are any shops in town that mass produce those bags, though," Zeph replied.

"No, but I'm pretty sure we have the fabric for them in the Embroidery Shop."

Everyone gave Marcus a funny look. This, in turn, made him blush. Since it seemed that Marcus knew his way around the Embroidery Shop, Zeph elected him to look into making the bags. Victor said he would buy the first shipment without the bags since it was a last-minute idea. All the arrangements were made to meet with Captain Victor again in two days. They also agreed on a name to call the glass balls, Sphere Lamps. It had a nice ring to it.

The four of them left the inn and headed for Gus' house. Almost like clockwork, the pressure vent blew when they rounded the road up to the house. This meant that the pressure chamber of the machine was at its max and Gus was venting excess pressure.

They walked up to the front door just as Gus opened it and stepped outside. He greeted the four of them and handed the glass bowl to Iggy. Iggy, of course, hadn't seen the bowl yet and was marveling at it. He threw it as hard as possible at the ground, making everyone jump except

Gus, who simply laughed. The rest of them glared at Iggy. He chuckled to himself as he picked up the perfect unscratched bowl.

"Well it looks like Iggy is in a great mood to get to work," Gus said with a chuckle, "How about the rest of you?"

Everyone nodded their agreement. Today would be a monumental day for them and for Daunt. Gus would be able to open a shop again in town. It would seem odd if the town council refused him a shop a second time. It had hurt Gus' business when the town council closed his shop. They had still allowed him to trade his inventions at the Trade Post by the docks. If not for that, Gus would have lost everything. Zeph thought it strange how much importance had been placed on the town's image at the cost of a man's business.

Since it would be loud in the lab, Gus went over the procedure of what they would be doing. Once in the lab, Marcus would create the ball. Iggy would then create the energy field around the ball. Once this was done, Marcus would maneuver the ball under the machine's nozzle, and Gus would apply the glass. Gus also suggested that Marcus make the ball a little smaller than before. The ball they had tried before had been about the size of a man's fist.

Pulling out one of the stones from his bag Gus handed it to Marcus. It was round and about the width of three fingers across and easily fit in the palm of your hand. In his other hand, Marcus formed a fireball of equal size. Gus nodded his approval.

Gus then walked over to Iggy. He told him to use his Focus as much as possible, and the rest would try to cool the ball as fast as possible. Focus was a term for an individual's mental energy when concentrating on and channeling their Abilities or Talents.

Breeze was next in line for Gus' pep talk. He told her to do her best, and he would do his best to help her. She was much more confident now than she had been earlier.

They entered the house and headed straight to the lab. There would be no wasting time today. Gus and Breeze took their positions by the glass extruder and cooling machine. Marcus and Iggy stood on both sides of the work table. Zeph slid open the large door leading outside. Gus gave him a thumbs-up.

Marcus spread his feet and took a solid stance. Placing his hands in front of himself he formed a single ball of fire the size Gus had requested. The ball floated forward and stopped when it was floating just below the nozzle from the glass extruder. There was a quick flash of light around the ball and the surface became smooth. All eyes looked at Iggy. He had a cocky smile and gave everyone a nod.

Seeing that kind of expression on Iggy's face was a rare occasion. Everyone knew he had it in him, but they rarely ever saw it. Iggy was very social with the other students in his class but became a little shy around adults.

Gus pulled the lever to release the molten glass. Grabbing the control stick he maneuvered the end of the nozzle back and forth. Marcus began to spin and rotate the ball so an even glass coating would form on the surface. A minute later Gus pulled the release lever back again. Breeze quickly opened the front of the cooling machine.

The molten ball of glass hung in the air. Despite the sweat dripping down their foreheads, Marcus and Iggy appeared to be holding up okay. Gus motioned for Marcus to place the ball into the cooling oven. Gus and Breeze took their positions as he did, and Zeph closed and locked the door.

The noise was more than Iggy expected as both father and daughter blasted wind into the machine. After several minutes, Iggy started feeling the drain on his mind. He grabbed Marcus' arm. Marcus looked down and then quickly ran over to Gus. Yelling into the inventor's ear, he informed Gus that they were running out of time. Gus looked over at Iggy and nodded to Marcus.

Zeph walked over to his little brother. It was evident that he was struggling to continue. Gus and Breeze stopped and Gus grabbed the ball out of the machine. It was still stable for the moment. It looked fabulous. Perfectly smooth and glowing. Everyone knew that if Iggy lost his concentration the ball would once again begin to overheat from the flames held inside before the glass had a chance to set.

Zeph reached his arm out to help steady his little brother but stopped as he glanced at his hand. The Omega symbol on the top of his hand was glowing. He pulled his hand away from his Iggy and the illumination faded.

This was not the time or the place for some weird mystical stuff to happen. Zeph moved his hand back towards Iggy and watched the symbol illuminate again. What did it mean? Zeph had no idea and wasn't sure if this was the best time to find out.

Breeze looked over at Zeph and noticed the illumination on his hand. Perplexed, she approached him as Gus pulled the pressure release lever. The loud boom caused Iggy to jump. Zeph quickly turned to him and motioned him to keep concentrating. Iggy nodded, although it was clear he wanted to give up. Even Marcus, who played with fire all the time, looked slightly drained from maintaining the ball for that length of time.

Gus ran outside, and the rest followed. Plunging the ball into the water basin, he shouted HOORAY! Everyone smiled and clapped their hands.

"In a few minutes, the ball will permanently cool," Gus said excitedly.

"How exactly will we know when that is?" Iggy asked with a distressed look on his face.

"Yeah, I was wondering that too, 'cause I'm also starting to feel the kick of overusing my Focus," Marcus said as he exhaled.

"It will be very soon. Don't worry boys, just try to hold out," Gus replied. They all stood by the water basin and waited. Both Marcus and Iggy looked weak but were pushing through it.

All of a sudden both boys grabbed their heads and let out cries in pain. They frantically tried to grab hold of something. Their legs began to buckle as it was clear they were about to pass out. Gus and Breeze's eyes quickly locked on the two boys.

The symbols on both of Zeph's hands instantly became brightly illuminated. The boys fell to their knees, and Zeph rushed over in what seemed like a fraction of a second. Without thinking he placed his hands on top of each of their heads.

Light burst from the palms of his hands, showering down on Marcus and Iggy. Energy poured from Zeph's hands and flowed down over both Marcus and Iggy like glowing liquid. Time seemed to slow down. Zeph felt as though he were floating. He could feel his whole body, inside and out. Light rushed past his eyes and the world began to grow dark. His head felt heavy as he let it start to slip backward.

The ground seemed to roll away and was replaced with the sky above. Zeph felt his hands slip off the boys' heads. His body arched backward. The sensation of falling overtook him as his knees became weak. The last thing he remembered was his head connecting with the hard ground, then only darkness.

DAY 4

> When I dare to be powerful, to use the strength that I know that is inside me, it becomes less and less important whether or not I am afraid to do so.
>
> ~Zeph

CHAPTER 4
MORE THAN A BOY

The morning was fresh as the family left the house. Dew sparkled on the grass as they headed down the path from their home. It had only been a few hours since the suns had risen. Both parents walked in stride as an energetic four-year-old bounced around them. The boy smiled up at his father. Shaking his head and smiling, the father picked up the boy.

As the family entered town, they met up with another family. This family had tanned skin and wore slightly different clothing than the first family. Both the men and women greeted each other. A mischievous two-year-old came bounding over to the first boy and jumped on him.

The two boys laughed as they rolled around in the dirt. Dirt was fun. Their mothers shot an evil look at them. Almost instantly, this put a stop to their fooling around. Heads hung low, they walked over to their mothers, who brushed them off.

Both families continued through town. Several shopkeepers greeted them as they passed by. A rather large man was waiting for them as they reached the path leading up to the Temple. He greeted the first family with great big hugs. He then chased the little boys around for several minutes until he caught the white-haired one. The boy giggled as the man tickled him. He then grabbed the little tan boy and placed both boys up on his shoulders.

The families arrived at the Temple and were met by the Uriym. He was the leader of the Temple in town. His name was Praotes. No one ever referred to him by just his name, though; it was disrespectful to refer to a leader without their title. Praotes had been with this Temple for many years, more than most of the townsfolk could remember. He had started as a Templar. Templars assisted the Uriym and helped them attend to their spiritual duties as Temple Leaders.

The old Uriym greeted them and showed them into the Temple. This was a smaller temple than most, but it was the only Temple out of all the neighboring villages. The main hall consisted of rows of stone benches. There was a stone pedestal at the front from which the Uriym would speak. Behind the pedestal stood seven lampstands representing the seven elements.

Everyone took a seat in the front row of the main hall. The two boys sat beside each other, their parents on both sides, keeping a close watch. The older boy looked over at his mother as she unwrapped the baby in her arms. It was his little brother, his brand new baby brother. He watched as Uriym Praotes took him from his mother's arms.

Worried, he tried to run over to his little brother, but his father grabbed him. The small boy began to cry. Even though he barely knew his little brother, he was very protective of him. His father told him that everything would be alright, that Uriym Praotes would give him right back.

Praotes smiled at the boy in his arms, slowly rocking him back and forth. There was no need for him to walk over to the pedestal for such a small gathering. He looked at both families, then began to speak.

"Friends and family, I welcome you on the happiest of days. A new life can only bring joy to this world. May I have the family stand, please?" Praotes asked as he motioned towards the first family. Both the parents and the little boy stood from the stone bench.

"Please state your names for the official record?" requested Praotes.

"I am Khoz, and this is my wife, Dawn," Khoz replied. Praotes also asked what the baby's name was. Both parents answered in unison.

"What a wonderful name; he will grow up to be a smart young man, of that I'm sure," Praotes exclaimed. A Templar stood nearby, writing down what was being said. The little boy wasn't thrilled that he hadn't been acknowledged. He pushed past his parents and walked up to Praotes.

"What about me? I'm here too, you know!" The little boy exclaimed without batting an eye. The old Uriym chuckled and looked up at his parents. They were embarrassed, but Praotes' eyes told them not to worry.

Praotes bent down so the little boy could see the baby in his arms.

"Is this your little brother?" he asked with a kind grin. The little boy nodded. "He's pretty special, isn't he?" The little boy smiled and nodded again. "Are you going to look after him forever and ever?"

"Uh-huh," the boy replied with an excited nod.

"Templar," Praotes called out, turning towards the young man off to the side. "Once the ceremony is complete, I want you to place this boy's name under the Official Guardian section on the record." Both parents looked at each other questionably; they hadn't even discussed who their newborn's guardian would be.

"Forgive me for speaking without consultation first. I know he is only a boy of four years old, but he displays true, genuine concern for his brother, which some people never achieve their whole lives. You should be very proud to be raising a son such as this. When he is old enough, I will show him your son's Christening Certificate and explain to him what it means."

The parents nodded their approval, and the little boy sat back down with them. The templar brought over a small vial and handed it to Praotes. The liquid in the vial was clear and glimmered with a faint light. At this point, Praotes asked everyone to stand once more. All the parents, the two boys, and the large man stood up. Praotes looked at the room of people.

"Witnesses, please give your names to the templar so that he may record them for the record." Everyone did as requested, and the templar wrote them down. Praotes then removed the cap off the vial.

"Every person in this world is special; every person is capable of great things. We are all born with a gift from Omega. Our Creator Omega blessed us greatly as a creation. As he cried our world into existence, so forth he left some of those tears behind. The Tears of God do not make us who we are; it merely proclaims to those around you how you are connected to Omega."

He raised the Tears of God vial over the baby and placed several drops on the baby's forehead. Several seconds passed, and a symbol appeared. Praotes walked over to the parents and handed them their baby back. Dawn was overjoyed to see the Light symbol on the baby's forehead. Khoz shook Praotes hand.

"Thank you so much, Uriym Praotes, for performing the Christening ceremony."

"It's not like you had any other temple to go to," the old man said with a chuckle.

"We are very overjoyed, thank you," Dawn said to Praotes.

The templar approached the family as everyone crowded around the new baby. He was skinny, and it took several tries to get Khoz's attention.

"I just need your oldest boy's name for the official record if I could."

Upon hearing the templar, the little boy burst through the crowd of people around his mother. He jumped right up to the feet of the templar. "My name's Zeph!" he exclaimed with a big grin.

THE DARKNESS SWAM THROUGH Zeph's head. Thoughts scrambled in every direction. He tried to open his eyes but found he was unable to. It felt as though he were encased in a thick, dark place. He fought to move, to open his eyes, to do anything. The frustration became too much, and he finally let out a tear-filled scream. Tears broke from his eyes as he breathed in and let out another cry.

He heard the sound of several footsteps rushing over to where he lay. His head was spinning, and he was unable to focus on anything around him. A muffled voice was heard amongst the confusion of his mind. "He's conscious; go and get his mother, quickly!"

His eyelids finally broke free from his state of darkness, and he found himself in a dimly lit room, staring at a stone ceiling. The walls were also stone. No windows were visible from where he lay. Candlelight bounced off the walls. Zeph looked around the room as he tried to move. Turning his body, he managed to sit up. This was short-lived as the dizziness overtook him, and he fell to the cold stone floor beside the bed. Before he even knew what was happening, vomit swelled up inside and splattered onto the floor beside his head.

Tears began to form in his eyes again. He had never felt so helpless in his life. He was lying next to a pile of his own vomit, and he was powerless to do anything about it. He began to cry as he ran his hand over the cold stone floor.

Uriym Praotes came rushing into the room and picked Zeph up. He laid Zeph back out on the bed and instructed him to rest. He gave Zeph a small vial and told him to drink it. The liquid tasted sweet at first but left a bitter taste in his mouth once he swallowed it. It did make him feel better, though. The spinning in his head was starting to fade.

Zeph realized he was in one of the side rooms at the Temple. He couldn't understand why he was here instead of the Healing Clinic. How long had he been unconscious? He was sure it couldn't have been more than a few hours. What had started this? They had just finished the first Sphere Lamp when Marcus and Iggy started to collapse.

Zeph held up his hands. He remembered placing his hands on Marcus and Iggy. Everything had gotten strange, and then he blacked out. Reaching behind his head, he felt the tenderness. That's right, he remembered hitting the ground.

The sound of the temple doors opening could be heard, along with footsteps running towards the room. His mother was the first to enter, followed closely by Iggy, Marcus, Breeze, and Gus. Along with the templar and the Uriym, the room was uncomfortably full now. Zeph's mother wrapped her arms around her son. The motion of quickly sitting up didn't help with Zeph's dizziness. Both Marcus and Iggy were eyeing the vomit already on the floor. They really didn't want to see anymore at this particular moment.

"I was so worried about you son," Dawn said through tears, "I kept expecting you to never wake up." She wrapped her arms tightly around him for several more minutes.

Praotes handed Zeph another of the vials he had given him before. Zeph drank it. He felt strong enough to stand up now. Everyone helped him up and walked him to the Temple's main hall. They all sat down on one of the stone benches at the back.

It seemed like a thousand questions flooded his head at the same time. He finally decided where to start.

"How long was I out?"

Everyone looked from one person to another. Finally, Marcus was the one to reply.

"I know you might find this hard to believe, Zeph, but you've been unconscious for the last two days."

It wasn't possible. Zeph couldn't believe it had been two days! What had happened to him when he blacked out?

"Why didn't anyone heal me?" he asked, frustrated.

"We tried. The healers at the clinic tried. Nothing worked. Finally, we brought you to the Temple. We told Uriym Praotes the specifics of what happened. He suggested it was connected to your Focus," Marcus explained.

Zeph moved his hand back and forth quickly in front of his eyes. Marcus chuckled, "No idiot, your Focus. You know, your mental strength, you use it when using abilities or talents." Zeph let out a sarcastic chuckle. The whole joke with his hand must have come across as a little melodramatic since nobody got it. He still didn't understand what had happened, though.

Uriym Praotes left and returned shortly with a leather-bound book. He flipped through the pages until he found the one he sought. Praotes handed the book to Zeph.

"I'm sorry, you'll have to read for me, Uriym. My head is still spinning a little," Zeph said, returning the book.

"Not a problem, lad," Praotes said as he located the spot on the page, "This book holds the accounts of all known ability manifestations. You never know if someone's 'new' ability is just a rare, not commonly known, ability."

"So, has anything like this ever been written down?" Zeph asked as he held the side of his head.

"Not exactly, but from what your friends tell me, I can tell you what happened. I'm not sure if it's connected directly to the Omega Element or not, but according to our books, you did a Focus Transference."

"How could I have done that? I don't even know what it is." Zeph was getting frustrated again. Just then, a gleam entered the eyes of both Iggy and Marcus. They motioned to Gus, and he motioned back. They whispered back and forth for a moment, deciding if now was the time and place. Taking a glance at Praotes, they motioned him over also. Whispering adults were not helping Zeph relax, and amid everything, it was only aggravating him further.

Gus walked over to Zeph. Still holding his head, Zeph looked up. Gus held a small, tied black bag that he handed to him. Everyone was now watching Zeph. He was starting to feel like he was some freak show. Zeph pulled the strings open on the top of the bag. Everyone held their breath as he tipped the bag upside-down. A glass ball rolled out onto his palm, illuminating the room.

Zeph was sure his heart had stopped just for a moment. The fire swirled inside the thin glass covering. It was like watching a rushing storm, glowing orange and yellow clouds expanding and rolling over each other. As he watched it, he noticed the light flickering like a small flame. He cupped his hands around the ball and looked at his glowing hands.

All of his frustrations had faded away in a mere instant. Zeph felt more excited than he had felt the entire time they talked about making the lamps. A look of distress fell across his face. Captain Victor! If he had been unconscious for the last two days, then that meant he had already left. As if reading his mind, Breeze reached into her bag and handed Zeph two silver kessas. His jaw dropped as he saw the money. She smiled back at him.

"After the first night you were still unconscious, we figured that we had to keep working. Of course, it was a lot more difficult without your whole 'transference' thingy," Breeze said, "We made six and sold five of them. I knew how disappointed you would be if we didn't save you one. If you can perfect your new ability, I'm sure we can make them at a much faster rate."

"Yeah, man, I have to say that's the best I ever felt. When you put your hand on my head, I felt so recharged that I could have made a fireball the size of this town!" Marcus exclaimed.

"So, you're saying I transferred my Focus Energy to the both of you?" Zeph asked, puzzled.

"That's correct," Uriym Praotes said, "but you transferred everything. You completely drained your Focus Energy and sent yourself into a deep coma. You should be proud, though. You now have the knowledge of your first ability manifestation."

'He's right!' Zeph thought. This was the first time in his life he had used an ability. He only hoped that his remaining abilities wouldn't be as detrimental to his health.

The next several hours passed by, and everyone remained in the Temple. Zeph spent most of his time pacing around the main hall. His expression was constantly changing. The others could only assume he was debating with himself. Gus, Breeze, Marcus, and Iggy all sat in a circle discussing the Sphere Lamp. Zeph's mother and Praotes stood off to the side, most likely discussing Zeph.

"What time is it?"

Everyone looked over at Zeph. It was an odd question since Zeph always had his pocket watch.

"You said it's been two days; that means today is the day we have our final exams." Breeze and Marcus looked at each other and then at Zeph. Their looks had begun to frustrate him. They looked at him like he wasn't even there.

"I don't think I've heard you ask 'what time it is' for the last two years, Zeph," Iggy said, stepping forward. Zeph rewound his words in his mind. Why had he asked that? He reached into his pockets and pulled out his watch. Opening it up, he noted the time. It was still early; they had almost an hour before they had to go to class.

Zeph sat down, and everyone followed suit. He felt so disillusioned. Nothing seemed to make sense. The two days that had felt like an hour before now felt like a lifetime. Heartbroken inside, he hung his head in his hands. Thoughts of his missing father flooded Zeph's mind.

Zeph had tried to push the memory out of his mind for years, but the thought of 'first' abilities brought it back. His memories brought him back to the day Iggy used his Light Abilities for the first time. Zeph had been so angry at his little brother. He had almost hated him. Zeph's father had seen that look many times in his life, but he never thought he would see it on his son. Darkness that should never enter a child had found its way into Zeph.

He remembered screaming at Iggy that he hated him, that he wanted him to die. Iggy was only five, and the little boy started to cry upon hearing his older brother's words. Zeph smiled a villainous grin and turned to walk away. Zeph's father was standing in the doorway with tears in his eyes. Zeph froze in his tracks. He had never seen his father cry before. He didn't understand; he had only meant to hurt Iggy. Why was his father crying, too?

Everyone sat silently as they watched the emotions swell inside Zeph; tears began falling from his eyes. He was not sobbing or weeping; he just had tears softly running down his cheeks. No one was yelling at him or telling him that they hated him. Zeph looked over at Iggy. "I'm sorry," he whispered, "I've never hated you."

Only the boys' mother knew what Zeph was referring to. Zeph's mother smiled softly at him. Iggy walked over and hugged his brother, as did his mother. Uriym Praotes walked over to Zeph.

"Young man, I have seen a great burden lift from you today. This spiritual atonement has brought you peace and closer to the path of Ascension."

"Thank you, Uriym," said Zeph.

Marcus slid over on the stone bench and wrapped his arm around Zeph's shoulders.

"I know this may sound a little weird coming from me, but let's head off to school early, seeing as you missed the last two days of studying. Come to think of it, so did the rest of us. If we head over early, Yad may help us out.

Everyone agreed. Even though Iggy didn't have a final that day, he also chose to join them. Praotes and Dawn watched as they walked away from the Temple. The two of them walked back into the main hall and sat down. It had been some time since she and the boys had attended a Gathering.

A Gathering was a weekly spiritual gathering, usually held on the last day of each week. The Uriym of a Temple would address the congregation at the Gathering. He would speak from one of the two great prophet's teachings. Ta'Hor and Sha'Kath, they had been brothers, the first recorded people born after the Ascension of The Uriel. They were born at the beginning of the First Age. Ta'Hor was born with Light and Sha'Kath with Shadow. Both men kept journals of almost every day of their lives. When the time came, and both men were lying on their deathbeds, they took different paths. Ta'Hor's body turned to brilliant energy, and he Ascended. However, Sha'Kath's body turned into a dark energy, and soon after, his body transformed into a Fiend.

From both men's journals, the teachings of Ta'Hor and Sha'Kath were created. Only through the knowledge of good and evil could a person hope to place themselves on the path to Ascension. There was, however, a third option. Many people did not Ascend or become Fiends at death.

When a person died, a small ball of energy would leave their body at the point of death, it was called their Gava. Their gava would rise from their chest and remain there for a moment. If it turned a bluish color and re-entered the body, the body would transform into a brilliant form of energy and disappear. This was a sign that the person had Ascended.

However, for most people, once their gava left their body, the body would be dispersed into thousands of strands of light. The strands would float up towards the sky and fade away. This was what most commonly happened when people died.

If the gava turned a reddish color and re-entered the body, the person would shortly transform into a Fiend. Black swirling energy would engulf the body and reform it into a fiend.

Fiends were dark creatures. They were the tormented echoes of the dead, trapped within a body of dark energy. Some would rise as fierce beasts and creatures, while others would rise in almost human forms. These fiends had the power to command and control lesser fiends. Lore and legend said that for Sha'Kath, it was almost as if he had never died. However, it became quite clear soon after that a great darkness had consumed all that was left within him.

Daunt was a peaceful town as far as fiends were concerned. There had never been a fiend attack within the town in its entire history. No fiend had ever formed from someone dying in Daunt either. The Temple in

Daunt was devoted to Ta'Hor. Despite the dark teachings, Temples that were devoted to Sha'Kath existed all around the world.

THE DAY CONTINUED, and the group went off to class. After spending an hour studying with Mr. Yad before class, the trio of youth was prepared for the final. The Elemental Final went well. Zeph was glad he could write something about his own abilities for the essay question. The rest of the final went as well as expected, having been in a coma for two days. After several hours, all of the students finished.

Zeph was finished before Marcus and Breeze. He decided to head home for the time being and told them he would meet them back at the school later for the Social exam. As Zeph walked through Daunt, everything seemed so different. It was as if he had been looking at the world through a dirty window that now had been cleaned.

Zeph pulled out the two silver kessas from his pocket. He had never had coin in his whole life. What should he do with it? He guessed that everyone in the group also had two silver kessas since they had sold five lamps. Pulling out the little black bag from his other pocket, he looked down at both hands. He found the link between the two items fascinating; that the item in one hand could bring the kessas in the other hand.

Continuing through town, Zeph stopped at the food market. The food market was a little different than the Trading Post. Even though food traded at the trading post would end up in the market, some people still preferred to buy it directly from the Trading Post.

Siah always brought Zeph's mother choice selections directly from the Post, rather than having her pick out lesser selections from the market. He was a lovely man and was like an uncle to Zeph and Iggy.

After spending several minutes browsing different items in the market, Zeph decided to save the coins. He wanted to have some handy for whatever he might need down the road. Plus, Victor would be back in two weeks. The thought of Captain Victor selling the Sphere lamps excited Zeph, and he wondered how people would react to them. Zeph wished he could be like Captain Victor, sailing around the world. Even to travel to Thai, as his father had done most of his trading there. Zeph wanted to see the advanced city with his own eyes.

Unlike Victor's voyages, his father's trips had been much longer than two weeks. Victor had a much larger ship with an odd sail configuration. He had told Zeph that the winds and currents were odd along his sailing route. Many sailors had lost their lives when sailing those currents. This was caused by a giant whirlpool where three main world currents had collided. It was called The World Vortex because of its massive size. Victor explained that the winds and currents in that area did not coincide with each other. His ship was designed to grab the currents from one direction and the winds from another. The ship would almost fly across the water when done perfectly.

Zeph loved talking with Victor. In some ways, it was like talking with his father again. He missed the stories that would fill the house after one of his father's voyages. Zeph knew now that some couldn't have been true and were only created for him and his brother's entertainment.

The walk home was charming that day. Zeph hadn't walked home alone, or anywhere for that matter, for quite a while. When he entered the house, his mother was sitting in the living room. She seemed surprised to see him but also glad. They began to talk about Victor; it seemed he was all Zeph could talk about since meeting the man. The sound in Zeph's voice made her smile, yet somehow hurt inside. Zeph hadn't spoken like this since his father had been in the house.

Dawn prepared lunch for both of them. They hadn't spent an afternoon together, just the two of them, for some time. Zeph enjoyed it. They talked about everything, including things from his childhood to things about his father and even about the book and scroll. It was only when they began to talk about the book and scroll that Zeph seemed to drift off in the conversation.

"What's wrong, dear?" his mother asked.

"Nothing, it's just...." Zeph's voice trailed off, "It's just that it scares me. The way Xa'an spoke about me. It was like I was someone I'm not, like I was someone of great importance."

were so, I don't think you'd be able to see them as well." Zeph took the book from his mother

"This must be how these symbols got burnt into my ceiling."

"What?! You have burn marks on your ceiling?" Dawn exclaimed. Zeph swallowed and, through a shaky smile, said,

"Yeah, didn't I tell you that the other day when I told you about everything?"

"You most certainly did not, young man!"

"Well, I don't think now is really the time or the place to get into that," he said, hoping that she would drop the topic for the moment. He was relieved as she did turn her attention back to the book.

Zeph touched the Omega symbol on the triangle. It disappeared from the formation, and the other two symbols moved farther down to the corners of the page. Words began to appear again.

'Greetings to you blessed with Omega. I am Mage Saphar. If you are reading my words, then you are the Omega Chosen One, and I am blessed that you are reading my words. Before I continue, two others must be present. Please bring the Fire and the Light so that I may reveal more to you.

The words and the symbols faded away, and the page once again turned blank. Zeph looked at his mother, slightly wide-eyed. He began flipping through the book; every chapter seemed to have several extra blank pages at the end. However, this was the only one Zeph saw anything on for the moment. Of course, the Omega symbol was still on the book's first page. Zeph was positive that the symbol was placed there specifically for him.

"Mage Saphar. Have you ever heard that name before?" Zeph asked his mother. She gave him a slightly odd look. The question now seemed strange once Zeph replayed it in his head. Why would his mother know that name? He would ask Mr. Yad about it later.

Zeph stood up from the couch. He held the Omega scroll in his hands. The look in his eyes caused concern in his mother's eyes.

"What are you doing?" she asked.

"I'm taking the next step," Zeph replied, placing his palms on the ends of the scroll. Bracing himself for the worst, he closed his eyes. The sensation he received was the opposite of what he was expecting. Rather than a painful, overpowering sensation, he felt revived. He opened one of his eyes and glanced down at the scroll. The Omega symbols on his hands had illuminated, but other than that, nothing else seemed to be happening.

"What's happening?" his mother asked cautiously.

"Nothing, I think. I mean... I feel a recharging sensation when I touch the ends, but this is completely different than last time." Zeph was highly puzzled. He touched the ends again, and the same feeling washed over him. The feeling was similar to when he drank the vials at the Temple, but it was far more intense. Still holding on to the scroll, he sat down.

"Are you sure you should still be holding it like that?" Dawn asked as she looked down at his hands. "I'm not really sure. This feels completely different. It feels like it's recharging my lost Focus."

Just then, Zeph had an idea. He stood up and told his mother to follow him. They walked to the back of the house where the garden was. Since his mother had Earth abilities and his father had Water abilities, it made sense that they would grow most of their food.

Still holding both ends of the scroll, Zeph looked around the garden for a specific plant. The garden was extensive for a house garden. It was twice the house's width and five houses' length. The growing season would end soon, and the harvest season would begin. During the harvest season, a gardener or farmer still grew plants, but it was a prime time to start harvesting the product from the last six months.

The first six months of the year were usually very fresh and wet, making it the best time for planting. The last six months were warmer and drier, making it much better for harvesting or growing plants that thrived best in warmer temperatures.

The plant Zeph was looking for was a Pirie plant. After several minutes, he spotted one and walked through the rows of plants toward it. The Pirie plant was rare and hard to care for, even for an Earth Elemental like his mother. It produced fruit about the size of a man's fist. It only produced only one piece of fruit at a time, producing a new piece of fruit only after one had been removed. The fruit had a hard outer shell with tiny barbs on it. Inside the shell, however, was liquid. The juice from the fruit was so expensive that a vial from one shell cost twenty gold kessas. That was almost a month's wage for the average person in Daunt.

Zeph bent down next to the plant. There was one shell on the plant. He noticed about a dozen pods where a new shell could grow once the current shell fell or was harvested. Only one pod would produce a shell at a time. Zeph looked over at his mother.

"I want you to make all those pods produce new shells."

She looked at Zeph as though he had just asked her to throw the Appagon Mountains into the sea.

"It can't be done, son. The Pirie plant does not respond to Growth abilities like other plants do. I planted this plant when you were a child, and it has only produced one shell a season since then. I'm sure it could produce more if we picked the shells, but you know the juice is bitter if you pick them before they fall off on their own."

Zeph finally let go of the scroll and placed it in his pocket. He felt energized beyond belief.

"That's one reason why I chose this plant. Do you know how Marcus said that after I touched him, he felt like he could have made a fireball the size of the town? Well, I believe he really could have. Now, I want you to concentrate on growing those pods into shells."

When Dawn said she believed in him, she meant it. So, she took a position over the plant, outstretched her hands, and began to concentrate. The plant's foliage began to become a brighter green and grew slightly. Zeph placed his hand on his mother's head. Energy could be seen traveling down Dawn's body and into her hands, which burst forth in glowing green light. Her hands began to shake as the plant started to grow at an accelerated rate. The pods on the plant burst forth into shells. The shells continued to grow until they reached three times their average size.

Zeph lifted his hand. He felt weak. Reaching into his pocket, he pulled the scroll out and touched the ends. The feeling didn't start instantly like before, but within a few minutes, he began to feel revived once more.

Dawn stood up and looked at her son. She held an expression he had never seen on his mother's face before. It was an expression of awe, not for the plant, but solely for him. She bent down and picked one of the oversized shells off the plant. The plant had also grown in size from only knee high at the beginning to now chest high.

They returned to the house. Zeph's mother went straight for the kitchen. She placed the Pirie shell on the table. She rummaged in the kitchen drawer and returned with a small metal spike and a hammer. After several firm taps, the spike pierced into the shell. She made a second hole so the liquid would drain easily.

"Zeph, can you grab the glass vial from the shelf in my room?" Zeph returned shortly with a tall glass vial. Its long, skinny neck bloomed into a large bottom base. She carefully poured the Pirie juice into the vial. Usually, a shell would barely fill the large vial a third of the way, but this shell filled it almost to the top.

Before capping the vial, she removed two small tin cups from the cupboard. She poured some of the juice into each cup and offered one to Zeph. It was highly unusual for someone of Zeph's age to drink Pirie juice. While the juice did not have the same intoxicating effect as the ale from the pub, it made a person appear to be drunk.

They both drank the juice slowly. For Zeph, it was a completely new experience. The liquid tasted incredibly smooth and sweet. He felt a strange sensation as the juice entered his stomach, the juice being absorbed and flowing throughout his entire body. He began to feel like he was floating. Zeph tried to sit down but fell over in the process. On the other hand, his mother had sat down before taking the sip.

"I've only had Pirie juice a handful of times in my life, but this is the best I have ever tasted!" His mother exclaimed. After several minutes of stumbling around the kitchen, Zeph found his way to the chair across from his mother.

"Is it supposed to make you feel like you're weightless?"

"I don't know if it's supposed to, but it does nonetheless," Dawn replied with a laugh, "If you're looking for something to sell to that Captain Victor of yours, I suggest you bring him some of this."

That was a great idea, Zeph thought. He was so happy that he could use his abilities for a helpful purpose. They placed the vial in the cupboard and returned to the living room. Both mother and son had once again regained their composure after the effects of the Pirie juice had dissipated.

Zeph sat fiddling with the scroll. He wanted to know why the scroll was reacting differently to him now than his first interaction. He didn't mind having something that could recharge his Focus, but it still left him with many unanswered questions. Something told him that the answers would come soon enough.

As if by instinct, Zeph suddenly realized how much time had passed since he had come home from school. Pulling out his pocket watch, he noticed it was almost time to return. Zeph was glad he had discovered more about himself, as well as the book and scroll. He couldn't wait to get Marcus and Iggy together to see what would happen with the book.

After thanking his mother for the fun afternoon, he headed back toward the school. As he approached the school, he saw Breeze, Marcus, and Iggy sitting outside under the shade of the large tree that had damaged the school only a few days earlier. Breeze and Marcus had probably gone there after the exam, and Iggy was most likely taking a break between classes.

Zeph ran over with a smile and jumped on the grass beside them. He lay on his back with the biggest smile ever on his face. Everyone glanced down at him; they were looking at him with questioning looks. After everything he had been through, they wondered why he was in such a good mood.

Placing his hands behind his head, he recounted the events that had happened with his mother that afternoon. Somehow, no one was shocked by the story. Marcus, however, had a disappointed look on his face.

"Wait, so you got to try Pirie juice," he asked with a pouty expression. Breeze rolled her eyes, and Zeph and Iggy laughed in unison.

"I have to say, gang, this feels so good. I know exactly how you guys must have felt when you first started using your abilities."

Everyone was happy for Zeph; it was refreshing to see this whole other side of him now. Most of the time, he came across as the strong, silent type, but no one would make that deduction now.

"So you ready for this Social exam?" Marcus asked Zeph.

"Yeah, I think so. It's just Trade, Marketing, Literary Representation, and an Essay. I think we have a bit of personal insight into trade and marketing after this week. I'm worried about the Literary Representation part, but other than that, it will be okay. It will be interesting in the next unit when the classes merge. Not having to worry about Initial will be nice."

"How can you complain about reading and writing? It's not like you've ever known anything different than Initial," Breeze piped up.

"I guess that's true, but I think it's the idea of writing in a language comprised of glyphs and symbols that intrigues me. In theory, a series of words in Initial could be created with a single Glyph."

They thought about Zeph's statement for a moment. Symbology was first, after all, as the ancients had created it. It wasn't until Ages later that mankind created the first alphabet and developed a written language comprised of the primary spoken language. Glyphs, on the other hand, were even more distinct. They were more like groupings of symbols; when combined, they could create greater expression and meaning. Combined correctly, they could even have elemental powers behind them.

"Well, let's do this thing," Zeph said as he quickly stood up.

"Yeah, I guess I should be getting back to class too," Iggy piped up.

"Hang around after, okay? We'll all head home together."

"Alright, see you later, Zeph." With that, Iggy ran off to class. Marcus and Breeze stood up and smiled at Zeph. Neither could remember the last time Zeph had this kind of energy or excitement.

Zeph smiled back; he knew he was acting vastly different than he usually did, but he didn't care. The energy he felt didn't come from the scroll but rather from his own self-esteem and newly discovered purpose. He put his arms around both Marcus and Breeze, and they all walked back to class together.

The test flew by faster than Zeph had expected. He was the first to finish. Mr. Yad followed him out into the hall so they could talk without disturbing the other students. Mr. Yad noticed right away several things had to have happened to Zeph. He told his teacher everything that had happened since he regained consciousness that morning.

"That's a lot to happen in one day, lad. I hope every day in the near future isn't so chaotic," the old teacher said with a chuckle.

"I'm not worried about that. I have a feeling that things will be okay. My life finally has some direction. I'm no longer afraid, and I think that was holding me back. I'm looking forward to these last two months of school, and of course, we have the Cronus-Solar Alignment only a month after that."

Mr. Yad was about to re-enter the classroom when Zeph stopped him. Zeph quickly asked him about Mage Saphar. The name seemed to cause a response from the teacher. Mr. Yad told him he would have to get back to him once he did some research. He did, however, mention that the likelihood of him finding anything was remote.

Since he had completed the exam so early, Zeph knew he had some time to spend on his own. He decided to visit the Temple, to thank Uriym Praotes for everything he had done for him over the last few days.

It was nearing sunset and the light was hitting the building just right as Zeph walked up the path to the Temple. An aura of orange and blue from the suns was cast over the Temple, making it look as though someone had poured liquid light on it. As Zeph reached the top of the hill, he was surprised to see Praotes standing just off to the side of the Temple. Zeph slowly walked up beside the old Uriym. He was staring at the suns. They would soon fall below the blue blanket of the sea. A gentle breeze brushed across Zeph's face, and he fell silent, listening to the waves washing over the shore at the edge of town.

Without turning to acknowledge Zeph, Uriym Praotes spoke up,

"I knew you'd come. Not to thank me as you believed your intentions were but for another reason."

Zeph was surprised, yet he somehow felt it was true. He placed his hand on Praotes' shoulder. If there was any man that Zeph could look to as a grandfather, it was Praotes. He was a spiritual leader and had been very empathetic toward Zeph's family when they were dealing with the loss of Zeph's father.

Still looking out towards the sea, Praotes lifted his hand towards Zeph. He held a parchment scroll. Puzzled, Zeph took the parchment and opened it. At the top, it said, *'Christening Certificate for Iggy, Second*

Son of Khoz and Dawn.' Zeph felt a lump build in his throat. Confused, he walked around Praotes to look him in the eye.

"Why are you showing me this?" Zeph asked with discomfort in his voice. Seeing his father's name brought back the pain and loneliness he still held deep inside.

"That day, you were only a young boy. Merely four years old. You were a young boy who cared for your brother more than anything else in the world. You made a very important promise that day; do you remember it?"

Zeph read the certificate over. His eyes stopped on a series of words. They read, *'Official Guardian: Zeph,'* the line just underneath it was written in Praotes' handwriting, *'I have seen today the purest form of concern and love for a brother that most do not see in a lifetime.'*

"I know those feelings for your brother still reside in you, Zeph. When you feel it is right, please tell Iggy about this. He should know that no matter what he will have to face in this world, you will be by his side." Praotes placed his hands on Zeph's shoulders. "A boy becomes a man the first time he makes a selfless sacrifice for another, when he would risk it all for another, when he places the concern of another before himself. After that day, whenever I saw you, I would think to myself, 'That lad is more than a boy,' and you really are Zeph."

The Uriym pulled Zeph in and hugged him. Zeph thanked him for the last few days and for the years of support the old Uriym had given him. They talked for a short while longer, and then Zeph left the Temple and returned to the school.

Sitting underneath the giant tree once again, he watched as the suns began to touch the water on the horizon. Many different thoughts ran through his mind. So he was Iggy's Guardian. The idea of it left a slightly ill feeling in his stomach. Of course, he loved his brother deeply, but being a Guardian was something a person could only hope to live up to in a lifetime. Whether you were family or friends, pledging to be someone's Guardian meant that you would give your all for that person.

The breeze brushed through his hair. The rays of light from the suns made his white hair glow softly. His blue eyes glistened like the sea he was staring at. Pulling his knees up, he wrapped his arms around them.

What to do now, he wondered. He figured it was time for the group to make more Sphere Lamps in preparation for Captain Victor's return. He was also going to take his mother's suggestion and offer Victor a vial of the Pirie juice. It was likely Victor would not add the juice to his regular inventory because of its high price.

Breeze stepped out of the school, and her eyes instantly focused on Zeph. She felt as though she were in a dream. The way Zeph was sitting caused the light to cast over his face in a way that highlighted all of his features. Until that moment, Breeze had believed only her mind could conjure up such a perfect image. She wondered how long it would be before they thoroughly discussed their feelings for one another, but for now, they would simply enjoy the pleasure of each other's company.

She walked over and sat down next to Zeph. He wrapped his arm around her shoulders, and she around his waist. They sat together silently, staring at the sunset and the sea. No words needed to be said as they sat in comfortable silence. She glanced up at Zeph's face. He seemed almost troubled and deep in thought. Something seemed different about his face. It was as though he had grown up a little more throughout the afternoon.

Soon after Breeze joined Zeph, Marcus and Iggy emerged from the school. They joined the two of them under the tree. Together they all watched the suns set. It was a peaceful moment they hadn't enjoyed together like that for some time. As evening turned into night, the four went their separate ways. Tomorrow they would all meet for a Gathering at the Temple. That was also something that they hadn't done for some time.

The light from the moons bathed the room with a soft blue glow. A gentle breeze crept in slowly from the open window. As Zeph lay in his bed that night, his thoughts were occupied with his newfound ability, Victor's return, the book and scroll, and Iggy. He knew he'd have to tell his brother sooner or later about the information he'd learned that day, but he wanted to wait for the right moment. He did not doubt that the upcoming week would be filled with new discoveries and life-changing events.

DAY 5

Knowing one's self is among the greatest goals in life. Do not think of yourself more highly than you ought, but instead, judge yourself by the measure of faith within you. For a man is nothing without a portion of faith to guide him.

~Praotes

CHAPTER 5
GLYPHS & GOLD

It was a bright day, slightly cooler than average. The odd person was wearing a vest on top of their everyday clothing. Daunt seemed busier than usual that day. Perhaps it was just because the town was experiencing a boost in visitors. The semi-annual festivals always brought in a lot of new visitors. However, this visitor boost was not caused solely by the upcoming festival but also by the Cronus Alignment that coincided with it this year.

Shopkeepers had placed out their best items in an attempt to draw in more 'out of town' folks to their shops. The docks were bustling. Most of the visitors to Daunt arrived by sea. There were several other towns on Appagon, but townsfolk from those towns did not usually arrive in Daunt until a week or two before the festivals. The earlier visitors tended to be those who had never been to Daunt before and had come to learn about the festival and alignment.

It was about mid-afternoon, and four figures were walking down the docks. They reached the end of the main pier. Two of the four people pulled out fishing rods from their packs and sat down at the end of the pier. The other two continued to pace back and forth behind them.

"He's three days overdue!" Zeph exclaimed as he paced back and forth. Both Iggy and Marcus glanced up slightly from their fishing rods to look at Zeph. They shook their heads and looked back to the water below. Breeze grabbed Zeph's hand, causing him to relax a little bit.

This was the third day in a row they had come down to the pier and waited for Captain Victor's return. Zeph knew that the day a merchant sets for return could always deviate slightly. After all, the sea does not always stay on time.

Siah came up behind them, "Any luck yet, boys?"

"He still hasn't arrived," Zeph answered, feeling discouraged.

"I was actually talking about the fishing, but it's good to know where the Victor situation stands," Siah said with a chuckle.

Siah had only just met Victor the last time he had visited Daunt. Victor hadn't come to Daunt to trade but rather to see the town, as Daunt wasn't on his usual trading route.

The World Vortex limited many traders and merchants from doing business beyond certain sections of the Southern Sea. Victor, though, used the Vortex and winds to his advantage. Of course, if Victor made one wrong course correction, his ship would be lying at the bottom of the ocean.

This same thought had haunted Zeph around the same time yesterday. He tried to shrug it off. Victor was, after all, a highly skilled merchant captain, perhaps the best in the southern seas. Building a ship to sail the World Vortex was a feat most captains wouldn't even attempt.

Zeph stopped his pacing momentarily and sat down next to Marcus and Iggy. Both boys turned to look at Zeph in unison. Needless to say, it was a little unsettling. His best friend and his little brother, what a combo, yet it seemed to fit in its own way.

It was the last day of the week, and Zeph had hoped that this would be the day of Victor's arrival. Other than attending the morning Gathering, they had the rest of the day free. The suns were still high in the sky. Perhaps Marcus and Iggy would finally catch something today.

Not a second after the thought crossed his mind, both boys were tugging on their lines in unison. Marcus was the first to reel his fish in. It was a Rainbow fish, a common fish around the coast of Daunt. The thick scales reflected bright colors in the light and were commonly used in different jewelry. Iggy was next to reel in his fish, revealing an Orange Sneer. It earned its name from its bright orange scales and elongated jaw, giving the impression that it was mocking you.

"That's so weird," Zeph said with a perplexed expression, "I was just imagining you catching those exact fish."

"That is a little weird, but so are a lot of things with you lately," Marcus said as he held up his catch. Iggy did the same. Both fish were a decent size and could easily feed the four of them. Siah offered to clean the fish, and they immediately took him up on his offer. He returned shortly with the meat wrapped in brown paper and two small bags.

"I'm guessing you boys will want to keep the scales," he said, handing a bag to Marcus and Iggy. They looked at each other, then nodded their agreement.

Zeph was still staring out to sea. He was standing at the end of the main pier with nothing but the ocean filling his view. A seamless tapestry of blue from water to sky. Breeze came up behind him and placed her hand on his shoulder. He instantly recalled the evening several weeks earlier when he had put his arm around her. He knew they would soon have to talk about their relationship and feelings for each other.

"Zeph, Breeze," Marcus called out, "Let's go to Sieve's and eat this fish, I don't think it will make Victor get here any slower." Marcus did have a point, so Zeph agreed, and the four of them headed over to Sieve's Grill and Meat Market.

Sieve's Grill and Meat Market was located at the center of the docks. It was an open-area shop. It had no walls and a simple straw and leaf roof. In the middle was a circular bar counter surrounding the large grill and meat rack. If you had just purchased some raw meat from the docks and wanted to eat it immediately, Sieve's was the place to go. A person could either bring their own meat or purchase something from Sieve's selection.

Marcus slapped the brown paper package down on the counter while the rest of the group sat at a nearby table. Sieve walked over and raised an eyebrow at Marcus.

"You haven't been around much, Marcus. I was beginning to wonder where you were," Sieve said as he opened the package. He was a foreigner to Daunt. Not much was known about him other than he had traveled from a distant land somewhere in the Water Realm. His accent was evident, especially when he stretched the vowel sounds in some words much longer than intended.

Sieve threw the meat down on the large grill. The coals sizzled as the fish began to cook. Marcus pulled out one of his silver kessas and handed it to Sieve. The little round man waved his hands and shook his head.

"No, no, Marcus, you know your coin is no good here," he said with a smile. Several years earlier, when Sieve arrived in Daunt, Marcus' parents had taken the man in until he could make a living. Sieve had told them that there was no proper way to repay a person for such generosity in his Realm. Instead, Sieve always offered free services to the family whenever they needed them. Marcus was the one who first started calling him Sieve. The man's full name was Tapsieve'Yow, but Marcus had simplified it so his customers had something easier to call him.

Sieve waved him off and told Marcus he would call him when it was ready. Marcus walked over and sat down. He spun the kessa on the table, and then a thought came to him.

"Hey, do you all still have your two kessas from before?" Everyone nodded in response to his question. "That's kind of weird, isn't it?"

"Well, to be honest, I almost spent them the first day I got them," Zeph replied. "But after I thought about it, I figured we might need them in the future."

"Yeah, and come to think of it, I'm pretty sure my dad still has his too," Breeze added.

"You have to wonder how much Victor is selling the Sphere Lamps for, or if he was even able to sell them."

"I'm pretty sure he was able to sell them, Marcus," Iggy replied.

"Well, I sure hope so, or it would have been a huge waste of the last two weeks, every day after school making more of them. How many are we up to now?"

"Thirty-seven," Zeph replied without hesitation as he reached down into his shoulder bag.

"See... now, how do you know that exact number?" Marcus questioned.

"Well, let's see. First of all, Victor said he would be back in two weeks. Two days ago, he would have been gone for exactly two weeks. Being that I didn't come out of my coma until two days after he left, we didn't start making them until two weeks ago today. We made three a day except on the last day of each week since we all felt pretty drained by the end of the week. Yesterday, we made four instead of three; therefore, we have made thirty-seven in the last fourteen days," Zeph closed with a somewhat triumphant look.

Marcus blinked for a moment, then shook his head. Everyone laughed at that. Sieve walked over with a platter of fish. It smelled great and caused all their mouths to start salivating with anticipation.

Zeph pulled his Glyph book from his bag. It was soft-bound with brown leather. All of the students in the class had received one on the first day of the new unit. They had also received a book of Symbols. Zeph had also studied that book, but he was far more interested in the glyphs than the symbols.

The main difference between a Symbol and a Glyph was how it was used and its meaning. Symbols were representations of objects or things. Words such as 'house,' 'door,' or 'path' were basic examples of symbols. Glyphs, on the other hand, were representations of actions or feelings. 'Burning,' 'protect, 'peace,' and 'anger' were prime examples of glyphs.

On each page of the book was a Glyph. Underneath it was a description of its meaning and its use. Instructions on how to draw or engrave it properly were also included. If you planned to simply write the glyph, detail and precision weren't that important. However, if you intended to use its elemental properties, you had to write or engrave the glyph precisely, or nothing would happen.

When Glyphs were written, they had no more power than a drop of ink. This was before they were written with the Tears of God. The Tears of God came from one of seven unique springs found around the world. It was said that Ta'Hor had found each of the springs while journeying across Arkhay. No one knew when Omega created these springs, but they knew they were instructed to place a drop on each of their children's foreheads. This, in turn, revealed a person's elemental alignment by creating a permanent symbol on the person's forehead. It wasn't until many years later that mankind discovered that writing glyphs with the liquid created mystical reactions and empowerments.

Rings and amulets were everyday items that could be engraved and empowered. A person would take a ring to the Engraving Shop, and have a glyph engraved on it. When several drops of the Tears of God were placed in the engraving, they would glow and seal the engraving, making it smooth. This, of course, would only happen if the engraving was done precisely. A black marking of the glyph would remain over the engraved area.

It was extremely expensive to have items or weapons empowered. Having just one glyph attached to an item could cost twenty gold kessas or more. The price varied between shops, and if you could provide the item and Tears of God yourself, most engravers would drop the price.

Zeph studied the book in his hands. He had spent a great deal of time memorizing the glyphs. After two weeks, he had more than several dozen memorized. His progress in studying the Symbol book was less extensive, but he had also made significant progress in memorizing them as well. Between the two books, there were nearly five hundred symbols to learn, and these were only the primary glyphs and symbols. There were several thousand overall. Students only needed to know the primary of both unless they planned to be a scribe, then they needed to know all of them.

The other three continued to eat and watch Zeph as they studied the page. He would hold the book in his left hand and let his right hand float in the air next to him. After several moments of studying one of the glyphs, he would draw it in the air with his fingers. He continued to do this as he flipped through the pages.

Finally, Zeph replaced the book in his shoulder bag and began to eat. Everyone else had already finished eating, so they continued watching Zeph.

"Do you all have to watch me eat?" he asked, sending awkward looks in all directions.

"Would you prefer us to watch you make your hand dance in the air some more?" Marcus asked in return. There wasn't anger in his voice, but Zeph could sense some frustration.

"Come on, you all know that Glyphs are one of the only things I feel I have a connection to."

"Yeah, we know; just leave the book in the bag once in a while, okay? Have some fun with us. A month ago, we could have never seen all this coming. First Xa'an and the scroll, then making the Sphere Lamps, and now we're trading with merchant captains. This is all really new." Marcus said, staring across the table at Zeph.

Finishing his food, Zeph stood up, and the rest followed. They walked back into town, away from the docks. The shops were bustling with the increase of visitors in Daunt. All the shops were set as 'open-air' shops for the festivals. All the shopkeepers would set up their best goods on tables just outside their shops.

Zeph walked over to the table in front of the Weapons Shop. The table had rows of all different kinds of swords, daggers, and blades. A rack off to the side had various types of bows lined against it. There was no plate armor selection, as the material to make plate armor was too expensive for such a small town shop. Zeph was about to turn and leave when he noticed a sword at the end of the table. It was a style he had never seen before. The blade was very jagged, with small points along the length of the sword. It looked like it would not only slice but also rip and tear whatever it was plunged into. Zeph shuddered at the thought and continued to the following tables.

Marcus had stopped by the table outside the Embroidery Shop. The vibrant colors of the fabric had drawn him over. His mother had been a seamstress since he was a small child. Perhaps that was the reason why he enjoyed looking at different fabrics. One of the fabrics at the end of the table caught his eye. It was black but reflected a deep shimmer of red when the light caught it from different angles. Marcus ran his hands over it and felt how incredibly smooth it was. He made a mental note of it as he continued browsing.

Iggy had made his way to the Alchemist Shop. Although the shop was minimal, Iggy still wanted to see what kinds of potions and remedies were on display. Each bottle on the table was labeled for easy reference. Iggy had been studying the process of alchemy on his own for the last little bit. The process of creating potions had always fascinated him since he first started using his Light abilities. Iggy stopped and picked up a potion, sitting off to the side. It was black and looked relatively thick. The label had a glyph on it rather than a name. Iggy made a mental note to ask Zeph about it later and continued to scan the shops.

Breeze had wandered from shop to shop, not finding anything that interesting. She soon came to the Fabrication Shop. It had once been her father's shop. That was before the town leaders had kindly asked him to close it down. Because of that, she had a natural dislike for this specific shop. A small device at the end of the table caught her eye. It was a black sphere with three rings locked in place around it. As she pushed one ring, another would start moving and rotating around the sphere. It was strange; she would have to ask her dad later what kind of contraption it was.

After a while, their disbanded group of four met up in the town square. Each talked about the shops they had been to. They were surprised to hear that each had found an item of particular interest. Iggy told Zeph about the potion with the glyph on the label. It meant 'shadows,' but in an action sense, like when a passing cloud would block the suns and cast a shadow. Zeph found it odd that a potion was named in such a way.

"This is a little strange, but that seems to be the new trend with us," said Marcus as he gazed from one person to the next within their group. "I have to say, it will be nice to have a bit more money when Victor returns. It was nice of my mom to buy the material for the Sphere Lamp bags, but she can't afford to buy any more black cloth fabric herself. Also, we should maybe think about..." Marcus' words were cut off by the ringing of the pier bell. The bell was in the Trading Post in the middle of the docks. It was usually rung if a ship could be seen approaching Daunt on the horizon. This way, the dockhands knew that their services might be needed.

The group took off running down towards the docks, quickly making their way towards the end of the main pier. They all looked out to sea but couldn't see anything. Zeph ran back down the dock to the trading post. Siah met him at the door.

"I don't see anything out there, Siah," Zeph said urgently.

"That's because you're not using one of these, boy," Siah said, tapping a finger on the metal pipe in his hand.

"What is it?" Zeph asked.

"I picked it up from a Thai merchant several months ago. It uses several glass lenses to make something in the distance appear much larger. He said it was called a Scope," Siah replied as he handed it to Zeph.

Zeph peered through the end of the scope and looked out to sea. It took him several minutes to locate it, but sure enough, the *Nephesh* was on the horizon. She looked beautiful. Siah told him that the ship would arrive within minutes at the rate the ship was coming in.

The excitement bubbled in Zeph as he ran back to Marcus, Iggy, and Breeze. They were all standing on the end of the main pier, looking out towards the sea with anticipation.

THE WAVES ROSE HIGH with every dip of the ship. The suns shone down without a cloud to block their light. The brilliant blue sea sparkled in the afternoon suns as water splashed over the deck of the *Nephesh*. Today, of all days, the ship held its name well. A *Nephesh* was a creature from the ancient time of the Uriel. Its name meant 'breathing creature'. The name bestowed a sense of power, like when a creature would take a massive breath before devouring its prey.

The ship had picked up a great deal of speed after the Vortex. The sea air and ocean spray blew across Victor's face. The red bandana on his head kept his long black dreads together. Ocean spray blew across his open white shirt and black pants; he was completely drenched. His tall black boots held him firm on the deck as he gripped the wheel.

The *Nephesh* gleamed on the water like a jewel. The long, sleek ship flew across the water. Light shone off of the polished wood paneling. Daunt seemed to be racing towards the *Nephesh*. Victor looked behind him at the men taking up positions to break. Usually, a ship this size would never move this fast. However, with the currents of the Vortex combined with the wind patterns, the speed could become almost unimaginable for a sailing vessel. As a captain, you would take advantage of it for as long as the ocean would carry you. But there would always come a time when you needed to slow down, and that was the tricky part today. The *Nephesh* flew across the surface of the water like a bolt of lightning; Victor gripped the ship's wheel hard and shouted out,

"Begin breaking procedure!"

"Alright, you heard the captain. We need to slow this beast down, and we need to do it in a hurry!" Koch yelled out across the desk.

He was short, no taller than an average man's shoulders, but built like a stone boulder. Koch had joined up with Victor several years earlier. Since then he had proven himself to be more than a man, and he had saved the captain's life on many occasions. Victor had made him his first mate in recognition of his great deeds.

The crew responded instantly to the first mate's words. They first brought in the wing sails. They were one of Victor's inventions. Sails that extended outward from the ship's sides in a wing-like fashion. These wings allowed the vessel to partially lift off the water at high speeds, and at that moment, the *Nephesh* was almost flying. The sails folded neatly into compartments on each side of the ship.

Next, the crew extended two long beams attached to smaller wooden arms from each side of the ship. The long beams ran parallel to the ship's hull and helped to steady and slow the ship down. They hit the water with a splash and locked into place. The speed was decreasing, but not fast enough. Daunt loomed ahead, and unless the ship could be slowed further, they would crash into the docks.

The ship began to ride on the water and less on the air. A loud rush came roaring up from the bottom of the boat as the hull became fully in contact with the water. Victor fought for control of his ship. The ship was rapidly slowing down, but still not enough.

"Release the breaking sails!" he yelled to Koch.

The breaking sails were a last resort. Victor had never needed to use them before, but with the speed the ship occasionally got up to, he felt it was necessary to have them. The men ran to the ship's stern and opened two large hatches. From each hatch came a large white shoot.

The shoots burst open immediately, causing the ship to wrench from the force. It began to shake violently. Lengths of rope held the shoots from down inside the bowels of the *Nephesh*. Fear gripped Victor as Daunt continued to race toward him. The ship had slowed significantly but was still moving fast enough to crash into the docks. Victor knew they had less than thirty seconds until the ship reached the docks. Knowing it would guarantee damage to the ship, Victor gave *The Order* anyway.

"Drop anchors!" he hollered.

Men on both sides of the ship pulled large metal levers as two steel anchors fell into the water on either side. The starboard anchor hit the water with a splash and immediately found the sea floor. The chain ripped backward violently, ripping the wood paneling off the ship's side. Debris struck one of the crewmen in the chest, sending the man flying across the deck. The second anchor had also reached the sea floor. Pulling backward violently, the chain broke through the port stabilization beam, snapping it in two.

A wave came rushing down the pier, drenching Zeph and the others as they ran from the looming vessel. They turned just in time to see the battered *Nephesh* drift softly into the docks. Marcus stood up, quickly dried himself off with flames from his palms, and then did the same for the rest of their group.

Siah, along with a dock crew, ran over to the ship. The damage looked quite severe in several places. Koch ran over to help the downed crewmen. Rather than waiting for the dockhands to bring the plank, Victor jumped down. Siah thanked him for his effort in not crashing into the docks, as several other smaller ships would have most likely been destroyed. He offered to help Victor with repairs and healing for the injured crew members. Victor graciously accepted.

A smile came over Victor's face as he walked down the dock towards the four youths waiting for him.

"Don't tell me you've been standing here for the last two weeks," he said with a chuckle. Zeph opened his mouth to speak, but Victor interrupted, "And before you start pointing it out, yes, I am three days later than I said I would be. However, my reasons will bring smiles to your faces." Zeph closed his mouth and smiled. It was great to have Victor back.

Victor spent the next several hours inspecting his ship and taking note of the damage. The chain from the starboard anchor had ripped off much of the outer wood paneling. It wouldn't be that difficult to repair. The port side was another matter, though. The anchor chain had snapped the port stabilization beam in two. That would take at least several days to repair. Other than that, the ship had handled relatively well.

All the sails were intact, which brought a great deal of relief to Victor. The wing sails were still carefully tucked away on each side of the ship. The three main sails were closed and functioning fine. The three main sail masts were on rotating bearings. This allowed for each mast to be turned and rotated. The masts needed to have such a function to catch the wind required to sail in close proximity to the Vortex.

Victor climbed down from the lookout atop the main mast and joined Zeph and the others on the main deck.

"She'll hold; she always does," he said with a grin. "Take the day off, boys. You can get an early start in the morning," Victor shouted to his crew working on the ship. They cheered and scampered off the ship.

Victor invited the group of youths into his cabin aboard the *Nephesh*. It was larger than Zeph was expecting. There was no bed, just a comfortable-looking hammock off to the side of the cabin. A table, relatively low to the floor, was in the center of the room. Several large pillows were placed around it. There was also a desk off to the corner of the cabin. Several large chests lay against the opposite wall. All in all, it was a rather impressive living space.

The group took up seats on one of the pillows around the table. Victor walked over to one of the chests and removed a fresh shirt. He removed his bandana and soiled shirt he had been wearing. Victor had a muscular look to his overall physique, as any man would after years of being a sailor. His Water elemental mark could be seen on his forehead. It was common for those born with Water ability, and in coastal cities, to become sailors.

Tying up the white shirt, he lay down in the hammock. His long black hair hung from the sides. It had started to form dreads in many places from weeks of not running a comb through it. Breeze wondered what he would look like if his hair was clean and combed. The one thing that was obvious about Victor's hygiene was his facial hair. Granted, it was a little rough at the moment, but it was clear that he shaved often.

Swinging his legs out, he sat with his back against the wall and looked at the four pairs of eyes staring back at him. He felt as though he should be some sort of a teacher with the amount of attentiveness he was being shown at that moment.

"So!" he exclaimed, clapping his hands together. "What have you kids been up to the last two weeks?"

Zeph tossed a small black bag from his satchel to Victor. There was no need for explanations. Victor let the ball fall out of the bag and onto his hand. The fire danced and swirled within the glass of the Sphere Lamp.

"These are revolutionary!" Victor exclaimed as he held up the glowing ball. "These are fantastic! I visited a much larger town than Daunt, and it mesmerized them. I sold them all within the first few minutes. Every family in the town wanted one, if not a whole handful, to place throughout their house," Victor said with a gleam in his eye as he held out the glowing ball. "You truly have no idea what you have created here."

"People are really that crazy about them?" Marcus asked with an astonished look on his face.

"Oh, you bet they are," Victor said, standing up, "I'm guessing that you have made more of them then?"

"We've managed to make thirty-seven more," Zeph spoke up.

Victor nodded for a moment. "Well, that is more than I expected, but the people of Krino want more than three dozen, much more. They could easily buy several hundred of them."

Everyone shot an odd look in Victor's direction. Iggy was the first to speak, "Krino?" he asked.

"Oh, right. I forgot you aren't familiar with towns other than those on Appagon. Krino is a city I have done much trading with over the last several years. It's located on the southern continent of Tsayla," Victor explained.

"Tsayla?" Breeze questioned, trying to pronounce the name the same way Victor had, with an odd 'tsss' sound.

Victor laughed, "I'm actually not that surprised you haven't heard of it. The people on Tsayla, well, let's just say, are very dark and secretive. The Shadow Realm is quite a different place compared to Daunt."

Victor joined the group around the table. Zeph brought up the topic of making more Sphere Lamps. The discussion continued until they heard a knock on the door. Victor shot everyone a questioning look and smiled as he walked over to the cabin door.

"I hope I'm not intruding; I just didn't have the time to stand around the docks all day," Gus said, shaking Victor's hand.

"Not at all; in fact, I was almost disappointed when you were not with the kids. I know that if I was even half the inventor you are, I could make a killing as a merchant," Victor said, showing Gus to one of the pillows.

This was the first time Victor and Gus had met. Although, with stories of each other being passed back and forth, the two men felt as though they had already met. Despite Gus being almost twenty years older than Victor, both men had a similar physique. If not for Gus' grey hair, he could have easily passed for a man in his thirties like Victor. Looking at the two men, Zeph wondered how people would judge his age once he was older. He guessed his white hair would throw many people off.

Zeph brought up the topic of the Sphere Lamps once again, and the conversation continued. In this conversation, everyone discovered why Victor had been several days late. It turned out that while he was in Krino, a messenger from a town in the mainland of Tsayla had asked Victor if the sphere could be made larger, ten times the size they were now. Victor told the man he was unsure, as the lamps were in an experimental stage. The messenger bought a sphere lamp and asked if Victor would remain for two more days. Victor agreed.

Two days later, the man returned, along with the mayor of his town. The mayor was a man by the name of Bain. Victor could tell by Bain's attire that he was exceptionally wealthy. Bain told Victor that their town was in the final stages of a lamp oil shortage, and that soon there would be no steady supply for their lamps. He had been sending out messengers to all the neighboring towns in search of oil reserves that would be willing to trade.

Victor wasn't sure how he could help the man, but he listened anyway. Bain asked if the spheres could be made larger, perhaps ten times larger. The larger spheres would be used as the town's street lamps, replacing the large oil-consuming ones.

Victor initially hesitated since he had yet to learn whether the lamps could be made larger. Bain seemed rather desperate, though. He told Victor that money wasn't an issue; he could pay whatever was asked. Victor felt quite sure the statement was true, as the man wore an exquisite black suit.

"What did the suit look like?" Marcus asked, cutting into the story. Everyone glared at him as Victor laughed and continued.

"So it was then that Bain asked what the price of a Sphere Lamps was. Now you kids know I gave you two silver kessas for them. Just so you know what the markup is, I had planned to sell them for five," Victor explained as he paced around the room. Everyone seemed okay with the price Victor gave. After all, he did have to go through a lot to sell them.

"However, the demand was much greater than I was expecting," he paused for effect, then continued, "I sold them for two gold kessas each."

Everyone's jaws dropped except Gus, who simply smiled. Opening one of the chests with a silver key from his waist, he removed a leather bag from it. Walking over to Zeph, he handed him five silver kessas. Continuing down the line, he handed everyone else in the room the same amount.

"Let's make it an even split. Those five kessas go with the two I gave you before. If I sell them for two gold kessas each, you deserve half the profits. I can pay you each seven silver kessas or one gold kessa; it's up to you." They agreed that since Daunt was such a small town, and rarely dealt with gold coins, silver coins would be more practical.

Victor jumped into his hammock and crossed his legs. It was almost like watching a little boy at times, Zeph thought with a smile. Everyone placed the coins into some sort of carrying bag and turned back to Victor. He had left them at the climax, and they waited anxiously to hear what Bain had offered Victor for the lamps.

After everyone quieted down, Victor continued with the story. Bain said he would give Victor any price he offered. Victor was a virtuous man and had no intentions of swindling the man's money, plus it was bad for business. He told Bain that if he wanted them to be roughly ten times the size of the current one, then he would charge ten times the price. Bain agreed and offered Victor some of the money upfront. Victor refused and told Bain to save the money for his return.

"So let me get this straight," Marcus said, "if we can make the lamps ten times bigger than this, Bain will pay you twenty gold kessas for them?"

Victor let out a mischievous grin, "That is absolutely right, Marcus."

Everyone took a moment for the reality of the situation to sink in. Iggy seemed to be discouraged, though. Victor watched Iggy's expression as thoughts ran through his head. His eyes caught Victor's. A concerned look came over Victor's face. As if reading Iggy's thoughts, Victor walked over to one of the chests and removed a handful of small vials.

"These are Focus Rejuvenation potions," Victor said, holding one of the vials for everyone to see. Zeph remembered those; he also remembered vomiting all over the temple floor.

"This project will be long, tiresome, and strenuous. That is why I purchased these vials. I wasn't sure if Daunt sold them, and I knew we would need them."

Iggy's expression quickly improved as he continued to listen to Victor. He knew that much of the project rested on his shoulders. Like many young boys Iggy's age, he was plagued with a lack of self-confidence.

"I, myself, will do what I can to help. I'm guessing that someone able to distort water could come in handy. I plan to stick by each and every one of you. I have seen many things in my life on the seas, but I have never seen a group of kids as extraordinary as the four of you." Everyone looked at Victor. The statement would form a new bond between everyone in the group, though none of them knew it yet.

The day grew to a close. Everyone stood on the docks and walked back into town as the suns set. Gus offered Victor a place to stay at his house, but Victor felt his crew staying at the Inn would be insulted, so he politely turned Gus down.

Gus and Breeze said their goodnights and headed out of town towards their house. Just Zeph, Marcus, and Iggy remained. Twilight colored the sky a deep bluish-orange. Villagers lit the lamps that lined the road through town. Zeph was full of energy, as were the other boys. Victor gave Zeph a feeling he hadn't felt since his father was around. Iggy felt it, too, even though he had only been four years old when their father had disappeared.

Marcus was about to head over to his house when Zeph stopped him. He invited him to spend the night with Iggy and himself. Marcus agreed, although he felt there was some sort of additional motive in Zeph's offer.

A chill found its way up Zeph's arm. The night had crept up fast. The pleasant conversation had drawn to a close, and the boys continued in silence. It was blatantly apparent that something was on Zeph's mind. Even as they entered the house, the chill seemed to follow the boys upstairs.

The house was dark. Their mother must have gone to bed early. Zeph entered his room, with Marcus and Iggy following close behind. The darkness was broken as Zeph removed his sphere lamp from its bag and placed it on the bed. The flickering light danced about the room. They could have stared at the ball for hours. The fire inside commanded their eyes' attention.

Zeph sat down on the bed and took off his satchel bag. Marcus had found it slightly odd that Zeph had taken his bag with him everywhere for the last two weeks, but never brought it up. Removing the history book from the bag, Zeph laid it open on the bed. The Omega symbol glowed softly on the inside cover. If only they could see what he saw, Zeph thought.

Turning his attention to the boys, he spoke up. "I have something to tell the both of you. Whether the two of you know it or not, I have been keeping a secret from you. I had no idea how you would react, especially after everything that happened with the scroll."

Marcus and Iggy shot glances at each other in the dimly lit room. Zeph's words were unexpected but also didn't take them by surprise, given everything that had happened over the last several weeks.

"These symbols," Zeph said, holding the sphere lamp up to the ceiling, "I think I know how they got up there." The two pairs of eyes staring back at Zeph were not confused as he was expecting, but rather intrigued.

Zeph flipped through the book until he was on the page where he had encountered the message before. Like before, he read the last paragraph out loud and watched as the glowing words appeared. Watching a book write itself with illuminated words was astonishing. Marcus and Iggy quickly sat on each side of Zeph and watched as the words continued to appear.

'The few, the chosen, one will come from every Age. The one chosen in the Seventh Age will bring forth the destiny of this world. They will be the last chosen and the last chance of Hope for the world.'

The words began to transform into strands of light, which spread to the opposing blank page. They moved along every crack and crease on the paper, reforming into the Omega, Fire, and Light symbols in the middle of the page.

"Whoa..." Marcus said with a gasp.

"Double Whoa..." Iggy said in return.

The symbols arranged themselves in a triangle formation with the Omega at the top, the Fire on the left, and the Light on the right. The boys looked at each other and realized that the symbols were in the exact positions they were sitting in.

The chill crept up the stairs of the house but would not enter the room with the boys. Wind rattled the window pane. A cold sweat had formed on the back of each of the boy's necks.

Zeph reached out and touched the Omega symbol. He had expected to see the greeting from the mage as he had before. The triangle grew, and the other two symbols slid down the page. Zeph looked at Marcus and Iggy. Both boys reached out and touched their symbol.

The symbols turned into bright strands of light, much brighter than before. They moved to the edges of the page, making a shining border of light. Then, at the top of the page, words began to appear.

'*Greetings to you, Zeph, Marcus, and Iggy. I am Mage Saphar. Let me start by saying that it was no coincidence that you came across this book. I developed the ability to see future events in my late youth. This is something that is found in the depths of the Omega abilities but does not commonly manifest.*

By our calendars, there are two hundred and seventy-eight years until the start of the Seventh Age. I have seen many visions of you since my youth, though I knew not who you were. I then came to the realization that you are the Omega Chosen One. I, too, was blessed with the gift of Omega. Though I can teach you a little about your abilities, there are things you must learn in order to face what is coming.

There is one thing I must tell you above all else. Marcus and Iggy, you must take great precautions to protect Zeph on the journey that will soon be upon him. You must ensure that no harm befalls him, or all will be lost.

There is a creature that will come amongst you. It will reach out with an arm of friendship and hold a dagger of deception behind its back. Its power is not of this world, and death has lost control to take its breath away. Beware of those that hide themselves in shadows.

I cannot tell you more of this without changing the path you must take. Please study the Glyphs on the next page; they will be crucial to your journey. They will guide you and, if need be, save your life.

I have received dozens of visions throughout the course of my life; most of them have been of you, Zeph. You will save this world; you will bring Hope. If the three of you wish to read this message again, you only need to close the book and touch the symbols again. The Glyphs I spoke of will remain on the next page.'

The page turned, revealing twelve glyphs. Under each was a brief description of their meanings and usage. Zeph had never come across them in his studies. He assumed they were not part of the prime glyphs in the school guide.

"This is starting to get a little heavy again," said Marcus as he placed his hands on his knees.

"Do you think this Saphar guy is for real?" Iggy asked as he glanced over at Zeph.

"Does it matter?" Zeph asked back. The question caught both Iggy and Marcus off guard. "Someone that lived over four hundred years ago has seen parts of my life. He says he wants to help me; I have to believe him."

"What about everything he said about a creature and all that 'friendship-dagger' stuff?" Marcus asked with a concerned tone in his voice.

"What am I supposed to say to that? I don't know what he's talking about." Zeph blurted out.

"Just the way he described it and his reference to 'hiding in shadows,' it almost sounds like Xa'an."

As soon as the words left Iggy's lips, they began to burrow deep into Zeph's brain. That couldn't be who Saphar was talking about, could it? Zeph's mind began to race as he played over the situation in his mind.

"There's no way... I mean, he couldn't..." Zeph's words sputtered out as his mind continued to race.

Marcus stood up from the bed, his body tense and head held high.

"You know what. I'm going to be the first to say that I don't think it's Xa'an. He looked after us when he was here. He showed us new things. If anything, he's our protector, not some creature of shadows that's going to betray us." Marcus' words rang out so profoundly that they put Zeph and Iggy's doubts to rest. Xa'an was their friend, and a cryptic message from the past would not change their opinions that easily.

Zeph closed the book and placed it in his bag, which he hung on his bedpost. Marcus pulled the additional bedding out of the corner chest and set up his bed on the floor next to Zeph. Iggy headed off to his room. Everyone seemed a little tense. It seemed like getting a good night's sleep was the best remedy for the situation. The boys began to fall into a deep sleep.

Zeph closed his eyes and tried to let his mind relax. A chill brushed past his face. He lifted his head towards the direction of the window; it was still closed. A shiver covered his body momentarily as though he were standing out in the cold. The darkness of the night crept around him. Fear gripped his chest that he hadn't felt since he was a small boy. His sleep was restless as he drifted off into his dreams.

THE AIR FELT FANTASTIC. Not as fresh as the sea air, mind you, but Victor enjoyed it all the same. He had risen early once again to work on the *Nephesh*. Two days had passed since they had almost crashed into the docks. The repairs were going well, and a lot of progress was being made. Victor estimated that only one more day would be needed.

Victor tugged on the rope around his waist. Pushing off from the side of the ship, he leaped farther down the wood paneling. He had spent most of the previous day attached to this rope, nailing the new siding onto the ship's hull. The last thing he needed to do now was stain and seal the wood.

Victor was grateful that the chain had not destroyed the engravings along the ship's stern. He ran his hands over the words carved into the wood. *Wherever this Ship may Roam, may the Sea always be our Home.* The words rang out in the captain's head as his fingers followed the carved lines in the wood.

"Captain, we're ready," Koch called down to him. Victor climbed up the rope and onto the deck of the ship. A row of men stood on the dock next to a very long beam of wood. It would be used to replace the port balance beam. Victor had worried that the wood would be of a different density than the starboard beam. Siah had assured him they had taken the necessary measures to ensure the proper weight.

Taking up the lead position, Victor and the other crewmen picked up the massive beam. It was close to thirty feet long and weighed nearly as much as a dozen full-grown men. The town folk watched as a dozen men carried the beam up onto the deck of the *Nephesh*. The crew began to mount the beam to the arms that would hold it in place. Shortly after, the men lifted the beam and threw it overboard. It floated on top of the water perfectly. The crew then attached it to the slots on the ship's side and rigged it back into place.

One more day and the ship would be able to get underway. Victor walked down the docks, glancing at the other ships in port. Most of them were much smaller than the *Nephesh*. He figured most of them were tourists' boats. The design of the ships led Victor to believe that most of them had come from Sire. He had visited the city of Thai on the coast of Sire maybe once or twice his whole life. It was extremely out of the way from his regular trading routes, so it was a rare occurrence.

Victor continued to make his way down the docks. A lone figure began to walk towards Victor among the figures walking the docks. His path carried him through the bustling dock like a stone falling in a pool of water. Without even a gesture or a shift in his body, the bystanders seemed to part to make a path for him. The boy's blue eyes sparkled in the morning suns, as did his pure white hair. His presence spread the path before him like dust blowing in the wind.

Victor had never seen a presence so strong from someone so young, not even when he had met with Bain, a man of great importance and wealth. The boy wore black boots similar to Victor's. Fine white pants covered his legs. A brass belt buckle shone in the light. His short-sleeved deep blue shirt enhanced the brightness of the white vest that lay over it. A strap of black leather found its way across the boy's chest and down to the bag resting against the boy's hip.

Zeph stood before the captain. Victor was speechless as he stared at him. Finally, a series of words came out.

"How did you pay for all that?" Victor asked, still astonished at the presence Zeph was exuding. Zeph was radiating confidence and causing people to stop and stare.

"You did, as a matter of fact," Zeph replied with a cheeky grin. Victor raised an eyebrow at his response. "Before your mind goes any further, we need to talk business," Zeph said, gesturing toward the *Nephesh*. Both of them boarded the ship and went straight for Victor's cabin.

"Let me start by saying that the bill for the boots, pants, belt, shirt, vest, and bag came to fifty-three sliver kessas. I told the merchant that if he allowed me to have these items, I would have his money for him within the hour," Zeph explained as he sat on one of the pillows.

"You're a good kid, Zeph, but you had better explain before I hand over that much coin, simply for a new outfit," Victor said with a hint of annoyance in his voice. He sat down in his hammock and waited for Zeph's response.

Reaching into his bag, Zeph pulled out a small vial of red liquid. It easily fit the palm of his hand. Offering it to Victor, he encouraged him to drink it. Though slightly hesitant, Victor felt confident that Zeph wasn't trying to poison him. He drank it down with a flip of the vial. Several seconds passed by before the effect hit.

Victor's eyes shot over to Zeph. "Where did you get this?" he asked as he steadied himself in the hammock.

"I learned several weeks ago that I can recharge people's elemental Focus. After an experiment with my mother, she caused a Pirie plant to grow three times its size and produce dozens of shells rather than one shell at a time. The shells were also much larger than what the plant would normally produce as well. Where one shell would normally fill three vials like the one you're holding, it now fills ten. This being said, and with your sampling of the product, I would like to make a business deal with you."

The air stood still in the cabin as Zeph came to his close. Victor tried to stand; even with experienced sea legs, he was no match for the effects of the Pirie juice and fell back into his hammock once more. He tried several more times before accepting defeat. He held the small vial above his face and spun it in his hands. It was the smallest vial you could buy, often called a two-shot vial by bartenders.

"I'll give you three gold kessas for vials this size," Victor finally said.

"I also offer a large size, equal to ten small vials. Are you interested?" Zeph asked.

"I'll give you the same markup, thirty gold kessas. Although, I think I'd only be able to sell one or two in that size to wealthy people," Victor replied as he tried to stand once more. This attempt proved worthwhile this time. He walked over to one of the chests and took out two bags of coins.

"Will that shopkeeper accept gold kessas?" he asked, glancing over at Zeph.

"He said he would."

"Good, then take him what you owe him for everything you bought and return quickly. We will talk about business more once you return," Victor said, handing Zeph the appropriate mixture of gold and silver kessas to pay the bill.

Zeph returned to the cabin a short while later. Victor was still lying on his hammock. The Pirie juice had taken its toll on Victor. Turning his head to Zeph's presence, Victor smiled. He sat up slowly, still experiencing some side effects from the juice.

"You are a shrewd businessman. Honestly, I never would have thought you would pull a stunt like this. I've never run up a tab and expected a business partner to pay for it. Was your father the same way?"

The question caught Zeph off guard. He thought about it for a moment, recalling memories of his father and stories he had been told by his mother.

"I would say yes. My father disappeared when I was nine, but I still remember a lot about him," Zeph couldn't recall the last time he had mentioned anything about his father to anyone besides those in Daunt who knew him personally.

"What was his name, if you don't mind me asking?"

"Khoz," Zeph replied.

"Do you think he's really gone?"

Again, another of Victor's questions caught Zeph off guard. No one had ever asked him that. Everyone had always told him to accept that his father was gone. Zeph stared up at the Water Element mark on Victor's forehead. His father had it as well. Somehow, Zeph knew Victor understood why he chose to keep believing.

"No, I think he's still out there... somewhere," Zeph replied softly. He then proposed a question to Victor. "Would you let the sea take you?"

"Not a chance. I know I never took the proper time to develop my Water abilities like most captains do, but I would never let the sea take me."

"What level are your abilities at, if you don't mind me asking?"

"I think I'm somewhere around an Emitter or maybe a Forger. So, not much more than what I learned in school, to be honest." As the words left Victor's mouth, he wanted to take them back. Zeph saw the reaction on his face and knew what the captain was thinking.

"Don't worry about it. At least I will finish at the Pupil level instead of nothing." There were seven ranking levels concerning an individual's knowledge of their Elemental abilities. Pupil was the first, demonstrating at least some knowledge of one or more abilities connected to your given Element. Master was the seventh and highest rank, representing that an individual had vast knowledge of their Element and the skills to demonstrate that knowledge.

Both of them stood. It was customary for traders to shake at the wrist when a deal had transpired. So that's exactly what they did. Clasping each other's wrists, they shook each other's arms.

Going with the theme of Zeph's new clothing, Victor also put on one of his nicer ensembles. They headed out of the cabin and back to town. They both drew the attention of the tourists. They didn't care, though. One could easily mistake them for father and son. Zeph had always wanted an exceptionally nice outfit, and now he finally had one. He couldn't wait to show his mother.

Marcus and Breeze would also be along soon. Mr. Yad had let him out early from the morning class today since he was excelling so well in his knowledge of Glyphs and Symbols. Zeph hadn't shown Mr. Yad his old history book yet or mentioned the new Glyphs that had appeared in it. For the time being, he felt it best to keep his teacher in the dark.

It was nearing midday. Victor and Zeph walked through town with no particular destination in mind. Zeph invited Victor back to his house for something to eat and to introduce him to his mother. Entering the home, Zeph called out to his mother with no reply. It was slightly odd but wasn't cause for alarm. Zeph went upstairs to look for his mother. Victor simply stood in the den for the moment.

The front door opened as a rather dirty and disheveled woman entered. She placed a large basket of vegetables on the floor and closed the door. Turning to pick up the basket, she noticed Victor standing in the den, staring at her.

Startled, she let out a loud gasp and grabbed her chest. Zeph came running down the stairs. His mother seemed overwhelmed as she looked from the well-dressed man in the den to her equally well-dressed son. She instantly became self-conscious, realizing the layers of dirt covering her body. She ran to her room, saying she would be out in a moment.

The two men caught eyes. It was all Zeph and Victor could do not to laugh. They took seats on one of the more oversized couches in the den. Teak came running into the room and jumped up on Victor's lap. He scooped her up in his arms and held her above his head. The combination of play noises that followed from the sea captain made Zeph shake his head and smile. Victor was a constant unraveling mystery.

Zeph's mother took longer than expected to prepare herself but finally emerged from her room. She was clean and appeared to have put on some makeup. Her hair was held neatly in a ponytail behind her head. For a woman of nearly forty, she still looked pretty youthful.

Zeph and Victor stood from the couch as she entered the den. She walked over and hugged Zeph, then looked him up and down.

"Did you buy these clothes for him?" she asked, looking at Victor.

"Surprisingly, your boy bought them himself after he swindled the coins out of me," he laughed.

"It's not what you think, Mom. I bought these with the coin I made from the Pirie juice deal," Zeph explained.

"I see," she said, raising an eyebrow. Zeph realized that the proper introductions had not been made.

"Mom, this is Captain Victor. Victor, this is my mother, Dawn."

"Like the morning rays, I'm sure you bring light into many people's lives, Dawn," Victor said, taking her hand. She blushed. Zeph let out a big grin and shook his head.

"Alright, you two. Mom, I need the rest of the small Pirie juice vials, and the large one as well."

"Uh...yes, they're in the kitchen, the small cabinet in the corner," Dawn replied, still staring at Victor. It had been a long time since she had found herself in front of such a handsome man. He reminded her so much of Khoz.

Zeph returned to the den with a brown sack and a large vial. The small glass vials were rattling around inside the sack. He handed them to Victor. In turn, Victor removed a bag of coins he had attached to his belt and handed it to Zeph. In the bag were one hundred gold kessas. That amount of coin was more than had ever been in the house at one time.

Shortly after they had eaten, Zeph left and started heading back to the school for his afternoon class. Victor remained behind and visited with Dawn for a while. Zeph wondered what would become of that. He hadn't seen his mother act like that since his father was around. Nonetheless, he saw it as a good thing. Victor was a decent, honest person whom Zeph trusted.

Zeph soon met up with Marcus and Breeze at school. Between classes, he told them about the deal he made with Victor for the Pirie juice. He offered the money he had earned to help finance their sphere lamp project. Besides, Zeph had no idea what he would do with one hundred gold coins.

The last class of the day went by fast. It was on the combinations of Glyphs needed to make Seals. Zeph had learned earlier that week that the elemental powers of glyphs changed when written in succession, like words following each other in a sentence. He remembered the series of glyphs that were inscribed on Xa'an's swords. *The Order* of the glyphs had to have been placed precisely on the blades. Zeph had asked Mr. Yad how an item could be mystically connected to a single person. Mr. Yad told him that the individual's blood was required for part of the enchanting process. Zeph realized that the mystical properties of Xa'an's swords must have cost him a fortune.

That night, everyone met at Gus' house. The large living room in the central part of the house was quite full. Marcus, Iggy, and Zeph sat on one of the couches. Gus, Breeze, and Dawn sat on the opposite one. Victor and Koch claimed the other two chairs. Victor had asked Koch to come with them that night. He respected the captain's request, although he was only somewhat comfortable in gatherings of unfamiliar people.

The repairs to the *Nephesh* were finished, and the ship was ready to sail the next morning. Victor would be missed, but everyone looked forward to his return in several weeks.

Gus stood up and walked to the middle of the room. He had a great smile on his face. He looked like a small child standing in front of the candy stand at the market.

"As you all know, the *Nephesh* will be leaving tomorrow morning. Again, we would like to thank you for stopping by Victor." Victor tipped his hat towards Gus as the old inventor continued. "We've worked hard on these two objects the last two days. I have to say that if it wasn't for Zeph's newfound abilities in conjunction with the Rejuvenation vials, we would not have been able to complete this new project in the time given," Gus paused for a moment to let his words sink in, as though he was giving a great acceptance speech for something.

He placed his hand on the black cloth covering the items on the table in the middle of the room and continued. "I know Victor would have liked to be involved in this project, but unfortunately, he had a ship to fix. So, without further delay, I present the Street Lamp version of the Sphere Lamp," he exclaimed, pulling the sheet away. The room was filled with bright light, causing everyone to shield their eyes momentarily. Two large sphere lamps sat on the table before them. They were about the size of a man's head, roughly ten times bigger than the previous version.

Victor and Koch stood and walked over to them. All Victor could do was smile while Koch stood with his mouth gaping. Victor picked up one of the spheres. It was incredibly lightweight, not much heavier than an ordinary sphere. It made sense; after all, it was nothing more than a thin layer of unbreakable glass with elemental fire trapped inside.

Victor placed the sphere back down and turned to face everyone. "This is truly amazing. I'm proud to have come to know all of you. Not just for the business you have given me, but also for the kindness and honesty you all possess. I look forward to many more years of trading with you."

"That goes for me too. The lot of ya are all right," Koch added.

They spent the rest of the evening sharing stories and enjoying each other's company. Everyone hung on to every single word of Victor's many stories. They knew most of his stories had to be embellished, but it made for a great evening.

The chimes on the large clock rang out. It was midnight. Dawn suggested it was time for her and her boys to head out. Zeph and Iggy protested at first but soon gave in, realizing how tired they were. The three of them headed out. Shortly after, Marcus, Victor, and Koch also made their way back to town. Gus had given them black sheets to cover the large glowing spheres so they didn't attract too much attention from the town folk.

The next day, everyone stood at the end of the docks bright and early. A round of goodbyes echoed from the group. Victor ordered the crew to cast off. Everyone watched as the *Nephesh* sailed off into the morning fog. Zeph was disappointed to see her go; he was sure everyone else felt the same. But he knew Victor would be back in just a few more weeks.

The group of youths headed off to class shortly after Victor's departure. The morning rays of light that shot through the fog fascinated Zeph as they walked through town. Occasionally, the fog would get thick like that in town. Zeph always enjoyed the patterns it created with the light. It was like a form of art.

Zeph continued his studies of the new glyphs in his history book. Marcus suggested Zeph give the book some sort of name since the book now had more to do with Zeph than it had to do with its actual contents. Zeph agreed, and from that point on, they all began referring to it as 'Saphar's Book.'

Over the next week, Zeph began to practice handwriting the glyphs with his purchased pen and ink. He had never owned a pen before. At school, they used either a piece of lead or, occasionally, a quill.

The wooden pen was beautifully hand-carved. It was amazingly smooth and precise. Zeph wasn't sure if he should attribute that to the fine-crafted metal needle tip, the rich smooth ink, or his own abilities. He decided on all of the above. As the week went by, Zeph's skills with glyphs grew exponentially. He could almost close his eyes and write any glyph perfectly.

An idea had entered Zeph's mind. He wondered about his Elemental scribe abilities. The glyphs he had written on the paper looked perfect, but were they? He would only truly know if he wrote them with the Tears of God. He knew there was no way the temple would allow him to use their supply. Perhaps it was something Victor could acquire for him.

Zeph sat at his desk, enjoying the night air drifting in through the open window. His sphere lamp sat on his desk; its light shone over the page before him. He had been studying the new glyphs for days now.

Why these twelve glyphs? The thought was a regular occurrence every time he looked at them.

He looked over at the handful of gold coins he had placed on his desk. The glyphs and the gold were two things he had no idea what to do with. The gold sparkled in the dim light. Zeph wished the glyphs would do the same.

Walking over to the calendar, he took a piece of lead and placed an 'X' on the day's date. Only a week left in the month, just one month more, and he would graduate from school. The thought both scared and excited him. Despite his academic struggles until recently, he had always looked forward to Graduation. What the future held for him, he still didn't know.

DAY 26

Lend an ear to the wise that would give you counsel.
For a life without counsel serves no purpose.
But a life with a multitude of counsel brings forth Truth
~The Book of Ta'Hor

CHAPTER 6
GRADUATION

The boy stood before the full-length mirror, staring at his reflection. It was as if, by studying his outward appearance, he would somehow understand the man he was becoming. He stared into his own eyes in his reflection. Perhaps there was something he could learn from himself.

The long blue robe hung just above his boots. The contrasting underlying white shirt worked well with the deep blue robe. He ran his hands over the buttons of the white shirt. The short, stiff collar pointed upwards from the top of the shirt. He had never worn a shirt with a collar before, or even buttons.

He turned around several times as he looked at his reflection in the glass. He couldn't believe this day was here. Amid everything that was happening, he wasn't quite sure how to feel. Something was tugging at his insides, but he wasn't sure what.

The knock on the door brought his attention back to the present, if only for a moment. He called out to enter. The door swung open as a tall, middle-aged man walked in. He wore a deep scarlet-colored coat that covered most of his body. The black collar and cuffs accented the red nicely. The man wore a white shirt in the same style as the boy. Shiny brass buttons lined the front of the coat down to the waist. The coat reached down to just above the man's knees.

The boy stared at the man for a moment. The feeling deep inside began rushing to the surface. Tears began to fill his eyes as he sat down on the bed. The man seemed confused as he walked over to the tear-filled boy.

"What's wrong, Zeph?" Victor asked gently.

Zeph pulled the tears back as he spoke, "You just remind me so much of my father, and I just really wish he was here today," he replied as the tears trailed down his cheeks.

Victor knew there was no way he could respond to adequately comfort him. He sat beside Zeph, placed a hand on his back, and waited for the young man to regain his composure. Several minutes passed, and then Zeph stood from the bed.

"I'm okay now, sorry about that."

"There is no need to apologize. Your feelings are perfectly justified," Victor's words came out softly and created a feeling of comfort around Zeph.

"I was wondering when you'd stop by. The ceremony is in a few hours, you know."

"Oh, I know. It takes a while for a man to get dressed, doesn't it?" Victor asked with a smile.

Zeph was glad that Victor would be present at the ceremony. This was the second time Victor had returned in the last month. Zeph couldn't believe it had been over a month since the incident with the *Nephesh*. Victor had created new sailing procedures so something like that wouldn't happen again.

Another knock came to the door. It was Iggy. He peered around the door.

"Is it okay if I come in?" he asked.

"Sure thing, little brother," Zeph replied.

"The robes look great, Zeph! Man, I can't wait. In two more years, I'll be graduating, too."

"Oh yeah, this is loads of fun," Zeph said sarcastically.

"You don't think this is fun at all?" Victor questioned.

"I didn't say that. I don't really know. I have a little bit of mixed feelings about this whole day," Zeph replied.

The three of them chatted for a while. The ceremony wouldn't start for several more hours. When it was time, several townsfolk would go from house to house, ensuring the graduating students were headed to the school.

Zeph talked about everything he had learned that school year. The most profound things happened near the end of the year. He attributed that to discovering some of his abilities. Finishing off the year with a unit on glyphs and symbols was also important to him. Finding a connection to something and having a lot of information on it dropped in your lap was a perfect graduation gift from Mr. Yad.

The house's front door swung open, and a loud voice echoed up the stairs.

"Where's my boy at?!" Marcus exclaimed, entering the house. When Marcus got excited, he would often talk in that manner.

"You think I have time to hide?" Zeph asked comically, looking around the room. Victor and Iggy both laughed. Marcus burst into Zeph's room. He had the biggest smile on his face. It was obvious that Marcus had been looking forward to this day for quite a while. He wore matching attire to Zeph's.

"I have to say, I love this little stiff collar thing. I have got to get some shirts made like this."

"That's actually a prevalent style amongst the noblemen and wealthy," Victor responded, looking over at Marcus.

"Well, I don't know about Noble, but we are definitely getting wealthy," Marcus grinned.

Marcus did have a point. Over the last month, trading with Victor had grown immensely. They had sold close to ten of the large sphere lamps to Mayor Bain. Victor was still buying the standard sphere lamps and a couple of vials of Pirie juice. The Pirie juice was bringing in the most coins. This, in turn, was making Zeph wealthier than the others. It didn't matter, though; he was willing to share all the profits. Shortly after that, they decided that any profit from the group's efforts would be returned to their projects. They were creating a little business empire in Daunt and wanted it to thrive.

Zeph looked over at the locked chest in the corner of the room. He had bought it several weeks earlier when they had started accumulating a large amount of gold coins. It was encased with metal and had a locking system built right into the front. It was no vault, but everyone was confident that their coin was protected. Zeph was in charge of most of the coin, but every group member also had a key. In case there was ever an emergency.

As Zeph sat and listened to the conversations around him, he found his mind drifted off to another place. Thoughts of the scroll were entering his mind. He held it almost every day, whenever he needed a mental recharge. The scroll itself remained a mystery, though. Sometimes, a cold wind would blow at night, and he would dream of the scroll. In every dream, he opened the scroll, and a blinding light would wash over him. Before anything else happened, he would always wake up.

The hour passed quickly, and the group realized they needed to leave. Everyone gathered in the den. Zeph and Marcus stood next to each other; their matching combination of blue robes and white attire was eye-catching. Zeph's mother stood with Victor as Iggy joined the boys. Together, they set out. They stopped at Marcus' house to pick up his parents along the way. Shortly after, Siah returned from the dock and joined the slowly growing group. Zeph looked around at everyone. The day was very similar to the day of Iggy's christening, except for Victor taking his father's place.

As the group continued through town, they saw many other groups and families heading towards the school. Blue-robed students were the dotting streets. Both Zeph and Marcus recognized all the other students from their class.

Skye came running up to Zeph. They had known each other since they were in First-class at school. When Breeze first moved to town in Middle-class, their friendship had fallen apart. Skye was a Wind Elemental, and being that Breeze was as well, he immediately tried to create some sort of a connection with her. However, in the end, it was Zeph for whom she fell. Zeph had never pursued her, which made Skye even more frustrated.

"Wait up!" Skye called out as she ran up behind Zeph and Marcus. Everyone stopped for a moment. Zeph told the group to continue; he would catch up with them in a minute.

"What do you want, Skye?" Zeph asked with a somewhat impatient tone in his voice.

"What? Can't we just have a friendly chat on Graduation day?"

"We haven't had a 'friendly' chat in years. What do you want?" Zeph replied, his tone getting tenser.

"I would like to finally claim defeat."

"What?!" Marcus interjected.

"I've been watching you and Breeze over the last month. For years, I saw her waste her affection for you. Then, one day, something happened; you started to return the affection. So, I would like to claim defeat. It seems the best man won."

Zeph and Marcus stood with their jaws hanging open as Skye walked away. The interaction was so baffling to both Zeph and Marcus.

"That kid's not right," Marcus said, shaking his head.

Zeph also shook his head and smirked. "Seriously, who claims defeat over an interest in a girl that started in Middle-Class years? That was five years ago."

"He was right about something, though," Zeph turned his head to listen to Marcus, "you are returning Breeze's feelings." Zeph blushed a little at the statement.

"We haven't talked about it. She and I know we have feelings for each other, but we haven't verbally expressed them yet."

"Don't worry about it, man. I see a grand future for the two of you," Marcus said, spreading his arms outwards.

"You'll be tagging along the whole way, I bet."

"Oh, of course," Marcus said with a grin. "I like *women*, but I don't think I'll ever get to the point where I'll like just one *woman*," he said, stressing the singular sense of the word woman, "there are just too many fish in the sea, bro." Zeph could only roll his eyes; Marcus had never had a steady girlfriend.

They laughed as they continued the walk to school. When they arrived, their families were waiting for them by the large tree in front of the school. Close to three dozen other students from the graduating class were already there. Several hundred family members and friends were also present with the students.

Zeph wandered around, talking to his classmates and their parents. Several families sympathized that Zeph's father couldn't see him on this day. Sometimes, Zeph forgot that his father's disappearance had affected others besides his own family.

Music began to play from the bandstand. A series of musicians had set up their instruments. Zeph wasn't very familiar with musical instruments, but he recognized several of the stringed ones. There were also a few horns and several drums. The melody floated across the breeze and filled the air on the hill. It would be a day he would remember for the rest of his life.

The music flowed over Zeph as he stood amongst the people. It was a soft melody, soothing but somehow tragic at the same time. He felt every note hit his skin and move along his body. The melody pulled within his heart like the kiss of a loved one saying goodbye. He felt a hand brush his shoulder. Turning, he saw Breeze standing there.

She wore the same blue robe he did. It was different; she was different. His eyes traveled down the glimmering silky white gown beneath her blue robe. The breath in his chest caught. Their eyes met. Never had he seen someone so beautiful in his life. Her eyes glistened in the morning suns. Long strands of black hair drifted softly in the wind. Gentle wings of light began to wrap their way around her gorgeous frame. No illusion could be so perfect; Zeph knew she must be real.

"Hi," the word came out slowly as Zeph released the breath he had been holding.

"Hey you," she said softly, hugging him.

"Wow, you look so perfect, Breeze," Zeph said, still astonished.

"You too. I have to say I love the way the robe feels over this gown."

Zeph continued to smile as she talked. It soon became apparent that his stare would not deviate in any direction. At this point, Breeze decided to take Zeph over to the rest of the group. Everyone greeted Breeze as she came over. Gus had already found his way over and was chatting with Victor. Marcus' parents were chatting with Dawn.

Two figures headed up the hill towards the gathering by the school. The ceremony would start shortly. The first person was Mr. Yad. He was followed closely by Uriym Praotes. The remaining two town elders were now present for the ceremony.

Siah joined the two men as they approached. Together, they walked up the bandstand stairs. Mr. Yad stepped up to the podium. Everyone slowly stopped talking and began to gather in front of the bandstand. The instrumentalists started to play the traditional graduation composition. The graduating students took their place in front of the crowd. Zeph, Marcus, and Breeze stood next to each other. They each had a smile on their face and a gleam in their eye.

The music faded softly as Mr. Yad raised his hand to the instrumentalists. The sound of the breeze blowing in the trees was all that remained. Light from the midday suns shone down on the crowd below. Mr. Yad scanned the crowd. His old eyes gleamed as he gazed down upon the overexcited students in the front rows. He had seen this day come and go many times. He never felt more proud than he did on graduation day.

"Welcome one and all!" his voice boomed over the crowd, "As you know, this is a wonderful day for the youth of Daunt. This is the first step towards grand futures for every one of the students here today. I could not be more proud of this graduating class. I know I say this every year, but this is my favorite graduating class."

Everyone chuckled at the remark. Zeph and Marcus smiled at each other as the ceremony continued. Mr. Yad spoke of the events of the last year. The parents seemed intrigued to learn about the success and progress of their children. The Elemental levels of the students varied. Some had grown to Guardians, the fifth of the seven elemental levels. Many only achieved the fourth level of Forger. On the other hand, Zeph was the only student to graduate at the Pupil level.

The ceremony continued as Praotes and Siah took turns speaking to the students and parents. This concluded the introduction part of the graduation festivities. It was now time for the Valedictory speech. This was a speech given by a student of the town elders' choosing. The student was usually the brightest and best student in the graduating class, although this was not always the case. Besides having to address their fellow students and parents, the student had no prior knowledge that they would be chosen.

My. Yad stepped forward once more. Every one of the students held their breath as they waited to hear who it would be. Many of the students were sure it would be Marcus. Despite his disruptions in class, he excelled the most. He was one of only four students who had reached the Guardian level. They knew that Elders didn't play favorites and that whoever was chosen would be for a good reason.

All eyes were on Mr. Yad as he opened his mouth to speak.

"We, as the town Elders, have spent the last month deciding on which student is most deserving of the title of Valedictorian. This is never an easy decision. The title is given to the student who has not only put a great deal of effort into their schooling over the years but will also be the most promising leader for years to come. That is why this year the student will be..." he paused for dramatic effect and waited for the impatient expressions on the students' faces to form,

"Zeph!"

Upon hearing his own name, Zeph felt as though his feet had somehow been transformed into lead. He could feel the blood draining from his face as everything seemed to slow down. A hand slapped him on the back, jolting him back to reality. Marcus smiled at him and pushed him toward the stairs to the bandstand. Every step up the stairs felt like it would be his last. He gripped the rail with all his might as he climbed them. Each of the Elders shook his hand as he walked to the podium. Mr. Yad felt the shakiness in Zeph's hand.

"Don't worry, lad. The words will come," he said as Zeph continued past him.

The feeling that his feet were made of lead was still there, along with the sensation that the bones in his legs had turned to pudding. Zeph gripped both sides of the podium to steady himself. He looked out at the crowd. The urge to vomit was swelling in his stomach. Looking down, he saw his mother and Victor standing together. Their eyes were both locked on his face. A wave of calmness seemed to wash over him, and he knew exactly what to say.

"I would like to start by saying that I have no idea why I'm up here right now. I haven't done anything special in my years at school." Some of the expressions on his fellow student's faces agreed with the statement, but the rest of the crowd did not.

"I guess I'm supposed to say why this school is great and what I've learned from my years here. Well, this school is great; I've had some of the best times of my life here. I've shared all eleven years with my best friend Marcus." A loud 'woot' came from Marcus upon hearing his name. Zeph smiled as he continued.

"I've greatly enjoyed my teachers over the years. I've learned a lot from them. And I've learned a lot from my classmates. I wish I had gotten to know some of you more. I'm thankful to have my friends here with me today. Marcus, Breeze, I couldn't have made it here without the support of both of you. Another loud 'woot" came from Marcus. This time, Zeph glared at him as he continued once more.

"So this is the part where I'm supposed to say what I've learned here. I honestly have to say I know almost nothing about myself. I've just barely achieved the level of Pupil several months ago." A murmur came through the crowd as parents whispered to each other. Zeph felt as though he was shrinking behind the podium. He turned his head to look at Mr. Yad. The old teacher just stared back; the soft sparkle in his eye filled Zeph with something new.

"But if I have learned something more important," Zeph said, raising his voice, "it is that abilities do not make you who you are. A rank cannot tell someone their place of importance. My teachers always had a place for me in their classes, which was right alongside my classmates." Mr. Yad began to grin as he witnessed Zeph's confidence unfolding before his eyes. "I have learned that true friends will stand by you through good times and bad. I have learned that knowledge, of any kind, is something to strive for and to be treasured."

"Right on, bro!" Marcus shouted out.

"Whoo!" Breeze shouted out as well.

"I would like to encourage all my fellow classmates to journey out into the world and find their place. I don't know where mine is, but I know I want to find it." With those words, the Elders stood up and began clapping, and the crowd of parents and students joined.

Zeph breathed a sigh of relief as he shook hands with the Elders again. He walked down the stairs and rejoined Marcus and Breeze. Hands from all sides padded him on the back as he walked past his fellow classmates.

"I didn't doubt for a moment that this young man was the perfect choice when we decided to make him valedictorian," said Mr. Yad to the assembly as he handed the podium over to Siah. The large man walked over to where Mr. Yad had been standing. The podium seemed much smaller, with Siah now standing behind it.

"Alrighty, we've made it halfway through this shindig. You've all been to a graduation before; you know what time it is. Trade Off! Parents, it's time to pull out those gifts for your bright young son or daughter," Siah's voice boomed over the crowd as people moved about.

It was the point in the graduation ceremony that was known as a Trade Off. It was not limited to events such as graduations but was always present at one. The parents of graduating students would present them with a gift in recognition of their achievement.

Marcus was the first to make his way through the crowd and find his parents. His mother had a smile on her face. It was something Marcus wasn't used to seeing, as he caused his fair share of trouble at home over the years. Next to her was his father. He stood tall and proud next to his wife. Marcus and his father hadn't always gotten along. Walking over to Marcus, he extended his hand toward his son. Marcus took it. His father pulled him in quickly and wrapped his arms around him.

"I'm proud of you, son," the words came out broken up. Marcus couldn't remember the last time he had heard the sound of genuine empathy in his father's voice. His mother came over and hugged both of them. She handed Marcus a small cloth sack, about the size of a hood.

Marcus looked around at the other students receiving gifts from their families. He wished his gift would be the ability to hold onto this moment forever. Moments like these were rare with his family. He looked down at the sack in his hands. He pulled open the top and shoved his hand inside.

He soon discovered there were several different gifts inside the sack. He decided taking them out one at a time was probably best. The first item was a coiled black leather belt. It had a brightly polished silver buckle on the front. Marcus's jaw dropped as they admired the craftsmanship of the belt. Next, he pulled out two silver arm bracers designed to wrap around his upper arms. Marcus wore shirts that often cut off at the shoulder, so the armbands would stand out quite well on his biceps. The last item he pulled out was a thick silver chain with two Fire symbols hanging from it. He wondered why two symbols were hanging from it. Looking up at his parents, his eyes immediately were drawn to the fire symbol on both of their foreheads. His question was immediately answered as he understood the symbolism behind it.

Marcus just stood there quietly for a moment, and then a grin began to form slowly on his face. Placing the chain around his neck, he hugged his parents. He would put on the other items later once he changed his clothes.

Breeze wandered through the crowd of parents and students. She couldn't find her father anywhere. Pushing towards the back of the crowd, she finally spotted him sitting under the large tree behind the school.

"What are you doing all the way back here? I almost didn't find you," she said, walking over to Gus.

"I have something very special for you, and only for you," Gus said, looking up at his daughter.

Rays of light broke through the leaves, bustling in the breeze. The light fell across both of their faces. Tears began to swell in Gus' eyes as he stared at his daughter. Turning, he looked out to sea. Breeze turned her gaze to match his.

"Your mother..." his voice trailed off as he choked back the tears, "your mother would be so proud of you today." He quickly stood and turned towards her. "I am so proud of you today." The words filled Breeze's ears as she wrapped her arms around him. They both stood there for a moment, remembering those who were not with them.

"I have something for you," Gus said, holding his daughter at arm's length. She expected him to pull something out of a bag or sack, but rather, he pointed out to the sky above the sea.

"Do you see it?" he asked with a smile.

Breeze scanned the horizon. She held her hand up in front of her eyes to focus better. Then, something caught her eye, sparkling in the sky out over the waters. A rush of excitement filled her even though she had no idea what it was.

Gus stretched out his arm to the sparkle of light in the distance. Breeze looked at him, slightly confused. He simply smiled and motioned for her to continue watching the sparkle. The object began to grow closer. It started to take shape as it grew more prominent in their sight. Breeze spotted an object attached to a chain. It raced towards her at great speed and then abruptly slowed.

Breeze stared at the object as Gus held it out. It was a beautiful silver chain. Attached was a brilliant green stone, unlike anything Breeze had ever seen. The chain and stone floated gracefully in the air above Gus' open palm.

"How are you doing this?" she asked.

"Over the last several years, I have begun to master the talent of Levitation. I wanted the knowledge of it to be part of this gift to you," he replied with a smile.

Breeze continued to stare at the stone. It seemed to be in a changing state of translucency, giving the appearance that it was constantly turning bright green. The chain was perfectly crafted. The rungs of silver reflected the sun's rays as though the metal would never dull.

Reaching out for the chain, Gus motioned for her to stop. She seemed confused. Smiling, Gus raised his other hand. Breeze felt her footing give way as her body lifted slightly off the ground. The feeling was unlike anything she had ever felt. Gus had often used the wind to make her float as a child, and even now, she could propel herself off the ground using her Wind abilities. This, however, was a completely different sensation. There was no wind, no blowing of her clothing, no rushing sounds in her ears; she simply floated in the air.

Moving his hand once more, Gus brought the chain up and over his daughter's head. He gently let the chain fall around her neck as he brought her back to the ground. She seemed flustered for a moment as she regained her balance. Then she turned to him and smiled.

"I love it, Daddy! And I love you," she exclaimed, wrapping her arms around him once more, "how did you ever afford a stone like this, though?" she questioned.

"When you were only a baby, a traveling merchant came to our town. The man claimed to be selling 'un-cut' gems. I was skeptical at first. He showed me the ordinary-looking stones he was selling and several precious gems. I was convinced, although your mother said I was wasting our valuable coin," he paused to touch the stone around her neck.

"I bought a bag of ten stones, using much of our savings at the time. Of those ten, nine of them were ordinary rocks. This one, however, was different. Jade stones don't exist on Appagon, not even up in the mountains. I remember spending hours staring at this stone's brilliant green color." They continued to talk as Gus told her more about the stone and the chain. Breeze was incredibly happy as she held the stone around her neck. She couldn't think of a more perfect gift to receive on her graduation day.

Zeph watched his classmates disperse in all directions as he leaned against the bandstand. He couldn't believe he had given that speech. His hands were still shaking. Three figures made their way through the crowd toward Zeph. Several moments later, the three of them stood before him. Zeph looked up at his mother.

"I'm very proud of you, son," Dawn said as she walked over and hugged him. Zeph could hear those words echoing from the groups of families that scattered the hillside. Victor and Iggy stood just behind them, quietly waiting for their presence to be called upon. Zeph waved them over. They all embraced Zeph in one enormous hug and then took turns congratulating him.

"I have something for you," his mother said, reaching into her dress. She pulled out what, at first glance, appeared to be a pocket watch. Taking it in her hands, she handed it to Zeph. It was gold and still resembled a pocket watch, only larger.

"It was your father's compass."

As the words left his mother's lips, it stung within Zeph's chest. He quickly located a series of buttons on the side. Pressing the most prominent button, one of the sides of the compass flipped open, revealing directional needles. He remembered his father holding the compass when he was a small child. Zeph tried to suppress the lump that was building in his throat.

"Why didn't Dad take this on his last voyage?" Zeph questioned.

"I don't know. Perhaps he was meant to leave it so that one day it would pass to you. Fate is not something we always understand," his mother replied.

Zeph closed one side and flipped the compass over. He pressed the large button once more. This time, it was the bottom side that was facing upwards that opened. Unlike the two needle points on the other side of the compass that joined in the middle to indicate north and south, this side had a three-pointed needle in a triangular formation. Each needle had a series of glyphs perfectly engraved along the center of each needle.

"What do these do?" Zeph asked with a puzzled look on his face.

"I don't know. I never actually noticed those before," his mother replied.

"Mind if I take a look at it?" Victor asked. Zeph handed the compass to him. After several minutes of studying the compass, Victor handed it back. Zeph wondered how the needles could correctly point to anything, being that there were three different points. At the moment, they didn't appear to be pointing anywhere specific. The triangle formation just floated on its axis, spinning slightly.

"I think out of the four of us, you're the best to tell us what those needles do," Victor said.

"Why do you say that?" Zeph asked.

"Well, you are the resident expert on glyphs and symbols, aren't you?"

Victor was right, of course. Zeph probably knew more about that topic than anyone else in town. He thanked his mother for the gift. It would be a challenge and an adventure to discover the purpose of the underside of the compass. Zeph found it strange that neither his mother nor he had ever known about the underside of the compass.

Everyone was returning to the bandstand. Zeph took his place at the front of the crowd with the rest of his class. Marcus and Breeze came and stood on either side of him. He quickly noticed the small sack in Marcus' hand and the sparkling green gem hanging around Breeze's neck. A smile formed on his face; he was very interested in learning more about his friends' gifts.

Uriym Praotes stood in front of the podium. His age was evident as he gripped the wood. Even though he and Mr. Yad were thought to be close in age, it was obvious that time had not been a friend to Praotes. Or that his age was far greater than he had ever let on. His skin bore the passage of time along with old scars from a life of battle. Few knew why the old Uriym had so many scars; even fewer dared to ask.

"I am proud to say we have reached the final stage of the Graduation Ceremony. Just as Faith is something a person carries with them throughout life, we present a symbol of recognition of your achievement to carry with you throughout your life as well. When you hear your name, please step forward and make your way up the bandstand."

Praotes began with the first name. The list was alphabetical. Zeph groaned upon coming to this realization; he knew his name would be the last one. The students began making their way up the bandstand. There were several long flat cases on the table. From these, the Uriym presented a ring to each student. Each ring had been previously fitted for each student's finger. Traditionally, the ring was made of fine silver, which the school paid for. However, there were several other metal options if the student covered the extra cost.

There were also three types of gold the rings could be made out of. Zeph paid for his, Marcus', and Breeze's rings to be made out of gold.

The engravings on each ring were made specifically for each student. Each ring was a simple, thick, round band. In the center of the ring was a slot in the shape of each student's Elemental symbol, and on either side were three round slots for stones. The symbol plus the six slots represented the seven Elemental levels a student could achieve.

Breeze made her way up the stairs. Praotes stood there with a ring in his hand for her. She had chosen green gold. It had a similar look to silver but with a greenish shimmer. Looking down at the ring, she gazed at the stones. Her symbol and three slots to the left were fitted with a shimmering clear crystal stone. This indicated that she was at the fourth Elemental level of Forger.

After a dozen or more students had gone up, it was Marcus' turn. He made his way proudly up to the stage. The Uriym held out the ring to Marcus. It was made of yellow gold and carried the same shimmering effect in the light. His elemental symbol and the three slots on the left and one on the right had been fitted with the clear stone. This indicated that he was at the fifth Elemental level of Guardian.

The minutes passed by as Zeph waited for his name to be called. Just as he had predicted, he was the last to be called. He made his way up to the stage. Walking over to the row of Elders, he accepted his ring from Praotes. Continuing down the line, he shook hands with Siah and Mr. Yad. Stepping down the stairs, he joined Marcus and Breeze, who were waiting for him.

"Well, let's see this thing," Marcus said, looking at Zeph's closed palm.

Zeph slowly opened his palm, exposing the ring. It was made of blue gold, a silvery look mixed with blue tones. Of the seven slots for stones, only his elemental symbol had been filled with the clear crystal stone. This indicated that he was a Pupil, the first elemental level.

"Awesome! I love how the gold has that bluish shimmer to it. These rings were worth the extra coin!" Marcus exclaimed.

Zeph placed the ring on the index finger of his left hand, as was the custom for graduation rings. It fit perfectly. Zeph had made sure the engraver had the exact measurements of his finger.

The ceremony came to a close, and the families began to disperse all throughout town. It was getting close to evening, and the suns were getting low on the horizon. The day had come and gone over the length of the ceremony. Dawn invited everyone over to their place for a meal. Zeph wondered how she planned to feed almost a dozen people, but he was glad to have the interaction.

The group of youth and parents made their way through town and up to Zeph's house. Zeph, Marcus, Breeze, and Iggy quickly made their way upstairs to Zeph's room and let the adults mingle amongst themselves in the den.

"Wow, that was a crazy day!" Zeph exclaimed as he collapsed on his bed.

"Awe, is the Valedictorian tired?" Marcus asked in a joking manner.

"Oh, don't even get me started on that," Zeph replied, lying on his bed staring at his graduation ring. The blue gold had a stunning effect. He had never seen anything other than white and yellow gold. When he heard of the blue gold and green gold, he immediately wanted the blue for himself. Breeze had quickly requested to have green gold.

"So, what do you guys think? Was the extra five gold kessas a piece worth it?" Zeph questioned.

"I love my green gold; it goes so well with my new gemstone," Breeze replied with a huge grin.

"Personally, I wished there was some sort of orange-gold, but I love this. Thanks for covering the extra cost for all the rings," Marcus added.

"Not a problem, we have too much gold anyways," Zeph laughed. "I guess now that school is done, we'll get even more since we can always work on the sphere lamps."

Just then, there was a knock on the bedroom door. Everyone turned to Zeph.

"Come in," he called out.

Victor entered the room. His presence was still as mesmerizing as it had been that morning. Zeph wanted to get a similar outfit sometime soon.

"How's it going, Victor?" Marcus asked.

Victor slightly chuckled, then sighed, "I don't think I'm made for adult conversation."

It was amusing to hear Victor talk that way. He was almost forty, yet he had many characteristics of a young man in his early twenties. It wasn't that strange that he preferred the company of the youths to the adults below.

He removed his long coat and hung it on the hook on the bedroom door. Since Zeph, Breeze, and Iggy had sprawled themselves across Zeph's bed, and Marcus sat on the floor, Victor took a seat on the wooden chair by Zeph's desk. The room glistened from the light of several sphere lamps placed around the room, while the light from dusk slowly faded into darkness through the window.

"What will you do now?" Victor didn't direct the question at anyone in particular.

"I don't really know," Zeph replied, "I guess I'll continue my studies of glyphs and symbols. I'm assuming that we're going to continue working with you?"

"I would like you to, but I would understand if you chose not to. You have a lot of opportunities now that you've finished school."

"Well, I know that Iggy and I are planning to continue manufacturing the sphere lamps," Marcus piped up.

"I thank you for that, boys. If you choose not to continue, I will still manage quite well. All of you have helped me earn a year's worth of trade in only a few months. I have enough gold to last me a long time."

Zeph looked at Breeze. Her expression conveyed the general consensus of the group. Everyone was in agreement that they would continue to work with Victor until a time came when something more pressing came into their lives.

Zeph pulled his father's compass out of his robes. This triggered a response, and Marcus and Breeze also glanced at their graduation gifts. Marcus emptied the small sack onto Zeph's bed, revealing the belt and the two arm bracers. His chain was visibly hanging around his neck.

"I have to say these are the most amazing gifts I have ever received," Marcus said, admiring his accessories. Breeze replied with a similar statement about the gemstone Gus had given her. She also told them about Gus's levitation talent. This came as a brief shock to the group simply because it had been such a well-kept secret on Gus's part.

"So, can he fly without Wind?" Iggy asked

"I'm not sure, but from what I've seen, he's very powerful at it. He was able to suspend the necklace and me in the air simultaneously while holding perfect concentration," Breeze replied.

"I wonder if we'll ever learn any Talents," Marcus pondered.

"I guess it is possible; we'd have to figure out which ones we are most susceptible to learning," Zeph replied.

The talk about their futures went on for some time, while Victor sat and listened to the thoughts of the three youths on their graduation day.

He remembered how many of the same thoughts had passed through his mind on his own graduation day.

After the meal, the families said their goodbyes and headed off. Victor was the only one to stay behind. Unlike his previous voyages to Daunt, he had planned to stay at Zeph's house this time. Dawn had set up a place for him in the den.

After a few hours of chatting, Dawn chased Zeph and Iggy up to bed. She and Victor continued to talk into the night. Zeph stood silently at the top of the stairs briefly, listening to their conversation.

"So what do you think of him, honestly?" Zeph heard his mother ask.

"I think he's an extraordinary lad," Victor replied, "He is lucky to have such a wonderful mother."

"May I ask you a personal question?"

"Of course," Victor replied.

"Why is it that you never married?"

"Ah, now that is a question I haven't been asked in some time."

Zeph could hear his mother stirring on the couch. He could picture her blushing.

"To say the right woman never came around would be a lie. I have had opportunities in the past to marry. But the life I have on the sea would make it difficult, especially for a wife waiting at home."

"I understand that. Khoz wanted to give it up many times, but I wouldn't let him. Now I wonder if I made the right choice in asking him to continue." The room fell silent as she spoke.

Zeph listened a bit longer, then quietly slipped off to his room. He got ready for bed quickly, throwing his clothes on the floor and his things on his desk. His compass slipped out of his robe and fell on the floor. Zeph rushed over and picked it up. It seemed fine. Pressing the large button, the cover on the bottom side popped open. He still had no idea what the three needles did or how they worked. Turning the compass on its side, he looked at the three other buttons along the rim. They were nothing more than mere bumps. He pressed one, but it would not indent. Perhaps the compass was simply old and out of use.

Zeph carefully placed the compass on his desk and then climbed into bed. Sleep soon overcame him. He awoke shortly after, his body jerking upright in his bed. Everything seemed different as he looked around. Swinging his feet off his bed, he tried to stand. His feet would not touch the floor; instead, he floated just above it. Stumbling forward, he threw his hands out to prevent the inevitable fall. Once again he found things were not as they seemed, as he floated gently out into the air. The walls looked distorted, as if they were made out of water.

It quickly became apparent to Zeph that he must be dreaming, but he had never had a dream that felt so real before. As he floated across his room, his eyes locked with the compass now floating off his desk. He reached his hand out, and the compass instantly flew into it. Opening the side with the three needles, he saw they were glowing and spinning quickly. The glowing needles formed three different rings. The rings of light began to float past the glass covering and out into the air. Zeph's gaze followed their every movement. They circled him several times. Before Zeph could react, they shot into the Omega symbol on his forehead. Pain resonated inside his head like lightning bolts. Losing his grip on the compass, it floated out before him. The pain instantly shot down into his chest. The rings of light burst from his chest as tiny balls of light. They made their way to the three small buttons along the rim of the compass. One by one, the series of small buttons popped outwards.

The weightless feeling Zeph had been experiencing disappeared. His body came crashing down to the floor. Zeph held his chest as he stood up. He wondered if it had all been just a dream. Uncovering a sphere lamp by his bed, he looked at the compass on his desk. The small buttons along the edge were now clearly raised from their previous positions. Picking up the compass, Zeph pressed one of the buttons. The tiny glyphs running up the center of one of the three needles lit up. The triangle formation moved slightly. Zeph tried the other buttons, and in each case, one of the needles lit up. Although he still wasn't sure of what the needles indicated, he figured that the glowing needle became the active one. The illuminated needle decided the direction of the triangular formation.

After playing with the compass for several minutes, Zeph crawled back into bed. Part of him began to wonder. Had his father known about the other features of the compass? Why hadn't he taken it with him on the voyage where he went missing? As Zeph drifted off to sleep again, he hoped no more dreams would come his way that night.

DAY 60

Education is but mere preparation for life.

A person's life truly begins once they have set foot out in the world.
No wonders of the classroom will ever replace the wonders of the world.

~Mr. Yad

CHAPTER 7
FESTIVAL OF FESTIVALS

The cool evening air blew through the tents lining the streets of Daunt. It was a blessing. The heat of the harvest season had finally set in over the last month. There would be five more months of heat, and then it would finally cool once more at the start of the next growing season.

The suns had set hours earlier, but the town continued to bustle with activity. Shop upon shop had been added to the handful already in town. Traders peddling their wares paced up and down the streets in Daunt. People from all over Appagon and other lands brought the best of both fine goods and cheap trinkets. More than a hundred extra shops crowded the streets.

The start of the festival had gone off without a hitch. This would be the first of three days where the quiet little town would not sleep. Daunt had already grown to ten times its size in the last week. The edges of town had been pushed out almost three times the regular size. People from all over came to Daunt for the festivals. Even people from the mountain village of Sanctus Spire could be seen among the crowds. Suddenly, the crowds began rushing towards a loud disturbance at the north end of town.

The flames of the torches danced across a man's angry face. It was Siah. Sweat beaded on his forehead and his massive arms. Drops began to flow down his wrists and onto the hilt of the enormous broadsword held tightly in his grip. The rage burned in his eyes as he raised his sword again and swung it.

A smaller man, yet still larger than most, quickly raised his arm towards the oncoming blade. The blade struck hard against the man's flesh. A quick burst of flame washed over the man's skin and sent Siah's blade ricocheting backward. It was as though the blade had come down on metal rather than flesh. The man sneered at Siah, who had become dazed for a moment. Taking the opportunity, the man shot an intense burst of flame toward Siah's face. It was so hot it could have melted stone. Siah released one hand from his sword and dispersed the flame with a blast of water that burst from his palm like a fountain.

The crowd of onlookers gasped at the display of elemental powers. Siah quickly brought the sword up in another attempt to strike the man, this time from the side. Even using one arm, the broadsword came up quickly, only to be caught by one of the man's weapons. They resembled axes more than anything else. Each weapon was a straight blade that curved outwards into a point at the bottom and two at the top. The points at the top made it easy to hook an opponent's weapon. A handle came out from the back of each blade near the bottom, allowing the user to have something to grip. Even though each weapon was only the length of a man's arm from elbow to fingertips, they were swift and accurate.

The man threw Siah's sword to the left, causing the crowd to scramble out of the way. Stumbling back, Siah threw his palms outward. Needle thin strands of water shot from his palms and through the shoulders of the other man; he cried out in pain. The man's face changed, and it was apparent to Siah and the crowd that adrenaline had quickly overcome the pain. Flames burst forward, covering the metal surface of the weapon in each of the man's hands. A woman standing near the crowd shrieked and covered her mouth. Slicing through the strings of water, the man charged at Siah, weapons blazing.

"Enough!" A voice boomed from above the crowd. Everyone's eyes immediately darted toward an old man in blue robes. The fighter continued to charge Siah. Everyone's eyes flew from Praotes back to the charging man. Siah shot blasts of water at the man, but they vaporized before reaching him. Quickly, Praotes turned to Gus, who was standing directly behind him on the podium. Gus nodded, and without even looking, he lifted the fighter off the ground. The man became startled and dropped his weapons.

"Thank you," Praotes whispered to Gus as he turned his attention back to the crowd, "This round has concluded due to poor sportsmanship by the fighter from Sanctus Spire."

The crowd seemed both disappointed and relieved. If the fight had continued for a few more moments, it could have ended quite badly. Both men picked up their weapons from the dirt floor of the arena. They shook hands; the anger present only moments earlier had already faded. Both men smiled at each other and then at the crowd lining the wooden seats of the stadium.

Marcus, Iggy, and Zeph had found a spot right against the boards at the arena's base while Breeze sat back with Zeph's mother and Victor farther up. Violence wasn't their thing, but it got the boys' blood pumping. They had never seen Siah fight before. When he first raised his sword above his head, all of their jaws had dropped. Holding the massive sword over his already massive body, he seemed almost as tall as a house.

The boys cheered for Siah. He smiled and waved in return as he left the arena. They quickly made their way out of the arena to track him down. Even though they heard the next fight beginning, they proceeded outside anyway. The night sky was filled with stars outside the arena. Siah was easy to spot as he stood only a few paces away from the arena fighters' entrance, just out of reach of the light from the torches. It was more than evident by the sweat dripping down the man's face that he was exhausted.

"How are you doing, Uncle Siah?" Iggy asked as they walked up behind him.

Siah smiled upon hearing the title 'uncle.' It reminded him that Khoz had been as close to him as a brother and that his sons were as close as nephews.

"I'm doing okay, lad. That fight was something new to me. The man was a formidable opponent, but what really scared me was the look in his eyes as his swords burst into flames."

It was strange to the boys to hear a man who was nearly three times their size talking about fear. They simply didn't expect fear to exist within the massive frame. He wiped a cloth over his face and down his arms as they continued to talk.

"The greatest warriors on Appagon come from Sanctus Spire. I can't really judge because I haven't fought others from there, but that man could be the best fighter I have ever met."

"Really?" Marcus inquired with somewhat of a skeptical tone.

Siah seemed almost insulted by Marcus' response. "If Gus hadn't caught the man when he did, I know I would have been killed. He was so focused that not even my abilities could have created a barrier to stop him.

They listened quietly as the words began to take meaning. The realization started to sink in that if the fight had taken place out in the wild, then Siah would have lost the fight and his life.

"There you boys are," a familiar voice said behind them. They turned to see Breeze standing there. "You men and your barbarianism, what will we do with you?" They laughed at her statement as she walked over. Zeph put an arm around her as she joined their little gathering.

The lights of the nearby arena were just far enough away from them that they were enveloped in darkness. The multitude of stars floated above their heads. The five of them lay down on the cool grass. It was very late, most likely past midnight. It didn't matter, though; none of them had to be anywhere but the festival for the next two days.

After a while, they got up and began to stroll around the campsites scattered all over Daunt and surrounding areas. Many of the people were foreign to them. There were many new cultures represented in Daunt for this Alignment Festival. As they continued through the campsites, a soft sound began to fill their ears. Everyone listened closely, trying to locate where the sound was coming from. They soon came upon a camp, discovering the source of the sounds. Staying out of sight to not offend the visitors, they listened to the hypnotic music beats.

"Hey! Hey!" one of the men shouted out. Several other men followed suit. Drums began to beat, and the women clapped their hands. A steady rhythm began to flow. A man stepped into the middle of the circle, holding a stringed instrument. It was different than the instruments that were typically found in Daunt. He began to play, his fingers moving so quickly up and down the neck of the instrument, it was as though it were a part of his body.

The drummers matched the rhythm of the man's songs. Those with sticks beat their drums harder, while others slapped their drums with their hands. Several men began to sing, not words, but deep sounds that simply faded into the music. It was intoxicating.

The group stood in the shadows, watching and listening to the people. The music made them feel so alive. They had never heard music like this before. Zeph looked over at Marcus and watched him bob his head to the beat of the music. He smiled and then realized that he was tapping his foot to the beat of the music. They had never encountered music with a beat so alive it involuntarily moved a person's body.

The man playing the stringed instrument noticed the group of them standing just in the shadows. He smiled.

"Come, my friends, dance with us!" he shouted to them.

The group was startled that the man had seen them but quickly took him up on his offer. As they emerged from the shadows, the people of the camp welcomed them. The beat began to flow again, and everyone continued dancing. It was not something that any one person could follow, but you simply allowed the music to guide your body. Some stamped their feet, while others clapped their hands; the women moved their hips in ways that no one from Daunt could.

After what seemed like hours, the music finally came to a close. Everyone was drenched in sweat. The string player walked over to the group from Daunt.

"Welcome to my camp. My name is Fernando," he said, extending his hand to Zeph.

"Thank you, my name is Zeph. This is my brother Iggy, my best friend Marcus, my girlfriend Breeze, and my Uncle Siah," Zeph replied.

Fernando's eyes fell upon Siah, "Ah, you were the man that was fighting in the arena earlier, yes?"

"Yes, I was," he replied.

"That was not a fair fight. Even though you are both powerful men, the use of rage cannot be allowed in a competition such as that. Even the calmest of men could break solid metal in a state of rage."

The group enjoyed the hospitality of Fernando's camp for a while longer. The depth of night had fallen on the town now. Even the late-night festival events had ended, and the town lay in slumber. The quietness of the night filled the ears of all that remained awake in the camp. The absence of sound seemed deafening to Zeph. He stood by the row of trees beside the camp and stared into the bonfire. Breeze sat on a log several paces in front of him.

His thoughts returned to a night shortly after graduation, when he had finally expressed his feelings to Breeze. If it hadn't been for the events of the graduation ceremony, he was sure that even more time would have passed before telling her how he felt. Zeph had felt somehow bolder by the events of that day and had chosen to tell Breeze. Even though he was almost certain she would express the same feelings, he had never been more scared.

It had been raining that night, and they were both enjoying it. The evening had come, and Zeph had gone to meet her. He stood in the rain outside her house. They decided to take a walk through town. Since Zeph was already soaked to the bone, he had no objections. The evening rain made the warmth of the harvest season bearable.

The town was quiet, and most people were indoors. The sound of the rain hitting the rooftops and the puddles in the road was all that could be heard. It was a calm rain; no thunder or lightning accompanied the evening.

The two walked hand in hand through the town, chatting back and forth. The topic of their conversation was about their feelings for each other. Zeph's white hair was soaked and clung to his face. The clothes he wore also similarly clung to his body. His pale blue eyes sparkled like the falling drops of rain. Breeze concealed her hair under a cloak. The rain began to seep through her cloak and soon started to soak her clothing.

Stars shone faintly on the horizon; the rain would pass soon. They made their way to the large tree by the school, and sat beneath it like they had so many times before. The branches held the raindrops at bay for a while. Breeze sat in front of Zeph, laying her head on his chest. He gently placed his arms around her. Together, they watched as the clouds slowly rolled away, giving birth to the great expanse of stars above.

A shooting star flew across the horizon. Breeze smiled, turning and tilting her head to look up at Zeph.

"Make a wish," she said, looking into his eyes. Zeph stared back. He leaned in and kissed her softly for the first time. A rush filled Zeph's body, starting at his lips and making its way through every single part of his body. He could only assume that the sensation was just as intense and memorable for Breeze as well. Their lips parted. Zeph finally found the air to breathe. It was more potent than any sensation he had ever felt. He wondered if every kiss after would feel the same way.

Crack! The campfire popped, pulling Zeph from the memory back to the present. He was no longer under the tree with his love. Looking down at her, he realized she had been staring at him for quite some time.

"What are you thinking about?" she asked, waving him over. He walked over and sat down next to her.

"About the night we first kissed," he replied. It was just what she wanted to hear.

"I was thinking the same thing when I saw you staring at me."

"I'll never forget that night, and I'll never forget how I feel about you."

"You better not," she said in a joking manner.

The night drew out longer than they had planned. The group soon said goodbyes to their host and headed home. The competitions started on the second day of the festival. Marcus loved the competitions almost as much as he loved clothing. Any opportunity to display brute force, and he was up for the challenge. Zeph and Iggy had always enjoyed the various competitions, too. Breeze was indifferent most of the time but tagged along nonetheless. However, this year, there was a competition in which each of the four youths wished to participate. Even though the night was late, the anticipation of the coming day made it difficult to sleep.

THE DAWN BROKE WITH force over Daunt. As the suns rose on the horizon, the townsfolk and tourists began to flood the streets. Much preparation was taking place for the daylong series of competitions. The clothing had changed from the previous day. Many people wore clothing that was drab and plain colored. The change in clothing was also in preparation for the upcoming day's events. Hours of competition were waiting, and no matter what a person was wearing right now, they would all be wearing the same thing by the time the competitions started.

Many Warriors had come to Daunt; it was the most basic title given. They were all men and women known for their strength and ability to protect others. The occasional Champion could also be seen amongst the crowds of people. A Champion was a well-known fighter, someone who fought to protect groups of people. Many town leaders were considered either Warriors or Champions because of their many years of protecting their towns.

The murmurs of the crowd began to quiet to a mere whisper. A single individual was seen leaving the Rolling Hills Inn. He was not a large man, but it was clear that he was fit and muscular. A silver-colored breastplate was strapped across his chest. His deep blue cloak hung behind him, held by silver chains connected to the top of the breastplate. The clothing he wore was tailored to allow for maximum movement while still presenting the image of a gentleman when he was standing still. His boots were also plate metal and reached the top of his knees. The elemental symbol for Wind was engraved in the center of his breastplate and on the top of his boots. It was a refined suit of plate armor, more minimalistic than most to allow for great freedom and movement. A glimpse of the man's Wind symbol could be seen through the long black hair that hung across his forehead.

All eyes fell upon the sword attached to the man's waist. It was an extremely well-crafted, long sword. It shone like a highly polished mirror. Several rows of glyphs ran upward along the blade, empowering it with several different properties. The weapon smith in Daunt just stared. He knew he could never make such a piece of weaponry if he worked on it for the rest of his life.

The man looked around at the eyes of the villagers staring at him. It didn't make him particularly uncomfortable; he was used to people stopping and staring at him. He began walking north towards the end of town near the arena. Several people started following him. It was like watching children follow their hero around. He allowed it for several minutes, then stopped abruptly and turned around. One of the men shrieked in terror, thinking the man had become angry by their following.

"If you're going to follow me, you could at least direct me to where I might find the Arbitrator and Presenter of the combat events," his voice was not harsh and angry as the men expected but relatively quiet and sincere.

"Well, I think Siah is already up at the arena; he's the Presenter, you see. Last night, though, Uriym Praotes took over for a short while during a match that Siah was fighting. And I guess Gus is the guy you're looking for if you're looking for an Arbitrator. I'm guessing he's probably up there too right now."

"Who is this man Gus?"

The tone of the villager's voice intrigued the man, and he wanted to learn more about Gus.

"Gus? Well, he's sort of an inventor. I remember a long time ago when he had a shop here in town."

"Why was he appointed as Arbitrator?"

"Not sure. I do know that he has Levitation talents. Last night, when a match in the arena wouldn't stop, he lifted one of the fighters right into the air to stop the fight."

"Impressive." The man's face ran through several emotions as he spoke. "Thank you, sir, you have given me a good amount of useful knowledge. Knowledge is just as valuable and protective as a suit of armor. Never forget that." With a simple gesture, he tossed a gold kessa to the man. Turning once again, he continued onwards to the north end of town.

"Wait! What is your name, good sir?" the villager called out.

"In my land, I am known as Sir Jarian the Hero, but you may simply call me Jarian."

The coin fell from the villager's hand, and his jaw dropped in unison. He quickly picked up the coin and ran to tell his friends that a Hero was in town.

Jarian continued through town; soon, he passed the final rows of houses and made his way up the last hill out of town. Reaching the top, he looked out towards the rolling green hills beyond the edge of town and the large arena set up before him. The arena stood tall in the early morning light. It was nothing more than groups of bandstands connected together in a large circular fashion. Despite its plainness, it was still an imposing structure in Daunt, and could easily hold several thousand people.

Jarian walked over towards two enormous wooden doors, which he deduced was the entrance to the arena. Voices came from the other side. Pushing on the large doors, they swung open with much more ease than he expected. Siah and Gus stopped conversing with the workers and turned their heads toward the doors. The heads of several workers poked around Siah's massive frame to see who had entered the arena.

"Can I help you, Sir?" Gus' question emphasized the word "sir." It was clear that this man was more than a mere Champion.

"Please, you need not call me by my title. I am no more a hero than a peasant working hard to feed his family," Jarian responded.

"Then I will call you friend and ask your name?"

"Jarian."

"Greetings, my name is Gus. What brings you to our quaint little village?" Gus asked as he reached out to shake Jarian's hand.

"I do not think that 'little' is a very accurate description of your village at this particular point in time," Jarian replied with a smile, "I have come for the Alignment, of course, but I was also hoping to participate in the Blade and Fist Competitions."

"You wish to compete?" Siah asked with a slightly wide-eyed look.

"If there is someone who wishes to challenge me, I will accept, but I was hoping more to help present the events."

"Siah?" Gus asked, looking over at the large man.

"It would be an honor to share my duties with a man such as you."

"Thank you, then I will help you with any preparations needed for the competitions," Jarian replied.

The large wooden doors of the gate swung open, again drawing everyone's attention in that direction. Standing there were four youths. Jarian looked each of them up and down. He couldn't place his finger on it, but the one with the white hair notably stood out in his mind.

"Jarian, perhaps you would like to meet four of Daunts most promising youth?" Gus asked. Jarian nodded as the group of four walked over. "This is my daughter, Breeze."

"Pleased to meet you, Jarian," she replied.

"I see she is gifted with Wind just as you are," Jarian noticed, "then we three share a common bond," he said with a smile.

Siah was the next to speak up, "Those two over there are my nephews, Zeph and Iggy."

"Let me guess, you are Iggy?" Jarian asked, staring down at Iggy.

"Yea, how did you know?"

"Just a feeling, so I guess that makes you Zeph."

Zeph was slightly hesitant but then nodded. The man was different from the other visitors he had seen in Daunt. The feeling that this man possessed great power was evident in how he held himself and his body language.

"Please don't let my appearance sway your views of me; I am no more different than you, Zeph."

Marcus let out a cough in an attempt to draw the man's attention. This caused Jarian to raise an eyebrow and turn his gaze toward the mocha-skinned young man.

"Those that seek attention will go unrecognized in life. A man's worth is not defined by the people that know him but by his ability to know himself." The words bore their way deep into Marcus. He tried to find the words to reply but found no words to speak back to Jarian.

"This is my best friend, Marcus," Zeph said, looking for some way to ease the state Marcus suddenly found himself in.

"A true friend he is, of that I have no doubt," Jarian looked at the troubled young man again. "Do not be discouraged by my words, Marcus; rather, learn what they mean to you." Marcus let out a small smile. "Good lad," replied Jarian as he squeezed Marcus' shoulder.

"Thanks for coming by, gang," Siah piped up, "but we still have a couple of hours before the first competition is ready. If you're planning on entering any of them, you need to sign up at the Weapons Shop," he explained.

"Alright, we'll go do that and be back later," Marcus replied as he regained his composure. With that, the four of them left the arena and began the walk back into town.

It was still early in the day, and the suns were only an hour or two above the horizon. There were some clouds scattered across the sky; these would be a welcome treat later in the day when the fighters would be worn from the warm rays of the harvest suns. Some would hope for rain; a fight could intensify during a rainstorm.

The group made their way through town; it took much longer than they intended. Even in the early morning hours, the streets were full of people. The street vendors had already started to peddle their wares, and people wandered from stall to stall from one side of the street to the other. A sea of brown and beige-clothed people ran through the town. Banners were starting to be hung from buildings and street lamps, featuring a variety of fighting stances and styles.

As they reached the Weapons Shop, they encountered a line of several dozen men and women standing in front. Within minutes, the line had grown to just as many people standing behind them.

"Wow, good thing we got here early," Marcus said, looking back at the line that had formed behind their group. The line moved at a slow yet steady pace. The minutes passed, and finally, they reached the front of the line. As expected, the line led to a man sitting at a table just outside the weapon shop.

"Name, Ability, and Competition?" the man asked. Marcus was the first to step forward.

"Marcus, Fire, and I would like to enter the Fist Competition." The man looked Marcus up and down.

"Well, you look strong enough for the Intermediate level, but for your own safety, I'm still going to have you take a proficiency test." After writing Marcus' information down, he handed him a card for the proficiency test.

"Who's next?" the man asked. Zeph stepped forward.

"Zeph, Omega, and I'd like to enter the Blade Competition." The man gave Zeph a skeptical look.

"Have you ever even handled a blade boy?" the question took Zeph by surprise; he had never thought of his skills coming into question. Before he could respond, Marcus jumped in.

"Just give him the proficiency test; he'll be fine."

"Alright, don't blame me if he gets hurt. And you, young lady, what will you be doing for us today?"

"Breeze, Wind, and I'll be entering the Bow Competition."

"Can you handle a bow, missy?"

"No disrespect, but a heck of a lot better than you could."

The man let out a bold laugh and smiled, "You got spunk, kid; you're in."

Iggy was the last to approach the man, something he wasn't looking forward to. His small stature had always made people question his age and capabilities.

"And what do you think you're doing, little boy?" the man asked.

"Iggy, Light, and I'll be in the Gauntlet Competition."

The man looked over at the rest of the group as if to say, 'Are you serious.' Due to Iggy's young appearance, he looked far too young to compete. Iggy slammed his hand down on the table, causing the man to jump halfway out of his seat.

"I may not be a strong fighter, but I'm fourteen years old, and I can damn well defend myself!" he shouted at the man.

"Alrighty," the man said in a shaky voice, handing Iggy his proficiency card. "And if I do say so, a boy your age should not be cussing." Everyone smiled as they walked away from the shop.

There were several different staging areas for the proficiency tests. They decided to split off and head to each of their tests. Breeze went with Zeph since she didn't have a test to take.

"So, can you really handle a bow, or was that just a bluff?" Zeph asked as they headed to his test.

"I actually can, just one of my many hidden talents."

"I see," he said with a smile.

It didn't take long to reach the staging area for the Blade Competition. It was in the north end of town. A large circle had been made by placing white stones into a shallow trench. Only a few men stood in line, it seemed that either not many had entered or most did not need to pass a proficiency test.

Zeph noticed Jarian standing off to the side of the ring. It seemed as though he was moderating the tests. Zeph wanted to know more about the man. He seemed to have so much knowledge and insightfulness inside. Perhaps he was someone else long ago, even though it was obvious that he had to only be in his early thirties.

Crack! The sound of the wooden swords clashing caused Zeph's eyes to dart toward the two men in the ring. One of the men resembled one of the arena workers Zeph had seen earlier. It made sense that the arena workers may also be skilled fighters. Zeph recognized the other man as a neighbor who lived nearby. He seemed to have good skills as a fighter.

Jarian raised his hand to the fighters. He then handed the man a card and sent him on his way. Even though Zeph couldn't see what was on the card, he guessed that it was the rank for the arena bout. After several more rounds, it was Zeph's turn. The fighter in the ring was visibly tired. Even though Zeph had never really fought with a sword, at least nothing more than play fighting with Marcus, he saw the man as an easy challenge.

"Wait!" Jarian called out. "I will test this young man myself." Zeph's eyes widened. One moment, he was fighting a notably worn-out fighter, and now he had to fight a genuine Hero.

"The easiest choices in life can often bring the hardest obstacles," Jarian said as he unhooked his cloak from his breastplate and picked up a wooden sword. Zeph also picked up a wooden sword. They stood opposite each other at the farthest points of the ring. The crowd gathered around the ring. This was the first time Jarian had been seen fighting, in any form, since his arrival in Daunt.

Zeph held the sword with both hands. He tried to concentrate on his opponent, visualizing Jarian not as a grand hero but as an average man. Opening his eyes, he stepped forward. Jarian lunged at him, Zeph quickly brought up his sword and blocked. A loud crack rang out. The wood vibrated violently in his hand. Zeph couldn't believe he had done that. His moment of triumph was lost as he felt the sting of Jarian's sword connecting with his ribs.

Stumbling back, Zeph raised his sword to block the next strike. He wouldn't make the continuing mistake of enjoying any of his accomplishments until the fight was over. Jarian lunged again. Zeph concentrated on the man's movements as he stepped forward. As Jarian lunged forward time seemed to almost slow down. Zeph quickly blocked Jarian's attack. Jarian tried several other fast attacks, but Zeph was able to block every single one. The crowd of onlookers followed each of Zeph's movements with intense focus. No one in the crowd had ever seen someone with such fast reflexes. After several minutes, Jarian raised his hand.

"A wise warrior knows when to strike and when to defend. You have proven that statement to be true, Zeph. Even though you have outstanding reflexes for blocking, you still have much to learn about taking an offensive approach. Your rank will be Novice."

"Thank you, Jarian, I look forward to seeing you later," Zeph replied. With that, he and Breeze left to find the others. It wasn't long until they ran into Iggy, who was also looking around for the others in their group.

"How'd it go, little bro?" Zeph asked as Iggy walked over.

"Pretty good, I think. I passed a series of small obstacles with little trouble. I was told that the real Gauntlet will be much harder."

"You'll do great, Iggy," Breeze said with a smile.

"I don't know about that. I didn't realize that people can be killed in the Gauntlet. I don't think even Gus could stop some of those traps at the last second."

The three of them continued to wander around. Marcus couldn't be too far behind. The Fist Competition was highly favored. It was the most participated in out of all the competitions held. Besides men, many women also entered.

It was nearing noon, which was when the Blade competition was scheduled to start. Zeph was nervous about the competition; he had never done anything like this before. The support of Jarian had encouraged him, though. If a hero said he had fantastic blocking skills, he must be outstanding. Visions began to fill his head; he saw himself defeating his last opponent and winning the competition.

"You haven't won yet."

The voice snapped Zeph's mind back to reality. He turned to see Marcus standing right behind them. Zeph began to open his mouth in protest to Marcus' accusation.

"Don't even think of denying it; I know you were daydreaming of your inevitable triumph in the arena." Marcus' words made Zeph stop his protest and simply chuckle.

As a group, they decided they would take the little time they had left before the first competition to browse the various shops in Daunt. They headed south, down the main road, and back into the center of town. Dozens upon dozens of shops lined the street, selling everything from jewelry to weapons to food. As they passed the many different shops, they all thought back to the Pythus Alignment festival nine years earlier. Iggy was too young to remember much, but the rest were sure it had not been this intense.

Zeph handed out small handfuls of silver kessas to everyone in the group. Heading to different shops on either side of the street, they bought themselves little trinkets from the merchants. It was more enjoyable than expected; they hadn't spent time together like this for months. No matter where life would take them, they knew they would always be friends.

A loud gong rang out over the town. It was time. The nervousness swelled up in Zeph again. He looked as though he might throw up the somewhat odd-looking food he had just eaten. Swallowing, he looked at Breeze.

"It will be okay. Remember, you can do this," she said in a comforting tone, "we'll be cheering for you from the stands, and I'll be waiting for you when you're done."

Zeph smiled weakly. Breeze leaned up and kissed him. It helped wash away the distressing thoughts floating in his head. The group made their way towards the arena. They pushed through the crowd as best as they could. Marcus shouted for people to get out of the way that a competitor was coming through. Surprisingly, it worked, and people let them through faster. Reaching the competitors' gate, the group parted with Zeph and made their way to some seats Siah had reserved for them at the bottom seats of the arena.

Zeph showed the arena worker his ranking card. The worker approached a nearby table and pulled a sword from its sheath. He handed it to Zeph. It was lighter than Zeph had expected. Running his finger along the blade, Zeph was surprised to find it sharp. He figured it wouldn't be much of a competition if the blade was dull.

A booming voice from up in the bandstands caught his attention. "Welcome, one and all, to the 6th Cronus Competitions of the Seventh Age. I'm sure we have at least several people in the crowd who were at the first competition of the Age, one hundred and eight years ago. I, myself, plan to see the 10th competition in another seventy-two years."

Zeph quickly realized it was Siah's voice he was hearing from his position beneath the bandstands. Other competitors stood nearby and listened to the announcements overhead.

"We have a guest in Daunt today; I'm sure many of you have already seen him." Zeph knew Siah was talking about Jarian. "He has come to help oversee the Blade and Fist Competitions. May I present, Sir Jarian the Hero." The arena began to clap and let out a loud series of cheers.

"Thank you, everyone. Before the first bout begins, I have a few words for the fighters standing beneath your seats at this very moment." A hush fell over the crowd. The fighters beneath the stands strained their ears to listen.

"Glory is for the unworthy, honor is for the poor, courage is reserved for the faint of heart, and victory is found only in the hands of the weak. For it is only when we have nothing left to lose do we see who we really are and what is worth fighting for."

The words continued to ring in Zeph's ears as he watched the first pair of fighters enter the arena. The sounds of the blades clashing and the cheers of the crowd seemed to fade away as his mind rolled over the words. Several bouts passed by as he stared into oblivion. The arena worker in front of him began to wave in his direction. Zeph realized it was his turn. He sauntered towards the man, dragging his sword behind him. Stepping into the bright noonday light, Zeph raised a hand in front of his eyes. A cheer rang out from the crowd.

"May I present Zeph, son of Khoz. Born and raised in Daunt, this is his first time in the arena," Jarian shouted out over the cheers of the crowd. Zeph looked up at Jarian, standing on a balcony across the arena from the fighter entrance. Hearing his name being called, Zeph saw Marcus, Iggy, Breeze, Victor, and his mother sitting at ground level a short distance away, waving at him. Smiling, he waved back and then to the rest of the arena.

"Let's see how this Novice level fighter fares against the current champion." Zeph looked across at the man he was to fight with. He was not a large man by any means; Zeph guessed he was maybe only a handful of years older than he was. Even though he had fought several bouts, he was full of energy. A winner of a bout was given a rejuvenation potion to drink. The potion would revitalize and bring the fighter back to regular strength. In this manner, each fighter would have an equal chance against the next.

The fighter raised his sword, and Zeph also followed suit. A hush fell over the crowd as they waited for the word. Jarian looked down at Zeph. Gus also stepped out from the back of the balcony and looked down at him.

"Begin!" both men shouted. The arena burst with shouts and cheers as the two opponents swung at each other. The man swung his sword towards Zeph's left shoulder. Zeph quickly blocked the first attempt and lunged at the man's stomach. He jumped back, avoiding the tip of Zeph's blade.

No protection was worn in the fight. Even though the blades were sharp, the point of the match was to make your opponent claim defeat, not to physically harm them or, in the worst case, kill them.

Zeph brought his sword above his head and brought it down fast. The man placed one hand on the tip of his sword and blocked the blow as it came down. Pushing off the ground, he threw Zeph several steps back. Swinging his sword from the right, he tried to connect with Zeph's left shoulder once again. This attack seemed to be the man's most powerful, and Zeph quickly anticipated it. Taking one step to his right, Zeph struck the man's sword, sending him spinning from the additional force added to his swing.

The cheers of the crowd rose at each clash of the blades. Zeph looked at the smiling and cheering faces of his friends and family. The man was not impressed with Zeph. He lunged at him. Zeph smacked the blade away, which caused the man to quickly lunge again. This time, Zeph stumbled back and fell. The crowd let out a gasp thinking Zeph had been defeated already.

Grabbing his sword, Zeph flipped backward and jumped to his feet once more. The crowd let out a cheer of approval that the bout had not ended quite so easily. Zeph felt a charge of energy run through him. He hoped it was simply adrenaline, not one of his abilities trying to manifest. The use of abilities and talents was prohibited at the Novice level of the competition.

Gripping his sword with two hands, the man quickly swung his sword up, trying to catch the right side of Zeph's body. Planting his feet, Zeph angled his sword downwards and caught the blade coming up. An instant lock of blades occurred as the hilt of Zeph's sword stopped the blade. The loud clash and grinding of metal that followed spurred the crowd even more. It was evident that this was their most favored bout in the competition so far.

Zeph began to grind his teeth as he pushed down with his sword. The man was also struggling as he tried to force the blade upwards towards Zeph's hip. A change in the man's stance caused Zeph to glance down at the man's feet.

Jarian's eyes widened as he watched the change in stance. Being a seasoned fighter, he knew exactly what the change meant. There was only one tactic for why a fighter would change his stance while in a pinned-down position. Turning to Gus, he blurted out, "Stop the fight!" but it was too late.

Zeph felt the downward pressure give out as the man pulled his sword back and quickly slid it across the ground, releasing all resistance. The man quickly spun around in one swift motion, his sword flowing around his body as he brought it up and swung at Zeph's unguarded left side.

The blade sliced into Zeph's garment, pushed past the skin and muscle, stopping abruptly at the bone. The crowd immediately became silent. Zeph's head began to bobble a little as he dropped his sword. It fell with a clang in the arena dirt. A burning sensation began to flow from Zeph's shoulder up into his head and down across his chest. His head dropped to his left as he looked at the blade suspended in his flesh. The man stared at the wound as he suddenly realized what he had done; he instantly let go of the hilt. Zeph watched as the weight of the sword caused it to slip out of the wound. It fell to the ground with a clank. Blood began to gush and flow profusely out of the wound. Zeph's gaze shifted upward to Jarian. Darkness began to cloud his vision.

Zeph saw Jarian leap into the air from the balcony atop the bandstands. Zeph's legs became weightless as he felt his body collapsing beneath its own weight. Expecting to feel the brutal impact of the ground, Zeph was surprised to find that in a split second, Jarian had managed to leap from atop the balcony and catch him on the arena floor.

"Get a Healer now!" Jarian shouted to the arena workers. His voice was unbelievably loud; it sent everyone in the arena jerking back. The workers quickly ran for town. There was no hesitation as Iggy leaped to his feet and jumped the bandstand wall. It was as tall as two men, but it was nothing compared to the jump Jarian had just made seconds earlier. He hit the ground with a thud. Running towards Zeph, Iggy slid through the dirt and skidded to a stop next to where Jarian held him. Two more thuds were heard as Marcus and Victor hit the arena's dirt floor.

Iggy tore the remaining portion of Zeph's sleeve off and quickly tied it around the wound. Gus, along with several guards, grabbed the other fighter. The man seemed stunned as he stared down at Zeph. He looked in shock at Jarian, "I didn't mean to... I'm so sorry. Omega, help him; he's not going to die, is he?" The man collapsed down to his knees and continued to stare at Zeph.

Jarian pressed his hands tightly over the wound. He watched as the blood completely soaked through the cloth and was now beginning to flow over his hands. Iggy held his hands outwards over the wound as he began to concentrate. Marcus and Victor removed their shirts and placed them underneath Zeph's head. Zeph's mother and Breeze ran into the arena through the fighter's entrance. They both tried to get to Zeph, but Marcus and Victor stopped them.

"Let Iggy and Jarian help him until the Healers arrive," Victor spoke softly to them. Tears filled both of the women's eyes. It had been no longer than a single minute since the incident happened, but it was already feeling like an eternity. Zeph's eyes began to flutter as he looked around frantically. A pool of blood was forming beneath his left shoulder. This kind of injury was extremely uncommon in the Novice stage of the competition. Several Healers were typically present, but not until the Intermediate bouts.

"Zeph, you have to stay with me!" Iggy said frantically. Zeph's gaze turned to his little brother. The soft glow on the palms of his hands comforted Zeph; he knew Iggy was trying hard. His skill, however, was not on the same level as the trained Healers in town. The pool of blood had doubled in size. Iggy fought back the tears that tried to break from his eyes. Marcus quickly rushed over, "How's he doing?"

"I don't know where to focus; I can't stop the bleeding fast enough," Iggy whispered as he began to cry, "and the healers won't get here in time." A wave of disbelief washed over Marcus. Zeph heard the words his brother had so carefully tried to hide from his ears. Reaching up, he touched the sleeve of Iggy's shirt. He turned and looked down at Zeph.

"Give me your hand," Zeph said as he reached up toward Iggy.

He concentrated on Iggy as he felt his consciousness beginning to fail. Even though Zeph knew his body was failing, he knew his mind was still powerful. A jolt of energy flew up Iggy's arm, startling the boy. Quickly, Iggy placed his hand directly over the wound. The soft, pale light emitting from his hands suddenly burst radiant white. The arena workers came rushing back into the arena, closely followed by two healers. The healers stopped in their tracks and stared at the young boy, who was emitting more energy than they could have produced together. Jarian removed the bandage as Iggy continued to concentrate on the wound. The wound was deep, and the bone and tissue were still visible, but it no longer bled as Jarian completely removed the bandages.

Zeph's grip on his brother's hand failed as he slipped into unconsciousness, breaking the transfer of Focus energy he had been passing to Iggy. The two healers quickly rushed over.

"We'll take it from here, lad; you did an amazing job," one of them said as Iggy stood to his feet. After several more minutes, the wound was completely healed, only a scar remained. Even with healers, significant wounds still left a scar from the healing process.

They gave Zeph several potions, and he was conscious and standing within moments. His mother embraced him and refused to let go. She told him that he had to stop scaring her like this. Zeph thought about it; she did have a point. He seemed to be getting into life-and-death situations regularly in recent days.

Jarian stood to address the crowd. "The competition will continue momentarily. The opposing fighter will not be disqualified or reprimanded since it was confirmed that the severity of this blow was not the intention."

Marcus and Victor took opposite sides of Zeph and helped him out of the arena. The group sat on the grass a short distance from the fighter's entrance. Zeph was still a little weak. His head felt oddly heavy and was still bobbling a little. Everyone else sat in silence while Zeph lay back in the grass. He looked down at the scar that wrapped around his left shoulder. His eyes caught the bright red color of all the blood that had soaked into his clothing. The skin and tissue were tender, but it felt like he had only been punched in the arm. The image of the blade slicing into his shoulder sent shivers up his neck.

Zeph sat up, "Thanks, Iggy."

Iggy looked over at Zeph and mustered a smile. It wasn't their first time in a place like this. They remembered back to the night at the inn, only a handful of months earlier. Ever since that day, Iggy had strived to become stronger in his Elemental abilities.

"I estimate about an hour longer till that competition is done," Victor piped up.

"How are you feeling, man?" Marcus asked in a concerned tone.

"Obviously, not the best, but I feel well enough to watch someone beat the brown off you."

Not many people could get away with throwing a joke like that at Marcus, but Zeph was like a brother to him. He poked Zeph in the scar,

"Oh, does that hurt? Oh, I'm sorry," Marcus asked sarcastically. Everyone couldn't help but laugh.

Victor, Marcus, and Iggy headed into town to gather food for lunch. Breeze and Zeph's mother remained. Each sat on the opposing side of him.

"You know you had both of us worried to death," Breeze glared. She was doing her best to hide how shaken up she still was.

"How was I supposed to know I'd get that injured? I figured a few bruises, some minor cuts max."

"Sometimes I wonder if you go looking for these things," his mother said with an equally intense glare. Her expression showed the distress and emotional pain she was still experiencing.

"Okay, look, you two are the two most important women in my life. Being that you both care a great deal about me, you'll just have to deal with worrying about me, just like I worry about both of you."

"I think Jarian would have put it more eloquently, but that will do for now," Breeze replied with a laugh.

"Mom?" Zeph asked, turning his head towards her.

"You know I will always worry about you, son; nothing will ever change that."

Zeph gave both of them a hug. The sounds of the arena drew their gaze back toward it. The competition continued on as planned. By the sound of the cheering, the next fight was going very well.

Victor began walking towards the three of them, with Marcus and Iggy following close behind. In their hands were several sacks. One could only assume there was food contained inside. They sat down and displayed all of the foods they had chosen. It was clear they had selected many different foreign cuisines. Over the next half hour, they enjoyed the foods of the other Realms that had come to the festival.

After the meal, the group continued to sit and talk amongst themselves. The next competition would be starting soon. As much as Zeph wanted to watch the remainder of the competition, he felt as though he needed a mental break. The day was progressing slowly. On a day of festivals, though, this was something sought after. No one ever wanted a day of excitement to flow by like a swift breeze.

The Blade Competition came to a close. A warrior from Sanctus Spire was named the winner of the Advanced. It wasn't surprising, though; most of the best warriors in town for the festival were from Sanctus Spire. Smaller prizes were given to the winners of the Intermediate and Novice categories. Marcus was already preparing for the next competition. He was off to the side, practicing his stances and punches.

Zeph walked over to him, "So you think you're going to win this thing, huh?"

"That's the plan."

"Well, I think you have a lot better chance of winning this competition than I did in mine," Zeph said with a grin.

Just then, a man came walking over to the group. It was the fighter Zeph had fought with earlier. He walked over to Zeph with his head hung low. Marcus raised an eyebrow as the man came close to Zeph.

"Looks like you didn't win either, huh," Marcus said with a look of annoyance at the man. The man held out his hand and offered Zeph the medallion in it. The medallion was inscribed: *Winner of the 6th Cronus Blade Competition of the Seventh Age. Rank Novice.*

"I cannot return to my family with this medallion, knowing what it almost cost me. If I had taken your life, I could not return to my village an honorable man." The man's head was still lowered as he could not look at Zeph.

Zeph took the man's hands and asked to see his face. The man slowly looked up at Zeph. He then repeated the words Jarian had spoken before the start of the competition, "Glory is for the unworthy, honor is for the poor, courage is reserved for the faint of heart, and victory is found only in the hands of the weak. For it is only when we have nothing left to lose we see who we really are and what is worth fighting for."

The man seemed to understand what Zeph was trying to tell him.

"In my village, you will be known as Zeph the Forgiving." With that, the man left. Zeph sat back down; the rest of the group was silent for a moment.

"That was a very honorable thing you did for that man, Zeph," said Victor. "You have more honor and forgiveness than many I have encountered in my travels."

The loud gong rang out again over the town, signaling it was time for the next competition. Marcus ran towards the stadium, and the rest followed close behind. Zeph waited as the rest of the group headed up to the bandstands.

"Good luck, bro," Zeph said, hugging his best friend. "You'll do great. I expect you to surpass the Intermediate category."

"Heck yeah!" Marcus let out. They clasped hands then Marcus headed into the fighter's entrance. Zeph joined the rest of the group up on the bandstand. The opening announcements were similar to those said in the last competition. After several more minutes of introductions, the first bout started.

The perspective was very different for Zeph. The fresh wood let out a soft fragrance from baking in the midday sun. The food and sweat of the hundreds of people in the stands also filled his nose. People in the stands waved banners with prominent symbols that Zeph could only assume were for a specific fighter or village. He enjoyed this perspective much better than in the arena.

Zeph took a seat between Breeze and Iggy. The three of them were excited. Zeph's mother and Victor sat in seats to their left. The first section of the competition ended. The remaining fighter was named the winner of the novice level. The fighter would now fight the first challenger of the Intermediate level. Even if the fighter was defeated, they would still receive the medallion for the novice rank at the end of the competition.

Marcus was the first to step out. The crowd cheered. Marcus quickly removed all jewelry from his body. He removed his ring, chain, and armbands and handed them to the arena worker. He also threw his shirt at the man. Zeph hadn't seen Marcus without a shirt for a while now, and it was quite evident that Marcus had been doing hard workouts for the last few months. His heavily toned, muscular brown skin shone in the midday suns. Women in the crowd sent out their coos to Marcus, who simply smiled and waved at them. In Marcus' opinion, there was nothing wrong with being the object of women's affection.

The fight began. Marcus was thrilled that he had the first shot at the winner of the Novice bouts. It was a middle-aged man who was fit, but it was apparent that he had the fighting abilities of a large stone. On that thought, Marcus made a mental note not to get into a position where the man could wrap his arms around him.

The man lunged at Marcus, taking a few swings. Marcus easily dodged them. In the competition, the use of hands and fists was the primary weapon, but an opponent could also use their feet and legs. This was something Marcus was hoping for. The man took a few more swings at Marcus. Grabbing the man's fist with one hand, Marcus delivered a brutal hit to the man's torso with his other. Holding his stomach, the man stumbled back. Marcus wasted no time; he quickly leaped up into the air. The loud smack could be heard as Marcus' right foot connected with the man's head. He fell to the ground, completely unconscious.

The crowd roared at the bold show on Marcus' part. Even Jarian and Gus, up on the balcony, raised their eyebrows at each other. Several workers took the man out of the arena. The next fighter, a young man, was announced, and the next bout began. Marcus quickly sized him up; he couldn't have been more than a few years older than himself.

The fighter charged at Marcus, leaping into the air; he connected both feet with Marcus' chest. Marcus did a complete backflip and landed hard on his stomach.

"Big mistake!" Marcus muttered under his breath.

Leaping to his feet, Marcus charged across the arena. He threw several quick punches at the fighter, who blocked them with surprising speed. He took a hard swing at Marcus, who simply ducked. Marcus sent his knee hard into the fighter's stomach. The young man stumbled back. Marcus threw a hard punch. He grabbed Marcus' fist and spun him around, pinning his arm behind his back. Reaching around with his free arm, Marcus grabbed the fighter's waist. Kicking hard off the ground, Marcus propelled himself upwards. The young man collapsed under the additional weight. Hitting the ground with a hard thud, the other fighter lay on his back, completely dazed, Marcus standing over him.

Jarian raised his hand and called out to the arena, "Defeated, Marcus is the winner." Gus and Marcus took a moment to talk; after several minutes, Jarian raised his hands to the crowd again. "We have decided to increase this fighter's standing rank to Advanced. Since he entered the Intermediate bouts, he will still have a chance to fight the last challenger." The crowd's response to the announcement did not sway one way or the other. Marcus waved to the crowd, which cheered him on even more. Marcus then headed back to the fighters' waiting area. The remaining bouts for the intermediate level proceeded. The bouts passed, some ending quickly, such as Marcus' first fight, and some taking longer.

The final Intermediate fighter stood in front of Marcus. A hush fell over the crowd. Nothing like this had ever been done before. Since Marcus had been pushed ahead to the Advanced ranking, he was now the first fighter to battle the winner of the Intermediate rounds. Now, everyone would see if he was truly worthy of being pushed forward.

Each fighter was given a rejuvenation potion to level the playing field. Each drank it down quickly.

"Begin!" Jarian shouted.

The man took a run at Marcus. Taking a swing at him, Marcus raised his hand to block. The man swept his leg underneath Marcus, knocking him off his feet. In a quick motion, Marcus flipped up onto his feet while narrowly avoiding several blows. In return, he delivered several fast blows that dazed the man momentarily. The man threw a punch, to which Marcus countered by catching the man's fist. This trick had been anticipated and was short-lived.

Smack! Marcus felt the man's other fist connect with the left side of his face. It burned as the blood rushed to the surface. Anger burned inside Marcus even more than the burning on his face. He swung his leg straight up as fast as possible, connecting hard with the man's chin. Using the same force, Marcus brought his leg down on the man's head. This, however, did not knock the man to the ground. The uppercut that quickly followed sent the man flying backward into the air. Marcus stood in triumph over the man where he lay motionless.

The cheers of the crowd rang out as Marcus was declared the winner. A brief break was taken before the next section of the competition started. Marcus strode around the arena, waving to the many fans he had acquired. He was so preoccupied with his musing that he didn't notice the large man enter the arena.

"Fighters take your place!" Siah announced from the podium. For the first two levels of the competition, Siah watched from the stands, but now that the competition was getting much more severe, he took a place on the podium.

Marcus turned around to see a huge man standing across from him. He was nothing compared to Siah but was an exceptionally large man nonetheless. Marcus swallowed hard. This would not be a very pretty fight.

"Begin!" Jarian shouted.

The man put up his fists. They were nearly half the size of Marcus' face. Marcus moved closer to the man, who seemed unwilling to move from his starting position. Taking several steps forward, the man took a swing at Marcus. He missed, to which Marcus was extremely thankful. Marcus rushed the man and delivered a hard kick to his ribs. The man groaned in pain. The look he shot Marcus made him almost wish he could simply apologize to the man. That thought was quickly wiped away as the man delivered both fists deep into Marcus' stomach. A cry of pain came blaring out of Marcus as he flew backward.

Dust flew up from the ground. The suns had baked the ground in the arena to a dry waste. Marcus stood, slumped over awkwardly, holding his ribs. Other than the pain from the initial blow, he could feel no breaks in the bones. Marcus looked up at the man, who was now taking several steps towards him. He looked as though he wanted to finish Marcus off quickly and continue to the next fighter.

Marcus quickly began running to the left, not away from the man but rather in a circular formation around the fighter. If there was something other than fighting, Marcus was amazing at it was running. He made several laps around the man before abruptly stopping. The distraction gave Marcus just the split second he needed. Giving a quick kick to the back of the fighter's legs, the man fell to his knees. Before Marcus could strike again, one of the fighter's arms caught him momentarily in the chest and sent him stumbling back.

The bout was becoming much longer than Marcus wanted it to be. He continued to look for a way to end the fight as quickly as possible. Placing one foot on the ground, the fighter began to stand. Marcus saw this as his opportunity. Running towards the man, he quickly stepped onto the man's knee. The man groaned as Marcus' weight landed on his bent leg. The expression of pain was quickly silenced as Marcus grabbed the man's head and embedded his knee into the fighter's face. A loud crack was heard as the blow shattered the man's nose.

The unconscious body of the man fell backward. Marcus stood in triumph. The crowd cheered once again. The arena workers removed the fallen fighter from the ring. Marcus took a moment to drink a rejuvenation potion. After that fight, he was feeling very drained. Within moments, his energy and focus returned. Even with the energy the potion brought, he had a strange feeling that this would be his final round.

A small, skinny man entered the arena. He was about the same size as Marcus but thinner and not quite as muscular. Marcus wondered how the man achieved the Advanced rank in the competition. They took up opposite positions in the ring. Jarian signaled for the bout to begin.

Marcus raised his fists just in time to feel the impact of the man's first three blows, one to his stomach and two to his face. Dazed, Marcus stumbled back. The man wasted no time and let loose a kick to Marcus' left temple, which was quickly followed by his other foot, delivering a power double kick to Marcus's head.

Blood splattered on the ground, and Marcus braced his fall. He could feel the left side of his head pulsing with every beat of his chest. The blood from his head quickly mixed with the blood he was spitting out from his mouth.

"Fight me!" the man shouted at Marcus, waiting for him to rise. The arena crowd looked down at the fighters with stunned expressions.

Rage quickly filled Marcus; he lunged at the man, knocking them to the ground. He threw several fast punches, all of which were easily blocked. Marcus' position on top of the man was quickly lost as the man wrapped his legs around Marcus and then wrapped his feet around Marcus' throat from behind, throwing him across the arena.

The feeling of impacting with the ground was starting to become all too familiar for Marcus' taste, as well as the taste of dirt in his mouth as he lay on his stomach. He wished for the fight to end. As he began to rise to his hands and knees, Marcus heard the rushing footstep of the other fighter racing towards him. Looking up, Marcus' last image was the man's foot launching upwards beneath his chin.

The crowd gasped as Marcus flew high into the air, doing a complete backflip. A small cloud of dust flew up around him as Marcus' body hit the ground. He lay motionless in the dirt of the arena. The arena workers swiftly ran over and carried him beneath the bandstands.

Zeph and the others quickly left the stands to find Marcus below. They found him being attended to by one of the healers. He was still unconscious and looked quite battered and bruised.

"Is he going to be okay?" Zeph asked with a skeptical look on his face.

"He's pretty banged up, but we'll take good care of him. That last fighter was more than he could handle," the healer explained.

"Uh...," Marcus moaned faintly.

"Looks like he's coming around," said the healer.

"Uh...my head," Marcus groaned as he lifted his hand to touch his forehead.

"That was a pretty crazy last fight. I guess you're not the best fighter in the world yet, bro," Zeph said with a smile. Marcus let out a weak smile. Zeph winced a bit at Marcus' bloody grin. Even though he didn't win the whole competition, Marcus was still happy to have won the Intermediate Medallion.

The Fist Competition came to a close. Each fighter was awarded a medallion. Marcus was given a commendation for his valiant efforts to hold on to the competition. He still looked somewhat bruised and battered from the competition even after being healed, but then again, so did all the other fighters.

There was another downtime between competitions; the next would start in an hour. It was getting near dinner time for most in Daunt. Many people returned to their homes or stopped by food vendors to find something to eat. The group still had a lot of food left over from earlier in the day. Everyone took a seat once more and ate atop one of the lush green hills near the arena. Breeze had returned home to gather her equipment for the next competition.

By the time the next gong rang out through Daunt, Breeze had returned with a finely crafted bow and a small quiver of arrows. The bow was simple, but not flimsy. Gus had crafted it when she was a little girl. Zeph and Marcus found it strange that she had hidden this skill from them for so many years.

After stringing up her bow, Breeze and the rest headed to an open area northwest of the arena. To the north of town lay rolling hills that went on for quite some time, but to the northwest of town lay open fields. It was the perfect place for the Bow Competition. Markers were placed at different points around the target areas, indicating where the crowd of spectators was allowed to stand and where not to.

Gus was entirely in charge of this competition. He waited for the majority of the crowd to gather before he spoke. The suns were making their way downwards on the horizon. The targets had been placed so that the suns' light would not affect the archers' abilities.

"Welcome to the Bow Competition. It is my great privilege to oversee this competition. Since we are a little behind schedule, I won't hold back the archers any longer. Archers, take your place."

The first row of archers lined up. There were about two dozen of them. A series of judges sat off to the side. Light Elementals were standing near the crowds that lined the course to help ensure that no one was accidentally hit by a stray arrow. If needed, they could project a barrier field to deflect oncoming arrows.

The first stage of the competition was Distance. It didn't matter if you hit the center of the target, just as long as you hit it. Different markers were set up along the ground in the distance between the archers and the targets. If an archer hit a target, it was considered a perfect score in that section of the competition. The competition consisted of five different sections. The first was Distance, followed by Strength, and then Accuracy. The two remaining sections consisted of different feats the judges created to narrow the final contestants down to one person. Only the top ten archers from the first three sections would advance to the last two sections.

Breeze stood on her marker. Placing an arrow against the edge of the bow, she raised the bow and pulled the string back. The target was nearly thirty paces away. She breathed in deeply. The other archers around her had already launched their arrows. Only several of them made it to the targets. She pulled the bowstring back and positioned the angle slightly upward. Zeph watched from the sidelines. He watched as her fingers released. A thin line of dust floated in the air where the bowstring had been. The arrow shot forward toward the target.

Thunk! The target shook as the arrow impacted. Many people watching near the targets were sure Breeze could have surpassed the target if she had wanted to. The crowd clapped for all the archers. Workers went out and changed the targets around for the next round. New targets replaced the old ones and were moved closer to the archers, only a few paces away.

The new targets were much thicker and consisted of several different layers. If the archer could pierce through the target to the last layer, they received a perfect score. After a shot was taken, the layers were removed one at a time to determine which layer the arrow stopped in.

Once again, it was Breeze's turn to shoot. She gripped the bow firmly and pulled the string back as far as possible. The string appeared to be unraveling as it seemed to grow longer and longer. She released the arrow. Bang! The crowd covered their ears as the sound of the arrow punctured through the back of the target and resounded out over the plains. There was no need to remove any of the layers as the arrow's point could clearly be seen sticking out the underside of the target. This was a true testament to the craftsmanship Gus had put into both Breeze's bow and the arrows.

Marcus and Zeph's jaws dropped upon inspecting the back of Breeze's target. This was, evidently, a side of Breeze that she had kept very secret from them, even more than Gus' Levitation talent.

"This is so unbelievable!" Zeph said with an unmistakable tone of shock in his voice.

"I know! I seriously don't understand how we didn't discover this over the years," Marcus added.

"She does look good holding a bow, though."

Zeph and Marcus looked down at Iggy. He simply smiled and glanced up at them. They shook their heads and turned their focus back to the competition.

The rows of targets had been set up for the last of the three opening segments. Breeze had been looking forward to this one since the competition started. Accuracy was her specialty, with Strength being a close second. Each of the archers had three chances to hit the exact center of each of the targets. There were three different targets. Each was set at a different distance from the archer.

Almost every archer hit the center of the first target, about half hit the center of the second target, and only a handful hit the center of the last target. Breeze didn't even need the three shots on each target, and she easily hit the center of each target on her first try.

A brief break was issued for the judges to compile their results. Breeze headed over to Zeph and the group, "So what do you guys think?"

"You are unbelievable!" Zeph and Marcus blurted out in unison.

"Thanks, I have been practicing for over eight years, though."

"Are you serious? Why didn't we ever see you?" Zeph asked with a perplexed look on his face.

"It's not something I thought you guys would understand. Being a girl, training in a form of combat, it's not that normal.

"Are you kidding me? This is so awesome. I can actually say I've known a female archer for most of my life," Marcus said with a huge smile. Just then, a gong rang out.

"They must have finished the judging; see you guys in a bit," Breeze said as she walked out to join the other archers. The judges quickly announced their ruling. Rather than announcing everyone who was out, they simply listed the names of those still in the competition. After the first nine names had been read, Zeph had almost given up hope that Breeze would continue in the competition.

"And the last contestant to continue is Breeze, daughter of Gus," the last judge announced. The group cheered as Breeze smiled and waved to the crowd.

The next section of the competition was designed to narrow the last ten remaining contestants down to two. It was a combination of speed, strength, and accuracy. A series of targets and dummies were set up in a maze-like fashion. Some had to simply be knocked over with the archer's shot, while others had to have a specific section of the target hit. Each archer was timed on how fast they could complete the course. The archers took their place in line; *The Order* coincided with *The Order* in which their names had been called. Breeze waited patiently since she would be the last of the ten to compete.

Finally, it was Breeze's turn. She walked into the middle starting point. One hundred eighty degrees of space was before her; she had almost three dozen targets to hit. The crowd had formed an equally large one-hundred-and-eighty-degree semicircle behind her.

She took off running, quickly pulling arrows from her quiver and striking the targets without hesitation. Reaching the midway, she refilled her quiver with the supplied arrows. The crowd couldn't believe how accurate she was and at the speed she was running through the targets. In half the time of any of the other archers, she completed the task of hitting all the targets. Everyone cheered as she walked back to the starting point.

The judges stood off to the side, discussing the results. Meanwhile, the last section of the competition was being assembled. The fighters waited patiently for the results to be given. After what seemed like an eternity, the judges stepped forward and gave the results to Gus. A young man from Tweedsmiur was called out, and to everyone's expectations, Breeze was also called out.

The last section of the competition would be like nothing they had done so far. They would run through a similar obstacle course as they had before. Each competitor would be given arrows with specific colored fletching that aligned to the color given to them by the judges. Both would run through the course at the same time. Once a target was hit, a point was claimed for that archer; any arrows by the other archer would not count.

Both Breeze and the other archer took their place on the starting line. Besides the stationary targets that had been in the last stage, there were also several series of moving obstacles and swinging targets. Breeze's arrows were green, like the color of the stone she wore around her neck. Her opponent's arrows were yellow. Several unique targets and dummies were placed within the mix of plain targets as well; they were color-coded to one of the two colors. If an archer hit their opponent's marked target first, they would get a point and steal a point from their opponent.

The field was a maze of targets, dummies, and obstacles. The crowd had been moved back to allow for more directional choices by the archers as they ran through the course. The series of judges were scattered around the edge of the course to keep track of the results as they happened.

A loud clang rang out. Both archers bolted from the starting line. Breeze's arm was almost a blur as she pulled arrow after arrow out of her quiver. Her opponent was not lost, though. He also kept up with her pace as they ran through the maze of targets.

Breeze spotted three green targets arranged in a row towards the end of the course. Taking a moment to aim, she quickly fired three shots, hitting each target square in the center. The crowd cheered at her display of accuracy. She noticed several dummies to her left that the other archer had not yet knocked over. Firing hard, she quickly knocked them over as she continued to run. For a moment, she lost track of the man; quickly spotting him up ahead, she picked up the pace.

The man reached the end of the course first. A smile of victory was on his face. Breeze joined him a moment after. A look of disappointment flooded over her. The judges went out into the course and tallied up the results of the hits. Minutes ticked by, and soon the judges returned. They spent several minutes debating the results before one finally stepped forward.

"An unusual turn of events has come to pass with the results of this last competition. Would the archer from Tweedsmiur please step forward?" The man did as requested. "With a finishing total of eighty-seven points, you have surpassed your opponent's tally by twelve." The man raised his hands in triumph; however, his victory was short-lived.

"Quiet down, please!!" The judge shouted to the man and the crowd. "However, upon inspection of the targets, it was found that even though the young lady hit fewer targets than her opponent, she hit the exact center of every single target and shot clean through the target on many. Even though this round is based on points, we are also keeping a watchful eye on the accuracy and skills of the competitors. Therefore, based not solely on her results but also her skills as an archer, we have chosen the competitor from Daunt to be crowned the winner."

The man from Tweedsmiur almost fell over upon hearing the final results. The crowd rushed out to where the competitors stood. One of the judges presented Breeze with a medallion similar to those presented at the earlier competitions. Engraved on it was: *Winner of the 6th Cronus Bow Competition of the Seventh Age.*

The enclosure of the crowd was becoming too much for Breeze. She and the rest of the group made their way out of the crowd and back toward town. Congratulations rang out from everyone in the group. Marcus and Zeph still couldn't believe how extraordinary Breeze was with a bow.

The last Competition of the day was the Gauntlet, a grueling obstacle course combined with a maze. Those who participated would have to make their way through the course while avoiding swinging beams of wood, arrows, spring traps, and many more devices. Like the other competitions, this was not designed to kill someone, but it was still possible for someone to be seriously injured or worse. In the past, there had been a few near-death injuries.

Zeph and Dawn weren't thrilled that Iggy was participating in the competition. As an older brother, Zeph felt it was his place to protect his little brother. After his conversation with Praotes about the commitment he made to take care of his brother, he felt it even stronger. As a mother, Dawn was not thrilled at seeing one of her sons placed in the path of danger, even more so after Zeph's incident earlier. Dawn could have easily stopped Iggy from entering the competition; he was under the age of sixteen, after all. Despite her fears, she wanted to allow her youngest son to grow and experience something new.

The Gauntlet would not take place for several hours. It was always a late evening competition. The darkness and the scattering effects of the torch light added to the intensity of the course. It wasn't common for more than a dozen or so competitors to enter the Gauntlet. This festival was no exception, and an announcement was made that only nine individuals were participating in the Gauntlet.

The group of family and friends came together and decided to go down to the south beach to eat their last meal before the final competition. The suns had set shortly after the Bow competition. The soft colors on the horizon were beginning to fade out into the deep blue of the night. The water lapping at the shore was relaxing. A gentle breeze was blowing over the beach. It was very calming. A person could easily drift off to sleep on the beach.

The group sat quietly, talking softly amongst themselves. The air was becoming cool, just as it had the night before. The cool evenings were always appreciated during the harvest season. A layer of fog began to rise over the water. The water released a somewhat unnerving feeling along the shore as the mist drifted onto the beach.

The last gong of the day rang out. Everyone gathered their things and began to head back. Everyone was heading towards the area west of town, between Daunt and where Gus' house sat. The area had been transformed into a massive obstacle course full of traps and various things designed to test the competitor's skills to solve problems and react quickly.

The nervousness was quite evident on Iggy's face as they neared the Gauntlet. Zeph placed a hand on his little brother's shoulder.

"You know, you don't have to do this if you don't feel ready."

"I'll be okay, Zeph, I'm just nervous."

They continued forward. Rows of bandstands had been set up all around the Gantlet. Zeph guessed that many of them had come from the arena since it would have most likely been dismantled to help with the construction of the Gauntlet. The seating would provide the crowd with an excellent view of the competitors within the Gauntlet.

The stands began to fill. Iggy gathered with the other eight competitors in a special area near the Gauntlet. The rest of the group found a decent place to sit in the stands. Zeph, Marcus, and Victor sat on the edge of their seats as they scanned the course Iggy would take. Some of the traps were triggered by pressure, but many were triggered by workers standing out of sight to the side. Zeph's outward expression quickly changed from excitement to nervousness.

"What is it, Zeph?" Victor asked.

"I'm just a little worried at the number of healers present there."

Victor scanned the areas where Zeph indicated. After several moments of counting, Victor spoke up.

"You're right; over a dozen healers are on the sidelines. Maybe Iggy doesn't understand what he's getting into."

"I'm just glad he won't be able to see anything while he waits for his turn," Zeph replied as he surveyed the Gauntlet. It was an extensive rectangular shape set about one story deep into the ground. This allowed the competitors to still see the crowds in the bandstands. The rectangular Gauntlet was a massive maze of winding corridors, traps, and puzzles. If any of the competitors were given the opportunity to study the course, it would create an unfair advantage against the others. For this reason, the competitors were waiting in a tent leading directly down to the entrance of the Gauntlet.

Several men stepped up to the podium. Praotes raised his hands to get everyone's attention. Siah, Gus, and Jarian were also with him. The crowd quieted down as Praotes began to speak.

"Welcome everyone to the last of this great series of competitions. This is by far the most trying of all the day's competitions. Not only do the competitors have to use their abilities to complete the course, but they will have to use their knowledge and reflexes to make their way past many obstacles and dangers."

Praotes stepped back, and Gus stepped forward. He wore a compelling expression that captivated everyone's attention, prompting them to listen intently to his words.

"This is a very dangerous competition. Even with my talents, I will not be able to stop many of the traps. Many healers are present to tend to anyone that becomes wounded," he paused for a moment before continuing, "There has not been a fatality in this competition since the Sixth Age. We all plan to keep it that way."

Gus stepped back, and Jarian stepped forward. The light from the podium torches glistened off his breastplate. He contemplated his words for a long moment before speaking up.

"Not all trials in life can be defeated, but all can be defied," he paused as he always did after speaking a proverb. "Some of you will win, and others will lose, but you will all be remembered that you were brave enough to try and give it your all."

The last to step forward was Siah. The other three men looked like children standing behind him. He raised his hands to the crowd.

"Light the Torches!!" He called out. Instantly, dozens of torches burst into flames all over the Gauntlet.

The crowd cheered as the first competitor stepped up to the gate. Iggy sat with the other competitors inside the tent. It led down a corridor of tapestry to the starting area. The gate opened and closed at the end of the corridor as the first man entered the Gauntlet. From his perspective, Iggy couldn't see what was happening inside, but he heard the sound of contraptions activating inside. He wondered how hard it would be; would he be able to complete the challenges?

It wasn't long before he heard Siah speak to the crowd. "The first competitor has dropped out of the challenge." This made Iggy all the more nervous. Saying someone 'dropped out' was a polite way of saying the contestant failed.

Iggy looked down at his hands; the leather gloves felt tight around his knuckles. Perhaps it was simply because he wasn't used to wearing them. He never liked the feeling of something covering his hands. This was something common among healers. The plain brown color of his clothes matched the color of his hair. It took all of Iggy's courage to simply sit and wait as other contestants 'dropped out.'

Finally, it was his turn. He looked at the several remaining contestants sitting on the bench inside the tent. As the candlelight bounced across their faces, they all gave him supportive smiles of encouragement. Everyone else in the competition was at least double

Iggy's age. Seeing their support made him feel a little bit better as he stepped through the gate.

Zeph and the rest of the group watched from above as Iggy entered the Gauntlet. Everyone cheered as he started the competition, then everyone fell silent. Zeph had already watched several other men fail the competition, and he badly wanted his brother to win. The crowd was required to remain silent while the contestant was going through the course and was not allowed to help them in any way.

Iggy looked down the stone path. It looked like a typical hallway in any regular building but had no ceiling or roof, as with the rest of the course. At the end, he could see a small pedestal. It was about a dozen paces away. Iggy knew that there had to be some sort of obstacle between where he stood and the pedestal.

Taking several careful steps, he began making his way towards the pedestal. The floor was made of interlocking stone, which Iggy could only assume concealed some sort of trap or mechanism. Taking another step, he felt something click under his foot. Looking down, he felt the floor lift beneath him, and he was suddenly thrown forward. A large wooden beam bolted out of the wall, blocking his airborne path. Reaching out, he used the beams to swing himself into the air and, with a quick flip of his body, landed safely on the floor again.

Breathing a sigh of relief, Iggy continued; he was only halfway to the pedestal. As he walked, he scanned the floor, looking for anything that seemed odd. Stepping forward, Iggy felt the floor start to slant downward toward his goal. He noticed a small lever on the wall to his left. After examining it for a moment, he decided not to pull it. Stepping forward, he felt something graze his chest. Looking down, he saw a thin, almost invisible string at his chest level. A loud click was heard as both sides of the wall opened up a few steps behind Iggy. Two large stone boulders came rolling out.

No hesitation was needed as Iggy took off running towards the pedestal. The boulders were gaining on him. Iggy noticed more levers on the wall and began pulling them as he ran. This caused wood beams to shoot out from the wall just behind the levers. The boulders quickly snapped right through them as they rolled ever closer. Iggy wondered if pulling the first level would have kept the boulders at bay. It was too late to think about that now. He burst into the open space around the pedestal. As he did, two large stone slabs closed behind him. A loud crash was heard as the boulders smashed into the other side of the slabs.

Eyes wide, Iggy breathed a sigh of relief. Sweat dripped off his forehead. He walked over to the stone pedestal. There were three small flat metal discs, each about twice the size of a standard coin. The stone pedestal had six round flat indentations, the exact size of each disc. Each of the indentations also had a horizontal slot. Iggy picked up the discs. He wondered which of the six spots he was to place the discs and if he should place them flat in the indentations or slide them vertically into the slots like you would a key. He decided to try placing them flat on the three circular indentations that made up the bottom half of the six. The discs drop perfectly into the indentations. A click was heard. A blunt arrow shot out from the wall, striking Iggy in the leg. He cried out in pain. Even though the arrow was blunt, it was still severe. The discs popped out of the indentations.

Iggy decided he would study the pedestal further before trying again. This time, he placed the discs into the slots in the indentations. A click was heard again. The arrow flew at the back of Iggy's head but bounced off an invincible wall before it could strike him. The crowd looked at Gus, to which he shook his head. It became clear that Iggy was utilizing his Abilities to protect himself, something he had become very talented at.

Retrieving the discs once more, Iggy continued to study the pedestal. He placed only one disc into the nearest slot. Next, he placed a disc in a slot two over, and the third two more slots over. The discs now made a triangle formation. A click was heard, and after a brief pause, no arrows were fired. Iggy examined the pedestal further. He tried to pull the discs out of the slots, but they would not release. As he tried to pull one of the discs out, he noticed that he could turn the indentation because the disc was sticking out of it. Turning the disc, it locked with a click when it pointed toward the center of the pedestal. Iggy quickly did the same with the other two discs. A loud click and rumble was heard as the stone wall in front of him slid open.

Iggy quickly ran through the door just as it closed with a loud slam behind him. The next room was more challenging to see as it only had a single torch in each corner, unlike the previous room, which had many torches on the wall. Raising his hand, he concentrated. An aura of light began to form around his hand. The room became much more visible now. The light from his palm revealed a thin walkway that weaved through the room. Darkness filled the gaps around the walkway. It had taken him a moment to realize that water was filling the darkness around the pathway. Iggy aimed the light from his palm downwards. He could see the bottom through the water. Nevertheless, it was deep enough that he didn't want to test it. He could understand how someone could easily miss this in the dimly lit room and was glad he could create auras of light.

Quickly looking around the room for any other signs of traps, he decided it was safe to walk the path. Taking a step outward, he stepped onto the stone path. It felt strange, as though it was floating. The sensation of falling quickly gripped him, and he took off running, holding his hand out to light the path. He quickly realized that the path was not made of stone but rather carefully disguised wooden squares. As he stepped on them, they slid and sank into the water, bringing him down with them. Iggy was light on his feet as he quickly went back and forth across the blocks until he reached the other side. The door on the far wall swung open into the next room.

In Iggy's opinion, the room was arranged strangely. Directly in front of him was a stone pedestal with a small stone tablet sticking out of it. He proceeded to scan the room before thinking about removing the tablet. Rows of torches lined the top of the wall. Beneath the row of torches were stone channels that ran horizontally along the wall, leading all the way to the far end of the room. Along the way, smaller stone channels branched off downwards and flowed down from the wall to a series of stone basins. From these basins, even smaller channels jetted out and down into grooves in the floor. The whole concept of the channels reminded Iggy of the vein pattern on a leaf. Iggy walked around the room; from his height perspective, it was unclear what purpose all these channels served. It reminded him of some kind of mini aqueduct system.

Reaching the large door at the far end of the room, he found that it had a strange locking mechanism in the middle of the door. The hole in the door evidently needed some kind of an object that functioned as a key. Scanning the room, Iggy noticed eight stone channels leading down from the large ones near the top of the wall, four on each side of the room leading to sealed basins. Then, four smaller channels lead down from each basin into the grooves all along the floor. It was like the way tree branches spread out and got smaller along the way. Iggy tried to remove the stone cap on the top of one of the basins, but it wouldn't budge. As he looked into the small hole where the stone channel connected to the basin, even shining light from his palms could not illuminate the contents inside.

Returning to the front of the room, he felt ready for whatever was coming. Pulling the stone tablet from the pedestal, he heard a loud click. The torches on the walls dipped downwards into the stone channels along the top of the wall. A whoosh sound was heard as flames quickly spread out along the whole length of the stone channels. A line of burning flame now lined the top of the wall on either side. Iggy realized that the stone channels must have been full of lamp oil. Fear quickly gripped Iggy as he realized where the flames would travel next. Looking down, he quickly read the words on the tablet.

"Only the swift will reach the path ahead without diving into flames."

Another series of clicks were heard, and the stone caps on all the basins flipped open. Iggy's eyes darted back and forth as he stared at the clear liquid in the basins. The sound of stone sliding filled his ears; Iggy watched in horror as the flaming oil began to flow down the channels along the wall toward each of the open basins.

Zeph's heart began to race as he watched his brother below. At this point in the competition, most of the others had failed. It was a test of swiftness but also luck of the draw. He hoped that Iggy would not be among those numbers.

Iggy rushed over to the first two basins, looking into the clear liquid, which he could only assume was oil; he saw no key of any kind in the basins. The flames were racing down the stone channels and were almost at the basins. He rushed to the successive two basins, still finding no key.

Rushing over to the following two, he saw within the first basin a long stone key of some kind. The image of the key quickly vanished as the flames covered the surface of the oil.

Adrenaline and anxiety overtook Iggy as he looked from the flaming basin, that he knew he must reach into, to the smaller channels that would cause the flaming oil to flow down into the grooves on the floor. Taking a deep breath, he reached into the oil. The first few seconds left him unphased, but then the pain smoothly flowed over his hand. His wrist bore the brunt of the burning sensation for the moment as his hand primarily remained untouched while submerged. Wrapping his fingers around the stone key, he quickly removed his hand from the oil. The flaming liquid covered his glove, wrist, and sleeve. It began to melt and burn away the leather and nipped at his flesh. Agony draped its way over Iggy's face. He looked as though he would scream, but no sound left his lips. Ripping off his burning sleeve, he used it to extinguish the flaming liquid on his hand.

Everything seemed to slow down. The flames seemed to almost stand still as Iggy looked down at his raw, bleeding, burnt hand. It was the first time in his life he had been hurt to this extent. He quickly began to channel his healing abilities into his hand. The flames had made their way down from the basins, and the blazing oil was starting to spread out into the patterns along the floor. Iggy rushed over to the far door. The flames licked at his boots and pants. He chose not to look down, but Iggy could already feel his boots catching on fire.

Reaching the door, Iggy tried several times to insert the key into the hole. The key was nothing more than a stone peg, but it had seven sides and was oddly shaped. It would only slide into the slot if inserted the correct way. The task would have probably been simple for Iggy if not for the pain and panic that was coursing through his body. The pain became more than he could bear as the flames crept up his legs. His scream echoed across the crowded bandstands that lined the Gauntlet. They watched in horror as Iggy fell to the floor, his body wrapped in flames.

Siah immediately jumped from the podium up in the bandstands and down into the Gauntlet. Gus used his talents to lift Iggy's burning body into the air, away from the flames. Siah burst into the blazing room and raised his hands. With his hands pointed at Iggy's floating burning body, he blasted a wave of water from his palms. Iggy quickly became encased within a layer of water that instantly extinguished the flames that had wrapped all around his body.

"Healers!" Siah cried out as he reached out and took Iggy's body. Several men had already jumped over the sides of the wall and took positions on either side of Iggy. Their hands burst with bright light that washed all over the boy. Everyone watched as the charred flesh reformed into smooth skin where Iggy's clothing had burnt entirely off. The rest of his body also began to regenerate quickly. Iggy's eyes shot wide open; wide-eyed, he gasped for air. The smell of burnt flesh filled his nostrils; tears filled his eyes as he looked up at Siah. The vivid images and sensations of burning alive mere seconds earlier were all that his young mind could process.

Siah quickly carried Iggy out of the Gauntlet. Zeph and the others rushed from the stands to the area below. Dawn wrapped her arms around her son and sobbed uncontrollably. Iggy, too, began to sob as he held onto his mother like an infant. Zeph stood nearby and watched. Tears filled his eyes, but he fought them back. He was trying with all his might to be strong for Iggy.

Soon after they left, a winner of the competition was named. He was a Water Elemental and a sailor. It made sense based on the traps and puzzles seen within the Gauntlet. The man walked across the water of the second room and simply extinguished the fire in the third. The man had also quickly mastered the other remaining rooms.

Rather than participating in the ending ceremonies, Iggy asked if they could simply go home. No one argued with him. The pain in his eyes and the echoing sound of his scream resonated in their minds. Zeph knew he would have the chance to speak with his little brother later, but for now, he simply let him be as they all returned to the house.

Iggy quickly went up to his room as they entered the house. Dawn and Victor went into the kitchen, and she began to make some tea. Zeph, Marcus, and Breeze stood in the living room. There was an uneasy quietness among the three of them. Marcus was the first to speak up.

"Do you think he'll be okay? I mean, like..., in the long run?"

"I honestly don't know," Zeph said with a sigh. "Does anyone become okay with the memory of being burned alive?"

The question made everyone seize up inside as the images of what had happened to Iggy flashed in their minds. Breeze and Marcus sat down as Zeph just stood in the archway. Zeph closed his eyes and listened to the sounds of the house. The sound of boiling water and soft conversation came from the kitchen. Zeph could hear the breath entering and leaving the bodies of his two friends in front of him. Faintly, Zeph could hear sobbing from the second floor of the house. Tears swelled in his eyes again; he found it more challenging to fight them back this time.

Breeze looked up, "Can you hear him?" she asked.

Zeph nodded as the tears softly fell down his face. She began to get up, but he raised his hand. Shaking his head, Zeph motioned for her to stay as he quickly made his way upstairs.

A small ray of light could be seen flowing down the hall. Iggy's door was open, just a crack. Zeph walked over to the door and slowly opened it. Iggy lay on his bed, face in his pillow. He continued to sob into it. Zeph quietly entered the room and closed the door behind him. He knew Iggy was aware of his presence but waited patiently for his brother to acknowledge him. After several minutes, Iggy lifted his face. Zeph walked over and sat down next to Iggy on the bed. Iggy rolled over and lay on his back. He raised his hands above his face; they wouldn't stop shaking. Not more than an hour earlier, he had felt the sensation of first his clothing and then his skin begin to burn away.

They sat in the room in silence for what seemed like hours. Iggy finally began to express everything he was feeling. His descriptions of the sensation of burning alive were almost more than Zeph could handle. He wondered how Iggy would endure the memories himself. They talked long into the night. Everyone else had either gone home or fallen asleep by this time. It had been a very long day, full of more life and death than either had ever wanted to experience. One day remained in the festival. More than any of the rest, Zeph wondered what kind of things the Alignment had in store for them on the final day.

DAY 103

If life was easy, where would the strong come from?
If life was simple, where would discoveries be found?
If life was long, where would the time go?
If life wasn't hard.....Where would the Heroes rise from?
~ Sir Jarian the Hero

CHAPTER 8
ALIGNMENT

The suns rose slowly as the townspeople rose from their beds. With no other events than the Alignment itself at sunset, it would be a busy day for the merchants. As dawn broke through the darkness of night, the many shops along the streets began to open up. Dew covered the ground, and the freshness of the morning slowly faded away as the warm suns rose. People began to weave their way into Daunt from the many tents outside the edge of town. The day quickly warmed, not only by the heat from the suns but also by the kindness of the villagers and travelers.

The day seemed to fly by quickly, like a pleasant breeze. The smells of many different kinds of food wafted in the air, reaching every corner of Daunt. Unlike the drab clothing of the previous day, the streets were now filled with brightly colored clothing. Today was a day for celebration.

Music flowed up and down the streets, as a group of traveling musicians played while they walked through the village. The mood of the town was upbeat and full of excitement. For many, this was their very first festival in Daunt. For the townsfolk, many familiar faces from previous festivals could be seen.

As the evening began to fall upon Daunt, energy slowly rose. People started chatting amongst themselves as they moved from the streets to the hills just north of town. An event like this only happened every nine years. This specific Alignment only happens every eighteen years. The town was bathed in a golden light as the suns began to reach the horizon. Shops started to close down in preparation for the event. The Alignment would take place in only a few hours now. Even at this point, long strands of light, like ribbons blowing gently in the breeze, could be seen flowing from the suns on the horizon up into the sky. This was a sign that the Alignment was beginning as the energy of both suns crossed and merged over each other.

Like watching majestic long golden hair blowing in the breeze, the strands of energy from the suns danced across the sky. Zeph stared up at the strands of light. He recalled a similar sight when he was only nine years old. Iggy had sat on their father's shoulders and reached up, trying to grab the strands. They didn't know at the time, but they had only a few months left with their father before they would never see him again. The memories still found their way to the surface, but not as much as they used to. Zeph realized that he spent a lot of time dwelling on the past and the hurt he held inside.

Shaking the thoughts from his head, Zeph looked around at the crowd of people gathering around. Hundreds of people were sitting all over the many hills. The rolling hills north of town were the best location to watch the event. The ocean could be seen; it was calm. The blue of the water seemed so much more brilliant than it usually did. Even the grass seemed that much more green as Zeph took in everything around him. The breeze from the ocean flowed over the ever-growing crowd of people. To see this many people all together was a fantastic sight in itself.

The Alignment would happen right at sunset, just as the suns slipped below the ocean on the eastern horizon. The difference between a Pythus Solar Alignment from nine years earlier and the Cronus Solar Alignment that was happening now was that the Alignment would occur exactly at sunset. With a Pythus Solar Alignment, the Alignment would happen in the morning as the suns rose over the mountains to the west. Appagon was positioned in the perfect spot on the world to watch either Alignment; Daunt especially for this Alignment.

Zeph and Iggy had found a spot at the top of one of the hills. Both sat with their backs to the tree atop the hill and gazed towards the ocean in anticipation of the coming event. Unlike many of the other significant events Zeph had been through in his life, this was a family event for most of the townsfolk. Looking around the hill they sat upon, Marcus could be seen sitting with his family. Breeze and Gus sat a little farther down, and Dawn and Victor sat closer to the bottom of the hill.

Looking down at his mother, Zeph watched her talk and laugh with Victor. It was nice to see. Even though it had been almost nine years, Zeph still knew that she clung to the memory of her husband. She had given up hope of her husband's return long before Zeph had. Perhaps it was time for everyone to let go of the past.

The boys talked amongst themselves. Other than the night before, it had been some time since they had done that. Zeph looked over at his little brother. Even Iggy was starting to grow up. His boyish appearance was beginning to change; Zeph was sure that he would eventually start to look his age before long. As time went by, the suns grew lower and lower on the horizon, and, in turn, the strands of light flowing from them grew in intensity and length. The light danced up and down the strands as they waved back and forth in the sky. It wouldn't be long now.

Reaching into his shoulder bag, Zeph took out the Omega scroll. He took it everywhere with him now. It continued to remain a mystery, other than its ability to recharge his mental focus.

"So, anything new with you and that thing?" Iggy asked, glancing down at the scroll in Zeph's hands

"Nothing more than usual. It's beginning to worry me, actually."

"How so?"

"I've been thinking about the voice I heard from within it that night in the inn, 'The journey of The Last begins Within. Seek the Six and stop the Sin.' Plus, there is all the other stuff, such as Saphar's book. "

Iggy took the scroll from Zeph; it was evident his hands were still shaky from the night before. Zeph sat back and rested his head against the tree, blankly staring at the suns. What did it all mean? Who was he supposed to be, to become? He let the energy flow from his head and into his hands. He then pulled it back and continued this process for several minutes. He had begun to do this daily as he found it helped strengthen his focus. He had become very good at controlling his only known ability. Iggy looked over at his brother's hands. Whenever energy flowed into Zeph's palms, they emitted a faint glow, similar to Iggy's when he used his healing abilities. The light would cover the palms of his hands, like watching some glowing liquid gather below the skin. This wasn't too far off, as even a faint glow could be seen traveling down the veins in his arms with each pulse.

"Why do you do that?" Iggy asked, looking at the flow of energy back and forth.

"I don't know; it's all I can really do," Zeph replied with a hint of discouragement. A murmur began to rise in the crowd. Both boys looked at the setting suns. They were half set; it would only be minutes now. The energy flowing from them was no longer limited to large strands here and there, but it had now grown to hundreds. The strands extended to the very top of the sky. The colors of blue, orange, green, and purple flowed within each strand of energy. The reflection of the suns across the ocean surface added to the intensity. It was truly an awe-inspiring sight to behold.

Zeph took back the scroll from Iggy. As he did, he felt a mild jolt of energy from it. He held it out at arm's length and shot a look at his brother.

"What did you do to this?"

"I didn't do anything. Why?" Iggy asked, puzzled as he looked back.

Zeph shook off the question as he looked over the scroll. Something was different. He let his gaze flow past the scroll to the setting suns in the distance. As he did, he began to feel a slight tingly sensation from the scroll. He quickly stood up, still holding the scroll with one hand. Iggy jumped to his feet as well.

"What's going on?" Iggy asked, slightly concerned.

"I...I don't know..." Zeph managed to slip out. "I...I feel strange..."

Everyone in the crowd of spectators now had their eyes fixed on the horizon. The suspense was building; it would be less than a minute now. Both boys, however, were fixed on the scroll. Zeph opened his palm to try and drop the scroll. The scroll simply floated in the air. Strands of light not unlike the ones currently painting the sky drifted out from the casing of the scroll. They reached out for Zeph's hand. Fear and confusion flashed over each of the boys' faces.

Vibrations rippled through the air, flowing over the plains. Waves of light emanated outwards from the suns and down the strands of energy across the sky. They rapidly began to get faster until they seemed to fold in over each other. The crowd began to chant a countdown. The energy was building on the horizon; the outline of the suns was no longer clearly visible, just strands upon strands of energy. Zeph's gaze drifted from the floating scroll just in time to see the burst of energy across the horizon.

Like Omega himself threw his mighty fist down upon the earth, the sky ripped open. The thousands of strands of energy seemed to explode from the suns, shooting outwards across the sky in all directions. Everyone held their breath as the brilliant display of light and colors filled the sky, turning dusk brighter than midday. After what seemed like an eternity, a tremendous bang was heard, shortly accompanied by a strong blast of wind.

The shockwave ignited the sky as it shot forward across the horizon. A multitude of light and color followed. The cheers of thousands of people erupted from the hills and were quickly followed by applause. The wave of energy rushed toward the town. It would soon pass over the town. Many people lay down to watch it pass over.

Zeph looked at the scroll. The strands of energy quickly flowed and wrapped themselves around his hands. He could feel the sensation of cold liquid covering his palms. The symbols on his hand began to glow brightly. It was all Iggy could do to simply watch and call out to the others. This got the attention of not only the rest of the group but also any of the onlookers nearby.

"It's happening," was all Zeph could muster through staggered breaths. Letting his resistance fade, he quickly gripped the ends of the scroll with both hands. Light burst forth from all three of his Omega symbols. His body jerked upwards into the air. People in the crowd suddenly ran in terror. Zeph's body floated in the air just above Iggy. Everyone else in the group had run over and stared at Zeph, who was suspended in the air.

"What's going on?" Zeph's mother asked frantically.

"I don't know; the scroll started reacting to him when the alignment started," Iggy replied. Zeph's hands released from the scroll, and his arms flung outward, causing a small shockwave to emanate from his body. He hung suspended in the air in a cross position. The Omega scroll floated in the air directly in front of Zeph. The strands of energy emanating from the scroll began to wrap around Zeph's body. His face shone with radiance like the suns. Many of the people nearby stood in awe as they gazed into his face. It was like staring into the face of Omega.

Iggy was the first to take action; he quickly took a knee below his brother and outstretched his hands towards him. The light glowed from his palms as he tried to encase Zeph in a protection field. Strands leaped from the scroll and flowed into Iggy's hands. He seemed as though he was in pain, but quickly, his body went limp, and he, too, floated gently up into the air opposite Zeph. Victor and Marcus took a step toward the boys but then hesitated. They still had no idea what was happening, and based on what just happened to Iggy, they had no plan.

The loud crackling of the shockwave quickly came upon them. Everyone turned to face the wave as it swept across the sky and over the town. As the wave of energy passed over Daunt, several large strands of energy like lightning shot down and struck the suspended Omega scroll. The energy instantly flowed from the scroll directly into Zeph. He let out a tremendous cry. It was not a cry of pain but a deep, guttural cry that you would hear a fearless warrior give just before charging into battle. Zeph eyes shone with brilliant white light.

ALL THAT COULD BE SEEN was white light, and then, as quickly as it came, everything plunged into total darkness. The floor felt hard and cold as Zeph's body impacted with a loud thud. He tried to open his eyes but could not distinguish if they were open or not through the complete darkness around him. Running his hand over the ground, he found it was completely smooth, like polished stone. Rolling onto his back, he lay there for several minutes. It was deafening silent other than his heart pounding in his ears and his muffled breathing.

A sound caused him to sit up abruptly. Was his mind playing tricks on him? He listened closely. Again, he heard the sound, like something stirring just off to his left. Fear began to take him as he decided whether to investigate or back away. Only one choice was drifting to the surface.

"Hello?" he called out cautiously. A slight groan came from the direction of the shuffle. He didn't know what to make of it. "Is someone there?"

"Yes," a faint voice echoed out into the room. Zeph immediately recognized his brother's voice.

"Iggy!" Zeph exclaimed as he moved toward the sound of his brother's voice. He quickly reached him. In the pitch darkness, he helped his brother stand. Both boys now stood in the darkness, trying to look around the room.

"Where are we?" asked Iggy as he tried to peer out into the darkness, keeping one hand on his brother's shoulder.

"Your guess is as good as mine. The last thing I remember is grabbing the scroll."

"I tried to place a protection field around you, but the energy from the scroll latched on to me. That's all I remember." The boys began shuffling together, trying to find something other than the floor below them. "I have an idea. I will create a beam of light, and we can look around."

"Good idea," Zeph said as he braced himself for the brightness to come. Iggy pointed his hand away from himself and lit his hand up. The expected parting of darkness never came, though. The light from Iggy's palm spread over him and Zeph, but the room remained in darkness. Only their reflections on the floor could be seen.

"This is impossible! There have to be walls and a ceiling!" Iggy exclaimed. Zeph knelt and ran his hand on the smooth surface of the floor. It was like touching cold black glass. Iggy continued moving his hands around the room, running several paces away from Zeph, yet there was still no evidence of any other surface besides the floor.

Zeph suddenly had a desire to channel his own energy. He pressed his hands hard against the floor, sending a burst of energy to his palms. Ring upon rings of glyphs and symbols appeared, bursting outwards from all around Zeph. They continued to travel outwards from where he stooped; it seemed like they would never end. A bluish glow from the never-ending sea of glyphs and symbols gave the room a great blue aura, but the boys still couldn't see any walls or ceiling. Iggy looked down at the floor all around him with amazement. Zeph began to read as many of them as possible, starting with the first ring that wrapped around him.

Each series of glyphs and symbols began to spin in the circles they had formed around Zeph. Each circle of glyphs and symbols started to spin in the opposite direction from the last as the reaction continued to expand outwards from where Zeph stood. Iggy rushed over to Zeph, and they stood in the middle together. The circles' speed increased until they appeared as solid glowing rings of light. Then, without a sound or a moment's notice, the expanse was again plunged into total darkness.

Light rushed towards the boys from every direction and wrapped itself around them as it filled the void. As suddenly as it came, it was gone. Opening their eyes, they found that they were standing atop an exceedingly high cliff. Laid out before them was a vast world, multiple landmasses with forests, rivers, and mountains. It was like nothing they had ever seen before. There were no visible suns in the sky above, but the world was illuminated as though there were. A rainbow of colors covered everything, from the most brilliant greens to the deepest blues. This world, this place, was perfect in every way.

Zeph peered over the edge of the cliff; he saw clouds below. It was then that he realized they weren't on a cliff but rather a single small piece of land afloat in the sky.

"Where are we?" Iggy spoke slowly and with a sense of awe.

"Is this Arkhay?" Zeph's question lingered in the air as he continued to look down at the world below.

A light in the distance caught the boy's attention. They turned to face it. It appeared to be a strand of energy similar to those seen in the Alignment. It flowed quickly towards the two boys. When it was almost upon them, it took shape in the form of a man. Like watching some eternal being's birth, the stands of light burst from all around the form, stretching long and high like the mighty wings of a bird.

The boys stared at the man as he floated in front of them. He wore fine clothing like none Zeph had ever seen. The material was white and had an aura about it. It was the finest suit of clothing he had ever seen. His hair was white, just like Zeph's. The man drifted over to the edge of the cliff and touched down. The magnificent wings of energy dissipated into the air. His appearance also changed; the radiance accompanying him on his arrival was now replaced with nothing more than your average man. His clothing turned to shades of blue and grey. His hair turned a light brown, and his eyes a pale green.

"Hello, Zeph," the words came out soft and yet bold at the same time. "I am Mal'ak, messenger of Omega." Zeph felt as though he should be kneeling before this man, and as the thought crossed his mind, Mal'ak took a brief knee before Zeph. Rising, he looked at Zeph with a smile of kindness.

Mal'ak looked puzzled as he looked at Iggy. "You are not the *Chosen One*. How is it that you have come to be here?" Iggy felt incredibly small as he stared at the ground. Not knowing what to say, he looked at Zeph.

"Not knowing what the scroll was doing to me, he tried to protect me, and in doing so, the energy enveloped him as well," Zeph explained as he continued to look Mal'ak right in the eyes.

"I cannot return him from this place without sending you as well. Therefore, he will also be charged with the task ahead, even though only you can carry it out," Mal'ak said as he locked his gaze on Zeph. It was clear that this man had great power behind him.

The man outstretched his arms, and the piece of earth they were on began to move and drift forward in the sky. It floated out to the beautiful world that lay all around them. Zeph turned his head to look in the opposite direction and was surprised to see a great veil of darkness that stretched far and wide. Wherever they were, this place was truly not of their world. Zeph turned his attention back towards the man. Mal'ak continued to face him. He had a soft smile on his face.

"You are the *Chosen One*, Zeph. By your hand, you will bring about Hope for all mankind and save this world from its fate." The words sent shivers up Zeph's arms.

"I don't understand any of this," he blurted out.

"You will, Zeph," Mal'ak replied, "From the time we ascended, your role for all mankind was already set in motion." One word stood out in the statement to Zeph.

"You're one of the Uriel?"

"I am," Mal'ak replied.

"Before my ascension, I was a messenger among our people. I let the light carry me anywhere in the world. And I continue serving Omega as his messenger of Light in this life."

Zeph continued to stare at the man, hanging on his every word. Iggy stood slightly off to the side and watched them speak. He also gazed out at the fantastic world below them.

"Your purpose is drawing near Zeph; you must be ready for it. Now is the time when the events that will change your world will begin. You must seek out the other *Six Chosen Ones*."

"I don't understand any of this; how am I a *Chosen One*? Who are the other *Six*?" Zeph asked, trying to grasp everything that was happening.

"*The Six* are just the same as you; in every Age since our ascension, there has been one *Chosen One* called from one of the Seven Elements. This is why the scrolls were crafted. When Omega saw that we were about to Ascend, he set forth the task of us to craft seven scrolls. We were then to scatter these scrolls to all the corners of the world."

"What do the scrolls do?" Zeph asked, puzzled.

"The six scrolls that came before you held a message to seek you out. Each scroll holder would carry it for the remainder of their life. Once they died, their essence and Elemental knowledge would be encased within the scroll to be passed to the next worthy chosen."

Zeph looked down at his palms. He hadn't noticed that they had been glowing for some time now. "What's happening to me?"

"You are starting to unlock all that is within you, Zeph. You have great power beyond what you can even comprehend. The road ahead of you will not be easy. I see much pain for you."

"You can see the future?" Zeph questioned as he looked at his hands.

"Only what Omega allows me to see. I have not seen all of what is to come, only the start of your journey. And the crossroads you will be faced with. " Mal'ak turned to face the world in front of them.

A thought occurred to Zeph as he thought back to the message Mage Saphar had left for him in the book. "Beware of those that hide themselves in shadows."

"Have you seen a glimpse of what's to come?" Mal'ak asked as he quickly turned to face Zeph. His gaze was strong and bold and pierced deep; Zeph knew he should not look away.

"A Mage from the past foresaw my future and sent me a message," Zeph replied.

"Show me."

Mal'ak walked past Zeph toward the center of the land they stood on. He placed a hand on one of Zeph's shoulders and gestured outwards with his other hand; strands of energy flowed from his palm. The energy formed into an image of an old man in long purple robes. As the image of the man's face formed, Mal'ak seemed to relax.

"Mage Saphar is the man you speak of. I had to know that your glimpse of what's to come was not a deception." The image of the man dissolved as the strands returned to Mal'ak.

"How are you able to do that?" Iggy asked. He had been sitting quietly off to the side for some time now.

"It is beyond your comprehension, Iggy, but there will come a time when you will understand, just not yet," he replied with the same softness on his face he had shown earlier.

"How would someone deceive me?" asked Zeph as he returned back to the statement Mal'ak had made. "There are forces out in the world, Zeph, that know who and what you are. But their plans for you are dark and nefarious. You must always be vigilant."

Mal'ak walked over to the edge of the cliff. They had moved far from the veil of darkness now. A beam of light could be seen rising from the ocean in the distance. Just then, the ground beneath their feet began to sway, and a piece of earth began to fall rapidly from the sky. Turning to face Zeph, he stepped forward. Mal'ak locked his gaze with Zeph as he spoke.

"The time is coming for you to make a choice, Zeph. Something is coming; I can't tell you more than that. A terrible event is going to happen; you MUST stop it at all costs, or I fear this world is doomed to be consumed and destroyed by the coming darkness. The one that seeks to destroy you will set in motion the events that will end the world. You MUST seek out the other Six. Only with their combined knowledge can you stop the coming storm." Mal'ak pointed to the veil of darkness that had moved from behind them and now covered the entire sky above them. Bolts of dark energy flowed from it. "This is but a glimpse of what will consume your world."

Fear wrapped itself around Zeph's chest as he stared at the void above them. The earth around them began to crumble. The wind rushed past them. The beautiful world began to fall and decay as they descended faster.

"Grow strong in the knowledge you have just been given," Mal'ak said as he pointed at the light flowing from Zeph's palms and throughout his body. "Take your brother and GO!" he shouted as the darkness rushed towards them. Zeph quickly grabbed Iggy's hand. A brilliant burst of light and energy exploded all around them.

Zeph felt the sensation of falling once more, and a moment later, he felt his body impact the ground. His hand moved over the long grass. Opening his eyes, he saw the wave of energy from the Alignment fading over the mountains. Rolling over, his first image was Iggy lying next to him. Marcus rushed over and carefully lifted Zeph to his feet. Zeph's hands began to glow; suddenly, both Zeph and Marcus were flung high up into the air. Quickly losing his grip, Marcus fell from Zeph. The breaking of branches was accompanied by Marcus' painful cry as he fell through the tree and hit the ground.

The crowds gasped as they had just witnessed a boy fall from several stories in the air. Zeph remained floating in the air. Clenching his fists, he tried to bring himself down. Slowly, he floated until his feet touched the ground. He looked over at Marcus lying on the ground; he looked like he was in pain. It wasn't a fatal fall, but it would have significantly hurt. Zeph's mother rushed over and wrapped her arms around him. Once again, Zeph's palms began to glow. Her smile was quickly replaced with distress as her body went limp, and then she lost consciousness. Victor quickly stepped forward and caught her.

Panic came over Zeph's face as he took several steps back.

"Get away from me!" he yelled at the crowd of onlookers. That was all they needed to start dispersing. His hands began to shake as fear started to consume him.

"Zeph, it's ok," Breeze said softly as she extended a hand to him.

"No, it's not! Stay back!"

Iggy helped Marcus to his feet. Victor stood by, still holding the unconscious body of Zeph's mother. Gus stood behind his daughter as she took several steps toward Zeph. He took several steps back and shouted again, "Stay BACK!"

"It's ok, Zeph; you didn't mean to do any of this. We'll help you figure this out."

Zeph looked around frantically, his heart racing, and he was in a state of panic. He spotted the scroll and his shoulder bag lying on the ground. As quickly as he thought about holding the objects, they flew from the ground and into his hand. He caught them quickly, placed the scroll in the bag, and slipped it over his shoulder.

"I don't understand what's going on," he stammered. "I don't even know what just happened." His voice was pitched and frantic.

"Ok, we understand, and we're here for you," Breeze said softly as she stepped closer.

"I told you to stay back." His voice was shaky as the words came out as almost a plea. She continued to step closer. Zeph raised a hand towards her; light flowed into his hand. A bolt of energy shot from his palm, hitting Breeze in the shoulder and sending her flying backward. Zeph stared in horror as her body spun rapidly in the air. He watched her limp body hit the ground with a thud. Wisps of smoke drifted from her clothing, which was accompanied by the smell of burnt flesh. Zeph took off running away from Daunt. No one in the crowds would stand in his way, and they all began to scatter as he ran.

DAY 104

> A Hero is someone that carries a torch of light out into the world, so that all men may see on the dark paths of life.
>
> A Chosen One is someone who walks through the darkest paths of the world, themselves a light to the world.

~The Uriel, Mal'ak

CHAPTER 9
CONTROL

Several days had passed since the festival's end. Most tourists had left, but repair workers were still seen on the streets throughout town. The large number of people had caused a high level of road degradation, so the roads had to be restored. New soil and stones were brought in and packed down, and the town returned to its normal state of quiet and peacefulness.

The hall was quiet as the meeting was called to order. Only the three town elders and six other people filled the school hall, which was the easiest place to have a meeting. This would not be an easy conversation. Even though the three elders, Praotes, Siah, and Yad, all knew and were close to Zeph, they couldn't forsake their duties.

"You know I love that lad as much as the rest of you, but something happened to him that no one here seems to be able to explain to me," Praotes said as he sat at the table across from them.

"I understand your concerns, but he's simply not himself," Dawn pointed out.

"And what are we to do? Simply ignore the fact that he greatly injured several people?" Siah replied, looking across at the group.

"But he wasn't trying to; he didn't even know what was happening," Iggy pleaded. Everyone took a quick look at Iggy. He knew exactly what their eyes were saying. Everyone expected him to have extra insight into this whole thing because he was there. He experienced the vision right along with Zeph. "I know you want more from me, but I've already told you everything I know about what Zeph and I experienced several times."

"I don't doubt you, lad," Praotes said softly to the assembly, "or the fact that Zeph was far beyond a simple state of confusion. Going on what we have heard from Iggy, we can only assume that the scroll in Zeph's possession unlocked much, if not all, of his Elemental abilities."

"The question still remains as to what is to be done," Yad pointed out, and he looked over the rims of his glasses.

Marcus stood up, "We'll go and find him."

"And what do you hope to accomplish if you do find him? You saw for yourself what he is capable of," Siah pointed out.

"I'll go with them as well," Gus said as he stood beside Marcus, "Perhaps he will listen to me. I have spent several years practicing meditation. Maybe I can reach him; maybe I can help him find the balance he desperately needs."

"Very well," replied Praotes. Both of the other men nodded their agreement. "It is our decision that you may go and seek him out."

Several hours went by. No one entirely seemed ready for what was ahead. Four figures stood on top of the hills north of town. A look of determination was in all their eyes. It was now the third day since anyone had seen Zeph. They weren't going to wait any longer. Marcus took point, followed by Iggy, Breeze, and Gus. The only clue to his whereabouts was that they had seen him run in the direction north of Daunt.

They set out over the first series of hills. The continuous rolling hills would be a decent trek for most of them. Clear skies and a gentle breeze accompanied them as they climbed hill after hill. The hills continued for several hours. There was minimal conversation along the way. More than enough had gone on over the last several days. Every single one of them only wanted to see Zeph alive and well. Of course, none of them knew how they would approach him if they did encounter him. They hoped that the last several days had somehow helped to calm him.

They reached the bottom of the last hill. Gus was perhaps the only one of them to have ever traveled this far north of town before. A small open plain lay ahead of them; beyond that, they could see some large rock formations.

"What do you think?" Marcus asked as he turned around to face the group.

Gus surveyed the area. Other than the vast open plains to the west and the ocean cliffs a short ways away to the east, the rock formations ahead seemed like the best option. The group continued north and soon reached the rock formations. Marcus motioned for Gus and Breeze to stay back as they proceeded through the tall rock formations. The rock ranged from smooth to jagged. Each of them oversaw their step as they continued on.

From a distance, the rock formation might not have seemed very formidable. However, once they had reached it, it had proven to be much larger than it had looked from a distance. It was not a mountain by any feat but a large section of rocks and cave formations. A large crack in the rock opened the path forward, giving way to the inner depths.

As they continued, they glanced upward at the vein of sky at the top of the crevasse. It was clear that the path through the rocks was on a downward slope. They continued moving slowly, watching their footing as they went. None of them wanted to be surprised if Zeph was somewhere inside the rock formations. Soon, the chasm widened and formed into a large open area. Looking up, the walls of rock now stretched several stories above them. It would be almost impossible to climb out from there.

Light from above created a solid pattern in the middle of the opening. The light enabled the view of several passageways that jetted off from the larger area where they stood.

"Where do you think we should head from here?" Iggy asked as he looked at the handful of cave-like openings in the walls. They looked at the passageways for a moment. It was decided that it was better to stay together; they chose the path that led off to the right. Iggy stood close behind Marcus, holding his hand out to light their path. After a short while, they began to see light up ahead and feel the ocean air.

Soon emerging from the passageway, they found a small open grassy area on the edge of the cliffs. The sea breeze hit their faces as they left the cave enclosure and stood on the cliffs. Water spray was in the air from the crashing ocean waves far below. The edge of the cliff was several paces in front of them. All their eyes were quickly drawn to the figure standing off to the side, only a single step away from the edge. He had his back to them, but his white hair was a dead giveaway. No one made a motion toward him or said a word. They simply waited.

"I can't go back...," the words trailed off as they fell from Zeph's lips, just loud enough to be heard over the breeze and crashing waves below. He stared at the waves crashing far below, watching his tears fall and join with the currents. How he wanted to do the same. It was Gus that stepped forward in front of the group.

"We're not here to take you back, son. We're just here to listen."

Zeph turned to face them, tears streaming down his face, his chin quivering. Thin, pale lines streaked down his face where the tears had washed the dirt away. His clothes were torn and filthy from the rocks and dirt in the caves. Looking down at his pulsing hands, they were in a constant state of flux, as though he had lost all control of his abilities. Holding them out, Zeph stared at his palms. The energy pulsed through his body, but he still had no idea how to control it.

"Look at me!" he screamed, "I can't do anything to stop what's happening. I don't even know what's happening."

Gus calmly spoke up, "Your subconscious has been opened up to all your abilities; your waking mind, however, is still trying to grasp what has happened." Breeze had carefully hidden behind Gus, so Zeph wouldn't see her. She was waiting for the right moment.

Zeph turned his attention back to the water below. "I can help you, Zeph," Gus continued, "I'm not saying it will be easy, but I'll help you in any way I can. Control of any ability is hard. Remember when you first learned Transference? You did it accidentally; you didn't even know what you were doing. But you didn't hurt anyone. In fact, you helped Marcus and your brother." Zeph turned his face half towards Gus as though he was beginning to listen to the words.

"All abilities can be used for good or evil, Zeph. You are NOT an evil person." Gus stressed the statement. Zeph turned to face the group. The anguish was still in his eyes. It was clear that he had been tormenting himself for the last several days with what had happened.

Breeze slowly walked out from behind everyone. Zeph's eyes immediately fell on the brace she wore on her right shoulder. He began to take a step back toward the edge of the cliff. The sight of her was more than he could bear. All the despair he had been holding onto for days. All of the heartache knowing that he had injured the girl he loved. It suddenly became too much at that moment, and he let everything inside collapse. Outstretching his arms, Zeph let himself fall.

The moment seemed to last forever. Zeph closed his eyes as he let his body fall backward over the edge of the cliff. The sensation of falling never overtook him as expected, though. Instead, a tremendous blast of wind sent him soaring upwards, and he fell to the ground atop the cliffs once more. Zeph felt an immense wall of wind directly behind him, blocking his way from the edge of the cliffs. Opening his eyes, he saw Breeze with her hand outstretched, palm glowing brightly. The tears were flowing down her face. The anger swelled up inside of her.

"How could you be so selfish?!" Breeze screamed, "To try leaving everyone that cares about you, everyone that loves you!" The anger and hurt burned in her voice as she kept the wall of wind to his back. All emotion drained from Zeph's face as he saw the anger on her face. He felt the wall of wind fade away behind him as she lowered her hand.

"If that's what you want to do, then fine; just jump. But then you will never, NEVER be the boy I knew!" Breeze spouted out as she stormed back into the caves. Zeph looked at Gus, his eyes pleading with him. Stepping forward, Gus took Zeph's hand. He could feel the energy pulsing in the young man's hand beneath his skin. The two of them sat down on the ground and crossed their legs. Marcus and Iggy returned to the cave to look for Breeze.

"I want you to close your eyes and focus on nothing else but my voice, Zeph," Gus said as he took Zeph's other hand in his. "Clear your mind as best as you can. Don't think about anything else right now, only this moment. Listen to the wind and the water crashing below. Feel your surroundings, the grass beneath you, the soil and stone beneath the grass, the rays from the suns above. Envision all that you are, everything that is within you. Let it gather in your mind; don't allow it to drift elsewhere."

Zeph sat there in silence for what seemed like an eternity; eventually, he opened his eyes and looked down. The glowing had subsided. As he stared at his hands, he felt the energy flowing down his arms. His hands quickly lit up once more. "You must concentrate, Zeph. This is not something you will master in a day," Gus said as he felt the energy between their hands again. Zeph nodded and closed his eyes once more. Gus continued to guide him as they sat across from each other.

Marcus and Iggy returned to the larger opening within the caves. They found Breeze sitting in the corner, crying. They slowly walked over and sat down on the ground on either side of her. She wiped the tears away with her sleeve. This caused a smear of dirt to appear across her face. Marcus smiled as he looked at her now dirty face. He pointed at her sleeve, and she noticed how dirty her clothes had gotten. A smile cracked on her face momentarily as she realized she must have smeared dirt all over her face. It quickly faded, however. In the dimly lit opening, it was clear that she was still in emotional agony.

"I'm not going to defend him, alright." Marcus started. "But I've been best friends with him since before I can remember," Marcus paused for a moment as she nodded. "I think I finally understand that expression 'being pushed over the edge.' You know Zeph has struggled with lacking Elemental abilities his whole life. And it seems like as soon as he finally starts to get a grasp on something and starts to feel good about himself, everything goes horribly wrong. I'm not saying he should take his life. I just can understand the torment he's going through. He doesn't deserve what's happened to him, and he doesn't deserve to live with the memory of how he hurt you. It doesn't matter where things go from here; he will carry that moment he hurt you for the rest of his life."

The three of them sat in silence for a while. Iggy got up and paced around the room for a bit. He raised his hand occasionally and shone a beam of light onto the cavern walls. Projecting light from his hands was becoming second nature to him by this point. He seldom really thought about it. He stopped for a moment and looked over at Breeze and Marcus. He had his head resting against the wall with his eyes closed. She had her hands wrapped around her knees with her chin resting on them. Her tears had stopped for a moment.

An idea popped into his head as Iggy walked over. Breeze looked up at him as he stopped in front of her.

"Are you wearing your Jade stone?" he asked. Of course she was; she never left home without it. She pulled the chain out from her clothing, revealing the stone attached to the end. "Can I hold it for a moment?" he asked. Marcus opened one of his eyes and looked over at Iggy as this was starting to pique his interest. She lifted the chain over her head and handed it to him.

Iggy walked to the middle of the room. Holding the gem, he cupped his hands around it so that the point of the gem stuck out from the top of his hands. Marcus stood up from where he was sitting and leaned against the wall. Breeze just continued to sit and watch.

"I've never tried this, but I'm thinking it will look really neat," Iggy said with a smile. Closing his eyes, he began to concentrate. The energy could be seen flowing down his arms. It seemed to stop at his wrists, which were starting to glow brighter.

"What are you...?" Marcus' words were cut off as a brilliant burst of green light filled the room. The gem in Iggy's hands was glowing with a brilliant green aura. The patterns of light shifted and flowed through the cavern walls just like they did within the gem. "Whoa..." was all Marcus could say as he looked at the brilliant green light that filled the cavern.

The light faded away as Iggy opened his hands. He walked over to Breeze and handed her the necklace back. Breeze seemed to be in somewhat higher spirits after watching the display. The three of them once again sat in silence. The mood was softening, though.

Hours later, Gus emerged from the passageway. The three of them had fallen asleep in a pile against the wall. Gus just shook his head and laughed. He was exhausted as well. Walking over, he softly touched Breeze on the shoulder. She began to stir and opened her eyes. She quickly looked past her father to the cave opening he had come through. There was no one else standing there. Looking puzzled, she caught Gus' eyes. He told her they had made significant progress, but Zeph said he wasn't ready to see anyone yet. Gus woke the boys as well. He quickly explained the situation to them.

"So Zeph is going to stay here?" Marcus asked with a perplexed look on his face.

"For the time being, yes," Gus replied. "He's been through a lot, and he doesn't want to return to town or see anyone until he's sure he won't hurt anyone again."

"What are we supposed to do?" Iggy asked.

"I need you to return to town. At the very least, give them an update. I'm sure Dawn will be grateful for the information. And if you could bring some food and supplies to last us a short while, that would also be very helpful."

The three youths reluctantly agreed and headed back to town. The hours seemed to go by quickly this time, and soon, they reached the edge of town. Making their way through Daunt, they stopped off at Zeph's house.

It was evening now, and upon entering the house, the smells from the kitchen filled their noses. Dawn was working over a large pot in the kitchen as she often was. Victor was sitting in the living room playing with Teak. He looked up at the three very dirty youths standing in the doorway. Even with the tenseness of everything going on, he couldn't help but chuckle. Dawn came rushing over, "So, did you find him?" There was an urgency in her voice as she spoke.

"Yes, we found him," Iggy replied.

"But he's going to need some work," Marcus added.

"What do you mean?" Dawn asked.

"He's very fragile right now," Breeze said. She went on to explain everything that happened when they found him. The pain overtook Dawn as the thought washed over her that her boy wanted to end his own life. After some time, she regained her composure. The group sat down to dinner. The three youths ate quickly as the long day had left them famished. Soon after, they cleaned themselves up and began packing supplies to return with. They packed food, water, rejuvenation vials, anything Zeph and Gus might need. After much discussion, it was decided that only Victor and Marcus would journey back since the night was falling fast, and it would take several hours to reach the caves.

As they headed out of town, dusk was already fading into night. Marcus once again led the way. When night was finally upon them, he removed two sphere lamps from the sack he carried and handed one to Victor. It was what they needed to light the way as they journeyed across the hills. The conversation was lively along the way; many of Victor's sea stories were told. Braving the sea wasn't something Marcus was overly thrilled to do, but visiting all these other cities greatly intrigued him.

After some time, they came upon the entranceway in the rocks that led down into the caves. Holding the lamps out in front of them, they carefully made their way inside. Upon entering the larger cavern, they were greeted by Gus, who was sitting quietly in the middle of the room.

"Where's Zeph?" Marcus asked, looking around.

"He's meditating out on the ledge," Gus replied.

"You left him by himself?" questioned Marcus.

"He has found a clarity for the moment that keeps him stable."

"Can I see him?" Victor asked. Gus shot him a skeptical look but then motioned for him to continue. Victor took up one of the sphere lamps and made his way through the passage. The sea air quickly found its way to him. Stepping out onto the grass, Victor gazed at the sea of stars above. He placed the lamp in his coat pocket to cover the light. The sky twinkled as millions and millions of stars shone down upon them. His gaze slowly fell on the young man sitting on the ground a short way from him. His hands were gently resting on his knees. Even though his eyes were closed, Victor was sure he was aware that he was standing there.

"Hello, Victor." The words were heavy, and it was obvious that Zeph was still burdened.

"Hello, Zeph," Victor replied as he took up the opposing position on the ground across from Zeph. "What a truly beautiful night, and this is a spectacular spot to gaze from."

Zeph opened his eyes and looked at Victor and then at the sky. It was clearer than any night he had ever seen in Daunt. There were no lights to prevent the sky from displaying its full splendor. As he stared up at the stars, it seemed like each one was calling out to him.

Victor pulled out the sphere lamp from his coat and placed it on the ground between him and Zeph. Looking down at it for a moment, Zeph slowly picked it up. He wrapped his fingers around the smooth glass ball. The light glowed through the cracks between each finger. Zeph stared down at it for several minutes.

"I know it's easier to run, to try and leave everything behind," said Victor as he broke the silence. "Perhaps you'll even find a place so far away that the pain can't catch up with you. But that's not you, and the pain will always find you. And trust me when I say that I speak from experience.

From the first day I saw you on the docks, Zeph, I knew you would do great things. I could see it in your eyes. I could see it in your excitement and the way you handled yourself. And I don't mean anything that the scroll has done to you; I mean you, Zeph, the person you are." And with that, Victor stood up and headed back.

"Thank you," Zeph said as Victor paused at the passageway entrance. Victor rejoined the group in the cavern. After some brief conversation, it was decided that Victor and Marcus should return to town. The question arose about how long Gus expected him and Zeph to remain in the caves.

"I really can't tell you for sure. We'll stay here until Zeph feels he is ready to return," Gus replied.

THE DAY WAS WARM AS the harvest suns were high in the sky. Even though it was only shortly into the ninth month, it felt closer to a month later. It was usually the warmest in the tenth month of the year. Many people had started harvesting from their gardens. Some had large sections of land behind their houses, while others had simple gardens. Only the plants that required the intense heat would be put off for another month or two.

Even in his absence, construction on Gus' in-town shop had already started. It was quite a prime location. The chosen location was a section of land at the crossroad between the main road and the road leading to the docks. The ground had been cleared, and the foundation was starting to be laid.

After everything that had happened in recent months, the town elders decided that Gus was an invaluable part of the town. Perhaps it was the change in times, or perhaps it was the extra commerce Gus was bringing back to town. Whatever it was, the town was happy with the idea of having a Fabrication shop again. Even though there was no ill will between Gus and the elders, they still expressed their deepest apologies for closing down his shop those years earlier.

The workers set the stones in the ground that would become the foundation. Other workers brought large pieces of wood. A small pile was slowly building up beside the work site. With all the help provided, the building construction would only take at most one week.

After visiting with Zeph, Victor returned to town and soon left Daunt for his next trip. Even though he wanted to stay and be there for Zeph when he finally returned, his responsibility to his crew and his trade had to come first. Daunt had become the center of his trading over the last few months. The production of the sphere lamps had become his primary piece of trade. Even the occasional Pirie juice sale helped boost his sales and spread the word of the fantastic Trader Captain Victor.

Breeze had spent much of her time staying with Marcus or Iggy since she did not want to return to her empty house outside town. Her shoulder had been healing well. The energy blast that had struck her had burnt a hole clean through her right shoulder. Even with the Healers, there was only so much they could do. Restoring flesh and bone was one thing, but there was still lasting damage that even the best Healers in Daunt weren't able to fully fix. Sometimes, the body just needed time to completely heal on its own. Even though it was still stiff, she no longer needed the brace.

It had been two weeks since they had found Zeph out in the cliffs on the north side of Appagon. The first seven days had passed very slowly, but the last seven days had passed more quickly. After the first seven days, more supplies were brought to Gus. They had been told that Zeph was beginning to make significant progress.

Dawn and Iggy were working in the garden, harvesting what was ready and checking on the ones needing more time. A short while later, Marcus and Breeze joined them. There wasn't much else to do. They had tried the first week to continue their regular work on the sphere lamps. Their progress was slow, however, since it was just Marcus, Iggy, and Breeze. Even with rejuvenation potions, their energy only lasted for so long.

Beads of sweat covered Marcus' forehead as the hot suns beat down on him. He had been growing increasingly quiet as the days had gone by. Zeph was like a brother to him. Marcus tried to fight his way through most of his battles in life, but in this situation, there was nothing he could do. There was no one he could fight with to resolve what was going on.

Dawn was on her knees in the soil, pulling weeds. Dirt covered all her clothing and clung to the sweat on her face. Her brown hair was in a tattered ponytail. It was the simplest image of a hard-working mother. She sat up briefly to catch her breath and wipe the sweat from her brow. It was clear that she was not only exhausted physically but also mentally. The last several weeks had taken their toll on her, night after night worrying about her son, plus days of working in the hot suns.

Sitting back on her heels, Dawn brushed the dirt off the plants. She looked over at the others as they worked at the soil. As Dawn looked out over the whole garden, something peculiar began to draw her attention. Looking at the rows of plants that stretched to every corner of the plot, she noticed that they were growing. She quickly jumped up as the plants in the garden grew to life. All the plants in the garden doubled in size. Even in the afternoon heat, they were bright green and fresh with dew. Everyone looked over at her, expecting to see some sign that it was her doing. She, however, simply shot back a look of puzzlement. Looking around, she searched for the source of the manifestation. Her eyes quickly fell upon the figure of a young man standing next to the house.

Slowly, he lowered his softly glowing palm. His crystal blue eyes seemed to shine with the light of the suns. While they had been working behind the house, he had been inside cleaning himself up. He wore the expensive white and blue outfit he had bought several months earlier. His hair and skin were washed and cleaned. The long white strands of hair hung down the sides of his face; it had been some time since it had been cut. A smile was on his face that no one had seen in ages.

Everyone quickly stood up and turned to face him. His gaze flowed over everyone and ended on Dawn.

"Hello, Mother," Zeph said softly. Dawn burst into tears as she ran over to him and wrapped her arms around him. It had seemed almost pointless that Zeph had cleaned up since he was now covered in dirt again. The minutes passed, and she finally released her grip but continued to hold him at arm's length. His face had changed somehow, as if he had left a boy and returned a man.

Brushing himself off, he moved towards the rest of the group. He put an arm around his little brother and smiled as he looked down at him. Marcus was the next on Zeph's path through the garden. He stopped before him, and they looked at each other for a moment. Marcus slowly lifted his hand. They clasped hands, wrapping their other arms around each other. "It's great to see you, bro," Marcus said as he fought back the tears.

Zeph smiled at Marcus and slapped him on the shoulder as he moved to the last person in the garden. Breeze had her head lowered as Zeph walked over to her. She slowly raised her head to look him in the eye. It was clear that there was still love behind her eyes. The recent incident, however, had put a wall up between them that would take some time to tear down. Softness was on his face. The words wouldn't leave his lips, but the apologetic look was on his face. She nodded in agreement. It was clear to everyone watching that it was a delicate situation. Dawn was the first to break the noticeably building uneasiness between the two.

"I think it's time we all went inside for a break," she said as she waved everyone towards the side of the house. Gus had been standing off to the side where Zeph had first appeared. He was still quite dirty and had a forceful smell about him since he had not returned to his house for clean clothing or to bathe. Wearing the same set of clothes for several weeks had built up quite a scent. Marcus and Iggy comically held their noses as they passed by.

Everyone entered the house and took seats in the living room. Zeph stood in the middle of the room as everyone else sat on the furniture and looked up at him. It was clear on everyone's face that a million questions were on the edge of their lips. Zeph simply smiled and raised his hands to them, "There will be a time for questions, but I have much to tell you first. You know more than anybody that a lot has changed for me, not just over the last several weeks but also over the last several months," he paused as everyone nodded.

"I'm here to tell you that I'm leaving."

"WHAT!" everyone blurted out at once; it was the reaction Zeph was expecting.

"I'm assuming Iggy has already told you about the events of the scroll and what I experienced in the vision. I know that I'm meant for so much more. I'll admit I don't understand it yet, but I know I must do this." The words hung in the air for several minutes. His mother was the first to speak up.

"Why do you have to go?" The hurt was evident in her eyes as she asked the question. Zeph walked over and knelt in front of her. Taking her hand in his, he said, "Mom, I know this will be hard for you. It will be hard for all of you. This is something I have to do. I wasn't asked to do this; I was born for it. I have to do it."

"You're not doing this alone!" Marcus blurted out as he jumped to his feet.

"I can't ask you to come with me. You have your own life, Marcus."

"I'm coming too," Breeze said as she also stood. Their eyes caught for a moment. There was something there, something he desperately missed. Zeph seemed to lose his place in what he had planned to say as he looked at the two of them.

"And I'm coming too," Iggy piped up as he also jumped to his feet. Zeph quickly shot him a look as if to say, 'No, you're not.'

"Don't give me that look, Zeph. You know more than anyone that I have to come with you. I wasn't supposed to see everything you saw, but I was there. Mal'ak said that I was charged with your task as well; I have to come."

Zeph looked over at his mother; the thought of both of her boys leaving was obviously hitting her very hard. This conversation wasn't going in the direction Zeph had expected it to. Gus seemed to be sitting quietly, watching everything.

"We have yet to hear from you, sir," Zeph said as he looked over at Gus.

"Perhaps even more than Iggy, I have a different perspective than anyone else here," Gus replied as he remained seated. Everyone else gradually settled back in their seats as it became clear that what he had to say was significant. "I know about what happened to you in the scroll through everything you told me, but I've also spent the last several weeks with you. I've seen your true character. You will do great things, of that I have no doubt. I will miss you, and everyone else that is planning on leaving. Omega knows that I don't want to see my daughter go, but she is a part of this."

Zeph slowly nodded his head in agreement. A smile formed on his face. He looked around at everyone in the room. Leaving might be hard, but he was no longer leaving alone. Dawn stood up and walked over to Zeph. Holding him at arm's length, she looked him up and down. Her eyes stopped on his long white hair.

"Well, you may have become a snappy dresser, but we'll have to do something about that hair," she said, forcing a grin. Everyone laughed.

"Alright, we're going to need supplies, and since there are four of us now, we're going to have to get enough for everyone," Zeph said.

"Well, what should we get?" Marcus asked.

"I think we should buy some more durable clothing; plain clothes just won't work in the long run. I also think it will be a good idea to have weapons of some kind; you never know what we'll come across. Of course, we'll need coins. We'll take what we can from the storage chest within reason. Besides that, I'm sure there are a variety of smaller items as well," Zeph replied as he looked at everyone else in the room.

"Sounds like a good start. We shouldn't rush into it. If it takes a few days to get everything ready, we'll know we have everything we need," Breeze suggested.

"Good idea," said Zeph.

The conversation continued for a while longer. The group's mood had changed, and excitement began to fill the air. Even though it would be difficult to leave, things seemed to be working out.

Over the next day, the four youths went from shop to shop buying supplies. Their first stop was the Weapons Shop. They weren't necessarily looking for suits of armor or anything of that sort. After browsing the limited selection, they bought some basic leather armor. The armor included leggings, shoulder pads, chest plating, and arm bracers. They could all easily be worn over their regular clothing. Zeph and Marcus found themselves looking at the weapons section of the shop next. Since Breeze had her current bow, she wouldn't need to buy a new one. Iggy was content to go without a primary weapon since he wasn't skilled in any field of combat. He did, however, purchase a small dagger that he could easily strap to his waist.

Zeph looked over the various blades hanging on the wall and the layout on the table. He knew he didn't need a very expensive blade but something that would do the job. Looking around, he spotted one that he liked. It was plain and had a thick handle wrapped with black leather. The width of the blade was about four fingers, and it was about twice the length of a man's forearm. The blade was smooth and perfect. It came with a black leather sheath.

Marcus was off at one of the other tables. Since he didn't primarily use swords, he was trying to find something to suit his style better. At the end of one of the tables, he spotted what he was looking for. Lying on the table was a pair of black fingerless leather gloves. A row of metal spikes lined each knuckle. It was precisely what he was looking for, something to add that extra damage to his punches.

Both boys paid for their gear and joined the others waiting outside. They talked briefly about where they should go next. It was decided that the Alchemy Shop would be next. It was several stores over from the Weapons Shop.

The four youths entered the basic shop; it had few potions outside the healing and rejuvenation. They bought what they could, including several extra vials of rejuvenation potion, which would be beneficial for Iggy as their healer. Daunt didn't have the means to have a large potion selection. Not like the village of Tweedsmiur did on the other side of Appagon. They didn't worry about food and other perishable goods, as they would purchase those on the day they left.

The group stopped by the future site of Gus' shop. Gus was up on one of the frame beams, working away. They waved up to him. He waved back with a smile. "How's everything going, gang?" he shouted down. They said it was going well and that they had bought most of the supplies they would need for the time being.

The shop would be a good size, well over twice as large as the shop Gus had created in his house. The shop was far enough away from most of the houses in Daunt that the noise it would generate wouldn't bother most people. Once the shop was completely finished, Gus would move and reassemble all his contraptions. He had already found several people in town who wanted to work for him. Each had been picked for their elemental abilities, which would be essential to creating the sphere lamps without the group's assistance.

Zeph had talked to Gus late the evening before about the financial situation that would occur once the group had left on their journey. After a brief discussion, Zeph appointed Gus in charge of the group's coins in their absence. Any coin they didn't take with them on the journey would be left in Gus' care. Gus assured Zeph that it would all be well taken care of. Since it was the group that had invented the spheres, Gus told Zeph that a part of all the profits from them would be set aside for the group to receive once they returned.

It was nearing the end of the week. They decided to wait until the seventh day and leave after the morning Gathering at the temple. Until then, the group spent the next few days hanging out together. It seemed as though it had been forever since they had done that.

DAY 123

> Omega gives power to the weak so that through time and endurance, they might find the strength they seek.
>
> Mount up in the strength given to you and soar above the clouds.

~The Book of Ta'Hor

CHAPTER 10
THE JOURNEY

Zeph sat on the long stone bench. The Temple was full. He looked around at all the faces, their eyes focused on the Uriym. Many thoughts stirred in Zeph's mind. It was always when he would sit and listen to the words spoken from the Book of Ta'Hor that he searched deep inside himself. Who was he? What should he be doing with his life? These questions and many more always filled his mind as he listened to the words being spoken.

"Understand this, my dear brothers and sisters! Let every person be quick to listen, slow to speak, slow to anger. Put away all evil things and humbly welcome the message I bring to you, which is the path to Ascension. But be sure you live out the message and do not merely listen to it and so deceive yourselves," the words echoed in the room as they left Praotes' lips.

It was moments like this when Zeph felt the weakest. In those moments when he looked deep inside himself, he knew something was missing. He had always been raised in the Temple under the teachings of Ta'Hor. Yet, as he listened to the words that had just been spoken, he knew there was so much more to it than he had ever realized. Most people simply tried to live good lives, but to live for the goal of Ascension was another level altogether. Of course, there were people in the world who lived by evil teachings as well, intending to live forever as beings wrapped in worldly power.

His emotions surged inside as he thought about how he was meant for so much more. Most parents tell their children that they are meant for great things. It's not so much a matter of whether they grow up to achieve greatness or not; it's about the inspiration that is implanted in the child. However, in Zeph's case, this went far beyond simple encouragement. He could, in fact, be one of the most important people in the history of the world.

The thought of leaving everything behind crept into his thoughts. He had been resisting it for the last several days now. It hurt to think about it. He tried to push it out of his thoughts again, but it would not be pushed aside this time. It scared him; it truly did. Just the thought that along the way, he might have to abandon everyone and everything he cared about to accomplish what he knew he had to do. He hoped this wouldn't be true, that the people that helped and supported him would always be there.

Zeph looked over at Breeze, sitting with Gus several seats over. Things had changed between them, more than he wanted to admit. There was a wall between them now, clear as glass but strong as steel. It was not a matter of forgiveness or restitution for anything he had done. Things were simply different now. It was the hardest thing he ever had to deal with in his whole life. Everything inside of him wanted things to be like they were. The memories of their life together still haunted him as he slept each night. Every moment he had with her now was a mix of joy and pain. He knew, however, that if she were to disappear altogether, it would hurt even more than it did now.

Breeze caught his stare as she glanced in Zeph's direction. She smiled softly at him. It was a moment of peace inside Zeph's heart, knowing she was still there for him. He didn't know what would happen between them in the future, but he had his own hopes and dreams for it.

Zeph heard his name among the words Praotes was speaking. He realized that the announcement of their journey was being given: "We will all miss these four young youths. But as they venture out into the world, let us remind them that they have our encouragement and prayers." Everyone looked over at them and gave a short round of applause. With that, the Gathering finished, and everyone stood up.

Zeph shook off all his thoughts and pulled a smile from deep within. 'Change is a good thing,' he told himself. People kept coming up to the group, shaking their hands and giving them embraces of support. It was the boost that Zeph needed right now. He was already nervous about the idea of leaving everything he'd ever known.

The lines of people trickled away until only the four of them, their families, and Praotes remained. They chatted amongst themselves for a short while. The suns were slowly getting high in the sky; they had planned to head out at midday. Praotes motioned for the four youths to step aside with him. They walked over to a large tree next to the Temple.

"This is a great honor for you, Zeph, to embark on such a journey. And for the rest of you, to be there to support Zeph in this manner is the measure of true friendship."

"Thank you, Praotes," Zeph replied as he embraced the old man.

"I'd like to pray for you before you go," Praotes said as he joined the group in a circle. Everyone joined together, wrapping an arm around the back of the person next to them. "Omega, watch over Zeph, your servant. Use him to complete what you have set before him. Protect these four children of yours and keep them safe. Give them the strength to endure trials, courage to overcome their battles, and wisdom so that they may always keep their minds and hearts true."

As Zeph opened his eyes and deeply breathed in the fresh morning air, an uncontrollable smile formed on his face. He felt as though he was floating, so he quickly looked down to check if he was. Everyone else was also smiling. This was the fresh start they needed.

No long goodbyes were needed; much of the last several days had revolved around that. Everyone gathered up their belongings. Zeph and Marcus each carried a larger sack full of sphere lamps on their backs. Breeze and Iggy both had a mix of food and other supplies. Except for Iggy, everyone was armed with their primary weapons, and all were wearing the new leather light armor they had purchased.

Nothing was left to do; nothing was holding them back now. They all turned and embraced their loved ones. After a moment, they turned and began the walk out of town. The families stood at the intersection and watched their children leave. Dawn, Siah, Gus, and Marcus' parents stood and watched as the group went farther and farther out of sight until they could no longer be seen.

The dust of the old dry road was stirred up as they made their way out of town. It wasn't long until they came upon Gus and Breeze's house since it was on the way. Soon after, the road tapered off to nothing more than a worn walking path. Not many people made this journey westward from Daunt regularly. They stood there for a moment, at the edge of all that they knew. Zeph stood in front of them as he eyed the open plains ahead. In the distance, he could see a large forest stretching out from the coast. He finally laid his eyes on the white peaks of the mountains, far at the top of the horizon. His gaze lowered back to the forest off in the distance.

"We'll make for the forest," he said without turning to face them. A smile was on his face. He knew that inside, he was still unsure of how his life would turn out, but he had his friends by his side. Reaching into his old shoulder bag, he felt the four other things that would help him along their journey. The scroll, his father's compass, Mage Saphar's book, and a copy of the Book of Ta'Hor Praotes had given him.

Zeph looked bold as he led the way out onto the open plains. His white hair had been trimmed, cleaned, and shone brightly in the suns. Light rays caught his crystal blue eyes just right to bring them to life. The clothing, weapons, and sacks made him the ideal image of an adventurer, which is precisely what he was going for. He was ready for some adventure.

The conversation was lively as they walked out into the long grass, which was fading to pale green in the heat of the harvest suns. Zeph walked to one side of the worn path and let his fingertips flow over the strands of tall grass as they walked. It was an interesting sensation, perhaps the simplest of all sensations. The constant flow of thin blades of grass created a slight numbing sensation on his fingertips. It was soothing in a way.

"So what should we talk about?" Marcus piped up.

"What do you mean?" Zeph said, glancing over.

"Well, we're going to have a lot of walking ahead of us, plus, I highly doubt this is going to be a short adventure. So, we gotta talk about something along the way, or it's going to be very boring." Zeph thought about it for a moment. Marcus did have a point; it's not like they could just walk in silence for hours.

"Who's nervous about this whole thing?" Zeph asked as he raised his hand.

"Really? That's the best conversation starter you got?" Marcus asked with a smirk on his face.

"Well, I'll be honest, I'm nervous about this. Let's set aside everything with my 'destiny' for a moment." It was starting to become a common habit to see him use air quotes, "We just left the only homes we've ever known. We're out in the real world. Who knows what kind of things we'll face or see?"

The words did seem to resonate in the minds of the other three. Zeph breathed in deep. The mixture of the dust from their feet and the flowers in the field created an interesting scent. The two scents intertwined in Zeph's head and brought forth a question.

"What is it that we do in life that will leave a legacy?"

The silence that Zeph didn't want to happen was now falling on all of them. Maybe it was too deep of a question for their afternoon stroll. Perhaps he should have asked something more comical, something less serious. Nevertheless, as he smelt the dust and the flowers mixing together, his mind envisioned how, in the future, those same flowers would die and dry up, turning into the very same dust on the ground.

"I think it all depends on how we affect the people around us," Iggy said, breaking the silence.

"How so?" Marcus questioned.

"Whether it's positive or negative, the level of influence you have on a person's life determines how you are remembered."

"Well, you can sure tell you two are brothers," Marcus laughed. "One asks a serious question, and the other gives a serious answer." Everyone else chuckled as well.

Several hours had passed since they had left Daunt. It was decided that it was time to stop for a break and eat. Walking off the path into the tall grass, Zeph took out his sword. It was beautiful, as only an adventurous soul could see a weapon. The sound was quick and smooth as the blade resonated from the sheath. Light danced across the mirror surface of the metal. With several quick swings, he cleared an area for everyone to sit down in. Zeph's face was gleaming as he looked down at the heaps of grass at his feet. Soft clapping turned his attention back to the others.

"Congratulations, you killed some grass," Marcus said as he slowly clapped. "Let's write this one down in the history books; we don't want to forget this day." The sarcastic tone in his voice was the strongest any of them had heard in quite a while. Zeph shot him a glare as he replaced the sword in its sheath. Taking a moment, he untied the sword from around his waist. When he first bought the sword, he considered wearing it behind his shoulder. Soon after, though, he switched the straps so it hung from his waist. It quickly became awkward to reach over his shoulder and realize it wasn't the best way to wear it.

As everyone else sat down, they removed parts of their armor. The light leather armor had become quite hot in the afternoon suns, and their shirts underneath were drenched in sweat. They knew they would have to get used to wearing it as adventurers. A soft breeze flowed over the plains and helped to cool them down.

Iggy removed several pieces of food from the sack he carried. He revealed bread, cheese, and dried meat. He passed it around the group, and everyone grabbed a bit of each. The bread and meat were just fine, but the cheese, on the other hand, was starting to show signs that it wouldn't last long. It was warm, and starting to sweat in the day's heat. They knew they would either have to finish the rest of the cheese off later that day or discard it. Water was something else that was on their minds. Each had brought a flask with them. However, the heat from the harvest time of year was starting to get the best of them. They knew they would have to be careful with the rationing until they reached another village or a source of fresh water.

Zeph sat in the little clearing he made, looking back toward Daunt. The hours of travel had placed the small village far out of sight. Looking over his shoulder, he glanced at the ever-growing forest in the distance. It was not so distant now, though; only a few more hours, he figured. The suns were still hanging overhead, beating down on his brow. The ocean reflected a brilliant blue towards them off the water. They weren't very far from the southern coast and could easily see the sea in the distance. Looking at the white, snowy peaks of the mountains helped Zeph imagine he was in a cooler place. Even though he had never seen or felt snow, he was told it was colder than the coldest water during the growing season. He looked forward to experiencing it one day soon.

"So, how do we plan on doing business once we reach the next village?" Zeph asked as he stood and began to pack his belongings.

"I'm guessing we should start by talking to the town elders," Breeze suggested.

"Hmmm, that's not a bad place to start. I'm guessing they might want to know who's selling what in their town."

"I have a feeling we'll sell most of the sphere lamps quite quickly," Iggy added.

"Yeah, I'm with the little man on this. If they've never seen anything like this before, everyone will want one," Marcus added.

They finished packing up and headed down the dirt road once more. The topic of whether or not they should sell all the lamps came up next. Obviously, there was a large market for this kind of invention. Other than the stories Zeph's father had told him about the lights in the cities on Sire across the Eastern Sea, everyone on Appagon used fires, oil lamps, or candles for light at night. Right now they had been selling the lamps for two gold kessas. Your average person made around seven silver kessas daily, equivalent to one gold kessa. Between Zeph and Marcus' packs, they were carrying roughly two hundred sphere lamps with them. They expected to sell every single one of them in no time at all. Just in case, though, everyone in their party had brought some sacks of coins, a mix of gold and silver kessas.

Not much was known about the other villages on Appagon. They knew that the next closest village was called Tweedsmiur and that they traded in potions. That was all they knew about it, though. A merchant from Tweedsmiur came to Daunt a handful of times throughout the year, but it wasn't very common.

The forest grew even closer now, and the suns began to slope down on the horizon. They would set in a little over an hour. The forest was visible now. It was a lot thicker than they had expected. The trees rose high into the sky. Stories upon stories of branches intertwined with each other. Black bark covered every tree. The four approached the forest with caution. It wasn't what they had been expecting at all. From a long distance away, it appeared very peaceful. Standing in front of it, looming over their heads, it seemed dark and ominous.

The path grew more worn as they neared the entrance to the forest. Remnants of small campsites were littered around the area. Perhaps these were left behind several weeks earlier by the travelers coming to Daunt for the Alignment. The four spread out and searched the various sites. Nothing useful was found. They gathered together again at the entrance to the forest. Next to the archway of tree branches that made up the entrance was a large wooden sign that read, "*The Forest of Light. Travelers beware, only enter at night and stay in the light.*"

"What do you think that means?" Marcus asked, pointing at the sign.

"Kind of sounds like a riddle to me, with the way it rhymes," Breeze replied.

They gazed up at the towering trees above them. The branches were so thick that they blocked almost all sunlight from flowing down inside the forest. Marcus walked over and touched one of the trees. The black bark was rough to the touch. The trees near the path bent and intertwined to form a large opening.

"How can trees like this even survive?" Breeze asked as she looked over the menacing rows of trees. "I don't even see any leaves. Do you think the forest is actually alive?"

"If you ask me, they should call this the Black Forest instead," Iggy piped up.

"Well, what do you say, gang? Shall we head in?" Marcus asked as he clapped his hands together.

"I don't know, man. The sign says to only enter at night. Plus, it's pitch black in there," Zeph replied.

"Well, we do have options, you know," Marcus said as he formed a small ball of fire in each of his palms. Iggy also stepped forward with rays of light emanating from his palm. Zeph's better judgment told him that they should stay and wait until nightfall. Everyone seemed ready to continue; they were just waiting for his signal. Reluctantly, Zeph gave in and waved his hand forward.

As they stepped over the threshold, darkness overtook them. It was unlike anything they had experienced before. Zeph fell to the ground. His bags, weapons, and armor all seemed to get much heavier. A sinking feeling of despair flowed inside him. It was as though the darkness within the forest was reaching deep inside, trying to force itself inside him. A cold chill shot up their spines, causing each of them to shutter. Zeph breathed in deeply as he felt his whole body tremble.

Marcus reached out into the darkness with his fire, but nothing separated the darkness. The hollow shell of branches flickered around them like bones, as though some great beast had consumed them. Zeph turned to face the entrance. Even though they were only a few steps inside the forest, it seemed so distant now. He wanted to turn back, to run back to the daylight. Iggy forced the light from his palms out into the forest's darkness, but it too quickly faded away with no effect.

They drew close to each other as they softly began to walk forward. The dirt beneath them welcomed their presence. A deep growl was heard in the depths of the darkness. Zeph felt his heart begin to race faster than he ever thought possible. He felt Iggy grip his arm and stand behind him. It was then that Zeph saw the eyes in the darkness—deep, piercing eyes glowing red in the consuming darkness.

The growl turned into a terrifying roaring scream. The sound was unlike anything they had ever heard before. No man or beast could produce such a sound like this. It was like a cry of pain and anger horribly mixed into one agonizing sound. They froze in place, fear holding them captive. Claws tearing through the rough dirt filled their ears. The sound of dirt being flung was quickly followed by Marcus' cries of pain as the beast launched itself and tackled him. The force sent him flying through the air and rolling out of the forest.

The suns were low but hadn't quite set yet. Orange light bathed the open plains. A gentle breeze flowed amongst the grass. It was a peaceful evening. The serenity was shattered as Marcus' screams echoed across the plains. The creature plunged its claw-like fingers into Marcus' chest. The duo impacted the ground hard, throwing dust up into the air. Marcus franticly clawed at the creature's arms, trying to escape its terrifying grasp. To Marcus' surprise, he gripped what felt like human arms.

The creature screamed in Marcus' face. He looked up at the creature in sheer horror. It was a man, or what had once been a man. The thin shell of a man could be seen beneath the blackness surrounding it. Its skin was a pale green and cold to the touch. Rough and worn, it felt like burnt wood. Wisps of darkness flowed out of the creature like fine hair. It wrapped itself around the creature, like thick fog clinging to its skin. Hot breath wafted over Marcus' face. The stench of rotting flesh filled his nostrils. He looked the creature in the eyes. Where would typically be the whites of an eye, there was only blackness. Where color would be, blood red filled its place. Its eyes glowed with a dark red radiance. A Shadow elemental symbol glowed red on the creature's forehead.

The pain was searing as Marcus tried to pull the claws from his chest. Even with the light leather armor, the end of the claws has still managed to pierce all the way through. He tried to find a way to burn the creature with his abilities but couldn't find the strength. Zeph drew his sword and ran towards them. The creature cocked its head in Zeph's direction. Pulling one hand from Marcus' chest, it thrust it in Zeph's direction. It seemed as though the arm stretched to several times its length. It hit Zeph in the chest, knocking him to the ground and gasping for air. Breeze quickly drew her bow, and without hesitation, she fired. The arrow impacted the creature's back. It screamed out in pain. The glowing red in its eyes burned like blazing liquid fire. Jumping to its feet, the creature threw Marcus into the air and let his body fly. It charged towards Breeze, its eyes blazing brightly.

Breeze began firing shot after shot at the creature. Each arrow went straight through it with a string of black fog trailing after. It was as though the creature simply let the arrows pass right through itself without a second thought. Her quiver emptied in seconds to no avail. The creature lunged out at her and wrapped its fingers around her throat, lifting her up into the air. It shook her violently as it screamed in her face. Pulling its free arm back, it quickly flung it forward and pushed its claws into her abdomen. She screamed out in pain as the long, slender fingers found their way deep into her flesh.

Zeph found his footing as he breathed deeply, trying to regain his composure. He looked over at Iggy. He could tell his brother was trying to think of something he could do to help with the situation. Iggy placed his hands out and sent a thin beam of pure white light toward the creature. It seemed to hit the creature with some force, but it looked like it was causing it very little pain.

Marcus had also gotten back on his feet. The three boys all looked at each other and rushed towards the creature, hoping they might have some advantage together.

"GET DOWN!" a voice boomed out across the plains. The boys skidded in their tracks to see Xa'an running up to them. He was racing toward them at full speed, arms and legs pumping rapidly like nothing they had ever seen before. His long black trench coat fluttered wildly as he ran towards them. Every impact from his boots stirred up dust clouds as he raced forward; it was as though the wind was beneath his every stride. Something in one of his hands was glowing. The creature quickly cocked its head in Xa'an's direction. Breeze began to go limp in the creature's grasp.

"Shield your eyes," Xa'an called out as he rushed forward.

Dropping to a knee, each of them covered their eyes. Xa'an flung the object. The round glass vial shattered as it impacted the ground in front of the creature. A brilliant burst of light emanated from it, causing the creature to screech and stumble back. Breeze fell to the ground and slumped over. Xa'an kicked off the ground, launching himself up into the air. Pulling both blades from behind his back, he sliced into the creature.

The cry of pain was silenced as quickly as it started as Xa'an's blades cut through the body of the fiend. It collapsed into four large pieces at Xa'an's feet. The body began to dissolve into hundreds of small glowing lights. They drifted up into the air and faded away. Only some small orbs of light remained on the ground. Iggy quickly rushed over to Breeze. She was alive and conscious. The pain was evident on her face as she tightly held her hands against her abdomen as blood seeped out. Placing his hands over the wounds, Iggy began to concentrate, and within moments, the bleeding stopped; she was healed enough to stand.

Xa'an knelt down and scooped up the glowing balls of light from where the creature had just been. He was careful not to wrap his fingers around them. Walking over to Zeph, he extended the orbs to him.

"What are they?" Zeph asked as he stared at the strange glowing balls of light. He knew that all beings dissolved into energy when they died, but he had no idea what this was.

"These are Essence Orbs. Contained within them are any number of attributes: knowledge, speed, strength, whatever was left behind in death." Xa'an's words sounded like a riddle. "All living things leave an essence behind, something of what they once were. Anyone can absorb these and, by doing so, obtain part of what it once was. You need to understand what this means. Please, each of you, take some of these."

Zeph reached out and took one of the orbs in his fingers. It felt almost completely weightless but still seemed to have density to it. Xa'an motioned for him to wrap his fingers around it in a fist; Zeph did as instructed. The orb easily dissolved right into his skin. A strange sensation flowed up his arm and over his body for a moment.

"How do you feel?" asked Xa'an.

"I feel....more agile somehow," Zeph replied with a strange look on his face.

"The orb has slightly increased your reflexes. Each time you absorb an Essence orb, its effects will be obvious. Just as you were able to distinguish that your agility has increased, you will notice that others will make you stronger or give you knowledge about something unknown before. This is how Essence Orbs work," Xa'an explained.

A small burst of light flooded the evening sky as the sun slipped below the horizon. The sky quickly changed from a soft orange to a deep bluish-purple. The four youths watched as the light faded away and then turned to face Xa'an. In the growing dim light of dusk, the soft orange glow of his eyes could be seen. It was one of his most fascinating characteristics. It had been months since they had seen him, and it was a first for Breeze. Even in the heat of the harvest season, he still wore a heavy black outfit. It was similar to what they remembered him wearing the last time, but his robes had been replaced with a trench coat. His long black trench coat flowed over his armored vest and down to his boots. The only thing to separate him from his scheme of black was his light brown hair, which had grown several lengths longer than the near-shaved length it had been before.

Iggy walked around, tending to everyone's wounds. It was a blessing to have him on the journey. He would be more helpful than any of them had ever thought. Doubts began to fill Iggy's mind as he held his hands over Breeze's stomach. The thoughts of being insignificant flooded his mind. He wished he could have done more to help and not simply clean up the aftermath. As if reading his thoughts, Breeze placed a hand on his shoulder. Iggy looked her in the eye. She assured him that what he was doing was very important and not to doubt himself. The time would come when he would know his role in the larger scheme of things.

A pale blue glow caught Zeph's attention from the corner of his eye. It was coming from the forest. Confused, he began walking over to the forest entrance. The group followed. Standing in the entranceway, Zeph stared up into the heights of the trees as he took several steps into the forest. Like watching the night sky come out at an accelerated rate, the very tops of the thick black forest canopy began to twinkle. Thousands upon thousands of points of light began to come into view. It was as though the forest was opening up to the night sky above. Zeph stood in awe of the display above him. The points of light began to drift down like feathers slowly falling in the air.

Xa'an smiled as he watched the young man gazing up at the trees as they entered the forest. The deep darkness of the void had faded away and had now given birth to a display so vast it felt as though they were walking amongst a sky of stars. The inner shell of the beast had now become a never-ending sea of tranquility.

"I don't understand.....what is all this?" Zeph asked, still perplexed by the display all around him. One of the specks of light floated down in front of him. Reaching out, he let it fall onto his palm; it was wet to the touch. He watched as the drop of light melted into his skin and faded away.

"You believed this forest was full of death because of its appearance when, in fact, it thrives much more than most others. At the very tops of the trees are large leaves. During the day, they gather the rays from the suns. When night falls, the leaves release this energy as a type of dew. It drifts down to the ground below and feeds the forest. This liquid is most commonly called Luminous," Xa'an spoke as they strolled through the forest.

"What does it do?" asked Iggy.

"If you drink it in its raw natural form, as you can see here, you will find it has a mild sweet taste and is quite refreshing. However, it is a key ingredient in most potions in Tweedsmiur, which is why most people collect it." After hearing you could drink it, Marcus was already walking around with his tongue out. Zeph just smiled and shook his head.

The Luminous liquid was lighter than normal liquid in the sense that it did not fall like a drop of water. Instead, it drifted down slowly like feathers. The drops began to make their way to the forest floor. As the group walked through the drifting rain of light, they began to feel refreshed—not just physically, but watching this grand display renewed their spirits. The whole forest was glowing brightly now; the path leading through it could clearly be seen as far as it stretched before them.

"So, where did that creature come from?" Zeph asked as he turned to look at Xa'an.

"That fiend came from within this forest," he replied.

"In a place like this? How can that be?" Zeph asked, puzzled.

Xa'an sighed for a moment, thinking about what he should say. "You are all still very young. In a sense, you know nothing about the world, about the nature of mankind. This forest is a perfect example of the nature of man. There are times when the goodness of man can shine so brightly that it is a beacon to all, and it heals those who seek it. Having said that, there are other times when a man allows the darkness to consume him and evil to dwell within."

It had been some time since someone had spoken to Zeph in such a profound way. It reminded him of the times Jarian had spoken to him during the festival. Zeph thought he understood what Xa'an was trying to tell him.

"That creature was a Fiend," Breeze said as the image of the creature's face flashed in her mind.

"Yes, it was," Xa'an responded.

"It was once a person, wasn't it?" she asked.

"At one time, yes."

She ran her fingers over her throat where the fiend had held her. "How did they come to be that way?" A look of distress washed over her face, not for herself but for the thought of what must have happened to the man.

"That, I don't know. It may have been something as small as they died in a tragic accident. But I'm guessing it's more likely they had been murdered," Xa'an said as he came up beside her.

"That's terrible," said Iggy.

"So why was it here?" asked Marcus.

"If someone becomes a fiend, it is most common that they dwell in the environment related to their elemental connection. Which is why that fiend lived in the shadows; it was where it was most powerful."

Zeph knew that they would all have to be on their guard in the future. In his mind, he tried to simply chalk it up to it being their first encounter, but he knew that was only partially true. This world was new to them all. The quiet town of Daunt was far behind them. Even though not every place would be full of danger, he knew they needed to be ready. It was comforting to have Xa'an with them again. With him around, Zeph felt like there was nothing that could touch them. On that thought, he turned to the mage once again.

"So why are you here? I mean, why now? How did you know to come?" Zeph questioned.

Xa'an stopped for a moment and looked Zeph straight in the eye. The falling drops of light danced across the soft glowing orange in Xa'an's eyes.

"Even from across the sea, Zeph, a day's journey away, I felt you unlock the scroll." Zeph began to say something, but Xa'an gestured that there would be a time and a place to discuss it further.

The terrain of the forest began to shift as they continued on. One moment, they would be going up a hill and then down the next moment.

They were starting to tire, but Xa'an assured them they would reach the village soon. The depth of night was beginning to fall on them. Even though the forest was brightly lit, the outside world lay in slumber. The effects of the Luminous gave them the energy to continue on.

Eventually, the sound of voices was heard up ahead. Laughter rang out into the night as they listened to the voices. They rounded a bend in the path to see a handful of middle-aged men by several rows of cauldrons connected by a series of pipes and funnels that led up into the trees.

"Well, hello, lads, oh and one lass I see," the man said with a wink and a grin. "What brings ya through this fine forest on this fine night?"

"We're travelers and merchants, of sorts," Zeph replied, stepping forward towards the man. The man jumped up from the oversized sack he was sitting on. Thrusting his hand out, he gripped Zeph's hand and gave it a good hardy shake. The man's long, wavy orange hair seemed slightly out of place with his round body and large potbelly. His clothes were worn and simple, and he had an old-rimmed hat atop his head. Even in the twinkling light of the forest, his Fire symbol was noticeable on his forehead just beneath the rim of his hat.

"Pleased to meet you, lad; my name be long and tedious, so the boys just call me Okies." His grin never seemed to leave his face, and there was a presence about him that you couldn't help but laugh about. "And if merchants ye be, then I'm yer man. I run one of the finest potion shops in Tweedsmiur."

Zeph took a few minutes to introduce everyone and tell Okies a little bit about themselves. The true nature of Zeph and the events surrounding him was not revealed. Okies invited everyone to take a load off their feet and have a seat with them.

"Now, Xa'an, I do believe I've seen ya passing through our village in times past, am I right?"

"It's been some time since I've been through, but yes, I have visited many times before," Xa'an replied.

"Ah! I knew it; I never forget a face, or someone as menacin' as yourself. Well, these are my boys; we've been together since we were wee lads. I'm guessin' in the same way that the lot of ya have been, too. Omega couldn't have blessed me with a finer bunch of scallywags to call me friends."

"So, what is it that you're doing out here?" asked Breeze.

"Well, lass, we use these contraptions of mine to catch the Luminous. I can't make my potions without it. So me and the boys come out here every night for a few hours and catch a couple of bottles worth," Okies explained as he pointed up to the rigging. The large funnels collected the falling drops, and the tubes brought them down to the cauldrons below.

"That's very interesting; I'd like to see the process of making a potion," Iggy piped up.

"Well, that shouldn't be a problem, young Iggy, but perhaps that might be something we could do in the mornin' part of the day." He replied with a chuckle.

The length of the day was finally setting in; everyone was exhausted. As they gathered up their belongings, Zeph's sack of spheres toppled over. A sphere lamp rolled out of the top of the sack and bounced across the forest floor, stopping at Okies feet. The man's eyes widened as he picked up the glowing ball. His usual grin was momentarily replaced by a look of sheer awe. The reflection of the sphere lamp could be seen in Okies' eyes. It was a sight like nothing he had ever seen before.

"What is this gleamin' thing?" he asked with pure shock in his voice. Zeph laughed at the man's expressions.

"That, Okies, is what we are selling. Tell you what, you hold onto that one for now, and tomorrow, we'll tell you all about them." That brought the big grin back to the man's face.

"When you get to the Inn, tell Flynn that I sent ya and to put your night's stay on me. I look forward to learnin' more about ya, Zeph," Okies said as he shook Zeph's hand once more.

The group gathered up their belongings and continued down the path. Before long, they came to the forest's exit; below the hill they stood on was the village of Tweedsmiur. The light from the moons scattered down over the many rooftops. It was larger than Daunt, but not by very much. It was clear by the town's layout that they were used to having visitors and merchants coming through. From their perspective atop the hill, they could see the grid-like layout of the town. The town itself sat in a massive bowl-shaped depression in the earth that led to the ocean. The forest wrapped around the north and east sides of the town, the sea lay to the south, and the west was rough open terrain that led northward up to the mountains.

The air was fresh and cool, which was surprising for the time of year. It may have been due to the forest and ocean surrounding most of the town. Small stacks of smoke rose softly from many of the houses. Even though it was late into the night, it was evident that only about half the town was slumbering.

As the group made their way down the path, music echoed down the street. It was lively and had a steady rhythm to it. There was something in it that caught Zeph's attention. It was a sound he had never heard before. They quickened their pace as they made their way down the street. Soon, they came upon the building where the ruckus was coming from. The sign on it read *The Wild Hooligan Inn & Tavern.*

They entered the building and found it full of people. Many people were sitting around the numerous small, round tables. Some were dancing together in the middle of the tavern. Almost everyone had a drink of some kind in their hand. Laughter and conversation rang out from all corners of the room. A small stage was in one of the corners of the room. Three musicians were on it, playing their hearts out for the patrons. The bartender noticed their party standing in the doorway and waved them over to the bar.

The man wiped his hands off on his apron and extended a hand to the group. After some quick, awkward handshakes, the man said, "My name be Flynn, and what brings you fine folks to my establishment tonight?"

"Okies told us to come find you. He said you would be able to give us a room," Xa'an replied.

"Oh, did he now? And I bet the bugger told ya to tell me to put it on his tab, didn't he?" Flynn replied with a laugh. "Alright, let me see what I can do for you," he said as he walked over to the Inn desk at the end of the bar. After a moment, he returned with several keys and handed them to Xa'an. "I ain't got a room that can fit the whole lot of ya, so these two will have to do."

Zeph slowly walked through the crowded tavern. The music had drawn his attention. He had always loved music. Whenever he heard different kinds of music, he felt connected to everything around him. Music produced a type of energy that nothing else in the world could. The sound flowed from the instruments and wrapped around him like long strands of ribbon.

Pushing through the dancing patrons, he stood in front of the stage. The music slowed down, and the young girl in the group took center stage. In her hands was a long wooden wind instrument. It had holes bored up and down its length. She softly blew into the end, moving her fingers over the various holes. The melody was soft and sweet like a child's voice calling out. Everyone quieted down for a moment as all eyes turned to the girl. For a moment, it seemed as though the whole room had faded away, and it was just Zeph and the young girl standing there. She looked up at him, and their eyes met. With a quick grin and a wink, the rest of the band jumped back in. With that, the whole tavern erupted into dance again.

Zeph laughed goofily as he smiled at the girl. Turning around, he walked back towards the bar and rejoined the rest of the group. Marcus asked what that was all about. Zeph explained that he was simply enthralled by the melody.

"And the cute little redhead over there had nothing to do with it?" Marcus asked with a laugh. Zeph blushed as he looked back over the crowd at the girl. She was dancing around on the stage as she played.

"I hadn't really noticed," Zeph said, trying to be coy.

Xa'an motioned for them to head upstairs. No one seemed to argue as they were exhausted from their journey's long first day. They reached the hall upstairs. Xa'an and Zeph took one room while the others took the adjacent. Zeph began removing his leather armor; he placed his sword around one of the posts of his bed. Xa'an was doing something similar. Not much was said, but they knew there would be time for talk in the morning.

DRUMS! ZEPH SHOT UP in bed. The sound of drums rang out through the streets of Tweedsmiur. It was a musical sound, filled with stringed instruments as well. Zeph squinted across the room as he tried to open his eyes. It felt like he had just laid his head on the pillow. He looked over to see Xa'an dressed and tying his boots up. Zeph let out a groan as he let himself fall back into bed.

"What time is it?" Zeph groaned out as he once again tried to focus his vision.

"It is midday, Master Zeph," Xa'an replied.

"Ah..da..dah..none of that now. You think because it's been months that I've forgotten about that. There is no 'master,' no 'chosen one,' and none of that nonsense. Just plain old Zeph will do," Zeph replied as he swung his legs off the bed and tried to sit up.

"I see you're becoming more assertive in your old age," Xa'an said with a chuckle. "You did celebrate your eighteenth birthday only a few weeks ago, didn't you?" The expression fell on Zeph's face for a moment. The day of the Alignment had indeed been his eighteenth birthday. They planned to return to his home and celebrate after the Alignment. A day that was supposed to be full of joy and celebration had turned into a day Zeph wished he could simply forget.

Xa'an sensed the pain and discomfort coming from Zeph. Even though they hadn't discussed what had transpired when Zeph opened the Omega Scroll, Xa'an could sense that the experience had been troubling.

"My apologies," said Xa'an. "I didn't realize the day had not been a joyous one for you."

Zeph shook the thoughts off for the moment and walked to the bathroom. Squinting at himself in the mirror, he tried to fix his hair. It had become a crazy mess of white strands that reminded him of how Gus usually looked. Pumping some water into the sink, he ran it through his hair and then proceeded to splash some on his face. It was quite cold, more than he was expecting. After several more minutes, he emerged from the bathroom, looking somewhat put together. The music he had heard minutes earlier had ceased. He walked over to the window and peered out.

"So please explain the drumming to me," Zeph asked, rubbing his face.

"Ah yes, the midday drums," Xa'an replied with a smile.

"The what now?"

"In Tweedsmiur, they announce midday of the first day of the week with a musical rendition. Sort of a kick-off to another week, you could say. I quite enjoyed it myself." A glare washed over Zeph's face, that he directed towards Xa'an, along with an additional mocking expression. He proceeded to dress himself, making sure to gather up all his belongings. With that, they left the room and headed downstairs.

The Inn was much quieter this morning than the night before. Everyone took a seat at one of the tables. Marcus and Iggy looked as tired as Zeph. Breeze, on the other hand, seemed very well rested. The boys weren't exactly sure how that had come about, but they didn't give it a second thought.

A young boy walked over to the table and offered them some menus. They had never heard of most of the food before, or at least not how they combined it in the pub. Zeph looked over the menu for something simple to start the day. He finally found it.

"I'll have eggs, please," he said, returning his menu to the boy.

"Would ya like a drink with that?"

"Sure thing; what would you recommend?"

"Try the rhubarb juice. It's great for the mornings," the boy replied.

"Sounds good to me," Zeph said with a smile, even though he had no idea what that was. If there was any time to try new things, now was the time.

Eggs were the running theme for everyone around the table. The boy handed Zeph a glass of dark red juice. He took a large sip of it, then almost immediately spit it out. It had a strong bitter taste but was also very rich and flavorful. The boy chuckled as he brought a small container over to the table.

"You might be wantin' some sugar to sweeten that up with." Everyone had a good laugh over it.

It wasn't long before everyone finished their food and stood up to leave. Another new day was upon the group. With each passing day, it seemed as though they learned more about themselves and the world around them. Some days, this was met with fear and others with excitement. However, being here in a new town filled them with the latter.

They walked the streets of Tweedsmiur, getting a feel for the town. Cobblestones lined every street and path. Most of the buildings were made from the dark wood of the forest, giving the town a rich, dark color scheme. There was a peace about the town that reminded Zeph of home. The air was different, the streets were laid out differently, and the people were all from various backgrounds, but it still felt like home in its own way. Maybe it wasn't so much the place you came from but the people you met that remind you of home.

Zeph ran his hand against the wooden paneling as they walked down the stone street. The wood was wet to the touch and felt as though it had been soaked for quite some time. Perhaps it was the weather patterns here by the ocean. Even though they were in the middle of the harvest season, the heat didn't seem to affect the town. It was a fresh day, and ocean spray was in the air. No beach was laid out at the bottom of the town like in Daunt. Instead, cliffs lined most of the town's base. A platform of piers and docks scaled part of the rockface down to a calmer part of the inlet below.

About a block down from the Inn, they found Okies' shop. The sign above simply read *Okies' Alchemist Shop*. A small bell on the doorframe rang out as they entered. The soft ring caused the man behind the counter to look up. It was one of the men they had seen the night before out in the forest. He welcomed them in and told them Okies would be out in a moment. In the meantime, they began to wander around the shop.

It wasn't an extensive shop. There were several small rows to the left and right of the store, and the counter was located in the center. A larger doorway on the right-hand side of the shop implied that there was more to the shop than what was currently visible. The shelves contained rows of small vials with various labels, different kinds of herbs, and other items used for potion mixes.

Iggy strolled down one of the rows, picking up almost every single vial as he went. He wanted to read every single label. He had always been very interested in Alchemy but had never had the opportunity to study it while growing up in Daunt. Marcus walked past Iggy, careful not to bump into the shelves.

"I wonder if any of these will help you grow taller," he asked sarcastically.

"Hey!" Iggy burst out.

"Just kidding around, little man; I'm sure one day you'll be bigger than me," Marcus said with a chuckle as he patted Iggy on the head.

Zeph couldn't help but overhear the banter between his best friend and brother. It brought a smile to his face. His spirits had been much higher recently than they had been in a very long time. It was strange, though, since so much tragedy had happened over the last few weeks since the Alignment Festival. He looked over at Breeze. They had hardly spoken since he had returned to Daunt only four days earlier. It had been a complicated series of circumstances that had effectively ended their relationship. Or perhaps it was merely a series of unfortunate events. Zeph was still working everything through in his head. She was the one thing in his life that gave him some of his deepest joy and also deepest despair.

A small explosion was heard in the backroom, causing everyone's attention to turn towards the large door at the back of the shop. The man behind the counter grimaced briefly and then shook his head. Everyone was quite surprised that the man took no action to check on what had just happened. He looked up from the counter to notice everyone was staring at him.

"Oh, don't worry about it. Okies blows something up on a daily basis. That's why he's the best Alchemist in town; he's always experimenting."

A moment later, Okies emerged from the backroom. His hands and face were covered with a bluish powder, and eye marks could be seen from where he had been wearing goggles before the accident. It was quite a comical sight. Marcus burst out laughing. He was easily entertained. On the other hand, Breeze had the opposite reaction, and she turned and left the shop flusteredly. Zeph went to go after her, but Xa'an stopped him, softly shaking his head as if to tell him to wait a moment.

"What? Has the lass never seen a man's face turn blue? I tell ya, I've seen many a woman's face turn blue waiting for me," he burst out with a laugh.

"She'll be fine. I'm sure she's just dealing with something personal," Zeph said as he walked over to Okies.

They exchanged a handshake as we wiped off most of the blue residue from his face. Throwing the towel at the man behind the counter, he continued to shake Zeph's hand firmly. Reaching into his pocket, he pulled out the sphere lamp. The gleam once again filled Okies eyes as he looked at it.

"You must tell me, lad, how did you make this?"

"That's a trade secret, my good sir," Zeph grinned. "But I have many to sell if you're interested."

"Oh, you know dang well I'm interested, boy!" Okies burst into a grin and slapped Zeph on the shoulder. "And you, being the sales genius that you are, made it all the worse by letting me have this one. So what are these worth to you?" Zeph thought about it for a moment. He looked around the shop at all the various potions. A thought occurred to him.

"Perhaps I'll give you a discount if you'd be willing to do some potion trading with us at an equal discount?" he proposed. Even though they had a good amount of coin with them, Zeph knew that it was still in their best interest to get deals along the way in their journey.

"You give them to me for half price, and I'll do the same for you. How's that sound, lad?" Okies offered.

"That sounds pretty good to me. What do you think, Marcus?" Zeph asked, looking in his direction.

"You're asking me?" Marcus asked, scoffing. "As long as we have food to eat, you know I'm good."

With a laugh and a handshake, they sealed the deal. Okies took Zeph up and down the rows in his shop, picking up vials here and there. He explained what was in each vial and how mixing them would create different results. Iggy followed close behind them. Pulling a small notebook from his sack, he carefully wrote down everything Okies said.

The combinations seemed infinite, and the ingredients never-ending. After they had gone up and down every row, Okies took them to the backroom. In the back of the shop was a highly complex alchemy lab with tubes connected to vials and bottles, which led to even more of the same. It seemed so chaotic to the group, but they were sure Okies knew what he was doing. At least, they hoped so.

Against the one wall was a large metal safe. This caught Zeph's attention right away.

"What's that safe for?" he asked. Okies went over to it, and after playing with the dial for a moment, he swung open the door. Inside were shelves stacked top to bottom with small glowing vials.

"This, my lad, is the fruit of my nightly labors. Now, of course, anyone could go out into the forest like me and collect Luminous, but if you noticed, it doesn't exactly fall at an astounding rate. Almost every potion I make needs some of it in the mixture, so it is a valuable commodity." He reached into the safe, removed a small vial, and then closed the door. Taking the vial, he walked over to his lab of tubes and beakers.

"Iggy!" Okies piped up. Iggy raised his eyebrows and cocked his head to the side to look at the man's face behind the lab equipment. "I could see you takin' an excessive inventory of my store during our stroll through it." Iggy awkwardly looked around the room. "Tis' not a bad thing, lad; in fact, I may get you to copy that list down for me. However, since you seem to know where things are, I need you to grab a few things for me." The young boy grinned at the idea of participating in a potion creation. He scampered off to the front of the shop and listened for what he was to grab.

"I'll need some Red Clover, Comfrey, and two Glowing Nettle," Okies shouted to Iggy. The boy scanned the shelves until each item was found and brought back. Placing the items on the table, Iggy couldn't help but be fascinated by the whole process. He watched as Okies rigged several of the beakers over burners, picked up the red clover, and added it to one of the beakers. It boiled up quickly, turning the water a deep red. Okies then placed the comfrey in a stone mortar and ground it into a fine powder with a pestle. After that, he took two long nettles from the container where they were stored. The nettles were about the length of a man's hand and had the appearance of quills made of glass.

Taking an empty glass vial from the shelf, he placed it on the table. Okies couldn't help but chuckle as he looked across at Iggy, watching the whole process with wide eyes. It was like watching a baby's fascination with their own hand, like nothing else in the world was more fascinating.

"Alright, young Iggy. I know you're dying to ask, so ask away before your head bursts." There wasn't a moment of hesitation before the boy started blurting out question after question.

"So why does the clover turn so red when you boil it? Why do you grind the comfrey? How are the needles used? What makes everything work together? Wha..."

Okies finally raised a hand to stop Iggy, or he knew the questions would just keep coming. Zeph and Marcus exchanged a glance and smiled.

"Alright, lad, let me walk you through this process 'cause this is the most basic of potions I can teach you. First of all," he said, pointing to the red liquid boiling in the beaker, "you need to boil the red clover in a wee bit of water. Just enough though so it doesn't burn, but not too much that it's diluted. Second," said Okies as he showed Iggy the fine purple powder in the mortar, "you need to make this into a fine power or it won't dissolve properly into the rest of the mix." Taking the empty vial from the table, he handed it to Iggy. Zeph leaned forward for a moment. "Ack, don't worry, Zeph, he ain't doin' anything that will blow him up." Okies said with a scoff.

"So here's what I want you to do. Pour about half of this Luminous into that vial." He said as he handed the glowing vial to Iggy. Setting both on the table, Iggy carefully emptied half of the contents from one vial into the other. "Good, now I want you to add the clover." Once again, Iggy carefully took hold of the glass beaker, careful not to burn himself. As he poured the vibrant red liquid into the pale glowing Luminous, he noticed that the solution caused the glow to instantly fade away.

"Did I do something wrong?" Iggy asked, disappointed.

"Not at all, lad, keep going."

Iggy continued the process by adding the purple powder to the vial. This caused the red liquid to turn almost black. Looking at the contents of the vial, he was sure he had made some sort of mistake. Okies just shook his head and smiled as he walked over to the table. "Alright, this next part is a little tricky, so watch carefully." Zeph and Marcus leaned in close as they also became intrigued by the process. It was actually quite interesting to watch. Okies took a small but very sharp knife from one of the drawers under the table. He then placed one of the glowing nettles on a stone slab at the end of the table. The nettle seemed so fragile, like a piece of tube glass.

"Now, watch carefully. You don't want to cut through the nettle; you just want to roll the knife over the middle section of it." They watched as he rolled the nettle on the stone slab while sliding the knife over the middle of it. He then held it up for Iggy to see. He moved in closer to see a fine line in the middle of the nettle. "Now your turn, Iggy," said Okies as he extended the knife to him. Carefully, Iggy placed his nettle on the stone slab and followed the instructions he had just witnessed.

"Perfect, well done, lad," Okies said as he slapped Iggy on the back. "Now for the final step. You see, that potion would be nothing without the Glowing Nettles. In every potion, you need a catalyst, that one ingredient that sets off a chain reaction with all the other ingredients. Watch me." Okies carefully held one of the nettles over the top of the vial. Placing his thumbs on either end of it, he applied some pressure.

Snap! The sound was unmistakable—like the sound of a small twig snapping. The nettle broke perfectly along the cut he had made in the middle. Two glowing drops fell from the plant's clear tubing. They entered the dark liquid in the vial and disappeared. It wasn't the reaction Iggy was looking for.

"Now, your turn, Iggy." Okies said as he pointed to the vial. Iggy took a deep breath as he held the nettle over the vial. He began to grimace as he applied pressure to the nettle. Once again, the snap was heard, and everyone watched as the two drops fell into the dark contents of the vial. Nothing happened for a moment, but then a spark of light was seen amongst the dark swirling liquid.

The sight was unlike anything any of the boys had seen before. It was like watching the birth of light itself. The simple swirls of light grew and spread. Colors formed: first orange, then red, and soon after, white. Clouds and strands of light formed and moved within the small vial until all the dark liquid was gone. The soft glow faded away to reveal a vibrant, translucent red mixture in the vial.

"And that, lads, is how you make a basic healing potion," Okies said with a smile as he crossed his arms triumphantly.

"That was fantastic!" Iggy exclaimed. Zeph smiled at his little brother's enthusiasm and patted him on the back.

Okies and Iggy sat and talked for a while about the art of Alchemy. You could see the liveliness in Iggy's body language as they compared different topics. It was like watching him in school again. Iggy always had so much energy when learning about something he enjoyed.

Zeph and Marcus strolled randomly around the shop for a bit. Xa'an stood in the corner, simply watching what the others were doing. He could see Zeph occasionally glance in his direction. You didn't have to be a mind reader to know what was on Zeph's mind. The continual glances in Xa'an's direction were almost a test of confirmation. It was clear that Zeph wanted to leave, to go find Breeze.

The pacing continued for a few more minutes until Zeph finally approached Xa'an. Their eyes locked for a moment. It wasn't frustration that Xa'an saw staring back at him, but pain. It was evident on the young man's face. He could see how much Zeph truly cared for Breeze.

"Go," he simply said.

With that, Zeph left the shop and headed for the south end of town. Even though Tweedsmiur was completely different from Daunt, Zeph knew Breeze would head for a beach or a cliff. She always did that when she wanted to be alone or needed a place to think.

One of the first times they had ever spent time together was shortly after she and Gus had moved to town. She was eleven at the time, and Zeph was thirteen. Most people were still under the impression Zeph was eleven as well since many didn't know that his parents had waited two extra years before enrolling him in school.

Zeph remembered leaving the school and seeing a girl sitting off by herself. It was under the large tree next to the school. Her long black hair was blowing in the wind. At the time, Zeph didn't know why, but he felt drawn to her. He walked over to her, and he could hear her crying as he drew closer. Coming up beside her, he sat down. There she sat, arms wrapped around her knees. The sobbing stopped momentarily as she noticed Zeph sitting next to her. The tears still streamed from her eyes as she stared at him. He didn't turn to face her; he just stared out at the blue ocean. Breeze wiped her face off on her sleeve. She was about to get up and leave when Zeph simply said, "Stay." The word was soft and sweet, and love poured out of it.

"I don't know why you're crying. And I know that even if I did, I most likely couldn't do anything to make it better." She stopped what she was doing and put her arms around her knees again.

The moments ticked by as they sat there in silence. Two kids who had never really spoken before, but in that moment, they needed to be together. Breeze kept staring at him, and Zeph continued to stare out at the ocean. His pale blue eyes mixed with the color of the water.

"You have pretty eyes." Breeze wasn't quite sure why she blurted that out, but it was what she was thinking as she stared at him. Zeph turned his face to meet hers, and their eyes met. His face was soft and kind, if not a little shy. But she could tell that underneath the shyness was a very loving person.

"What's wrong?" he asked softly.

"My mom died a few months ago," Breeze replied as she fought back the tears that begged to break forth upon speaking the words.

"I'm sorry to hear that."

"My dad and I moved here a week ago. I didn't want to come. I didn't want to leave my home."

Zeph knew that feeling. It had been the same when his father had died. He didn't want anything that reminded him of his father to be moved or put away.

"You'll never forget her," Zeph said quietly. She turned to look at him once more. The tears built up again and began slowly running down her face. Zeph watched as the clear drops fell from her chin. He turned to face the sea once more and then continued speaking.

"When someone you love goes away, part of you goes with them. What's left can only hold part of the person. You can either try to remember everything wonderful about your mother, or you can remember the pain you're feeling right now. But the memory of her can only hold one of those, not both."

With that, Zeph slowly stood up and walked away. Breeze sat there as the words of what he had said began to sink in. She closed her eyes, and the tears stopped.

Zeph breathed in deeply as the memories from that first day came rushing back as he saw Breeze once again sitting alone on the cliffs. He walked over and sat down next to her. This time, however, he was staring at her, and she was staring out at the sea. Her eyes were bloodshot, as it was clear she had been crying for some time. She had one hand wrapped tightly around the Jade crystal on her necklace. Zeph began to realize what she was going through as he watched her. She was reliving what she had gone through five years earlier.

"He's not gone, you know," Zeph said softly as he played with some strands of grass between his fingers. "He misses you just as much as you miss him right now. But he's not gone, Breeze. He's standing there in the doorway of your home, waiting for his little girl to come running into his arms again." The tears once again began to break from her eyes. She did miss her father, so much that it pained her deeply. They had never been apart since her mother had died, and even though it had only been one day, it felt as though she would never see him again.

"I'll be here for you, Breeze," Zeph said, placing a hand gently on her shoulder. "I'm going to need you on this journey. What you're feeling right now will pass, but until it does, you don't have to do this alone." She shuffled over underneath his arm and placed an arm around his back. They sat there for a long time. Their embrace was a comforting reminder that they could still rely on each other no matter what may have happened between them.

A while later, Marcus, Iggy, and Xa'an found their way to the cliffs. They watched Zeph and Breeze sitting together. Marcus was glad to see that. He knew how much recent events had hurt their relationship and was happy to see that there was still a connection of some kind between them.

The three of them walked up behind the two youths. Zeph turned his head slightly to look up at them. There was a calm sense amongst the group as the five of them took in the view of the ocean and breathed in the mist from the crashing waves below. They spent the rest of the day touring the town, taking in the scenes, and experiencing what Tweedsmiur had to offer the wayward traveler.

DAY 125

I believe the day will come when sorrow reigns no more.
I believe hope will return to this world.

> I believe that the time is coming when the life of one will change the life of many...

I believe that I will see my sons again.
~ Dawn, Mother of Zeph

CHAPTER 11
WORDS IN A BOOK

It wasn't long before everyone in Tweedsmiur had heard about the Sphere Lamps. Within several days, they had sold dozens of them. Between the supplies that both Zeph and Marcus had brought, they were down to half. In return, they had significantly increased their supply of gold and silver kessas. Rather than selling their whole supply of sphere lamps, they encouraged the townsfolk to journey to Daunt to buy more.

Okies was true to his word, and they traded for many potions. Iggy spent most of his time in the Alchemy shop, learning as much as he could from Okies. The group's reputation grew all over town. Many of the townsfolk would greet them as they walked down the street.

The first few days had been a time of rest and reflection for the group. Most of all, Zeph had time to dig into the books he had brought with him. He had spent much of his free time with Iggy and Marcus. They would get together to study parts of Mage Saphar's book. He would also read from the Book of Ta'Hor when searching for wisdom.

The teachings of Ta'Hor began to open up a brand new perspective for Zeph on the world around him. Looking at the world around him now, he saw so many new possibilities. It was clear that during his lifelong quest to discover more about Omega, Ta'Hor had seen so much of the world. Just reading the words in the book gave Zeph a greater understanding of the world's true nature and how people should treat their fellow man. The teachings were so simple but perhaps more challenging to live out.

Zeph sat reading by a tree near the cliffs by the docks of Tweedsmiur. He had started coming to this spot often; it resembled the old tree by the school back in Daunt. He turned the pages, skimming over the content.

The book was divided into many sections, each relating to different principles of how one should live. There was a particular passage that caught Zeph's eye this afternoon. It read: *'Therefore be content with weakness, with insults, with troubles, with persecutions, and with difficulties. The body is but a shell for the greater glory Omega has intended. Do not become a fool and rely on the strength found within the world, for it is Omega that gives true strength to the weary and peace to the lost.'*

Closing the book, Zeph laid it on the grass next to him. He closed his eyes for a moment. Letting his mind reach out to the world around him, he felt peace. A sensation flowed up over his shoulders and down his arms. Opening his eyes, he looked at the glowing energy building in his veins. He let it continue down his arms until it reached the palms of his hands. Holding one of his hands out in front of his face, he watched as the energy slowly pushed its way through the pores of his skin. It was like watching sweat bead, small drops of pure light began to form and spread. Small pools of liquid light filled both of his palms.

Xa'an stood a ways off to the side, watching the display. His curiosity got the best of him, and he slowly walked over to Zeph.

"What are you doing?" he asked in a soft tone.

Zeph began chuckling, which quickly turned into laughing and tears. He regained his composure slightly and blurted out, "I honestly don't know!" The smile on his face was uncontrollable. Raising his hands towards the sky, the energy shot from his hands, bursting forth in long, thin strands. It reminded Xa'an of the energy released from the body when a person died and their body dissolved away.

Zeph jumped up with a start. "I have no idea what I was doing. All I know is that I was happy and content, and as I felt those feelings, the energy flowed into my hands." Xa'an smiled and nodded. He wasn't quite sure what to make of it, but nevertheless, it was amazing to see Zeph as happy as he had become since the first day they had arrived.

They made their way through town. It had been just over a week since they had arrived. In those eight days, they had made a great impression on Tweedsmiur. The town elders had been incredibly excited to finally meet them. The mere idea of being the first town on Appagon to buy this new invention had greatly thrilled them. Once they had introduced the spheres to the whole village, business exploded. The group had begun to think that they would quickly run out and not have any left to sell elsewhere. That's when they decided to redirect the townsfolk to Daunt for more of the sphere lamps.

After the sales had died down, they couldn't help but look in awe at the piles of coins they had accumulated in such a short amount of time. They had converted as much as they could into gold kessas to make it easier for transportation. Including the gold they had brought on the trip to begin with, they now had almost one thousand gold kessas. Okies had offered to store it in the safe in his shop for the length of their stay. The quirky alchemist had proven himself to be very trustworthy, and they weren't worried about the safety of their coins.

The group used their time in Tweedsmiur to learn about the local culture. This town was very different from the small, simple town they were all used to. Whether it was the drinking and dancing at Flynn's, to which Xa'an monitored the group's consumption carefully. The many trinket shops that lined the stone streets of Tweedsmiur had also caught their eyes.

Zeph and Marcus were the first to embrace the local dress of the town. Not two days had passed before they purchased new attire in a clothing shop. There wasn't a lot of choice in style or color. Most of the clothing had only a variety of forest colors to choose from. Shades of greens and browns adorned the clothing shop. For the men in the town, the standard dress was a plain long-sleeved shirt of some kind with a vest over top and a pair of straight pants. This was precisely what the two boys had bought. When the two boys emerged, Iggy and Breeze had been talking with some of the townsfolk outside the shop. A brief chuckle ensued as they looked the two of them up and down. The only difference between their matching outfits was the color. Each wore a long-sleeved white shirt, although both boys had rolled up the sleeves. On top of that was a simple vest with brass buttons up the front and straight, long, blank pants. Zeph's ensemble was composed of green colors, whereas Marcus' was composed of brown.

The green was a change for Zeph, as he usually enjoyed blue tones in his clothing. Nevertheless, Breeze thought he looked particularly dashing, even though the look was quite a change for him. There was an ease between them now. The day Zeph sat with her on the cliffs had opened her eyes to his kind nature once again. It wasn't as though she had been ignoring it or pushing it away; she had simply removed it from her mind as a place to seek refuge. They were still a very long way from being anything more than friends, but there was a closeness that was beginning to form once again.

Zeph walked with Xa'an along the cliffs for a while. Their conversation was light. As they continued their journey, it became increasingly clear that something was troubling Zeph.

"I can tell there is something on your mind, Zeph, something that you want to ask me about," Xa'an said with a puzzled look.

"There is Xa'an," he paused momentarily, considering what he would say. "You know I respect you, and I trust you. With everything you have done for us, I feel you have earned that, at the very least. But there are things I haven't told you about recent events. Don't get me wrong, I have wanted to tell you about everything that happened. Before I do, though, I need to know where you stand."

Xa'an studied Zeph's face for a moment. He wasn't trying to probe Zeph's mind but simply trying to understand where the young man was coming from. Zeph was careful not to let his thoughts slip as he saw Xa'an looking over his expressions. His gatherings with Iggy and Marcus had been done in cautious secrecy. The warning from Mage Saphar's book still troubled him. Zeph wanted to be sure that Xa'an wasn't the one Saphar had warned him about. They had only looked over the specific passage once since coming to town to refresh what they knew already. Nothing new had been revealed yet within the book's pages.

"I want to show you something, but I need to know I can trust you." Again, Xa'an was puzzled by Zeph's words.

"I sense thoughts of betrayal on your mind, Zeph. I can't say I will always be able to stand by your side, but I will not betray you." Zeph looked into the man's soft, glowing eyes. He looked past the soft glowing orange and into the very heart of the man. There was something there, something he couldn't deny. Zeph slowly pulled Saphar's Book out of his bag and handed it to Xa'an.

"What is this?" the mage asked as he took the book from Zeph.

"You're not the only one that's been guiding me about my destiny."

MARCUS AND BREEZE STROLLED down the main street in Tweedsmiur. They were enjoying their time in the quaint little town. With each passing day, they had become more accustomed to it, and the thoughts of returning home to Daunt weren't so prevalently on their minds. Their conversation today was about Zeph, however. Breeze had been seeking out Marcus' advice since their arrival in town. The situation between her and Zeph had been troubling since the incident where Zeph tried to take his own life. The events of the Alignment hadn't bothered her as much, since she understood that those things were out of Zeph's control. But the moment Zeph completely gave up on living, something deep within her had changed.

Somewhere inside, she wanted things to be like they had been before. The memories of their years of friendship together and the joy and love she felt with Zeph still lingered deep in her mind.

"Have you talked to him about any of this yet?"

"No. It's still too complicated right now," Breeze replied to Marcus.

"I guess I can understand that. But at some point, he needs to know that you haven't walked away from him. He may not show it as outwardly these days, but you have to know that inside he still loves you. He just doesn't know how to live with what he's done."

She stopped for a moment and took in Marcus' words. Knowing that Zeph still loved her somehow gave Breeze an extra sense of security.

"My boy Zeph is strong, and you know what, Breeze, even if you two never get back together like before, he will be okay. Having said that, I do know that there is still no one else in this world that he'd rather be with. From my own experiences, I know people can fall in love, be together and happy for a time, then go their separate ways and still be happy."

"Maybe things will be like they were before, one day," she pondered.

"I know that no matter what you two decide, you'll still love each other. I don't think that will ever change."

Time seemed to move at such an uneven pace now for her. The weeks they had been apart while Zeph was learning to gain control had felt like months. The days she spent with Zeph now almost seemed to go by in a blur. It pulled her emotions back and forth. In fact, in many ways, it was hindering her emotional healing. For the moment, though, she tried not to think about it.

Soon, Breeze and Marcus came upon Okies' shop and decided to go inside and see how he and Iggy were doing today. Over the last week, they had seen very little of either of them. They spent most of their time in the shop. Iggy was learning quite well under Okies' tutelage from what they had gathered in their brief encounters.

Entering the shop, they found Iggy at work in the back. He was in the middle of, what they could only imagine, was a crazy experiment of some sort. Marcus went over and stood by the young boy and watched the concoction play out. Breeze, on the other hand, went and talked with Okies. After the incident where she had stormed out of his shop, she returned later that day to explain herself. She told Okies that seeing him covered in blue powder reminded her of the antics her father would do. It had brought up a swell of emotions that had left her homesick. Okies had understood completely. Being far from home and family, it was entirely understandable for one so young to be homesick.

The four of them lollygagged around the shop for a while. Iggy continued to experiment with different potions and mixtures. Marcus noticed that Iggy looked a little rough around the edges and had a twitchy look about him. He asked Okies if everything was okay. Okies simply laughed and explained that Iggy had already blown up several mixtures earlier that day, trying to perfect his experiment.

"I tell yeah, that kid is starting to take after you crazed inventor types more and more," Marcus said with a grin.

"And what be wrong with that?" Okies asked with a smirk.

"Oh, nothing at all; I just figured that there might be an easier way to blow yourself up on a daily basis," Marcus said with a wink.

The doorbell chimed. Everyone's attention was redirected towards the front of the shop. Standing there were Zeph and Xa'an. It was clear by the look on Zeph's face that this wasn't a simple social call. Marcus walked over to him, "What is it?"

"It's time," Zeph replied. Iggy quickly asked Okies to look after his experiment for the moment as they left the shop. No talk or discussion was spoken along the way as the group headed for the inn. They entered and quickly headed upstairs to their rooms. Once everyone had entered Zeph's room, he locked the door behind them. Somehow, this situation seemed all too familiar. It reminded Zeph of the night months earlier when he had first met Xa'an. Marcus walked over and closed the curtains, casting the room into a dim light. Iggy removed a handful of spheres and placed them around the room.

Zeph motioned for Xa'an to sit at the table. Pulling Saphar's book out, Zeph placed it on the table and sat down opposite the man.

"I don't believe this book came to me by chance. Just like when you found me, I believe I was destined to have it. It was written almost four hundred years ago. Someone in the past saw my future and sent me a warning," Zeph explained.

Opening the book, Zeph flipped to the section where Saphar had first introduced himself. Xa'an watched as the glyphs began to appear and glow on the page. Without hesitation, Marcus and Iggy reached over and touched their corresponding symbols on the page; the text unlocked. Turning the book to Xa'an, Zeph allowed the mage to read what had been written. He scanned the page as the words continued to flow with soft, glowing light. Suddenly, he stopped and looked up at Zeph and then at all the other pairs of eyes locked on him. It was clear to all what part he was now reading. The page read,

'There is a creature that will come amongst you. It will reach out with an arm of friendship and hold a dagger of deception behind its back. Its power is not of this world, and death has lost the control to take its breath away. Beware of those that hide themselves in shadows.'

"You fear this 'creature' spoken of in this prophesy is me?" asked Xa'an.

"Actually, I don't," Zeph replied, "But I needed you to see where I'm coming from. This isn't something I've taken lightly. This man, Mage

Saphar, saw my life hundreds of years before I was even born. He saw what I would become and what had to be done."

Xa'an continued to scan the pages, reading what else had been said. He then fell upon the pages of glyphs. As he looked them over, it was evident on his face that they were not foreign to him. Zeph noticed his expression immediately.

"You know what they are, don't you?" Zeph questioned.

"They are control glyphs," Xa'an replied.

"Control glyphs? What does that mean?" Zeph asked, puzzled.

"Think of them like the punctuation at the end of a sentence. When enchanting an object, or anything else for that matter, you need to have control glyphs in order for the enchantment to become active." Xa'an pulled out one of his swords and placed it on the table next to the book. Running his hand along the side of the blade, he stopped on two of the glyphs; he then matched them with two of the twelve glyphs in the book. "See, these two here are part of my enchantments."

"How do they work?" Zeph asked as he compared the glyphs to each other.

"This first one here is the glyph for Union. In the most basic of explanations, it means that there has to be physical contact. And this second one is the glyph for Impinge. It is what caused the force of Marcus' blow to backfire against him when he tried to use my sword."

"I understand now; it has to do with your blood, right?" Zeph asked as he studied the other glyphs and symbols on the sword, "The Union glyph is what activates these other ones in the enchantment, and the reason why the enchantment only works when you're holding the sword."

"Okay, wait a minute. Maybe I missed something. I agree with most of what you're saying, except for that last part," Marcus piped up.

"Since the enhancement only activates when Xa'an holds his swords, he would have needed to mix his own blood in with the Tears of God when the sword was being enchanted," Zeph explained. "The enchantment made it so that the swords would only be sharp while Xa'an was holding them. The Impinge glyph part of the enchantment made it so that if someone other than Xa'an tries to use his sword, the force of their blows would backfire. Just like when you first tried it that night, Marcus."

"That's actually incredible," said Marcus with genuine awe as he ran his hand over Xa'an's sword. He was also impressed at how far Zeph's knowledge of glyphs and symbols had progressed.

"Zeph is quite correct in his analysis. The Impinge glyph also has some other applications; it can also be used to activate the enchanted only when the object strikes something."

"How exactly does that work?" Marcus asked, slightly puzzled again.

Xa'an smiled momentarily, then continued, "Think of it this way, Marcus; what if someone wanted to imbue a sword with fire? Now, they wouldn't want the sword to always be ablaze. Furthermore, they wouldn't want it to necessarily ignite every time they touched it either. That could cause problems if your sheath burst into flames before you even drew your sword. So, the Impinge glyph would be used in conjunction with other symbols. This would allow the sword to only burst into flames when it struck the surface of something with force."

At that moment, Marcus' jumbled mixture of thoughts became clear. He understood what Xa'an had been saying. The idea was quite intriguing to Marcus as he looked down at the spiked gloves he wore. He pictured flames bursting off the gloves with every hit.

Just then, the pages of the book suddenly began to flutter, drawing everyone's attention to the center of the table. Rays of light began to stream forth from between the pages. The fluttering finally stopped as the book lay open. Blank pages lay open before everyone's gaze. There was a pause as they all leaned slightly to examine the pages.

With a force like someone slamming their fists onto the book, the Omega symbol appeared in the middle, spanning both pages. Two more symbols appeared on the corners of the outer pages. It took a moment for everyone to realize that the four symbols in each corner of the pages corresponded to their elemental Alignment.

This was new, that was for sure, but Zeph knew that it must be for a purpose. He had searched the book daily and it had not reacted again until now. Reaching out, he placed his palm over the Omega symbol. The symbol on top of his hand shone brightly, giving the appearance that the light from the pages was shining directly through his hand; even the Omega symbol on his forehead gave off a slight glow. Everyone watched as untold power flowed through the young man. He shot everyone a glance. With a deep breath, everyone else reached out and touched their corresponding symbol.

A rush of wind burst from the book, and light scattered throughout the room. Zeph felt the energy from everyone else in the room flowing through him. Images began to flow into his mind. He saw a vision of an old man writing in the pages of an old book. The man stopped for a moment and looked up at Zeph. The man smiled and extended a hand, gesturing for Zeph to take a seat.

The wind and light flowing from the book instantly stopped as everyone staggered back slightly from the table. Not Zeph, however, he was sitting on the chair holding the book in his hands. Everyone walked up behind him and watched as words of light appeared on the pages.

'Zeph, I greet you once again. It was nice to see you face to face, or as close as we will have in this lifetime. I am glad your companions are present as well. You need not fear Xa'an; he is a worthy ally. Those that you keep close to you will serve you well in your life. '

Xa'an raised an eyebrow at seeing his name appear in words written with light by a mage from hundreds of years ago.

'My visions of you have changed, Zeph. The outcome of your future is no longer what was first foretold to me. But be forewarned, a great tragedy is coming! You know this, Zeph; it has been shown to you by the scroll. Darkness will soon come; it will devour and consume. Power, unlike none this world has known, will be spilled out over it, a power that man was not meant to ever touch or hope to control. There is still Hope, though; there is always hope. You have not pierced the veil of your mind yet, but you have the ability to do so.'

Confusion washed over Zeph's face momentarily as he tried to understand what Saphar meant. Xa'an placed a hand on Zeph's shoulder and raised a hand to indicate he could help explain later.

'They will come for you soon, Zeph, go with them. You must pierce the veil of your mind that separates who you are from who you must become. I cannot prepare you for what you will experience. You must search within

yourself. You must truly believe in the depths of yourself that there are no limits to what you can do, Zeph. Mal'ak has shown me the same thing he showed you in the scroll. You must seek out the other Six; it is only by joining together that this world can be saved. The Seven of you were to be the protectors of all of Arkhay. This future can never be Zeph, but never forget my words...There is always Hope.

This is the last you will hear from me, Zeph. Omega has not shown me how your life will unfold, but I have hope in you. Seek the power within you, Zeph. Omega has given you a piece of himself; use it. Close this book now; they are knocking at your door.'

Just then, a heavy rap was heard on the door of their room. Zeph quickly closed the book and placed it with his belongings. Xa'an carefully walked over to the door, one sword drawn. He looked over at Zeph, to which he quickly nodded back. Xa'an opened the door cautiously, only to be greeted by a familiar face.

Standing before them were two men in black robes. Their heads were shaved, and the Shadow symbol was on their foreheads. Unlike Xa'an, they wore simple mage robes and nothing else. No weapons or extra armor of any kind could be seen. They also did not wear a pair of goggles as Xa'an did. Xa'an seemed almost puzzled as he looked them up and down.

"Why are you here, brothers?" asked Xa'an.

"Master Sotiris has asked that you bring the boy before him," they replied, raising a hand towards Zeph.

"What does your master want with me?" Zeph asked, stepping towards them.

"You fear he wishes you harm; he does not," one of the mages replied.

The sudden arrival of the mages had set Zeph's senses on high alert, but then he remembered Saphar's words telling him to go with those who would be coming for him. He waved for Xa'an to stand down and for everyone else to gather their belongings.

After quickly stopping by Okies to gather supplies and their coin, they said their goodbyes and headed for the docks by the cliffs. They assured him that everything was okay. Anxiety was visible on his face at seeing his newfound friends being escorted out of town by men in black robes. The group walked to the cliffs and descended the platforms and docks to the water below. Waiting for them was a black sailboat.

It was long and sleek with a pointed bow. The wood of the boat had been stained almost black, and the sails looked as though they were made from the same black fabric as the mage's clothing. It wasn't a large ship by any means, and it looked as though it was designed to carry no more than a dozen men. A series of glyphs and markings were visible on the vessel's hull.

Everyone made their way onto the boat and took up seats along the inner hull. Xa'an took a place near the stern of the ship. Marcus, Breeze, and Iggy huddled together near the midsection. On the other hand, Zeph took a place near the bow of the boat and looked out as the ship made its way out to the open ocean.

Many thoughts were going through Zeph's mind as they got underway. Anxiety was the first thing that came to mind. He wasn't exactly sure where it was coming from; it was a feeling that he hadn't felt in many weeks. It wasn't from the sudden arrival of the shadow mages either. The thoughts rolled over in his mind; something was troubling about all of this. Placing a hand on his neck, he checked his pulse; it was quick and steady. Why was he so on edge? Taking a deep breath, he held it in for a moment before letting it out slowly. It didn't help as much as he had hoped. He closed his eyes for a moment. A gust of wind came by; Zeph felt the boat quicken its pace as the wind filled the sails and propelled them on their way.

Reaching into his bag, he pulled out the book of Ta'Hor and began scanning the passages for something that might help him understand his feelings. He had found comfort in the pages of the book before, and turning to it had become a regular reaction when he was unsure of something. Ta'Hor had lived thousands of years before him, and yet, when reading the words, he felt as though he knew the man.

Letting his fingers guide his eyes, he ran them over the pages. He stopped for a moment and read the passage above his finger,

'Can all your worries add even a single moment to your life? Will the anxieties of this world stop the actions of men from being pressed upon us? We are pressed on every side by troubles, but we are not crushed and broken.

We are perplexed, but we don't release our convictions. We are hunted down, but Omega never abandons us. The humble will see their Creator at work and be glad. Let all who seek Omega's help live in joy. For He hears the cries of His needy ones; He does not despise His people who are oppressed.'

The words flowed off the page and into his mind. Closing his eyes, Zeph leaned back against the side of the boat. The light from the sun passed through his eyelids. Ocean spray washed up the sides of the vessel and rained down on his face. In silence, he offered up a prayer to Omega, that the next step of his journey would give him a greater understanding of his calling.

The trip continued throughout the day as the boat cut its way through the crystal blue waters. Several hours into the trip, one of the mages picked up an instrument and began to play. He told them it was called a Lute. It was odd at first, but as the melodies began to flow from the strings, a peace started to fall over the boat. The mage explained that this kind of instrument had been used by their order for many generations. Music was commonplace in *The Order*. The rest of the group, besides Xa'an, was surprised to learn this fact. They enjoyed the tune he played, though, as the boat continued.

Hours went by, the trip becoming much longer than Zeph had expected. It was sunset now. The light from the suns shone through the water on the eastern horizon. Orange light bathed the boat. Zeph rested his arms on the side and stared out across the sea. Thoughts of his father began to surface. Zeph realized he hadn't been on a boat since losing his father. Looking down over the rail, he peered into the water below. His gaze bored down into the depths of the sea until the darkness overtook the crystal water. Returning his gaze toward the setting suns, he listened to the music the mage was playing. He had been playing for hours, but he did not tire.

Xa'an came up beside him and rested his hands on the rail. They didn't look at one another, just stared out to sea.

"You're thinking about your father, aren't you?" Xa'an asked. Zeph nodded. "How did he lose his way?"

Zeph simply shook his head, "No one knows; he just never came home."

"Do you believe he is out there somewhere?"

"I want to...," Zeph answered as his voice trailed off. "I was always told that when a loved one dies, you can feel their presence leave as their energy fades and joins with the Elements. I don't know where he is, but I've never felt my father's presence ever leave me."

Xa'an simply nodded and placed a hand on Zeph's shoulder, "Hold onto that."

Night began falling on the sea, and the winds were slowing down. Zeph was starting to wonder when they would reach Tarn. Just as the thought entered his mind, he saw a small flicker of light across the dark horizon ahead. He squinted and tried to make it out. As they grew closer, he saw that the light was not just one source but several. The boat began to draw near the island. Soon, Zeph realized the light was coming from torches lining a dock. The dock was located inside the mouth of a cave at the base of the high cliffs that lined the island.

"We're here," Xa'an said as he pointed ahead.

The boat entered the cave, and, to everyone's amazement, the cave was huge. Docks spanned the inside of the cave with many piers on each. There were at least a dozen or more boats throughout the cave, just like the one they were on. Light from the torches danced inside the cave. Several mages were waiting for them at the end of one of the piers. They docked the boat, and everyone disembarked.

One of the mages approached the other two that had journeyed to Tweedsmiur. They spoke quietly for a moment, and then one returned to the group.

"I know the journey has been long, but it seems that Master Sotiris wishes to speak with you immediately upon your arrival. If you would follow me, I will take you to him."

Zeph looked at Xa'an, who simply nodded that proceeding was okay. Gathering up their belongings, they followed the mage. They made their way up a stone staircase that took them to the top of the cave. The smell of the wet stone filled Zeph's nostrils. It was something he wasn't overly familiar with. Scents of earth and water filled the air and mixed with the oils burning in the cave lamps.

They continued on their way to the very top of the cave. Once there, a hallway cut into the stone led them into a large room. Much of the interior of the caverns had been carved right out of the stone itself. Down the hallway were rows of doors; most were closed, and those that were open seemed to be used for storage. They reached a very large spiral staircase at the end of the next hallway. It was much larger than the one down at the dock, with enough room for four people to climb it side by side. The climb was long. Zeph wasn't exactly sure how high they were going, but he knew it was a reasonable distance. The darkness of the night had hidden the size of the island from Zeph when they had first arrived.

A grand hall opened before them as they reached the top of the staircase. It was unlike anything Zeph had seen before. The room was truly massive. The ceilings rose several stories to the carved rock above. He couldn't believe they were still within the island's rock, even after the long climb. The rest of the room was wide and long. It seemed as though part of it was used as a temple of sorts, with rows of stone benches arranged like the temple back in Daunt. The rest of the grand hall seemed to be a meeting area as well as a general gathering area.

The moment they entered the grand hall, the glyphs caught Zeph's eyes. Rows of glowing glyphs and symbols lined the walls up to the high ceiling above. A path of glowing glyphs led from the stairs directly to the middle of the room. Xa'an watched carefully as Zeph followed the path, studying it as he went. Everyone else began to wander in the hall, examining what the different mages were doing. Some of the mages were simply meditating, while others were at tables studying over piles of books. Off to one side, there was a group of mages sparring. There were at least fifty or so mages throughout the grand hall.

Xa'an walked over to Zeph. He was now standing in the middle of the room, staring up at the glyphs on the ceiling. They moved outward in a bursting pattern, not unlike the ones on the floor. They joined together like a massive seal. It was like looking at the room's foundational structure. Several rows of large stone columns were spread throughout the room. They also had markings that wrapped around them.

"What is it you're looking at?" Xa'an asked as he stood behind the young man.

"I'm just blown away by all the glyph work. It must have taken years to enchant all of this," Zeph's words caused several mages nearby to turn their heads. Xa'an shot a quick glance in their direction.

"What exactly do you see, Zeph?" Xa'an asked with a cautious tone in his voice.

Zeph's smile quickly turned to confusion as he saw the look on Xa'an's face. "I...uh...I don't know..." The words came out awkwardly as the confusion set in further. Zeph looked around the room once more.

"Ask your friends what they see," was all Xa'an said in response. Confused even more, Zeph walked over to Marcus.

"This place is pretty amazing, huh?" asked Zeph.

"It really is, bro. I can't believe how huge this room is," Marcus replied as he paced around it.

"The glyphs are pretty amazing, too, right?"

"Oh really, show me."

The words didn't make sense as Zeph stared back at Marcus. Did none of the others see what he saw? "I'll show you in a bit; I need to talk to Xa'an."

"Yeah, ask him when we're going to meet with this Master."

Zeph walked back over to Xa'an. The mage met the young man eye to eye. No words were said; Xa'an simply nodded to what he already knew Zeph was thinking. As he looked around at the rest of the group, he knew that no one else could see the glowing glyphs that lined the walls of the grand hall. Reaching into his bag, Zeph pulled out Saphar's book. He scoffed momentarily and shook his head as he saw many pages of glowing text and glyphs within the book.

"This isn't just because I'm here, is it?" Zeph asked with a somewhat displeased look, as though something had just been revealed to him that everyone else had been keeping secret. He seemed to be seeing glyphs and symbols everywhere.

"I think not. If my Master called for you, it was most likely because he has received a vision."

Just then, several mages entered the hall from the west side. Everyone in the hall stopped what they were doing and took a simple stance of attention. Xa'an waved the rest of the group over to him and Zeph. The mages walked up to the group. One of them was noticeably different. He wore plain black clothing underneath a long black cloak. The cloak itself was lined with a silky, shimmering red material. He wore matching silver bracers on his wrists, and a large silver chain with *The Order*'s symbol was around his neck.

The man walked up to the group of arrivals. To be honest, it wasn't what Zeph had been expecting. The man was not muscular like Xa'an, nor had the divining look of wisdom like some of the other mages. He was tall and thin with a defined facial structure. His head was shaved like most of the other mages. His eyes had a similar orange glow that never dimmed, just like Xa'an's.

Reaching out toward Zeph, he offered his hand; Zeph took it. Then, the mage did something completely unexpected: He took a knee in front of Zeph. The shocked expression on Zeph's face was not limited to just himself; he saw it appear on the faces of many of the other mages in the room.

"I am honored to greet you, *Omega Chosen One*," the man said as he stood again. Their eyes locked for a moment. Despite the man's frailties, it was obvious that he had great power inside him. "My name is Master Sotiris; welcome to *The Order of Seeing Shadow Mages*."

"Thank you," was all Zeph could muster up. He was still very confused by everything that was happening.

"Walk with me, will you?" Sotiris asked. Zeph nodded and motioned for him to lead the way. The group left the grand hall and proceeded down a large corridor.

"Do you know why I have asked you here, Zeph?"

"Not really, but I suppose there is more to this than I understand."

"You are right in thinking that there is more to this, but understanding cannot be easily grasped."

They rounded a bend in the corridor and continued on. Everyone else followed several paces behind. Every now and then, they noticed Zeph shoot a quick glance behind, just to make sure they were close.

Soon, they came to an open courtyard. It was the first time they had seen the outside since their arrival. The night sky was upon them now. Light from the moons cast shadows across the courtyard, even in the dead of night.

"You see the moons. Even they balance out the night. A simple reminder that man was not always meant to live in shadows," Sotiris said as he stared up at the night sky. They walked over to some stone benches in the middle of the courtyard. It was then that Zeph saw the mountain they had just walked out of. Even in the light of night, a quick survey of the island showed that it looked like nothing more than a seemingly useless huge chunk of rock in the sea. It would be very easy for any ship to sail by without giving a second thought.

The others stayed close to Xa'an and sat a few paces away from Zeph and Sotiris. This situation was far beyond what any of them had dealt with before. They knew that Xa'an would give them direction as needed.

Zeph sat down on the stone bench across from Sotiris. The man locked eyes with him once more. The silence seemed to last forever, but Zeph never flinched for a second. He didn't know what the master was doing but just went with it. Looking away momentarily, Sotiris spoke up, "Have you ever had a vision, Zeph?"

"I don't think so; I mean, I'm not really sure." Zeph's thoughts drifted to when he had first opened the Omega scroll, when he and Iggy had been taken somewhere else.

"I have," Sotiris continued. "I have had many in my lifetime. But so few have I had where I've been shown the future."

"What did you see?" the question just seemed to come out of Zeph's mouth before he even knew why he had asked it.

Sotiris smiled and replied, "I saw you, Zeph, sitting here with me under a night's sky." Zeph simply nodded as he listened. "You are an amazing young man, Zeph. You stand at the first step to becoming something this world will never understand, and you do it with complete trust in your fellow man. The world would view this as ignorance, and many will mock you for your kind nature, but do not let them. It is not ignorance; it is a plain and simple desire to see the good that all mankind can achieve if sought out."

Zeph listened as the man spoke. The words were soft and had a measure of truth to them. He began to understand the enticing quality this man had with those in *The Order*. They talked for a while longer, and then Sotiris stood, and everyone returned inside. The corridor echoed with their footsteps as they proceeded down the hall. Zeph tried not to call attention to the fact that he could see all the glowing glyphs and symbols that lined the tops and bottoms of the corridor. After his and Xa'an's brief exchange in the grand hall, it was obvious that he was not supposed to be able to see them.

They rounded another corner and headed down a set of stairs. These stairs seemed much older than some of the others. Once they reached the hall below, it was obvious that they were in a much older part of the island. Dust and cobwebs were everywhere along the hall. It caused Breeze to grimace, as she was a bit of a clean freak at times. They walked down the hall; Sotiris had lit a torch and carried it in front of the group. Zeph wondered if he even actually needed it. From his perspective, the hallway was bathed in light from the glowing glyphs; he only assumed it was the same for Xa'an and Sotiris.

They reached the end of the hall. Sotiris turned to Zeph and asked, "So where do we go from here, Zeph?" The question confused Zeph momentarily, but he followed his basic instincts.

"Through that door," Zeph replied, pointing to the archway just past them. Everyone except Xa'an and Sotiris shot him an odd expression. Sotiris simply smiled and said, "You're ready."

Touching the wall at the end of the hall, Sotiris pressed his fingertips against several of the glyphs on it. Light shot through the stone like bolts of lightning, giving it the appearance it was cracking to pieces. The stone wall pieces crumbled and faded away to dust in an instant.

"How did you know there was a door here, Zeph?" Sotiris asked.

"I...uh..." Zeph wasn't sure how to respond, but he figured there was nothing else left to say. "I saw the doorway, just like I can see everything else enchanted on the walls within *The Order*." Marcus and Iggy gave him puzzled looks, but Breeze began to understand instantly.

"It's like the symbols in your book, isn't it?" she asked. He nodded in return.

"It has begun then; you just need to take the next step," said Sotiris.

"What do you mean?" Zeph questioned.

"In my vision, I saw you, Zeph. I saw you both outside in the courtyard and in this room. Do you recognize this room?" Sotiris asked, waving his hand in the direction of the open archway. Zeph took a step forward into the room. The rest began to follow, but Xa'an quickly raised a hand to stop them. It was a large room with many shelves of parchment and scrolls. There were rows of tables leading down the center of the room. Obviously, this was some kind of an archive room, and a very old one at that. Zeph walked past the tables, running his hand over them. The dust drifted up into the air.

Something quickly brushed past him, causing Zeph to spin around. A glimpse of something caught his line of sight for a split second, and then it was gone. It was then that Zeph noticed that everyone else was standing just outside the doorway. The sensation brushed against Zeph again; it was more like an image, this time within his mind.

"What's in this place?" Zeph asked as he tried to grasp what was going on.

"More than scrolls and manuscripts are held here; there are memories trapped within its walls," Sotiris simply answered. His eyes were almost filled with despair as he looked back at Zeph.

It was then that something clicked within Zeph's mind. Memories rushed back from the first night he had met Xa'an. The story filled his mind of what Master Desiree had done in *The Order* a thousand years ago. A chill went up Zeph's spine. He stopped and looked all around the room; his eyes scanned the tables and floors. The sensation brushed past him again, and a series of images filled his mind. It was then that he saw the blood and the lifeless faces.

"This is where it happened, isn't it?" Zeph asked with a mix of anger and fear in his voice as his hands began to tremble. "This is where Desiree killed them all?"

"It is," the words came out softly from Xa'an standing in the doorway. Zeph shot him a look, and then Sotiris.

"Why have you brought me here?" Zeph flinched as another image shot into his mind. A slight sensation of pain followed, causing Zeph to touch the side of his head for a moment. Marcus didn't like what was happening and turned his attention toward Sotiris.

"He asked you a question," Marcus spat, his voice displeased. Sotiris looked at Marcus and then back at Zeph.

"There comes a point when those gifted with Seeing, the ability to glimpse beyond the world around them, must pierce the veil of their mind. It is usually done when a person has been found ready. At this point, they are taken to a place that holds strong memories for many people. A memory anchor of sorts." Horror flashed over Zeph's face. He began to shake his head.

"No....not this, not this place, please not this place!" Zeph grabbed his head with both hands as another image flashed before his eyes. "Please, I don't want to see this! I don't want to watch it happen!" he shouted as he fell to his knees. Sotiris rushed over and knelt with him.

"Zeph, look at me," he said, gripping Zeph's face. "I am truly sorry that this is what you must endure. In my vision, I brought you to this place. Believe me when I say I wish it could be any other place. I can't hope to understand why it must be this place, but Omega wanted you to see something. Please trust that this is what it is supposed to be."

Zeph nodded slowly. Reaching around his waist, he unhooked his sword and handed it to Marcus. He also removed all of his other belongings and gave them to Iggy. He paused momentarily and looked at the others standing in the doorway. Flinching again, he twitched his head to the side as another memory fragment drifted into his mind. As he opened his eyes, a faint blue glow briefly burst over them before fading.

"Zeph, you're eyes..." Breeze trailed off.

"I have to do this." Everyone could see the tears forming in his eyes.

"No, no, I'm not letting them do that to you," Marcus said with determination. "You don't have to do this, Zeph."

"Marcus, please," the sadness was evident as Zeph spoke.

Sotiris backed away from Zeph and motioned for the others to follow. They stood outside the archway. Placing both his hands on the symbols on either side of the doorway, the stone began to rematerialize as Sotiris sealed the door. Breeze and Zeph caught a final glimpse of each other, and then the wall of dust and stone formed.

Zeph turned and began walking farther into the room. Taking a deep breath, he let his mind flow completely open, just like Gus had taught him. There was nothing at first, but then another image shot into his mind. It was like someone was pushing something hot and white into his brain. He held his breath for a moment, trying to brace the pain. A dull energy began to build up in the room around him. It was so vivid Zeph felt he could almost reach out and touch it. There was a pause for a moment. His eyes widened. The breaths came in quick and deep as he saw a wall of energy come at him from every side of the room. Throwing his arms out, he let the energy flow into him.

The group stood outside the room in silence. Even though they had many questions, they held them at bay. Time dragged by, and an odd sound was heard, perhaps the shuffling of footsteps. The silence was shattered as a cry of pain came from within the room and echoed through the hallway. The sound flooded out into the hallway, as though the stone covering of the archway did not exist. Upon hearing the cry, Breeze slid down the wall to the dirty floor. The cries continued; some were small, and others frightening. When they started to hear the words 'Please! No!' Marcus could no longer hold his ground. He walked over to the archway; Sotiris and Xa'an stood before it.

"Let him out."

"Marcus..." Xa'an said, raising a hand.

"I wasn't asking, let him out!" Marcus bellowed as he raised his voice.

"Please stop!!" the words rang out loud and clear from behind the wall of stone. Marcus grabbed Xa'an by the chest. Flames flowed up Marcus' arms as he gripped the man.

"You open that door right now, or I swear..."

No one had ever seen Marcus act like that before. The flames began to flow out over Xa'an's robes, but Marcus kept them from igniting the clothing, if only for the moment.

"Marcus." It was Sotiris who spoke up; Marcus' eyes darted from Xa'an to the old Master. "I can see that you truly care for Zeph as more than a lifelong friend; to you, he is your brother. But if you listen to his cries, painful as it may be, Zeph is not asking to be let out." Marcus thought about the words for a moment and then slowly loosened his grip on Xa'an. The flames that had begun wrapping themselves around the mage dispersed.

"What do you think he's seeing in there?" Breeze asked as she ran her fingers through the thin layer of dirt on the ground. It was the complete opposite of her natural demeanor. It was clear that she was trying to block out the sounds from the next room. Iggy sat down on the floor next to her. He wrapped his arms around his knees and buried his face. It was then that Breeze snapped out of it. She wrapped her arms around Iggy and let the boy cry.

The minutes ticked by for what seemed like hours. They began to wonder if everything was okay. Sotiris said not to worry; Zeph would come when he was ready to leave. While they sat, he tried to explain what Zeph was going through to help them understand.

He told them it was like dreaming. Sometimes, you have those dreams where you're not really sure if you're asleep or awake—those times when you don't even realize you were dreaming until you wake up. You always feel a vision coming on, though. Sometimes, they can be painful, but that's more so at the beginning before a person's mind has adjusted to receiving them.

Iggy was the first to ask what was on their minds. Why do people start having visions? Sotiris paused for a moment, as it was not a simple answer. He explained that, for most, visions were of the past. For people with Light and Shadow abilities, it was as simple as developing your own skills to a point where the ability of Seeing develops naturally. Usually, coming into contact with a place of strong memories will trigger the first vision. After that, it's entirely up to Omega's will.

"Visions aren't something that can be forced," he explained, "It is not like reading someone's feelings or thoughts. Even though those things are part of Seeing, visions are something that cannot be controlled. Omega is the one that sends visions, so whatever is shown to a person is the will of Omega."

"So it's Omega's will that Zeph sees what he's seeing in there right now?" Marcus asked, frustrated.

"I have to believe that Omega wanted him to see what he's seeing in there. What happened in there nearly broke the foundation of our Order. But it also changed the life of one brilliant young girl forever. No one alive in *The Order* today has been given a vision of what happened in that room over a thousand years ago. All we have to go on are the accounts and texts that survived. When you take a life, it changes you, Marcus." Sotiris paused for a moment as he considered the nature of why Omega chose this place for Zeph. "Perhaps Omega wanted Zeph to see something of this girl, Desiree, that we have not. Perhaps there is much more to that tragic event than we have ever known."

DAY 133

> A man with true vision will see more than the world before him.

When he looks outside, he dreams.
When he looks inside, he awakens.
~ Sir Jarian the Hero

CHAPTER 12
BEHIND RED STRANDS

The rain fell heavy against the window, strands of water making their way down the glass. Darkness covered the room, shadows filled every corner, and the cloud-covered sky offered no relief from the darkness. Like a heavy drum, the rain continued to beat down on the house. The smell of wet wood made its way into the depths of the house, and sickly sweet scents filled the air. A silhouette could be seen against the glass.

A five-year-old child sat next to the window. Expressive eyes darted back and forth as she watched the villagers run around outside. Her eyes were the color of green plants after rainfall, with dark and brilliant tones. Her skin was pale, like that of a porcelain doll, smooth and perfect. The strands of red hair hanging past her face were red like silk dipped in scarlet dyes.

The thought of blood filled her mind. Perhaps the terror had already gripped her as she watched the carnage just outside her window. Maybe this was why she made no sound. The movements of her eyes told a different story. Wide-eyed, she watched as the beast leaped into the air and pounced on one of the men. His body fell into the mud; the cries from within were quickly silenced as the beast began to devour the man. The girl watched as the man's Gava left his body. It was hard to see past the beast's claws digging into the man's back, but she spotted the small ball of energy. Her father told her what happens to people once their Gava leaves them. Eyes locked on the man's body, she waited. Within seconds, she saw his body dissolve into thousands of strands of energy and drift away.

The village was in a panic. A pack of ravenous fiends had descended upon the town. It wasn't uncommon for a fiend to be spotted in the area or even right outside the village. They were usually taken care of relatively quickly. This time was different, however; a pack of lukos had made its way to the village. This kind of behavior was not known of in fiends. Lukos were large beast fiends that walked on all fours, with thick black coats of fur and long pointed teeth. Next to their teeth, their claws presented even more danger as they often lunged at a person, lacerating them deeply. The lukos had attacked in a pack, which had never been heard of before. More than eight had attacked the village at the same time.

The woman's breath came out quick and deep as she pressed her body against the door. Her eyes drifted down slowly from the ceiling to her child sitting by the window, watching everything; she had wished her daughter would never witness such a thing in her lifetime. Their eyes met, and the moment lingered. It was then that the girl's eyes made their way slowly down her mother's body. The patterns of red grew within the fabric of her dress. Drops of blood dripped slowly from the ends of the dress and joined the puddle of water on the floor.

She watched as her mother slowly slumped down to the floor. Rushing over, the little girl wrapped her arms around her mother.

"I'm sorry, baby," the woman said slowly and softly as her breathing began to slow.

"Where's daddy?" the little girl questioned. Her voice was shaky as she spoke. Tears filled her mother's eyes, and she began to sob. It was then that the girl knew her father was gone. She knelt beside her mother and watched as she slowly began to slip away. The screams of the village disappeared in her ears as she saw the light in her mother's eyes fade away. Looking down at her chest, she watched her mother's gava begin to form. She could almost reach out and touch the small ball of light floating just above her mother's chest, and she nearly dared to. Terror quickly gripped the child as she watched the ball turn a deep red color, turn to dark strands of energy, and make its way back into the body.

The little girl jumped up and quickly stumbled back. She had been raised to always watch for this if someone died. She was unsure how quickly the transformation would happen, but she had nowhere else to go. Running to the kitchen, she looked around frantically for a knife. Her chin just barely made it over the counter. Darting her eyes back, she continued to look at her mother, who remained unchanged for the moment. Pushing a chair towards the counter, she climbed up. Several knives were hanging on the wall. Scanning the knives, she chose the one with serrated edges. Standing on the chair, she turned to face the direction where her mother lay. Her body was still lying against the front door.

The change started, black veins spread out underneath her skin. Her body became pale, almost white. Her eyes shot open. The little girl jumped in horror at seeing what her mother had become. The whites of her eyes had now become blood red. She watched as her mother climbed to her feet, but it wasn't her mother anymore. A Corpse fiend now stood before her.

Still holding onto its human form, a Corpse was a human-like fiend. They were slow-moving at first but became fast and violent as the rage built. The basic desire to consume flesh was what drove them forward. A sound like a gargled growl came out of her. She looked around the room and quickly locked eyes with the little girl on the chair in the kitchen. Cocking her head to the side, she began to stagger forwards, dragging her feet as she moved.

"Mommy, please don't!" the girl pleaded as she held the knife out in front of her. The frailty of the small girl became evident as the knife began to shake in her hands. Tears flowed freely at the sight of her dead mother slowly coming towards her. She leaned back against the counter. It was then that the most basic of all emotions kicked in.

"Help me! Someone, please help me!" the little girl shouted. The look in the corpse's eyes changed as though it had turned to anger upon hearing the shouts of the little girl. It lunged at her, and the girl shrieked, thrusting her hands out. The serrated blade found its way into the neck of the fiend. Blood sprayed in all directions from the wound, splattering across the little girl's face. She closed her eyes and flinched. Opening them, she looked eye to eye with the fiend. The gargles came out with the blood. It wrapped its hands around the little girl's neck, but the mortality of the wound began to overtake the fiend. If it hadn't just freshly been formed, it would have taken more than that to bring it down.

The blood dripped slowly down the little girl's face as she watched the fiend fall to the floor. Reaching up, she touched her face. The sensation of warm, sticky blood was beneath her fingertips. The fiend fully collapsed on the floor. It was then that the front door of the home burst open. Standing there was a man dressed in black, wearing tightly bound robes and holding a curved sword in each hand. His eyes quickly fell upon the little girl. The man had known killing most of his life, but something stirred in him as he gazed down at her. Her frailty and innocence were apparent as he looked at her delicate, doll-like features. Their eyes met, blood still covered the one side of her face.

The house was still now. The screams of the village had stopped, and all that could be heard outside was the rain. Faint sounds of blood gurgling could be heard from the fiend on the floor. Blood pooled underneath it. The man looked down at the fiend as he slowly walked into the house, but the girl refused to and just stared straight ahead. With a quick flip of his blade, he thrust the tip into the head of the fiend. It shrieked out for an instant, causing the little girl to shutter. Then, the fiend began to dissolve into strands of energy. Touching her face, the little girl felt the blood on her cheek fade away as well. Nothing remained of the person or fiend when they died, not even their blood.

The man slowly knelt before the little girl, extending his hand toward her. She stood on the wooden chair, still holding the knife out and shaking. "I'm not going to hurt you, little one," he said softly. The fear had consumed her, and she stood there wide-eyed, not making a sound. "You can't stay here; it's not safe. We'll take you somewhere where it will be okay." His words were soft, as though he was speaking to his own daughter.

She let the knife slip out from her fingers. It landed with a thud as the tip stuck into the wooden floor. Slowly, she reached out and took his outstretched hand. Taking it, he gently wrapped his other arm around her and picked her up. She wrapped her tiny arms around his neck as he carried her in his arms.

They left the house and walked out into the rain. Mud squished beneath the man's boots. Minutes ago, the village streets were full of bodies and blood. Now, nothing remained but the rain. They were shortly joined in the middle of the village by several other men in black robes. Each man was dressed the same. The little girl clung to the man more as they approached the others.

"Who is she?" one of them questioned. The man looked down at the girl in his arms.

"She's the only one left," he replied.

"Orestes, we can't bring her back to *The Order* with us. You know that," protested one of the men.

Orestes hung his head down and looked into the girl's eyes. The rain had soaked through her hair and was now clinging to her face. Her eyes were big and beautiful, their green depths standing out boldly against her pale skin. She continued to hang onto him like a daughter would with her father.

"This girl just watched her mother turn into a Corpse, and when it attacked her, she killed it," he paused for a moment as he let the words sink in. The expressions on all their faces agreed with his own; there was no place left for her here.

They gathered up their things and made a final sweep of the village. The town would fade away now, wiped clean of life. Perhaps someone would come again and once more fill it with life. It was in a remote mountain location, so it would likely remain abandoned.

It was still unclear as to what had happened. Orestes and his men had been staying in a small village farther down the mountains. A man had come screaming into the village, bleeding badly. Before he succumbed to his wounds, he was able to tell them of the attack on his village. Orestes and his men quickly ran to the village. When they arrived, many of the villagers were already gone.

In their place, the village was swarming with Lukos fiends, powerful and terrifying fiends that resembled a large rabid wolf. The lukos turned their attention to the new arrivals, but they were no match for them. Orestes sliced through the fiends quickly, his men following suit as they went through the village. Once they had cleansed the village of the fiends, they went from house to house checking for survivors. Some of the houses still contained fiends from the recently departed villagers.

Orestes and his men returned to the village farther down the mountain. The five of them walked into town, Orestes still holding the small girl in her arms. Men and women came out into the streets as they entered. They began to question them about what had happened. In his mind, Orestes knew that it couldn't have been just a regular fiend attack, not with the numbers that had attacked the village, but he had no other explanation at the moment. He knew that there were people in the Realm who had become powerful enough to command the will of beast fiends. A talent that was most common in the Shadow Realm.

The villagers wanted to keep the child with them, but Orestes objected.

"This girl cannot live among you. What she has witnessed today will not leave her mind for many, many years. At *The Order*, we will give her purpose and the ability to overcome."

"By raising her as an assassin!" a man shouted out. Orestes looked in the crowd and spotted the man. He walked through the crowd and right up to the man, still holding the girl in his arms.

"We do the calling of our Order and do not take death lightly. A village was massacred today. If it was this village, would you still question our methods?" he asked, staring the man down. The man slowly shrunk away. Orestes held the girl close in his arms. She still clung to him and hadn't let go since he first picked her up.

"We will be leaving your village soon. If you have the means to tell others about what has happened here, then I suggest you do."

They returned to the inn and gathered up the rest of their things. Orestes sat on the bed in his room and gently sat the girl beside him. She refused to release her arms from around his neck.

"It's okay, little one, you're safe now."

She shook her head and made a whimper. He picked her up again and held her in front of himself so they could look eye to eye. She was a beautiful little girl, so young, so innocent. Brushing her hair away, he saw the Shadow symbol on her forehead. Reaching behind his head, he undid the black bandana he wore around his head.

"You see, I'm just like you," he said as he revealed his Shadow symbol to her. Slowly, she reached up and touched it. To his surprise, her gentle touch stirred something within him. Looking down at her, there was an instant connection of love. She had just watched the massacre of her village and been forced to kill the twisted fiend of her mother, and yet she was finding comfort in his arms. Tears seemed to come from nowhere; Orestes fought them back. He had never known the love of a child, nor had one return the feeling to him.

"What's your name?" he asked, looking deep into her innocent green eyes. She stared at him for a moment as though he had just asked her a huge secret.

Her eyes darted away before she whispered softly, "Desiree." He smiled softly at her and ran the back of his fingers down her cheek.

"That's a beautiful name. Hello Desiree, my name is Orestes." She slowly released her grip from around his neck and stared back at him.

The room felt so big to her as she looked around, even though it wasn't much bigger than her room at home. She slid off his lap and let her feet touch the cold wooden floor. It felt rough to her bare feet. She took several steps from the bed; Orestes just sat and watched her. The connection he felt to her he couldn't explain. He had never taken a wife or fathered a child, but looking at her now, he found that those feelings were stirring in him.

Desiree walked over to the window and peered out. She loved to sit by windows. The ripples in the glass distorted the view slightly, which she liked. As she looked through the glass, she would slowly move her head from side to side, watching the images distort as they passed through the ripples in the glass.

The dirt on her clothes was evident, and the mud still covered her feet. She would need some new clothing before they left. Desiree watched as Orestes stood up and walked towards the door. Fear gripped her once again, and she ran over to him, wrapping her arms around his leg. He smiled softly down at her,

"It's okay, little one, I'm not going anywhere. I'm just going to see if we can get you some clean clothes."

It was then that she looked down at her clothes. She ran her little hands over the dirt, trying to brush it away. After several attempts, she gave up and looked back up at him and smiled,

"Okay," she said, reaching up and taking his hand. Once again, Orestes felt his heart melt at her tiny hand slipping into his. Picking her up again, they left the inn and headed to one of the shops in the village.

Desiree had never had a new outfit before. The clothes she was wearing were one of only two sets she had ever owned. It was nothing more than a simple gray dress. She watched curiously as they made their way down the street. Some villagers stared at her; she still didn't understand why. Soon, they entered the Embroidery shop in the village. Orestes placed Desiree on the floor and let her wander around the shop as he talked to the shopkeeper.

She looked up and down the racks as she wandered through the shop. The clothes were plain and straightforward, and there wasn't very much for little girls like her. Her eyes caught a little faded red dress at the end of the row. Going over to it, she ran her hand over the fabric. It was pleasant to the touch, and she smiled as she ran her fingers over it. Orestes watched from the counter, and a soft smile formed on his face. He told the shopkeeper he would take it. They walked around the shop for a little bit longer. Orestes also wanted to find her shoes or something for her feet. Sadly, nothing was found. He knew that she would have everything she needed once they returned to *The Order*. Many talented mages in *The Order* handcrafted all the clothing worn.

They returned to the inn and gathered up the rest of their belongings. Desiree looked at the other men in the group. They smiled down at her. Most of them had never been fathers or been around children this young. Even within *The Order*, most children were brought to it, not born into it.

Everyone boarded the ship as they prepared to leave the docks. The journey back to Tarn would take several weeks. Desiree held Orestes' hand as they walked down the docks. She pointed to the ship. Orestes smiled and nodded, saying it was the ship they were leaving on. It was long and black, with black sails. Supplies had been loaded, and they prepared for the trip ahead. The sails caught the wind, and the ship took off.

Desiree watched Tsayla grow smaller as they journeyed away from the Shadow continent. She had never been on a ship before, which was an exciting experience for her. The land behind them was quickly removed as they passed through fog. At this point, she began to stroll around the small ship. She couldn't wander very far as the ship only had enough room for a dozen men at the most.

As she walked around, her eyes followed everything. The men watched as the curious little girl made a complete sweep of the ship. Shortly, she found her way to the front where Orestes was sitting. She climbed up the steps and stood at the bow with him. He smiled down at her as she looked out to sea. The fog they were traveling through would break soon, and there would be much for her to see. In the meantime, he took a seat by the rail and let her look around.

Desiree held onto the wooden rail and looked out into the fog. She was used to the fog back in her village and wondered if the fog was everywhere. The day was always cloudy and grey, something common in the Shadow Realm. Light was not strongly present across the Realm, whether it was overcast skies or thick fog. There was always something to dim the day.

The ship soon broke free from the fog and sailed smoothly out to the open sea. Desiree's eyes widened as she looked at the clear blue sea. She had never seen the ocean before. In fact, she had never left her small village a day in her life. She happily bounced up and down, gripping the railing as she looked at the horizon of blue water. The suns shone down over the waters. Desiree looked up at them; it was perhaps the first time she had seen them clearly in her whole life.

Just then, something splashed the side of the ship, startling Desiree. She carefully peered over the side of the railing. What she saw mesmerized her. It was a school of fish. They were a mixture of blue and purple, with a rainbow shine to their scales. Keeping pace with the ship, they jumped in and out of the water as they followed beside it.

"What are they?" Desiree asked as she looked down into the water.

"They are called Rakaf fish," Orestes said as he peered over the side to where she was looking, "You see them traveling alongside ships out here in the ocean. They get their name by the way they flutter alongside ships." Desiree stared down at them. They did look like they were fluttering as they jumped out of the water. The long fins on their bodies made it look like they had little wings. She continued to watch as they journeyed on.

As the next several weeks went by, Desiree began to open up more and more. She even started to talk to the other mages on the ship. The ocean crossing was coming to an end. In the distance, an island could be seen on the horizon. Orestes explained to Desiree that the island was where they were going. The ship docked within the depths of the island, and they disembarked.

The Order was happy to see their brethren return, but Desiree's arrival was causing a stir within *The Order*. Orestes explained the situation to the others, stressing that this was the best course of action for the girl. After some convincing, the others agreed, and it was proclaimed that she would train with them to become a Shadow Mage. At the time, Desiree had no idea what that meant; she just stood there holding Orestes' hand.

Orestes took her to the living quarters section of the island, where he made a room for her. It was evident that she didn't want to leave his side, so he took her to his room. After he showed her all around the inside of *The Order*, he showed her how to find her way around and where to go if she was ever looking for him.

The hallways seemed so big to her as she walked them with Orestes. The smell of wet stone was a different change from the smell of damp wood she was used to. Dim light bounced down the halls from the oil lamps. This place was strange to her, but it was all she knew now. She gripped Orestes' hand as they walked down the halls. Turning into a small room, Orestes led her to several closets. Opening them up, she saw they were full of cloaks and other clothing accessories.

"Are these for me?" she asked, eyeing everything.

"Well, not all of them," Orestes said with a chuckle. "You would need to grow some more before you'd fit into many of these." She stuck her little lip out as only a little girl could. All he could do was smile down at her adorable face. "Let's see if we can find something that will fit you." After several unsuccessful tries, they found one outfit that would work. He slipped the black cloak over her head. The sleeves fell past her hands, and the train of the cloak bunched on the floor. She waved her arms around, flapping the sleeves as she did. Orestes smiled; he could not believe how much the little things she did melted his heart.

"Well, it's not quite your size, dear, but you'll grow into it," he said with a smile.

She nodded her agreement, and they headed back to her room. She sat on her bed, and Orestes knelt on the floor next to it.

"Do you know why we have brought you here, Desiree?" Orestes asked in a soft voice. Desiree nodded slowly. She didn't say a word, but by the look on her face, it was clear that her young mind was fully aware of what had happened weeks earlier.

"Mommy and Daddy are gone," she said, looking deep into his eyes.

"Yes, they are, dear. But things will get better. That's why you're here. You will learn much here; I will help teach and train you."

She reached out and hugged him. He wrapped his arms around her fragile little frame. The day had turned to night, and it was time for her to be getting some sleep. Orestes tucked her in and said that if she needed anything, all she had to do was go to his quarters down the hall. He ran his hand through her scarlet hair as she drifted off to sleep.

Sitting there a while, he listened to the sounds of the corridors. Even the gentle sound of her breathing filled his ears. She looked so peaceful as she slept. Kneeling beside the bed, he said a silent prayer for her and blew out the lamp before leaving.

BLOOD. SHE COULD SMELL the blood. Touching her face, she felt the warm wetness on her skin. The body fell to the floor and began to bleed out. She looked down at it. It was her mother, lifeless and dying once again. The knife fell from her hand. Kneeling down, she looked into her mother's eyes. They weren't those of the creature that she remembered, but they were her own. Reaching out, she touched her mother's face.

Desiree awoke with a start. The images of the dream were still vivid in her mind. She took a deep breath and held it for a moment. When she could no longer hold it in, she let it out and began to sob. Tears flowed through her fingers as she cupped her face. It had been four years since that night, yet the memories wouldn't fade.

Swinging her feet off the bed, she let them touch the cold stone floor. Removing her night garments, she put on her traditional robes. Kneeling by her door, she strapped on her boots. She turned and walked back towards her bed, stopping at her nightstand. She picked up a silver chain and placed it around her neck.

She caught her reflection in the mirror. The Shadow symbols were visible on her forehead and dangling on the chain.

She left her room and proceeded to head down the corridors. Those that passed her by didn't make a sound, and she gave none back in return. Over the last four years, she had learned much, but opening up to others was a skill that still escaped her. She continued down the hall, hands tucked into each of her sleeves.

Before long, she arrived at her destination. The outside air was a little fresh that morning. Other students had already arrived; at least she wasn't the last to arrive. Orestes stood off to the side while waiting for the rest of his students to arrive. Desiree smiled over at him. When Desiree looked at him, it was the only time others saw real happiness coming from her.

At the still young age of nine, Desiree had advanced quickly. The first thing she had dug into was the ancient archives in *The Order*. One of the few things her mother taught her was how to read. She found a place to escape from the memories and the world around her in the archives of scrolls and books. Once she began her physical training at age seven, it became apparent that she was naturally skilled in basic combat. She would watch different fighting techniques, and with only minimal practice, she could duplicate them perfectly.

Orestes walked over to the center of the courtyard from his position near the stone wall. The group of students followed. They created a large circle around him as they prepared for their next lesson. There were about two dozen students in his class. Desiree followed suit and stood with the others. She didn't like standing next to students she didn't know very well, which was most of them.

The lesson began. Orestes demonstrated several new techniques to disarm an opponent. Everyone watched and listened closely. Desiree, on the other hand, tracked every moment of his body. She noticed the subtle movements and shifts in stance far more than the other students did. It was the little details, like how he curved his fingers or the position of his toes as he made a move. Next, it was the students' turn to try out the lesson. Everyone was paired off, and the sparing began.

Desiree stood across from a boy slightly older than her. They had sparred often during class. He was one of the few students not overly intimidated by her. They took their positions and commenced. As usual, Desiree quickly took the boy down. They switched back and forth, but Desiree took the upper hand each time. Her ability to learn what she was taught was unmatched by the other students.

"Desiree," Orestes called out. She turned her head to see him waving her over. He also called out to another student and waved her over. "I'm going to have these two girls pair up against each other," Orestes said to the class. "I want you to watch how they perform the techniques they have learned." Some of the students scoffed a little; they knew exactly how well Desiree could fight.

The girls paired off as everyone moved back to give them some space. Desiree didn't really like confronting others, so she was glad when the other girl made the first move. Throwing several quick punches, she lunged at Desiree. Catching them with her hands, she blocked them and swung her leg over the ground in an attempt to knock the other girl off her feet. The girl jumped up quickly and kicked Desiree in the shoulder. Stumbling, she shook it off and faced the girl again. Desiree took several quick steps towards her and let a flurry of small punches go. She was surprised to find that every one of her punches connected hard against the girl.

Orestes cocked his head and narrowed his eyes for a moment as he watched. Something wasn't quite right. The other girl tried to connect several blows against Desiree but missed every time. It was then that the other students were beginning to notice what Orestes had. Desiree's movements were almost a blur at times. It was more than reflexes; this was something ability-based.

Great speed and agility were common in Shadow and Light Elements, but they didn't manifest themselves until a person was usually much older. It might start with something as simple as catching a falling object without effort or pushing oneself physically without tiring.

Orestes nodded to two other students and motioned for them to join the fight. He had to be sure it was what he was seeing. The two other students came at Desiree from behind. She spun around and delivered several quick blows to both of them, sending them staggering back. Turning around, Desiree looked back at the girl. Taking a step towards her, Desiree suddenly felt her body lurch forward.

The other students gasped in surprise as they watched Desiree fly across the courtyard in a long black streak. She connected hard with the girl, sending her flying and knocking her to the ground. The girl lay on the ground, staring wide-eyed at Desiree. Moving her arms back and forth, Desiree watched as her arm movements were nothing but a blur. She clenched her fists and tried to control what was happening.

Stumbling back, Desiree looked at Orestes with a pleading look in her eyes.

"That's enough for now; everyone return to your quarters," commanded Orestes.

Everyone backed away from Desiree as she walked towards the archway. Tears began to fill her eyes as she ran down the hall. Bursting into her room, she shut the door and fell on her bed, sobbing.

The minutes passed, and then the gentle sound of her door opening and closing entered her ears. She turned her head to see Orestes standing there. He slowly walked over to the bed and sat down. Desiree still lay with her face in her pillow. Running his hand over her head, Orestes began to stroke her hair gently. The long red strands flowed between his worn, strong fingers.

"What's wrong with me?" the muffled question came from beneath the pillow.

"Nothing is wrong with you, dear. In fact, what just happened is a sign that you are growing," Orestes explained.

Desiree rolled over to face him, "But everyone's afraid of me now," she said, choking back the tears.

"Many people, even those here in *The Order*, can be afraid of things they don't understand. You did something today that most shadow elementals won't achieve until they are much older."

"I don't even know what I did!" Desiree blurted as she threw her arms on the bed in frustration.

"It's called Gravitate," he explained. "It's the ability to will one's body forward simply with the mind. To the observer, they will see the person move only as a blur or streak."

"Why is this happening to me?"

The question lingered in the air for some time. Orestes took her hand in his and looked down at her.

"You are my daughter, and I love you, Desiree. I will always be proud of you."

She looked back up at him as soft tears rolled down her face. Orestes didn't have the ability to read minds like most Shadow Elementals, but with Desiree, he didn't have to. Over the last four years, they had become closer than he had been with anyone his whole life.

"You're still having the nightmares, aren't you?" he asked as he rubbed her hand.

"Yes," was all she could muster. Desiree sat up on her bed and wrapped her arms around her knees as she pulled them into her chest.

"If you need to talk about it, I'm here for you, dear."

"I have it almost every night. I see her there lying on the floor," the tears started again as she spoke. "That's the last image I have of her. I've tried to remember her differently, but I can't. I can't even remember what my father looks like anymore."

Orestes listened to her words, waiting for the moment to say something, but it never came. He moved over and held her in his arms; it was all he could do. Her abilities were something that couldn't be predicted. Most students developed at around the same pace, but Desiree seemed to take leaps forward.

"I'll help you control your abilities, Desiree," Orestes said, looking over at her.

"I just wish they were gone. I wish I was normal and that no one even noticed me."

"You're here for a reason, Desiree. I know it was Omega's will that we found and saved you that day."

They talked for a while longer, during which time Desiree expressed more of her frustrations with adjusting her rapidly growing abilities. Orestes said he would see about setting up private training with some of the higher-level mages in *The Order*. The idea of that comforted her a little. It would help her to train with others who understood her manifesting abilities.

Orestes smiled at her as he closed the door and left the room. Desiree sat there on her bed, still in the fetal position. The light of her candles danced around the room. She felt a cold chill flow up her neck. Shuddering, she looked around the room. As she breathed out, she could see her breath in the air as though the room had grown cold.

"Who's there?" she called out. There was no answer. She called out again, this time jumping up from her bed. Something in the corner of her eye caught her attention. In the dark corner of her room, she saw a figure move.

The man stepped out of the darkness and into the dim candlelight. He was tall and thin, with a dark quality about his features. Thin black hair and a bony face sat atop his gangly frame. The clothes he wore were those of a wealthy, well-dressed man. What caught Desiree's attention first was that there was no mark on his forehead.

"Hello, Desiree," he said in a sinister voice that sent more chills up her spine.

Throwing her hands towards him, she tried to hold him in place. She had been practicing her telekinetic talent for some time now. The impact of it hit his clothes, but he simply shook his shoulders and walked through it.

"You'll have to do better than that, deary."

Desiree clenched her fists as she concentrated on him. This was something relatively new she had read about in some of the archive scrolls. The ability to mentally paralyze your enemy with pain was a valuable skill to have.

The man stopped for a moment and twitched his head. Desiree smiled as she saw her efforts working. With his head down and eyes locked on her, the man coughed and shook his head with an evil smile as he continued to step closer.

Nothing was working on him. So Desiree tried a desperate approach. She lurched forward at him, trying to connect several blows. The man stopped and waved his hand. This caused Desiree to fly backward, hitting the wall. She landed on the floor, quickly scampered to her feet, and ran at him again. Once again, with a flick of his hand, he sent her smashing into the wall again.

"Now listen, little lady, I can do this all day. Can you?" he asked, leaning over her.

She staggered to her feet, stood in the corner, and locked her eyes with him.

"Sit," he said as he twitched his head to the side. Instantly, Desiree felt her body move toward the bed and sit down. She didn't try to fight it but simply let it go. The man walked over to her bed and stood in front of it.

"Who are you?" she asked.

"Now that is the question of the day, isn't it; who am I, who am I, who am I? I think the real question is, who are you, Desiree?" the man asked with a confident swagger to his step. He quickly crouched down beside her bed and looked her in the eye. She was able to get a better look at him now that he was close and fully in the light. The clothing he wore was the finest she had ever seen. A long black velvety coat was on top of the shirt, vest, and tie combination underneath. The vest and tie were scarlet-like, like her hair, and the rest were all velvet black.

"My name is Mizimmah," he said as he looked at her with a crooked grin.

The name sounded familiar to her. She searched her mind for a moment, trying to recall where she had encountered it before. Then it hit her, and her eyes got wide.

"You're one of the Uriel!"

"Indeed I am, pretty lady, and I've had my eye on you for some time now."

"What do you want with me?" she questioned.

"I'm here to help you. See, I've been around for quite some time. And every now and then, I come across someone who truly needs my help. So I am here to show you more of yourself, of what you are, and what you can become. I can show you how to grow and control your abilities and be more powerful than you could ever imagine."

She sat there, slightly confused at his words. "How do I know you're who you say you are?"

Mizimmah smiled that crooked smile of his and shook his head. With a flick of his wrist, his body dissolved into stands of thick black smoke. He darted around the room, taking shape in several spots before dissolving again. Manifesting directly behind her, he whispered in her ear, "I can do more than you've ever dreamed of." Turning around quickly, she looked at him boldly.

"I don't want to become more powerful. I just want to be like every other person here in *The Order*. I want to have friends and have everyone not be afraid of me."

"Ah, I understand your predicament. I was not unlike you back in my day. Well, here's my counter-proposal. I will teach you what you need to know in order to control your abilities. Then you will be able to pass as just a regular ordinary girl. How does that sound?"

Desiree stood there and thought about it for a moment. The idea of it all seemed so sudden. Why would one of the Uriel appear to her and offer to help? She looked back up at Mizimmah. He simply stood there with that crooked grin of his.

"Okay, I'll do it."

"Fantastic, deary. I do have just one little condition, though."

"What's that?" she asked wary.

"That you keep my involvement in your development a secret."

"Alright, I can do that," she replied with a curious look on her face.

"Good," he said with an evil grin, "let the training begin."

THE ROWS OF STUDENTS paired off and took up sparring positions. At the front of the line stood a bold young girl. Her long and flowing red strands blew in the breeze. A moment passed, and then she gave the signal to begin. Each student opposite the other advanced. They had become an extremely well-trained group under the guidance of their Head Mage.

It took a lot of skill to become an instructor. Desiree had worked hard for the last five years to get where she was now. At age fourteen, she was now the youngest Head Mage in *The Order*'s history. She taught multiple classes every day. With each class, she brought up new students to a higher level of learning. Those who made it through her rigorous training became some of the finest students in *The Order*.

Behind her obvious skills, there was a secret side to her. She only allowed the teachings from Orestes and the other mages to show through. In reality, though, her skills had far surpassed everyone in *The Order*. Mizimmah had opened her eyes to so many things. At first, it scared her, but over time, she began to seek out the new skills he would show and teach her. The skills and abilities she now possessed would make even the skills of someone like Orestes look like a child's by comparison.

The class finished up and headed back inside. Desiree stood in the courtyard for a while. She liked to walk to the edge where the cliffs were. Resting her hands on the stone wall, she looked out to sea. The sound of the waves below calmed her. Her youthfulness had not faded over time, but it had matured into a beauty unlike any other. The strands of her red hair, her pale soft skin, and the deepness of her hauntingly green eyes made her an actual work of art.

Orestes came up beside her. They stood there for a moment and looked out to sea together. He smiled down at her. She tried to keep a serious face but soon gave in and smiled back up at him.

"How are you today, my dear?" he asked.

"Things are good; the students seem to be training quite well."

"But not as good as you, right?" he winked.

They both laughed. It had been hard for her to keep Mizimmah a secret from him over the years. There were so many times she wanted to show him what she had learned. The fear of what that would mean for her in *The Order* still held some weight inside her, though.

"I'm going down to the archives. Would you care to join me?" he asked.

"You know I've been down there hundreds of times," she said with a smile.

"Ah, but this is different. I'm going to take you to some of the more ancient archives." Her eyes lit up at hearing that. Reading the old scrolls was a fun pastime for her as a little girl, but in recent years, she has been reading them to gain knowledge and advance her skills.

They made their way inside and headed down the stone corridors. Grabbing some torches, they headed down the old stone staircase leading them into the depths of the archives. Desiree had only been to this part of the archives several times before, but she knew that more archives were hidden even deeper. Thoughts of everything she could learn filled her head as they entered the corridor.

Many rooms could be seen down the hall, but their destination today was the first archive room on the left of the staircase. Like most of the other archive rooms, it was rows of shelves with chests and lock boxes on the floor. In the middle were tables and chairs for the mages to study the manuscripts. Torches were on the walls, although none were lit at the moment; oil lamps were on the table.

Desiree walked over and lit some of the torches. They went from row to row, looking up and down the shelves. Orestes ducked into a few and rummaged around. On the other hand, Desiree walked around the room, looking at the sections listed on the ends of each shelf. There wasn't a particular one she was looking for; she just loved to familiarize herself with the sections listed. There was something that caught her eye, though. Walking to the end of one of the rows, her eyes fell upon a large chest on the floor. She loved to open chests because they often contained more than just a scroll or manuscript.

Opening the chest, she found it full of journals and clothing. The clothing was at least several hundred years old, to be sure. She had just begun to pick up a journal when something else within the clothing caught her eye. It was silver and smooth. Pulling it out, she held it in her hands. It was a beautifully crafted silver scroll case.

Orestes stood at the end of the row watching her. She looked at the scroll for a moment before his silhouette caught her attention. Quickly standing, she walked over to him and handed him the scroll.

"What is this?" she asked with great curiosity.

"That's an excellent question," Orestes said as he looked the scroll over. It was beautifully crafted, but there didn't seem to be any way to open it. Walking over to the chest, he examined it as well. Finding things within the archives that no one knew about wasn't uncommon. The archives went back several thousands of years to at least the Third Age. It has only been fifty-seven years since the start of the Sixth Age.

Orestes looked through the chest as Desiree looked over the scroll once more. There was something about it; she was drawn to it. There was no latch on it of any kind. Wrapped around the length of the scroll were embroidered patterns within the metal.

"These were obviously the possessions of a mage. Based on the age of the other things in this chest, I'd say they were from around four hundred or so years ago. Based on some of the manuscripts with it, it seems that no one in *The Order* was ever able to open this scroll, so it was simply placed with the other belongings," Orestes said as he walked back over to Desiree.

"Have you ever seen a scroll like this before?" she asked. He took the scroll and looked at it once again.

"Not one crafted like this. It seems perfect in every way."

As Desiree looked at the scroll, she began to notice something. Perhaps it was just her imagination, but for a moment, she thought she saw the Shadow symbol appear on the end of the scroll. Orestes placed it on the table and got up to look through the archives more. Desiree took hold of the scroll; there was something different about it; she was sure of it. As she looked at the end of the scroll, she saw the shadow symbol appear. Turning the scroll over, she saw that the symbol had appeared on both ends. Running her fingertips over the end, she felt something, like a warm, tingling sensation. Desiree held the scroll, fingertips holding either end. She pulled the ends closer until her palms touched the ends.

Closing her eyes, she gasped as energy began to flow into her. Shadow symbols appeared on the top of her hands and began to glow a soft red. Her grip on the scroll increased. The energy within it was like no other. The shadow symbol on her forehead also began to glow red.

The strain almost seemed too much. Desiree stood quickly from her chair, still holding onto the scroll. Orestes was drawn by the noise and walked out of the row he had been standing in. His eyes quickly darted from the scroll to Desiree's glowing elemental symbols and back again. Rushing over, he stood by her and watched. The symbols on her hands began to glow brightly as her body started to levitate.

It was too much for Orestes; he reached out and tried grabbing the scroll. A field of crackling energy formed around the scroll, making it untouchable. He looked at Desiree, something was disturbing about her expression. It was something he had never seen on her before. Looking around frantically, he did the only thing he could think of. With a quick fling of his hand, he sent a wave of energy against Desiree. Her body flung into one of the shelves, causing her to drop the scroll. Orestes quickly scooped it up.

"Give me that!" she bellowed at him. Orestes was taken aback by her reaction. The look in her eyes was nothing short of pure lust for power. The commotion had caused several other mages to come down to the archives. They stood beside Orestes.

"Escort Desiree back to her quarters, please," he said as he motioned to the mages.

A look of anger flashed across Desiree's face as she lowered her head. It looked as though she might put up a fight. Relaxing, she took a deep breath and walked away with the mages.

Orestes looked down at the scroll; it was still warm to the touch. He returned to the grand hall and gathered some high-ranking mages. They joined together in one of the meeting rooms. Orestes placed the scroll on the table and explained what had happened.

"What do we know of this scroll?" one of the mages asked.

"Not very much; I looked through the other belongings with it and found that it belonged to a mage from the fifth age and that no one has ever been able to open it," Orestes said.

"I have a theory," said one of the other mages as he looked over the scroll.

"Go ahead," replied Orestes.

"It has been long since anyone has spoken of it in *The Order*, but perhaps this scroll belonged to the *Chosen One*."

The room fell silent at his words. Everyone looked down at the scroll on the table. Everyone knew the story he spoke of. Over half an Age ago, there was a young mage who was given a scroll by Omega, or so the story goes. He was told to pass the scroll down through the generations, and that one day, it would meet with six others. It was said that the scroll gave him untold knowledge of Shadow abilities.

"You don't actually believe this could be that scroll, do you?" Orestes questioned.

"The story tells that the scroll marked his hands, and you said that her hands now bear the Shadow symbol."

The hours went on as they discussed it further. It became quite clear that the scroll must have belonged to the *Chosen One* of Shadows. What to do with it now was a whole other question.

Desiree paced around her room for what seemed like an eternity. Her mind was racing. The feeling of holding the scroll was slowly fading away. All she wanted to do was hold it again. There was something so powerful about it. It was like a whisper in her ear now. She couldn't make out the words, but she wanted to hear more.

There came a knock at the door. Desiree opened it to find Orestes standing there. He asked if he could enter, and she welcomed him in. They sat and talked for a while. Orestes wanted to make sure she was okay. It was new and confusing; she didn't understand what the scroll had done to her. He assured her that everything would be fine, that she just needed to put it out of her mind. That was something much more complicated than he knew. Power was something she had become accustomed to over the last five years. Mizimmah had seen to that.

Later that night, Desiree decided to go for a walk out past the courtyard. Besides the view from the cliffs, she also enjoyed the garden section, which was more in the southern part of the courtyard area. The freshness of the growing season made all the trees and plants smell sweet.

Unlike most trees, several large trees in the garden produced fruit during the year's growing season. It was the vines that Desiree loved. How they grew and wrapped around things added so much to the object, in her opinion.

Sitting under one of the trees, she gazed up at the stars. She didn't notice the man standing just off to her left.

"Well, deary, did you have an interesting day?" Mizimmah asked from the shadows.

"You know very well what happened today; I know you watch everything," Desiree replied slightly annoyedly.

"Now, now, don't be like that; if it wasn't for all my training, that scroll wouldn't have even nudged you when you held it."

"What do you mean?" she asked puzzled.

"Oh, never you mind. Just know that the scroll was meant for you. You are the *Shadow Chosen One*." He walked slightly into the light so she could see his face. There was always that sparkle in his eye, as well as his crooked grin.

"What am I supposed to do? They're not going to let me touch it again. Not after what happened," she pointed out.

"Oh, I beg to differ. As a matter of fact, I think you should meet with your precious Orestes tomorrow and ask to see the scroll again. All you need to do is hold onto it long enough to open fully."

"How do you know all this?" she asked.

"I've been around a very long time, deary. I've seen others in the past who had a chance to be great; the cards never fell the way they should have for them. I'm just trying to help you. They will say that you're not meant for the scroll, especially if you tell them you're the *Chosen One*. But don't you listen to that."

Thoughts of holding the scroll drifted back into her mind. She could almost feel the energy flowing in her again. The marks on her hands hadn't faded away as she thought they might.

"I don't want to defy Orestes' wishes," she said softly. It wasn't what Mizimmah wanted to hear, but he knew it was coming. He strolled around the tree she was sitting under. Reaching up into the branches, he plucked a piece of fruit and held it in his hand. Tossing between his hands, he extended it to her. "Care for a bite?" he asked. She shook her head no, to which Mizimmah chuckled and smiled his sly grin.

"Orestes just doesn't understand you the way I do, deary. If you get that scroll, you'll have all the knowledge you've ever dreamed of. There is still so much we haven't unlocked yet, and you'll have it all."

He made everything sound so enticing. Desiree knew she shouldn't, but there was something about his words. She wanted to know more about the scroll; a short while later, she headed back inside. Mizimmah just stood there in the shadows of the garden. He took a bite of the fruit in his hand and smiled, "Good girl." Dissolving into black strands, he disappeared into the shadows.

That night, Desiree's sleep was restless. Thoughts of the scroll kept filling her mind. She wanted to know what it held and what it would do to her. She awoke early and got ready quickly. There wasn't a moment to waste; she wanted to meet up with Orestes. Typically, she would find him knocking on her door, so it was a change for her to knock on his for once.

Desiree stood outside his door for several minutes. She still wondered if she should confront Orestes about the scroll. After several more minutes had passed, she decided to simply knock. Movement was heard inside, and soon, the door opened, revealing Orestes standing in the doorway.

"Can we talk?" she asked.

He welcomed her in, and they sat down at his desk. The room served not only as his quarters but also as a personal study. Because the whole complex was built inside the mountain of the island, there were always candles or lamps burning in any given room. They sat across each from each other. Orestes knew exactly why she had come to his quarters, but he wanted it to play out for the moment. Silence hung in the air for some time before Desiree spoke.

"I need to know more about the scroll," she said softly.

There was a pause in the air. It was clear that Orestes was going to say something in return; he was just searching for the words. Folding his hands on the desk, he looked across at her. So much time had passed since that day he rescued her. Some days, he wished for that little girl to return again. She was growing up so fast, more than he wanted to admit.

"We don't know much about the scroll, but we know it holds great power."

There was a pause as Desiree took a deep breath. It was evident that her thoughts were entirely focused on holding the scroll again. Orestes continued, "We also know that it was meant for the *Shadow Chosen One*."

"I know, I'm the *Chosen One*," she blurted out.

Orestes stared at her with confusion. Knowledge of the *Chosen Ones* hadn't been taught in *The Order* for several hundred years. So, to hear her speak of it was unsettling.

"The bearer of this scroll lived hundreds of years ago, Desiree. You can't be the *Chosen One*."

"Well, you're right, but so am I. It's hard to explain." She fumbled over her words as she spoke. "It spoke to me."

"What did it say to you?" Orestes questioned at the unexpected turn of events in the conversation.

"It told me to 'Learn Within to Find the Last.'"

Orestes thought about it for a moment. The decision could not be made lightly. Up until the day before, he thought he knew her. However, when she held the scroll, there was something there he hadn't seen before, something dark.

"I can't allow you to hold the scroll again; we don't know what it's doing to you. And until we do, it will remain locked in the Sacred Archives."

Desiree fought back the frustrations that were building inside of her. She stormed out of the room and headed back to her quarters. Slamming her door, she walked over to her bed. Looking down at her hands, she saw that they were shaking. She tried to take deep, steady breaths to calm herself down. What was going on with her? She had never gotten angry at Orestes like that before.

The minutes passed, and she sat in silence. Walking over to her closet, she opened the door. Inside were her different sets of clothing, but it was her weapons that she was eyeing. A belt of small throwing knives hung at the back. On the shelf below was a set of two curved blades. They were shorter than most in *The Order*, and the blades were curved outward. She touched them; they were still sharp as always.

Closing the closet door, she began to pace around her room. The thoughts in her head were beginning to trouble her, and she whispered under her breath for help.

"You called, deary?" Mizimmah asked as he stepped out of the shadows.

It wasn't surprising anymore. Desiree had quickly learned that he could travel between shadows at will. This meant that he could be stepping out of some dark corner at any moment.

"I don't know what I should do. I can't escape how the scroll is drawing me in. But they've locked it away and told me I'm not allowed to go near it."

"Well, now, that is a predicament. Perhaps you've forgotten you are the most powerful mage in *The Order*."

"What is that supposed to mean?"

"Oh, I think you know," he said with an almost evil grin on his face.

An involuntary twitch went up the side of her neck, a representation of the struggle that had just occurred in her brain. Closing her eyes, she ran her hands through her hair. Mizimmah slid behind her and whispered in her ear.

"This is your destiny, and these people are just getting in the way. Whatever the cost, even to the point of shedding blood..." the words trailed off.

Typically, those kinds of words would faze Desiree, but not this time. The thought of having the scroll was too great now. She had to have it. Walking over to her closet, she quickly grabbed her weapons. Strapping them to herself, she stopped and looked at Mizimmah. He just stared back at her, almost like a proud father. With that, she left her quarters.

"Now we'll see what you're really made of," Mizimmah said as he stepped back into the shadows.

Desiree stood at the end of the hall. She could hear voices at the other end. Although it was a long distance, the path was straight. Reaching into her cloak, she ran her hands along the handles of her blades. Breathing in quickly, she took several deep breaths. Like the snap of a finger, she was off, racing down the hall at full speed. Every boot fall echoed off the walls like some pounding anthem of death. She knew that the mages in the archive were aware of her presence, but it was too late to turn back. Bursting into the room, everyone around her jumped at the sudden entrance.

Orestes stood at the far end. He had a feeling this was coming, so he had come down to the archive immediately after their altercation, along with a handful of the best-trained mages in *The Order*. Desiree locked eyes with him and then focused on the scroll in his hand. As she took several steps forward, she noticed the other mages were slowly walking out of the stacks. There were perhaps eight or more mages in the room. Orestes looked at her with great love and pain in his eyes. The look on his face pled with her not to do what he knew she was thinking.

"Give me the scroll," she said in a low voice.

"Please don't," he whispered with a hint of fear in his voice, not fear for him but for what she was becoming.

"Give me the scroll!" Desiree screamed into the room, causing everyone to step back.

"Desiree, what's become of you?" Orestes asked with pain in his voice.

She didn't satisfy him with an answer; instead, she began to advance. The mages, in turn, began to advance slowly on her. This was not going to end well. There was nothing else to do, so Orestes motioned for the mages to restrain her.

Four mages approached her from all sides. She stopped her advancement and took a stance. They all knew of her incredible fighting abilities but had no idea they were greatly undermatched. Desiree wasted no time and delivered several strong blows to the mages. Her speed was unlike anything they had ever seen in her lessons. With a flick of her hand, she sent out a wave of telekinetic energy, knocking the mages off their feet.

They slowly staggered to their feet once more. The other mages took up positions, surrounding her on all sides. Orestes watched silently. He had given the mages one order before Desiree entered; they could restrain her by any means except the use of weapons. Harming her wasn't the goal of taking her down.

One of the mages slowly reached into his cloak. Desiree caught the gesture out of the corner of her eye. In less than the time it took to blink, one of Desiree's small throwing knives found its way into the neck of the mage. Desiree stood there with perfect positioning, one leg extended outwards to her side, one arm extended lengthwise in the direction of the fallen mage. The pose was elegant in a frightening way. Everyone in the room wasn't sure what had just happened, and then all eyes darted to the mage staggering backward. He gripped his throat as the blood poured out. Desiree didn't even turn around to watch him die. Falling to the floor, he collapsed in a heap. Orestes looked in horror as the man's body dissolved into energy.

"You just killed a man!" he blurted out, eyes locked on her.

"Give me the scroll," Desiree said in a low growl, "I won't ask again, Father."

It was chilling to hear her address him in that role after what she had just done. Orestes threw his hand out, sending a telekinetic blast that pushed her to the floor. The mages drew their weapons and advanced on her.

Desiree erupted from the floor. Drawing her two curved blades, she sliced upwards through the bodies of the mages on either side of her. Instantly, their bodies dissolved. Spinning swiftly, she let her blades slice through anything in their path. Pressing forward, she slew two more mages. Dropping her blades, she reached out and lifted the mage into the air that was blocking her path to Orestes. Still suspended and unable to move, he could only watch in horror as Desiree stepped closer. Clenching her fists, the mage screamed out in pain. The sounds of his bones snapping could be heard. She let his body fall to the floor, and within moments, he, too, disappeared.

Only two mages remained. They stood close to the archway where she had entered the room. It looked as though they might run; Desiree quickly spun around. Reaching into her cloak, Desiree threw two of her knives at them. Each blade found its target in their chests. They both slumped down to the floor and began to fade away.

There was a chilling silence in the air as Desiree stepped up towards Orestes. He extended his hand towards her. She stopped in her tracks. Pain began to build up inside and spread throughout. The weakness spread through her body. Anger burned on her face. She threw her hands forward towards Orestes and yanked him to the ground in front of her. This display of ability was something Orestes had never seen from her before.

"I'm not some puppet you can control!" she shouted with burning anger in her voice. Orestes held a firm grip on the scroll and sat on his knees in front of her. Desiree began to pace around him. With a wave of her hand, all the throwing knives from around the room instantly flew toward him. They stopped and floated in the air just in front of him.

"You will give me what I want," she said, kneeling beside him.

"You mustn't give in, Desiree," said Orestes as he greatly struggled through the pain she was inflicting.

There was that twitch again in her neck. Something inside of her was still fighting her lust for power. She shook it off. With anger in her eyes, she let the knives plunge into his body. The cries echoed down the hall. Each knife had found a place in his body to inflict a tremendous amount of pain but not a fatal strike. His blood began to flow out onto the floor.

Desiree knelt next to him and grabbed the back of his cloak. Orestes began to cough blood as several of the blades had struck him in the chest. Reaching towards him, she tried to grab the scroll from his hand. Even in his dying weakened state, his grip held firm. She looked him in the eye. Another scream echoed down the corridors as all the fingers in Orestes' hand shattered. The scroll dropped to the floor in front of him. Desiree picked it up and stood in the middle of the room.

Orestes watched as she gripped the ends of the scroll. Light burst from her hands and forehead. Her body lifted into the air. The scroll drifted out in front of her as strands of light left the scroll and wrapped around her body. A moment passed. He didn't know what was happening to her, but he knew it could never be worth the price she had just paid. A moment later, she stood on the floor once again. The glow faded from her eyes, and she looked at him.

Orestes sat there on the floor as the blood slowly drained from his body. He knew that within minutes, he would be dead.

"No matter what, I'll always love you, Desiree."

The words came out broken as he sat there dying. Desiree closed her eyes and shook her head for a moment. There was something deep inside her, deeper than all the power she had just received. It was screaming and clawing at her from somewhere locked deep inside. It wasn't strong enough to run over to Orestes, to hold him in his dying moments. The only thing that managed to escape to the surface was the tears softly rolling down her face. Desiree slowly raised her hand; a swirl of dark energy wrapped around her, and she was gone.

THE SIXTH AGE, 54th Year

> It shall come to pass in the coming days Omega will choose his people.

Your sons and daughters shall prophesy,
the old will dream dreams,
and your young men shall see visions.
~ The Book of Ta'Hor

CHAPTER 13
A COLD TRANSITION

The stone was cold to the touch. The moisture in the air clung to the surface of the stone floor. If not for the scent of dust and dirt, it was like the aroma of an old sea cave. Musk was the dominant scent. Stale air mixed with many other smells. The perfectly cut stone of the floor had worn with time and was uneven to the touch in many places.

Drips of water were heard in the hall. Sometimes, when the rain fell heavily outside, it worked its way down to the very depths of the mountain. The stone walls were always cold, though, no matter the temperature outside.

The sounds of a young man screaming echoed throughout the old hallways and could be heard in all corners of *The Order*. It was a relief when the screaming finally stopped. The silence left more unanswered questions for those who had listened to the screams. It was not a normal thing to behold, even in a place such as this.

The mystical seal across the stone doorway began to crack and break. Everyone held their breath as they waited for what would happen next. Stone dissolved into dust and dirt. All eyes looked into the room. Sotiris held a torch towards the archway. In the dim torchlight stood Zeph.

Zeph hung his head as he stepped forward. Lifting it, he revealed blood dripping from his nose, ears, and eyes. The sweat on his forehead had caused his hair to cling to his face. He looked as though he had just been in a horrible fight. Everyone took a step back at the sight of him. Everyone except Iggy, he was the first to step forward and offer aid. He reached out to Zeph, offering to heal him. Even though the gesture was kind in nature, Zeph quickly pulled away. Tears filled his eyes, and he shook his head. Holding onto his sleeve, Zeph wrapped his arm around himself as he momentarily leaned back against the wall.

Xa'an led the group as they walked slowly down the hall. Nothing was said as they walked. A short time later, they brought Zeph to a room and let him rest. A bath was drawn for him, and clothes were set aside. With that, everyone left the room and waited for him to come to them.

Zeph sat down on the bed. You would think a million thoughts were racing through his mind at a glance. He clung to his sleeve and gently rocked back and forth. The glazed expression on his face continued. There was something different about him now, though. The rocking stopped, and he took a moment to blink. He looked down at the clothes next to him. Reaching out, he was about to pick them up when he noticed the blood on his hands. The images rushed into his head again.

Slowly, he stood up and walked over to the large copper tub in the corner. Reaching down, he let his hand graze the water. It wasn't a particularly warm temperature, but it would do. Slowly, he removed all his clothing. Even though he had no physical injuries, he moved as though he did. Climbing into the tub, he let his body slip into the water. Reaching into the water, he began to cup it and pour it on his face. Running his fingers over his face, he felt the blood begin to wash off. Sliding back, he let his head slip under the water. The sound of nothing filled his ears. It was peaceful.

The story Xa'an had told him was nothing compared to the firsthand account he had just witnessed. Some of the details were similar, but all the little nuances no one else knew about stood out so vividly in his mind now. There was so much more to her story than history had ever recorded. He wondered if people would also have misconceptions about him one day after he was gone.

Getting out of the tub, Zeph quickly dried himself. Walking over to the bed, he put the clean clothing on. It was similar to what everyone else in *The Order* wore. Sitting again on the bed, he let his hands rest on the sheets. The long black sleeves of his cloak flowed over his hands. The connection between his body and mind seemed so frail at that moment. He remembered the things Gus had taught him out at the cliffs.

Zeph sat on the floor and crossed his legs. Placing his hands on his knees, palms facing up, he began to meditate. He let the pools of energy form in his hands. Opening his eyes, he allowed the energy to disperse. In his mind, he reached out to Iggy. He knew they had a mental connection because of their shared experience with the Omega Scroll.

Iggy sat in a room down the hall. The others were talking amongst themselves. Xa'an and Sotiris had begun to discuss the significance of Zeph having such a traumatic vision.

"The boy is meant for so much, this much is sure," Sotiris said, looking over at Xa'an.

"This is true," Xa'an replied, "I just wonder how this vision has affected him. In all my years here, I have never heard of someone bleeding due to a vision."

"Neither have I. Then again, if the vision was indeed what we believe it was, no one here has ever had a vision so brutal," Sotiris concluded.

Iggy listened to their conversation, but soon, his mind began to drift. Within the mix of his thoughts, something else was there. It wasn't as distinct as a voice, but it felt like Zeph was calling to him. He quickly stood up.

"Zeph is ready for us," he announced.

Everyone stopped what they were doing and looked at him. Breeze and Marcus shot odd glances at him, but Sotiris and Xa'an understood. They left the room and walked down the hall. Marcus was the first to enter. He slowly opened the door, and the rest followed. Zeph looked at everyone, but his eyes stopped on Iggy. They locked eyes as only brothers could. He simply nodded his approval that Iggy had heard his call.

Zeph stood and, in turn, offered his bed to everyone else. Even though he had cleaned himself up physically, there was still evidence of significant mental strain. He held onto his sleeve, his hand shaking slightly. Every time he opened his mouth, the words wouldn't come. Like a wave, his emotions began to wash over him. His lip began quivering, and the tears filled his eyes. Gasping, he tried to hold back the tears. Holding his hands together, he began to shake. Breeze was the first to take action. Quickly rising to her feet, she approached him with open arms. There was no resistance as Zeph let her embrace wrap around him.

Sotiris and Xa'an said they would give the four of them time to rest. Marcus, Breeze, and Iggy sat around Zeph, one on each side. He didn't open up or start telling them what he had seen; he just sat there enjoying their presence. The hours passed until the morning came. Zeph had finally regained his composure. He told them it was time to talk to Sotiris and get to the bottom of what he had seen.

They left the room and headed up the stairs. The Grand Hall was full of mages. Silence quickly fell upon the huge room upon Zeph's entrance. By this time, all in *The Order* knew who he was and what had transpired. Sotiris waved the group over from the far side of the grand hall.

Xa'an, Sotiris, and a handful of the elder mages stood there. They were all very interested in hearing Zeph's account of his vision. They left the hall and headed to a smaller meeting room. Inside was a large oval table. The walls were lined with torches, giving a bright atmosphere to the room.

Everyone took seats around the table. Without even trying, they divided themselves from one end to the other, with Zeph sitting at one end and Sotiris at the other. The table seated twelve, and every seat was filled. All eyes were on Zeph now. Little did he know that everything about to come from his mouth would contradict everything in their ancient records.

Standing, Zeph looked at everyone at the table. Taking a deep breath, he began. He intertwined his fingers and held them in place so no one would see how nervous he was.

"She was just a sweet, innocent girl who watched her family destroyed before her very eyes," Zeph said as he began to speak. "I was shown a vision of the person you know as Master Desiree." There was a stir amongst the elders present. Sotiris and Xa'an simply listened.

Zeph went on to speak of the entirety of the vision; the attack on her village as a child and how Desiree was forced to kill her own mother after she had turned into a fiend. Sotiris found it intriguing how Orestes had taken her in as his own. Zeph went on to talk about Desiree's struggles as she grew up. When he mentioned Mizimmah's first appearance to Desiree at age nine, there was a stir among the elders again, including Sotiris.

Xa'an stopped Zeph for a moment and pulled him close.

"What are you planning on saying about the Uriel?" Xa'an whispered cautiously.

"What do you mean?" asked Zeph, confused.

"We value the Uriel quite highly, particularly the one you speak of," he explained.

Zeph's look of confusion turned to frustration. He continued speaking to the room, telling them about Mizimmah's offer to train Desiree in secret. At this point, Zeph hadn't revealed anything negative about him, but it was coming.

"Are you sure this man you saw in the vision was indeed Mizimmah?" Sotiris questioned skeptically.

"Yes, I'm sure, I saw everything," Zeph replied sharply.

He continued his story, going into the details of Orestes and Desiree finding the scroll. As he described Desiree's experience with the scroll, Iggy and Marcus couldn't help but look at each other and see the similarities between the experiences. Xa'an listened intensely, hanging onto Zeph's every word. The involvement of Mizimmah in Desiree's life was very apparent in the story, and it caught people's attention. It was the small details, such as her not wanting power for herself, but rather, it was Mizimmah pushing her down that path.

The moment was coming; Zeph had just finished telling of Desiree's encounter with Orestes when she asked to see the scroll again.

"Mizimmah was the one who told her to take the scroll at all costs. He was the one that twisted her and put that lust for power in her."

Sotiris slammed his hand down on the table.

"How dare you!" he barked at Zeph. "I will not stand by and listen to you disgrace the Uriel, and certainly not one of the Shadow Uriel. *Chosen One* or not, how dare you make such accusations!"

All eyes were now on Zeph. Sotiris had come down on him pretty hard. The whole room had fallen deathly silent. Against all odds of what everyone thought Zeph would do, he did the opposite. He slammed his hand equally hard down on the table; a flash of energy from his palm spiked across the surface and scattered like sparks.

"She was young and innocent, and she was on the path to becoming a wonderful person until Mizimmah stepped in and turned her into a monster!" Zeph bellowed back across the table.

"You insolent child!" spat Sotiris as he quickly jumped from his seat, "I will not have you speak such slander here. Xa'an, remove him from *The Order*. Take him back to Appagon at once!"

Xa'an and the others stood. He quickly escorted them to their quarters to gather up their belongings. Before long, they had boarded one of the ships in the sea cave. Nothing was said as they disembarked. The turn of events had rapidly changed from what everyone had been expecting.

Zeph was quiet as they headed out. He sat near the front of the ship and looked out to sea. It was clear that he was still infuriated about the whole situation. He sat there with a cloak pulled around himself. It didn't matter that those in *The Order* had made him out to be a liar; he knew what he had seen, and he knew it was true. If Omega had meant for him to have that vision, then he knew it was imperative.

An hour or so passed by. No land was visible in sight. Zeph had sat in silence. In his hands were the scroll and the book of Ta'Hor. Slowly, he opened the book and searched the pages. His mind was heavy with all he had seen, and his heart was distressed by what had just transpired. Turning the pages, he let his fingers run down over the words.

'Beware of turning to evil, which you seem to prefer to suffering. Omega is exalted in his power. Who will show you the wonders He has in store for you? No power of this world can compare.'

He read the words over and over again, trying to let them sink in. How could he see the vision as a good thing? It was the most traumatic thing he had ever experienced. Following the page some more, he stopped at another passage.

And I saw Omega in my vision, and the words were spoken to me: 'I have bestowed strength on a warrior; I have exalted a young man from among the people. I have found My chosen servant; with My tears, I have anointed him. I will raise him up in the Seventh Age.'

Zeph felt a strength rise within himself as he read the words. These words were written over seven thousand years ago, yet they spoke to him like they had been written that day. Closing the book, he tucked it away and continued to look out to sea. The whole experience with Sotiris brought up some memories from his childhood. After his father had disappeared, Zeph was the only one who said he was still alive. No one believed him then, either.

Xa'an approached Zeph slowly as he walked up to the ship's bow. Zeph didn't turn or acknowledge his presence, but Xa'an knew he was aware of him. Taking a seat across from Zeph, he looked at the young man. This young man had just done something that no person had done in over a thousand years. He defied *The Order*'s beliefs and rulings. Something had stirred in Xa'an when he saw Zeph slam his hand on the table. The burst of energy had caught his attention. Only someone with true beliefs and convictions would have shown something like that.

Finally, Zeph turned his head and looked at Xa'an. The man's face was stricken. It was clear that something had very much changed within him. Turning, they sat facing each other now. It seemed as though Xa'an was trying to put the words together, but they wouldn't come out.

"I need you to tell me everything, Zeph," he said softly.

Zeph looked back at him for a moment. His voice showed genuine sincerity, and he knew that Xa'an actually wanted to hear him out and not simply dismiss what he had to say. So Zeph retold his account of the vision, right to the very brutal, bloody end.

Everyone else watched as the two of them continued to talk for a while. Marcus, Breeze, and Iggy sat together near the midsection. Two other mages had also joined them to navigate the ship on its journey. They watched Zeph speak. There was passion in his voice and body language as he spoke. It was something they had never seen before. Even when they had heard him speak at the graduation ceremony, he had not shown even a hint of the passion they were witnessing now.

"I truly do believe you, Zeph. I can't imagine why one of the Uriel would twist that girl in such a way. And I don't believe that act was part of Omega's plan for her. I want to help, to join you now but I can't. For the time being, I must return to *The Order*. I will plead the case again on your behalf. Perhaps in time, Sotiris will see reason," Xa'an said as he stood with Zeph.

The hours went by, and soon, land was once again visible on the horizon. They made their way for Tweedsmiur. Once they arrived, the ship quickly departed once again.

"Head north, up into the Appagon mountains. Make for the village of Sanctus Spire," said Xa'an as they left.

The group made their way up the catwalks and stairs of the pier until they reached the base of the village. They had come and gone in only a little over two days. For Zeph, it felt like it had been weeks since they had left.

It was getting late in the day, so it was time for dinner. They decided to head to the pub for some food. Along the way, they were sure they'd run into Okies. The streets were quieter than Zeph remembered. Everything seemed different to him now, like he had been wearing something in front of his eyes his whole life, and now it had been removed. Perhaps there was some truth to the expression about piercing the veil.

Entering the tavern, they took a seat at one of the tables. Not more than a second had gone by when a large man came rushing over to them. To the surprise of no one at the table, it was Okies.

"Oh, thank Omega!" he exclaimed, "I never thought I'd see the likes of ya again."

"It's good to see you too," Iggy said with a smile.

"Now, what's the trouble with the lad here?" Okies asked as he looked Zeph up and down. Everyone fell silent at the question. Okies instantly realized he had touched a sensitive topic. "Ya know what, 'tis none of me biz. I say, though, 'tis great to see the lot of you again." They ordered a large amount of food and drink, and they all ate and drank into the night. Zeph remained quiet for the most part, though, and Okies asked no further questions about the subject. He knew the time would come, and he waited with most eagerness.

The next morning came quickly. From the moment he jumped out of bed, Iggy was off to Okies' shop. He didn't want to pass up a chance to learn more about Alchemy before they left town once again. Breeze went with him at Marcus' request. It was clear that Marcus wanted some time to talk with Zeph alone. They hadn't had a chance to speak alone since everything had happened.

The two of them watched as Iggy and Breeze walked down the street. After that, they walked to the edge of the forest on the north side of town. It brought back feelings of their childhood together. Their mothers had always told them to be home by dinner, which only happened half the time. They would be off playing on the hills north of Daunt or down by the seashore. Those were good times, some of the best either could remember.

Reaching the edge of the forest, they stopped to talk. The conversation had been light on the walk, but now it was apparent that Marcus wanted some insight into everything that had been going on.

"I just want to know what you're going through," Marcus explained.

"What do you want me to say? I watched the most horrific thing I have ever witnessed in my life. It wasn't like it was just an image flashed in my mind, Marcus. I was standing there right next to her the whole time. It was as real as us standing next to each other right now," Zeph said as he struggled to control the swell of emotions rising inside.

In times like this, Zeph would start to break down, but it became increasingly apparent that he was fueling his frustrations into anger. Marcus wanted to get to the bottom of this.

"I know it all must have been so hard for you. And I just want you to know that I'm here for you. We're all here for you, bro."

"Thanks," Zeph said with almost a scoff in his voice. "You know what gets me; you know what really gets me?" Marcus could see the anger once again rising to the surface as Zeph spoke. "That Sotiris is too blind to see that one of his precious Uriel might actually be evil." Zeph began to pace. He ran his fingers through his hair and let out a shout in frustration. Marcus wasn't exactly sure what to say or do now.

"I just wish I could have done something; I wish I could have stopped Mizimmah." The anger was evident in Zeph's voice.

"It happened a thousand years ago, man; there's nothing you could have done."

Zeph let out a frustrated shout again and threw his hands out. A nearby tree exploded as a bolt of energy shot from Zeph's hands like lightning. Pieces of wood scattered everywhere as Marcus ducked for cover. Marcus looked over at Zeph; his palms were glowing. Looking down at his hands, Zeph aimed his palms toward the pieces of wood on the ground. Several of them began to shakily rise in the air. There was no control, though, and they quickly fell to the ground.

"Well, that's new," was all Marcus could come up with.

It was clear that Zeph was at ease now. His face showed a calmness that had not been there moments before. Turning to Marcus, Zeph offered him his hand. Marcus gripped it firmly and pulled Zeph into a hug.

"I guess there's still a lot I need to learn," Zeph said as he began to relax.

"That's my bro," said Marcus as he slapped Zeph on the back. They headed back into town. Soon, they would continue their journey once more. Looking to the north of the village, the mountains loomed above them. Before long, Zeph knew they would be at the top, and he couldn't wait for the experience.

THE WEEK HAD GONE BY quickly. While Zeph, Marcus, and Breeze had spent much of their time together, Iggy was always at Okies. They knew he was learning so much during his time there. His knowledge of alchemy would be a great asset in the coming journey. Besides what he was learning with Okies, he was also pushing his Light abilities, becoming stronger with them every day. If only their mother could see them now, how far they'd come in only the handful of weeks since they left. Zeph was sure that the visions were something she would not want to know about.

The trio of youths headed down the street towards the shop. It was early morning, and once again, Iggy had left at the crack of dawn. He had also spent the night with Okies out in the forest, gathering Luminous. They entered the shop and headed for the back. The man behind the desk just waved his hand at them; he was used to it by this point. Voices could be heard coming from the back room. Entering, they found Iggy and Okies tinkering away with the lab setup.

"Ah, Zeph, good to see you, lad," Okies exclaimed. Zeph truly loved Okies' exuberant nature. He was always so excited to see them.

"Hello, Okies. How are things going with you and Iggy?"

"Oh, things couldn't be better. He's a brilliant lad. I never thought someone could match me wits, but the way he experiments 'tis unbelievable."

Zeph walked around to the other side of the large table. Iggy had continued to focus on his work when the group had entered the backroom. It was his preoccupation that Zeph wanted to study further.

"Whatcha makin'?" Zeph asked in the most childish way he could.

Iggy shot a glance of annoyance over at his big brother, to which everyone just chuckled. He turned his attention back to his work.

On the table were a handful of vials with different colored liquids in them. Some were over lamps and boiling away. At the moment, Iggy was combining some herbs together. Near the end of the table were a handful of potions in a row. These were potions that Iggy had already finished. He had been spending much of his time making potions to take with them when they journeyed up the mountains.

Zeph picked one up; it was greenish in color. Removing the cork on the top, he was about to smell it. Quickly, Iggy reached over and snatched the vial out of Zeph's hand.

"Ah! I wouldn't smell that unless you want to be unconscious for the next several hours," Iggy said as he quickly replaced the cork and set it back on the table. Zeph simply raised his hands and backed away; everyone else smiled and laughed. Iggy stopped what he was doing and looked at everyone.

"Alright, I guess you want to know what I've been working on." Everyone nodded their agreement, even Okies. "I've learned much about all these different herbs and ingredients. So I set out to make more or less a 'super' version of some of the more common potions." He walked over to the row of vials on the table and picked up the first one. It had a reddish color to it. "This is more than a healing potion. It heals tissue, repairs bones, and increases blood production." The next one he grabbed was blue. "This is like a rejuvenation potion, but besides increasing mental strength, it also increases alertness, stamina, and endurance."

Everyone seemed very impressed. Iggy had taken what he had learned from Okies and used that knowledge to create more advanced versions. Next, he picked up the green one Zeph had just picked up.

"This one is a special creation of mine. Add a few drops to someone's drink or breathe it in, and they'll be unconscious for several hours," Iggy said proudly.

"I do greatly enjoy that one," Okies grinned. "Perfect for those nights when ya just can't get to sleep. I had made several potions like that before, but nothing as strong as what young Iggy has created," he added.

"My last one is what I've been working on most of the week," Iggy said as he walked over and took the large vial from where he was working. "I tried and failed many times to get it to finally turn out the way it did." The vial was full of clear liquid, even though it seemed like all the various tubes of colored liquid flowed into it. The liquid in it sparkled like it was full of light and silver flakes.

Iggy held the potion up proudly. Looking around the room, he gestured for Marcus to come over. With some reluctance, he finally did. Iggy offered him a small sip of it. Raising an eyebrow, he looked skeptically at Iggy. After several moments of convincing, Marcus reluctantly took a sip.

Everyone watched as Marcus became disorientated and took a step back. The effects of the potion instantly took effect. His hands shook for a moment, and then he breathed deeply. The feeling was so intense; he felt amazing. Throwing his hands upwards, he made coiled strands of fire shoot from them. Swinging his arms around, he noticed his reflexes were incredibly fast. Unnoticed by Marcus, Iggy had picked up a small knife and was standing behind him. Without warning, Iggy sliced down Marcus' arm. He cried out in pain and turned around quickly.

"What the heck, Iggy!" Marcus blurted out.

Before anyone else could react, Iggy pointed to the wound on Marcus' arm. Everyone watched in amazement as the blood pulled back into the wound, and it closed within seconds.

"This is my crowning achievement, the Invincibility Potion," Iggy said proudly.

Okies' jaw had dropped, and he stood there in shock, eyes wide. Everyone was also stunned, but they had become accustomed to all things strange and surprising.

"That is truly amazing, lad!" Okies exclaimed. "I can't believe how much ya've learned in the last several weeks."

"Well, I couldn't have done it without you, Okies. I've wanted to learn Alchemy for so long, and as soon as I had the chance, I put everything I could into it."

"Oh, that much is evident, lad," Okies said as he patted Iggy on the back.

"I have something for you," Iggy said as he walked over to the corner and grabbed a stack of papers. He handed them to Okies.

Okies looked over the papers, his eyes darted back to Iggy.

"Oh, I can't take these, lad! These were your creations."

"I used a lot of your most expensive ingredients in the mixtures. Ones I know you cannot easily replace. You deserve to share in this. And I wouldn't have even been able to create this if it wasn't for all your instruction and teaching. We're heading out today, and I want you to have it. I've made copies of all my notes as well. Continue, and make more of it."

"Thank ya, young Iggy. And thank ya all. You have brought somethin' truly special into me life these last few weeks. I can't even describe it properly; let's just call it hope," he said as he embraced them all.

It was time for them to gather their belongings. They gathered up the remaining sphere lamps and the coins they had stored at Okies. Traveling with such a large amount of gold wasn't the best idea, but they had no other choice. Each carried a sack of more than two hundred gold kessas. The journey to Sanctus Spire could take at least a few days, depending on the conditions in the mountain pass. They quickly stopped by the shops on the way out, buying bread, dried meats, and other foods they could easily transport.

The last place they had to stop was the expedition shop leading out of the north side of town. Cold temperatures would come into play as they journeyed up the mountain, and they needed to have the necessary protection. Reaching the shop, they entered it and looked around. It was small, about half the size of Okies shop. There were a variety of heavy cloaks and other garments to protect against the cold. Each of them bought a heavy fur cloak, as well as some gloves and scarves made from the fur of the mountain wolves. This was something that was commonly worn by the people in Sanctus Spire.

"Do ya have a compass?" the man behind the counter asked.

It had been a while since Zeph had thought about his father's compass. He felt inside his pack and was relieved to find it was still with him.

"Uh, yes, I do. Why do you ask?" Zeph questioned the shopkeeper.

"Well, if ya get caught in a snowstorm up there, 'tis very easy to lose which direction ya're headin'," the shopkeeper replied.

Zeph pulled his father's compass out of his pack and showed it to the shopkeeper.

"Wow, now this be a fine compass indeed, one of the finest I have ever seen."

"Thank you," Zeph replied as he replaced the compass in his pack.

Once they were sure they had everything they needed, the group set out. The cloaks were heavy and warm, but they knew they would need them once they got higher up into the mountains. For the time being, they just wore them tied behind their backs. Everything else was in the bags on their waist or sacks on their backs.

After leaving town, they passed through a small forest clearing and an open field. The field stretched out and quickly sloped upwards. The mountains loomed above them. They had seen these mountains on the horizon their whole lives, but they never dreamed they would be climbing them one day.

Zeph took the lead, and they continued forward. A wide, worn path led from Tweedsmiur up the mountainside. For the first little while, it was an easy trek. After several hours, the slope of the mountain became evident. They felt the incline taking shape with each step up the dirt path and stopped for a few minutes to rest. Tweedsmiur was far below them now, but they could still see the village from their perspective.

"Well, this is a bit more than I was expecting," Marcus said as he sat on the grass.

"Yeah, who could have known climbing a mountain would be so hard," Zeph said sarcastically.

"So what's the plan now anyways?" Iggy piped up.

"I guess that's a good question," Zeph said, "The only thing we know for sure is what Saphar told us in the book, that something bad is going to happen, and that I need to find the other six *Chosen Ones* to stop it."

"Oh, and let's not forget that someone or something is seeking you out to try and kill you," Marcus added.

"Yeah, I guess that's true too," Zeph replied as he remembered Saphar's words in the book.

"Then perhaps Sanctus Spire is just where we need to be. There are warriors there; maybe we can train and learn from some of them," Breeze suggested.

"Mhm, good point, Breeze," Zeph said as they all stood and continued the climb.

The dirt path became rocky as they continued upwards. The temperature also began to drop the higher they got. Journeying up into the rock was more complicated than they had imagined. Because they had all lived in a town by the seashore, climbing mountains had never happened.

Nightfall was coming fast, and they knew that they would have to make camp soon. A small outcrop in the mountain was visible up ahead. This would provide a place for them to sleep for the night. Marcus quickly made up a fire as Breeze and Iggy prepared some food. Zeph had returned to the path and looked up the mountain again.

Surveying their path, he saw that it led to a huge snowy pass farther up the mountain. The temperature had become colder but wasn't freezing yet, similar to a fresh, cool morning in the growing season. Zeph knew, however, that they were in for much colder temperatures the following day.

The sound of a lone wolf howling echoed in the distance. Light from the moons bathed the side of the mountain. The four of them sat around the fire. Thoughts of those they left back in Daunt filled their minds. From their vantage point, they could just barely see Daunt far off in the distance. It was just a few flickering lights at the far corner of the island, but they knew it was Daunt. The realization of how small Appagon really was had finally set in as they gazed out over the island's southeastern part.

Each made their bedding and headed off to sleep; they would need their energy for the climb tomorrow. They all huddled close to each other around the small fire.

The morning hit them quickly. Cold wasn't the right word for what they were experiencing. Marcus awoke to the sensation of frost on his cheeks and eyebrows.

"Ah, what the heck is this?" said Marcus as he brushed his face off. Everyone else did the same. Looking around, they were surprised to see a film of white over everything. Since none of them had ever seen snow before, it was a fascinating thing to behold. The morning suns shone over the fields and made the frost on the ground sparkle.

"You think this is snow?" Breeze asked as she shook her cloak off.

"Um, I don't think so. I think it's just some kind of frozen dew," Zeph replied.

"Well, whatever the heck it is, it's cold!" Marcus exclaimed as he shivered and wrapped his cloak tight around himself.

They made a quick breakfast for themselves and headed out once again. A few hours went by before they began to encounter snow. It was cold, wet, and white. Iggy was the first to realize its unique properties. He quickly made a ball out of it and whipped it as Zeph. Startled, Zeph promptly looked around. He realized what had happened when he saw Iggy laughing. With that, everyone took cover and began whipping snowballs at each other. Maybe snow was going to be more fun than they thought.

The day continued. The warm suns shone down on them, a pleasant blessing. The air was still cold, but the warmth of the suns took the edge off it. This was short-lived, as a storm front began to move in over the mountains from the east. The light from the suns faded away, and a cold wind picked up.

Zeph pulled the compass out of his bag. Opening the top, he quickly got his bearings to ensure he knew their direction. Turning it over, he popped open the bottom. He pressed each of the buttons on the side. With each one, the symbols on one of the three needles lit up. It wasn't until he pushed the third one that something caught his eye. The needle lit up and immediately moved and pointed in a direction.

Zeph quickly motioned for them to stop. The needle was pointing off to the left. There was some sort of movement in the trees. It was then that they saw a black figure moving through the trees. A deep, low growl came from the creature. Zeph looked down at the compass. The needle tracked the movements of the creature. Quickly drawing their weapons, the group took a defensive stance. The creature snapped and growled, eyes glowing red. It wasn't that much bigger than an average wolf, but this was no wolf. It was quite clear that this was a fiend of some kind. Nothing like what they had encountered back in the Forest of Light, but a problem nonetheless.

Just as they were about to attack, they heard the sound of something else running through the forest off to the right. Zeph's eyes quickly darted in that direction. He saw nothing at first but then spotted the white figure running through the trees and snow. It leaped into the air and came crashing down on the fiend. There was a commotion of growling and snapping at each other. As quickly as it started, there was a loud yelp from the fiend, and it dropped to the ground before rapidly dissolving away.

The second beast turned to face them. Unlike the fiend, which was dark and menacing, this creature was the exact opposite. It was a magnificent creature. It was white with black spots and had soft, glowing blue eyes. It walked over to them slowly. Everyone else backed away, but Iggy stepped forward towards it. It was easily three times the size of the Iggy. Reaching out, Iggy gently touched the creature on the head. Everyone was stunned as they watched the small boy touch this fearsome creature. It stayed for a moment and then darted into the forest again.

"What the heck was that?!" Marcus exclaimed.

"I think that was an elemental creature," Iggy replied.

"A what?" Zeph questioned.

"Okay, seriously, did you ever read your textbooks, Zeph?" Iggy remarked. "An elemental creature has elemental ties just like people do; they are connected to one of the seven elements," Iggy explained. "I think that was a snow leopard, one of the Beasts of Light. That might be why it let me touch it."

"I think the real question here is how you knew something was coming, Zeph? We didn't even spot the fiend until it came out of the trees," Breeze inquired.

Zeph looked down at the compass in his hand. Perhaps his father had intended for the compass to be passed onto him for just such an occasion. If they hadn't known about the fiend, it could have easily attacked and killed at least one of them.

"It was my father's compass. Those needles on the bottom—I didn't know what they meant; well, I know now that one of them points towards fiends," Zeph said, holding the compass out for everyone to see. The needles slowly spun in place, and they assumed it meant no other fiends were nearby.

A blast of wind drew everyone's attention back toward the top of the mountain. The storm was slowly growing above them now, and soon would be heading down the mountain pass. Zeph suggested they get moving quickly. The group still wasn't sure how much farther they had to go until they reached Sanctus Spire, but they assumed there was still a reasonable distance to cover.

They push slowly but steadily up the mountain pass. Snow piled around their feet as they trudged forward. The fur cloaks proved very effective, but with the coming storm, there was a sense of urgency amongst them. Snow began falling heavily, and the wind blew hard down the mountain. They had never experienced temperatures like this before. Marcus was the one to take point. Holding his hand out, he placed a thin flame shield before them. This, in turn, protected them from some of the blisteringly cold wind. As the hours ticked by and the mountain grew darker, his strength slowly failed.

Reaching the top of the pass, they knew the village couldn't be much farther now. Visibility had drastically dropped over the last hour. Wave after wave of snow came down. They did the best they could, wrapping the cloaks around themselves. Gloves were on, and scarves wrapped around their faces, but it was becoming just too much for them. Each tried to use their abilities the best they could. Marcus placed a fire shield, Iggy tried to light their way, and Breeze attempted to part the wind around them.

It was dark now, and they had been braving the storm for hours. Ice and snow clung to their cloaks and any exposed clothing. Zeph continued to pull them forward. Several times, Iggy had collapsed in the snow. Zeph used his abilities to give him some energy, but even he was beginning to fail. They held onto each other as they pressed on. The snow was up to their waists. Zeph searched the darkness ahead, trying to see some sign of the village. They couldn't have gotten lost, could they?

In the darkness, there was a faint glow. Zeph pushed forward, trying to reach it. It seemed to almost be calling to him. As it grew closer, he made out the form of an animal. It looked like the snow leopard they had encountered farther down the mountain. Amongst the raging blackness of the storm, it was glowing in the darkness. Zeph almost wanted to cry as he saw it. It waited for him as he continued to follow it up the mountain, the rest of the group in tow. Soon, Zeph began to see what looked like torches up ahead. Zeph took one last look at the leopard, and then it ran off and disappeared into the storm.

"I see it! Just up ahead; we're almost there!"

Zeph pulled everyone along. They had all huddled behind him, trying to stay warm and not become separated. Following the light of the torches, they soon came upon an inn. Bursting through the door, the four stumbled in and collapsed on the floor. The innkeeper looked at them slightly wide-eyed from behind the counter. It wasn't that uncommon to have visitors at all times of day or night, but to see four snow-covered teenagers was something new. He quickly came over and helped them up.

Digging into his bag, Zeph placed a handful of gold kessas on the counter. He had no idea how much the rooms cost, but he knew that would cover it. The innkeeper took the money gratefully and helped them all to their room. He gave them a large suite at the back of the inn. It had four beds and a large fireplace against the central wall. As they removed their ice and snow-covered cloaks, the innkeeper started a roaring fire for them. Zeph thanked the man for everything, and they headed off to bed. Nothing was said between them; they were all exhausted and quickly fell asleep.

The next morning, a loud pop from the fire stirred Zeph awake. He lethargically opened his eyes to see Marcus crouched over the fire. Slowly glancing around the room, he saw that Breeze and Iggy were still asleep in their beds. The bed was exceptionally soft and comfortable, the blankets fur, and the mattress feathered. The light coming through the window suggested that it was morning and the storm had passed.

Slowly, Zeph sat up in bed. Marcus tossed him some clothes. They had been hanging near the fire to dry for the night. Getting dressed, Zeph walked over and joined Marcus. He could see Marcus playing with the fire. It was common for people with fire abilities to not even be affected by fire. This meant that they could touch and hold fire freely without getting burnt. Zeph knew that Marcus had never been burnt his whole life. He wondered what that must be like as he watched Marcus freely move his hand through the flames.

"Some night, huh," Zeph said in a soft tone so as to not wake the others.

"Oh, you're telling me. I didn't think we were going to make it for a while there. I have never been so cold in my life," he replied.

"Think we should go check out this village?"

"Oh, you bet; we have a whole new market here after all," Marcus said with a hint of excitement in his voice.

They woke Iggy and Breeze and quickly gathered up their belongings. The fire had dried everything that had been frozen from the night before. After getting dressed, they grabbed a sack of sphere lamps. Finding out who was in charge was their first task. They were sure the innkeeper could point them in the right direction.

Locking the room, they headed for the front of the inn. It was the same innkeeper as the night before. He took one look at Zeph and chuckled. "I thought the frost had done that to your hair, but I guess I was wrong." Zeph smiled at the innkeeper's playful jest.

"Nope, always been like this. Could you direct us to whoever is in charge of the village?" Zeph asked.

"Oh, you bet. I'm guessing this is your first time here? You're looking for Korak. He lives in the large house towards the north end of town; you can't miss it."

"Thank you," Zeph replied, "I hope we gave you enough for the room."

"Oh, much more than enough; you could stay here for a week on what you gave me."

"Depending on how things go, that's a realistic possibility."

With the quick exchange, they headed out. The suns seemed extra bright as they stepped outside into the cold mountain air. The white snow that lay all around them seemed to intensify the brightness of the light. It wasn't just that, though, as they quickly noticed. Even the trees, including the leaves on their branches, were white.

Sanctus Spire was at the very top of the mountain. The village sat in a small crater-like depression at the summit. Rows of houses went straight north up the village. Homes and shops were built side by side, and there was only one main road that led up through town. The style of the houses was that of large log cabins. Snow covered everything in the village all year long. It wasn't a substantial village, no more than a few hundred people.

They stood outside the inn and breathed in the fresh, cold air. It was cold, but they were becoming accustomed to it. One thing they realized was that they would need better boots. Other than their cloaks, gloves, and scarves for extra warmth, they still wore the regular boots they had left Daunt with. Nevertheless, they began to truck through the snow, making their way north through town.

The very first thing they noticed was the color of the wood. All the buildings in the town looked almost translucent, as though they were made of some sort of fogged glass rather than wood. It was clear that the insides had been painted so anyone couldn't simply look inside someone's house. Zeph understood why it was hard for someone to find the village in a snowstorm.

They made their way through town. The smell of meat was in the air, making everyone salivate. They decided to stop to eat before they headed to Korak's house. Food seemed to be a way of life in the village. There were a handful of shops making food. As the villagers left their homes, they could be seen heading to one of them.

Heading over to the closest one, they ordered some food. The cook was a rather large man, and he greeted them happily. Travelers in their town meant more trade and more coin. The smell of the meat cooking completely filled their nostrils. Each ordered a large piece of roasted meat. It was served to them within minutes, and they quickly began to chow down. It wasn't until they started eating that they realized how truly hungry they had become. Because of the storm, they hadn't been able to eat very much along the way.

Marcus was the first to notice the meat's unique taste. He couldn't place his finger on it, so he turned to the cook.

"What kind of meat is this exactly?" he asked.

"Oh, that is some of my finest wolf; I killed it just yesterday," the cook replied.

Marcus stopped chewing for a second and looked down at the piece of meat. There was an awkward pause, and then he simply shrugged and continued eating. Everyone laughed at that. After they finished eating, they asked the cook if he knew which house was Korak's. Leaning out his shop window, he pointed to the large house just a ways down with a statue atop the roof.

Pushing through the snow was harder than they had expected. Their legs were still quite worn out from the trek up the mountain. The snow in town varied from ankle to knee-deep in places. Before long, it would become compacted from the villagers' foot traffic.

Reaching the front of the house, they climbed the steps to the front door. They quickly looked at each other and ensured they weren't too disheveled. Zeph grabbed the large metal ring and knocked hard on the front door. A moment later, the door swung open, revealing an exceptionally large man.

The man stood several heads taller than any of them. He had a large, bushy beard and massive forearms. There were many similarities to Siah; they could have easily been brothers. There was a pause as he looked down at the four youths at his doorstep. It was obvious to him that they were not from his village or Tweedsmiur. The very fact that they had made the trip to the village intrigued him.

"Good morning, young'ens, and what can I do for you?" he asked in a commanding voice.

"Morning to you, sir," Zeph said, "We've come from the village of Daunt. We're adventurers of sorts, and we have items to trade."

"All the way from Daunt, you say," he said with more intrigue in his voice. "Well, come in then, and let's see what you have to offer."

Everyone entered the house and stood in the front hall. They quickly realized that not only the buildings themselves but everything inside them was transparent. The furniture looked as though it was made of ice, and even though it was cold to the touch, it was clear that it was not ice.

Korak offered them a seat around a small meeting table. Furs were draped over the chairs and throughout the house. As they took their seats, they all introduced themselves.

"My name is Korak, chief of the village," said Korak as he extended his hand to all of them. Zeph made his usual sales pitch to the man, asking questions revolving around their dependence on oil lamps or candles. As usual, there was a need for a better system. At this point, Zeph removed a sphere lamp from his bag and handed it to Korak.

Holding it in his hand, he was mesmerized by it. The reaction was nothing new to them, though, as they had seen it on the face of every person who had gazed upon a Sphere Lamp. The lamp, which usually filled Zeph's palm, looked like only a small ball in Korak's massive hands.

"This is truly a brilliant creation you have here. I'll take twenty personally," he said, looking over at Zeph. That was the response they had wanted to hear.

"How do you think the rest of the village will respond to them?" Zeph questioned.

"Oh, I'm sure equally as well," Korak replied.

"We require new clothes and weapons; perhaps we can do some straight-up exchanging?"

"Oh, without a doubt, I know several of the weapon makers will jump at the chance to trade with you."

"Perfect," Zeph said with a grin on his face. They quickly exchanged the lamps for the coins. They were slightly surprised that Korak had eighty gold kessas just sitting around his house. Then again, they all had several hundred in their sacks, not that anyone else needed to know that.

They were just about to head out when Korak stopped them. He took Zeph aside for a moment, and everyone else became uneasy at this sudden change. Zeph waved them off and followed Korak to another room of the house. He turned and looked at Zeph; it seemed as though he was sizing him up.

"You're more than what you seem to be, aren't you?" Korak asked and pointed at Zeph's hands. It was easy for Zeph to forget that he bore his Omega symbols on his hands as well as his forehead. Zeph covered them up quickly. "Oh, you have nothing to fear from me," said Korak gently. "However, our whole meeting brought something to mind. Outside the village to the northwest, there is an old Master. He is a great warrior, that much is clear, and if he had been living in the village, he would have most likely been made chief over me based solely on that alone. Perhaps that is why he chooses to live outside Sanctus Spire. That aside, he came to me several weeks ago with a message."

Zeph paused and held his breath. The alignment had been several weeks ago, and that was also when he had opened the Omega Scroll.

"He told me this simple message, 'When the boy comes who brings the light, send him to me.'"

Silence hung in the air. Zeph was starting to get frustrated with everyone around him knowing more about his life than he did. Like everything else that had happened, this couldn't be ignored, not while they were seeking out the other *Chosen Ones*.

Korak quickly gave them directions to the old Master's house, and they departed. When the group asked him where they were heading, Zeph simply shook his head, "We're going to see someone who probably knows a lot more about me than I do." His frustration, mixed with sarcasm, was evident in his voice.

They made their way up the snowy path away from the village. The fresh snow made the path hard to make out, but it seemed they were headed in the right direction. The suns shone down on everything around them, causing them to squint as they walked through the bright snow. It wasn't long before they noticed a path leading through the trees to their left. As they headed down the path, seeing the white trees all around them was bizarre. If not for their shadows, they would have nothing but a flowing sea of white all around them.

Zeph walked over to one of the trees and ran his hand over it. The bark wasn't rough as expected, but instead, it was smooth to the touch, like ice. Even though the trees were clearly still wood, they almost appeared to be formed of white crystal. Perhaps the trees simply grew this way in the cold mountain climate. Looking up at the branches of the trees, Zeph noticed that some of the leaves had turned from the milky white of the trunks to the almost crystal-clear look of the buildings in the village. One of the leaves fell off the high branches and quickly dropped to the ground. Stooping down for a closer look, Zeph picked it up. It looked like a regular leaf but was almost as clear as glass. He tried to bend it but found that it was incredibly resilient, further adding to the sensation that he was holding a glass leaf. He would have to ask Korak about the trees when they returned to the village.

They continued through the forest for a short while. Small talk bounced around the group as they walked. It was exciting to be in such a different place. Only a handful of weeks earlier, they had been in Daunt preparing for the alignment festival.

Soon, they reached a clearing in the forest. There, they saw a house. It was different than the houses back in the village. For starters, it appeared constructed with translucent and dark brown wood. A swept stone path led up to the front steps. They found it curious how the path was cleaned with all the snow around. A large deck wrapped around the whole outside of the house. There was wood paneling running around the outer walls of the entire house. No visible windows or doors could be seen, but based on the look of the house, the wall panels could slide and open up.

The roof had dark-colored shingles, which appeared to be made of clay. Overall, it was a very unique house.

An old man stood on the front deck watching them. He wore white robes that were tightly wrapped and bound in place. It was similar to the robes and cloak Xa'an wore, just white.

"Hello, young man, I've been waiting for you," the old man said as they approached the front steps. Zeph raised an eyebrow, but it was becoming too familiar for him to worry anymore. The man had his hands behind his back and bowed to Zeph as they approached him. Zeph bowed in return.

Marcus leaned towards Iggy and whispered, "A gold kessa if this guy had a vision of Zeph."

"You're on," Iggy whispered back.

"My name is Sensei, and you are Zeph. You're an extraordinary young man, and I'm privileged to meet you." After a quick series of introductions, the attention was turned back to Zeph.

"How do you know who I am?" Zeph questioned.

"Several weeks ago, I was watching the alignment from the outskirts of the village. As I looked down to the southeast coast, a flash of light came from near Daunt, and I received a vision." Iggy discreetly handed Marcus the coin. The two of them chuckled, and Breeze smacked them both on the back of their heads.

Sensei continued, "In the vision, I saw you standing here, exactly how you appear now. I was instructed to train you and your companions up to be warriors," he explained.

Marcus scoffed at the notion that they needed to be trained. Sensei glanced past Zeph and looked Marcus up and down. He waved Marcus over. They stood at almost the same height. Sensei looked very old, perhaps even older than Mr. Yad or Praotes.

"Perhaps you would care to have a quick spar with me, Marcus?" Sensei asked as he gestured to the clearing beside the house. Again, Marcus scoffed at the notion that a man at least five times his age could best him. They walked over to the clearing and took up stances; the rest of the group watched from the deck.

Sensei quickly rushed towards Marcus, catching him completely off guard. He moved amazingly fast for someone his age. Before Marcus could even reach Sensei with his first punch, the old man delivered several fast, hard punches to Marcus' chest and swept his leg across the ground, knocking Marcus down. The rest of them couldn't help but smile from the deck as they watched Marcus fall into the snow.

Marcus jumped to his feet and decided to take the fight to the next level. He was tired of playing it safe. Thrusting his hand out, he sent a blast of flames at Sensei. It didn't faze him in the slightest. Quickly waving his hand, Sensei wrapped the flames in a protection field and hurled them to the ground. The mastery of his Light abilities was a fantastic sight to behold. Making a series of motions with his hands, Sensei thrust both hands forward and aimed his palms at Marcus. A wave of brilliant white light shot from his palms. It hit Marcus hard, sending him flying to the far side of the clearing.

Sensei walked over to Marcus, who was groaning in the snow. He extended his hand to him. Reaching up, Marcus took it humbly.

"Are you ready to learn what it means to be a real warrior?" Sensei asked with a grin on his old face. Marcus slowly nodded, then smiled back. They joined Zeph, Iggy, and Breeze on the deck. This would be the start of the most intense training they would ever experience.

DAY 142

It is misguided to believe that men succeed through strength;
more often, they succeed through failure.

Advice, direction, and preparation could never have taught them without the experience of failure.

~ Sensei

CHAPTER 14
THE WARRIOR PATH

The following week passed by quickly. Much of it had been spent at Sensei's house. Each morning, they journeyed back through the forest to the house, returning to the village in the evening. The sphere lamps had been a great success once again. Every person in the village now owned at least one. For some exchanges, they traded services with the merchants. New clothing had been the first thing on their list. They all had brand-new mountain attire.

The mystery of the trees had also been solved. The trees up on the mountain were all white but were just as normal as any other tree. However, they had an interesting property once they died. Once a tree was cut down, it was quickly cut into whatever was needed. The urgency was because once the wood fully dried and hardened, it would turn transparent like glass and become as strong and durable as steel. Even weapons such as swords, spears, and arrows were made from the wood of the trees.

The swordsmiths in Sanctus Spire did not slave over a hot pit of coals and slam a hammer down on an anvil. A more accurate comparison would be that they were master carpenters and craftsmen. Within several hours, they would carve a perfect sword out of the wood and hang it outside, allowing the wood to dry fully. It was an interesting process to watch as the hanging weapons transformed from solid white to almost crystal clear in a matter of days. The drying process was considerably accelerated compared to how most wood traditionally dried. It was a meticulous process because adjustments could no longer be made once the wood was fully air-dried. The extra bits of wood were cut into small chips and pellets. When thrown into fires, they acted much in the same way as charcoal. They would heat up and retain their heat for hours, even after the fire died. Over time, they would eventually burn up and turn to ash after many uses.

Light from the midday suns shone down in the forest clearing by Master Sensei's house. Gentle snow drifted down from the trees. Bird songs could be heard, and the air was calm. The group of five sat in a circle in the clearing next to the house. It was time for meditation. Zeph had become accustomed to this because of his time with Gus, but meditation with Sensei was on a completely different level.

Over the last week, Zeph's appearance had changed somewhat. He had cut his hair, for starters. It wasn't overly short but it was more clean-cut and less shaggy than it usually was. They had all changed their clothing and now wore simple robes like Sensei. Of course, they still had all their newly purchased fur clothing for the cold nights. The robes they wore were dark blue with white underneath. Marcus had completely shaved his head, which he had done from time to time in his life. Breeze had kept her hair long, just the way she liked it, and had it in a tight braid that hung down the back of her robe. Iggy always seemed to have the hood of his cloak up over his head, only revealing his face.

Meditation was something Sensei took very seriously. He said it was not only a way to find oneself but also brought a person closer to Omega and, by doing so, a greater understanding of their Element. There was no temple in Sanctus Spire, but the teachings of Ta'Hor were present and embraced by most. Sensei had been very pleased to see that Zeph carried a copy of the Book of Ta'Hor with him at all times.

Sensei stood, and everyone followed. His features told the story of a man who had lived through many years and many battles. The short white beard accented Sensei's bald head. There was a look of wisdom about him, and he carried it well. Age was only a state of mind to him, and though his body showed great age, he still moved with the grace of youth. Perhaps it was because he was a Light elemental, or maybe it was from the years of mediation.

He instructed them to take up specific poses, a common daily exercise. He would walk around and observe their technique. Along with these exercises, he would teach them principles to live by.

“A gem cannot be polished without friction, nor can a person’s true perfection shine through without trials,” he said slowly as he walked around them. It reminded Zeph of the sayings Jarian would say.

“Sensei, when will we begin to learn skills to fight with?” Zeph asked as he tried to hold the pose that was required.

“When I see that you are ready, Zeph, and that time has yet to come.”

That was not the answer Zeph was looking for. He had tried to be patient over the last week, but it was starting to wear on him. They had done nothing but meditate, learn different standing poses, and listen to Sensei spout proverbs. The frustrations that had filled his heart and mind from *The Order* were still present within Zeph. They had mixed with his memories from the past and brought about a great deal of inner turmoil. He had kept it hidden, but it was starting to bubble to the surface.

“I’m ready; we’re all ready,” Zeph said as he stopped holding the pose and gestured to everyone else. They all looked over at him but continued to hold their pose.

“Are you ready to let go of your anger, Zeph?” Sensei asked, looking him dead in the eye.

The question caught Zeph slightly off guard. He had tried to cover his reaction, but it wasn’t effective.

“I just want to learn how to fight for myself!” Zeph blurted out.

“I can see we can’t proceed further until you’ve dealt with your feelings. Very well.”

Sensei walked over to the nearby weapons rack. Removing two long staffs, he walked back and tossed one to Zeph. The others backed out of the way and stood by the circle’s edge.

Sensei stood across from Zeph, one hand holding his staff firmly planted on the ground. Zeph held his staff horizontally, gripping it with both hands. The staffs were made from the wood of the mountain trees. This also meant that they were extremely strong, just as strong as staffs made of metal.

“Well, I’ll make this simple for you, Zeph,” said Sensei as he raised a single finger on his hand. “You only have to hit me once. If you do, I will grant you permission to start your combat training.”

Marcus looked at Zeph, their eyes caught for a moment. He shook his head 'no' to Zeph; he shouldn't be doing this. Ignoring it, Zeph stepped forward. Sensei kicked the bottom of his staff, quickly flinging the end upwards. It caught Zeph's staff in the middle, causing him to lose his grip and sending it flying upwards into the air. Zeph's gaze followed the staff upwards. As Zeph looked up, Sensei quickly thrust his staff forward and caught Zeph hard in the ribs. Zeph cried out and crumbled to the ground; his staff fell to the ground next to him.

Zeph stood up slowly, using his staff for support. Getting a firm grip on the staff, he lunged at Sensei. After several quick attempts, Sensei sent a hard blow to Zeph's staff, pushing him back.

"What's wrong, Zeph?" The question had almost a mocking tone. "You want to fight, but you put no heart into it?"

Zeph again tightened his grip on his stain and clenched his jaw as he stared Sensei down. Quickly spinning, Zeph let the staff slide through his fingers. This was an attempt to catch Sensei's feet and throw him off balance. Easily anticipating this move on Zeph's part, Sensei kicked his feet off the ground, almost twisting his body completely horizontally. He lunged with his staff toward Zeph. The end of the staff connected hard with Zeph's chest. He cried out in pain and gasped for air as he fell back in the snow.

Sensei looked down at him mercilessly. There was not a look of anger on his face, but fierce determination.

"Fight me, boy!" he barked down at Zeph. Marcus and Iggy exchanged worried glances with each other. Both of them knew from their weeks of training that Zeph was no match for Sensei, but how far would he push before claiming defeat?

The anger began to flow to the surface now; it flashed across Zeph's face. Kneeling in the snow, he gripped his staff and lunged forward with it. Energy crackled over the surface of the staff and burst from the end as a blast of energy. Quickly placing his staff vertically in front of him, Sensei formed a protection field. Zeph's wave of energy hit it, pushing him back slightly. He smiled at Zeph, but it was more of a malicious smile.

"Good!" Sensei spouted across the clearing. "I'm going to hit you now, Zeph; stop me if you can," he demanded as their gaze locked. Everyone else just stood silently and continued to watch. They began to fear what the outcome of the fight would be. Over the last week, they had seen a gentle old man spend his time training them. There seemed to be a different man standing before them now who was neither weak nor frail; he commanded strength and even fear.

Lunging at Zeph, he took several quick swings with his staff. It was much faster than Zeph had anticipated. He tried to block them to the best of his abilities.

CRACK! The sound echoed through the trees. Breeze quickly gasped and covered her mouth. Zeph's head spun to the side as his nose shattered. The blood sprayed onto the clean white snow. Just as Zeph thought he might black out, he suddenly felt the pain disappear as his nose instantly set and healed itself. Zeph's eyes quickly darted to Iggy, and he pointed back at Sensei. The old Master's palm was glowing brightly.

"You're not going down that easy, boy!" The old man's face was almost angry now. "This is what you wanted, isn't it?" he scoffed. "To fight someone? I'm right here. Hit ME!"

Zeph ran full speed at him. Their staffs crossed violently, sending loud echoes throughout the forest. The rest of the group watched in silence. They had never seen Zeph act this way before. The fight continued on as blow after blow echoed in the trees. It was clear that Zeph's abilities were manifesting once again as he seemed to get faster and faster. The speed of his blows was almost a blur. Sensei didn't seem to be at a disadvantage, though; he continued moving equally fast and matched blow for blow with Zeph. Loud cracks of the wood colliding were still echoing through the forest. Anger was fueling Zeph, and hate was burning in his eyes.

With every swing of Zeph's staff, bursts of energy could be seen like the sparks from a blacksmith's hammer falling on hot metal. There was no control, just intense bursts of energy. Sensei was easily blocking these attacks, and he also seemed to absorb or disperse the energy from each blow. The time was coming for the fight to end, and he needed to inflict significant pain on Zeph to finally stop the building rage.

Sensei flung the end of his staff forward with full force, slipping between Zeph's attempts to block and connecting hard with his ribs. Those watching grimaced as the sound of bones snapping was drowned out only by the gargling cry as Zeph coughed up blood onto the snow. He could feel that the rib had punctured his lung.

Breeze was about to call out, but Sensei raised a hand to her. For a moment, his expression shifted to a gentle kindness as he looked from Zeph to her. She didn't know what to do, but something told her that the situation was still within the old Master's control.

Zeph knelt bent over in the snow, holding his side. Blood dripped from his mouth as he struggled to breathe. The pain was too much for his anger to overcome, and he gave in, letting the heartache pour out. Gentle stretching out his hand, Sensei used his mind to raise Zeph up to his feet. Zeph held his breath as he felt his ribs shift back into place. Iggy watched and marveled at Sensei's power and control with his healing abilities.

Sensei dropped his staff and grasped hold of Zeph, pulling him in close.

"I understand your frustration, boy," he whispered softly. "It's not that you want to fight. You simply want to win, to be heard."

Zeph slumped back to his knees. Sensei could tell the young man's mind was working a mile a minute, and the flood of memories was beginning to rush to the surface.

"No one would believe me; they just told me to accept the fact that he was dead," Zeph said as he choked back the tears. Iggy was perhaps the only one who instantly knew exactly what Zeph was talking about.

Sensei reached and helped him up. Everyone gathered together, and they headed inside. As they sat at the table, everyone watched Zeph, which wasn't making him feel particularly comfortable. The anger they had seen him show in the fight had turned to pain. Perhaps it was the physical pain of the battle that had brought it on or Sensei not backing down. Either way, what was done was done now. Sensei brought some tea for everyone. He sat down next to Zeph and placed a hand on his shoulder.

"A warrior cannot fight and ever hope to win if he carries burdens with him. A memory can weigh a person down even more than heavy weights strapped to their body."

Zeph nodded at his words. He had been carrying these memories for so long that he had almost forgotten about them. They would have stayed deeply buried if it hadn't been for the incident with Sotiris.

"My father disappeared when I was nine. Everyone told me he had been lost at sea. I never believed them. But they kept telling me the same thing over and over. No one would believe me," Zeph said as he hung his head. Sensei nodded. It would be hard to let something like that go.

"Why did you never give up hope, Zeph?" he asked.

"My father would not die at sea; he was a Water elemental." This surprised Sensei, and he pondered Zeph's words for a moment. It was not common for someone to perish by their own Element. The room fell silent. No one really knew what to say. Sensei stood and walked over to a nearby shelf. Removing a book, he set it on the table. After a minute, he found the page he was looking for. Turning the book to face Zeph, he spoke the words aloud.

O to be a prisoner of Hope! To be bound to it alone, and the fears and doubt of the world will have no hold over me. But hope for what is seen is no hope at all; who hopes for what they already have?

"I believe your father still lives, Zeph. I do not know where he is, but don't lose heart or hope."

Zeph laid his head in his hands and allowed himself to cry. It was not out of anguish but the simple act of letting go of all the long-held pain. A multitude of memories of his father flashed across his mind as he cried.

THE MORNING WAS BRIGHT as an excited nine-year-old Zeph jumped out of bed. He bounded down the stairs of their family house. His mother was making breakfast in the kitchen. It smelt so good; maybe it was pancakes and bacon, which he loved. In the den were his father and Iggy. Iggy was sitting on their father's knee while he read Iggy a book. Glancing up, he saw Zeph standing there. He couldn't help but smile and laugh at his boy. Stands of white hair were sticking out in every direction. The large shirt he wore belonged to his father; it almost looked like a woman's nightgown on him.

"Good morning, sleepyhead," his father said with a smile.

"Morning, Dad, morning, Iggy," he said as he plopped down on the couch beside them.

Khoz wrapped his arm around both of his boys and embraced them lovingly. They were the most precious thing in his life, something he told them daily. He had been reading to Iggy out of the Book of Ta'Hor. The truth within its pages was something he wanted to pass on to his children. Both boys huddled into their father as he continued to read.

Dawn stood in the archway and watched them. She was a proud mother and a loving wife. The day Zeph had been born was truly wonderful. She had always been worried about having children or if she even wanted to. It wasn't until she held Zeph in her arms for the first time that she realized what had been missing in their lives. Once Iggy had come along four years later, it had just added that much more joy to their lives.

Khoz noticed her standing there in the archway; he smiled softly up at her.

"Hey, who's that pretty lady?" he asked the boys.

"That's not a lady, that's mommy," Iggy piped up. It was all Khoz could do to not burst out laughing. Dawn glared back at him.

"Alright, boys, come get some breakfast in you." With that, the boys jumped off their father's lap and ran into the kitchen. Khoz stood and walked over to his wife. Slowly, he wrapped his arms around her and kissed her softly. She smiled back and pushed him towards the kitchen. Zeph and Iggy were already sitting at the table, eagerly awaiting food. They all sat, and after a short blessing over the food, they ate.

Zeph looked at his father across the table. He loved him very much. When Zeph had started school several years earlier, his father would walk him to class every day. That was when he wasn't off on one of his voyages. Even though Zeph missed his father when he was off at sea, he loved it when he returned because he often had toys or trinkets for him and his brother.

Today was another day that his father would be leaving. After breakfast, they would all head to the docks to see him off. Uncle Siah would often go on trips with him. Today, though, they were told that he was staying behind. The boys were excited, as it was nice to have him around when their father was away.

Zeph watched from the kitchen table as his father packed up his belongings and placed his sack on the floor by the front door. It was almost time. He knelt down by the door as Zeph came bounding over. Wrapping his arms around him, he gave him a big hug.

"Are you going to be good for your mother while I'm away?" he asked.

"Uh huh," Zeph replied.

"And you're going to look after little Iggy?"

Zeph nodded his agreement, and his father smiled back at him. The four of them got together and headed down to the docks. Khoz placed Iggy on his shoulders and held Zeph's hand as they made their way through town. It was a great day for sailing. The sky was clear, and there was a decent breeze.

As they began walking down the pier, Siah greeted them. Even standing next to Khoz, who was above average in height, he still looked huge. The boys ran over to him, and he quickly scooped them up and hung them upside down by their ankles. They giggled and wiggled about.

"Hey, if those two vomit on you, I'm not cleaning it up," Khoz said with a chuckle.

Siah quickly set the boys down. They headed down the pier to Khoz's ship. It wasn't very large, but it could hold a handful of men quite well and was sturdy enough for an ocean voyage. Several other men were already rigging the boat up to sail. It was time. Khoz turned to Dawn and embraced her. She looked him in the eye and told him to be safe, just as she always did before every voyage.

Next, it was the boys' turn. They ran over to him and hugged him at the same time. He ruffled their hair and told them to be good for their mother. Throwing his sack onto the deck of the boat, he climbed onboard. They pushed off from the docks and unfurled the sails. This journey was to Thai across the Eastern Sea. Zeph loved it when his father would return from Thai because he always had exciting stories to tell. Zeph and Iggy waved from the docks as they watched the boat sail out of sight. Dawn took them to the school right after so Zeph could get to class. Afterward, she went home with Iggy.

The following two weeks went by quickly. Before long, they were all once again down at the docks, eagerly waiting for Khoz's ship to return. Siah was there with them as well. They sat at one of the outdoor restaurants on the pier all afternoon and waited, but Khoz's ship never came in. Siah said there must have been some delays in the trip; it did happen from time to time. He told them to head home and go about their everyday tasks, and he would come get them as soon as Khoz returned.

Zeph watched as his mother sat in the den. She looked dreadful. Iggy had already been put to bed for the night, and Zeph was supposed to be up in his bed as well. Slowly, he crept into the den. It took a moment, but she noticed him standing there.

"Dad's okay, Mom, don't worry," he said softly.

She waved him over and wrapped her arms around him. It was comforting to see such faith from her son.

"I sure hope so, baby," she said in return.

As the days went on, though, the hope began to fade. Days turned into weeks. It had been almost three weeks since Khoz would have usually returned. Zeph watched as his mother went down to the docks every day. At night, he could hear her crying from his room.

The month drew to a close, and the news came. Several other ships had returned from Thai with no trace of Khoz or his ship. It was on this day that Zeph remembered his mother taking him aside. Her eyes were red from crying. Praotes had come and joined her at the house that day. The old Uriym sat in the den next to his mother as Zeph stood in front of them. Praotes was the one to speak up.

"I'm sorry to be the one to tell you this, Zeph, but your father was lost at sea. Do you know what this means?" he asked softly, looking down at Zeph.

Zeph slowly nodded. Confusion flashed across his face as he looked back at Praotes and his mother.

"Dad's not dead," Zeph said back to them.

"I'm sorry, Zeph, but your father is dead," Praotes replied back to him.

"No, he's not. I know he's not. Mom, listen to me," Zeph pleaded as he went to his mother. She embraced him and tried to comfort him through his tears.

"He's gone, sweetie, and we just have to carry on."

Zeph quickly pulled away from her; frustration was written on his face.

"I told you, he's not gone. Why don't you believe me?"

"Your father has been missing for over a month, Zeph. It is most likely that he perished," Praotes explained.

"I don't care what you say; I know he's alive," Zeph shouted as he stormed upstairs.

Slamming his door, he jumped on his bed. Tears began to fill his eyes. He didn't care what they said; he knew his father was still alive. Even if it was only a feeling inside, he knew he had to hold onto it. Iggy slowly opened the door. He was holding onto his favorite blanket.

"What's wrong, Zeph?" he asked.

Zeph sniffed and waved his little brother over. Picking him up, he placed him on the bed beside him.

"You're going to hear a lot of things, little brother. But I don't want you to believe any of them." Iggy nodded in response. "People are going to say that Dad is gone, but I don't want you to believe them." Iggy began to look upset at hearing his brother's words. "Just don't believe them, Iggy; Dad is just fine; he just won't be home for a long time. But I'll be here to look after you, okay?" Iggy nodded slowly and hugged Zeph.

ZEPH LOOKED UP SLOWLY and stared at Sensei from across the table. Everyone had been sitting quietly around it. Zeph took a deep breath in and held it for what seemed like forever. Finally, he breathed out slowly, and as he did, he felt as though a huge weight was being lifted from his chest. Sensei looked at him proudly. Zeph remembered how strongly he had held onto hope that his father was alive. Where had that hope gone over the years, he questioned himself.

"I'm sorry, everyone, I didn't realize how my memories were affecting me," Zeph apologized.

"This is something you all should take to heart. If you are holding onto pain, hurt, or anger, then your enemy has already struck a blow against you without even lifting a finger," Sensei explained as he stood and slowly walked around the room.

"What must we do to clear our minds, Sensei?" Iggy asked.

"First of all," he said, pointing to the book of Ta'Hor on the table, "Read that Book and know it inside and out. If you know the story, you know that Ta'Hor sought out Omega as he walked this world. He listened to Omega and followed the visions that were sent to him. In turn, his brother Sha'Kath chose a different path. He journeyed across the world and sought to find all the world had to offer. And we know how they both ended. Ta'Hor was raised up by Omega and Ascended. Sha'Kath, on the other hand, was consumed by worldly power and transformed into an Immortal Fiend."

"So if Sha'Kath became an Immortal Fiend, does that mean he is still somewhere out in the world?" Marcus asked, intrigued.

"I have been asked that many times, and in all honesty, I don't know Marcus," Sensei replied. "Perhaps there are still places on this world that men have not tread since the time of the Uriel."

"What do we do now?" Breeze asked.

"You will continue in your training. Once you have cleansed your minds, we will progress to the next step. I hope you all see now that fueling your abilities with hate or anger is never the answer. It makes a sickness deep inside a person." Everyone nodded at Sensei's words. They all stood and returned outside.

The fresh air of the day was starting to become a wonderful experience. One needed only to breathe in the cold, refreshing air to feel exhilarated. Watching the snowfall in the forest was a relaxing sight as well. They had spent much time in the forest, and much more would come. Having snow around their feet was a sensation they had gotten used to as the days went on. Most of the snow was light and easy to walk through.

Sensei gathered them in a circle once more. The mood had changed as they took up their poses. A sense of unity was felt among them. Perhaps this is what it was supposed to feel like. Sensei walked around them, watching their form. He was impressed; they were all learning so quickly. When the vision had come to him, he had no idea when they would arrive. Now that they were there, he felt a greater calling to not simply train them up but impart the blessing of Omega on them.

As the weeks passed, they took to his teachings with great fervor. Sensei was more than a Warrior in the sense of the title. His skills were far greater than that of a mere warrior, though. Even the next title rank of Champion seemed to fall short. In Zeph's eye, he deserved the title of Hero.

Iggy took great care in Sensei's teachings, particularly regarding the lessons on Light abilities. Until now, Iggy had never pictured someone with Light abilities ever being a great warrior. It was the way Sensei so easily mixed his elemental abilities with his fighting styles. Placing a projection field to deflect or attack was as effortless as waving his hand. Soon, Iggy learned that there were many offensive characteristics to Light abilities as well. The ability to create a field and throw it at someone was something he had never considered before. Sensei spent a great deal of time with Iggy, one on one, teaching him the depths of his abilities.

Even though Sensei fought primarily with a staff, he showed them how to fight using their preferred weapons. Zeph learned quickly with the sword. The basics he had acquired during the last several years quickly went out the window as he learned from Sensei. He discovered that any weapon is nothing more than an extension of one's own body. When swinging and striking, you can easily allow your own elemental energy to flow over the weapon. This was evident during their fight before when Zeph caused his energy to burst from his staff while striking. In the same way, Sensei taught him how to control these bursts and focus them with each blow.

Marcus had learned new ways to fight with his fists. Sensei also taught him the importance of using his feet to attack. He also introduced a new type of weapon to Marcus, something that would still allow him to use his particular fighting style while maximizing the damage. It was called a Blastano, and the name simply meant to spring up. It consisted of a thin blade concealed in a sheath strapped to the top of the forearm. Straps were attached around the wrist, hand, and forearm. The locking mechanism released when the wearer made a fist and angled their wrist down. Marcus had to only throw his arms down for the blade to slide out of the sheath and lock in place. The length of the blade matched the length of the wearer's forearm.

The first time Marcus put them on, they felt strange and awkward. He made a fist with each hand and heard a small click. Quickly throwing his arms out, the blades shot out of the ends and locked in place. Then, his eyes lit up, and a big grin appeared on his face. Reaching up, he turned the latch on the Blastano and slid the blade back inside the sheath. It was exactly what he wanted in a weapon. It was something an assassin would wear, and that was intriguing to Marcus.

Along with the weapon, Sensei also showed Marcus how to master channeling fire with his strikes. With each swing of his arms, fire flew over the blades and shot off the ends. Out of everyone in the group, Marcus mastered this skill the fastest. He was a natural-born fighter, and everyone knew it.

Breeze had received a new bow from Sensei. The frame of it was incredibly thin. Since it was made of the same wood as the other weapons, it had to be very thin so the bow would have some flex to it. He also gave her a quiver of arrows. Each arrow was crystal clear, which sometimes made it a bit of a hunt to find them in the snow. Her skills with a bow were unmatched. Sensei had never trained with a bow before, but after watching Breeze's skills, he knew she already had a powerful mastery of it.

At Iggy's request, Sensei gave him a staff to train with. After watching all the various lessons Sensei had taught, Iggy knew it was the weapon for him. They practiced together day after day for many, many hours until Iggy had a solid mastery of the staff. Besides training Iggy to fight, Sensei also taught him everything he knew about Light abilities. It was a lot for Iggy to take in and even more to practice. His ability to create different types of fields and absorb energy grew significantly under Sensei's teachings.

Sensei also wanted to show Iggy something very special about his staff. He had placed a small gemstone fragment in the middle of the translucent staff. It was green like the gem around Breeze's neck. If Sensei hadn't pointed it out to Iggy, he may not have even noticed it.

Gripping the staff and placing his hand over the green shard, Sensei produced a beam of light from his palm. It struck the shard inside the staff, causing light to bounce and refract all along its length. The whole staff lit up with a brilliant, bright green aura. It was a truly amazing sight. Sensei showed Iggy the staff he had given him; inside, there was a blue shard, and when light was projected into it, the whole staff shone with a bright blue aura.

"This is almost more amazing than our Sphere Lamps," said Iggy as he gripped his staff firmly and stared in awe at the bright blue aura coming from it.

"I have found that it can be much more effective at lighting up a large area rather than channeling light directly from my hands," Sensei explained. "I hope that in dark times, it will also help to light your way, young Iggy."

They all trained together in the courtyard daily, practicing attacks, blocks, and various stances. They were all becoming warriors, and by the time they were ready to continue their journey, each would be granted the title rank as well. For now, though, the training continued.

DAY 150

If there is love, then there can also be heartache.

Should we refuse to love for fear of the pain that may come our way?

Or should we find a way to shorten the bridge of anger that connects the two?

~ Sensei

CHAPTER 15
PIRATES, WENCHES, & TRADERS

The forest was quiet, too quiet. Zeph cautiously moved through the trees. His eyes darted left and right. The attack could come from any direction. Sword drawn, he pressed forward. Something caught his eye to the right, and he swung his head. It was gone. He knew they were coming, and it would be soon. Slowly making his way through the snow, he kept a watchful eye near the tree tops. Sometimes, they liked to attack from above.

Without warning, the end of a staff swung at the back of his head. His heightened reflexes kicked in, and he quickly swung around and blocked the attack. Locking eyes with his attacker, Zeph threw them back into the snow. Not a second went by, and then he heard the quickened footsteps coming up behind him. Pushing off the nearby tree, the sound of his attacker leaping into the air could be heard. Swinging around once again, Zeph looked just in time to see the attacker coming down on him. Planting his knees in the snow, Zeph thrust his hands out; a shockwave of energy burst from his palms and sent the attacker flying backward into the air.

Whoosh! Zeph blinked for a second as an arrow flew right past his shoulder. Now, things were getting interesting. Zeph knew his attacker had to be up in the trees; he just didn't know where. Then he spotted her. Swinging his body around for extra momentum, he thrust his hands out at her. She jumped out of the tree just as the blast hit where she had been positioned.

Running at full speed towards him, she fired arrow after arrow with fantastic speed. He blocked several of them with his sword and dodged the rest. The three attackers surrounded him now. There was nothing left to do. He took a knee and thrust his fist into the ground as hard as possible. A shockwave burst from around him, sending the attackers flying in all directions.

The sound of clapping could be heard as Sensei slowly made his way over to the group. Marcus, Breeze, and Iggy picked themselves up and out of the snow and made their way over to Zeph.

"Well done, all of you," Sensei said as he joined them. "You have all learned very well over these last few months. Well done, Zeph, on your ability to control and channel your energy," he said with a smile.

As the weeks passed, Zeph had shown increased control and skill over his telekinetic abilities. It wasn't until several days earlier that he could push that ability even further to include a burst of energy as well. It was an outstanding achievement on his part. The rest of the group had also significantly increased their skills and elemental knowledge. Building up their elemental strength had been a key point in Sensei's training. He had told them that weapons and armor can only do so much, but when you have nothing left, it will be left to your abilities to save you.

Zeph smiled and patted everyone on the back. He had greatly enjoyed coming out and training every day like this. They began walking back to Sensei's house. As Zeph started walking, Iggy noticed he was oddly shuffling his feet.

"Did we actually manage to hurt you this time?" asked Iggy with a chuckle. Iggy's comical disposition quickly changed to one of alarm as he saw the pained expression on his brother's face. "Zeph, what's wrong?" There was a pause as Zeph stopped in his tracks. The symbols on his hands and forehead began to glow.

"I....I don't know. I think tha-" Zeph stopped abruptly and gripped his head as he dropped to his knees.

The vision came on fast and hard as images flashed before his eyes. He was standing in a dark and dingy alleyway. He didn't recognize the city or any of his surroundings. It was dirty, and the stench of booze hung in the air. The sound of screaming drew his attention. Running down the alley, he came around a corner to see four large men beating a young girl. He couldn't make out their faces, but he saw hers clearly. She was young, couldn't have been more than sixteen. Her hair was a mix of black and purple. They continued to kick her as she lay on the ground, struggling to move. Zeph rushed over to try and help but was shocked when he simply passed through the attackers as though they were made of nothing.

Zeph opened his eyes to find himself once again kneeling in the cold snow. He quickly stood to his feet. After several deep breaths, he regained his composure. It was nothing like the intensity of his first vision or even his experience at *The Order*. This was quick and almost smooth. It had lasted for only several moments, and it had only been painful for a split second at the beginning.

"What did you see, Zeph?" Iggy asked.

"I saw a girl being attacked in an alley. It was in a strange city I'd never seen before. It was dirty and drab, walls and buildings made of stone bricks, and it kind of smelt like stale booze," Zeph replied.

"The city of Iy Ra'Kal is where you speak of," Sensei spoke up. "It's on the northern coast of Appagon, down the northern mountain pass from here."

"What do you think it means?" asked Marcus.

"I don't know, but I feel this strong urge that it hasn't happened yet."

"That's quite interesting; not many people blessed with visions see things of what's to come," Sensei pointed out.

"Well then, perhaps we should head to Iy Ra'Kal," Breeze suggested.

Zeph looked over at Sensei. They had spent many weeks with him, and even though they had all learned much, he wondered if they were ready. As if knowing what Zeph was thinking, Sensei turned to them and said, "This is a sign that your training is complete. This vision signals that it is time for you to continue on your journey and follow whatever path Omega has set before you."

"Do you really think we're ready?" questioned Marcus.

"You have all come so very far in such a short amount of time. I am pleased to call you Warriors," Sensei said proudly.

The rest of the day was spent preparing for the mountain trip. Although journeying down the northern side would be easier than climbing the southern pass, it would still take time. The skies were clear, though, which was a blessing.

The next morning, they set out. Supplies weren't a big concern. The remaining sphere lamps were brought with them as well. Between all they had sold at both Tweedsmiur and Sanctus Spire, they were down to only a couple dozen. They still had their gold, though, which would become more important now that they were getting low on lamps. A selection of meats, cheeses, and bread were packed as well. They were more prepared than ever before to venture out on the next leg of their journey.

"Thank you for everything," said Zeph as he embraced Sensei.

"The pleasure was truly mine, lad," Sensei said as he gripped Zeph firmly. "I will pray every day that what you have learned during your time here will serve you well." He stopped and looked Zeph in the eye as he held him at arm's length. "Never let despair and anger consume you, Zeph. I know part of the pain still resides within you. Never allow that pain to grow again. Take the lessons you learned here to heart, and find peace in dark times."

"Thank you for everything, Master Sensei."

They left Sensei's house and headed for the main path that led away from the village to the north. The trek was easy at first as they continued north through the snow. Sensei had assured them that before long, they would reach the northern pass and would be able to see the coast and the city far below. True to his word, they reached the pass. From their perspective, it felt like they were on top of the world. Even though they couldn't see the southern part of Appagon anymore, they could see all across the northern horizon. Ocean was laid out before them as far as the eye could see.

Standing at the top of the pass, they looked down. They could see what looked like a large city on the edge of the coast, and they could barely make out the many sailing ships that dotted the harbor. It was, without a doubt, the largest city on Appagon. They were told that it was the main trading port on Appagon, with most of the trade coming from the Earth Realm to the north across the ocean. What the people would be like, they still didn't know, but the vision had not filled Zeph with confidence in the quality of the citizens.

The journey down was slightly more complicated than they were expecting. It was much steeper near the top of the pass than anticipated. As they journeyed down, though, it became more of a long slope. They made camp for the night. The mountains loomed over them in the light of the moons. Below them, they could now see the city's lights in the distance. It was like a sparkling jewel. They would make it there by midday the next day. Excitement filled them as they went to sleep. As dawn broke the next morning, they were already on their way. As they grew closer, they were able to scan the layout of the city. It was, in fact, a city, and not like the villages and towns they had visited so far. It was vast compared to what they were used to, perhaps twenty thousand people or more, plus a few thousand more in visitors and traders.

Once they reached the city, they planned to sell their mountain fur clothing. Now that they were no longer in the frigid areas of the mountain, the temperature had once again returned to the warmer climate they were used to. There were only a few more weeks until the end of the year, and the growing season would start once again. So much time had gone by since they had left Daunt; it had almost been four months now.

The path turned from rough rock to dirt as they approached the city. The buildings were drab, as was most of the city. Everything looked like it was covered with a film of dirt. Brown apparently was the color scheme overall. A large sign on the side of the road read: *Welcome to Iy Ra'Kal.* Underneath, someone had pained the words 'get your drink and get out.' They scoffed at the sign and shook their heads as they walked by. That alone said a lot about what they should expect.

They continued on and made their way through the city streets. Shops seemed to be everywhere, and they sold anything you could think of. They made for the nearest clothing shop and sold their mountain clothing. The shopkeeper was very grubby and smelt like it had been some time since he bathed. They asked him for advice on where they should travel in the city. He listed off more than half a dozen pubs. It wasn't quite what they had in mind. They asked for directions on how to get down to the harbor. Using the same pubs as landmarks, he gave them a series of directions on how to get there.

Iy Ra'Kal was the only actual city on Appagon. It was positioned along the northern coast and had a large harbor to facilitate constant trade. Many people from the Earth Realm would journey to Iy Ra'Kal since it was a short trip of only a few weeks across the ocean. The city's layout went from the higher class of inns and shops near the harbor to the poorer, more shady areas expanding outwards the farther you went into the city. Besides the legitimate traders, the city was also a haven for those who would call themselves pirates and thieves. There was no significant law enforcement in the city, at least none that they had seen, but it was plain to see which sections of the city should be avoided unless you were a pirate or had a death wish.

They walked the streets for a while. There were many people all about. The smells in the air were a tangled mixture of many different foods, drinks, and people. Oh, how they could smell the people! It seemed as though most of the city's residents hadn't heard of the concept of daily bathing. The question now was where they should go. They had come to the city based solely on Zeph's vision. How would they find a single girl out of the thousands of people?

They first decided to find an inn to stay the night, a respectable, clean inn, to be more specific. This took them on a journey through the city. They soon realized that they needed to head for the harbor if they wanted to stay in a nicer inn. Perhaps it was because the center of trade was based around the harbor. An hour or so passed before they came upon the Joyful Goblet Inn. Entering it, they saw that it was a clean establishment and decided it was their best bet for a safe place to stay.

White walls and dark red carpets lined the halls as they entered. It was by far the fanciest inn that any of them had come across before. The rooms were laid out in a simple fashion. Two beds and a full bathroom were in each of the two rooms they booked. It was more expensive than any inn they had stayed in before, costing nine silver kessas a night per room. The inn back in Daunt charged only three. At least they would stay in comfort, though. After they had settled in, they decided it was time to walk the city streets again. They had to find the girl in Zeph's vision before it was too late.

Zeph knew that if he had received a vision of her, then she must be important for what was to come. He tried to remember back to his vision. There had to be some other clue as to where they could track her down. As he played the vision back in his mind again, he caught a glimpse of a sign hanging beside the alley. It was a white gazelle jumping, most likely the sign for a pub. That's where they would start their search.

On their way out of the inn, they asked the innkeeper if he knew of any pubs or taverns that had a sign with a white gazelle on it. He said it didn't ring a bell with any of the pubs he knew about in their district. He suggested it was probably one of the many pubs in the city's slums. It made sense with Zeph's vision. In the vision, the alley seemed very run down and dirty. A sense of urgency was starting to fall over Zeph as he didn't know when the events of the vision would happen. He hoped that they could find the girl before the event in question took place.

"So where do we go from here?" Marcus asked.

"We need to head for the slums, I guess," Zeph replied.

As they walked on, the city changed. It was no longer a place of respectable trading. The streets became darker, the people shadier. Music could be heard coming from the pubs and taverns, as well as the occasional bar fight. The smell of booze, blood, and urine was in the air. This was not a part of the city where a person wanted to find themselves alone. Sailors and pirates alike walked the streets. On some of the street corners and outside the pubs, scantily dressed women stood selling their bodies to anyone who would give them the coin they desired. It was a new experience for the group and something they had never had to deal with growing up in a peaceful, respectable village like Daunt.

Several hours passed, and they were deep in the slums of Iy Ra'Kal now. They passed pub after pub. Finally, they came across a bit of luck. One of the passersby said he saw a tavern with a gazelle on the sign several blocks over. They ran down the street and stopped at the intersection. There it was, the white gazelle Zeph had seen in his vision. The name of the tavern was *The Dancing Gazelle*. Music was coming from the tavern, and there were many people inside. At a glance, Zeph didn't recognize anyone from the vision, although he hadn't been able to make them out very well.

"I'm not sure what to do now," Zeph said as he stood against the outside wall of the tavern.

"Any idea when this is supposed to happen?" Breeze asked.

"Not a clue," he replied.

"Well, let's go check out the alley for now," Marcus suggested.

They walked down the street and around the side of the building. There didn't seem to be any alley that went behind the tavern. Puzzled, they continued on. Perhaps this wasn't the right place after all. Zeph looked at the sign that hung above the tavern and then thought back to the vision. It was facing the wrong way from the perspective he had seen it. Gesturing for everyone to follow him, Zeph went a block over and behind some other buildings. It was then that they saw a dark alley leading behind the strip of shops and pubs. As they walked over to it, a large man blocked their path.

"Run along, kids; you have no business here," he said in a deep raspy voice.

Just then, they heard a girl's scream coming from farther down the alley. Zeph ran forward, but the large man shoved him away.

"I told you this is none of your business. Now leave unless you want to get hurt," the man said as he reached for his dagger. Before Zeph could react, Iggy reached into his cloak and quickly removed one of his potions. He held it up to the man's nose; before the man could even react, he collapsed to the ground almost instantly. Placing the cork back on the vial, Iggy stowed it back in his cloak.

"Wow, that was amazing!" Marcus exclaimed. "I can't believe how strong that stuff is."

"No time, let's go," Zeph said as he took off running down the alley. Rounding the corner, he saw her. It was exactly as it had been shown to him in the vision. She was being held by two men and being beaten by the other two. They dropped her to the ground as they saw Zeph round the corner.

"Who the 'eck are you?" the one man asked.

Zeph delivered his answer by grabbing the man and punching him in the face as hard as he could. He kept beating the man repeatedly. The other men quickly turned their attention away from the girl and rushed Zeph. Iggy was the next to come running down the alley.

"Oh, look at tis' little lad," one of the men scoffed. Iggy quickly twirled his staff and struck the man several times, flipping him up into the air and landing hard on his back. Marcus and Breeze promptly joined in, and within a few moments, the remaining men took off running. Zeph's focus quickly shifted to the unconscious girl lying on the ground. She was beaten badly. The bruises on her body indicated that this wasn't the first occurrence either. Zeph gently sat her up, and Iggy held his hands over her. The bruises quickly began to fade. She gasped and coughed as she regained consciousness. Her eyes frantically darted around as she looked at all of them. Fear was in her eyes.

"It's okay; you're safe now," Zeph said softly as she scampered into the corner and tried to hide herself. "We're not here to hurt you; we're here to help you."

"Why?" she responded with a bewildered look in her eyes.

Zeph debated what he should say. After thinking about it for a moment, he decided to simply tell her the truth.

"I saw a vision of you being attacked several days ago, and we came to try and rescue you."

She stared at him blankly. It was not at all what she was expecting to hear. Slowly, she stood, bracing herself against the wall. Her injuries had been healed, but her body was still frail.

"Will you come with us?" Zeph asked. She was hesitant as she stared at the four strangers before her, but eventually, she slowly nodded. They left the alley; there was no trace of the men that had attacked her. Zeph offered her his cloak as they went through town. They arrived at the inn and gathered in Zeph and Iggy's room. The girl huddled beneath Zeph's cloak as she sat on the bed. Zeph walked over and knelt on the floor beside her. She looked over at him, her hair half covering her face. He offered her a moist cloth to wipe her face. Taking the cloth, she quickly cleaned herself up. The cloth returned to Zeph, covered with dirt and blood. It was a sad sight to behold.

After the group returned to the inn, Marcus and Iggy left to buy clothing and food for the girl. Before long, they returned. She accepted the food without hesitation but refused the clothes. They left it on the bed for her regardless. The rags she wore as clothing barely covered her body.

"What's your name?" Zeph asked.

"Violet," she said softly.

It was fitting for her. Purple strands were mixed in amongst her black hair. She was thin and pale. They guessed she was used to hiding and rarely ate.

"Violet, my name is Zeph," he said as he smiled softly at her. "This is Marcus, Iggy, and Breeze." She quickly glanced at each of them in response. The puzzling part now was why Zeph received a vision of her. She continued to look around the room cautiously. Perhaps it was her first time in a room as fancy as this. Marcus and Iggy sat at the nearby table. She watched them as they sat. They tried not to stare back at her and simply let her take in all her surroundings.

Violet looked over at Zeph and studied his face for a moment.

"I've never seen an Omega elemental before," she said as her eyes locked on the symbol on his forehead.

"I'm told we're not very common," Zeph replied as he sat on the floor beside the bed. Breeze sat near the head of the bed.

"What can you do?" asked Violet between rather large bites of her food. Zeph smiled and chuckled. It was an interesting question since he had only just started to tap into his abilities.

"To be honest, I don't really know. I grew up in a place where there wasn't any knowledge of Omega elementals. I can do a few things, though," he said, holding his hands out towards her. Cupping his hands together, he allowed the energy within him to flow out of his palms and pool there. It was something he had done many times, but it was a first sight for her. Her eyes widened as she stared at the glowing liquid in his hands. He smiled at her, then let the liquid dissolve and float into the air like vapors.

"I can also recharge other people's Focus," he added.

"Can you do that for me?" she asked. The question caught Zeph slightly off guard, but he proceeded. Standing, Zeph placed a hand gently on her head. At first, she looked uncomfortable, but that quickly changed to a sense of relief. Zeph let the energy flow from his hand and wash over her. Everyone watched as Violet began to change before their eyes. She looked healthier and revitalized, the exact opposite of the frail girl they had rescued. As Zeph removed his hand from her head, he noticed the shadow symbol on her forehead.

"Where are you from?" he asked.

"I was born on Tsayla. My parents died when I was very young. One of the orphanages in a nearby village took me in. Traders took me here to Appagon several years ago. I stayed here in Iy Ra'Kal at one of the orphanages until I was fourteen. Since then, I've spent the last two years living on the streets," she explained.

"Who were those men that attacked you," asked Marcus.

"They're just part of the gangs here in Iy Ra'Kal. They find street kids like me, kidnap us, sell us, force us to work for them, or even worse."

It was a hard truth for the group to swallow. They had grown up with loving families their whole lives. It was hard to imagine life without them or having to always be on guard for fear of being kidnapped and sold. Not to mention living life on the streets and in back alleys.

"So what can you do, Violet?" Zeph asked as he gestured to her Shadow mark. Reaching up, she parted her black and purple hair and touched the elemental mark on her forehead. It had been a long time since she had shown her abilities to someone new. She used them all the time to defend herself on the streets. Overuse without resting had made her weak, though.

Standing up from the bed, she took up a pose, holding her hands out. Zeph's pack against the wall rose and floated over to them. Violet smiled as she watched the bag float to her. It had been some time since she had the strength to do something like that. She placed the bag on the floor in front of Zeph and walked to the closet. Opening the door, she stepped inside. Everyone watched, wondering what she was planning on doing. As she stood in the shadow of the closet, they were amazed that she seemed to fade away and disappear completely. They heard her giggle from the closet. Then, she stepped out of the shadows and became visible once again as the light from the room fell over her.

"That's pretty much all I can do. That's all I've used over the years. Either to hide or to fight," Violet explained.

"Impressive. Disappearing into shadows would be a convenient skill to have," Zeph noted. "We do share some similar abilities, though," he said as he waved his hand and his pack flew over to him. Reaching into the bag, he tossed Violet one of the sphere lamps. Grasping it out of the air, she stared at it intensely. It was the expression everyone seemed to have when they first saw them. Zeph explained everything there was to tell about the sphere lamps, starting when they first created them to the events of the journey so far since they left Daunt. It was when he mentioned *The Order* that her ears perked up.

"What's *The Order*?" she asked.

"From what I understand, it's an ancient order of shadow mages that educate and train Shadow Elementals to become assassins. I'm sure that if they had crossed your path when you were younger, they would have also taken you in," Zeph explained.

"Will you take me there one day?"

The question seemed to catch Zeph off guard again. It was unexpected, but the sincerity in her voice rang with truth. Zeph said that perhaps one day they would be able to take her there. It wasn't a place a person could really visit unless they were invited. Plus, Zeph wasn't sure if he would even be allowed back after what had transpired the last time.

"Perhaps you can show us Iy Ra'Kal?" Zeph suggested.

"That is something I can do. Where would you like to go first?" asked Violet.

"Where would one go to get information on recent events and perhaps old folklore?"

"Why old folklore?" she asked with an intrigued look on her face.

Zeph paused for a moment. He knew he shouldn't be telling people about the Omega scroll or that he was the *Chosen One*. He also knew that if he had any chance of finding out what happened to the Shadow Scroll, he would have to trust some people. Perhaps she would have some insight into it since she was from the Shadow Realm. They had nothing to go on but the old stories of Desiree, and Zeph's vision of what had happened a thousand years ago. The last thing he had seen in the vision was Desiree disappearing with the scroll, but that was centuries ago. Who knows where the scroll had ended up or who the current *Shadow Chosen One* was.

"Have you ever heard the name Desiree before?" he asked Violet. She shuttered for a moment.

"Since you're asking about folklore, I'm assuming you mean the legend of Master Desiree," she replied.

"You know of her?" Zeph asked with a sense of caution. Everyone else gathered around the bed, waiting to hear what Violet would say.

"Well, yeah, it's a pretty common story parents tell their children. She lived over a thousand years ago. She was the *Shadow Chosen One*. It's a story that's told to scare children. I remember it being told to me when I was younger."

"How does the story go?" questioned Iggy.

"It's kind of like a poem," Violet explained, "It goes like this:

There once was a girl all dressed in black
With long red hair all down her back
With eyes of darkness and blade in hand
She brought us death across the land
The power held inside the scroll
It fed her deep and bled her soul
For in the shadows, she would find you
And steal all the good inside you
She will take the life within you
To stop all time and make her life new
A lust for power did consume her
Searching for one to defy her
She walked across the faceless lands
Where deserts lie and no one treads
She walked beyond the world we know
And into darkness deep below
And if you ever hear a whisper
Feel a chill, or sense a shiver
Beware 'cause she is at your door
Run and hide or be no more

The room fell silent after Violet finished the poem. The content was much more chilling than they were expecting, and some of the imagery was disturbing. The mention of the scroll was a clear indication that the poem was indeed referring to the same Desiree that Zeph had seen in his vision. A reference to time having lost its hold over her was another aspect of the poem that caught Zeph's attention. Marcus was the first to say something.

"So...that was a children's poem, huh?" he asked with a slightly disturbed tone in his voice.

"Yes," Violet replied, "it's a very common one back on Tsayla, actually. I remember my mother telling it to me when I was little."

"Well, that's not really facts to go on, but most folklore is based on some truths. I think one thing we can assume for sure is that the scroll made Desiree one of the most powerful people in the world," Zeph stated.

"Is there anything else you could tell us about her from lore and legends?" Breeze asked Violet.

"Ummm, well, not a whole lot is really known. I mean, she was something of an unstoppable terror back in the Sixth Age, or so the legends go. She's probably the most renowned figure in Shadow Realm folklore besides Sha'Kath himself."

That also sent shivers up their spines. Sha'Kath, after all, was the father of all Dark Teachings on Arkhay. The fact that Desiree was remembered on the same level as him was unnerving. Violet continued to tell them all she could remember about the legend of Desiree. There wasn't much to go on, but it seemed there weren't many tales of her journeying outside the Shadow Realm. Based on that, they assumed that the Shadow Scroll had to still be somewhere on Tsayla. It was still a whole continent to search, but at least that narrowed it down to only one-seventh of the world. There was also the possibility that whoever had been chosen next had taken the scroll somewhere else in the world after Desiree had died. However, there were no recorded accounts of who came next in succession. The tales of Desiree were all they had to go on for now.

"How well do you know the lands of Tsayla?" Zeph asked Violet.

"Well, it's been a few years since I was last there, but I traveled across the realm many times before being brought here. At the very least, I think I could help you on your journey," she said with a pleading look on her face. She clearly didn't want to stay in Iy Ra'Kal any longer.

After some discussion among the group, it was decided that Violet would join them. After all, it would be beneficial to have someone of another elemental alignment in their party, and she did have more knowledge about the Shadow Realm than any of them. It would be handy to have a guide of some kind once they reached Tsayla.

At this point, Violet finally took the clothes Marcus and Iggy had bought for her. She returned from the bathroom shortly, wearing the outfit. Her face and hair had been cleaned, and she wore the new clothes. They were a mix of black and purple. Since those colors were already naturally in her hair, Marcus and Iggy thought it would be best to match them. She wore a black short-sleeved button-up shirt and purple vest combination, with matching boots and skirt.

Zeph stared at her from across the room. There was something about her. He couldn't quite put his finger on it. It may have been the vision of her that sparked a desire to be close to her. Violet looked over at him, their blue eyes locked for a moment. Even though they shared blue eyes, hers were paler and not as brilliant blue as Zeph's. Violet blushed as she saw Zeph staring at her. Blinking, Zeph shifted his gaze and smiled back.

"So where do we go from here?" Iggy asked.

"Well, if we're going to head to Tsayla, we need a ship. Maybe we can charter one down at the harbor," Marcus suggested.

"Hmmm, that might be the best bet," Zeph agreed. "Since we'd have to travel up and over the mountains again, I'm guessing it would take almost two weeks to reach Daunt."

"Daunt?" questioned Violet with a puzzled look on her face.

"Oh, it's the town we come from. It's at the southeastern tip of Appagon," Zeph explained.

The five of them gathered their belongings and headed out. Violet hadn't spent much time in the city's richer sections, so it was a nice change for her. Even the shops had much more class to them as they neared the harbor. Well-dressed businessmen manned the counters of the various shops the group passed. Children ran past them as they walked the streets. Soft melodies filled the air. The suns shone down on them, and a gentle breeze blew through the city, filling their noses with all sorts of pleasant aromas. The most pleasant of these were the scents of food and flowers.

They made their way toward the docks. It wasn't far from the inn, no more than ten minutes farther north. They could already see large masts as they approached. The streets opened up to the harbor in front of them. Dozens of ships were docked. Some were beautiful, with amazingly detailed side paneling, while others were ragged and worn. They ranged in size from small fishing boats to large ocean explorers.

The docks were extensive and ran the whole way around the harbor. Larger ships had priority in docking right against the central piers, bringing them closest to the Trading Post and various shops. The wood was worn by the constant travel of many visitors. Rope railings lined the edge of the piers and docks. The harbor was shaped like a giant crescent moon.

Zeph absorbed it all as they continued down the docks. The marvel of this city was not lost on him. On this side of the city, many of the buildings were white, and red roofs lined the tops of the buildings. Birds flew overhead and could occasionally be seen diving into the waters, only to emerge moments later with a fish in their beaks.

Looking over at Violet, Zeph couldn't help but stare. In the light of the midday suns, the stands of purple in her dark hair stood out vibrantly. She seemed just as excited to look at everything as they were. He guessed that while living in the city's slums, she had never been able to visit this side of the city. Once again, their eyes caught.

Breeze watched their glances transpire. It had been weeks since she had romantically thought about Zeph. Seeing his attention drawn by another girl filled her with a twinge of jealousy and a nagging hurt. She knew this eventuality would come at some point, but it was not something she wanted to endure. The thought that Zeph might move on to someone else filled her mind. She tried to push the thought away. It was hard, but she reminded herself that the decision to end their relationship had been hers, and no matter how hard it was or how she felt, this was the way things were now.

They quickly reached the Trading Post. Unlike the small building on the docks of Daunt, this was huge by comparison. It consisted of a huge square building with a courtyard in the middle. Captains of the various ships were checking in with the Post Masters. Like most trading ports, it was customary for captains to sign in after they docked. It was an easy way for the city to know who was visiting and what kind of wares were being traded in their city.

The five of them stood nearby and simply watched the people come and go. People all over were shopping at the various seaside stores. It was then that the thought hit them. They felt the purses of gold strapped on their waists. Perhaps it was time to do some shopping. They didn't know when their next chance to shop at a place like this would come.

They headed past the Trading Post down the main street. These were some of the finest shops in the city. The shops held anything and everything a person could want. Several jewelry shops caught the girls' attention, and they quickly headed over to them. Zeph, Marcus, and Iggy continued down the street. They had all agreed to meet up with each other in an hour.

Marcus wanted to find some new clothing for himself; the idea had also crossed Zeph's mind. They entered one of the shops. The display featured a variety of clothing from around the globe. The shopkeeper explained that most of his wares came from the Earth Realm. Marcus typically wore short sleeves or cut-offs, but with his new weapons on his forearms, he started wearing long sleeves to conceal them. The shopkeeper caught a glimpse of the blade sheaths.

"I have a feeling you're looking for something to keep those hidden, aren't you?" the man asked. Marcus looked around cautiously, not wanting to draw attention to them. "Oh, don't worry about me," the merchant said, "I see all kinds here. But if you're looking for something better than sleeves to hide them, I might be able to help you out with that." He went into the back and returned shortly with some black leather bracers. They looked as though they were explicitly designed to cover the Blastanos. They consisted of two pieces: the top strapped around the shoulder and down the arm, and the second was the length of a man's forearm from the wrist to the elbow. It had a slot to access the locking pin on the blade mechanism. Gesturing Marcus over, the merchant strapped it to his arm and down over the top of his Blastano. Marcus pulled his hand into a fist and jerked his arm down sharply. The blade slid out perfectly. Marcus smiled back at the shopkeeper. It was just what he needed.

Zeph and Iggy continued to browse the store. Iggy was content with his blue cloak and wasn't interested in getting anything new. Zeph, on the other hand, wanted something a little more adventurous. They quickly learned that you didn't need a lot of armor to protect yourself. In fact, it wasn't necessary to have any at all if you were skilled enough. Zeph felt as though he was at that point. Something caught his eye on one rack. It was a dark blue shirt with a white collar. String ties were going up the front of it. Matching grey pants were hanging with it as well. They looked light and comfortable. He still had his black boots which were serving him well. Picking up the clothing, he walked over to the counter. The shopkeeper looked at the clothing in his arms. Walking over to a nearby rack, he returned with a fine leather belt. It had holders for potions as well as clips for money sacks.

"You'll need one of these to go with those fine clothes, young man," the shopkeeper replied as he neatly folded the clothing Zeph had picked. "The clips on this belt are practically thief-proof." The cost of everything was more expensive than Zeph had expected it to be. The shirt, pants, and belt came to six gold kessas. The three of them stood outside the shop. Zeph looked over at Marcus.

"Looking good, bro," he said as he looked over the dark leather bracers.

"Thanks," he said with a grin.

A disturbance down the street quickly caught their attention. It was hard to see, but it seemed like a group of people were aggressively pushing their way down the street. As they drew closer, it became clear that these men did not belong in this part of the city. They were dirty and had a stench about them. Even though they had heard the stories and seen some shady characters, they hadn't actually expected to see what they were seeing. These men were fearsome pirates.

As they walked down the street, they began grabbing bystanders who hadn't already fled at their sight. They took anything they could grab and threw them aside. Both Zeph and Marcus couldn't believe they were witnessing assault and robbery right in the middle of the day.

Zeph glanced back at the shopkeeper. He was quickly closing up the shop.

"Who are those men?" Zeph asked, running over to the counter.

"They're part of Captain Domm's crew," he replied nervously. "They pass through this part of the city on their way in and out. They leave us alone the rest of the time and stick to the slums."

"So they just come through ransacking the city on their way in and out?" Zeph asked with a tone of annoyance.

"Yes, and you would be best not to get in their way if you value your life. I have watched them kill a man in the street for nothing more than his coin purse." With that, the shopkeeper closed and locked the windows of his shop.

Zeph gestured to Iggy and Marcus to follow him, and the three stood in the middle of the street. People ran past them as the pirates drew closer. The gaggle of pirates stopped abruptly as they noticed the three young men standing in the middle of the street. Everyone else had cleared the way.

"Out of our way, you little brats, or taste the sting of my blade," said their pack leader as they stopped in the middle of the street, a few paces away from the trio. Seven or eight large men were facing the three boys. Zeph stood in front with Marcus and Iggy to his left and right.

"What gives you the right to torment these people?" Zeph challenged the man. The man drew his sword, and the rest of his men followed suit. They were a grubby bunch. Most of them had a bandana around their heads and wore beads in their hair and around their necks. Each carried a similar sword, a cutlass of some kind. Their elements differed from man to man, but it seemed like most were Water, except for a few Wind and one Fire.

Zeph reached for his waist and drew his sword. Iggy gripped his staff firmly. Marcus made fists but did not trigger his blades yet; flames flowed over the spiked leather gloves. People watched in pure shock from their windows. They had never seen someone openly defy Captain Domm's men before. Silence hung in the air, a moment's pause before the battle.

"Last chance, drop what you've taken from these people and leave," said Zeph boldly as he gripped his sword.

The leader looked back at Zeph with a scoff. Lunging forward, he swung his sword at Zeph. It was all that was needed for the situation to erupt. Zeph clashed hard with the leader's sword. All the other men behind him rushed forward. Iggy leaped forward, spinning his staff wildly. The end connected with several of the men's heads. Jumping into the air, Marcus brought his fists down hard against two of the men. Several of the other men in the back began forming large spheres of water in their hands. They flung them at the boys. Marcus thrust his hand out, and flames wrapped around the sphere in the blink of an eye and turned it to vapor. Zeph continued to battle head-to-head with the leader, their blades clashing wildly. He was quick, but Zeph was far faster. Iggy was holding his ground with only two men trying to attack him.

Marcus, on the other hand, was surrounded by four men now. Thrusting his arms down, Marcus locked his concealed blades into place. The rage in Marcus' eyes matched the intensity of the flames that wrapped around each blade. The pirates looked at him with a hint of concern now. He rushed forward, swinging the flaming blades at them. They returned in kind. It was not a casual fight like the kind they had experienced during their training. Unlike other battles they had fought before, these men were actually trying to kill them.

One of the men caught Marcus in the shoulder just between his leather armor. Blood flowed from the wound. Pain and adrenaline filled Marcus. Swinging at the man, flames shot from the end of the blade like bolts from a crossbow, catching the man in the face. He screamed and dropped to the ground as the flames scorched his eyes. As Marcus had his back turned, one of the men leaped into the air, ready to bring his sword down. Before Marcus could react, a massive blast of wind sent the man flying several stories up into the air. Marcus swung his head in the opposite direction to see Breeze and Violet running up the street toward them.

Bow drawn, Breeze sent off a handful of arrows. Several of the pirates were able to block the arrows, but a few of them found their targets in the flesh. Violet had no weapon to speak of, but she had her abilities. Thrusting her hands out, she blasted two of the pirates to the ground with her telekinetic abilities. It was quickly becoming a fair fight. One of the pirates noticed Violet and took off running towards her. Fear gripped Violet as the man was almost upon her.

Violet threw her palms toward him. The pirate stopped abruptly and fell to the ground. Dropping his sword, the pirate gripped his head and began to scream out. The other pirates looked over. Violet's palms were glowing, but no one was really sure what she was doing. Iggy was making quick work of those who were attacking him. His small size had made the pirates greatly underestimate his ability to fight and hold his own.

Zeph continued to battle the lead pirate. With a quick flurry of his sword, Zeph finally knocked the pirate's sword from his hand; it skidded to the side of the street. The pirate leader staggered back. Most of his men were groaning on the ground. Anger burned in his eyes as he looked at Zeph. Dropping his sack of stolen goods, he quickly picked up his sword and motioned for his men to do the same. After they had dropped all they had taken, they staggered to their feet and headed towards the harbor.

"I won't forget this, boy!" the leader screamed angrily. "You've made a powerful enemy today. If my captain had been here, he would have torn you to pieces!"

They quickly disappeared down the street. Slowly, people began coming out of their shops and homes. The contents of the sacks were dumped in the street, and everyone came to collect what was their possessions. Rounds of thanks rang out from everyone that came over. It was a display that most had never seen on their streets before. There had always been an unwritten understanding between the pirates and merchants on *The Order* of things. Today though, that order of things had been challenged. Future pirates would now know that some would challenge them.

The boys met up with the girls. The girls were glad the commotion had drawn their attention from a neighboring street. Breeze asked what had started the whole thing. She knew how the boys could easily get into trouble. After Zeph took a moment to explain the situation, it was clear to her that they had made the right decision in defending the citizens.

The sound of clapping caused them all to turn their attention up the street. A figure of a lone man could be seen slowly walking towards them. He was a well-dressed sea captain. The combination of his large hat and the light from the midday suns hid his face.

"Now that was something truly unexpected. I see you have come far in the last four months," the man said in a familiar tone.

Everyone else was confused by the man's words. Not Zeph, though. He instantly recognized the man's voice. Placing his sword back in the sheath, Zeph ran happily towards the man. They grasped hands and embraced each other. The rest followed Zeph over. As they grew closer, they suddenly recognized him as well and rushed over. It was the fancy attire that had thrown everyone off at first glance, everyone except Zeph.

Victor removed his hat and embraced them all. He looked over at Violet with a questioning glance. They quickly explained the situation that had caused her to join their party. Victor was sure the brief explanation was just the tip of the iceberg. He invited them all back to the *Nephesh* to share their stories.

They all walked up the street together. It was an unexpected pleasure to see Victor again. The months apart had gone by quickly, but their time together with him had always stayed in their minds. As they reached the central piers, they quickly looked around for signs of the pirates they had encountered. They didn't want to have another confrontation so soon. With so many ships in the harbor, they wouldn't likely cross paths on their way to Victor's ship. They continued down the docks and soon reached the *Nephesh*.

Zeph stopped and looked at the ship. It was different. There had clearly been a great deal of modifications since they had last seen her. Much of the vessel was reinforced with brass joints. New sails were strung on the masts. Overall, it almost looked like a brand-new ship. Victor caught Zeph looking the ship over. He came up behind him and placed a hand on his shoulder.

"She looks great, doesn't she?" he asked.

"She really does. I see you've been busy too," Zeph said, turning to Victor.

"Mhm, everything has been refitted and rebuilt. If it hadn't been for Gus' help, this project would have taken well over twice as long."

"He's doing well then?"

"Who? Gus?" Victor questioned, "Yes, he's doing very well. The shop has never been better. In fact, much of Daunt has had modifications that were in no small part due to Gus' influence. Every person in town has a sphere lamp now."

That was surprising to Zeph. Daunt was a simple town, and it was hard to picture the whole town having modifications made to it. It was exciting to discover that their invention had spread throughout the entire town. Perhaps they would be able to stop back at Daunt before they journeyed to Tsayla.

They boarded the *Nephesh* and headed for the captain's cabin. Koch came over and greeted them. He seemed shorter than before somehow but still looked tough as nails. Everyone entered and sat down on the pillows. Victor hopped into his hammock and swung his legs over the edge. It had been a good while since they had all sat in the cabin together.

Victor looked each one of them over. With the exception of Violet, they were all as he remembered, and yet somehow different at the same time. It was quite clear that much had transpired since they left Daunt all those months before. The last time Victor had seen them was when they had walked out of town on their journey for Tweedsmiur. As he stared at them now, it almost seemed like years had gone by.

"Well, I think for once I need to be regaled with some amazing stories, and I'm sure you all have some interesting ones for me," Victor said with a smile as he leaned back in his hammock with great anticipation.

Zeph laughed, as did everyone else. He wasn't wrong. Zeph started from the beginning, with the fiend encounter outside the forest. He also told of the forest and the events in Tweedsmiur. Victor listened closely.

As the stories continued, he leaned forward, hanging onto Zeph's every word. He was amazed at what they had all been through in such a short period. Violet was also on the edge of her seat as these stories were a first for her as well.

Once Zeph reached the part of the story where they met Sensei, Victor began to understand why they were so well trained. Several hours passed, and Zeph finally finished telling all that had transpired. Victor leaned back in the hammock. It was a lot to take in. He simply smiled and shook his head.

"That's more than I've experienced in the last year. Although, I do have to say that my life has become much more eventful since meeting you, Zeph," Victor said with a chuckle. "So it sounds like the next place you're heading to is the continent of Tsayla?"

"I'm thinking so," Zeph replied. "We're still trying to track down what happened to the Shadow Scroll. At this point, all we have to go on is my vision of Desiree and myths and legends that are centuries old. Perhaps there is more we can learn in the Shadow Realm that will help."

"So, do you have any better understanding of your role, Zeph?" Victor asked curiously.

"Not really; I can only guess that our combined purpose will become clearer as I find the other Scroll Holders in the world. I'm sure that they are searching the world for me as well. Or I may continue to receive visions to guide me along the way."

Victor nodded as he listened to Zeph's words. The young man was taking on a huge task. From what he had just learned, Zeph seemed to be taking strong leaps towards his destiny.

"I know this might sound like an odd question, but what are you doing here, Victor?" Iggy asked.

"Ah! Now, that is a good question. Of course, you know I don't normally ever sail this way; I keep my trading around the Eastern Sea and the World Vortex regions. But since I've been spending so much time in Daunt, I decided to branch out and visit some of the other cities on Appagon. My main source of trade has been nothing but lamps and Pirie juice for several months now. In some ways, I have almost started to call

Daunt my home," Victor said with a smile. Everyone else seemed to like that answer.

"How's my father?" Breeze questioned.

"Oh, Gus is doing fine, dear. He misses you very much, though. His shop is doing fantastic. They're thinking of making him one of the town elders. Can you believe that?" Victor said with a laugh.

"Oh, well, he must be making a good impression then," Breeze said as she smiled and shook her head.

"I was going to suggest we spend a few days in Iy Ra'Kal selling sphere lamps, but after that incident with those pirates, our best course of action would be to leave. I don't want to involve my crew in that conflict. Don't get me wrong, I completely agree with what you did back there, but there will be consequences."

They all looked at each other for a moment. The thought had never really crossed their minds. Perhaps doing the right thing was not as simple as it had seemed at the time.

"What do you suggest we do then?" asked Zeph.

"I say we swing around the northeast point of Appagon, head down for Daunt, and then on to Tsayla. Who's with me?" he asked with a mischievous grin. They all smiled. Their next adventure was just beginning.

DAY 208

> Setting an example is not the main way to influence others; it is the only way.
>
> You are only as strong as your convictions.
>
> For even the strongest amongst, you will falter without a cause.
>
> ~ Praotes

CHAPTER 16
I CAN SEA HOME

After loading up some supplies for the journey, the crew headed out the next morning. There was no sign of the pirates from the altercation on the previous day. Victor had informed them how dangerous it could be to cross paths with pirates. Some were nothing more than scavengers who would rather steal and run. Others were to be avoided at all costs if you valued your life. Victor informed them that the pirate known as Captain Domm was, without a doubt, the latter.

Zeph had never been on the *Nephesh* when it was actually out on the seas before; it was a fantastic experience for him. He stood on the front deck of the ship. The sails had caught the wind, and the ship had taken off quickly. Every time the ship caught a wave, he felt himself lift from the deck slightly. It was an exhilarating sensation. It instantly brought back all the memories he had as a child on his father's fishing boat. It had been so long since Zeph had stepped foot on a ship that he was starting to understand why his father had found it so freeing.

Water sprayed up over the bow of the ship. The wind was strong today, so they were off to a good start. Clear skies were overhead, and the warmth of the suns shone down on them. Flocks of birds flew overhead. As they headed east along the Appagon's northern coast, the shoreline could be seen off their starboard side in the distance. For the journey to Daunt, there wasn't any need to travel far out to sea, just as long as they stayed away from the reefs and coastline.

Victor came up behind him. Zeph turned around, smiling with a big grin. All Victor could do was shake his head and laugh.

"I see you're enjoying yourself," Victor said as he slapped him on the back.

"This is fantastic. It's nothing like the smaller boats I've been on before."

"Well, that's good because I'm going to teach the whole lot of you how to sail. I have a feeling you're going to be with me for a good while, so you might as well know your way around the ship."

Zeph's eyes lit up, and he quickly ran to the other side of the ship to grab the others. After being practically dragged to the ship's bow, Victor made them all stand at attention. The other sailors onboard the ship momentarily stopped what they were doing to watch what was about to happen.

"If the five of you are going to be on my ship for any length of time, you'll have to know how this ship runs and how your skills can be used for the overall benefit of the ship and crew." They stood patiently and listened to Victor's words. "First of all, can any of you tell me what kind of ship the *Nephesh* is?" he asked.

Iggy quickly raised his hand, "It's a Barquentine, Captain."

"That is correct, Iggy. A Barquentine is a sailing ship with three or more masts. This ship has a main square rigged foremast," Victor said as he pointed to the large mast above their heads. They all craned their heads to look up. There was a series of large square-shaped sails going up the mast. "These sails are called jibs," he said, pointing to the sails that ran from the main mast to the front of the ship.

"The rest of the sails are fore-and-arc rigged sails. You will also notice the sails I have created for the sides of the hull," Victor said as he directed them to one of the ship's rails. Everyone looked down at the wing-shaped sails protruding from the side of the ship. "These are designed to create lift and reduce drag created by the ship cutting through the water. At high speed, these allow the ship to hover over the water for brief periods. You will also need to familiarize yourself with the different sides of the ship and their names. Can someone tell me what they're called?" Iggy raised his hand again. "Someone other than Iggy."

"The front is called the bow, the back is called the stern, the left is called port, and the right is called starboard," Violet replied.

"You, young lady, are correct. I see you have some basic knowledge of sailing vessels," Victor said as Violet blushed a little.

With the introduction to sailing out of the way, Victor put them to work. They spent the rest of the day working the rigs and learning how all the sails worked together. It was a very long day. The hours passed, and the energy and excitement they had felt in the morning quickly faded. As night began to fall, the crew again took over all the tasks. The winds were calmer that night, so keeping the ship sailing onward didn't require much effort. The group headed down below. Rows of hammocks were strung up below deck for the crew to sleep in. Over a dozen people were onboard, including their group and the regular crew.

No argument was needed before they all climbed into a hammock and quickly fell asleep, knowing the morning would bring just as much labor. The ship rocked back and forth with the movement of the sea. Zeph let himself rock gently back and forth. He looked over at everyone, fast asleep. A lot was going on, but he felt good about it. For the first time in weeks, he felt as though he had no cares in the world.

The second day started quickly. It felt like they were up again as soon as their heads had hit the pillow. The rest of the crew was busy doing their tasks around the ship. Zeph and the gang climbed up from the lower deck. Victor took one look at them and shook his head. They were a ripe bunch when it came to sailing. He was surprised that no one had thrown up yet. No sooner had the thought crossed his mind when he saw Marcus run for the railing.

Victor decided to be a little lighter on them today. The tasks were simple, most of which revolved around scrubbing the ship. After the previous day, they were all glad to do it. Around midday, they broke for lunch. The food was actually rather tasty. It was common for the different crew members to take turns cooking for the ship.

Zeph spotted Violet near the bow of the ship. He walked over and sat down next to her. She was still a little timid, but that was to be expected. It had been a while since she had been on a ship. Being surrounded by complete strangers didn't help either. Zeph was different, though. There was something attractive about him other than his boyish good looks.

Violet turned to look at Zeph sitting across from her. He was looking out across the sea to the coast in the distance. She wondered what he was thinking. He looked so deep in thought, as if his mind were thousands of miles away.

"What are you thinking about?" she asked in a gentle tone. There was a pause before Zeph spoke.

"Do you see those cliffs?" he asked, pointing at the coast. She nodded. "I almost did something truly horrible up on those cliffs months ago."

"You tried to kill yourself, didn't you?" Her question caused Zeph to immediately turn his head and lock his gaze on her. "I can't read your mind or anything like that; I just know that look. When you grow up on the streets, you see that look a lot. I'm sure people saw that look in my eyes many times as well."

Zeph nodded slowly as he turned his gaze back towards the open waters. Memories of that day on the cliffs entered his mind. The torment and despair he had felt that day still stung deep inside at times. Closing his eyes, he took a deep breath and pushed the thoughts away. There was no need to dwell on the past.

"Can I ask you something?"

"Sure," she replied.

"What exactly did you do to that one pirate during the fight back in Iy Ra'Kal?"

"I...I don't really know," Violet said slowly as her gaze shifted to her hands. "I've done it before, but only when I'm really emotional. I've never been able to do it by just concentrating."

"What is it exactly?"

"I really don't think you want to know, Zeph. It's a darker ability associated with Shadow Elementals."

The look on his face showed that he still wanted to know more. Violet sat there for a moment and looked down at her thumbs. She had never opened up to anyone before, at least not like this.

"It's most commonly called Pain. You take all the emotional pain inside yourself and inflict it on someone else as physical pain."

The sound of the men working on the ship and the voices on the deck was all that was heard. Water sprayed into the air from the bow of the vessel. Violet kept her head down but looked up slightly towards

Zeph. Through the stands of purple hair hanging in front of her face, she saw that he was simply holding his hand out to her. Hesitantly, she took it.

"I understand," was all he said.

Conceivably, if Zeph had grown up in a different place at a different time, he would have also developed such destructive abilities. All elements had the potential to be used in detrimental ways. A person with Light abilities could choose to light a path or blind someone. It was entirely up to the individual to decide how to channel and use their abilities. During his struggles, Zeph had hurt people, people he loved. It didn't matter if it was unintentional or not; he still felt the weight of those actions.

Breeze watched Zeph and Violet sitting together from farther down the ship. Once again, she felt that sting inside. Seeing the two of them holding hands intensified the feelings she desperately didn't want to have. With every passing day, she felt a little better and then a little worse. Parts of her were healing, while other parts were still breaking. She knew the time would come when she and Zeph would be happy for one another, and no pain would be involved. It seemed as though Zeph was rapidly moving away from her, and she feared that she would lose him altogether. She was about to start walking over to them when she felt a gentle tap on her shoulder. It was Marcus standing behind her. He, too, had been watching Zeph and Violet's interaction.

"I know what you're thinking, Breeze, and all I can tell you is don't lose hope," he said as he put an arm around her shoulders.

"I just don't know what to do. I feel like it was all a mistake," Breeze said, almost in tears. Marcus turned her around to face him.

"You were his first love, Breeze. No matter what happens, he will always remember that. He'll remember the first time you smiled at him, the first time he held your hand, the first time you kissed under that tree. I know that he feels like he has destroyed everything good he had with you because of what happened that day. I don't want to say letting go of him is the answer, but if you do, just know that it doesn't mean he won't still be there for you."

After Marcus finished speaking, he wrapped his arms around her again and held her close. This was the first time Marcus had really seen Breeze heartbroken like this. He hoped that this would not become a recurring situation. They had all been through a lot. Marcus knew all the stories about their relationship. Zeph would tell him everything that happened between Breeze and him. The three of them had been so close over their years together; Marcus hoped it would continue for many more.

Victor stood at the wheel of the ship. Even though he could have any of his crew steer the vessel, he always preferred to be the one behind the wheel when possible. Iggy walked down the deck and stood beside him. He had been wearing his cloak without the hood pulled over his head for several days. His light brown hair looked even lighter out on the open seas.

"I have to say, Iggy, you've come a long way since we last met," Victor said as he glanced down at him.

"I never thought I would," he replied.

"Oh?" asked Victor, slightly puzzled by the statement.

"I just never really thought I could make it, that I could really be someone," Iggy said as he leaned on his staff.

"Now that does puzzle me, Iggy. Size should not be a thing that defines you. Do you remember back at the Festival? When Marcus was fighting that smaller man?" Iggy nodded. "Marcus thought he could beat him simply because he was larger and, therefore, somehow tougher. But we both know how that ended."

Iggy smiled at hearing his words. As he looked up at Victor, he imagined this was what it would have been like to sail with his father. Victor looked down at him with a mischievous grin. Stepping to the side, he offered the wheel to Iggy. Never had he seen a face light up like Iggy's did just then. Carefully, Iggy took hold of the wheel as Victor instructed. He felt the subtle pull on the wheel as the ship moved forward, and the sails caught the wind. It was very exhilarating for him.

The voyage was going quite well since they left Iy Ra'Kal. The wind was with them, as was the weather. They would round the northeast point by nightfall. From there, traveling south would take less than a day to reach Daunt. They were all very excited about it. No one knew they were coming back with Victor. In fact, no one in Daunt knew precisely when to expect Victor back.

Nightfall came upon the sea. Zeph stood on the front deck of the ship. He loved to stare out at the night sky. There were so many stars to look at. The moons were not visible at the moment, so nothing but the night sky hung above his head. He leaned on the railing, head craned upwards. Breeze slowly came up behind him. She leaned against the railing next to him. Looking up at the stars was something they both loved to do together. It was something they hadn't done together in a while now.

Zeph looked over at her. She was beautiful, just like the very first day he met her. Sliding his hand over the railing, he let his fingers drape over hers. It was comforting, more comforting than she was expecting it to feel. He leaned over and softly kissed her cheek. She breathed in deeply and closed her eyes. The conflict in her arose again. Feeling him there with her brought back all the memories they shared. It was then that she knew there would always be something between them, even if they never got back together. She would try her best to stand firm in the choice she made until the time came that fate might bring them together once more. They stayed there on the deck for a while longer before they headed off to bed.

There was always something to be done on the ship. Stories of Victor's past voyages began to surface among the crew. Despite Victor's objections that some of his more embarrassing stories not be told, they still found their way out. He would shake his head and laugh as his crew would share some truly absurd and over-exaggerated stories with the group of youths.

The *Nephesh* rounded the northeast point of Appagon and began heading south. As they began heading south, Zeph looked up at the cliffs. After searching for a while, he spotted the cave on the cliffs where he had spent those few weeks with Gus. He was excited to see Gus and everyone else once they returned. Seeing his mother had been on his mind since he climbed into his hammock. They would be at Daunt before long.

As the suns rose in the west over the Appagon mountains, the crew was already hard at work. They would reach Daunt only in a few hours. Preparations were underway for the ship's arrival. As they traveled down the coast, the towering cliffs slowly gave way to the rolling hills. Everyone was on deck as they began the final run toward Daunt. Due to the reefs, they would have to come away from the coast and spin around to make their final approach.

Siah sat alone in the Trading Post tower. Since it was the last day of the week, almost everyone else in Daunt had headed off to the Temple for the weekly Gathering. Not many ships came to port on the last day of the week. It was a nice, slow day. There were still several dockhands around in case something came up. As he glanced out on the horizon, a sail caught his eye. Picking up his scope, he looked out to sea. After a few moments of focusing the scope, he made out the *Nephesh*.

Siah and Victor had become good friends during the months he had been traveling to and from Daunt. After Victor set up Daunt as his primary village to conduct trade, they began spending even more time together. Both being men of the seas, they swapped many stories. Many of them were of Khoz and Siah's voyages together. It was through these stories that Victor began to get a greater understanding of who Zeph's father had been. Victor was proud that Zeph had come to think of him in a similar way to his father.

Siah marched down the docks and waited for the ship to pull into port. As the *Nephesh* drew closer, the figures standing on deck caught his attention. He probably wouldn't have recognized them if not for the shining white hair on one of the figures. Siah's heart leaped with happiness as the ship came to rest at the dock. The deckhands extended a plank to the ship. Zeph stood at the top and looked down at Siah.

"Hello, Uncle," he said with a smile as he walked down the plank. Siah rushed over and wrapped his massive arms around him, picking him off the ground.

"Oh, how I missed you, boy!" he exclaimed.

Iggy and Marcus were next down the plank. Dropping Zeph, he, in turn, scooped them up in unison. Breeze and Violet followed after them.

Once again, Siah dropped the two boys and scooped the girls up in his massive arms.

"Violet, this is Zeph and Iggy's Uncle Siah," Breeze said, trying to breathe within the massive squeeze he was giving them both.

"Nice to meet you," Violet replied with an awkward look of confusion on her face. He quickly set them down. Violet leaned over to Breeze, "That's not how everyone says hello in this town, is it?" she questioned nervously. Breeze just laughed and shook her head.

They began walking down the pier towards town. Siah told them all about how everything had changed since they left. As they left the dock and began to enter the town, the changes became more and more evident. It appeared as though the whole town had undergone some sort of renovation since they had left only four months earlier.

The first thing that caught their attention was the extensive shop at the end of the pier, where the dock joined the main road in town. It was Gus' shop. The shop size did not reflect the frame they had seen being put up when they had first left Daunt. Siah explained that Gus' shop had quickly become a source of many beneficial things for the town. Not only did his inventions produce a great deal of trade, but he also helped to upgrade many features throughout the village.

As they stood outside the shop, they glanced up and down the street. Siah was right; much had changed. The look of the buildings had been upgraded to include new windows, stronger side paneling, and much more. The tall metal poles on the corners caught Zeph's attention. He walked over to one of them and examined it. On the top was a large metal ball. It didn't make sense at first, but then he spotted a small crank handle on the side of the pole. Grabbing hold, he started to turn the handle. Shutters around the ball began to open, revealing a brightly glowing ball of fire contained inside. Zeph looked at the surface of the glass; it was amazing to see the sphere lamps at that size. He then looked up and down the street. Every corner had one of the poles. A sense of accomplishment he had never known before bubbled up inside of him. He couldn't believe that their small little invention had grown this far.

"It's amazing, isn't it?" Siah asked as he came up behind Zeph.

"I just can't believe how much the town has advanced. I mean, there's a huge sphere lamp on every corner," Zeph said as he shook his head in disbelief.

"Oh, there is much more than that, but I'll save that for Gus to show you."

"Speaking of which, where is he?" Zeph questioned.

"Oh, I'm sure he's at the Gathering with everyone else."

Zeph pulled out his pocket watch. It was that time. Everyone would be down at the Temple. That also explained why the town seemed so empty and quiet. They gathered together and began heading for the Temple. Everything seemed brand new. It wasn't just from the paint on the buildings or the new stones that lined the main streets. The town seemed newer overall; it was refreshing. Violet was the only one in the group who was not mesmerized by the changes to the town. Then again, she didn't have anything to compare it to, and even though it had a more polished look now, it was nothing like the upscale feel of the trade district in Iy Ra'Kal.

As they climbed the hill leading up to the Temple, they could hear Praotes speaking. It was a comforting feeling to hear his voice once again. The Temple's windows and large front doors were open, allowing the breeze to flow through. Once it was filled with people, it would often get hot in the Temple. It could sometimes become quite uncomfortable if not for the windows and some Wind Elemental's abilities.

Zeph stopped them for a moment outside the doors. He wanted to listen to what was being said before they entered. Once they walked through the doors, everyone in the Temple would turn to face them, and Zeph just wanted to listen to what was going on before that happened.

"If one man says to another, 'Go, I wish you well on your journey; keep warm and stay fed,' but does nothing about his physical need, what good are his words? In the same way, faith by itself, if not accompanied by action, is dead. Faith cannot be fulfilled without actions. For it is by the evidence of your faith that it is made complete." Zeph heard Praotes pause for a moment. He could picture him holding onto the stone pedestal, looking at the faces of everyone inside.

"If anyone is in trouble, they should call out to Omega. If anyone is joyful, let them sing songs of praise." Zeph slowly walked towards the entrance, and the rest of the group followed. Praotes was the first to spot them. Even though the light flowed in from outside, he still made out their faces. A soft smile, warmer than the suns, appeared on his face. Everyone else turned and looked. The shock was on many of their faces. A figure near the front quickly jumped from their seat and raced over. Dawn threw her arms around Zeph.

"Oh, thank Omega!" Dawn cried as she tried to hold back the tears. She cupped his face in her hands and started to cry. Tears of joy were never sweeter than those. Praotes came over and offered his hand to each of them. When he came to Violet, he took her hand softly. There was a kindness on his face she hadn't seen in many years. Gently, he pulled her close and embraced her. She offered no resistance as she, too, put her arms around him.

"There is something special about you, young lady; I feel as though you are meant for great things," Praotes said in his soft, gentle voice.

Breeze looked around but saw no sign of Gus. Disappointment flooded her face, and then a hand touched her shoulder. Turning, she saw her father standing there with tears in his eyes. She quickly clutched him and held him tightly.

"It is so good to see you, dear," he said shakily.

"I missed you so much, Daddy."

Marcus also found his parents in the crowd. Zeph and Iggy brought Violet over to meet Dawn. They figured she could stay with them since Violet had no family or other connections in Daunt. Dawn held her like a daughter. There was an instant connection between the two of them.

The whole congregation left the Temple and flooded outside. Everyone wanted to see the group and hear their stories. Zeph assured everyone that there would be time for that later. The townsfolk dispersed back throughout the town. Only the family members of the group remained. Victor walked over to Dawn and wrapped his arms around her.

They had no idea where to start first. So much needed to be said and shown to them. Dawn and Gus were particularly interested in hearing all that had happened. It was clear that much had transpired along their journey. Zeph had a look about him now that his mother couldn't quite place. He had more confidence and strength than she had ever seen before.

After gathering some food, they all sat on the hill behind the Temple. No house was large enough for everyone to fit in, so the idea of an outdoor picnic was the best they could muster. Everyone sat in a large circle. Zeph began the tale of their adventure so far. The hours went by quickly. For the group, listening to the story was like hearing some fantastic tale by a grand storyteller. It wasn't, though; it was a true tale of their children's lives. Zeph wondered how they were taking it. He had to live it, and at times, he felt he could never become the character his life's story was beginning to tell. Their triumphs, struggles, and perseverance were all evident throughout the story.

"I'm very proud of you, Zeph." Gus had spoken up. "You have overcome your struggles far better than most people I have known. There was a time when you learned from me, but now I feel we could learn from you."

Everyone in the group nodded in agreement. Zeph simply sat there in the grass, his fingers slipping in between the strands. Sitting there, it felt like home again, surrounded by his friends and family. They took the rest of the day to relax and spend time with their families. The next day, they would take a tour of the 'new' town.

Sleep came quickly for them that night. Each had gone to their own home. One difference was that Gus now had a house in town. He had not abandoned his grand house outside of town but instead moved much of their belongings to the new house. This was part of why his shop in town had seemed so much larger than expected. Not long after the shop had been completed, Gus began producing the sphere lamps regularly. He then asked if he could build an attached house. The town elders welcomed the request with open arms.

The setup of the house was similar to that of the house outside of town. It had a large open hall and a loft as well. He had separated the loft into two parts. Each part had a different staircase to allow for completely separate accommodations. This was made so that when Breeze was home, she would have privacy even though they shared the same section of the house. From the living room, it also connected directly to Gus' shop without having to go around to the main entrance. After Gus gave Breeze a quick tour, they headed off to bed.

Zeph and Iggy gave Violet a tour of their family home. Dawn went straight to work setting up a nice bed for her in the den. Violet liked the fact that she was staying with Zeph since he was the only one she really felt comfortable around at the moment. Zeph went up to his room and opened the door. Other than being tidier than when he left, it was exactly the same. It was nice to be home and actually sleep in his own bed again. He was surprised at how much he missed it.

As he lay down in his bed, he looked up at the burn marks on his ceiling. They hadn't crossed his mind for a while now. After the final message from Mage Saphar in the book, he hadn't really turned to it anymore. He was still uncertain about the whole purpose of the page of control glyphs. Zeph had taken it upon himself to memorize them so they would be recognizable if he saw them on anything. He was sure that their purpose would come into play at some point.

Rays of light came flowing in through the window. Zeph lay sprawled across his bed. One leg hung off one side while his opposing arm hung off the other. A pool of drool was on his pillow. He slowly opened his eyes a crack. Standing there in his doorway was Violet and Iggy. Both had their heads cocked sideways to match Zeph's awkward position. Zeph simply groaned and pulled the blankets over his face.

"What do you two want?" his muffled voice came from under his blanket.

"Oh, this just seemed like an interesting study in sleeping positions," Iggy said mockingly.

"Your mom told us to come and get you up," Violet piped up.

Zeph rolled onto his back and tried to blink. He was sure that it wasn't that late in the day. Perhaps just being back in his own bed once again made him love the feeling of sleep so much. He let out a big yawn and slowly sat up. His hair was a mess, as always, and he had a sluggish look about him. Violet smiled at him as he walked by. He gave her a smile and a nod between half-closed eyes as he walked past her and headed for the bathroom. They headed downstairs, and Zeph joined them shortly afterward.

"Good morning, sleepyhead," his mother said as she looked over at him.

"Mhmmmm," Zeph replied, still trying to fully wake up.

"It's good to have you boys home," she said with a smile.

Both Zeph and Iggy exchanged glances. They hadn't told her yet that this was just a stop along the way. She crossed her arms and stared intensely at them as if reading their minds.

"You're not staying, are you?" Dawn asked, a sense of hurt in her voice.

Zeph walked over and took his mother's hands. He saw in her eyes how much this was hurting her. Even though he didn't want to put her through any more pain, he knew he had to. She looked back at him. It was the same look she used to give his father every time he left. Zeph never expected to receive that look from her; he could see the pain that look carried.

"I'm sorry, Mom, but we have to go again. We won't be heading out for a few days, though," he said, trying to comfort her.

She walked out of the kitchen and headed to her room. The kitchen fell silent. Zeph just stood there and leaned against the counter. He never intended to hurt his mother by leaving. In fact, he never intended for any of this to happen. However, that did not change anything, and he had to continue with the quest that had been handed to him. Iggy looked up from the table at Zeph. Both he and Violet seemed to be looking at him for direction. Zeph just simply sighed. He knew his mother and knew that she would be fine in time, but for now, she needed to be alone.

They finished up their breakfast and cleaned the kitchen. It was a small gesture, but a gesture nonetheless. They grabbed a few things and were just about to leave when Dawn came out of her room and walked over to her boys.

"You're all I have left. I can't lose you," she said, holding them in her arms.

"You won't, Mom," Zeph said as he gently rubbed a hand against her back.

She forced a smile and waved them off. They headed down the dirt path from the house onto the main road. Looking down the street, the old packed dirt road had been replaced with a much more durable cobblestone layout.

The three of them chatted as they began to walk through town. Zeph pointed out many things to Violet as they walked. She was enjoying the village. It was small and simple and seemed like a great place to grow up. All the buildings now had a white and brown theme. Zeph assumed it must have something to do with Gus' paint, which Siah had mentioned. Looking at the sphere lamp poles on every corner, Zeph wishes he had gone out in the middle of the night to see what they really looked like.

"So you lived here your whole life?" Violet asked as they walked.

"You bet. I never really knew anything else about the world. Well, at least, nothing besides the stories my father would tell me about his voyages," Zeph explained.

"Can I ask you something personal?"

"What do you want to know?" Zeph asked.

"What's your relationship with Breeze?"

Zeph smiled awkwardly and nodded his head as they continued walking. It wasn't an easy question, but he figured he would give it a shot. He told Violet about their past together and how their friendship over the years slowly turned into something more. Then, she wanted to know how things had gotten to the state they were now.

"Well, that's a little complicated. After I opened the Omega Scroll, I lost control of my abilities," Zeph paused for a moment as the images flashed in his mind from the day he had struck Breeze with his uncontrolled energy, "I hurt her physically; I could have easily killed her. Which I think was something she could have forgiven me for, given the accidental circumstances. But when I tried to take my own life, that was something that broke us, I think. I know it's not because she doesn't love me anymore; it's just that things are different now."

"I think I actually understand all of that," Violet replied. "Just let things play out on their own for now and see where life takes you."

Zeph had to admit it was good advice. They realized that they were now standing in front of Gus' shop. It was early, but they could see movement inside. They walked up to the front door, and before they could even knock, the door suddenly swung open. Gus stood there, goggles on his head and a work apron strapped around his waist.

"Welcome, gang!" he exclaimed, "Come right in. I can't wait to show you around."

They entered the shop and were utterly blown away. It was truly amazing. The front portion was a shopping area and a front counter of sorts. The rest of the shop was completely open. Behind the desk were several other townsfolk working on different devices at various stations. Zeph recognized the machine in the corner. It was just like the machine from Gus' old house. It was bigger and better than ever before, though. There was a large table in the middle of the work area. It was metal and had many different parts and pieces of contraptions scattered across it. All kinds of inventions were scattered throughout the shop. The whole shop was as big as Gus' old house, meaning it was at least four times the size of Zeph's house.

Gus encouraged them to walk about and take a look at everything. In the meantime, he returned to one of his workstations off to the side. Zeph took a look around; there was so much to take in. A series of large drawings pinned to the wall on the far side of the room caught his attention. He walked over and began to study them. They were of the *Nephesh*. It showed the various changes Gus had made to it already. There were more layouts as well, showing even more modifications.

"Are you planning on adding more to the *Nephesh*?" Zeph asked as he studied the blueprints. Gus rolled over on his work chair and lifted his work glasses.

"That I am. Victor and I have been going over these for quite a while. We've made all the initial modifications to the ship, basically just reinforcing the overall structure and whatnot. The next stage is to make major changes to the ship."

"What are these long tubes you have in the diagram here?" Zeph asked, running his hands over the paper.

"Those are something I've been working on. Just like how my pressure machine has to build up a lot of steam for the melting process, these tubes would channel similar steam out the back of the ship. I believe I can make the ship travel across the water using this as a method of propulsion."

The idea sounded amazing to Zeph. He was sure that if anyone could make it work, it would be Gus. Iggy continued to look around as they talked. Glancing up, he happened to notice a set of wings hanging up in the rafters. They reminded him of the wing sails that came out of the sides of the *Nephesh*.

"What's the plan for these Gus?" Iggy asked, pointing upwards.

"AH! Perfect timing, Iggy. Going along with what I was telling you, Zeph; I think that once those release tubes are installed in the *Nephesh*, the main sails could be removed, and all that would be needed is a series of sails like these. With the speeds the ship could reach, it could pretty much fly over the water all the time," Gus explained excitedly.

"Wow, so you're talking about, in essence, making some sort of a flying ship?" Iggy questioned with equal excitement in his voice.

"That I am, my boy!" Gus replied with a huge grin. "Granted, it won't soar through the sky, but it will fly over the water."

Just then, Breeze walked in through the doors that led from the house to the shop. She still looked a little tired but awake enough. Zeph smiled over at her, and she smiled back. Gus went over and gave her a hug. It was quick and caught Breeze a little off guard. Everyone just chuckled a little. She joined the rest of them and looked around the shop some more. Iggy had a million questions for Gus. That was his inventor curiosity coming out.

"I'm guessing Daddy already told you about his flying-thingy," Breeze said, shaking her head.

"Yes, he has," Zeph replied with a laugh.

"I'm guessing you got the short version. At the crack of dawn, I started hearing about all his inventions," she said as she blinked and opened her eyes wide for a moment in an attempt to clear her vision.

"Are you glad to be home?" asked Violet.

"Mhm, it's nice to see my father again. I know he's been missing me terribly. That's probably why so much got done while we were gone."

"What do you mean?" Violet asked, puzzled.

"Well, when Daddy is distressed, he works. It's been that way ever since Mom died," Breeze explained.

They continued to look around the shop. It had many half-finished inventions lying everywhere. Blueprints for future inventions were also scattered around. Gus introduced the other workers to them. Several men and women from town had always wanted to invent but never had the opportunity. It also worked out perfectly for Gus, since two of them were Fire Elementals and the other was Wind. Working on the sphere lamps had been very easy with their help. Hearing that, a handful of questions came up in Zeph's mind.

"So, how many sphere lamps have you made?" he asked Gus.

"Oh, I stopped counting after a thousand," he grinned.

Everyone's jaws practically hit the floor. They couldn't believe that Gus had produced that many. Gus motioned them over to a nearby chest. It was an enormous, long chest, large enough for two full-grown men to fit inside. He swung the top open. Light burst from inside. Everyone peered inside, and to their amazement, they saw hundreds and hundreds of glowing sphere lamps inside.

Gus looked back at them with a twinkle in his eye. He then waved them over to a metal chest in the corner. After playing with the locks for a moment, he also opened that chest. Inside, they saw thousands of kessas, both silver and gold.

"Daunt has completely stopped using oil lamps and candles of any kind. Every home has at least five spheres in it. And, as I'm sure you've already seen, we now have large sphere street lamps," Gus said proudly.

They all looked at each other. Not in their wildest dreams had they ever thought their crazy idea would grow into what it had become. It was one invention, and a simple one at that. Seeing how it had grown into something so much more was absolutely amazing to behold.

"We've been able to use the revenue from it to help the town and produce commerce that Daunt has never seen," Gus explained.

"So what are you going to do now?" asked Marcus.

"Well, we've put off the production of more lamps for the time being, as we have more than enough in storage for a while. There is talk that we will start production on a larger pier and dock system. I am also very interested in sitting down with Victor again and reviewing the new *Nephesh* modifications."

"That will be a large undertaking, won't it?" Iggy asked.

"Oh, no doubt it will be. Once I have all the parts and machines built, installing and modifying the ship will still take weeks. I've already started collecting the parts to build the machines. Some merchants from Thai have been very helpful. It seems they use steam-powered machines a great deal in that part of the world," Gus said as he led them around the shop some more. He liked to walk while he talked.

"Perhaps it will be done by the time we return again," Zeph suggested.

The room instantly fell silent. Gus stopped what he was doing and stood there with a blank expression on his face. Breeze had already told him that they would only be in town for a short while before continuing their journey. It wasn't something he really wanted to think about quite yet. He had missed his daughter greatly in her absence.

After a moment had passed, Gus took a breath and shook it off. Forcing a smile, he led them from the shop and into the adjoining house. They began to reminisce about the last few months. Gus was eager to take a look at their new weapons. It wasn't often that such different materials came to Daunt. Since they all had clear translucent weapons, it attracted more attention than typical metal would have. It was strange to look upon a sword that had the appearance of fogged glass.

Iggy's alchemy skills were another thing that piqued Gus' interest. Even though he had never researched that field himself, Gus still possessed some basic knowledge of it. Being an inventor, he was used to developing different mixtures for his crafting. Iggy took out his notebook and showed him everything he had learned from his time in Tweedsmiur.

The day continued. After they ate lunch, everyone went their separate ways. Each had family and friends to visit while they were back in town. Iggy stayed at home with his mother and Victor. Breeze helped Gus at the shop. Marcus met with his parents. Zeph went for a walk by himself. Violet had wanted to join him, but he said he would meet up with her shortly. She returned to the house with Iggy.

As Zeph walked through town, he breathed in deeply. It was the smell of the sea, of the shops, of the food; It was the smell of being home. He headed towards the southern shore. The road led him to the paths to the Temple and the school. Glancing up the path, he saw Praotes sitting outside the Temple. Slowly, Zeph walked up the path toward him. It seemed that he was always either inside or outside the Temple. The old man liked the view, perhaps. He could sit and stare out at the ocean from the benches outside the Temple.

Praotes noticed Zeph walking up the path toward him. He smiled and waved him over. They sat together, looking out to sea. It was the southern sea and the next leg of their journey. Even though he couldn't see it, Zeph knew that the land of Tsayla, the Shadow Realm, was far over that horizon. He felt prepared for the journey. Praotes simply watched as Zeph lost himself in his thoughts. The old Uriym was very proud of the young man he saw before him now.

"Lost at sea?"

Zeph scoffed as his thoughts snapped back to reality, "I sure hope not," he said with a laugh.

"You've come so far, Zeph. You've amazed everyone so much," Praotes said softly.

"I've amazed myself, too. The things I've seen and the places I've been, it's just so much to take in. Some days, I still feel like it's all a dream."

"You've held firm in your faith, I see," Praotes said as he noticed the Book of Ta'Hor sticking out of Zeph's bag. Removing it from his bag, Zeph opened it to a random section.

"I have found it very comforting, and it has been my guide in times of trouble," Zeph replied.

"As it was always meant to be," added Praotes. "It was Ta'Hor's hope that the book would be a shining light to the lost and broken of the world."

"Things are going to be different on Tsayla, aren't they?" Zeph asked as he continued to stare out to sea. There was a pause in their conversation. Praotes had an answer to Zeph's question, but he wasn't sure if the young man would grasp the weight of his answer.

"Things will be different, Zeph. Tsayla is a land where the teachings of Sha'Kath are the basis for all spiritual teaching. You will see many things that will test the beliefs you have spent your life surrounded by."

"What do you know about Sha'Kath?" asked Zeph as he shifted on the bench to face Praotes. As soon as the question slipped from his lips, Zeph saw those twinkles in Praotes' old eyes fade away, if only for a moment.

"I do not believe the teachings of Sha'Kath to be inherently evil. But I have seen through my own experiences that any teachings that encourage a lust for power do indeed bring about evil. People will do unspeakable things in their quests for power. But I have faith that you will stay strong as you always have, Zeph."

"Thank you, Praotes," Zeph said as he took the man's old hand.

Zeph left the Temple and headed back home. As he neared, he saw Violet sitting on the front steps. She was playing in the dirt with her feet. It wasn't until he was almost there that she looked up and noticed him. A smile came across her face. Zeph smiled back and joined her on the steps. She asked where he had been, and he told her about his meeting with Praotes. It was all very different for her. She didn't hold firmly to one belief or the other. During her time on Tsayla when she was young, she had never really learned about the teachings of Sha'Kath.

As their conversation continued, she began asking more questions about the Omega Scroll and the events of the Alignment. Zeph explained the best he could. It was still something he was trying to figure out. Their world was on the verge of changing forever. If Zeph and the other scroll holders didn't come together soon, he feared all might be lost.

Violet held the Omega scroll in her hands. It was perfect in every way. The Omega markings on the ends almost looked like engravings now. The scroll still provided Zeph with increased energy like it had before. He still wasn't sure what level his abilities had grown to. The ability to transfer focus and move objects was what he used the most at the moment. His thoughts drifted back to the day of the alignment. When he had struck Breeze, a bolt of energy like lightning had shot out of his hand. He guessed that was something he could tap into as well;

for the time being, it seemed that he could only channel a small burst of energy across his sword when striking. Maybe when they had more time, he would begin to practice and push that ability more.

"How does it feel to be a *Chosen One*?" Violet asked as she handed the scroll back to Zeph.

"Not really all that different," Zeph replied, "and yet completely different at the same time. I don't know if I would have believed it myself if not for my encounter with Mal'ak."

"Who's Mal'ak?" The name caught Violet off guard.

"He was the Uriel that appeared to me when I opened the scroll. He showed me what the world would become if I didn't stop what was coming."

"What's coming?" she asked intrigued.

"I honestly don't know. But there is a darkness coming, I can feel it already. Sometimes, I can feel a chill flow up me, like a presence is right here with me. I know there is a darkness coming, and I'll stop it if I can," Zeph replied as he looked down at the scroll in his hands.

It was still hard to believe that this scroll had brought about everything that had happened. He often wondered what would have become of him if Xa'an had never shown up that night. Maybe he would still have no knowledge of his abilities. Maybe they would have never left Daunt.

The thought of leaving Daunt once again crept into his mind. He understood that they could only stay in town for a few days. They still had no idea what they were seeking out, but with each passing day, a sense of urgency was growing inside Zeph. The trip to Tsayla would take several weeks across the open ocean. That was considerably faster than most sailing vessels. If not for the speed the *Nephesh* could travel, it would take them much longer to cross the seas.

Zeph took Violet inside. They sat in the living room with Iggy and Dawn. The four of them talked late into the night. It was clear that Zeph had some sort of infatuation towards Violet, but no one said anything. They headed off to bed. Violet stood at the top of the stairs with Zeph. She held his hand and thanked him for everything he had done for her. As Zeph headed off to his room he felt a chill go up his spine. Even as he entered and sat on his bed, he couldn't shake the feeling that there was a presence there that didn't belong.

As he lay on his bed, he ran his hands over the scroll, letting his fingertips feel every groove. There was power within it, to be sure. Gripping the ends, he felt the charge fill his body. Breathing in deep, he held on until he felt the flow of energy fade. Holding his palm above his face, he allowed the energy to flow into and fill his palm. It looked as it normally did, like a pool of glowing water in his hand. His hand hanging upside down over his face was a mesmerizing illusion since the energy didn't drip from his hand like real liquid would.

Zeph thought back to the moment he had struck Breeze in the shoulder. A small spark of light jumped from the center of his palm to one of his fingertips. Zeph continued to let the memory fill his mind. Soon, another spark jumped, and then another. The sparks turned into strands that traveled from the center of his palm to the tips of his fingers. It was like watching small bolts of lightning flowing from his palm.

Pulling the energy back into his hand, Zeph rolled over. Perhaps it wasn't as simple as focusing one's mind to channel abilities; perhaps there was an emotional element to it as well. Slowly, he allowed his mind to calm down; he needed to get some sleep. The next handful of days would be taxing, not only for him but for everyone.

IT WAS THE MORNING of the fifth day since they had returned. Preparations were already underway for their departure. The mood was a mix between excitement and somberness. For Dawn, it was like she was reliving all her worst fears all over again. It had been hard enough when Zeph had left the first time. Seeing him on a ship brought back memories of Khoz's departure. Victor assured her that he would care for him as long as he could. The seas were not always safe, but knowing that Victor would be there did help calm her fears. Victor reminded Dawn of Zeph and Iggy's skills and that they weren't the fragile boys she was still picturing in her head.

Zeph dropped the last sack of his belongings on the deck of the *Nephesh*. The ship looked ready to go. The last handful of days had been spent with family and friends. On the previous day, they had begun to load up the *Nephesh* with what they would need for the coming journey. Much of their provisions were simply for the sea voyage. Once they reached the towns and villages on Tsayla, they would be able to get more supplies.

Their destination was the town of Krino. It was the port town Victor had traded with in the past. It was also the first town on Tsayla to receive sphere lamps. From there, they would journey inland toward the city of Araphel. This was the city that first inquired about obtaining large Spheres for street lamps.

Everyone was gathered on the docks. It was time to say farewell once again. This time, though, the town was more excited. They had watched the group of young adventures return, listened to their stories, and helped them prepare to head out once again. This brought a sense of community to the town since they were all part of the village. Many villagers were on the docks as the group boarded the ship.

Zeph's mother took him and Iggy aside. She was stronger than before, but she was also their mother. The feelings of worry and doubt she had would never leave her, just like her love for her boys. They assured her that in time, they would return and not spend her days looking out at the ocean.

Gus held his daughter close. As the months went by, his work had consumed him. It was the only thing that kept him sane, at least emotionally. He prayed that it would not be as many months before he saw her face once again.

"You look just like your mother," Gus said with tears in his eyes as he held her face.

She touched his hand on her face. It was rough and worn, like that of a farmer or a blacksmith. He worked hard for her and her mother. The years without her had hurt them both. Pulling her closer so their foreheads touched, he said a prayer for her.

"You'll see me again, Daddy. Have faith in that, and never forget that it's true," Breeze said as she held him close. "I love you, sweet daughter," he said in return. Holding each other at arm's length, they took a final look at each other. Her long strands of black hair blew in the breeze. The smile on her face could light up any room. His grey hair was sticking up all over the place, making her smile. It had become even greyer in recent months, and she feared it was because of her.

The rest of the group said their goodbyes. This leg of the journey would be longer than their last. After Victor dropped them off at Krino, he was to return to Daunt, where he and Gus would start the process of applying his modifications to the *Nephesh*.

They pushed away from the docks and began to head out to sea. Victor instructed the crew to carry out the task as he took the youths down to his cabin. As they entered, Victor told them all to take a seat. He stood by his desk and looked at each of their faces. They were a brave bunch; that much was true. Even if they didn't know it themselves, they were venturing out into the unknown for the second time. Taking the first step was always hard, but continuing the journey forward took very special individuals.

"We've just left your home," Victor said, looking around at all their faces, "I hope you understand how blessed you are to have come from such a place as Daunt. We are heading to a land where, in more ways than one, is the opposite of the world you know." They all listened intensely as he spoke. It wasn't common for Victor to take them aside like this or give a speech in this manner. "Tsayla is a dark land, not only because it is the heart of the Shadow Realm but also because of the teachings there. You will feel separated from everything you hold dear. You must always be on your guard.

"I have not had a place to call my home since I was only a little older than most of you. I made the sea my home. That being said, Daunt is the first place in a very long time that I feel a sense of loss every time I leave it. I know the road ahead will most likely not be an easy one for you, but I want you all to know that this ship will always be a home for you. My crew and I created the ship's motto a handful of years ago, and it remains true today." Zeph remembered the words inscribed on the side of the ship as he continued to listen to Victor,

'Wherever we may roam, may the sea always be our home.'

They all left the cabin and returned to the main deck. Taking up positions, they helped to get the ship fully underway. It wasn't long before Daunt disappeared on the horizon, leaving nothing but the open ocean all around them. The wind began to pick up. Victor ordered the men to get ready for the increase in speed. The group was excited to once again see the ship in action. Slowly, the wind began to pick up speed as they ventured farther out to sea. The crew launched the wing sails. There wasn't a significant difference at first, but the ship lunged forward as the wind began to hit them. The ship's masts weren't particularly tall, which helped make the ship more aerodynamic. Before long, they were flying over the water. It was a rockier ride than they were expecting. Every time the ship caught a wave, they could feel it lift off the water's surface, if only for a moment. Victor simply smiled and laughed as the group held onto what they could. The next couple of weeks were going to be a fun ride.

DAY 219

The bond of family is not limited to blood.

> You need only to open your arms and your heart to bring someone into the bonds of family.
>
> One needs only to look at the depths of true friendship to know this is true.

~ Praotes

CHAPTER 17
A SHADOW UPON YOUR HOUSE

The fog was rolling in, signaling that they were getting close. Even though the crew had done this trip many times before, there was still a slight uneasiness among them. There was something different about the voyage this time; they could all feel it. The winds were dying down as the ship slowly disappeared into the fog. They would reach land within the hour.

Zeph leaned against one of the rails, peering out into the fog. It seemed almost unnatural in a way. The fog not only flowed around the ship but also over the deck like smoke. Everyone was quiet as the ship slowly drifted forward. Just as Victor had predicted, just under two weeks had passed since they had left Daunt. Krino would soon be visible through the fog.

Overall, the trip had gone smoothly, without any problems. Zeph had been surprised at how much the currents had increased as they reached the halfway point of the voyage. Stories about the World Vortex had been told to him since he was a child, but he never expected it to have such power over the seas. They were still a ways away from it, more than a day's journey, and yet the flow of the water could be felt as the ship picked up even more speed. At this point, it didn't matter if there was wind or not, as the strong ocean currents kept the ship moving. There was the danger of getting off course, though. Since the currents revolved around the vortex hundreds of miles away, over time, any ship would be pulled towards it if it didn't constantly correct its heading.

As everyone peered into the fog, they began to see lights in the distance. Victor ordered the crew to prepare to dock. Within minutes, they broke through the fog. The village was only a few minutes away.

Zeph looked back at the vast veil of fog that was behind them. It was a strange phenomenon.

The ship slowly approached the docks. They were nothing fancy, and judging by the look of the docks, they weren't used to having a lot of traders or visitors. However, there was one familiar sight throughout the town. Everywhere they looked, they could see sphere lamps: in shop windows, on dock posts, even in children's hands as they played catch with them. It was a fascinating sight.

Everyone disembarked. Victor gave them directions to the inn where they could stay. The trade master seemed happy to see Victor again. It appeared as though Victor was beginning to make a grand name for himself everywhere he went. Victor introduced Zeph and everyone else in the group. The man was thrilled to meet the inventors of the sphere lamps. He told them about how the lamps had changed the town. Although looking around, the town still appeared pretty run-down.

It was clear that it had rained recently due to the mud on the roads. The smell of wet wood also hung thickly in the air. Clouds covered the skies above. This was a dark and dreary place. Zeph guessed that it wasn't likely to change either. Appagon wasn't part of any of the Elemental Realms. In fact, it lay in the middle of the ocean between four of the Realms. Therefore, there was no specific elemental effect on its land. On Tsayla, though, everything seemed to be darker and gloomier. This was undoubted since somewhere on Tsayla, the Shadow Tear lay, its power flowing over the land. In the distance, they could see forests and mountains, most of which appeared dark. The land gave no sign that the suns ever broke through the clouds.

Zeph looked down at his boots as they squished into the mud. They walked down the road through town. Victor had joined the group to give them a brief tour. Krino was a simple town, maybe half the size of Daunt. It seemed as though most people were left to fend for themselves. Not many shops were present. There was no evidence of a school or a temple. Just rows of houses lined the road leading through town.

Krino was on the northeast point of Tsayla. Even though there were much larger coastal cities they could have headed for, they chose Krino because they already had a connection to the people there because of the sphere lamps. Once they got used to the lay of the land, they would venture out for the larger cities on Tsayla. Besides the central continental mass, Tsayla also included a huge desert island to the west, as well as a few smaller ones. It wasn't until Victor took out some maps and explained the size of the landmasses that they fully understood that Appagon was nothing more than a small island out in the middle of the ocean by comparison. Tsayla was well over two hundred times larger than Appagon and was still considered one of the smallest continents in the world.

After settling into the inn, Victor sat them all down. The five of them looked back at him. His sit-downs were becoming more frequent. He told them to prepare themselves for anything that could come their way. Tsayla wasn't a civilized place in the broadest sense of the word. After seeing them in Iy Ra'Kal, he was confident they could handle themselves without a problem, but he still wanted to warn them.

Zeph watched from the docks as the *Nephesh* disappeared back into the fog. They were on their own now. After visiting the single pub in town for a quick meal, they returned to their inn rooms. Gathering together, they began to decide their next course of action.

"I think we can all agree that we should head for Araphel," Zeph said as he looked around the room.

"What's our best method of getting there?" Marcus asked.

"Ideally, by carriage, but I'm not seeing that as an option right now. The innkeeper said that the carriage from Araphel only comes every few weeks or so," he replied.

"I guess we could start out on foot?" Breeze suggested.

"I wouldn't recommend that," said Violet.

"Why's that?" Zeph questioned.

"You may not be used to it since you come from a very peaceful land, but many fiends roam the lands of Tsayla," she explained. Zeph paced around and thought about it for a moment. Their safety was his primary concern, but he also knew how skilled everyone was.

"We'll just have to hope for the best. We'll head out tomorrow," he said.

Much of Zeph's apprehensiveness had faded over the months of training with Sensei. He was starting to show clear signs of leadership in his daily life. In many ways, Zeph felt responsible for everyone in the group, even though he knew they could all handle themselves in a fight.

Their sleep was a restless one. Too much was on all of their minds. As morning came upon them, they felt little refreshment from the night. It was hard to tell morning had come at first, as the day was heavily overcast and dark. After gathering up their gear and supplies, they headed out. The path leading out of town was wide, with worn wheel marks from countless carriage trips. If they were lucky, they would see the carriage along the way. They weren't sure how long the journey would take on foot, but they knew it would take at least several days by carriage.

The road was lined with patches of forest and trees. Many of the trees seemed twisted, like the branches had chosen to grow in any direction they wished. Perhaps this was from the lack of sunlight. They walked on either side of the road, trying to avoid the mud as much as possible. Zeph led on one side of the road with Iggy, while Violet led on the other with Marcus and Breeze. They were relying on Violet to help guide them now since she was the only one in their party with any knowledge of the land.

Hours went by. It wasn't long before they reached a clearing. The road continued on, but the forest pulled back to create an open area off to the side. It was quiet. They decided it was as good a time as any to take a short break. A mist drifted through the trees of the forest. Zeph listened to the group chat with each other. He was quiet for the time being. A lot was on his mind. As they continued to chat among themselves, Zeph began to realize something. It was far too quiet. When they had first sat down, they could still hear the birds and other animals in the forest, but now everything had gone completely silent.

Standing up, Zeph slowly drew his sword and motioned for the others to stop talking. They gave him several odd looks before realizing the odd silence around them. Drawing their weapons, they all quickly stood back to back in a small circle.

"Fiends?" Marcus whispered.

"Maybe, but I don't think so. They would have attacked by now," Zeph whispered back.

They scanned the forest, but it was hard to make anything out through the dim light and the mist. Movement was spotted, but no figures could be made out. They saw men stepping out from the trees at several points around them. They wore leather armor and were well-armed. The look in their eyes said only one thing: their intent was to rob them.

Everyone pressed closer together, forming a solid circle. The group of bandits began to form a circle around them as well. There were five of them, so it was an evenly-matched fight. Zeph and the others had never encountered this kind of situation before. It was hard to believe that there were people who made a living by preying on travelers.

"If you drop your belongings and continue on your way, no one will get hurt."

It was a line you would have expected to hear from one of the bandits. However, the words had come from Zeph as he stared down the bandit directly across from him. The bandits simply scoffed and exchanged glances with each other.

"We were actually thinking of letting the lot of ya live, well, most of ya. But not after that remark," said the bandit directly across from Zeph. The man thrust his hand out, sending a blazing streak of fire toward Zeph. Throwing his palm up, the fire impacted Zeph's protection field. Everyone turned their head to look at Zeph. Iggy was obviously the most surprised. Before they could even ask how Zeph did it, the other bandits launched their attack as well.

Weapons weren't the favored tool of the fight. The bandits lashed out with their elemental abilities. The group returned in kind. Blasts of flames, water, and wind flew back and forth. The ground beneath them shook as one of the bandits flung his palm against the soil. This was a very different fight from what they had been expecting.

A blast of flame shot through the group, hitting Marcus in the arm. The flames absorbed directly into his skin. This was common for very skilled Fire Elementals. They were able to absorb their own element without even thinking about it.

The fight continued. These bandits seemed quite powerful in their respective elements. Everyone had paired off, and each fought person to person with one of the bandits. Violet was the only one who seemed to have the upper hand. She had no weapon to fight with, but her ability to cause the bandit Pain quickly caused him to drop to his knees. It seemed as though they were winning the fight one moment and losing it the next.

Zeph fought hard, but his attacker came at him repeatedly with just as much determination. The thought had crossed Zeph's mind that they might have to kill these men in order to survive. He knew that they wouldn't simply let them go if they won the fight; they would not hesitate to kill them. Taking a knee, Zeph threw his arm out. Even with the sound of different elements clashing all around, the sound of crackling lightning echoed through the trees. The bandit looked down at the smoking hole in his chest just before his body dissolved into strands of energy and light.

Lesser men may have stopped fighting at this point, having just seen their comrade die. Not these men, however, they were fueled by aggression and anger, which they brought down with full force. Zeph may have been the first one to realize how the fight would have to end, but the others quickly came to the same conclusion. Marcus extended his hidden blades from their sheaths. Running at the bandit, he quickly plunged the blades deep into the man's sides. A gargled breath escaped from his lips just before he too quickly faded away.

Drawing an arrow, Breeze fired. The bandit quickly raised his hand, and a chunk of stone burst from the ground and deflected the arrow. While his view was momentarily obstructed, Breeze sent a blast of wind from her palms and launched herself into the air. Without hesitation, she fired another arrow downward at the bandit. It quickly found its way through the man's neck. Clutching his neck with both hands, he fell to the ground. Breeze turned her head and looked away; she didn't want to witness the first life she had been forced to take come to an end. Iggy swung his staff with all his might, striking the bandit across the neck. A crack was heard as the man's neck snapped. He collapsed in a heap on the ground and dissolved away.

The rest of the group watched the man kneeling in front of Violet. He wasn't bold like the other men had been; he was sobbing for his life like a small child. She looked down into the man's eyes. Slowly placing the palm of her hand on the man's forehead, he gasped out and fell backward. Violet watched as his gava left his body like all the others, and he faded away. There was a look of shock on all their faces. It seemed so dark and cold to kill a man who was begging for his life.

"He wasn't begging for his life," Violet explained. "I was forcing him to relive a time I had once had. I made him feel every moment of that memory. If I had stopped inflicting Pain on him, he would have risen up once more and tried to kill me." It sent chills up everyone's spine.

They all looked around at the glowing essence orbs scattered across the ground where the bodies had lain moments earlier. Carefully, they gathered them all up. They had almost forgotten what Xa'an had taught them about Essence Orbs. Placing them all together on the ground, they sat around them. Each person slowly reached out and took several at random. The orbs quickly absorbed directly into their hands. It affected each person differently. For Zeph, images of the forest and the path leading from Krino to Araphel flashed through his mind. It was like he had traveled the road many times before.

Each person in the group received various aspects from the orbs. Iggy said that he felt more powerful now, like he could produce more energy for his abilities. They each shared quickly what they thought they had learned. Zeph's knowledge of the forest was perhaps the most beneficial.

They stood, and after a moment of silence, they continued on. It was Zeph's idea to have the moment. Even though they were all perfectly aware they had been fighting for their lives, the knowledge that they had just killed five men weighed heavily on them. It was something they didn't want to take lightly. They would never forget this place and what had happened there.

There was little to no conversation among them for the next several hours. Zeph guided the group along the road. The information he received from the essence orb made him the most knowledgeable about the specific region. He spoke very little. The image of the man's expression was still fresh and vivid in his mind. It seemed so simple to take a life. This wasn't a feeling he wanted to become familiar with, or even worse, something that didn't faze him at all. Zeph wondered if this was one of the aspects of the Shadow Realm that Praotes had warned him about.

Iggy came up beside him as they continued walking. The other three fell behind a few paces, allowing the two brothers to talk freely. Zeph already knew what was on his little brother's mind. Zeph had used abilities they had never seen before, some of which Iggy possessed.

"What happened back there?" asked Iggy.

"We did what we had to do," Zeph said without turning his head to look at him.

"Did we?" There was an abruptness in his tone. "Did we have to kill those men?"

The words hung in the air like the smell of stale food. They couldn't change it now.

"I didn't want to be the one to make the call, but being here in this place, in this land...," Zeph paused for a moment, struggling to find his words, "I feel what's coming."

"You're not the only one, Zeph."

Zeph stopped in his tracks. The others, a few paces back, also stopped and waited. Zeph looked down at his little brother.

"What do you mean?"

"I was pulled into the scroll with you, remember, I saw everything you saw. Ever since we were pulled into that vision together, I've had some sort of connection to you. I felt what you felt back there when you killed that man. You were afraid, afraid at how easy it was to take his life." The other three stood off to the side, trying not to listen in, but the topic drew their attention. Iggy was right, of course. The idea of how easily he killed the man was stuck in Zeph's mind. It was the same type of energy Zeph had accidentally hit Breeze with after he opened the scroll. This time, it was no accident, and proved even deadlier when directed properly.

"We need to continue on. I can't tell you there won't be costs along the way. What's the alternative, little brother? Do we let the world fall?"

"We don't, Zeph, we fight for what's right. Otherwise, what world will we have to go back to?" Iggy said as he looked Zeph in the eyes.

They journeyed on until nightfall. Once the suns had set entirely, the haze of fog and clouds seemed to lift. Before long, they could see the stars above. It was almost as if the land kept a veil of darkness around it. After setting up camp, they gathered around the campfire. Everyone was quiet. Zeph was their leader, and he had a lot on his mind right now.

Zeph sat there, his gaze locked on the fire. It helped to calm him as he watched the flames dance. Marcus was roasting some meat over the flames as everyone else sat quietly. Their gaze would drift back and forth from the fire to Zeph. He knew they were all looking to him for direction. The minutes continued to drift by. Finally, Zeph spoke up.

"I don't know what the best course of action is for what's coming," he let the words hang in the air for a moment before continuing. "Praotes said this land would change all of us if we let it. So, let us agree that our goal will always be to save lives, no matter who they are. Agreed?" Everyone nodded their approval at his words. It was a noble goal to have. Everyone seemed to rest easier after that. It was the closure they needed for the situation.

Zeph went over the images in his mind of the road to Araphel. It would be exhausting on foot. At least a full week of travel on foot was ahead of them. They had enough supplies to make it, but the journey would still be challenging. The terrain would become rocky and harder to travel through in several days. The road would still be a good advantage if they stayed with it. Fiends would also be a problem as well. It seemed this was the reason that the majority of the travel between the two villages was done by carriage.

As each day went by, they encountered many different things. A fiend attack came upon them once or twice a day. Sometimes, it was nothing more than a single fiend scurrying out of the forest. On the third day, they were attacked by a pack of Lukos. Zeph remembered the beasts from his vision of Desiree. Like ravenous wolves, the pack of fiends had attacked them. With weapons drawn and abilities in hand, they made short work of the fiends. They knew that if the average traveler had encountered the same fight, it would have resulted in death. Tsayla was a dark, untamed land to be certain.

They rested after the fight. The beasts had been fast, and it had taken a great deal of agility and speed to fend them off. Even though it was only midday, they set up camp anyway. Reaching into his sack, Zeph removed several small vials of Pirie juice. Everyone shot him odd glances. He handed one to each of them. They still seemed confused by his gesture.

Looking down at the vial, he thought about everything he had learned that year. It had been the greatest year of his life, as well as the most painful. He discovered that life, most of the time, was seldom fair. Raising the vial up, he looked at everyone.

"I know it may have slipped everyone's minds, it did for me until a few moments ago. Today is the first day of the new year," Zeph said as he held the vial in his hand. Everyone looked at him, then at each other. It took them a moment, but they realized he was right. It was easy to forget with everything that had happened, or the fact that they were out in the middle of nowhere in a strange land.

"A lot has happened this year. Almost three hundred days ago, a man named Xa'an changed my life forever by giving me an ancient scroll. And almost five months ago, I left my home for the first time in my life and began this journey that was asked of me. Today starts the one hundred and twenty-third year of the Seventh Age. I don't know what this year will bring, but I'd like to raise a toast."

Everyone opened their vials and raised them up as Zeph had. They looked at him to start the toast.

"Here's to discovering what's inside us all," said Zeph.

"Here's to adventure," said Marcus.

"And friendship," Breeze added.

"Here's to those waiting for us," Iggy said, looking over at Zeph.

"Here's to the start of something that will change the world," Violet said, closing the circle. They all said cheers as they clinked the vials together over the fire. Tilting their heads back, they all downed the juice. After giving themselves a while for the effects to wear off, they headed out again. They were amazed that Zeph had so meticulously kept track of the timeline of events, but then again, they were some of the most important things to happen in his life.

Several more days went by. Their supplies had all run out. Zeph assured them that they would reach Araphel before nightfall. The forest had continued to line the road on either side for their whole journey. Zeph guessed that it must have been cut down and cleared to make the road in the first place.

The fog grew heavy as they continued down the road. A faint light in the fog ahead caught Zeph's attention. As they grew closer, he saw a faded blue glow on either side of the road. After several more minutes of walking, they discovered two large stone pillars on either side of the road. Glowing symbols flowed up and down each of them. Zeph began to walk around them, trying to make sense of the engravings. Everyone else just watched him with confused expressions on their faces.

Zeph finally noticed the odd looks he was being given. Looking back and forth from the pillars to their faces, he finally made the connection.

"You can't see anything, can you?" Zeph asked while awkwardly pointing to the pillars. They all shook their heads no in unison. Zeph simply sighed and nodded. "Well, they are covered with a series of glowing symbols. They don't seem to serve any real purpose other than being landmarks."

"Well, if they're landmarks, how come only you can see the symbols?" asked Marcus

"Hmmm, good question. From what I gather, Araphel is just up the road. Perhaps they are like signposts of some sort, maybe for the carriage driver."

They continued on and, just like Zeph predicted, they soon came upon the village, although 'village' might have been an understatement. It was substantial, with hundreds of houses and dozens of shops—at least four or five times larger than Daunt.

Walking into the town, they passed under a large stone archway. A stone wall surrounded the whole city with only several different entrances. Townsfolk wandered around, seemingly not caring that new travelers were in town. After the group passed through the archway, they realized that the streets in the city were made of interlocking stones. A statue drew their attention. It stood in the middle of the circular courtyard area they had entered. It was a statue of a man, and in his hand was a sphere lamp. It was one of the larger ones they had made. They could only guess that the statue portrayed the town's mayor, Bain.

To their left, they saw the carriage that was most likely used to travel back and forth to Krino. They all shot glances at each other, it was clear they were all thinking about how useful that would have been. Walking over to the statue, they set their belongings down for a moment. It was an exceptionally well-carved statue. They wondered if it had been made before or after starting their dealings with the town for the street lamps.

As they glanced around the town, they observed that it was quite affluent. From the paved streets to the street lamps on every corner to the clothing of the townsfolk, everyone in Araphel was quite well off. Almost every window seemed to have a sphere lamp in it as well. The women all wore fine dresses, and the men wore suits in a variety of styles. Looking down at their clothing, they all felt very underdressed compared to the townspeople.

The buildings in the town all had a similar style. They had tall roofs that pointed upwards. Most of the buildings in town were made of wood, but some of them were made of stone as well. They mainly had dark brown colors, not unlike the buildings in Tweedsmiur. The windows on the buildings were made of fine glass. It was the most extravagant town they had visited so far, even more than Iy Ra'Kal.

A street vendor approached them and asked if he could be of any assistance. They asked where a good place was to spend the night. He pointed to a large pub at the far right of the courtyard. They took a moment to browse his product before continuing on.

As they walked into the pub, they noticed that it was crowded with numerous people. It seemed as though the townsfolk enjoyed congregating with a drink in hand. Making their way over to the counter, they booked a room. It quickly became apparent that the bartender doubled as the innkeeper as well. They made their way up the stairs behind the bar and quickly found their rooms. For rooms above a pub, they were quite extravagant. Fine carpets were on the floor. The furniture was crafted out of dark brown wood and had brass trim on most of it. Paintings of different scenes hung on the walls. Their rooms were across the hall from one another, which made it easier to interact. They put the boys in one room and the girls in the other.

After they had all settled in, they met in Zeph's room. It was decided that the most effective course of action was to arrange a meeting with Bain. Iggy also suggested that if there was a Uriym in the village, they could speak with them; there was a chance he had some knowledge of the lore and legend of Desiree.

They headed back downstairs. The number of people in the pub still surprised them. It wasn't very late in the day either, so seeing so many people drinking before the evening arrived was odd. Walking over to the bar, they motioned the bartender over. He was a tall, skinny man with orangey-red hair. His clothing consisted of a white button-up shirt, a faded red vest, and striped pants. The sleeves of the shirt were rolled up past his elbows.

"What can I do for ya?" asked the man,

"We're looking for Bain," Zeph replied.

"Oh, Mayor Bain. You should be able to find him at his manor. Just cross the bridge up the main street, head up to the left, and you'll see it a little ways from there."

"Thank you," they said as they began to turn and leave.

"Why not stay and have a drink before you go?" the bartender asked as he began pouring a drink for them.

"Oh, thank you, but we really do need to be going. Perhaps next time," Zeph replied.

"Your loss," the man said as he downed the freshly poured drink.

They shook their heads slightly as they left the pub. It was strange to find people who conducted themselves in such a manner. Even though there was a pub in Daunt, it was more of a casual establishment. In Araphel, however, it seemed that the townsfolk spent much of their time drinking. There was a pub on almost every street corner.

As they made their way down through town, they stopped on the bridge for a moment. A stream ran through the whole town, most likely providing fresh water. They stood in a row and looked down at the stream below. It held peacefulness in this strange land. The bridge was made of stone and had a wooden trim along the railings. Everything in town seemed to have been made with a great deal of craftsmanship.

The street split in several directions after the bridge. They followed the left path. It led up a gentle slope. Another bridge passed over their heads, connecting two other streets. The town was awe-inspiring. Soon they reached the top of the hill. Before them stood a courtyard of sorts, with a large fountain in the middle of it. They walked around the fountain and stood before the dark, majestic building. There was no mistaking it, this was Bain's manor.

The manor was monumental. It was primarily dark brown with black trim. It towered two stories high, with tall roofs extending even higher. Stone steps led up to the large double doors of the manor. It looked as though it had at least twenty rooms or more. They all wondered why anyone would need a house like this.

Climbing up the steps, they stood in front of the doors. One of the doors had a large brass ring on it. Reaching up, Zeph lifted it and rapped it against the door. A moment passed, and the door opened, revealing a tall, thin man with white hair. He wore a black suit and white gloves.

"May I help you?" he asked with a slight look of disgust

.

"My name is Zeph. We're here to see Mayor Bain," Zeph replied.

"And you are?" the man asked, the look of disgust remaining on his face.

"My name is Zeph, we are the creators of the sphere lamps," he replied. The man raised a questioning eyebrow and looked them over.

"I highly doubt that, but I will inquire as to whether my master will see you. Wait here a moment, or don't." And with that, he abruptly shut the door.

Everyone looked at each other, unsure what to say after that. They wondered if Bain would be a similar man. After a few minutes had ticked by, the door opened once again. The man swung both doors open, "You may enter." The monotonic sound of disgust had not left his voice.

As they entered, they were all taken aback. The manor was magnificent. They were standing in a large entrance hall. The ceilings reached the full height of the manor. A large chandelier hung over the heads. They were amazed to see it had been crafted from sphere lamps and various crystals. Two sets of curved staircases flowed up from either side of the main hall and joined together on the second floor. A large archway was straight ahead under the staircases. Hallways also led to the left and right. Sphere lamps hung along all the walls of the manor. They could only imagine how many lamps Bain must have ordered just to furnish his own home.

The floors were polished stone with a greenish color. Paintings hung on the walls leading up the stairs and down the halls. To say Bain was wealthy was a tremendous understatement. They slowly entered the hall and stood silently, waiting for further instruction. The tall, thin man gestured them towards the large archway straight ahead.

"Master Bain will see you in his study," he said, not making eye contact.

They walked forward and through the archway leading into a relatively wide hallway. They continued down it and soon reached the study. It was covered with bookshelves. There had to be hundreds of books in the room. To the one side was a large wooden desk. This room had a more miniature sphere lamp chandelier compared to the one in the main hall. The ceilings didn't rise to the height of the main entrance but were raised higher than standard nonetheless. Zeph figured that all the ceilings in the house must have been built to a higher standard than what they were used to.

A moment passed, and then they noticed a man sitting at the desk. His face was focused on the book in his hands. They walked over and stood a few paces from his desk. Several minutes passed. Finally, Zeph let out a slight cough, announcing their presence. The man looked up at them from over the rim of the book. His eyes looked back and forth momentarily, studying each of their faces. Setting the book down, he leaned back in his chair.

"So, you're the supposed creators of the sphere lamps?" he asked skeptically. They all looked at each other, unsure what to say to him.

"We are," Zeph replied.

The man stood from the desk and walked over. He was well dressed. A black suit jacket was over a white shirt and purple vest combination.

Long black slacks went down his legs to the polished black shoes on his feet. He had short brown hair that was combed back but still stuck up a little bit. He put his hands in his vest pockets and looked them over again. It was starting to become uncomfortable.

"I've had many people coming to my town, claiming to be the inventors of the sphere lamps. Mostly just to get some of my gold. What makes the five of you any different?" he asked boldly as he stood directly across from them. They looked at each other for a moment.

"Well, in all honesty, Mayor Bain, we don't want any of your gold. We've made plenty of our own. I'm pretty sure that a lot of the gold currently in our pockets already came from you," Zeph replied with a hint of a grin.

There was a pause in the room. They weren't quite sure how Bain was going to react to that statement. Placing his hands behind his back, he slowly stepped forward. Bain stood toe to toe with Zeph. The others simply stood by and watched. After another moment, he extended one of his hands to Zeph, to which he took and shook it firmly. A smile appeared on Bain's face, and then he let out a laugh.

"It is a pleasure to meet all of you!" Bain said in an enthusiastic booming voice. "I can't tell you how much your invention has completely changed the face of my town," he said as he led them over to his desk. "So what can I do for you; Zeph was it?" he asked as he sat and gestured for Zeph to do the same. After a quick introduction, Zeph began to explain why they were there.

"Well, we're actually looking for information on Tsayla, specifically some of the history and lore," he replied.

"Ah, then you've come to the right man. As you can see, I have a great deal of resources on hand that could help you. What is it that you're specifically looking for?"

"Well, let me ask you this. Do you know anything about the stories and legend of Master Desiree?" Zeph asked. Bain's face turned a little white at hearing the name.

"Why are you interested in the legend of Master Desiree?" Bain asked in an almost nervous tone.

"We're trying to track what happened to her before she died. We're looking for a possession she carried," Zeph explained.

"The Shadow Scroll," said Bain as he stared across at them. They all stopped for a second. It was strange that Bain knew precisely what they were looking for.

"You seem surprised, Zeph. The legend of Desiree is commonly known all across Tsayla. She spent much of her life here before disappearing from our lands. And everyone knows of the scroll she carried. She was the *Shadow Chosen One*, after all."

Standing, Bain walked over to one of the bookshelves and removed a handful of books. He gestured for them to follow him to one of the other tables in the study. Placing the books on the table, he told them that the information in the books was a good place to start. They all sat around the table and picked up a book. Bain called for his butler. The thin old man entered the room.

"Please set up rooms for our guests. They will be staying with us for a while," Bain said. Zeph tried to protest, saying they already had rooms at the inn. But Bain wouldn't hear of it; they were his guests.

The afternoon turned into evening quickly. The group spent all of their time in the study poring over the various books Bain had shown them. There seemed to be a lot of blanks in the story of Desiree. But from what they could piece together, it appeared that she had come to Tsayla after she left Tarn. The one discrepancy that kept coming up was the dates of different accounts of her presence. Many of the records were decades apart, but they still continued to describe her physical appearance in the exact same fashion.

Based on the different historical records, it seemed as though she had been searching the Shadow Realm for something. Zeph looked over the various accounts and could only assume she was trying to find the other scroll holders. Besides the bits about Desiree, there was also a lot of history about Tsayla.

As impressive as Araphel was, it wasn't the grandest city on Tsayla by any means. A vast city called Tamay was considered the 'capital' city of the Realm. Getting there would be another thing altogether. It was located on the far west side of the continent, a journey that would take weeks even by carriage. Perhaps there was another way. Zeph continued to read up on the city.

It was the oldest city on Tsayla, created by the original founders almost seven thousand years ago, back in the First Age. From what Zeph was reading, it was incredibly advanced. Glyph enchantment was commonplace in every aspect of daily life within the city. It was located at the mouth of a large bay area that stretched for miles. The book said that thousands upon thousands lived in this great city. Zeph knew that if they couldn't find the answers they were looking for in Araphel, Tamay was the next best bet.

Placing the book on the table, Zeph stood and walked over to the wall of shelves. He began walking up and down the rows, slowly reading the titles of each book. In all his travels so far, he had never encountered a collection of knowledge such as this. He found it even more peculiar that it was in a personal library, not some grand archives. There were hundreds of books in Bain's study, maybe even thousands. It was clear that the man was well-learned.

After a few moments more, Zeph's eye abruptly stopped on a single book. It sent shivers up his spine. The spine of the book read *'The Book of Sha'Kath'*. Slowly, he removed it from the shelf and brought it back to the table. The others were still reading through the books before them and didn't notice what Zeph was doing. Placing the book on the table, he stared down at it. The book represented the opposite of everything he believed in. He wondered if he should dare to open its pages. What kind of things would he find inside?

Slowly, he opened the front cover and began flipping pages. As he read a passage here and there, a sick feeling started to fill his insides. The book's message was dark compared to the teachings of Ta'Hor, with which he had grown up.

'Let us eat, drink, and be merry. For none knows what tomorrow will bring. Gather up possessions before your fellow man is given the chance. Nothing in this world comes without a cost, and everything has its price. If you should find the means to bring happiness into your life, do it away from the eyes of your fellow man, lest he partake in what you have found.'

The words seemed so cold as Zeph read them. He couldn't believe that there were parts of the world that followed these teachings. As he scanned the pages, he stopped on another passage.

'Power is found in the riches at your feet, and strength is your ability to wield them. For nothing is gained by the equality of man, there must always be a strong to rule the weak. Take what you need to survive, and then take again to rise above all those around you.'

It wasn't exactly what he was expecting; it was worse. The book was a guide on how to consume yourself with nothing but the world, at whatever cost it happened to be for you. That thought caused Zeph to begin flipping through the pages, searching for some reference as to the point of following Sha'Kath's path. It wasn't long before he found a section on it. The words flashed across his eyes as he read.

'Be consumed by the world's power, so that when your life ends, you will be reborn and continue to live on through the power you have obtained. Let the weakness of your body fade away, and let the flesh reform into your new being. Let the power you sought in life bring forth new strength beyond death. Only those who have truly followed this path will never disappear from this world.'

Zeph abruptly closed the book. Everyone glanced up at him, as it had been louder than he intended. Marcus shot him a questioning look. Zeph looked back and simply shook his head. He got up and walked over to the window. Marcus grabbed the book from across the table and slid it over. Looking down at the title, he understood Zeph's reaction.

Breeze got up, walked over to the window, and stood beside him. The moons loomed in the large window, their light bathing the two of them.

"Are you okay?" Breeze asked softly. He nodded and took a breath. Something about reading the words in the book stirred something deep inside. It was an uncomfortable, sickening feeling. A moment passed before he spoke.

"I just can't believe people follow the teachings on those pages. They truly believe that the more corrupt they are, the more they allow themselves to be consumed by lust, greed, envy, wrath, whatever it may be; that somehow the greater they will become. They believe it will make them stronger, so they will become immortal fiends when they die. Even with the fiends all around them, the evidence of what they will become, they still follow the path with hopes that they will simply never die. That somehow, by putting their faith in the power of the world, they will be spared death." There was an ache building in Zeph's throat that he couldn't swallow.

Breeze simply nodded and placed a hand on his shoulder. Zeph had always had a heart for people. Even his gesture on the first day they met had gone a long way over the years. She knew it must be hard for him to be so far from home and from those who had taught him the path he now followed. Even though they hadn't always attended Gatherings, they were all still brought up with the teachings of Ta'Hor.

The evening turned to night. It wasn't long after Bain announced that he was going to bed that they all felt the gentle tug of sleep pulling at them as well. Each headed off to their own room. They had thought the rooms in the inn were extravagant, but it was nothing compared to the rooms in the manor. Red carpets lined the floors. Wood paneling and wallpaper flowed up the walls. The sheets on the beds were so soft and the blankets so comforting. It was easy to lose yourself in all the possessions at your fingertips. Sleep found them easy that night. The long journey to reach Araphel had worn them out.

The next day, they awoke and continued their research in the study. This continued for several more days. Each day, Bain chose to interact with them a little bit more. He wanted to get to know them, and they wanted to get to know him as well. There was a charming quality about him. Something else was also there, something they couldn't quite place their finger on. Perhaps it was the way he conducted himself; it was always very proper. Bain had taken them to the tailor shop in town and purchased them all new clothing. It was nice not to draw so much attention in the streets anymore, and they did enjoy the feel and quality of their new clothes.

The next morning, they all sat around the large table once more. Bain walked around the study recounting tales of his youth and how he came to be mayor of the town. Oddly enough, it involved a great deal of trickery on his part. He had found oil on a businessman's land that the man had not discovered. Offering to pay the man a great deal more than the land was worth, the man agreed. Soon after, Bain began to process the oil and became very wealthy because of it. He was appointed the mayor since he had risen to become the most powerful man in town.

As he listened to Bain's tales, Zeph realized that the man was the way he was simply due to his upbringing. He had been taught to cheat and swindle others at a very young age to gain favor in the eyes of others. Zeph wondered if situations had been different, would he have turned out just the same?

The hours went by slowly that day. Information on Desiree was quickly running out. The timelines of the various entries still conflict with each other. They already knew she was born within the first hundred years of the Sixth Age. Some of the accounts of her deeds spanned as far as the third and fourth centuries of that Age. It didn't seem possible that she could have survived for several hundred years. Zeph looked for any sign of a connection with the Shadow Scroll, but there were very few accounts about it other than that she possessed it. Zeph looked down at the scroll in his bag and wondered if being the *Chosen One* would somehow allow him to live longer than a normal person.

Their attention was drawn to the sound of a bell ringing. Bain informed them that it was the bell for the Gathering at the Temple. Once again, the chill went up Zeph's spine. He could tell from looking at the others that they felt it, too. Violet was the only one who didn't seem fazed by it. It was most likely because these teachings were familiar to her since she was from Tsayla.

Reluctantly, they left the manor and headed to the Temple. It wasn't much different from what they were used to back in Daunt. It was obvious that the Temple itself was very old, as it was one of the few buildings in town still made entirely from stone. It was also much larger than their Temple back in Daunt, holding over a thousand people rather than just a few hundred.

A young-looking man approached the podium. He looked no more than thirty years old. Zeph found it slightly odd that a man so young was already a Uriym and not a mere Templar. He wore black robes with a dark purple sash. He bore the shadow mark on his forehead. Everyone began to settle down as he stood behind the podium. He opened with a traditional greeting. As he did, his eyes fell upon the group sitting with Bain.

"I see we have some guests in Araphel today. From what land do you hail?" he asked. No one really wanted to speak up. Finally, after an awkward silence, Zeph spoke up.

"We come from the village of Daunt on Appagon," Zeph replied.

"I can't say I've heard of it, but we're glad to have you here today."

Zeph breathed a sigh of relief as the man didn't ask any more questions. As expected, he opened up the Book of Sha'Kath and started to speak from it. It wasn't until he started speaking about Transfiguration that Zeph became noticeably uneasy. Talking about being transformed into a fiend as a glorious event wasn't something he could handle.

The Uriym stopped speaking as he noticed Zeph's increasing discomfort.

"Do you have a problem with the teachings?" the Uriym asked as he stared Zeph down. The whole Temple fell silent, and everyone else in the group also remained quiet. Zeph looked around; the entire Temple was now looking at him. Slowly, he stood to his feet.

"I don't believe that to be reborn as a fiend is something any person should strive for," Zeph said boldly. Murmurs filled the Temple. Bain remained quiet through it all and simply watched Zeph; this was a side of the young man he was interested in seeing. The Uriym raised his hands to quiet the congregation.

"And what do you believe is so wrong with the desire to live on after death?" the Uriym challenged.

"It is a good desire, but cannot be achieved by becoming a fiend."

The Uriym tapped his finger on the podium as he continued to stare at Zeph. Scanning the crowd, he spotted a couple and motioned for them to stand. Zeph turned his head from the Uriym to the couple. They were a middle-aged couple; there was nothing particularly special about them. Something strange about the husband quickly caught Zeph's attention, though. He seemed unusually pale, and there was something about the man's eyes. They were a brilliant shade of pale green, almost unnatural.

"This man is a farmer. Several years ago, he suffered a fatal accident while working. He was reborn as a Dhampir, a fiend."

Zeph's eyes widened as he locked his gaze on the couple. He remembered his vision of Desiree as a small girl. This fiend was nothing like the undead humanoid creature her mother had turned into, but it was plain to see that the man was no longer human. It was then that Zeph decided to turn the tables.

"If he is now immortal, as you claim, how does he survive?" Zeph questioned the Uriym as he turned his gaze back towards him. The man held the sides of the podium firmly. It was obvious that Zeph's remarks were beginning to frustrate him.

"We feed him." It was the man's wife who had spoken up. "My children and I give him our blood. It is what Dhampir survives on."

A look of horror flashed across Zeph's face, as well as Marcus, Breeze, and Iggy. Zeph's look was intensified even further as the woman pulled the collar of her dress down, revealing multiple bite marks all along her neck.

"You would allow a fiend to live and feed on your own people, Uriym?" The anguish was evident in Zeph's voice as he threw the question out.

"We help him to continue to live on in his new form," he replied with unsettling neutrality to his tone.

"The man is dead!"

Zeph's voice echoed off the walls of the Temple. He hadn't intended for his voice to be as loud as it had been, but nevertheless, it was.

"Death is only the beginning. Now, you will please remove yourself from the Temple so we can continue on," the Uriym said as he gestured towards the doors of the Temple. There was no argument on Zeph's part. He quickly shuffled down the row and stormed out the doors.

Rain was pouring down as he left the Temple. It was cold. He needed it to help calm the blazing fury growing inside him. Moments later, the rest of the group walked through the doors and followed Zeph out into the rain. Bain was close behind as well.

Zeph stood in the center of the large stone courtyard, holding his face in one of his hands. The water had soaked through his clothes. His hair clung to the sides of his face. Pulling his hand away, he looked up at the thick dark rain clouds that hung in the sky above. The water ran down his face. Reaching into his bag, he pulled out the Omega Scroll. Gripping the ends, he held it at arm's length in front of his chest. Strands of energy began to flow from the scroll and over his hands. They had never seen him do something like this with the scroll before and were unsure what exactly he was planning.

Zeph opened his eyes. They were glowing with brilliant blue light. Stands of energy wrapped their way up his arms. No one knew what he was doing. Letting go of the scroll with one hand, he gripped it firmly with the other as he let the energy flow and wrap around his arm. Suddenly, he thrust his arm up into the air. A bolt of energy flew from his fist and up into the dim midday sky. Everyone's gaze quickly darted upwards. They watched as the energy from Zeph's hand shot up high into the clouds. Without warning, a burst of light illuminated the sky. In the thick dark clouds, they saw a massive glowing blue glyph seal appear across the whole sky. A moment later, a tremendous concussive bang was heard, and a shockwave of wind washed over the entire town.

People came swarming out of the Temple, only to see Zeph standing there. His hands now hung at his sides, scroll still in hand. The Omega symbol on his forehead was glowing brightly. Their attention was quickly drawn from him to the massive glyph seal suspended in the clouds above.

"What is the meaning of this?" demanded the Uriym.

"You have clothed yourself in darkness, allowed your minds to forsake your calling. Will you stand in the light?"

Zeph's powerful voice resonated off the buildings like the echoing claps of thunder. The voice seemed to not come from Zeph himself but from some greater power dwelling deep inside. The words echoed off every corner of the village, and people began to run out of their shops and homes.

The glyph seal overhead burst with light and faded away. The clouds began to vanish in the center of where they had been, and a small opening in the sky appeared. Brilliant rays of light found their way down to the ground. The courtyard all around where Zeph stood was bathed in light. The townsfolk quickly backed away. The crowd's expressions clearly showed that they had never seen sunlight such as this before. The light was beautiful, more brilliant than they had ever seen.

"I ask again, will you stand in the light?" Zeph's voice boomed out once more.

The townspeople looked in awe at Zeph but kept their distance from him. They looked at the Uriym, trying to find direction as to what they should do. Zeph's eyes had not wavered as he continued to stare boldly at the Uriym. This time, though, there was fear on the man's face. In the blink of an eye, Zeph was suddenly right in front of the man, gripping him with both hands.

"Please spare my life, good sir!" the Uriym stammered.

"Why do you beg for your life if you believe you will be reborn, Uriym?" Zeph asked as he looked deep into the man's eyes. The man could see the glowing strands of energy filling the deep blue of Zeph's eyes. Quickly spinning around, Zeph threw the man into the middle of the courtyard. He slid across the wet stone and into the circle of sunlight. His cries of pain echoed across the village as the townsfolk simply stood and watched. The suns bathed his body with their warmth. The man tried to shield his eyes from the rays but could not. His screams stopped, and he simply sat on his knees and stared up into the sky. His hands began to shake as he reached up toward the light.

The crowd of people grew around the circle of light. Each of them kept their distance, ensuring they didn't enter it as well. The rain continued to pour down everywhere except within the circle of light.

Zeph motioned for the others to step forward. Marcus, Iggy, and Breeze stepped forward and stood in the light beside him. Violet stood at the edge of the light and watched them. Together, they stood in the light as the townspeople watched in awe. Everyone's attention was quickly drawn back to the Uriym kneeling on the ground. He began to cry out and clapped his hands over his eyes.

Kneeling beside the man, Zeph took his hands in his. The man was weeping. He slowly raised his face to look at Zeph. It was then that Zeph saw the man's eyes. They had turned completely white.

"I'm blind, I'm blind!" the man stammered out as he wept.

Iggy began to walk over, but Zeph raised his hand, gesturing him to stop. Zeph held the man's hands firmly in his own.

"You have seen more than the light of the suns, you have seen the truth. Your blindness is not something that can be healed by man. You will journey to the village of Daunt, north across the ocean from Krino; there, you will find a man named Praotes. Tell him everything you have seen and heard, and you will find your sight again."

With that, Zeph stood and walked towards Bain. The rest followed suit. Suddenly, the clouds returned overhead, and the rain continued to fall on the entire courtyard. The townspeople helped the Uriym to his feet. They asked what they should do now. He told them to lock the doors of the Temple until his return.

Zeph led the way as they headed back to Bain's manor. There was silence as they walked. Only the sound of the falling rain on the stone streets filled their ears. Upon entering the house, they all went to their rooms to put on dry clothes. A short while later, they gathered in the study once more. Even though they all had questions, it seemed proper to let Bain be the first.

"I've never been a man of belief, Sha'Kath or Ta'Hor. I don't know who you are, Zeph, but I know there is great power that follows you. And it isn't any sort of power that man can wield, only channel," Bain said as he sat across from Zeph. The glow in Zeph's eyes had faded, as had the energy flowing over his arms.

"I lived my whole life being taught there was darkness in the world. I never really believed it until I came here. In a land covered in shadows, I discovered the real darkness is what dwells in the heart of man," Zeph replied.

"What will you do now?" asked Bain.

"We need more answers. I had hoped a vision would have come to guide us by now, but nothing has."

"A vision?" questioned Bain. "I thought people only had visions of the past."

"I receive visions of both the past and future," Zeph replied.

"Who are you, Zeph?" Bain asked with a mystified look on his face.

"If you had asked me six months ago, I wouldn't have been able to give you a straight answer. But now....," Zeph paused for a moment, "now I know I am a *Chosen One*. I still don't know what that fully means, but I know there are six others somewhere out in the world just like me, and I have to find them before it's too late."

"Then I will wish you luck, Zeph. If you are looking for more answers, I suggest the city of Tamay is your best bet. Getting there from here will be challenging, though," Bain replied.

Tamay was several weeks by carriage, and who knew how many months on foot. They literally had to travel from the east side of the continent to the western shore. It wasn't the best option. This opened up the conversation for ideas. Violet said she somewhat knew the lay of the land, but there was still vast land between them and Tamay that was unknown to her. As they continued discussing the best way to reach the city, something Zeph had read in one of the books came to mind. In one of the books about the history of Tsayla, there was talk about points across the land that a person could instantly travel between. They had been referred to as Topos Gates. Zeph didn't really understand what the book meant when it referenced them.

"What's a Topos Gate?" Zeph asked, looking over at Bain. The man looked deep in thought for a moment, and then his eyes lit up.

"Yes! That could work," he said with a gleam of hope in his eye.

"What is it exactly?" asked Iggy.

"Topos Gates were commonly used in the First and Second Ages. They were believed to be constructed based on instructions left behind by the Uriel. They were stone platforms engraved with glyphs and symbols. It was said that all someone needed to do was to touch the corresponding series of glyphs for the desired gate and then step onto the middle of the platform."

"Why aren't they used anymore?" questioned Marcus.

"No one really knows for sure," Bain replied. "Perhaps they function or no longer exist."

"Do we know where the closest one is located?" asked Breeze.

Bain went over to the bookshelf and searched for a moment. He retrieved the book that referenced them. After several minutes of searching the pages, he closed the book in frustration. There were a great many references to the gates, but no specific references to their whereabouts. Bain paced around for a moment, thinking about where they could find the information. His collection was the most extensive in the area; there had to be an answer within it.

Everyone paced around the room, giving Bain space to think. Iggy walked over to a large map of Tsayla on the wall. It was almost the size of the whole wall, wider than he could outstretch his arms. After a few minutes, he located Krino on the coast and Araphel farther in. He looked at the distance on the map between where they were now and Tamay. As he studied the map, he began to notice different icons all over the map. The map legend on the side told him what most of them were, but there was one symbol that he couldn't seem to find anything for.

"Zeph, what does his symbol mean?" he asked, waving his brother over. Zeph walked over and looked at the symbol Iggy was pointing to. He recognized it right away. Explaining it would be another thing. Zeph had a great deal of knowledge of glyphs and symbols, but they weren't always the easiest to explain.

"It's a little hard to explain, the symbol basically means 'a single point.'"

Bain's ears perked up when he heard the boys speak. He quickly went to the map and looked at where they were pointing. Sure enough, the symbol was there, but not just there. The symbol was scattered in a handful of other spots all across the map of the Realm.

"How did I never see this!?" he exclaimed, smacking his forehead.

"Huh?" Iggy asked, confused.

"Topos Gates were sometimes called Point Gates because they let a single person travel from point to point. I don't know why I never noticed them on this map before."

"How far is this one from here?" Zeph asked, pointing to a location on the map near Araphel.

"On foot, that's about two or three days. Some of which might be a little rough since it's up in the mountains."

"Oh, I think we'll be fine. It's not the first time we've climbed a mountain," Zeph said with a grin.

There wasn't a moment to lose. They quickly gathered up their belongings and headed out. The townsfolk gave them strange looks as they made their way through town. Every person kept their distance from Zeph. He knew that in time things would change; he hoped for the better.

As they left the outskirts of town, they didn't look back. They were the ones who had illuminated the city with the sphere lamps. Perhaps Zeph had repeated this act once again. Ahead of them, not too far off, stood black hills rising through the fog. This was their destination and the next leg of their journey.

DAY 235

> See how the faithful have fallen and become nothing more than harlots.

The righteous once dwelt here; now only murderers remain.

> They have forsaken Omega and sought strength in the weakness of the world.

~ The Book of Ta'Hor

CHAPTER 18
DARK MEMORIES

After a day's travel, they finally reached the base of the dark hills. The fog that seemed everywhere across the land also followed them. It was truly a dreary place. The lack of direct sunlight hadn't been that much of an issue when they had first arrived in the Shadow Realm. However, after weeks of being under the thickness of the clouds, they welcomed even the slightest thinning for the suns to try and break through.

They stood at the end of the path and looked up as far as they could. Rough rocks and jagged stones lined the path leading upwards into the hills. The blanket of fog prevented their gaze from reaching farther than a few dozen paces. They all breathed in a deep sigh before they continued onward. The path was rough, and the dirt gave way as they walked up the hill. Mud was still present in some spots, causing them to slip and fall.

Bain had given them a map of the surrounding area to help guide them. The scales weren't completely accurate, but if they made good timing, they might be able to make it to the Topos Gate by the next morning. In some ways, they almost missed the cold of the Appagon Mountains. At least there they could see and had a better footing.

As they continued to journey up the slope, the terrain became rougher. Before long, they could no longer simply walk; they had to climb the rocks as they went. Fog in the air clung to the rocks, making them sometimes slippery to grab hold of. After a while, they could no longer see the ground below or the path they had come in on.

Zeph was leading the way up the mountain. Since the walk had become a climb, he doubted how soon they would reach the gate. He couldn't seem to shake the sense of urgency that seemed to be building within his mind. The air was moist and had a strange scent to it. He couldn't quite place his finger on it, but it held an almost unpleasant stench.

As Zeph reached up to grasp the next rock, a dark, twisted face seemed to lung out at him from within a crevasse between the stones. He instantly became startled and jolted back. Losing his grip, Zeph's heart froze as he felt himself falling. He quickly found relief as Marcus caught and steadied him.

"What happened?" asked Marcus.

"I don't know exactly," Zeph said as he panted heavily, "I was just reaching for the next rock when this weird image of a face came at me."

"A face?" Marcus questioned. Zeph simply shook his head; he didn't know what it was or how to explain it. They decided it was best to keep going. Hopefully, they would be able to reach some level terrain soon.

The climb continued for several more hours. They were all quickly becoming exhausted. Pulling themselves up over the next cliff, they finally breathed a sigh of relief. The fog still prevented them from seeing how far the top was, but it was clear that there was a flat path leading through the rocks now.

They flopped on the ground as each pulled themselves up over the cliff's edge. The soil was damp and cool—refreshing. Zeph lay there on the ground. Reaching up, he pressed his fingertips to his temples. There was an ache in his head that just seemed to be getting worse. He wasn't quite sure when it had started, but he knew he wanted it to stop. A sense of pressure followed as he pushed on his temples.

An image flashed in his mind. It was the day he had met Breeze. Zeph closed his eyes for a moment. It felt like he was having a vision; just something wasn't quite right. The imagery continued to play out in his mind.

Zeph saw himself walking over to Breeze just as he had all those years ago. The same uncomfortable feeling continued as his mind drifted through the memory. As he looked around, everything was a blur; the only thing he could focus on was Breeze. The colors around him seemed flat and grey, unlike those he was used to experiencing in a vision. He had never had a vision from his past before, so it seemed odd that he would have one now.

Zeph stood there for a moment. The only thing he could really do was approach Breeze, so he did, just as he remembered doing before. Walking over, he sat beside her and looked out to sea. A moment passed, and he turned to look at her. The pleasant memory was suddenly shattered as Breeze quickly turned and plunged a dagger into his chest.

The five of them were lying quietly on the cliff's edge, catching their breath, and enjoying a moment's rest after the climb. The peacefulness of the moment was violently broken as Zeph let out a blood-curdling scream and grabbed his chest. Everyone immediately jumped to their feet and looked over at Zeph. Blood was soaking through his shirt where he was holding his chest. Iggy quickly ripped the shirt open. To the astonishment of everyone, there was a gaping wound beneath the clothing, even though there was no cut in the shirt itself.

Zeph looked into the eyes of the person he thought was Breeze. The illusion faded away around him. Her face turned into the dark, twisted one he had seen earlier while climbing. Zeph looked down at the dagger being pushed into his chest. Rays of light began to shoot out from all around the dagger. The creature screamed at Zeph and pulled it out. Darkness wrapped itself around him as everything went black.

Iggy pressed his hand firmly over the wound. Rays of light shone through the cracks in his fingers. Lifting his hand, he saw that the wound was healed. Zeph remained motionless on the ground, however. Iggy shook him gently but to no avail.

Opening his eyes, Zeph found himself sitting on the docks of Daunt. Standing behind him was Iggy. It wasn't the Iggy he knew; this boy was no more than five years old. Zeph peered down at his reflection in the water. The face reflected back confused him even more since it wasn't the young nine-year-old face Zeph knew he should have in the memory.

Looking around, he saw his mother and father standing nearby. Zeph's heart sank; he remembered this day. It was the day his father left and never came back. The memory was strange. It wasn't how he remembered it. A slight sting caused him to run his hand over his chest. There was an odd sensation he had just been somewhere else a moment before, but he couldn't remember anything about it. When he looked up, he saw his father sitting next to him. They looked into each other's eyes. It was then that Zeph knew something was wrong. His father's eyes turned completely black, and he lunged at Zeph, throwing them both into the water.

The group knelt around Zeph as he lay motionless on the ground.

"What's wrong with him?" Marcus asked with a hint of angst in his voice.

"Your guess is as good as mine," Iggy replied as he rested a hand on his brother's forehead.

"What do we do now?" asked Breeze.

"I seriously have no idea what's wrong with him. Any ideas, Violet?" Iggy asked as he turned to look at her. She was just about to open her mouth when Zeph opened his.

Water spewed from Zeph's lips and poured over his face. A gargle deep inside his throat brought up more water.

"Help me!" Zeph gasped as he continued to cough up water.

Popping his head above the water for a brief second, Zeph gasped. The hands around his neck were those of his father. He looked up at his mother and Iggy standing on the edge of the dock. Once again, he pleaded with them. They looked back at him with lifeless black eyes. He quickly turned his attention back to his father, who was trying to drown him. Grabbing hold of his father's arms, he sent a blast of energy out of his palms. The energy shot through his father's body. Zeph looked in horror as his father's face turned into a twisted creature before everything slipped into darkness once more.

In the darkness, Zeph began to focus. Images of four faces standing over him came into view. Zeph tried to open his eyes fully but couldn't find the strength. This didn't feel like before; he felt awake now. Lifting his hand, he reached out for Iggy. Zeph pulled him close and whispered to him.

"My memories are killing me," Zeph said as he collapsed and lost consciousness once again.

Everyone looked over at Iggy.

"What did he say? Is he having a vision?" Marcus asked.

"He said 'My memories are killing me,'" Iggy replied.

Violet's face went white, and her eyes got wide. Breeze noticed her expression and grabbed her.

"You know what's happening to him, don't you?" she blurted out angrily as she held firmly onto Violet.

"I...I think it's a Nytemare," she stammered, still wide-eyed.

"Nightmares don't kill you," Marcus said with a look of confusion.

"No, not like a bad dream. It's a kind of fiend called a Nytemare," Violet explained. "It has no solid form; it enters your mind and turns your memories against you until you die from them."

"The face!" Marcus exclaimed.

"What?" asked both Breeze and Iggy.

"A little while ago, when Zeph slipped, he said he saw a face come at him from between the rocks."

"How do we kill the Nytemare?" Breeze asked, turning her attention back to Violet.

"I...I don't know," she stammered, "We can help him by healing him if he gets hurt. But I think the only way he can prevail is from inside his own mind."

They all looked back down at Zeph's body on the ground. Fear began to slip into their hearts as they watched his eyes dart back and forth beneath his eyelids.

Zeph breathed a sigh of relief as they stepped outside Gus' house. The heat from the machine had made them all very sweaty. He watched as the glass ball glowed under the water in the basin. Both Marcus and Iggy looked exhausted. Panic was on Iggy's face. He told Gus he didn't know how much longer he could hold on. Looking down at his glowing palms, Zeph rushed behind Iggy and Marcus and placed his hands on their heads. Energy flowed into them both like a lightning bolt.

Marcus let out a cry and threw his arms out. A ball of fire began forming between his hands.

"What are you doing, Marcus?" Zeph said with a look of horror on his face. Marcus looked back, but it wasn't him anymore. The creature's twisted face was in his place.

"Oh, but this is what happened. Don't you remember?" the creature replied with a deep, sinister voice and an evil grin.

The ball of fire grew rapidly. Within seconds, it was larger than Gus' house. It towered high in the air overhead. Then, without warning, the creature let go. The ball began to fall quickly toward the house and the town. It was like one of the suns was falling on the world at that very moment. All Zeph could think to do was hold his arm out to the coming flames. Fire wrapped around him as they were engulfed within the massive ball of fire. The creature's malevolent grin instantly faded as he saw Zeph holding the flames back with a protection field around himself. It was an obvious struggle for him, though. Running over, it grabbed one of Zeph's arms and pulled it out of the field.

Everyone was kneeling around Zeph. It was all they could really do at the moment. Iggy held his brother's hand, while Breeze held the other. Marcus and Violet sat quietly at his feet. With each minute that passed, they became more worried that Zeph was losing whatever battle he was going through.

Iggy looked down at Zeph's hand; it was starting to feel strangely hot. Zeph lurched upwards and threw his arm out. Blisters burst from his skin, and the flesh began to peel. The smell of burnt flesh filled their nostrils. Breeze gasped and covered her mouth. Marcus staggered to his feet as he stumbled back from Zeph's reach. Iggy quickly grasped the burning flesh in his hands. It was hot and began to burn him as well. He didn't care. Throwing all his strength into it, he began to heal the flesh as quickly as possible.

Zeph's eyes shot open. They were covered entirely in black. He was breathing heavily. The skin on his arm was in a constant state of burning and healing.

"Zeph, listen to me. You have to fight it. It's not real!" Iggy yelled. Tears began rolling down Zeph's face.

"I can't, it's too strong," he choked out through the pain and tears.

His body once again went limp. Iggy finished healing the arm, then stood and turned around momentarily. The others looked at him and then lowered their heads. They all knew what had to be going through Iggy's mind. He and Zeph had always had a close brotherly bond, and their shared experience with the scroll had only increased that bond. They knew this must be destroying Iggy emotionally right now.

Opening his eyes, Zeph saw he was sitting at a table. He felt very dazed. He was starting to remember what was happening, that everything wasn't real. Slowly, he looked around. It wasn't quite clear where he was. Running his hands over the table, he found it to be rough. Bookshelves lined the walls and came out from them as well. Candlelight lit the room. The walls were made of stone. It seemed familiar somehow, and yet not at the same time. Standing from the chair, he realized he was wearing black robes. He looked up from his robes with a hint of confusion. Reaching into his robe, he found several small swords strapped to him. Again, he felt more confusion.

The door burst open, causing Zeph to spin around. Standing there was a young girl with long red hair. Their eyes locked. Her eyes were completely black. It was at that moment that Zeph remembered what had been going on. A fiend of some kind had trapped him within his own twisted memories. Zeph quickly became aware of what memory the fiend was now causing him to relive. It was not one of his personal memories but a memory of a vision he held within his mind. It was the vision of Desiree's massacre in The Order.

Zeph suddenly realized that he would not be able to escape this memory this time. In the guise of Desiree, the fiend quickly slaughtered the other monks and then set its eyes on Zeph. He quickly realized he was standing in for the role of Orestes.

"Time to die, boy," the creature said as it approached him. Its current persona, a twisted form of Desiree, truly brought to life the kind of tales told in the lore and legends about her.

Closing his eyes, Zeph began to concentrate. Reaching out with his mind, he tried to connect with Iggy.

Iggy quickly turned around and looked down at Zeph. Everyone else looked over at Zeph, wondering what had drawn Iggy's attention. Iggy simply raised a hand to them and turned his head sideways as though he was listening intensely. Whispers seemed to drift out of Zeph and into Iggy's mind. He quickly jumped back from his brother and held his palms out in a defensive stance.

"It's coming out! Marcus, get ready!" Iggy shouted.

Zeph opened his eyes and stared directly into the creature's dark, twisted face. The fear inside Zeph quickly faded and was rapidly replaced by anger. The creature stopped for a moment and cocked its head sideways.

"What are you doing, boy?" it asked in a deep, raspy voice.

"You don't know who I am, do you?" Zeph said with a smile on his face. "You picked the wrong person's mind to mess with."

Throwing his arms down at his sides, energy flew from his chest and down his arms. The energy crackled as it moved from the center of each palm to each fingertip. Eyes wide, the creature looked at Zeph. Then, Zeph saw exactly what he had hoped for: fear. Thrusting his arms out, he let the energy shoot from his palms like crackling bolts of lightning. The creature let out a scream as it flew across the room. This time, everything turned bright white.

Everyone watched as energy began to build up beneath Zeph's skin. It looked as though his very blood was starting to glow blue. His body lurched up again. With his head cocked back, he let out a scream. Black strands of smoke flew out of his mouth. Iggy quickly wrapped the strands in a stasis field.

Floating above Zeph's head was now a sphere of black smoke. Iggy looked over at Marcus; he nodded back at Iggy. Stepping up to the sphere, he placed his hands on either side. They could see a dark, twisted face in the swirl of black smoke. It was pressing against the sides of the field, trying to break free. Marcus' palms became intensely bright orange as he let the flames burst from his hands and engulf the sphere. Iggy waited a split second before he let the field collapse.

The creature's loud shriek lasted a mere second before they saw the black stands burn away. Zeph lay panting on the ground, holding his chest. He opened his eyes, and to everyone's relief, they looked normal. He shuddered as he breathed out. Reaching out, he took their hands as they helped him to his feet. His face seemed pale, and he was still breathing heavily.

"Are you okay, Zeph?" asked Iggy. He nodded as they helped him over to the rockface so he could lean against something.

"I see you heard me," he said with a smile. Everyone looked over at Iggy with a questioning look.

"Well, not exactly, I didn't know what you were saying, but I got the message that you were going to expel the fiend."

"Fiend?" Zeph asked with a puzzled look on his face.

"Yeah, I'm pretty sure that was a type of fiend called a Nytemare," Violet replied.

"Well, I'm glad it's out of my head," Zeph sighed. "I know we want to keep moving on, but is it okay with everyone if we stop here for a bit?"

There were no objections. Breaking out some food, they all rested for an hour or so. Each kept a watchful eye on the fog. They didn't want another Nytemare to find its way into one of their heads.

Another hour went by, and the fog seemed to lift a bit. They decided it was time to move out once again. The path they found led through the rocks up the side of the mountain. They took one last look out over the clifflike rockface they had climbed. It was hard to tell how high they were since the fog blanketed the ground below. They guessed that they were quite high based on the time they had spent climbing.

As they continued on, the fog seemed to lift more and more. Soon, they could clearly make out the rock formations. The mountains they were on weren't like the Appagon Mountains. It had taken them less than a day to get to the top of these mountains. Temperatures hadn't dropped very much either, which was also very convenient for them. It would have been complicated if they had needed to bring another set of clothing.

Zeph stopped for a moment. They had reached some sort of clearing. He pulled out the map and his compass, then tried to compare anything on it with their surroundings. After a few moments, he decided on a direction, and they were off again. They still had no idea what to do once they got to the gate. Everyone hoped that Zeph would have some sort of an answer; after all, he was their glyph and symbol expert.

The terrain went up and down, but it didn't seem overly rough anymore. As night slowly fell on them, the fog lifted. The stars came out as the dead of night came upon them. A suitable campsite hadn't crossed their paths yet, so they continued on. The sound of water trickling caught their attention. Soon, they discovered a mountain spring. They set up camp nearby and settled in for the night. The gate had to be close; Zeph could feel it.

As morning arose over the mountains, the fog had returned once again. It remained relatively light, though. They refilled their canteens and moved on. Their sleep had been surprisingly easy. Perhaps it was the fresh mountain air, or the previous day's journey had been long.

Following the map, they continued to head west. They wished it were a bit more accurate, but so far it was taking them the right way, they hoped. The rock formations rose to their left as they walked. Reaching the top of a small slope, they looked down below. In the fog, they could see what looked like old structures off in the distance. They guessed that was where they were heading.

Not long after, they came across a small circle of stone pillars. Time had done its fair share to them. Some of them were half broken, and one was on the ground. Only several of the pillars still remained erect. In the center of the pillars was a large, round stone platform. Engravings were etched around its edge. They all walked around it, trying to study it.

Violet just stood there, staring at it. Zeph finally noticed her gaze locked on the platform. He walked over to her and cocked his head sideways. There was something about her expression. It was pulling at something deep inside him.

"It's the altar...," she whispered softly, still looking at the stone.

"What do you mea..," Zeph's words were cut off as her eyes darted to the right. He quickly turned his gaze to match hers. He could see some other ruins in the fog, a short distance away. Violet took off running towards them. The rest of the group quickly looked over, just in time to see her racing past them toward the ruins.

"What the heck is she doing?" asked Marcus.

"I don't know, but we should follow her," Zeph replied as he took off running. The rest of them looked at each other and then followed suit.

Violet raced towards the ruins. She stopped abruptly as she entered them, and her eyes darted all around her. It was clear that the ruins were once part of a small village. She slowly walked through the village's ruins. It was obvious that it had been long abandoned. The buildings were nothing but foundations and some chunks of rubble.

Zeph finally caught up to the ruins. He was surprised at how quickly Violet had reached them. Catching his breath, he scanned the ruins for any sign of her. The fog was stronger in the ruins, so it was harder to make everything out.

Marcus and the others caught up to Zeph as well.

"So do we know what's going on?" Marcus asked through panting breaths.

"I don't know, it was so strange. Violet was just looking at the gate, and then she ran off. I thought I heard her say something about an altar." Zeph replied as he scanned the ruins.

Violet walked from ruin to ruin. It seemed as though there was a specific remnant of a building she was looking for. She heard Zeph and the others calling out for her, but she didn't reply. The rubble of the buildings made it hard to tell what had been there before, but she knew it had been a village. Stepping into one of the ruins, she paused. Her eyes were drawn to an object on the ground.

After anxiously searching for her, Zeph finally spotted Violet in one of the ruins. As he walked over to it, he saw her crouch down and pick something up from the ground. Slowly, he stepped into the ruins and stood by what looked like it had been a doorway. He watched her for a moment. There was something about her, and something about this place. A shiver went up his spine that Zeph couldn't shake off.

Slowly, Violet turned around to face him. There was something small in her hands. He couldn't quite make it out. The footsteps of the others caused him to turn his head for a moment. Violet looked at him with pain in her eyes. Zeph's gaze quickly fell from her eyes to the object in her hands. Zeph's eyes widened as a wave of confusion and disbelief washed over him.

"Two hundred...., two hundred years I looked, and I never found this place again, until now..." Her words seemed to fade away as she spoke.

Everything around Zeph began to shake. Light and colors burst from all around him. He grabbed his head as he felt a vision coming on fast and hard. The pain was only for a moment. Opening his eyes, he realized he was standing on a mountaintop. In the distance was a magnificent-looking city, larger than anything he had ever seen or imagined. He looked to the sky above and saw the clouds stretch far and wide. He knew he was still in the Shadow Realm.

The ground beneath him seemed to give way, and he found himself racing forward. The wind rushed past him at incredible speeds. He felt as though he was flying. The city raced towards him in his field of view. He expected a sensation of slowing down to occur as he flew towards it. In a matter of seconds, he had burst through the entire city, and he found himself gliding through the air above the open sea. The water sprayed up underneath his feet. Land was rushing towards him. His feet hit the sand, and he glided to a stop. Before him was a barren wasteland like nothing he had seen before. A desert of sand was all around him.

He began walking forward, not knowing where to go. Soon the ground began to tremble. The sand in front of him began to sink. The ground started to shake violently, causing Zeph to stumble and topple over. A structure quickly rose out of the sand. It was like a grand ancient temple, towering up into the sky. The sensation of falling overtook him as he slipped through the sand. Everything went dark all around him. He hit the ground hard. Slowly, he staggered to his hands and knees. What he saw next took his breath away. Somehow, he was now deep below ground, and a massive cavern lay before him.

In the middle of the cavern was a towering pyramid structure. A single beam of light shone down on the top of the pyramid from an opening high above in the cavern. Zeph looked up at the ceiling of the cavern. It towered dozens of stories up into the air. He couldn't believe that he was underground and there was still so much above him. Without even having to be told, part of Zeph already knew what was at the top of the pyramid. Something about this place indicated to him that it was not where he would find the Shadow Scroll, but rather something much more powerful.

A small flash of light in the distance caught Zeph's eye. At the very top of the pyramid, there was a flickering light. Zeph felt his heart begin to race like it never had before. He started running towards the pyramid. The flickering light began to get brighter. Then it happened.

Brilliant light pushed away all darkness from within the chasm's depths, illuminating it with the purest light Zeph had ever seen. This was followed by a deafening sound so intense that Zeph felt it resonate every bone in his body as it washed over him. A wave of energy burst from the top of the pyramid. Zeph knew what that meant. The shockwave hit him, sending him flying backward. This was it. Zeph knew this was the start of the end of everything.

Violet looked across at Zeph as he held his head and gasped to breathe. His body flew backward, and he slammed into the crumbling bits of ruins. The sound of Zeph hitting the wall caused the others to run over. Even with the fog, they were there within seconds.

"What happened, Violet?" asked Iggy as he knelt beside his brother.

"I think he just had a vision," Violet said as she kept her distance.

Zeph began to move, as though he were trying to speak. He was still dazed by the vision and its impact.

"What did you see, Zeph?" asked Breeze as she knelt beside him.

"There was a large desert island to the west, past the city of Tamay," he struggled for a moment to catch his breath, "A temple rose from the sands, and beneath it was a pyramid. At the very top...," Zeph stopped and gasped for a moment, trying to fully understand what he had just witnessed within the vision. "I think it was the Shadow Tear."

Violet's eyes widened at hearing his words. Zeph's head bobbled as he stood up. The vision had thrown him off his train of thought. Once his eyes fell on the object in Violet's hand, he suddenly remembered what had transpired the moment before the vision started. A veil seemed to lift from Zeph's mind as he began to put the pieces together. Everyone else followed Zeph's gaze to Violet's hands.

She looked down at the rusted, crumbling remains of what had once been a small serrated blade. The wooden handle had worn away long ago, just like the wooden floor it had fallen into. Tears were still running down her face as she held it close.

"Even after a thousand years, I never found my home again," Violet said as she looked over the rubble.

Everyone else looked confused, except Zeph. He lowered his head and took a defensive stance.

"That's not Violet, there never was a Violet," Zeph said as he locked eyes with her.

Violet looked back at Zeph with a confused expression. A moment passed, and then a small, malevolent grin slowly crept across her face. With a wave of her hand, the facade finally ended. Her clothing changed to an elegant black and red dress. Tall black boots lined her legs from her feet to her knees. On her hands, she wore small black fingerless gloves.

She flicked her head to the side, and the short black and purple hair they were accustomed to seeing suddenly grew in length and turned a vibrant blood red. Her eyes changed from blue to a bright pale green. The sweet girl who claimed to be Violet was now gone, and in her place stood the malevolent being known to the world as Master Desiree. She still looked no older than Zeph, even though she had to be over a thousand years old.

"I can only assume that your vision showed the Shadow Tear breaking?" Desiree asked in a sickly smooth voice; she already knew the answer, of course. Zeph remained silent, but the fear that flooded his face was unmistakable. "Good to know. I'll meet you there, Zeph," Desiree said with an evil grin and a wink. Stands of energy like wisps of smoke quickly wrapped around her whole body, and she disappeared.

DAY 237

Visions are the tools of Omega to guide the faithful.

Some are to direct us, others to correct us, but all are from Him.

I pray mercy on those who hear His words and do not follow.
~ Mage Saphar

CHAPTER 19
IMMORTALITY

The air was calm in the field. Overhead, the suns were shining down on the plains. As time passed, an occasional cloud blocked the rays from coming down. A lonely tree stood amongst the tall grass. Beneath the tree stood a man. He was tall and thin with short black hair. Clearly, he was out in the field simply to wait for something or someone. Moments passed by, and then it happened.

Out of nowhere, a burst of black smoke appeared. It faded away quickly, revealing a young girl dressed in black. Her long red hair flowed down her back. The man smiled at seeing her. His evil grin was unmistakable.

"How'd it go?" he said, waving her over. Tears were still streaming down the girl's face. She had just killed the only father she had left and slaughtered the closest thing she had to a family.

"I don't want to talk about it," she said with pain and anger in her voice.

"Oh, come now, child. We both knew that obtaining the scroll was more important than anyone or anything," said Mizimmah as he watched Desiree's movements closely. He had spent the last five years molding and shaping her for this moment; he wasn't going to let it fall apart now.

Desiree paced in a circle by the tree. She held the scroll in her hands. The knowledge felt as though it was pressing firmly on the inside of her skull. It was a lot to take in. She knew everything about the Shadow element now; any questions she had ever had about her abilities had now been answered in only a few short moments. She looked down at the marks on her hands; the Shadow symbol on top of each.

The message in the scroll ran through her mind again and again. She knew her job now. It was to seek out the next person to pass the scroll down to, until the coming of the *Omega Chosen One* in the Seventh Age. The start of the Seventh Age was just under nine hundred years away. She had all the power in the world now, but nowhere to go with it. There was more, too. She knew her first task was to seek the other scroll holders out, but she had a sense of a greater task ahead.

There was an image in her mind. She imagined a great black pyramid. Something was glowing at the top, but she couldn't make it out. Out of everything she learned within the scroll, the pyramid was the only thing that seemed to have pieces missing. There was something special about it, though, and she knew she had to find it.

Mizimmah simply leaned against the tree and watched her. He could read everything that she was thinking. When the image of the pyramid flashed in her mind, he stood up abruptly. Desiree shot him an odd look at his reaction. He tapped a finger on his lip and turned his head to the side as if to indicate he was deep in thought. She had known for some time that he could thoroughly read her mind, even see her thoughts, although they had never actually spoken of it.

"What is it about the pyramid?" Desiree asked as he continued to think.

"It just might be what we're looking for," he replied.

"Why? What is it?"

"I'm sure you know the story of the creation of this world," Mizimmah said as he began to stroll through the field. Desiree followed suit. "Then you will also know of the seven tears." She nodded as they continued to walk through the open field and head across the plain. "Many people believe that the tears are just a symbolic representation of how Omega made the world. But they're not," he said as he continued on.

"So what are they?" Desiree asked. Mizimmah stopped and turned to face her. His eyes always had a glimmer that went perfectly with his twisted grin.

"They are everything, sweet girl. Within each Tear is the very essence of each Element. If that scroll you're holding gave you complete knowledge of the Shadow element, then within the Shadow Tear would be the limitless power of the Shadow element. Understand?"

"Why don't you take us there then?" she questioned.

"Ah, now see that's the catch. After we ascended, Omega hid the Tears from us. Not in the physical sense, but in our ability to locate them. You might remember at the end of the story where it says that Omega cried the seventh Tear and it scattered across the world, creating seven beacons of light?" Desiree simply nodded as she continued to listen to Mizimmah's story. "Well, the historians got that a little bit wrong," he said with a tone of loathing. "The seventh tear didn't shatter until after we ascended."

"How long were you living on the world before you ascended?" Desiree asked curiously.

"You mortals mark your time in days, hours, minutes. We didn't do anything like that. Let's just say it was more than a single lifetime," Mizimmah said as they continued on. It was unclear where they were going. Desiree wasn't even sure where she was. After opening the scroll, she simply willed herself to return to Mizimmah. She still wasn't exactly sure how she did it either. Teleportation was still entirely new for her.

"For all intents and purposes, we were immortal on this world; we did age, but differently than people do now. After we ascended, though, we truly became immortal. As you can see, I'm still here six thousand years later." There was that evil grin on his face again.

"So why do you want to find the Shadow Tear again?" asked Desiree.

"There is power in it, power that can be used to rule the world, or shape it as you please."

Hearing his words, something stirred within Desiree. Mizimmah had spent years turning her into exactly what he needed for his purposes. The lust for power was strong now, and Mizimmah knew he could control her with it. Now that she had opened the scroll, it was all coming together. He could see her processing his words as they walked. All he had to do was wait for the string of words to come out of her mouth.

"I want the Shadow Tear."

It was all he could do not to beam at hearing those sweet words leave her lips. He turned to face her. Raising an eyebrow, he leaned in close.

"Then all you have to do is take us there," he said, looking deep into her eyes.

Desiree pictured the pyramid in her mind. Holding her hand out in front of her, she focused on the place. Black strands shot from her hand and wrapped around her and Mizimmah. In the blink of an eye, they were both gone.

It was a cold sensation as the blackness covered them. Desiree opened her eyes but saw nothing. It was different than when she had first jumped to Mizimmah. Suddenly, a bright light filled her vision. She stumbled and fell to the ground. Sand slipped between her fingers. She squinted as she looked around. The suns were brighter than she had ever seen them. The ground seemed dead of all life. Picking up the sand, she let it run through her fingers. Her gaze moved from the sand running through her fingers to the sea of sand that was laid out before her.

The heat from the suns baked down on her. She had never spent much time out in the suns during her life, but this place was by far the most intolerable of any place she had ever been. Looking around, she saw Mizimmah standing behind her. He had a look of disgust on his face.

"Why did you bring us to this desert?" he blurted out angrily

"I thought about the pyramid from the vision, and this is where it brought us," she shouted back.

Mizimmah began to walk out into the desert. Desiree stood by herself for a moment and then began to follow after him. She didn't have anyone else to travel with. There was only sand as far as the eye could see. No sign of the pyramid was on the horizon anywhere, just sand. After a few more minutes of walking, Mizimmah stopped.

"You won't find it on your own. There's a piece of the puzzle you're missing," he said as he sighed in frustration.

"What do you mean?"

"You won't be able to find it without the *Omega Chosen One*," he replied.

"And what am I supposed to do now? I'm not giving this up to someone else," Desiree said, clutching the Shadow Scroll close.

Mizimmah thought about it for a moment. All of a sudden, his eyes lit up. He walked over to her, head down, face looking mischievous as ever. Gripping both of her shoulders, he looked her straight in the eye.

"Well then, we'll just have to make sure you're still around in a thousand years, won't we?" he said with a sinister grin and a wink.

RAIN WAS COMING DOWN hard. The steady banging of the blacksmith's hammer could be heard throughout the village. His shop was the only one open on rainy days like that. For the most part, the town was dark and closed up. No one wanted to work on a day that was so dark and dreary. The heavy raindrops bounced off the stones in front of the shop. Cold air blew through the open areas. No other form of shelter was attached besides a roof and a back wall.

The refreshing scent of the rain filled the blacksmith's nostrils as he continued to bang his hammer down on the anvil. Sweat dripped down his massive arms. Removing the blade from the anvil, he plunged it back into the coals of his furnace. With a wave of his hand, flames burst from his palm and fueled the fire. He sent several more blasts of flame into the coals before removing the blade and placing it on the anvil again.

He brought the hammer down several more times before he noticed the figure standing just outside his shop. The cloak they wore was dripping wet. Drops of water poured onto the stone around their feet. The blacksmith stopped and looked at the stranger for a moment. It was an odd thing to have visitors in their town, even odder to have one in this kind of weather. Rain or shine, he always worked on his weapons.

The stranger stepped beneath the cover of the roof. They began looking over the finished weapons on the racks off to the side of the shop. If not for the cloak, the blacksmith might have been able to see the stranger's face. Not to let his work be interrupted, the blacksmith continued to bring his hammer down on the hot, glowing blade. Turning around, he placed the blade back into the coals. Something from the corner of his eye caused him to spin around. The stranger was directly behind him now. He could see a pair of brilliant green eyes staring back into his eyes just below the hood of the cloak.

"What can I do for you, stranger?" he said with a hint of anxiety in his voice.

"I need your blood," the hooded figure replied in a cold, empty tone.

Before he knew what was happening, the blacksmith felt the burning sting of a blade plunged into his chest. He tried to struggle, but with a wave of his attacker's hand, he found that he was unable to fight back. Slowly, he collapsed onto the cold stone floor. The stranger knelt down beside him, hand still gripping the blade. Pulling back the cloak, the image of a young girl hung in front of his face.

"Do you know who I am?" asked Desiree. The man nodded in pain. She looked down at the blade sticking out of him. His hands were shaking as he looked up at her. There was a darkness in her eyes that he had never seen before; not in man or fiend.

"Why are you doing this?" he stammered out.

"You come from a pure Fire Elemental bloodline going all the way back to the First Age. I bet you didn't even know that, did you?" The man shook his head no. "Your blood is very special," Desiree said as she looked down at the blade handle. The handle was, in essence, a glass vial that connected to a thin hollow channel within the blade. The glass handle was now full of blood. It had rows of glyphs and symbols wrapped all around its surface. Twisting the vial, it sealed itself as it detached from the blade's hilt. Blood began to flow freely out of the opening in the hilt.

Desiree stood and looked down at the man. Her eyes showed no remorse or regret; she was simply focused on her task. The pool of blood grew around the man as he continued to bleed out. Within moments, he would be dead.

"There is one more thing I need from you," she said as she lowered her head toward him. His body was weak, and he could no longer lift his arms. All he could do was stare into her cold eyes. Soon the light faded from his eyes. Reaching down, Desiree placed her hand in the pool of blood that had formed, letting it coat her whole palm. She then reached out and placed her hand above the man's chest. Just as expected, the small ball of light rose from his body. It was his gava, his very being, his essence. Desiree clutched it in her hand before it could return to his body. Her blood-soaked hand allowed her to hold the gava without it simply passing through her. Gently, she opened the collected vial of blood and let the small glowing ball slip inside. The man's gava remained suspended within the blood and did not fade away.

Standing up, Desiree looked down at the body. It was strange to see a body in this manner. Most people would have faded away or transformed into something else by now. She looked at the vial of blood. The man's gava began to draw in all the blood; within moments, the blood had been transformed into some form of glowing liquid. Reaching into her cloak, she placed it next to three other glowing vials.

Placing the hood back over her head, Desiree walked back out into the pouring rain. The villagers would have a horrific discovery later that day, one that they would not be able to explain or understand. Without the energy of his gava, the blacksmith's body would not dissolve away. It would be nothing more than the meat of a dead animal left to rot in the streets.

Almost two years had passed since Desiree first opened the Shadow Scroll. In that time, she had traveled around the world, visiting many lands. Mizimmah was always close by, keeping an eye on her progress. He had devised a way to give her immortality. It was a heavy price, more than she wanted to pay at first, but over time, she sought out what was needed to accomplish the task.

Before the Uriel ascended, they had lived long lives, exceedingly long lives. They did age, but not on a scale that a mortal could comprehend. There were still people out in the world who had pure blood. Meaning that over the thousands of years since the dawning of the First Age, they never had children with someone of a different Element. It was this blood that Mizimmah directed Desiree to seek out. The blood alone would not be enough. The essence of life itself was not found in just the blood but also within the body's energy. A person could not live without their gava, and their gava would always try to give the body life. This was demonstrated in how it absorbed the blood in the vial and turned it into the very essence of life.

Mizimmah said that for her body to stop aging, she would have to collect the gava of a pure-blood from each of the seven elements. Once she had all seven, nothing in the world would have a hold over her anymore. She would absorb each gava, and their life-giving energy working in unison would give her immortality.

Tracking down actual pure-blood elementals had proved to be a challenging task. Over time, Desiree began to see people differently. At first, she had sought out various research and bloodline records. The first person she stumbled onto was purely by accident. An old man had been working in a library archive in the Earth Realm. If only he hadn't let it slip that his bloodline had remained unbroken since the dawn of the First Age, perhaps his life would have been spared. Almost two years later, she had four of the seven gavas she needed.

Desiree continued to walk down the muddy road leading out of the village. She always wondered what the people would do with the body. Would they bury it? Perhaps burn it? In a world where the body always transformed after the point of death, what would be done with those bodies left behind?

Glancing down inside her cloak, she gazed over the four glowing vials in her satchel. These four were not the first people she had killed, and they would not be the last. Her name was becoming known in different lands. Perhaps one day they would write stories about her. In her travels, Desiree always kept an ear open for someone else just like her, but no stories ever crossed her path. She began to wonder if there really were other *Chosen Ones* out in the world. If the legends were true, there should be at least four others somewhere else in the world. Desiree was always listening for the arrival of the *Light Chosen One*, which was foretold to rise in the Sixth Age. Of course, they could be chosen at any time within the Age.

In the beginning, Desiree's quest for the purebloods had been slow, but as she traveled the world, she began to acquire the knowledge she needed to track them down. If she could find four of them in two years, she was sure she could find the remaining three she needed within the year. It wasn't as though she was starting to count her age; she was only sixteen after all. But the vanity of her youth and beauty drove her to accomplish the task as soon as possible.

She and Mizimmah traveled the world many times over the years. Some places he took them by teleporting. For many destinations, though, Mizimmah let her travel there by more practical means. It allowed him to develop his control over her even further. Once Desiree had visited a location once, she could always teleport back to it again; she just had to focus on the memory of the location. At times, she would find her newfound Shadow abilities quite draining. It was after this that she discovered the regenerative abilities of her scroll. All she had to do was hold it for a few minutes, and it gave her the energy she needed. The more she pushed herself, the more powerful she became.

As she walked through the rain on her way out of the village, Desiree noticed a figure standing by a tree in the distance. It was Mizimmah. It didn't matter that he was too far away to fully make out; she knew it was him. Desiree walked over and stood beneath the tree as well. In his hand, Mizimmah was cutting up a piece of fruit. As he took a bite, he looked down at her cloak. She opened it, revealing the four vials. He smiled at her.

"Good girl. Just Wind, Light, and Omega left," he said with a wink.

"How do I find a pureblood Omega?" she questioned.

"Ah, now that one will be a little tricky, and yet all too simple. You see, the people in the Omega Realm rarely travel out to the other Realms. I would say that at least three out of five are purebloods already," he explained.

Desiree had discovered through her research that if both parents shared the same Element and had a child within the Realm of their Element, there was an exceptionally high chance the child would be born of the same Element. Throughout the seven Elemental Realms, as the Ages had gone by, the people of Arkhay had spread out and mixed through every Realm. But there were always some who could trace their elemental bloodline all the way back to the First Age.

"Your real challenge will be Light," Mizimmah said in that sly tone as he spoke up.

"Why Light?"

"Shadow and Light are opposites, my dear. The only way you'll get into their Realm is on foot. Either Element can't teleport into the opposing Realm," he explained.

"We're close to the Wind Realm, let's head there for the time being," Desiree said after thinking about it for a moment.

"I like your thinking, lead on."

They headed south from the Fire Realm. The village they had just come from was on the far southwest part of the Realm. It was an easy southern trip across the continent to the Wind Realm. Desiree no longer viewed traveling as the passing of time. The days all seemed to blend together, and all that mattered was her goal of becoming immortal. Over the previous several years, they had traveled thousands and thousands of miles over land and sea. The world was large and full of so much more than she had ever imagined. Despite it all, her lust for power had caused her to still view all those around her as lesser beings.

It was interesting to see how the different parts of the world had grown throughout the ages. Overall, the Shadow Realm remained a dark and barren place with only a handful of large, successful cities. In the Earth Realm, their ability to control the Earth around them was amazing. Whole cities had been formed out of the ground. Their use of glyphs and symbols for elemental enchantment was impressive as well. They were people who, as a whole, had truly embraced the Earth Element.

While Desiree was in the Water Realm, she could see that their path was slowly taking them away from focusing solely on the Water Element and had started to branch off into the art of Invention. Perhaps in a thousand years or so, they would have merged the two.

The Fire Realm was the most different of all the realms she had visited up to that point in her quest. Culturally, they were on the verge of abandoning their elemental ways completely. They had begun pursuing the art of Invention over an Age before, and the center of their society was based around technology. It was clear that they would completely abandon any remaining elemental ways as time went on. If not for the village she had stumbled upon on the edge of the Realm, it may have been a much longer search for the Fire pureblood since their culture had been mixing the bloodlines for generations already.

The days turned into weeks. Before long, they were in the heart of the Wind Realm. It seemed to have a very similar quality to that of the Earth Realm. The people were very focused on the Wind Element and the art of enchantment with glyphs and symbols. The most amazing aspect was the land within the clouds. At a glance, on their journey into the Realm, it looked like nothing more than an elevated landmass poking out above the clouds. It wasn't until Desiree was farther into the Realm that she realized what she had actually been seeing. Large chunks of land, the size of mountains, hung suspended in the sky above the Realm. She guessed it was only by the power of the Wind Tear that it was made possible.

As the weeks went on, there was a defining characteristic between those who dwelt on land and those who lived on the landmasses in the sky. The more common folk seemed to live on the land below, where the monarchy and those of wealthy descent lived in the clouds above. If there was a better example of the wealthy looking down on the poor, she couldn't think of one. It was clear, though, that she would have to journey to the land above to find a suitable person.

After searching across the land, she found their method of travel between the land above and the land below. The people of the Realm had created elemental gates of some kind across the Realm. These were different than the Topas Gates she had used in the past. Once a person stepped onto the platform, they were launched into the air, connecting to a similar platform on the land above the sky. This was another thing that separated the people of the Realm. In order to use this method, a person had to have great control over Wind abilities to guide themselves through the air. Not only to rise above, but also when a person wanted to journey down, they had to control their descent as well.

Rather than having to journey to the land above, a situation came across Desiree's path, eliminating the need to go to the Highlands. She had been staying in a town near one of the transit gates. On a particular day, a nobleman descended down to the town from the Highlands above. At the very first glance, Desiree knew he was pureblood. It wasn't something she could fully explain, but after she had killed the first two, she could just tell by looking at someone. From her perspective, it was almost as though they had an aura that only she could see.

The nobleman was coming to check on the progress of the crops, since most of the food for the Highlands was grown in the Lowlands. He was a younger man with good looks and a charm about him. Desiree knew exactly how she would play him. Her beauty was something of her legend, second only to her cruelty.

Introducing herself, she asked if he would have a drink with her at the local tavern. Caught up in the infatuation of the moment, he agreed. After several rounds of drinks, they headed upstairs to one of the rooms. It was, in fact, his own depraved nature that led to what was about to happen. With only the thought of getting her into bed on his mind, he failed to see the blade she drew from behind her back. It quickly found its way into his chest. His eyes were wide and full of panic as he coughed blood down the front of his finely crafted outfit. Slowly, he slumped down against the wall of the room. His death came much faster than Desiree's last kill. Completing the same ritual as the last, Desiree placed the fifth vial in her cloak and left the room.

For the next part of her journey, they would need to book passage on a ship. After reaching a port city, she and Mizimmah headed off. If he didn't stay with her on the ship, he wouldn't be able to join her in the Light Realm. Even for someone as powerful as a Shadow Uriel, the elemental restriction of the Realm still applied to him as well. It was a journey that would take them several weeks across the seas. Desiree wasn't used to having Mizimmah around for that amount of time. The majority of their time together, up until that point, had revolved around small visits here and there, to teach or train her.

Mizimmah was a mystery, but then again, so was she. Only he really knew the person Desiree was inside. All the years of training she had received from him had brought her to this place. Once she had the Shadow Tear in her hands, her powers would be unmatched by anything else in the world.

They reached a port in the Light Realm. Everything seemed so perfect. It was almost like living in a dream. The land itself was nothing short of beautiful. As they traveled through the land, they were greeted happily by everyone. The contrast between her Realm and the Light Realm was blatantly evident. Light shone everywhere, not all the time, of course, there was still night, but the very nature of the land explained why she couldn't simply teleport. With the absence of Shadow energy, it would be impossible to use Shadow abilities to get there.

Desiree began to realize something about the people as she traveled through the Realm. They were old, not in mere appearance, though. The majority of the people in the Realm were at least several hundred years old. The Light Element sustained those with it and those who could wield its healing properties within themselves.

Like in the other Realms, Desiree simply had to scope the land and see where the oldest parts were. As it had been in the previous realms, the person she needed was always found in the most ancient part of the land. It made sense since it was in those places that the people of the Realm first developed and spread out. The Fire Realm had been the only real exception to this.

A grand ancient city was in the center of the Light Realm. The city was white and, at times, seemed to be made of light itself. This time, it wasn't an issue of finding a person. It was finding a place to do it. The people were so open and friendly that it was hard to find a single person off somewhere on their own.

Something else Desiree had to be mindful of was keeping her mind clear of the dark thoughts that would cross it. Many people in the Realm were Seers, those gifted with strong abilities to read the thoughts and minds of others. If she wasn't careful, they would read her mind and her plans. Days went by as she tried to complete her task. If she were to be found out before it was complete, it would jeopardize all the efforts of the last three years.

It had been almost a year since she left the Fire Realm. True to her predictions, she was just about to get the sixth vial she needed. After the Light Realm, it was an easy journey to the final person in the Omega Realm. At seventeen, she felt it was the perfect age to stop aging.

Desiree watched the various people throughout the city. Other girls looked around her age, but she knew that they were most likely two or three times her age. Once she had all seven gava, she wouldn't need anything like healing abilities to prolong her life. She would simply cease to age.

Desiree found her victim by befriending one of the local girls. Through their friendship, she offered to show Desiree one of her favorite spots in the forest beyond the city. It was the perfect opportunity Desiree had been looking for. They ventured out from the city and into the forest. It was a calm and tranquil day. The birds were singing, the suns were shining, and all was right with the world.

That world came to a horrible crash as Desiree's blade found its way deep into the side of the girl. Startled, the girl quickly spun around and pulled the blade out of the wound, throwing it to the ground. She stared wide-eyed back at Desiree. The blood continued to pour out of the deep wound. Desiree looked back at her, trying rapidly to figure out the best course of action. This had never happened before. The haunting look of betrayal was in the girl's eyes.

Placing her hand over the wound, the girl quickly began to heal it. Desiree picked the blade up from the ground and lunged at her. The girl threw her hand up directly in front of her. Desiree bounced off the invisible field that the girl had produced. Fear was starting to grip Desiree now; she couldn't leave without what she needed. Throwing both of her palms toward the girl, Desiree used her abilities to fling the girl across the clearing. She connected hard with one of the trees and slumped over. Wasting no time, Desiree gravitated over to her. Dazed, the girl couldn't prepare for the coming blow. The blade dug deep into her chest. She gasped out and gripped Desiree's arm.

Even with the blade plunged into her chest, it was clear that she was resisting the mortal blow. Desiree's gaze darted rapidly from the girl's eyes to the blood filling the handle of the dagger. All she needed was a moment more. The edges of the wound began to glow. The girl gripped Desiree's arm hard, trying to force the dagger out. Looking down, Desiree saw that the vial was full.

Quickly, Desiree placed a hand on the girl's forehead. She let out a scream and began to shake as Desiree held her down. The need to use her more devastating abilities didn't come up often, but in this situation, Desiree knew that if she didn't, the girl would keep regenerating herself.

The pain was evident in the girl's eyes. It was by far the cruelest way Desiree could kill her. She rarely needed to use Pain on a person. Eventually, the pain Desiree was inflicting would kill the girl. If it wasn't for the dagger lodged in the girl's chest, the process might have taken quite a bit longer. However, within minutes her strength failed, and her lifeless body collapsed against the tree. The midday rays of the suns bathed the forest clearing, as well as the scattered remnants of blood. Desiree looked at the blood on her hands. It was still warm. The girl's face stared back at her, eyes still wide open in fear. It was haunting. Desiree had never struggled to kill someone before. What had transpired couldn't even be considered a fight.

Desiree had been in many fights. Swords clashing, arms swinging, the very scent of battle in the air—that was what she had experienced in the past. However, this time had been different. Only fear, the very essence of fear, had been in the air. The girl knew she was going to die and fought Desiree to her very last breath.

Desiree finished the ritual, wiped her hands clean, and fled the forest. She needed to return to Mizimmah quickly. They needed to flee the city before the girl's body was discovered. Desiree lifted one of her feet off the ground, holding one arm outstretched, she willed her body in the direction she wanted to go. The ability of Gravitating was something that anyone could learn with enough practice. Many people perceived it as a blur since the person usually traveled very quickly. It was similar to teleporting in a way, but the caster didn't fully disappear.

Back in the inn, the room door burst open. Mizimmah was sitting at the table reading a book. He glanced over at her from his position with his feet propped up on the table.

"Troubles, darling?"

"We have to leave, right now." The tone in her voice left little argument. Mizimmah jumped up from his seat, throwing the book on the bed.

"What did you do?" he asked with anger in his voice.

"What I had to do!" Desiree returned equally as angrily. His expression turned to one of satiric surrender as he raised his hands and stepped back. "You might not be able to die," spat Desiree. "But if these people find that girl's body, they are going to hunt me down and kill me."

"Oh you're worried about these little cretins," Mizimmah said in a mocking tone.

Angrily, she held her palm out towards him. A flood of images filled his mind. It was an ability Desiree had developed after she opened the Shadow Scroll. Mizimmah had shown her how it could be used to manipulate and influence people. However, in some situations, it did allow for the fast transfer of specific thoughts and memories. The images of what transpired in the forest filled Mizimmah's mind.

Mizimmah blinked and shook his head, it was a bit of a rush and unexpected.

"I see," was his reply.

"If they come after me, I can't hold them back if they can heal like that," Desiree said as she finished gathering her belongings.

They left the inn and exited the city as quickly as possible without drawing attention. Once they were out of the city limits, they both gravitated across the land. They traveled northeast up a long peninsula that jutted off from the main continent of the Light Realm. They continued on until they reached a port city on the northernmost tip. From there, it would take them no more than a couple of days by sea to reach the Earth Realm.

The moment they set foot in the Earth Realm, they teleported away. Desiree had to admit, it was a good feeling to have the freedom to move where she pleased again. One of the things Mizimmah had done during their travels was take her to specific places in each of the other six Realms. This enabled Desiree to establish reference points for future teleportation. Although she often didn't do excessively long jumps, teleporting to the other side of the world drained her for days, even with the Shadow Scroll to help recharge her focus.

They were now in the Omega Realm. It was the one Realm that Desiree knew the least about. Much of the abilities of Omega elementals were shrouded in mystery. The land itself wasn't overly lush in any sense.

Each of the other Realms had characteristics of the Element that resided within it. By the look and feel of the Realm, it was unclear as to what aspects of the Omega Element had been infused into the landscape.

In the blink of an eye, they were both standing on a rough road in the middle of an open plain. Desiree remembered this place. Only a few hours north was a small village. She knew that they would find what they were looking for there. Desiree had grown tired and wasn't able to gravitate, so they decided to walk on foot for a bit.

"What will I have to do once I have all seven gava?" Desiree asked as they walked.

"You will have to mix all seven with your blood. They will bond to your blood and become as one. Once this is done, you will have to place the final result within your body."

"There is something I've been wondering."

"You want to know why you needed the gava from a Shadow Elemental?"

"Yes," she replied as they continued on.

"You are a Shadow Elemental, but your blood is not from a pure bloodline. The other six gava wouldn't have bonded to yours, but your gava will bond to the pureblood Shadow gava. The merging of the two Shadow gava is what will make the whole process bond," he explained.

They could see the village now. It would be less than an hour until they reached it. Desiree hadn't encountered very many Omega elementals in her journeys. She still had no idea what to expect from them regarding their abilities. After reviewing all the possible actions and outcomes, she decided that quick brute force was the best course of action. She only needed one more gava, and if she had to kill the whole village to get it, then that's what she would do.

It was a tiny village, nothing more than a large settlement. A few dozen people lived there in tents or small huts. A large fire was in the middle. It was set up as a communal place to cook and warm oneself. As they approached, Desiree could see an old woman sitting by the fire. She stopped a few paces away from the fire. Their eyes caught for a moment. A moment passed by, but it felt like an eternity. Mizimmah watched the scene unfold from a distance. The speed at which Desiree moved was faster than he had seen; even he had trouble distinguishing her movement.

Like the blur of a streaking arrow, Desiree gravitated across the open area and burst across the fire pit, flames flying left and right. The dagger plunged into the woman's chest as Desiree lifted her off the ground with the sheer force of the impact. All the other villagers dropped what they were doing and ran at Desiree. Reaching into her cloak, she threw several small daggers in all directions. This instantly dropped the villagers to her right, and they soon dissolved away. Turning her head to the other group approaching from the left, she inflicted Pain on all of them at once. With a twitch of her head, they all screamed out in excruciating pain before they collapsed and faded away. Mizimmah watched the impressive show of skills.

"You will be judged one day by what you do here today." The words came out weak and staggered from the old woman's lips.

Desiree turned her head to face the old woman. There was something about the words she spoke. They caused a shift within Desiree; they were spoken as almost pure prophecy. It rang out with a sound of truth that she couldn't put out of her mind, no matter what she did. Desiree looked down at the dagger; the handle was now full. She didn't want to take any chances like the last time in the Light Realm. Pulling the dagger out she quickly slit the woman's throat and then plunged the dagger into her heart. The life disappeared instantly from her eyes. Before her body could even fall to the ground, her gava left her. Desiree grasped it as the body slumped to the ground. Turning to Mizimmah, he watched as she placed the gava in the vial.

The moment had come, and Desiree finally had all seven gava. If any ordinary person could have gazed into Desiree's eyes at that exact moment, fear would have filled every part of them. Mizimmah, however, looked down at her and displayed an evil, twisted grin of approval.

There was no need to go anywhere else to do the next step. They searched through the camp until they found a bowl. Mizimmah held it in his hands as Desiree carefully poured each of her seven vials into it. She watched as the liquids blended and merged with each other. Each gava bonded with the next until only one remained. Desiree looked down at the glowing bowl of liquid. It was the potion of Immortality. If any person in the world took it as she was about to, it would also give them the ability to live forever.

"What happens now, do I just drink it?" asked Desiree, looking back at Mizimmah.

"Oh, not quite deary," he said with a malevolent expression. He thrust his hand deep into her abdomen. Desiree gasped and collapsed to her knees. Blood dripped off Mizimmah's hand as he stood over her. She clasped her hands tightly over the gaping wound.

"What are you doing?" she managed to spit out as she fell backward onto the ground. Suddenly, the faces of the seven people she had murdered in the pursuit of this quest flashed through her mind. They had all been lying on the ground just like she was now. The same fear she was feeling now must have coursed through their veins just before Desiree had taken their lives.

Mizimmah knelt down beside her and held the bowl over the wound.

"Lie still and don't fight it," Mizimmah told her as he moved her hands aside; the blood began to flow again. The wound was deep and wide. Slowly, he poured the glowing liquid into the gaping wound. It flowed into the wound like water going down a drain. Desiree held her breath. A moment passed. She could feel the liquid flowing into her body. Suddenly, she gasped out in pain, and her body arched up into the air. Light shone from her eyes and her elemental symbols. Within her chest, a bright glow began to form beneath her clothing. Her gava was merging with the liquid. The feeling was indescribable. It was the sensation of having your very being burned away from the inside out, only to be replaced with another at the same time.

A few minutes passed. The gaping wound in her abdomen began to slowly close and heal. Typically, only someone with Light abilities could recover at that rate. Since she now had the combined natural healing properties of seven people, her body would now heal much faster. Mizimmah just stood beside her and watched the process happen. A moment later, Desiree sat up abruptly.

"How are you feeling?" he asked. Desiree ran her hand over her abdomen's smooth, freshly healed skin. Her gaze darted to his as their eyes met. Mizimmah could tell she was furious with him for not telling her what he would do.

Desiree stood up. It looked as though she was going to attack him. After a moment, the feelings passed. She looked down at her hands. Balling them into fists, she breathed in deep. The feeling was intense, refreshing, and powerful. Her body felt strong and perfect.

"Say goodbye to aging, pretty lady," Mizimmah said with a wink. "You're just like me—well, minus a few extra abilities that this world can't offer."

"What happens now?" Desiree asked as she looked around the abandoned camp.

"My work is done for now. You wanted to live until the *Omega Chosen One* comes forth. You just have to wait until the Seventh Age rolls around now. Might I suggest you spend the next few centuries taking in all the world has to offer?"

That's just what Desiree did. First, she returned to the Shadow Realm. Her first several hundred years were spent roaming the Realm. The name Desiree soon struck fear into the hearts of all those across the land. With her newfound sense of superiority, she began to view regular people as nothing more than playthings. It didn't matter who they were, young or old, rich or poor. If they had something she wanted, she got it. It wasn't until several hundred years had passed that she moved on.

Word had reached her that the *Light Chosen One* had emerged. The Light Realm was still a place that she didn't want to tread, but she sought it out anyway. Her quest to find the other *Chosen Ones* began. She knew they existed out in the world, and now she had all the time in the world to find them.

Despite her best efforts as the centuries ticked by, she couldn't find any trace of the other five like her. Since she was the only one who was immortal, it made it difficult to track. She knew that each scroll would be passed down to another Scroll Holder every eighty to one hundred years or so.

Over time, Desiree grew tired of her appearance. She often changed her looks to match the local attire as she traveled to different Realms. It wasn't until several hundred years before the dawn of the Seventh Age that she realized she had the ability to manipulate people's minds to believe she looked like anyone she wished. This allowed her to blend in and conceal who she really was everywhere she went. At first, maintaining the illusion with those around her had taken constant mental concentration. After a few centuries, it was so second nature that she could maintain the illusion for as long as she wished without it draining her focus. It was nothing more than a trick of light to her.

The dawn of the Seventh Age was a momentous occasion for her. In her mind, it brought her that much closer to the day when the *Omega Chosen One* would emerge. A hundred years passed by. She tried to predict where in the world the person would come from. It seemed logical to her that the person would come from the Omega Realm.

The first thousand years of Desiree's life came and went. The only thing that still drove her forward was that one day she would hold the power of the Shadow Tear in her hands. She could only imagine what it would feel like to have the power of every Shadow elemental at her fingertips.

As Desiree slept one night, she awoke with a start. Energy was flowing out of the Shadow scroll. As she picked it up, she heard a voice from within. It was telling her that the *Chosen One* had come and to seek them out. Over the next several weeks, she teleported all across the world. By chance, she happened to hear of an island out in the middle of the ocean. It was said that it didn't belong to any of the realms. She knew that she had to see this place for herself.

Boarding a small ship from the port city of Thai, she set out across the sea to this new land. It was quite rare that she came across a place in the world that she had not previously visited or explored. She departed the small merchant ship and walked down the docks. The town was called Daunt, and it seemed simple enough. As she walked down the docks and headed into town, she realized that her attire was drawing more attention than she wanted. She wore mostly black clothing with a silky cloak. It was apparent they weren't used to seeing people in that kind of attire. Even though she did enjoy the clothing, she thought it best to trade it in. She could have easily used her illusion abilities, but if the *Omega Chosen One* was nearby, she didn't want to risk being discovered sooner than she wanted.

She visited several shops, where she traded her clothing and a few small items she had in her possession. She also sold her sword, which wasn't one of her favorites; it was simply something she had been carrying around for centuries. The sword had a black hilt and serrated edges along the length of the blade.

The owner of the Embroidery Shop was very excited to trade for her silky black cloak. There were two other items Desiree had been carrying for some time that she decided she didn't need anymore. The first was a cloaking potion. If a person drank the thick black potion, it would allow them to blend into the shadows for a short period of time. Since she had that ability naturally, it wasn't needed any longer.

The other item was a small device she had gotten during her time in the Fire Realm. To that day, she had never really figured out what it was supposed to do. It was a small black ball with interlocking rings that moved around it. Perhaps it was some sort of puzzle or a child's game, and since she didn't really know, she discarded it as well.

Now that she had rid herself of her dark attire, she looked no different from one of the townsfolk. This was exactly what she was going for; it would allow her to blend in and learn about the village and its people before she moved on to the next village.

A commotion at the docks caught her attention. She went running down with a handful of other people. A ship was coming into port extremely fast. It looked as though it was going to crash. Everyone on the docks began to flee at the sight of the impending collision. The only people who didn't seem fazed by it were a group of four youths at the end of the docks. Moments later, a large wave washed down the docks as the ship came safely into port. Desiree stood with the crowd of onlookers. The group of youths standing at the end of the pier was drenched. One of them was drying everyone off with flames from his hands. She quickly noticed the young man with white hair. Despite the many different hair colors she had seen in her travels, it was surprising to see someone so young with a full head of bright white hair.

Desiree continued to watch for a moment with the crowd but then dispersed when they did. The feeling that she was close to the person she was looking for wouldn't leave her. Whoever the *Omega Chosen One* was, they had to be somewhere on the island of Appagon.

After a few more days in Daunt, she set off toward the mountains. The townsfolk had told her that there was a village farther along the coast and another up in the mountains. Within several days, she reached Tweedsmiur. Their knowledge of potions was intriguing. She had been to many cities in the world that specialized in potions; each seemed to have something unique to offer.

From there, she headed up into the mountains. The village of Sanctus Spire was the kind of village she liked, full of warriors who would offer a good fight on request. Their way of making weapons from the unique wood of the trees was something she had never seen before throughout all her travels. It was quite impressive.

As Desiree journeyed down the mountains towards the city of Iy Ra'Kal, she was sure that the person she sought would have to be there. It was the largest city on Appagon, after all. Weeks passed, and she began to get a good layout of the city. Desiree knew that if the person was in the city, it would be by chance that she found them. Nevertheless, she felt it was her best bet of running into them. They still felt close.

Desiree chose to live in the slums to avoid drawing too much attention to herself. After being there for several weeks, she decided a new look was in order. She used her abilities to change her appearance, starting with shorter black and purple hair and the clothing of a street urchin. On many occasions, she would lure a group of pirates or gangs into a back alley where she would slaughter them and take any valuable belongings. It was a sick game she used as a way of entertaining herself. She loved to play with their minds, letting them beat on her for a short time before she would overpower and kill them.

On one particular day, however, things played out quite differently. As she was letting the men get in the first few punches, a young man came bursting down the alley in an attempt to rescue her. Nothing like that had ever happened before. He fought off the pirates quickly and effectively; it was obvious he was well-trained. Instantly, Desiree remembered where she had seen him before. He was the boy with white hair back on the docks in Daunt.

As he was fighting off the pirates, she quickly altered her appearance. If she were to infiltrate their group, she needed a way in. Desiree added the look of bruises to her body by manipulating the blood vessels in her skin. The ability to change her appearance had grown from a mere mental illusion to actually being able to change the physical look of her body. After she applied the bruises, she slumped over and waited for them to finish their valiant rescue.

They sat Desiree up and tended to her wounds. As she looked at them, she devised that playing the role of a scared little street girl was the best approach, so that's what she did. When Zeph started to talk about his vision of her, she began to wonder if he was the one she was looking for. A glance at the symbols on his hands confirmed it. She knew that she had to follow him until he revealed what she needed to know. When Zeph asked her what her name was, it caught her slightly off guard. She had almost forgotten what her appearance looked like. Thinking quickly, she said the name she had always liked: Violet.

As the weeks went by, there seemed to be a connection forming between the two of them, more than she could understand. Desiree had never had a friend before, or even someone to spend time with across her vast lifetime. The way Zeph looked at her was something that had never happened before. Back when Desiree was mortal, she had never drawn a boy's attraction, especially when she wasn't even trying to.

Hearing Zeph talk about his vision of Desiree was intriguing for her. Hearing about her mortal life through someone else's eyes wasn't something she ever expected to experience. The one thing that seemed to catch her attention was every time Zeph spoke about her, he was truly devastated about how she had been so used and twisted. Desiree couldn't quite understand how Zeph saw her that way; perhaps the centuries had completely changed her perspective on herself. Her memories of who she had once been a thousand years ago had long faded.

After they returned to Daunt, Desiree started to see everything in a different light. She watched the town's happiness at being reunited with the group. No one had ever greeted her with open arms like they did. They treated her just like anyone else in the group. When the group agreed to head to Tsayla, Desiree was excited. She hadn't returned to her homeland for centuries.

The darkness felt good as they traveled across the Realm. In some strange way, Desiree was actually beginning to enjoy her connection to the group; even if it was under the guise of Violet. When the bandits had appeared on the road to Araphel, it was all she could do to restrain herself from destroying them without a moment's thought. She couldn't let on that she was something more than she appeared to be. When she used her Pain ability, it had caused a bit of concern within the group, but it seemed to pass quickly.

Desiree began to notice how uncomfortable Zeph was becoming from just being in the Shadow Realm. During their time at Bain's manor, it escalated further after he read from the Book of Sha'Kath. Desiree knew the book inside and out, but it didn't really matter to her anymore. What she was doing superseded the teachings of Sha'Kath in her mind. After all, she was already immortal and didn't have to be reborn as a fiend to do it.

As their time together progressed, Desiree began to wonder when some sort of connection would form between her and Zeph. If they really did have a connection to each other because they were both *Chosen Ones*, why hadn't something happened yet? She knew she couldn't ask Zeph directly about the ancient temple from her vision, at least not without revealing that she was more than the persona of Violet. Over a thousand years had passed since she first set out to find him, what harm could a few more days do?

Zeph didn't seem to have the same Scroll-given knowledge she had. He had no grasp on his abilities other than a few small traits. Desiree's experience with the Shadow Scroll had been the exact opposite since it had unlocked vast knowledge for her. It wasn't until the day at the temple in Araphel that she began to see that there was indeed great untapped power within Zeph. To part the very skies over Tsayla and strike a man down blind; it was clear that there was much more to him than what she could perceive on the surface.

Desiree was glad when they headed out into the Realm once again. The more they journeyed together, the closer she felt to getting the answer she wanted. Their climb up the mountain had been a little rougher than expected. Desiree hadn't had to do anything like that for years. As they climbed the mountain, she devised a way to see how much Zeph could handle. If he really was the *Chosen One*, he should be able to overcome anything that came across their path. Within the cracks of the rocks, she noticed several Nytemare fiends hiding in their depths. They could clearly sense her power and cowered in fear. Her abilities had given her a great deal of control over various types of Shadow fiends. They could see the power emanating from her immediately and kept their distance. She mentally took hold of one of them and commanded it to enter Zeph's mind.

Desiree and the others watched as Zeph battled the fiend within his mind. She was very impressed with how he overcame each attack and eventually expelled the fiend from his mind. Zeph never ceased to surprise her. Their journey was going very well. It seemed tedious to track down the Topos Gate since she could have teleported them all in the blink of an eye. It wasn't until she saw the gate for herself that everything changed.

She had no way of knowing that the gate they were searching for was actually the altar from her childhood village. Her village had used it as a place to kill and clean animals. It was a large stone slab, so it worked quite well for the task. When her eyes had fallen upon it, a rush of long-forgotten memories came flooding back into her mind. In all her centuries and travels, Desiree had never again stumbled upon the village of her birth.

As she searched through the rubble of what had once been her home, she found the one thing she knew must have survived the passage of time. The rusted fragment of metal was all that was left of the kitchen knife she had used to kill the fiend form of her mother. The pain flooded up from deep inside Desiree. It brought with it many memories she had forgotten centuries ago. Turning, she saw Zeph standing there. She wasn't sure what it was, but something she had done triggered his vision.

Finally, Zeph began to say the words she had waited a thousand years to hear. The temple had sunk below the desert sands when the knowledge of it had been wiped from the Uriel. Even if she didn't know exactly where to look, she had a reference point now, and that was all she needed.

She watched as the expression changed on Zeph's face. It was clear that he could see through her disguise, to who she really was underneath. There was no need for it any longer, so she used her abilities to discard the persona of Violet and reveal her true form. It gave her a sweet feeling of satisfaction for the group of them to look on her true form in all its perfection. The race was on, and with Zeph's vision to guide her, she was sure she'd reach the Shadow Tear first. Desiree gave Zeph a wink and teleported away.

THE SIXTH AGE, 57th Year

> There are those that will seek out ways to prolong their lives, no matter the price.
>
> Despite the heavy cost, life will always fade away.
>
> For nothing of this world will ever replace what Omega freely gives.
>
> ~ The Uriel, Mal'ak

CHAPTER 20
THE GATHERING SHADOW

Zeph fell to his knees and began pounding his fists into the ground. The stone foundation of the ruins started to crack with each impact. It was understandable for him to feel frustrated, but it was unusual to witness such a strong display of emotions from him. He paused for a moment and then sat back on his heels. His chest rose and fell quickly as he breathed in deep and fast. Fury burned in his eyes. His hands were shaking as they hung at his sides. He looked up to the overcast sky and screamed out a cry of frustration.

"It's okay, Zeph," Breeze said, trying to calm him down.

"No, it's not okay!" he blurted out as he jumped to his feet. "She was right here, under our noses this whole time. Just waiting for me to give her that one little piece of information she needed. And the worst part is I could have prevented this if I had just paid attention!"

"What are you talking about? You couldn't have prevented this," said Marcus.

"Oh really, really?!" Zeph fumed as he walked over to Marcus. Reaching into his bag, he whipped out Mage Saphar's book. Flipping open the pages, he shoved it into Marcus' hands. Running his hands through his hair, Zeph paced around as Marcus read the page. There was a sobering look on Marcus' face as he read the words written as a warning to them over four hundred years earlier.

'There is a creature that will come amongst you. It will reach out with an arm of friendship and hold a dagger of deception behind its back. Its power is not of this world, and death has lost the control to take its breath away. Beware of those that hide themselves in shadows.'

"Do you understand what she's going to do?! She's going to break the Shadow Tear," Zeph said as he tried to calm himself down, to no avail. Even as he said the words out loud, Zeph felt a surge of fear swell up inside.

"What will that do exactly?" asked Iggy.

"She believes it will give her unlimited power."

"But you're pretty sure something else will happen?" asked Breeze.

"All I have to go on is what I saw in my original vision from the Omega Scroll. The first thing that happened was the wall of darkness. I don't think the power is going to flow into her. I think when the Tear breaks, it will spread a wave of darkness over the whole world."

"Then I guess we have no time to waste, let's go!" Iggy said as he took off running, motioning for the others to follow. It caught everyone off guard for a moment, but they quickly followed.

They all went running back to the Topos Gate. If they had any chance of stopping Desiree, they would have to get to Tamay as quickly as possible. Zeph's heart felt like it was beating out of his chest as he caught up with his little brother. It wasn't the fact that he was running but the reality that the very fate of the world was in his hands. Iggy slowed to a stop as they reached the gate. Now came the hard part.

Zeph walked around the platform looking at all the glyphs and symbols that were engraved on it. He was starting to wish he had a textbook of some kind for it. Knowing glyphs and symbols was one thing, but knowing the inner workings of a device controlled by them was a separate circumstance altogether. Once glyphs and symbols were combined into a Glyph Seal, their purpose was usually evident.

Reaching down, he touched one of the glyphs on the stone. It began to glow. He wasn't sure if that was from being touched or specifically from him touching it. As he looked around the platform, he marked out thirty different symbols and a handful of glyphs. From what he knew of the two different markings, he suspected that the symbols had to do with geographical locations and the glyphs had to do with controlling the platform itself.

An hour passed by. Zeph continued to walk all around the gate, pressing different glyphs and symbols as he did. The rest of the group sat on the ground, leaning against the old pillars. It was easier that way, allowing Zeph to work without getting in his way. He was starting to feel like he had a handle on it. It seemed like the glyphs in some way powered the gate itself. This wasn't that odd of a concept once he explained it to the others.

The glyphs powered the gate by drawing energy from the Shadow Realm itself. There were six glyphs positioned at equal points around the engraved ring on the platform. In between them were the symbols. He noticed that the glyphs were two sets of the same three glyphs. As he continued experimenting, he discovered that they activated the platform. He guessed the reason there were two of them was because one set of three activated one platform, while the other three activated the destination platform. With that out of the way, he just had to make sense of the symbols.

Symbols were a little trickier. They commonly represented places or things, while glyphs represented actions. Zeph just had to make sense of the symbols. As he looked over the symbols, one seemed familiar to him. It wasn't anything he remembered learning back in school; this was something more recent. All of a sudden, it hit him. The stone pillars in the forest, just before they reached Araphel, had the same symbol on them. Zeph was starting to understand how the gates worked now.

"I think I might know how these work," Zeph said as he looked at the others. They looked up from the meaningless activity each was doing to pass the time.

"Do tell," replied Marcus.

"The glyphs activate this gate, as well as the destination gate. But, without the specific gate's location, it doesn't matter. That's where the symbols come in," Zeph said as he opened up the map Bain had given them. On it, he had marked the location of the gate from what they had seen on the large map in his study. There were nine gates all across Tsayla.

"I think all we have to do is choose the specific number of symbols closest to the gate we want and then simply activate it."

The rest of them didn't find it very simple. There were several dozen different symbols, and they knew nothing about Tsayla or where each symbol could be located. Zeph sat down in the middle of the platform and looked over the map. If only he could figure out where each symbol was on the map. He already knew where one was because they had passed it on their journey.

Closing his eyes for a moment, he hung his head. He hadn't realized how exhausted he was until that moment. When he opened his eyes, everything around him had turned a grayish tone, and looked as though it was made of water, like something from a dream. The marks on his hands were glowing brightly. Looking around, he saw the others sitting by the pillars; they looked almost frozen in time. Suddenly, he remembered being in a state like this before. It was the night he had the dream about his father's compass.

Quickly, he pulled it from his pocket. Turning it over, he noticed one of the buttons was glowing. He pressed it, and one of the needles lit up. The glyphs running down it were glowing blue. At first, he wasn't exactly sure where the needle was pointing. It wasn't until he held it up to the map that it drastically changed direction. The needle was locked on the city of Tamay, as indicated on the map. As Zeph moved the compass closer and farther from the city's location on the map, he noticed that the point on the map began to glow as he brought it closer. Placing the compass directly over top of the city on the map, the compass needle began to spin quickly in a circle.

Stands of light jumped from the compass to a series of symbols on the gate platform. They began to glow. Zeph moved the compass over the map until it was over the gate they were standing at. Once again, strands of pure light flowed down from the compass to a different set of symbols on the platform. All Zeph could do was shake his head and smile. He wondered if his father had ever known what the compass could truly do.

The veil of the dream collapsed around him, and everything returned to normal. The glowing symbols on Zeph's hands caught everyone's attention.

"What just happened?" asked Marcus as he quickly stood.

"Uh, that's a little hard to explain. In short, I discovered what another one of the needles does on the compass."

"Oh, really," Iggy said excitedly.

"I think this one here points to enchanted objects nearby," Zeph said, pointing to the glowing needle.

"But how did you know which symbols you needed to activate?" asked Breeze.

"I just had a dream or vision of some kind. The compass showed me which symbols we needed to use. So I guess there's only one way to find out."

Zeph quickly wrote down the symbols he had seen in the dream. Since only one person could go through at a time, they would need to have them written down. Zeph guessed that the destination gate had to be activated first, since that's how it was shown to him in the dream.

Standing in the middle of the platform, he reached down to the different symbols. Each time he touched one, it began to glow. Five symbols needed to be activated. After he pressed them, he pushed the three glyphs as well. Nothing happened. Of course, Zeph wasn't really sure what to expect.

Each symbol Zeph touched was still glowing, so he was sure he hadn't messed anything up. Perhaps he needed to do both sets before anything would happen. He handed the paper to Iggy for safekeeping and proceeded with the next set.

As Zeph reached down and touched the final glyph, the ring around the platform instantly lit up. What could only be described as a large blue flame shot up from the glowing ring and engulfed Zeph. They had only a split second to watch before suddenly he was gone. Marcus was the first to act. He jumped on the platform and began pressing the same sequence as quickly as possible. Before Iggy or Breeze could protest, he, too, was gone in a brilliant display of blue energy. Iggy shrugged and handed the paper to Breeze. He wasn't quite as fast as Marcus but finished the sequence nonetheless. There was nothing left for Breeze to do but follow after them.

The sensation of the energy wrapping around her was like jumping into the ocean on a fresh morning. It was a frigid and watery sensation. Everything went black for a moment, and then suddenly very bright as she appeared at the platform in Tamay. Looking around, she quickly spotted the three boys standing just before her. It was hard to focus;

everything seemed incredibly bright. She guessed it was due to the disorientating effect of teleporting, but then she noticed the sky. There was sunlight here.

Zeph stood with Iggy and Marcus at his sides. They were standing in a massive city, with large stone buildings everywhere. The fact that there was sunlight also greatly confused Zeph at first until he saw the ring of clouds wrapping around the edge of the city. Obviously, the city's rulers had somehow created the parting of the clouds for their people.

When Zeph first stepped through the gate, there had been many people around. It looked like he was in the middle of a large outdoor market of some kind. Seconds after he stepped through, everyone had scattered and run off. It was an unexpected reaction, Zeph thought. Perhaps they just weren't used to people using the Topos Gates anymore. Zeph began to turn to see how the trip had been on Breeze when he heard the sound of footsteps running towards them from all directions.

Bursting out of various side streets and corridors came rows of men in armored uniforms. Each had a silver breastplate and was armed with a long, thin sword. They quickly fanned out and surrounded them. More than three dozen soldiers filled the open-air market. Zeph backed up, and the rest of the group followed suit until the four stood back to back.

"What have you gotten us into now, Zeph?" Breeze asked with an irritated tone in her voice.

"Me?!" he blurted out.

Just then, the circle of soldiers began to part, revealing a tall man walking towards them. He wore a similar uniform to the rest of the soldiers, but it was apparent that he was a higher-ranking soldier.

"My name is Captain Krima of the Tamay City Guards, and you are all under arrest for unauthorized use of the ancient Gate."

"Oh, this is so not what we need right now," Zeph muttered under his breath.

THE DESERT AIR WAS hot and dry as Desiree appeared atop one of the dunes. Even though it was the start of the year's growing season in most places, that didn't affect the temperature much in this place. There was a steady wind blowing across the sand at the moment. The desert overall was relatively flat, with the occasional dune here and there. Now began the task of finding where the Temple was hidden out in the desert. If the pyramid was indeed somewhere below the sands, the Temple would be her way down to it.

She began to gravitate out across the desert, leaving a trail of blowing sand in her wake. Even with the speed at which she was flying across the sand, it would still take a great deal of time to search the desert. The desert was roughly twenty times the size of Appagon. Nothing of value was on this desert land, only the sand and hot air. A day came and went. The night air came quickly to the desert, dropping the temperature rapidly.

As the suns rose over the horizon the next morning, Desiree was already on her feet. Reaching into her bag, she held onto her Scroll for a few minutes before heading out again. Any normal person would be practically crawling on the ground from exhaustion. If not for the rejuvenation power of the Scroll, there was a chance that she would have been too.

The winds kicked up just after midday. Taking part of the cloth from her cloak, she wrapped it across her face. Sand was blowing everywhere, making it hard to see anything in the distance. There was no way she could gravitate across the desert with the sandstorm upon her, so she decided to take the alternative. She sauntered through the sand.

By the time the third day dawned, she was beginning to wonder if it was somehow all a ruse on Zeph's part. Perhaps he had already seen through her deception before saying anything about the vision and had sent her out into the desert on a fool's errand. She began to get angry at the thought of being tricked when she spotted something on the horizon. As she headed towards it, she started to distinguish it more clearly. It appeared to be nothing more than a pile of stones. As she neared it, she reduced her speed, a wake of dust and sand followed in her wake.

The pile was no large than a house. It seemed odd that a pile of stone would be out in the middle of the desert like this. By this point, she was certain she had reached the exact center of the desert isle. It would have taken any normal man weeks on foot to reach this point, but with her ability to gravitate, it had taken her only days. Even if Zeph somehow made it to the desert, she would be long gone by the time he caught up with her.

Climbing the pile of stone, she quickly reached the top. Looking out at the horizon, she could see no sign of the ocean in any direction. She was now sure it was the exact center of the desert. The island was almost completely round, so being unable to see the sea was a good indication of where she was.

As she sat atop the pile of stone, she happened to glance down at the stone she was sitting on. It was white and very smooth from centuries of weathering from the sand. Running her hand over the stone, she gazed down between the cracks. A round metal ball about the size of a fist caught her eye about an arm's length down into the gap. It seemed odd that a metal ball would be inside a pile of rocks in the middle of a vast desert.

Reaching down to grasp the ball, she noticed that the Shadow symbol on her hand had begun to glow. A smile appeared across her face as a slight flutter of excitement filled her. This was what she was looking for. Grasping the metal ball in her clutch, she felt the ground beneath her begin to shake. Quickly, she jumped down from the pile of stones and backed away. The desert all around her was vibrating heavily. She backed away even farther. The pile of rocks began to topple over. A point began to jet and rise out from within the center of the pile.

Sand shot up violently from the desert as a structure began to rise from the depths. The ground wouldn't stop shaking as the structure continued to rise. Desiree held her arms outwards, trying to maintain her balance. After a few more minutes, the sands beneath her finally came to rest. Standing tall before her was the Temple. The whole structure stood more than five stories tall. A spire could be seen coming from the top and stretched further towards the sky.

A dome structure was at the spire's base and covered most of the top of the Temple. The remaining portion leading down to the base was square. Pillars were carved into the sides, going all the way around. In between the pillars were tall stone statues carved into the outer walls. Desiree guessed that the small metal ball she had touched was the spire's top point. It was hard to make out from the weathering, but Desiree guessed the statues could be depictions of the Uriel from the First Age.

Desiree looked at the large stone steps that led up to the huge archway of the front of the Temple. It was time; she had waited long enough. Trudging through the sand, she soon set foot on the hard stone of the steps. The large square archway was above her head. Even though the Temple had been underground for untold centuries, it still looked as though it had never been buried beneath the sands. As she entered the Temple, she quickly realized that the entirety of the inside was a massive open hall.

Standing tall against the inner walls were rows of statues. Their height reached almost halfway to the dome's ceiling, at least twice the height of your average man, if not more. The statues inside were different from the decorative ones carved into the Temple's outer walls. These statues inside were carved in the stances and poses of warriors and heroes. Light from the dome shone down through colored glass and into the Temple, casting an arrangement of colors across the floor. On the walls behind the statues were murals depicting the story of creation. They spanned all around the Temple. The bright colors and imagery were awe-inspiring.

Besides the rows of statues and the murals, the only other thing that caught Desiree's eye was a small shrine at the center of the Temple. She walked towards it until she was directly beneath the center of the dome. Looking around at the Temple, she guessed it had once been used for prayers or meditation. She could picture the rows of monks or mages all sitting in rows around this center shrine.

Pacing around the shrine for a moment, she took it all in. It was a collection of small statues with what looked like a dried-up fountain in the middle. It wasn't overly large and only rose to chest height. The fountain had multiple tiers with a basin at the top. She was sure the shrine was the key to reaching the depths below the Temple. Looking at the dried-up fountain, she wondered if it was as simple as pouring water into its basin. She poured a canteen of water from her bag into the basin at the top of the fountain. Desiree watched as the water flowed down from the basin to the one below and so on until it reached the bottom level.

Nothing happened. Once again, she was becoming frustrated. Puzzles weren't her strong suit. She also found it strange that Mizimmah hadn't shown himself to her in quite a while. It was making her a little nervous. She figured that with the discovery of the Temple, he would have joined her by now. Perhaps he was testing her.

Desiree looked down at the fountain again. The small statues that were wrapped around it depicted people embracing the fountain. Taking a closer look, Desiree began to notice that each of their hands were in a specific place around the fountain. She began to walk around the small shrine. As she did, she noticed that underneath one of the basins was each Elemental Symbol carved into the stone. The fingertips on the hands of the statues all seemed to be pointing to one of the seven symbols, except for one of the statues. The hands ran along the rim of the basin, making it appear to be holding it up.

Looking over the statue, Desiree noticed that the stone pendant in the carving looked odd. Running her fingers over it, she pressed down. The pendant pushed into the statue. A loud click echoed throughout the Temple. Desiree felt the floor shift slightly. Cracks were now clearly visible in the smooth stone floor. Taking several steps back, Desiree watched as the small fountain shrine slowly rotated, and the floor around it began to separate into small brick-like pieces in a ring formation.

The shrine spun around and then stopped with another loud click. Even though the way the bricks had separated on the floor gave the impression that it would reveal a passageway, nothing happened. The sound of stone grinding filled Desiree's ears. It wasn't coming from the floor this time but from the statues that lined the Temple's inner walls.

It was an interesting sight, and one that she could honestly admit she had never seen in the hundreds of years she had walked the world. The statues began to move from their positions and step towards her. She guessed that she must have done something wrong, and this was some sort of failsafe.

There were at least twenty statues as tall as a two-story house marching their way toward her. In their hands were huge weapons, from swords to spears. It didn't matter, though. Desiree sent a blast of telekinetic energy at one of them. The wave of energy that would have normally sent one of her enemies flying across the room simply washed over the statue, leaving it unfazed. There was no way she could fight them off, but she wasn't going to back down now. Reaching into her satchel, she grabbed the Shadow Scroll. As she pulled it from the satchel, the statues abruptly stopped advancing.

Desiree looked down at the Scroll and then at the statues. She had done everything right. It was a test to see if she was worthy to enter the depths of the Temple.

"Kneel!" she boomed out into the Temple. Her voice echoed off the walls. Each of the statues took a knee on the floor of the Temple before her. She smiled with an evil grin, not unlike Mizimmah's. The statues stood and returned to their original positions. As each finished taking up its pose, another click was heard throughout the Temple. Desiree looked over at the fountain shrine. The ring of bricks around the shrine began to sink into the floor and lock in place. It was like watching a staircase burrow down into the ground. She started to descend the stairs, slowly making her way into the depths below.

MARCUS GENTLY BANGED his head on the bars of the cell. It had become something of a meditation process for him. The coolness of the metal relaxed him, and the gentle repetitive banging numbed his head. On the other hand, the repetitive banging was beginning to wear on the nerves of the other three cellmates. Gripping the bars firmly, Marcus let his body fall back. The stretching of his forearms felt nice. They had been cooped up in the cell for two days now.

Zeph sat on the nearby bench and stared out the barred window. He could see the harbor from their perspective. It was massive, at least five or six times larger than the harbor in Iy Ra'Kal. Looking up at the sky, he still couldn't believe they had parted the clouds over the city. It was such an odd sight to see, the edge of the clouds cast a dark shadow on everything just outside of the harbor.

Breeze sat on the floor across from Zeph, her back against the bars. Iggy was lying on the floor with his legs propped up on the other end of the bench Zeph was sitting on. The last two days had been nothing but questioning and interrogations. The Topos Gate was extremely off-limits to the citizens in Tamay, and use of any of the gates was restricted all across the Realm. Of course, they hadn't known that when they used it. So far, they had spent most of their time trying to explain who they were and convince Captain Krima that they were not spies of some sort.

At first, they all wanted to use their abilities and skills to fight off the guards and escape, but after careful contemplation, they decided it wasn't their best course of action. Of course, that meant they had to spend their days in a small prison cell. Despite their situation, though, they were still well taken care of. Meals were brought to them three times a day.

Footsteps coming from down the hall caused everyone's ears to perk up. Perhaps they were finally getting released. Just as expected, it was Captain Krima. Iggy remained on the floor and tilted his head farther back to look at the man through upside-down eyes. Krima pointed to Zeph in the corner.

"Come with me, Zeph," he said as the accompanying guard opened the cell door.

Zeph did as he was told; it was starting to become a regular occurrence. Over the last two days, they had been questioned as a group and individually several times each. This was precisely what Zeph was expecting to happen once again.

This time was different, however. Krima didn't cuff him when they left the cell. They walked down the hall together. The sound of their footsteps echoed off the walls. Mostly, every building in Tamay was made out of stone, not just plain stones. All the building materials were finely crafted. Tamay was a magnificent city. Its architecture was an extraordinary feat of engineering. Most of the buildings towered more than four or five stories. The larger buildings in the city reached a height as high as twelve stories. Zeph had never seen anything so amazing.

They rounded the corner and headed in a different direction than they usually went. Zeph looked puzzled.

"Where are we going?"

"Thane Akuo wishes to see you," Krima replied.

Zeph wasn't quite sure how to respond to that. He had no idea who that person was, but he got the distinct feeling that it was someone of importance. The way Krima had said 'thane' seemed to indicate that it wasn't a name but some kind of title. They continued down the hall, which opened up into a courtyard. People were sitting on benches talking. Several trees were growing right out of the stone. The leaves on them were a faded red color. Zeph had to admit that there was a lot of beauty within the city walls.

Continuing on, they entered another archway on the other side of the courtyard. This led to a huge hallway with a distinct feeling of leading to somewhere important. Zeph glanced over at Krima as they walked. The Captain's armor was finely crafted, and in many ways, it reminded him of Sir Jarian's armor.

"So, why no cuffs this time?" Zeph asked as they continued down the long hallway.

"If you are foolish enough to try anything in the presence of the Thane, we will simply kill you."

Again, Krima had used that title. Zeph was becoming curious.

"I don't mean any disrespect, but what is a Thane?"

Krima stopped in his tracks. Zeph immediately got the impression that he just asked the strangest question in the world, or perhaps just the dumbest. Krima just stared back at him.

"Do you really not know what a Thane is?"

"No, I don't," Zeph replied awkwardly.

"The Thane rules all of the Shadow Realm. You really are not from these lands, are you?"

"That's precisely what we've been trying to explain for the last two days.

"Well, perhaps Thane Akuo's ears will be more attentive to your words than mine have been," Krima said as he gestured for Zeph to continue.

The hallway joined a grand white hall. Red carpets lined the floors. The ceilings towered high into the air. Large arches curved together at the very top. Open windows standing several stories tall were carved into the walls. Light bathed in from outside. Rows of shelves lined the walls and towered several stories high. Ladders were attached, and people were on them at various points throughout the hall. It was hard to believe that this city was the heart of the Shadow Realm. Zeph had always guessed it would be dark and menacing, based on everywhere else they had seen in the Realm.

"Not everywhere in this land is menacing, young Zeph."

Zeph looked around, trying to find the location of the voice. The grand hall seemed to be a meeting area, a throne room, and a library all at once. Besides Zeph and Krima, a handful of scholars walked around with books throughout the grand hall. Zeph's eyes fell on the old man sitting at one of the nearby tables. It was his robes that had caught Zeph's attention. They were a mix of black and red and made of the same kind of fabric he had seen on Desiree's garments.

"Ah yes, my robes," the old man said as he ran his hand over the edge. "They are made from some of the finest fabrics our land has to offer."

Zeph was taken aback by the old man's words. Slowly, he walked over to the table. Krima stayed a few paces away but kept a watchful eye on Zeph. Sitting down at the table, Zeph looked across at the old man.

The man was indeed quite old, how old Zeph could not be quite sure. People did age differently in different realms; Zeph had come to realize. Nevertheless, the man had long white hair loosely tied down his back. His long white beard flowed down onto his lap. He was slowly flipping through a rather large book that was sprawled on the table in front of him. On his face was a small pair of eyeglasses. He glanced up over his glasses for just a moment, so he could catch a glance at Zeph. It was then that Zeph saw the pale orange glow in the old man's eyes. He was a Seer.

"Yes, I am a Seer, Zeph," Akuo replied. "I can read so much from so many, but you, on the other hand, are a mystery."

"What do you mean?" asked Zeph.

"With you, I can only read what's on the surface, and not what lies deep within."

There was a pause in their conversation. Zeph wasn't quite sure what he should say next. He looked down at the book Akuo was reading.

"What are you reading?" he asked.

"Everything that has ever been recorded about this," he replied as he pulled the Omega scroll from his robes and slid it across the table. Zeph breathed a sigh of relief as he reached over and took it. It had been confiscated along with the rest of their belongings when they were first captured. Zeph had been worried, but also had a feeling that the Scroll would be returned to him.

Akuo watched Zeph's expressions as he held the Scroll again. He could tell that the Scroll meant a great deal to Zeph; he held it like a charished possession. Closing the book, Akuo crossed his fingers on the table and looked over at Zeph. There was kindness in the old man's eyes.

"I've read all I can and I've listened to what my Captain has told me of you. Now I want to hear your story, Zeph."

Zeph looked back at him. It had been a while since he had recounted his tale. Zeph began on the day he unlocked the Omega Scroll and the vision it had shown him of what would befall the world. Akuo listened very intensely as Zeph spoke. There was definitely something in Zeph's voice that drew an audience. Even the other scholars in the hall stopped what they were doing and stretched their ears to listen in as well.

Several hours passed by. The story continued to grow in length each time Zeph told it. So much had happened in just the several weeks since they had arrived on Tsayla. Desiree's reappearance in the story was the focal point of the tale. Akuo had been genuinely surprised to hear that Desiree was still alive after all the centuries. Her legends of terror and cruelty were well known all across the Realm. Hearing that she was still alive was like finding out one of your worst fears had become a reality.

Once Zeph began telling Akuo of his latest vision, the old Thane leaned forward and listened closely. A specific detail had caught his attention.

"So we're trying to get to this temple in the desert in the hope of stopping Desiree," Zeph concluded as he finished his story.

"And do you know how you will accomplish this?" Akuo asked with a slight grin.

"No, I don't. I'm worried that we're running out of time."

Akuo stood, and Zeph followed suit. He gestured for Zeph to follow him. They walked farther into the grand hall. Zeph spent most of it looking up at the ceiling and the bookshelves. Krima followed several paces behind them.

"You are an extraordinary young man, Zeph. Some of us are called into greatness, like you. Others are born into it, like me. When I was a young boy, my father was the current Thane. I knew that one day the responsibilities would be passed down to me. As a young man, no older than you, I spent my days in this very hall. This was my classroom, my sparring room, whatever the need might have been. In all that time, there was only one thing I wanted to do once I became Thane."

"What was that?" Zeph asked as they continued to walk at a slow pace.

"I wanted to bring light to my people," Akuo replied.

Zeph looked at the rays of light flowing in through the massive windows. Ahead of them was a large stained glass window. The colors of the light danced across the floor.

"How did you do it?" Zeph asked.

"I did nothing; it was my people that accomplished it. It was gradual, but over several decades, the darkness pulled away."

Zeph stopped and looked at the man. He wasn't quite understanding what Akuo meant by all that.

"If a man wishes to cower in the darkness, to be covered by it, to have it consume him, then the darkness will find him. If a man seeks the light, it too will find him," Akuo replied with a smile. "I showed my people that we don't have to be consumed by darkness simply because we are born of Shadow."

Akuo placed a hand on Zeph's shoulder and took a good, long look into the young man's eyes. Zeph wasn't sure if he was trying to read his mind or simply staring at him. The old man sighed and patted him on the shoulder.

"Remember my words one day, Zeph, the darkness is only there because we embrace it."

They turned and began walking back toward the front of the hall. Akuo's words still resonated in Zeph's mind. There was a great deal of wisdom in the old man. He wondered if he would have that kind of wisdom and knowledge when he reached old age. They reached the archway that led back the way Zeph had first entered.

"So what happens now?" asked Zeph.

"There is still one thing you need to discover before you may leave," Akuo replied.

"What would that be?" Zeph asked with a slight tone of irritation in his voice.

"Return to your cell, think about what we have discussed, and think about your vision, Zeph. You will understand when it happens. I have seen things in you that you have yet to see in yourself. It is time for you to stop looking at the world around you and start looking at the gifts inside yourself."

With that, Krima escorted him out. Zeph still didn't understand. Shortly, Zeph found himself back in his cell again. It was late in the day now, and everyone was beginning to get a little tired. Food came to them shortly, and they all ate.

"So what are we supposed to do now?" asked Marcus.

"That's really the question of the day now, isn't it?" Zeph replied.

"What do you think Thane Akuo meant when he said there was something you had to discover?" asked Iggy as he curled up on the floor.

"I'm pretty sure he knows more than he's letting on. I just don't know what about. There was a look on his face when I was telling him about what I saw in the vision, about us traveling here, then to the Temple in the desert."

"Well, let's all get some sleep, and we'll figure it out tomorrow," Breeze said.

The guards provided blankets and pillows. The cells had no bedding, but they made do. They all drifted off to sleep quickly. The nights seemed cooler here in Tamay compared to some of the other places they had stayed in Tsayla.

As Zeph slept, the vision flashed through his mind again. He felt the wind wrap itself around him as he flew across the waters of the sea and across the sands of the desert. The sensation was cold and wet as he felt his body fly through the air at speeds he could never dream of achieving. He watched the Temple rise from the sands. It towered up into the sky.

Zeph quickly sat up. The others were still asleep next to him. Something about the vision was pulling at him. The sensation he felt as his body flew over the world was familiar. Standing up, he walked over to the bars of the cell. The metal was cold as he ran his fingertips over them. He felt as though he was so close to an answer. It was a nagging sensation in the back of his mind. The worst part was he was sure that Akuo knew what he had to do.

Resting his head against the bars, he let out a sigh. He wanted to leave, to reach the Temple out in the desert. An image of the Temple flashed through his mind again. He remembered feeling cold as he stood before the Temple, which he found odd since he was out in the desert. He gazed at the stone wall from his cell on the other side of the hall. What did he have to learn in order to leave?

Closing his eyes, he took a deep breath. The sensation that he had just taken an icy drink of water suddenly filled him. It was a cooling sensation that spread from his chest out towards his body. Eyes still closed, he leaned forward. Suddenly, his hands were pressed against a stone wall. Immediately, Zeph opened his eyes. His face was hovering just in front of the wall opposite his cell. Spinning around, Zeph looked at the locked cell directly across from where he stood. His mind kicked into overdrive as he tried to comprehend what had just happened.

No guards were standing near the cell; they were posted farther down the hall. It was a good thing, too; he didn't want to have to explain this one to them. Zeph looked at his brother lying on the floor under the bench. He wanted to be back in the cell with him. The cold sensation filled Zeph again. Looking down at his chest, he saw a glow emanating from it. Everything around him blurred for a split second, and then he found himself back in the cell, standing over Iggy.

Zeph shook his head and took a deep breath as he sat down on the bench. Iggy began to stir, then slowly looked up at his big brother. The look on Zeph's face made Iggy wake up quickly. Sitting up, he looked at Zeph and asked what was wrong. Zeph looked down at him with a slightly glazed-over expression. Without answering him, Zeph walked over to the bars of the cell. Iggy watched as Zerh held his hands out, energy like smoke wrapped around Zeph in an instant, then suddenly he appeared on the other side of the bars. Iggy's eyes widened.

"How did you do that?" he whispered.

"I have no idea. I just put some of the pieces together in my mind," he replied.

Zeph teleported himself back into the cell again. It was a fascinating sight. They hadn't gotten a good look at Desiree when she disappeared. Looking at Zeph now, it was as though his body had collapsed in on itself, turning into stands of energy and smoke as it did.

Walking over, he placed his hand on Iggy's shoulder. Before Iggy could even ask what Zeph was about to do, he found himself on the other side of the bars. Iggy paused for a second and then took a deep breath. The sensation was more than he was expecting. It was like he had just jumped into freezing cold water. It was similar to the sensation they had all felt when teleported by the Topos Gate, but much more intense.

Zeph understood now what Akuo had wanted him to find out. This was how they were going to get to the desert. He teleported them both back into the cell. They would wait until morning before they set out. Zeph was certain that Akuo was aware of what was coming and that he would be waiting for them in the morning. Zeph and Iggy lay back on the floor and went back to sleep.

The light from the morning suns bathed in through their window. Both Marcus and Breeze were awake and sitting on the bench. After some time, Marcus began softly kicking Zeph to get him up faster. Zeph rolled over in an attempt to ignore him, but to no avail. He sat up and rubbed his eyes. Iggy let out a big yawn and got up as well.

"So what's the plan now, Oh fearless leader?" Marcus asked as he leaned back against the wall.

"Today, we leave," Zeph replied.

"Oh, really, and how are we supposed to..." Marcus' voice trailed off as they heard the footsteps of several people coming down the hall. It was Thane Akuo and Captain Krima. Several guards also followed. They stopped in front of the cell. Akuo had a soft smile on his face, to which Zeph returned in kind.

"Good morning, my friends," greeted Akuo. "For those of you who are unaware, I am Thane Akuo, ruler of the Shadow Realm." Everyone nodded their heads respectfully. "So Zeph, are you and your comrades ready to leave this cell?"

"Yes, we are," Zeph said with a look of confidence.

"Show me," Akuo replied.

Zeph held his hands out and concentrated for a second. In the blink of an eye, he stood on the other side of the bars. Both Breeze and Marcus looked at Zeph with bewilderment plastered on their faces. Marcus was beginning to feel like Zeph was keeping secrets from him again. As if reading his best friend's mind, Zeph assured him he had just discovered it the previous night.

"These abilities have always been within you, Zeph, not that Scroll or anything else made you the way you are. You have the Omega Element inside you. You can do anything you put your mind to. And on that note, I bid you safe journeys," Akuo said, gesturing towards the guards carrying their belongings. They unlocked the cell, and everyone loaded up once again. Akuo walked with them to one of the large balconies that looked out over the city. Zeph hadn't realized how vast the city really was until that moment.

"Do you know what will happen? Will I be able to stop her?" Zeph asked Akuo, almost afraid of the answer.

"No eyes have seen, no ears have heard, what Omega has planned for you on this day," he replied. "Your story is your own, Zeph. Whatever happens, it is what was always meant to be. Remember that."

Taking the Scroll from his bag, Zeph pressed his palms against the ends. The surge of energy began to fill him. He knew that he would need all the energy he could get for this jump. Everyone else gathered around him in a circle. Linking arms, they joined with Zeph. They exchanged glances from inside the small circle they had made.

"Take a deep breath," Zeph said with a smile. As each of them did, they felt the cold sensation wash over them. Everything blurred around

stop and then slowly headed down the spiral staircase to whatever lay below the Temple.

Iggy shone light from his staff as they went, illuminating their path. The staircase led down into a small hallway. The walls were black and very smooth, like polished stone, and the floor was as well. Both Zeph and Iggy looked at each other. This place reminded both of them of where they had arrived when the Omega Scroll pulled them into the vision during the alignment. The group continued, knowing their greatest challenge might be just down the hall.

DAY 240

Everyone is born with a path and purpose.

> Some will find it simply by not following it, while others will seek it out and embrace it.
>
> Humbled is the man who walks the path Omega sets before him, no matter what it leads through.

~ Thane Akuo

CHAPTER 21
BREAKING

The light from Iggy's staff bounced off the walls as they continued down the cold, dark, black hallway. It must have been carved by hand, or the stone wouldn't have been so smooth and perfect. They continued down the hall for some time. Their hearts were pounding in their chests. Everything they had set out to find was coming together. It wasn't exactly how they had imagined, though.

Zeph's thoughts were of Desiree as they walked the dark hallway. Because of the vision, he had a unique understanding of her. There was a longing inside of him to help her. In the depths of the vision, Zeph had been given the rare opportunity to see how she had once been an innocent girl. The monster she had become was never something she had wanted to become.

A nagging thought had already crossed Zeph's mind: He may have to kill her to save the Tear, but it was the last choice in his mind. His mind drifted back to the various things that Praotes had taught him. If he could be there right now, Zeph was sure that he would tell him that no matter how lost someone had become, they could always come back to the light. Zeph wondered if, after a thousand years, was there any humanity left in Desiree?

They began to see a glimpse of light at the end of the tunnel. As they moved closer, the hallway widened in width and height. Soon they were all standing under a large archway. Before them was an enormous underground cavern, and in the middle stood a large pyramid, its height stretching at least ten stories up into the air. It was very close to the archway, much closer than it had appeared in Zeph's vision. They saw a light shining brightly at the very top of it; they knew it had to be the

Shadow Tear. Their eyes next fell upon the figure about halfway up the pyramid, racing their way to the top. It was Desiree.

Zeph took the lead, and everyone else followed suit. To the confusion of everyone other than Zeph, they all hit an energy barrier and stumbled to the ground. A ripple of glowing blue light emanated from where they had impacted. Marcus looked up at the field blocking them from Zeph; he then noticed the soft glow coming from Zeph's hand. Confusion turned to anger as Marcus jumped to his feet and pounded his fist against the field.

"What are you doing?! You can't do this alone!" Marcus shouted at Zeph from behind the barrier. Iggy and Breeze noticed what Zeph was doing and quickly jumped up as well.

"I'm sorry," Zeph said as he touched the field, "I have to do this myself." Zeph took off running; it was even faster than they had seen in the past. He took off up the stairs, leaping several stairs at a time. Desiree noticed his approach and began to quicken her pace. Just as she reached the top, Zeph tackled her from behind. She quickly threw him off as he slid to the other side of the platform.

They stood a few paces across from each other on the top of the pyramid. The top was larger than Zeph had expected. It was about the size of a large courtyard. In the middle was a small pedestal with what looked like a brightly glowing crystal in the shape of a teardrop floating above it. They both eyed each other, and then the Tear. Desiree gravitated towards it, but Zeph knocked her out of the way before she could touch it. She was surprised to see that he could also gravitate and that his speed was comparable to hers.

From within her cloak, she pulled out a sword. Zeph recognized it from back in Daunt; it was the one that had sent shivers up his spine. The blade was slightly curved and razor-sharp; the back side had serrated points running from just below the tip, all the way down to the hilt. It was the perfect twisted weapon. One side sliced while the other side ripped and tore.

Zeph reached down and drew his translucent sword, which he had received in the mountains of Appagon. He held it out with one arm pulled back, taking a defensive stance.

"I can't let you break that Tear, Desiree."

"What makes you think you can stop me?" she asked as they moved slowly back and forth.

"It doesn't matter if I can or can't, I have to try."

"I admire your commitment," Desiree said with a sarcastic tone.

Desiree took the first lunge. Her blade slipped just past the left side of Zeph's ribs as he quickly dodged the attack. Zeph returned in kind, swinging his blade towards her left shoulder. She quickly spun around and blocked the strike. From there, it began to get faster with every blow. Each person was fighting with all their strength. Soon, Desiree realized that she had to mix things up a bit.

Taking several quick swings at Zeph to push him back, she threw her hand out. The shockwave hit Zeph hard, sending him spinning into the air. The look of satisfaction was quickly wiped off Desiree's face as Zeph landed on his hands and feet, then quickly pushed himself up again. Zeph locked eyes with her; he was trying not to become angry during the fight; he wanted to fight with strength and not anger. Throwing his hand out, he sent a shockwave across the platform towards her. There was no distinct difference between either of their telekinetic abilities. There wasn't even a color or glow of energy from the wave, just a ripple in the air like heat rising off the hot ground.

Marcus, Breeze, and Iggy stared up at the top of the pyramid from behind the barrier below. They could see the sparks flying off the blades, and shortly after, came the bursts of energy. Clearly, the fight was getting more intense with every passing moment. There was nothing they could do, not until Zeph dropped the barrier.

"Why would he do this?" Marcus said as he banged on the barrier again.

"I think a bigger question is how," Iggy pointed out. "I didn't realize that his abilities had grown so much."

"I have a feeling he was keeping a lot from us," suggested Breeze.

"I don't care how he's doing it, I just want him to stop so we can help," Marcus growled.

A burst of light like a crack of lightning caught their attention again. Just as they saw the burst of energy, they felt the barrier fluctuate slightly.

Zeph was beginning to push himself. If he drained himself too much, the barrier would fall. In many ways, it was what they wanted and didn't want simultaneously. If the barrier fell, that could only mean one of a few things, and they didn't even want to think about that right now.

Zeph ran towards Desiree, energy crackling over his sword. He swung his body rapidly in a circle and struck hard against her blade. The force pushed her across the top of the whole platform. Zeph cringed as he felt a burst of pain shoot all throughout his body. It was like his very bones were on fire. Looking up, he saw Desiree's palm glowing as she pointed it at him. As he began to collapse to his knees, Zeph let out a blood-curdling scream and threw both hands out. His sword dropped to the ground, and bolts of energy like lightning flew from his palms and connected with Desiree.

Her projection field held back one of the bolts, but the other burned through the tissue on her right arm. Desiree dropped to one knee and grabbed her arm. She looked down and watched the tissue slowly healing itself. Within minutes, the wound would be gone. Reaching into her cloak, she quickly threw a small dagger towards Zeph. It found its mark on the side of Zeph's left thigh. Wrapping his hand around the handle, Zeph yanked it out and threw the dagger to the ground. Blood soaked through his pants as it ran down his leg.

Desiree leaped towards him, sword thrust forward. Zeph quickly rolled out of the way, but not out of reach of Desiree's blade as she quickly swung it up behind her. The searing heat that flowed through his body wasn't because of a mind trick this time. Zeph felt the wound running down the length of his back. It wasn't very deep, but it ran almost completely from top to bottom. Zeph gasped and collapsed to the ground. Desiree shuffled her feet and stood a couple of paces away.

Out of the corner of his eye, Zeph caught a burst of black smoke at the platform's edge. He turned his head to see the tall, thin figure of Mizimmah standing off to the side. Anger began to fill him now. It was the kind of anger he had been taught about by Praotes, the kind someone should feel when they see something they know is truly wrong.

"You're doing great, little lady, but I think that boy has a bit on you," Mizimmah said with a chuckle.

"Get away from her!" Zeph shouted as he jumped to his feet and threw a bolt of energy at Mizimmah. In the instance it took for the energy to reach the spot, Mizimmah had already reappeared on the other side of the platform.

"Now, now Zeph, I'm not the enemy here, she is," Mizimmah said as he gestured to Desiree, running towards him. Zeph quickly raised his sword and blocked the attack as Desiree brought her sword down hard. Rolling backward, Zeph flung her over himself and jumped to his feet.

"There's someone else up there with them," Iggy said as he squinted at the top of the pyramid.

"Who is it?" asked Marcus.

"I don't know, but I have a bad feeling they're on Desiree's side."

Zeph looked down at the bottom of the pyramid; he could see the rest of the group waiting on the other side of the barrier. A part of him wanted to drop it now, but he couldn't risk any of them getting hurt. No one was going to die today. His attention quickly turned back to Desiree.

They each took a fighting stance and held their weapons firmly. Mizimmah just stood by; it looked as though he wasn't going to interact one way or another. Zeph and Desiree locked eyes and then gravitated at full speed. They connected hard, and the ringing of their blades echoed throughout the chasm. Both blades clashed against each other as they remained in a deadlock state. Zeph grabbed the front of Desiree's cloak and, in a bold move, kicked her hard in the ribs.

Desiree gasped and crumpled over slightly. Zeph let go of her cloak and punched her in the jaw as hard as he could. She collapsed down to one knee as blood sprayed from her lips. Before Zeph could deliver another blow, she quickly reached into her cloak and plunged a small dagger into Zeph's side. His eyes went wide as he felt the blade slip between his ribs. Staggering back, Zeph took a deep breath, increasing the pain further. It was evident that the blade had punctured his left lung. Pulling the dagger from his side, he threw it off the side of the platform.

The dagger sailed down over the edge. It reached the ground and bounced before sliding over to the edge of the barrier. The trio all looked down at the bloody dagger as it skidded to a stop a few feet on the other side of the barrier. Their eyes went wide. Marcus' face was a mix of anger and pain as he looked down at the bloody weapon.

"Can you do anything, Iggy?" Marcus asked as he choked back his words.

"He's too far away; I can't heal him from here."

Zeph stood on the edge of the platform. He felt the blood clinging to his clothing, but he wasn't ready to give up. Desiree slowly stood to her feet. She was battered and bruised as well, but slowly healing nonetheless.

"You want to do this forever, or will you let me take what's mine?" she shouted across to Zeph.

"It's not yours, Desiree; it never was," Zeph replied, once again taking a fighting stance.

She rushed forward at him faster than he was expecting. Dropping his sword, he threw both of his hands out. There wasn't the expected burst of crackling white energy bolts. Rather, she felt the hard impact of her body colliding with the protection field Zeph had placed in front of himself. Dazed, she staggered back. It was clear that Zeph was beginning to weaken; she just had to keep pushing him.

"You don't have to do this, Desiree, you never had to," Zeph pled.

"You don't know me, or anything I've been through!" she blurted back.

"That's not true, Desiree. I saw you as a little girl; you were forced into this. And if it wasn't for him," Zeph spat angrily as he pointed to Mizimmah, "you wouldn't even be here. He turned you into what you are now."

"He's done nothing but be a father to me."

"You had a father!" the pain poured out as Zeph shouted back, "Orestes loved you. Mizimmah twisted you so much that you felt your only choice was to kill him to get what you wanted."

Desiree hung her head for a moment as the memories came flooding back. Mizimmah watched her closely.

"It's too late for me," Desiree said as she shook the memories.

"No matter what you've done, it's never too late, Desiree."

Taking a deep breath, Zeph decided that it was time. He pulled his sword behind him as he gravitated toward her. Sparks flew from the end as it ran over the smooth black stone. Quickly flinging his sword upwards, it caught Desiree's sword. The force of the blow lifted Desiree right off the ground. Zeph threw his palm out towards her chest. Her eyes widened as she saw the energy charge up across his fingertips. Kicking off his chest, she did a complete backflip in the air as the bolt of energy passed beneath her. While still in the air, she teleported behind Zeph. He had anticipated this and swung around quickly, slicing through the side of her arm. The blood splattered across the stone.

Desiree let out a scream of anger and pain. She grabbed the side of Zeph's head and sent a blast of concentrated energy out of her palm. Zeph's head took the full impact as it jerked to the side, pulling his body down with him. There was a ringing coming from his ear, and he knew it was bleeding. His eyes started to roll back as he collapsed backward. Desiree lifted her sword above her head as she watched Zeph collapse to the floor. Nothing was stopping her, and one swing would mean his death. Desiree's eyes quickly jumped from Zeph to the Tear on the pedestal. Dropping her sword, Desiree walked over to it. Mizimmah joined her as well.

From their perspective at the bottom of the pyramid, all they could see was a series of quick flashes and bursts of energy, and then the barrier blocking them fell. Their hearts instantly sank. Wasting no time, the trio took off, running as fast as they could towards the top of the pyramid. They didn't have the advantage of gravitating to the top like Zeph did.

Desiree walked over and stood in front of the Tear. It was like a beautiful gem. It was no bigger than two fists wrapped around each other. Mizimmah watched as she reached out for the Tear. All his years of influence were about to enact his perfect plan. Desiree slowly placed her hands on either side of it and cupped it in her hands. She clenched her teeth and gripped it harder. Throwing her head back, she let out a scream. The energy of the Tear flowed into her at tremendous speeds. Her wounds instantly healed, and her feet began to lift off the floor as she continued to grip the Tear firmly between her hands. The power coursed through her veins; it was even more amazing than she had ever dreamed it would be.

Zeph slowly opened his eyes and lifted his head to look at Desiree. Blood was running through his eyes and stung as he tried to focus. He saw the Tear in her hands, its energy being drained. Zeph's gaze noticed something within the crystalline structure as he tried to stand. There was a crack forming in the Tear. As Desiree gripped the Tear harder, he saw the crack grow bigger.

"You have to stop," Zeph sputtered out. "You don't know what it's going to do!"

Desiree paid no attention to his words. It wasn't even clear if she could hear him at that moment. Marcus and the others climbed the last stair and rushed over to Zeph. Iggy quickly worked on healing him, and Breeze knelt by his side. Marcus took up the defensive pose between them and Desiree.

Mizimmah looked over with an evil grin. He looked directly past them to Zeph and mouthed the words, 'Too late.'

"Get down!" Zeph shouted at the top of his lungs. Everyone around him dropped to the floor. Desiree looked wildly from the Tear to Zeph, then back to the Tear. Suddenly, the cracks in the Tear fractured across the whole structure of its form.

The moment seemed to almost be frozen in time; all sound and light were absent from all reality. The split second of total darkness was shattered as the Tear exploded in Desiree's hands. Blinding light filled the underground chasm. A deafening sound like a thousand claps of thunder reverberated off every wall. A ring of light shot out from the Tear. The wave of energy knocked Desiree to the ground. It passed over the rest of the group. Each had their eyelids squeezed tight and their hands cupped over their ears. The ceiling of the chasm gave way in an instant as a massive pillar of energy shot up through the rock and sand into the sky high above the desert isle. A colossal dark cloud formed in the sky over the desert. Lightning cracked down from the sky all over the land. The cloud shot out in all directions and began to spread across the whole world.

Desiree was on her hands and knees beside the pedestal. She gripped it firmly and tried to pull herself up. The energy that had filled her only seconds before was fading fast. She cried out in pain and gripped her chest. It was glowing brightly. Something inside of her had shattered as well. Her efforts to rise to her feet failed as she collapsed beside the pedestal.

Mizimmah slowly walked over to Desiree. He looked down with that evil grin of his as he crouched beside her.

"Thank you very much, deary. You did what I wasn't able to do for seven thousand years."

Confusion and betrayal flashed across Desiree's face as she looked up and listened to his words. She threw her head back and screamed as the painful sensation in her chest became unbearable.

"What's happening to me?" she shouted through tears.

"Oh, well, you remember that little potion of immortality we made for you all those years ago? Well, it seems that without the power of the Shadow Tear, those extra gava can no longer intertwine with yours. No Tear, no power," Mizimmah spoke in a mocking tone.

Desiree looked up at him with pain in her eyes. The tears streamed down the sides of her head and dripped on the stone floor. Light burst from her chest in the form of long strands of energy. They shot up into the air and burst into thousands of tiny lights. It was the seven gava that had been trapped inside her. Now that they were no longer bound together, they were able to finally be released.

Mizimmah leaned down and whispered in her ear.

"You're mortal once again, deary, enjoy it while you can."

"Why did you do this to me?" Desiree asked as she struggled to stand up.

"Well, you see, we Uriel, as you call us, we can't touch the Elemental Tears. I didn't even know where to find the Shadow Tear after the knowledge was wiped from my mind. But you, on the other hand, could find it. And you could destroy it for me," he explained. "This was always my plan from the very beginning; you were nothing more than a tool to accomplish it," he said with disgust in his voice.

As Desiree slowly staggered to her feet, anger built up inside her. The look of betrayal on her face was quickly replaced by rage. Mizimmah looked over at Zeph.

"Until we meet again," he said with a wink, and then he teleported away.

Desiree's breath came out fast and heavy as she wrapped her hand around her sword. She looked over at Zeph and the others. It didn't matter that Mizimmah had betrayed her; she wanted someone to pay.

Zeph's eyes widened as she gravitated towards them. Marcus and Breeze split in opposite directions, leaving Zeph and Iggy in the middle. Iggy stepped forward with his staff in hand. Desiree's sword connected with the staff; to everyone's surprise, the sword sliced clean through it. Iggy quickly spun out of the way as the blade came down and cut off the side of his robe. Zeph threw his hands out and pushed her back with a shockwave.

Marcus and Breeze took up opposing points across from Desiree. Both launched an attack simultaneously, Breeze with her arrows and Marcus with blasts of flames. Desiree quickly deflected the arrows away from herself, but Marcus was able to hit her several times in the back. Her cloak instantly caught on fire. She threw it down to the ground and let it burn. Beneath her cloak, they saw that she was heavily armed. Across her chest were rows of small throwing daggers. At the small of her back were two short curved blades.

Iggy looked down at the two halves of his staff in his hands. It was a disappointment but not a total loss. She had cut it at almost the exact center of the staff. Zeph stood side by side with his brother. They had Desiree partially surrounded. Of course, she could teleport away at any time she wanted. They knew she was out for blood, though.

Kicking off the ground and flipping into the air, she threw a dagger in either direction. Both found their marks in Breeze and Marcus. For Breeze, it had connected with her shoulder. With Marcus, on the other hand, it had lodged itself on the right side of his chest. As he breathed in, he could feel the blade in his lung. He worried about what would happen if he tried immediately pulling it out.

Desiree landed just in front of Zeph and Iggy. She quickly swung the sword, and both boys arched backward, narrowly missing the blade. Pieces of the boys' clothing that couldn't escape the blade fell to the ground. Iggy sent a blast of light toward Desiree that caused her to stumble back. Zeph shot a bolt of energy at her, which she quickly deflected, catching Iggy in the side. Iggy took a deep breath and shook it off. It was excruciating, but hadn't hit anything vital.

Breeze fired off several quick shots at Desiree. They were aimed at specific points on her body. She knew that if she could at least get one to connect, it would help turn the fight in their favor. As if sensing the coming projectiles, Desiree quickly spun around and deflected the arrows. Reaching out, Desiree clenched her fist. Breeze began to scream and dropped to the floor. Everyone else watched in horror as Desiree started to inflict Pain on Breeze; they knew that within moments it would be fatal. Marcus threw his arms down, locking the blades on his forearms into place. He took off running towards Desiree, and flames wrapped around the blades as he did.

Dropping her large sword, Desiree reached behind her lower back and drew one of the small curved swords. Looking towards Marcus, she let Breeze drop and grabbed the other from behind her back. They began to go toe to toe. She would take a swing, and Marcus would block it. Fire burned in his eyes as he thrust the blades toward her. The fire within his body burned brightly over the surface of his blades. With each swing, he came close to connecting the smoldering hot blades with her flesh.

Zeph and Iggy rushed towards Breeze. She was still kneeling on the ground off to the side of the platform; the intense pain had significantly weakened her. Marcus was perhaps Desiree's greatest challenge next to Zeph so far. As they fought, she eyed the small dagger still sticking out of his chest. She delivered several quick blows, which Marcus blocked perfectly. It gave her the opening she wanted. Punching through the gap in his blocks, she slammed her fist against the end of the dagger. It plugged deep into Marcus' chest. His eyes went wide as he staggered back and choked back the blood. Iggy leaped into action and rushed for Marcus.

Thrusting her hand out, Desiree lifted Iggy up into the air with her mind as he ran towards her. With a swing of her arm, Iggy flew through the air and off the edge of the pyramid. Zeph's gaze darted towards his brother, his face white as he watched Iggy fly far over the edge. With his concentration distracted, Desiree knelt down and wrapped her hand around the handle of her large serrated sword. Her eyes locked on Zeph's back as he quickly scampered towards the edge to scan where Iggy had fallen.

Breeze watched in horror as she saw what was about to happen. Bursting up from the ground with a blast of wind from her palms, she threw her body forward. Desiree gravitated across the platform in the blink of an eye. Zeph turned his head around just in time to see her thrusting her sword forward.

The sound of flesh ripping filled Zeph's ears. Everything seemed to slow down around him. He looked down to see Breeze standing right in front of him. The bloody end of the sword was protruding from her back. Everything around Zeph seemed to collapse, as if all he knew was shattering in that instant.

Breeze had moved so quickly that Desiree didn't realize who she had impaled until she was looking directly into Breeze's eyes. Desiree locked eyes with Breeze as their faces stood only inches apart. Breeze tried to speak, but the words only escaped her lips as small gasps. The look of anger and rage instantly faded from Desiree's face as she stared deep into Breeze's eyes.

Over the thousand years and the hundreds of people Desiree had killed, she had never witnessed someone willingly sacrifice themselves for another. Desiree let go of the hilt and stumbled back. It was the way Breeze continued to stare at her. There wasn't fear or even anger on her face; just a simple expression of acceptance. She was happy and willing to give up her life. In that moment, it was something Desiree's mind couldn't process.

Zeph quickly caught Breeze as she began to collapse to the ground. Even if they could remove the blade, there was no telling if Iggy was in any condition to help her, or if he was even alive. Zeph looked down at Breeze's gentle face in his arms. Her beautiful, long black hair hung to the sides. Pure red lips parted the pale sea of her skin. Her shining blue eyes looked deep into his sparkling blue. Zeph held her face in his hands as his tears began to fall.

"Please don't leave me," Zeph pleaded through tears. "I'm so sorry for everything."

Breeze reached up and placed a hand softly on his cheek. Zeph's tears slowly made their way over her fingers. They looked into each other's eyes for what seemed like forever. Breeze glanced over at Desiree, crouched on the ground a few steps away. She just sat there with a stunned expression on her face as she watched Breeze slowly bleed out. Something had broken in her. The shell of darkness that had surrounded her for over a thousand years had cracked. Mizimmah's deception, combined with the Tear shattering, had broken something deep inside. When Desiree's sword unintentionally found its way into Breeze, the shell shattered and fell apart completely.

Breeze looked up into Zeph's eyes again. She could see the pain and heartache pouring out along with his tears. The boundless love he carried for her was evident in his eyes as she watched the internal battle flash across his face. All the years they had spent together were coming together in a single moment. As if leaping past the veil of time, she saw the broken person he would become. She desperately didn't want this moment to define the man he would become. It pained her more than the blade within her abdomen. She gently reached around his neck and pulled him close.

"Forgive her, please forgive her, Zeph. Don't carry the pain with you," Breeze whispered softly to him.

Zeph looked over at Desiree. All that was in him right now was pain, more pain than he had ever experienced. He didn't believe it was possible for a single person to feel what he was feeling at that very moment. All that pain would turn into anger and hate if he let it. Zeph looked over at Marcus. He was lying on his side, coughing up blood. He had seen everything transpire but was unable to do anything to help. They were all in bad shape.

Breeze began to take in slow, staggered breaths. She finally looked down at the sword sticking out of her abdomen. When it had entered her body, she had felt it not only slice but also tear through her. The pain didn't even matter anymore. Within moments, she would be gone, and she knew it. Reaching around her neck, she grabbed hold of the green gem.

"Bring this back to my father," she whispered. Zeph gently slipped it over her head and held it in his hand. The pool of blood beneath them grew larger with each passing moment. Zeph wanted to do something, to remove the blade, to make it all go away. He would have given everything at that moment to trade places with her. He would have died a thousand times over if it meant she could stay.

Zeph held Breeze close in his arms. Her breathing became shallow, and then it slowly stopped. He looked down into her beautiful blue eyes and watched as the last flicker of life left them. Zeph held her head against his chest and let out a loud sobbing cry.

"Please just take me!" he cried out, as his voice echoed across the cavern.

A moment passed, and then Zeph saw Breeze's gava slowly rise from her chest. The glowing ball of light was all that was left of the girl he loved. It was so close Zeph could reach out and touch it. It made the pain rise even more inside because he knew she could never come back now.

As Breeze's gava floated there, it began to glow brighter. Strands of energy flowed out of it and back down into Breeze's body. They weaved their way throughout her entire frame until her whole body began to glow. Zeph felt all the weight of her body wade away, as Desiree's sword fell to the ground with a clang. Breeze opened her eyes and floated upwards until she was standing before Zeph. Her body was radiating pure light. Zeph reached out to touch her, but his hand passed right through. She looked down at him and smiled.

Desiree watched as the radiant, ethereal image of Breeze walked over to her. Reaching down, she placed her hand on Desiree's forehead. Like a dam breaking, all the guilt trapped within Desiree's mind came pouring out. She remembered the faces of every person she had killed while immortal. The darkness that had clouded Desiree's mind for over a thousand years instantly released its hold. A great cry of pain left Desiree's lips and echoed across the cavern.

The sound of someone shuffling caused Zeph to turn his head. There, he saw Iggy slowly climbing up over the edge of the platform. Tears of happiness sprang from Zeph's eyes as he saw his brother still alive. Iggy looked over at Zeph and then instantly past him to the glowing figure of Breeze standing over Desiree. He then noticed the way Zeph was sitting and the blade lying at his feet. It took a moment to process before Iggy assembled the pieces of what had transpired.

Breeze lifted her hand from Desiree's forehead. She sat there in front of Breeze on her hands and knees, sobbing. The words 'I'm sorry' kept spilling from her lips again and again. Zeph slowly got to his feet and walked over to Breeze. She turned to face him. Reaching out, she pressed her hand against his chest. It was warm and felt like nothing he had ever felt before. As though love and joy had become tangible and were pressing firmly against his chest.

"You were right, Zeph. No one can escape redemption, no matter how far they've fallen," Breeze said in a voice so soft and sweet it made him want to cry again. Zeph knew what he had just witnessed, but to actually watch someone ascend was something he thought he would never observe.

"What happens now? Where will you go now?" Zeph asked, not wanting to know the answers.

"Wherever Omega wills me to go. Keep strong in the faith that this life is not the end, it is just the beginning."

"I love you, Breeze. I always will."

"I love you too. You will always have my heart, Zeph."

With a gentle smile, Breeze let her body rise up into the air. They all watched as she dissolved into thousands of tiny bits of energy and dispersed across the chasm. It was like looking at the night sky, which she and Zeph both enjoyed so very much. Moments later, they completely dispersed, leaving only the light from the opening above in the cavern.

Zeph turned his attention to Desiree, still kneeling on the floor. He walked towards Desiree and stood over her. With her head down, she continued to sob and rock back and forth.

"Just kill me, please," she begged softly through the tears.

"Why do you want to die?" Zeph asked as he knelt down in front of her.

"There's nothing left for me. My whole life has been a lie. I killed so many people without a second thought. I killed the one man who truly cared about me, and the other just used me for hundreds of years until he got what he wanted. I'm worthless, there's nothing left for me," she said.

Zeph looked down at her and pushed away the pain that still lingered within his heart. He had just witnessed the death of the girl he loved most, and yet there was peace in knowing that she had ascended. Zeph extended a hand toward Desiree. She looked at it for a moment. The strands of her long red hair were hanging in front of her face. She shook her head violently, no.

Looking at her now, Zeph saw a completely different person before him. The thousand-year-old monster had been slain. And from the belly of the beast emerged the scared little girl. It was the same way Zeph remembered her from his vision.

"Please take my hand," Zeph said in a tone so soft and gentle that Desiree lifted her head and stared at him through strands of red hair. Slowly, she reached out and took his hand. Zeph pulled her to her feet and gently brushed the hair from her face. The subtle gesture made her feel like a small child for the first time in countless lifetimes.

"Others may not understand or be so quick to let go. But I've seen your life; I've seen the person you wanted to become all those years ago. I was taught that no matter what someone has done, they can always return to the light. Breeze's dying wish was that I forgive you. So I forgive you. Not because she asked, but because I hope that someone would do the same for me if I had fallen from the light," Zeph said as he looked down into her bottomless green eyes.

As Zeph stared into her eyes, he saw something there. Whether she truly knew it yet or not, she had changed. Her face was softer now, less beaten down by the world. All she needed was for someone to believe in her; believe that she could be a good person.

Iggy slowly made his way over. Desiree tried not to make eye contact with him. The last time she had, she had thrown him to his death. Iggy wasn't looking the greatest, but he was walking. It was clear that the fall had been nearly fatal. Zeph reached into his bag and pulled out the Omega Scroll. Placing his hands on either end, he let the energy flow into him. Desiree watched the process; she had never seen someone else use the scroll to recharge their elemental abilities. When Zeph was finished, he placed a hand on his brother's head. The energy transfer could be seen throughout Iggy's body; the tissue beneath his skin began to glow as the energy traveled from his head down into his chest.

Clenching his hands into fists, Iggy began to heal himself. The energy transfer was so strong that it only took seconds for his body to heal completely. They walked over to Marcus, who was lying on his back a short distance away. To their relief, he was still alive and breathing.

"Thanks for leaving me until last, guys," Marcus said jokingly to take his mind off the intense pain he was still experiencing. They both knelt beside him; he wouldn't make eye contact with Desiree. It was understandable based on everything that had just happened. Zeph and Iggy looked at the wound in his chest. The small dagger was still within the flesh, even though the hilt wasn't visible. Iggy placed his hands on either side of the wound while Zeph reached down slowly.

"Take a deep breath, this will probably hurt a lot," Zeph said as he looked at Marcus.

Zeph pushed his fingers into the wound until he felt the dagger. Marcus laid his head back and began to cry out in pain. Seconds later, Zeph dropped the dagger on the ground, and Iggy healed the wound.

Marcus was shaky as he stood to his feet. He ran his hands over the small scar that was left from the wound. It would always be a reminder of what Desiree had done to him. She hung her head as Marcus glanced over at her. Zeph wanted to say something to him, but he understood that he couldn't force someone to forgive; it had to be their own choice.

The four of them headed for the platform's edge and slowly descended down the pyramid to the archway below. All they could do now was return home to Daunt and take it from there. The story would be hard to tell when they got back. Zeph already knew that some of the townsfolk would not accept Desiree; not after what she had done. As they walked through the archway, Iggy held out his hand and shone a light down the dark passageway back towards the temple.

The massive cavern was quiet now, with only the sound of drifting sand pouring down from the opening above. At the top of the pyramid, a pillar of black smoke appeared. Mizimmah appeared and watched as Zeph, Iggy, Marcus, and Desiree disappeared through the archway at the bottom of the cavern. He grinned that crooked, evil grin of his. Just behind him, there was another appearance of black smoke. A woman dressed in a flowing black dress appeared. She stood beside Mizimmah and watched.

"What do we do now?" she asked.

"It doesn't matter, the girl served her purpose," Mizimmah replied.

"What if Zeph had killed her?"

"The boy didn't have it in him; that's what made her perfect for the task. He would rather save the life of one pathetic little girl than save the world," he said with a smile.

"All your years of work on her over the centuries have all been undone. All the darkness within has left her."

"It doesn't matter anymore, she still broke the Tear. That's all I ever needed her to do."

"What happens next?" asked the woman.

"Everything has been set in motion. They can't stop what's been set in motion. All we have to do now is just watch it unfold." With that, they both turned into black smoke and teleported away.

The group emerged at the shrine inside the temple. They stood in the huge archway of the entrance and looked out into the desert. The sky had cleared from the cloud of darkness that had appeared overhead before. Everything looked different, though, as they looked out into the desert. The sky was darker somehow, and the shadows blacker. If all the power of the Shadow Element had been contained within the Tear, it had now been released out across the whole world.

Desiree looked at Zeph. He was the only one who wouldn't look at her with disgust.

"Where do we go from here?" she asked.

"We'll return to Tamay for now, and then we'll head back to Daunt."

"Can you teleport us back to the city from here?" asked Marcus.

"Yeah, I think so. Is everyone ready?" Zeph asked as he looked at the others. They all nodded their agreement. They formed a small circle. Marcus ensured that Zeph and Iggy were on either side of him so he didn't have to touch Desiree.

"Ready, one...two...three!"

DAY 241

> Whoever guides those lost in darkness back towards the Light will save them from death,
>
> And bring forth the forgiveness that covers all things.
>
> Let us rejoice for the lost that have been found.

~ The Book of Ta'Hor

CHAPTER 22
FAMILY TIES

People lined the balconies and rooftops of every building across the city of Tamay. A great burst of light in the western sky had drawn their attention. Moments later, an enormous dark cloud swept across the sky heading to the east. The separation of the clouds over the city no longer held, and the city plunged into darkness. Lightning began to strike down all across the city and continued across the Realm in the wake of the cloud of darkness. As the minutes passed, slowly the sky began to lighten again. For the first time, the people of Tsayla saw the unnatural cloud cover over the Shadow Realm disperse entirely, only to be replaced with a dim sky.

Thane Akuo stood on the balcony near the library and looked out over his city. He knew what had just transpired. The burst of energy to the west was a clear sign of it, and even more so was the sky itself. The suns still shone down, but they were somehow dimmer now. The power held within the Shadow Tear was now spreading out over the entire world.

A flash of light and a cracking sound of energy caused him to turn around. Standing in the middle of the library were four youths. Guards immediately rushed over and surrounded them. Akuo rushed over as quickly as he could for an old man. Once he saw that it was Zeph and the others, he told the guards to stand down. As he looked them over, he quickly realized that only three of them were from the four that had initially left.

Desiree stayed close to Zeph as the four of them stood together. Marcus' and Iggy's body language clearly indicated they did not want to be near her. Their clothing was ripped, torn, and bloody. It was apparent to all in the grand hall that they had come from the scene of some tremendous battle.

As Akuo walked over to them, he began to feel Desiree's presence fill the grand hall. His old eyes widened as he locked his gaze on her. Her mind was completely blank to him; he couldn't even get a slight sense of her thoughts or feelings. However, the power emanating from within Desiree was quite easy for him to sense, as it radiated like none he had ever felt.

"Tell me what has happened," Akuo asked Zeph, gesturing the group towards the tables near the bookshelves. They sat down at one of the tables. Akuo called for food and drink to be brought at once, as they looked about ready to drop from exhaustion. Zeph told him everything that had transpired. Desiree sat with her arms wrapped around herself, her long red hair hanging in front of her face in an attempt to hide herself from Thane Akuo's gaze.

The Thane listened to the whole story. Zeph was worried about what he would think about Mizimmah's role in the series of events. As he was one of the Uriel and a Shadow Elemental, he might react similarly to how Master Sotiris had when Zeph mentioned his vision.

"Mizimmah is a trickster. His very name means to plot evil," Akuo explained. "Why he wanted the Tear broken; that I cannot understand."

"The world is changing now, isn't it?" Zeph asked.

"It is. It has started to become a darker place. I don't know how the world will be changed by this, but I can tell you that we have all become much more powerful."

"What do you mean?" asked Desiree in her first effort to speak freely among them.

"We, as Shadow Elementals, have grown stronger by the breaking of the Tear. My guess is that since its power is no longer constrained to a single point, it has spread out among all the Shadow Elementals across the world."

Desiree thought about it for a moment. It did make sense to a certain degree. The power held in the Tear was too much for any one person to contain. Squeezing her hands into fists, she let the energy charge up in her arms. Thane Akuo was right; she felt much stronger.

Marcus watched her closely as the energy traveled down her arms and to her palms. It was like watching Zeph when he channeled his energy, except that the energy was a reddish color rather than blue. She noticed Marcus eyeing her and stopped immediately. There was enough reason for him to hate her; she didn't want to give him an excuse to attack her.

The food came and they all ate. Hunger hadn't seemed to hit them until the very moment food was placed in front of them. Once it was in their hands, they began to eat like they hadn't eaten in days. For Desiree, it was true. After they had finished eating, Akuo offered them some quarters to rest for the time being. He knew they would soon be heading back towards the eastern coast. They took him up on his offer and retired to their assigned quarters.

Desiree lay on her bed and closed her eyes. She flinched as the faces of her victims once again flashed through her mind. The darkness that had consumed her had also blocked their countless faces from her mind. They were haunting her now like she had never experienced before. When she was a child, her mother's face used to haunt her at night. That was the last time she could remember being haunted by the face of the dead. Her sense of self had been shattered with the reveal of Mizimmah's deception. But it was when Breeze had placed her hand on her head that everything changed. Maybe it was because she was an ascended being; in that moment, all the darkness that had consumed her had been pushed from every cell of her being.

Walking over to the closet, Desiree opened it. Inside, she found an assortment of clothes. Looking down, she realized her clothes were destroyed and in rags from the fight. They were ripped, torn, bloody, and burnt. She flipped through the clothes for a few minutes before deciding. Taking the clothes, she laid them on her bed. Walking into the bathroom, she began to run the water. Desiree noticed glyphs that started to glow on the one handle as she turned it. She quickly realized they were applying heat to the water, allowing a person to run warm water into the bathtub.

Removing her clothes, she slipped into the water. The dirt and blood on her skin began to slowly drift off and mix with the water. She slid lower until her chin was just under the surface. Her memories seemed to speak to her like whispers that she couldn't shake no matter how hard she tried. Questions filled her mind as well, about Zeph, about Mizimmah. How could she have been so blind?

Desiree heard a knock at her door as she exited the tub. Quickly, she wrapped herself up in a robe and went to the door. Opening it slowly, she saw that it was Zeph standing there. He glanced down at her and noticed her damp hair and the robe she was wearing. Slightly embarrassed, he looked away and asked if he could come in. She opened the door and gestured for him to enter.

Desiree walked over to the bed where she had laid her clothes. Again, Zeph became embarrassed as Desiree dropped her robe and began to dress. Out of the corner of his eye, he caught a glimpse of her back. It was covered with all kinds of scars and burns, some of which were still fresh from the fight. It was the old ones that caught his eye, though. He knew of her natural healing ability over the last thousand years, so he knew that anything that left those kinds of marks would have to have been unimaginable.

"You can look now if you wish," Desiree said as she sat down on the bed.

She was now wearing a simple, wrapped dress of black and red fabric. It was functional but also elegant. Zeph had seen other women in the city wearing similar clothing. The fabric wrapped around her slender, youthful body, accentuating her curves. Zeph had to keep reminding himself that she was, in fact, over a thousand years old. In his eyes, though, he still saw her as the young teenage girl from his vision.

"How are you feeling?" As soon as the words left his lips, he knew they were a dumb question.

"Better, despite all the circumstances," she replied.

"We're going to head out tomorrow. We'll take the Topos Gates to the eastern side of Tsayla. From there, we'll journey by ship back to Daunt. We both know that together could simply teleport the whole party back to Daunt, but I'm pretty sure we all need time to process everything that has happened."

Desiree nodded at his words. It did make sense. There was a lot that had happened that needed to be explained, and none of it was going to be easy. She thought back to the time she and Breeze had spent together while they were in Daunt. For the first time in Desiree's life, she had felt like she had made a friend, even if it was under false pretenses.

As if by reading what she was thinking, Zeph walked over and sat down next to her. He paused for a moment before he chose his words.

"She liked you, and she would have liked the real you if given the chance."

Desiree's lip quivered at hearing Zeph's words. It was true. Breeze had been so nice to her, even her moments of jealousy hadn't changed how she had treated Desiree. Tears softly rolled down her cheeks and fell onto Desiree's lap as she stared down at her hands.

"So many people must hate me for the things I've done to them and their families. And they have every right to," she whispered softly. Zeph thought about her words for a moment. There was no easy answer to the situation.

"Yes, I'm sure some do. But there will always be those who will forgive you. For some, it might take longer than others."

"Will Gus forgive me?" she asked softly. The anguish flooded her face as she asked the question and held her face in her hands.

Zeph hadn't thought about what he would say to Gus yet. Breeze had been his whole world. Since the passing of his wife, she was his greatest treasure. He knew that Gus would take comfort in the fact that Breeze ascended. Knowing that a loved one ascended when they died was something that brought great happiness amid grief for many. For him to look his daughter's killer in the eye would be something completely different, though. Zeph hoped that he would have the chance to explain to Gus how Breeze died before he made any rash decisions.

"I believe he will, ...in time," Zeph replied.

"Why did you forgive me?"

"You took someone from me that I loved. Before she died, Breeze whispered to me, she asked me to forgive you."

"So you did it just for her, then."

"No, I did it because she once forgave me for what I had done to her. She saved my life, even though I had hurt her. And by doing so, she showed me how powerful forgiveness can be. There's enough hate and anger in the world already. I'm not going to add more to it. There are two paths a person can take in this world. I chose the one that I think few tread.

It's easier to give in to pain; it's easier to run from it all. I've been there, and I will never forget the look in her eyes that day I tried to kill myself. I thought about it as she was dying in my arms. I chose to forgive you, because in that moment you didn't understand what she did for you. The look in your eyes showed it clearly; you've never seen sacrifice like that before."

They continued to talk as the hours went by. Slowly, Desiree began to open up to Zeph more and more. Her perspective on her past and the world around her drastically shifted with each passing minute. Somehow, long ago, she had become dark and cold to the world around her. It was around the time Mizimmah had sent her out on the quest to make the Immortality potion. Once she had finally consumed the potion, the darkness that had been building in her finally took hold and held its grip on her until the moment Breeze released it.

The more Desiree looked over her life, which was many lifetimes, the more she saw that her short time in Daunt had been the best experience of her life. There was something about the people there. Perhaps it was because it was such a small town, but the people had a sense of family among each other. She worried how they would treat her this time around.

As the evening dragged on, Marcus and Iggy joined them in Desiree's room. It was clear that they were both still holding her at bay. They had lost a dear friend, in many ways a sister, because of her. Looking at how Zeph was reacting to her was helping to change their opinion. If he could look past who she had been to the person she wanted to be, then maybe they could, too.

The expected nightmares didn't come as Desiree drifted off to sleep that night. There was a slight peace and comfort from her time talking with Zeph. Everything was changing for her now. She was no longer the immortal seventeen-year-old girl. The thought of aging did scare her slightly, but it was also intriguing. It was something she hadn't done in a very long time.

The next morning, they all awoke close to midday. All the events of the last few days had left them drained. It was nice to sleep, though, Zeph thought, as he dressed and gathered his belongings. Iggy was still very disappointed at the loss of his staff. As they were greeted by Akuo, Iggy noticed that he came to them with a tall metallic staff in his hand. At the top of it, a red jewel sat in the center of the vine pattern that wrapped its way along the whole length of the staff.

"This is for you, young Iggy. I had my personal weaponsmith work through the night. No man should be without his staff," Akuo said with a smile. Iggy took the staff with a smile of appreciation.

After a quick meal, they headed for the Topos Gate. It wasn't as though they couldn't teleport their way across Tsayla, but it was significantly draining. Even for someone as experienced as Desiree, she would never have been able to teleport the whole group in a single trip.

They gathered together around the gate and said their farewells to Akuo. Zeph was the first to step on the gate. He reached down and began pressing the symbols. To the puzzling curiosity of everyone there, nothing happened when Zeph tried to activate the gate. After several more attempts, Akuo had one of the city's elemental specialists called in. It was then that they made a shocking discovery.

"What do you mean it's useless?" asked Akuo.

"We always assumed that the gates drew energy directly from the Realm in order to activate. But from what I can gather, they must have drawn their energy directly from the Shadow Tear," the man explained.

"So what you're saying is that none of these gates across the whole Realm will work anymore?" asked Zeph.

"Not just the gates, anything that's elementally empowered with glyphs that draw power from the Shadow Element," the man replied.

"I guess that rules out a fast trip across the land," Marcus sighed.

"With Zeph's help, I think I could get all four of us as far as the gate up in the mountains near Araphel," Desiree suggested.

It was different when Desiree was only teleporting herself around. After all, she had easily made the jump from the mountains to Tamay and across the sea to the desert island. The difference now was that there were four of them. Even with her increased mental strength, it would be challenging. Zeph did have the ability to teleport as well, but was still very new at it.

"Are you sure?" asked Iggy.

"I'm pretty sure. After all, we did make it here from out in the desert," Desiree replied.

"I'm up for it; let's go," said Marcus as he spread his arms and gestured for them all to come and huddle in. He still wasn't too thrilled about being close to Desiree, but at least he was fine with being in contact with her now.

They all join in a huddle like they had before out in the desert. Everyone else backed off and gave them some space. Strands of energy jumped out of Zeph and Desiree, wrapping around the group in the blink of an eye, and with that, they were gone. The transition felt rougher than when they had traveled from the desert to the mainland. Then again, it was almost twice the distance.

As they felt their feet touch solid ground again, Zeph and Desiree stumbled over. It was a very draining experience for both of them. They had reached the gate platform up in the mountains near Araphel, though. As they looked around, it seemed as though the whole face of the land was different. The heavy fog that had always seemed to be everywhere before was no longer present. Also, the constant veil of clouds had lifted, allowing the rays from the suns to bathe down. Despite the sunlight, the light seemed dimmer now, like a slightly overcast day.

The group sat down to rest. Marcus and Iggy were fine, but Zeph and Desiree needed to recharge for a bit. They both reached into their bags and pulled out their own scrolls. After a few minutes, they felt refreshed. Standing to their feet, they were about to head out when Zeph caught Desiree eyeing the path to her village.

"Do you want to stop by the village one more time?" he asked in a comforting tone. She wasn't sure at first, but then Desiree slowly nodded. The group walked down the path from the gate to the ruins of the village. Desiree seemed almost nervous as they walked. Without the fog blanketing everything in the area, it was much easier for them to spot the ruins from a distance.

Anything of value had been taken or worn away to nothing long ago. Nothing more than foundations and bits of rubble remained. Desiree went over to the ruins of her house. She stood in the middle of it as the boys stood a few paces away. Kneeling down, she ran her hands over the worn stone foundation. Her back was to them, but they could tell by the movements of her shoulders that she was crying. They simply let her be. It had been over a thousand years since she had been in this place. From what Zeph knew of the vision, she had never had a chance to truly mourn the loss of her family. The nightmares of the ordeal had haunted her for years and had not allowed her to move on.

The minutes went by, and soon Desiree stood from the ground. She wiped the tears on her sleeve and walked over to them. Her breath was shaky as she walked over.

"Are you okay?" asked Zeph. She nodded slowly.

"I remember my mother's face, the way she was....before."

Zeph offered his embrace, and she took it. Whatever she had been in the past, she was starting a new path in her life now. Closure was something so important to the process.

"So what do we do now?" asked Marcus.

"We could make for Araphel," Iggy suggested.

"Yes, that will work for now," said Zeph. He knew that with an additional teleport, they could be in Krino and ready to set sail for Daunt. However, with Desiree being a new addition to their group and with the recent events still fresh in their mind, Zeph wanted to prolong the trip for a bit. He wanted her to adjust to being with them as Desiree and not in her Violet persona. It would have been easier for her to put the veil over everyone's eyes once again and take that form. She and Zeph had talked about it the previous evening in her quarters. Zeph told her she couldn't start new by building on an old lie.

They teleported to Araphel. The city limits were in view from where they had materialized. As they walked up to one of the city gates, they were greeted by several of the townsfolk. It seemed that much had changed in the week since they had been gone. After Zeph's outburst in the Temple and the events of the town square, the townsfolk had feared and shunned him. Now it seemed that their perspective had changed entirely.

Soon they reached Bain's manor. The old butler greeted them with as much zeal as he had the previous times. Bain greeted them in the main hall of the manor. They retired to the library, where Zeph told the story of what had transpired. It was a fantastic story to hear.

Bain's gaze fell on Desiree. He wasn't exactly sure what to make of her. Based on everything he had just heard from Zeph, she was the most powerful person he had ever encountered. Looking at her now, though, he couldn't picture the person they had all fought with just days earlier.

"Well, it is good to see all of you despite the tragic circumstances that have transpired. I was wondering if you could tell me more about what this means now for the Realm. I want to be able to tell my people something about the effects of the Tear shattering."

"I wish we could tell you more. So far, all we've been able to discern is that any localized manifestations of the power of the Tear are no longer present," Zeph replied.

"Well, that much is evident with the parting of the clouds. I can honestly say that I have only seen direct sunlight several times in my life. I find it strange now to see it every day."

"How have the townsfolk adjusted to what happened after we left, as well as everything happening now?" asked Marcus. Bain walked over to one of the large chairs in the corner of his library and sat down. He gestured for the rest to sit with him as well.

"They are very lost and confused. I've never made it a town law for people to attend Gatherings every week; they just did. After you marked our Uriym, the people began questioning everything they believed in."

"And what of you, Bain?" Zeph asked.

"Well....," he trailed off for a moment, "I'm not sure what to believe. Until the day you left, I had never seen any reason to put my faith in the path of Ta'Hor. After what you did, though, I can't deny that it has more merit than I had first thought."

Zeph nodded as he listened to the man. He knew Bain was a proud man who wouldn't change his ideals overnight. It was clear, though, that something had stuck with him, and in Zeph's mind, that was a significant step forward. If he followed the teachings of Ta'Hor, the rest of the town would most likely do so as well.

Bain offered them the hospitality of his home, and they took him up on his offer. It was the nicest place they had stayed during their time on Tsayla, including their rooms in the palace at Tamay. Desiree spent the day walking through the town. She went from shop to shop, looking at the different clothes the people had for sale. It was something she hadn't done in a very long time. Usually, she would just take anything she wanted and kill anyone who protested. It had been a very effective method for hundreds of years.

Several of the people stopped and talked with her. Zeph watched from a distance. He wasn't spying on her so much; he was simply there to support Desiree if he saw her in a situation that she didn't know how to handle. In many ways, she was becoming a young, timid seventeen-year-old girl once again.

At one of the shops, she met a kind old woman. She was one of the town's bakers. The smell wafted out into the street and drew Desiree into her shop. A fresh batch of sweet bread was sitting on the counter. The old woman saw Desiree eyeing it.

"Would you like a piece, dear?" she asked. There was a soft kindness in her voice. Desiree wasn't quite sure how to respond. After a moment, she replied with the only thing she could think of.

"I don't have any coin."

"Well, that's no problem, dear. Just take a piece," the old shopkeeper said with a gentle smile. Desiree quickly picked out her piece and took a bite. The bread was light and fluffy with a sweet taste. She had eaten many foods from around the world, but something about the bread felt like home to her.

"Is this bread common in this area?" asked Desiree as she enjoyed another bite.

"I would think so; it's very simple bread that has been made in these parts for many generations."

"It's very good."

"Oh, well, thank you, sweetie. You know your appearance resembles something of a legend around here," said the old woman as she looked Desiree up and down.

"Oh?" replied Desiree with a hint of nervousness in her voice.

"Just old wives' tales going back hundreds of years," she said with a smile. "You are very beautiful, though, dear."

"Thank you," Desiree said as she hung her head. Zeph watched the conversation transpire from the shop's door. It looked as though Desiree was starting to become a little uncomfortable.

"Oh, is that young strapping lad at the door your man?" asked the old woman as she looked over at Zeph. Desiree turned and looked over at Zeph, then blushed momentarily. Zeph walked over and placed his hand on her shoulder.

"No, we're just good friends," he replied with a smile. Desiree looked up at him and forced a small smile. It was nice to be referred to as a friend.

"Are you enjoying the bread?" Zeph asked as he looked down at the last little bite in her hand. She nodded. "We'll take three full loaves," Zeph said, placing a handful of gold kessas on the counter. The woman looked down at the coins and shook her head.

"That's far too much for the bread, young man!"

"Please, keep the coin. My gift to you so you can continue to make your delicious goods," Zeph said as he took the bags of bread.

"You're far too generous, but I thank you. Please come visit me again."

They left the bakery and walked through town a while longer. The air was fresh; it felt like rain might be coming. Zeph looked over at Desiree as they walked. She was holding onto the loaves of bread.

"What is it about the bread?" Zeph asked.

"I think....I think my mother used to make bread just like this when I was little," she replied.

It was good to see that some of her childhood memories were coming back. Zeph hoped that in time, they would replace the hundreds of years of bad memories. For now, though, they would take it one step at a time. She was beginning to adjust very well.

They stayed in Araphel for two more days and left on the third day. It was a quick jump to Krino. As expected, they had to find a ship that could take them all the way to Daunt. It would have been a perfect coincidence if the *Nephesh* had been there waiting for them. After spending most of the day trying to find a ship, they finally found one willing to make the long trip. It was a local trading ship, but for the right price, they convinced the captain to take them all the way to Daunt.

They set sail after paying the captain three times more than the trip was worth. Even the fog over the waters that surrounded Tsayla had mostly lifted. They could see all the way out to sea from the shore of Krino. The trip would be longer than if they were on the *Nephesh*.

Over the next several weeks, both Iggy and Marcus began to make an effort to get to know Desiree. It was a slow process the first few days, but they began to see more of who she really was over time. It was the first time in her life that she felt she had a choice about who she could become. They were glad that she was choosing to take the path away from the darker life she had led. Time would only tell as to what kind of person she would become.

As each day came and went, Desiree began to get more nervous. She knew what she would be facing once she got to Daunt. It wasn't even the townsfolk she was worried about—it was Gus. She had taken away the most precious thing in the world to him. All three boys tried to reassure her that things would be okay and that they would be there for her.

After a few weeks, they could see land on the horizon. As Daunt grew closer, they saw the *Nephesh* docked in the harbor. It was completely different from when they had last seen it. In the last several months, a great deal of refurbishing and rebuilding had been done to it. From the look of it, though, it was clearly not ready for the open seas yet.

Their ship pulled up to the docks. As they began to disembark, one of the deckhands recognized them instantly and took off running to get Siah. As they stepped off the docks, they noticed Desiree was still standing by the ship's rail. She was gripping it tightly. Zeph walked over to her.

"It will be okay," he said softly.

"I don't know if I can do this," Desiree said as she took a deep breath and fought to keep the tears from coming out. She could feel her heart racing.

"Take my hand," Zeph said as he reached out and took her hand in his. They walked onto the docks together. She remembered everything about the town from her previous visits. The boys looked up to see Siah coming down the docks. He had a great big grin on his face. As expected, he picked each of them up in one of his great big hugs. When it came to Desiree, he looked puzzled.

"And who do we have here?" he asked as he looked Desiree over.

The look of puzzlement turned to fear rather quickly as he noticed that Breeze wasn't with the others.

Zeph took him aside for a moment. He didn't have time to explain everything right at that moment. All he could do was say it in the simplest way he could. She's gone. Zeph could see the man's massive heart break as he said the words.

Down at the far end of the docks, they could see Victor and Gus jump off the *Nephesh* and begin making their way toward them. One of the dockhands must have informed them that they were back. Zeph glanced from them and back to Siah.

"This is going to be traumatic for him," said Zeph as he gripped Siah's massive arms firmly.

The man knew what he had to do. Even with the two men a good way down the docks, Siah began to order the people to clear off. Gus and Victor knew something had to be wrong as they saw the various dock workers and other people start to walk away from the end of the pier.

Zeph walked over and stood with Desiree. Marcus and Iggy stood by her side as well. Gus came running over but was stopped by Siah. They couldn't hear exactly what he said, but they saw Gus look frantically from Siah to the group standing at the end of the pier. Gus walked over to Zeph and looked him straight in the eye.

"Where's my baby girl?" he asked in a shaky voice, tears forming in his eyes. Zeph looked down for a minute, trying to find the words to say.

"I'm sorry... I'm so, so sorry," Zeph replied as he also began to cry.

Gus ran his hands through his hair and looked away in disbelief. His body movements were erratic as he took fumbling steps back and forth. His breaths became rapid as he pulled each one in quickly. Disorientated, he spun around several times. The expression on his face twisted across a wide range of emotions. Finally, he just collapsed to his knees and began to sob. Desiree stood behind Zeph and watched the man's anguish pour out. It was like reliving what she had seen Zeph go through back in the cavern, just a hundred times worse.

Victor and Siah stood on one side of him, while the four youths stood on the other. Never before had they seen such pain. Even when Zeph's mother was grieving over the loss of her husband, she hadn't shown the kind of emotions being poured out by Gus. A crowd stood at the far end of the docks, closest to town. They kept their distance so as not to intrude.

Desiree looked down at Gus as he sobbed with his face in his hands. She couldn't take it anymore. She pushed past the boys and knelt down in front of him. Siah looked as though he was going to protest, but Zeph shook his head no. Desiree's eyes filled with tears as she looked at the broken man before her.

"I'm sorry," she whispered. "I'm sorry for what I took from you."

Gus lifted his head to look at her. His eyes were red, and tears were streaming down his face. Both his hands and lips were shaking as he looked across at her. The heartache was too much, and she burst into tears. Desiree sat back on her knees as Gus stared across at her. The moment hadn't fully set in yet; he was still in shock from the news.

"What....what did you say?" he sputtered.

"I'm sorry I took your daughter from you," she managed to get out between sobs.

Gus looked up at Zeph standing behind her. His old eyes pleaded for answers. Zeph placed a hand on Desiree's shoulder and looked down at Gus.

"Breeze requested two things of me before she died. One, that I would give you this," Zeph said as he reached into his pocket and handed the green gem to him. Gus grasped it in his fingers and pulled it into himself. "The second was that I would forgive Desiree for taking her life."

Gus rocked back and forth as he held the stone in his hands. It was the last thing he had of his daughter. He looked up at Desiree, kneeling across from him.

"She...she killed my baby girl?" Gus asked as he sucked the words in through the tears.

Desiree could only nod and continue looking down at the wooden planks. Zeph could see the anger starting to build up in Gus just as it had in him as well. Zeph didn't want him to live with the pain and anger.

"There is one more thing you should know, Gus," Zeph said as he knelt down in front of Gus, separating his gaze from Desiree. He placed a hand on Gus' shoulder and squeezed gently.

"Breeze didn't simply die; she ascended."

Gus quickly looked into Zeph's eyes. Even as the words had left his lips, Zeph could see the hate beginning to subside in the old inventor's eyes. He wrapped his arms around Zeph and pulled him close. Zeph held him in his arms. Marcus and Iggy walked over and placed a hand on either side of Desiree. She continued to kneel on the docks with her head hung low. Siah and Victor came up behind Gus and did the same.

A few more minutes passed by, and then everyone except Desiree stood. She had taken hundreds of lives, but this last life she had taken was different. It was the one that had changed everything. She didn't want to stand with them; she didn't even want to exist anymore. Marcus and Iggy knew what she was feeling and wanted to help. They helped her to her feet.

There would be much time for mourning, but for now, they all needed to rest. Siah and Victor took Gus home to his house, which was attached to his shop. The remaining four headed into town. Their destination was Zeph and Iggy's home. By now, there was a good chance their mother knew of their arrival, but they hoped not. Entering the house, they found something so warm and familiar about it. Their mother was cooking over a pot in the kitchen. She turned to see who had entered and almost dropped the bowl she was working with. Rushing over, she embraced her boys in her arms. Tears of joy filled her eyes as she held them close. They knew that soon enough they would be tears of sadness.

The rest of the day went by slowly. Desiree asked if she could rest for a short while, so Zeph took her to his room and let her sleep. He rejoined the rest of the group down in the den. Dawn was still recovering from the news of Breeze's death. She knew that the news would spread quickly throughout the town. There hadn't been a death from anything other than old age in Daunt for generations, other than Zeph's father, Khoz. Dawn knew that once word reached Praotes, he would begin to plan a memorial service.

Zeph spent the next few hours telling his mother all about what had happened during their absence. Strangely, she was proud of what they had accomplished with Desiree, even if killing her meant they could have stopped the darkness from being released. Dawn listened to the story and found her son's actions very honorable.

The creaking of the stairs caught everyone's attention. It was Desiree. She wasn't looking very well. The stress of everything was clearly taking its toll on her. She quietly entered the den and sat down. The awkward silence she was expecting from everyone didn't come. In fact, it was the opposite. They all asked her how she was feeling and if there was anything they could do to help her. Even Zeph's mother offered to help her in any way she could. Desiree had never known such kindness, not since she was a very small girl, and a man dressed in black rescued her from the monsters.

"What will happen to me now?" Desiree asked as she huddled on the couch.

"What do you mean?" Zeph asked.

"Will the town judge me? Pass sentence on me?"

The room fell silent. It was hard to believe that even with all her abilities, she was willing to be locked away or worse for her crimes. They told her they weren't entirely sure what would happen. Many would forgive her, and others would need more time. They guessed that within the next day or two, the town would gather for a memorial service for Breeze.

Gus was nowhere to be seen over the next several days. He had locked himself away in his shop. Both Victor and Siah would stop in to see how he was doing. They also wanted to make sure that he didn't do anything to hurt himself. Zeph knew firsthand how powerful grief and despair could be. He hoped that the man who taught him how to deal with his own emotions could find the strength to rise above his own despair.

Gus and Victor had been working side by side on the *Nephesh* for the weeks following the group's departure to Tsayla. During that time, they had become very good friends. Victor tried to be there for Gus as much as he could.

The group had gone to see Praotes on the second day. They wanted Desiree to meet him and have him understand what had happened. To their surprise, they found an unexpected guest staying with him in the Temple. It was the Uriym from Araphel. He had arrived in Daunt several days before they had. As soon as he stepped on the docks, he asked the people to take him to the man named Praotes. Once in the Temple, he told Praotes everything that had happened in his encounter with Zeph. It came as a great shock to Praotes to hear of Zeph's deed in Araphel. Obviously, his judgments of Zeph were significantly understated.

Praotes had prayed over the man, and as soon as he was finished, the man's sight returned to him. It was a revelation for him, and he chose to stay on as a Templar under Praotes to learn the teachings of Ta'Hor and bring them back to the people of Araphel.

Praotes took Desiree's hands and sat with her on one of the temple benches. The light from the sphere lamps bounced off the stone walls, creating a peaceful place of meditation. He looked into her eyes for what seemed like forever before he spoke.

"You are not an evil girl as the world has perceived you. Rather, you have followed the only path you have ever known; a path that was laid by evil men. If a sword is used for evil, it does not make the sword evil. From what Zeph had told me, I see now where things changed for you.

In the teachings of Sha'Kath, the concept of self-sacrifice does not exist. Perhaps this is why watching it unfold before your very eyes was so incomprehensible. In the teachings of Sha'Kath, it is better to save yourself than to save another. Perhaps if every follower of these dark teachings watched someone sacrifice their life for them, they too would see the light," Praotes said, looking across at her. His words stirred something deep within her that she had never felt before: Hope.

"What do I do now?" Desiree asked. It became a constant question on her mind with each passing day.

"You will continue to live, grow, and love. And you will tell others what has happened to you, and by doing so, you may help save others from the same path that you walked for so many years."

"But I've wronged so many people, Uriym. I don't deserve to live."

"Indeed you have, my dear. But on the value of your life, you are quite mistaken. Every life is precious. I have seen those consumed by the darkness of this world before, people I loved very much. And if the day should ever come, I would gladly give my life to save the lost."

Desiree sat there in silence as she let Praotes' words sink in. She still couldn't understand how a life that had caused such pain and misery for others was somehow worth saving. Perhaps one day she would understand.

As they left the Temple, they saw several villagers working on a stone near the slope behind it. It was about waist-high and about as large around. They were slowly carving it into a four-sided pillar. It was to be Breeze's marker. It wasn't a common custom to create a marker for those who had died; this was to honor the person's memory. With Breeze, there was another reason behind it. She was the first person in the history of Daunt to ascend.

On the evening of the third day since their arrival back in Daunt, the town gathered together on the hill behind the Temple. Gus stood there in a long black suit. The coat of it flowed down to the back of his knees. A pressed white shirt was underneath it. His long black slacks draped over the polished black boots on his feet. His hair was neatly combed back. He stood with Praotes, next to the stone pillar on the side of the hill. The rest of the town circled them as they covered the hillside.

It was a calm evening; a gentle breeze was in the air. All eyes were on Praotes as he placed a hand on Gus' shoulder. Zeph and Marcus' families lined the circle's edge closest to Gus. Desiree stood with Zeph and Iggy. Victor and Siah stood on either side of Gus. The service was beginning.

“On this day, we gather together to remember a special young woman from Daunt. To say she was only known by some would be a lie; she was known by all. Breeze, daughter of Gus, came into our lives just over five years ago. From that point on, she reached out to each and every one of us. Her cheerful nature brightened our days whenever we saw her.” The townspeople nodded their agreement as Praotes spoke. There was a pause as the words soaked in.

“Today, we come together to remember her life and her sacrifice. Breeze died saving Zeph’s life, who we also all know as well. But in reality, she saved two people’s lives.” Praotes gestured for Desiree to step forward. The eyes of the crowd followed her as she walked forward toward him. She turned to face the crowd as she stood just before him. Praotes placed both hands on her shoulders.

“This young woman is the one responsible for Breeze’s death.” There were murmurs in the crowd as Praotes spoke. Gus looked away from her, still unable to make eye contact.

“Breeze did not simply die in battle; she died protecting someone she loved; she sacrificed herself to save Zeph’s life. That kind of sacrifice is what we are called to do. We are indeed asked to love everyone we encounter on our journey through life. But to sacrifice ourselves for another, to lay our lives down to save another, that is the greatest gift we can offer. Breeze saved this young woman, Desiree, from a life of darkness. Shouldn’t each of us be so grateful to have our last act in this world be so monumental?” The villagers nodded once again at his words.

“I ask you now, not to look upon this young woman with contempt or ill will. For she was once lost, but has now been found. Let the forgiveness that Breeze gave to Desiree also pour from your hearts as well.” Praotes released his hands from her shoulders, and Desiree returned to Zeph’s side.

“We have great cause to rejoice as well. For our daughter, Breeze did not simply fade away. No, she served Omega to the fullest and was raised up in death. Rejoice and take comfort in the fact that Breeze ascended when she left this world,” Praotes said as he placed a hand on Gus’ shoulder.

Among the many looks of sorrow on the faces, there was also much happiness at hearing of Breeze's ascension. Gus tried to remain strong throughout the whole procession. Praotes continued speaking for a while longer and then allowed those who wished to speak to say something about Breeze. The service continued even after the suns set. So many of the townspeople had so many good things to say about their memories of Breeze. As they wrapped up the service, Gus began to speak to the gathering.

"I loved my daughter with all my heart. The world seems somehow darker now without her light in it," he paused and looked over at Desiree. His choice of words was profound to all there. They had seen the dark cloud sweep across their land as well. It was clear to them all that the effect of the Shadow Tear breaking had spread across the whole world.

"My daughter's last request of me was that I would forgive her executioner." There was a long silence as he gathered the strength. Everyone in the crowd looked at Desiree. Many had already decided in their hearts and minds to forgive her as well. Tears began to fill and fall from Gus' eyes as he looked at Desiree. He had lost his wife and now his daughter. Despite all the pain that was still inside him, he wanted to honor his daughter's wishes.

"May Omega grant me the strength to forgive you," he whispered softly, looking away.

The service came to a close. People walked by the stone pillar as they left and headed back to their homes. On it, it read:

Wonderful friend, loving daughter, servant of Omega.
May she continue to grace the world with her presence
As she continues to serve Omega as an Ascended.

Desiree stood with Zeph as they both looked down at the pillar. Zeph let his tears gently roll down his face. He knelt in front of the pillar and gently kissed it.

"I'll see you again in another life," Zeph whispered as he wiped the tears away. After a moment longer, he ran his hand over the pillar and stood. Everyone in their group said their goodbyes and returned to Zeph's house.

The home was once again full of people, totaling almost a dozen, all of whom were considered family. Everyone was spread all throughout the house. The young people had gathered together in Zeph's room. It was still strange to think of Desiree as a teenager like they were. By all accounts, she was the oldest person in the world aside from the Uriel.

Nevertheless, they still embraced her as one of their own. Her appearance was that of a seventeen-year-old. Since she would begin to age from this point on, it was like she was starting her life anew for the first time.

They continued to talk among themselves for a while. The topic was mostly about how breaking the Tear would affect the world overall. Zeph also brought up the topic of his destiny. They all agreed that his initial quest to seek out and find the other *Chosen Ones* in the world was still the best course of action moving forward. Searching for five people across the face of the whole world would not be an easy task by any means. Desiree had a great deal of knowledge of the world, although some was sure to be outdated since she hadn't visited some of the Realms in several centuries.

A knock at the door caused a pause in their conversation. They called out for the person to enter. It was Praotes. He asked for a moment to speak with both Zeph and Desiree alone. Iggy and Marcus left the room and stood just down the hall.

"The path you both are taking now will take you in different directions," he said as he sat down on Zeph's bed. "But it will also join you two together." Zeph and Desiree shot glances at each other as he spoke. "You made a specific choice, Zeph, when you chose not to kill Desiree in that cavern. By allowing the Shadow Tear to be broken, you allowed a series of events to begin." Zeph knew his words were true. Even the Uriel, Mal'ak, had implied as much when he had spoken to Zeph from the vision in the scroll. As much as Zeph wanted to believe that the quest before him was simple, he knew it wasn't.

"What are we to do now, Praotes?" asked Zeph.

"Seek the other *Chosen Ones* out in the world. I'm sure they are seeking you as well. I believe your purpose for this world isn't known yet, not even to Mizimmah."

Praotes was a wise old man, and Zeph always valued his counsel. There was always something prophetic about the way he spoke. As they sat on the bed together, he turned to Desiree.

"How are you, young lady?" he asked with a soft smile. Hearing him call her 'young lady' forced a smile onto her face that she couldn't hide.

"I'm doing well, all things considered. I know what he said at the ceremony, but do you really believe Gus will forgive me?" she asked, hesitation in her voice.

"Right now, he is a man who has lost all hope. It is the greatest thing any one person can lose in this world. In time, he will come to see that there is still hope left in the world. Perhaps this is something you can show him?" Praotes suggested. It was not a small task by any means, but something Desiree wanted to try and accomplish if possible.

"Will you help to guide me during my time here?" she asked.

"Of course, I will, my dear. It seems that there are many seeking the light these days. Perhaps the darkened sky has opened the eyes of those who did not realize how much they were in darkness."

Marcus and Iggy rejoined them in Zeph's room. The night was getting late, but only a few guests had left. Zeph's mother, Dawn, and Victor remained close. Siah stood by Gus as a supportive friend. Praotes had gone back downstairs to rejoin them. Zeph made a mental note to ask his mother and Victor how their relationship was going. Despite the denials that he was sure would come from both of them, he wanted them to be happy together.

Everyone within their home's walls right now was considered family. Zeph's time away from home made him realize how important that truly was to him. There was still an ache within his heart for Breeze. He was sure that much time would have to pass before it left him. For now, though, he chose to embrace the good feelings within.

Even at the late hour, Zeph wanted to speak to everyone. The four of them headed downstairs and joined everyone else in the den. As expected, most of the conversation was about Breeze. Each person had different memories to share and tell about her. Zeph stood up and walked to the center of the small room. Everyone quieted down as they waited for what he might say.

"Breeze was one of the most wonderful people I have ever known in my whole life. I can truly say she was the first girl I ever loved. She was special to me beyond words, and I loved her each and every day. I have to believe that what has happened was for a purpose, a reason. I may not understand it now, but I'm sure I will in time." He paused for a moment as everyone listened to him speak.

"I would like to say..." his voice trailed off as he blinked his eyes. "...like to say..." Again, he pressed his eyes together and shook his head slightly. Zeph opened his eyes and looked down at his mother. Her gasp was enough for him to know something was wrong. Zeph held his hand up to his eyes. Everyone else had seen what Dawn saw as well. The pale blue of Zeph's eyes had begun to glow. Iggy and Marcus already knew what was about to happen and jumped to their feet just in time to catch Zeph as he fell backward.

Everything faded away around Zeph as he felt his body drop to the floor. The impact was not against the wooden floor of the den as expected. Instead, the impact was against hard, warm metal. Slowly, Zeph began to stand up. The warmth of the suns bathed down on him. He quickly realized he was on the roof of a tall building, at least five or six stories tall. Below him was a bustling city. Most of the buildings were made out of stone.

Slowly, he walked over to the edge of the building. The city streets below were full of people. The city was foreign to him, and yet, somehow all too familiar. As though he had been told stories of it before. Noise from the streets below caught his attention. A large enclosed metal carriage of some sort was running down the street. No horse was pulling it. Zeph noticed the metal rails that ran down the street as he looked down from the rooftop. The metal carriage followed the rails around the corner. Steam puffed out of small stacks along the back of the carriage.

The streets were paved with large, smooth-cut stones. Zeph began to look for a way to get off the rooftop. He spotted a door nearby, which he assumed was the way down inside the building. It was locked. He was very sure he was in a vision of some sort, so he didn't think anyone would mind if he used his abilities to get where he needed to go. Pointing his palm at the hand of the door, he shot a bolt of energy at it. A flash of light appeared over the door in glyph patterns, indicating that the vision's purpose was not to enter through the door.

Just by the construction of the buildings and the city's layout, it was clearly far more advanced than Daunt. They seemed to have a grasp on some technology. As Zeph looked down at the street below, he observed the people. Most were finely dressed. On the corner, he spotted a young boy who looked a lot like Iggy, handing out newspapers to passersby.

Looking out over the city, Zeph took it all in. The harbor was down to the west. The city spread far and wide. It was nestled right along the coast. Behind him, Zeph noticed that the mountains to the north were only a short distance from the city. They towered over him up into the sky. The white peaks dotted the tops as he watched the mountain ridge continue on to the east.

As if being struck by lightning, Zeph finally placed the city within his mind. His father had told him countless stories of this place. It was the city of Thai on Sire in the Fire Realm, east across the ocean from Appagon. If what he was seeing was truly how the city looked, then Zeph was very impressed by its engineering advancements. Even Tamay didn't come close to Thai. Granted, Tamay was focused a great deal more on architecture than Thai appeared to be. As Zeph looked out towards the harbor, he saw a tall structure with an arm sticking out from it. It was lifting cargo off and on the ships.

Suddenly, there was a brilliant flash of white light across the horizon. Zeph had to shield his eyes from the light. Holding his fingers over his eyes, he looked between them. The light was not coming from the sky but rather from over the water and the ocean's depths. The ocean glowed a soft blue leading up to the horizon's edge. Soon after, a wave of energy rapidly washed over the skies above, heading in all directions.

The building beneath Zeph shook for a moment. The people below had scampered all over the streets, many running towards the coastline to see what was happening. Zeph just stood on the rooftop and looked out to sea. The light slowly faded away. As he stood on the roof, the air seemed to grow colder. The gentle breeze picked up and began to blow harder. Eyes still fixed out to sea, Zeph watched as the very horizon seemed to grow.

His heart began to race as the ocean on the horizon began to rise up into the sky. Soon, the people on the streets below saw what he was witnessing. They began to scream and run for the northern part of town. All Zeph could do was watch as the wave began to form. Fear shot up his spine as he saw the wall of water on the horizon lift higher and higher up into the sky. There had been fierce storms that hit the coast of Appagon before. Waves had crashed into Daunt, causing some flooding. They were nothing more than a splash in a bathtub compared to what he was witnessing now.

The wave grew closer to the city. As it did, it grew even higher in height and began to slow its approach. Darkness washed over the city as the wave blocked out the very rays from the suns in the sky. Zeph looked up as the wave towered so high into the air that it stood level with the mountains behind him. The fear he felt in his chest at that moment was nothing like he had ever experienced.

Screams echoed through the streets as the wave came crashing into the city. They were quickly silenced as the water rushed through the streets, covering anything in its path. Zeph threw his hands out as the water rushed towards him. He felt the water impact him hard as he flew across the rooftop, and then everything went black.

Zeph collapsed to the floor in the den. Both Iggy and Marcus let go of his arms. His breath was quick and came out in gasps. His hands shook as he tried to sit up, to no avail. Everyone else in the room stared down at him on the floor. Most had never witnessed Zeph have a vision before, other than Iggy, Marcus, and Desiree.

With every breath, Zeph tried to speak. There was no strength in his body as he struggled to sit up. He held his head in his hands. It was by far one of the most intense visions he had ever experienced.

"What did you see?" asked his mother.

"There's going to be a horrible disaster," Zeph managed to get out through his gasps. Everyone quickly looked at each other. They all wanted to be sure they heard him right. He managed to sit himself up as he knelt on his feet.

"The ocean is going to burst," Zeph said as he looked at each of them with anguish in his eyes. "Cities everywhere are going to be destroyed;

tens of thousands will die." Tears filled his eyes, and he ran his hands through his hair as he leaned forward again.

Everyone's expressions fell even farther than the events of the day had created. Praotes looked at the young man sitting on the floor before him. He found it hard to believe that Zeph continued to endure everything life put him through. There was a light within him, not something tangible but real nonetheless. It was strength and hope manifesting.

Just as Zeph began to regain his composure and breathe normally, once again, he gripped his head. This time, the light shot out brightly from his eyes and the symbols on his head and hands. He cried out in pain, as someone would when trying to lift a heavy object. Everyone moved back slightly. They weren't sure what was happening, but it looked like he was having a second vision.

Light wrapped itself across Zeph's gaze, and he found himself in darkness again. He collapsed hard onto the floor. It was cold and smooth, like the floor in his vision with the scroll. Reaching out, he felt a wall and slowly stood to his feet. What he saw amazed him beyond words. He ran his hands over the glass of the large window as he stared out into the city. Even though it was night, a grand city of lights was spread out before him. Buildings towered high into the sky from the streets far below. It was unlike anything he had seen before, even grander than his vision of Thai.

The buildings towered many stories into the sky. Light came from the windows on every story. Rows of colored lights lined up and down the structures. The streets below were lined with rows of lights. Zeph couldn't even count how many lights he saw across the city below. He ran his hand over the window's glass as he gazed at the sea of sparkling colored lights.

Turning around, he looked down the hallway he stood in. The floor-to-ceiling glass windows spanned all the way down the hall. He could only assume that the whole building was covered in glass windows. As he walked down the hall, it was like something out of a fantasy. His gaze was still constantly looking out over the city. From his perspective, he was at least a dozen stories or more above the city streets.

Doors lined the hallway as he walked. He began to try to open different doors but found he was unable to do so. As he rounded the corner, he walked into a bed on wheels sitting in the hallway. A woman was walking down the hall towards him. He called out, asking if she could tell him where he was. She didn't seem to be able to see or hear him. Her clothing was pale blue and looked like pajamas a grown man would sleep in. Her forehead bore the Light symbol.

Zeph continued to follow her down the hall. He soon realized that this place was like the Healers clinic back in Daunt, just on a scale like nothing he could ever have imagined before. As he once again rounded another corner on his path to follow the woman, he noticed a series of glowing glyphs and symbols lining the floor in the hallway, making a path of some kind. The woman didn't seem to see them, or didn't care, as she walked over them. She continued down the hall, but Zeph stopped in front of the door that the path led to.

Reaching down, Zeph slowly turned the handle on the door. A pattern of glyphs and symbols lit up across the door's surface. As they faded away, the door clicked open. Zeph slowly stepped inside. The room was obviously a place for people to stay while they recovered from injuries. There was a large bed against the far wall of the room. Zeph slowly walked over to it. Odd-looking devices were on either side of the bed and were connected to the person. They seemed to have lights indicating different things that Zeph didn't understand. The room was dark since it was the middle of the night. As Zeph looked around the room, an object on the bed caught his eye.

Stepping closer to the bed, the object began to glow softly. With each step closer, it began to glow brighter. Zeph instantly recognized the object. It was one of the seven elemental scrolls. The Water Symbol on the end was clearly visible. This man was the *Water Chosen One*. Walking up to the bed, the light from the scroll began to fill the whole room now, as its intensity seemed to grow with Zeph's presence.

Zeph's eyes slowly drifted from the scroll to the face of the man lying in the bed. His hands began to tremble, and he took a step back. Their eyes met as the man slowly opened his eyes. Tubes were running underneath the man's nose to help him breathe, as well as tubes running from the man's arms into the devices next to the bed.

The Water Symbol on the man's forehead glowed softly, as well as the symbols on his hands. It was clear from his appearance that he was very sick. He was aged farther than his years should have taken him. The sickly state of his appearance might have masked his features from someone else, but Zeph saw right through it. Everything seemed to slow to a stop around Zeph, as though time no longer existed. They looked into each other's eyes for what seemed like an eternity. The man softly smiled. Tears began to form in Zeph's eyes as he walked closer and stood beside the bed.

"Dad?"

"Hello son," Khoz said softly.

The world around Zeph blurred and pulled away in a bright display of color as Zeph once again collapsed to the floor in the den of his home. He cried out with a mix of pain and heartache. With every breath, he let out a sob. No one dared to ask him yet what he had witnessed. The flood of feelings from within the vision quickly flowed from Zeph into Iggy. Their connection seemed to be getting stronger with each passing day. The feeling was enough that Iggy didn't need to see the vision for himself. Iggy stumbled back from Zeph's side.

"What is it, Iggy? What's happening?" Dawn asked with great concern in her voice. Everyone else was also anticipating his response. Zeph lay in a fetal position on the floor, still holding his head in his hands. He was unable to speak, so Iggy did it for him.

"It's dad...he's alive."

DAY 258

Every man believes his son is meant for great things.

But what do I do when my son's destiny is greater than anything I could imagine?

What do I do when I'm told my son can only save the world if I never return home to him?

~ Khoz, Father of Zeph

THE STORY CONTINUES IN BOOK II TIDES OF DARKNESS

Zeph's relentless quest across the treacherous seas leads him to the brink of despair as he clings to the hope that his long-lost father might still be alive. When the long-awaited moment arrives and father and son finally come face to face, the truth reveals itself with shattering consequences. Zeph's world unravels as he uncovers the dark forces that have been orchestrating events from the shadows since his childhood.

Guided only by a vision, Zeph, along with Victor, Gus, and their loyal companions, ventures into the perilous Water Realm. Their journey is fraught with danger as they are ambushed by a vengeful old enemy, forcing them into a fierce battle for survival to save their ship from destruction. Amidst the chaos, Victor's hidden past comes to light, compelling him to make a heart-wrenching choice between his own survival and the lives of his newfound friends.

Gus grapples with his unresolved grief over his daughter's loss, a pain that creates an emotional chasm between him and Desiree. Despite her attempts to make amends, their strained relationship persists until they find themselves in a dire situation where the truth must be confronted. Only by bridging their divide can they hope to escape their perilous predicament.

As Zeph and Iggy's mystical bond deepens, Iggy discovers a side of his brother he never imagined. With the fate of the Water Realm and their hometown of Daunt hanging in the balance, the brothers must race against time to thwart a catastrophic chain of events set in motion long ago. Together, they must navigate treacherous waters and unravel a web of deception to safeguard everything they hold dear.

About the Author

Growing up, my mind was always brimming with possibilities. From the melodies of musical instruments to the visuals of photography and graphic design, creativity has been the constant thread throughout my life. But it was the quiet act of writing, starting with early poems, school newspaper articles, and short stories, that truly captured my imagination.The world of the Tears of Omega series first took root in 2004, a small spark of an idea that quickly grew into a vast, seven-book epic. Life took a brief detour while I pursued a degree in Photography, but the pull of those characters and their stories remained strong. By 2011, the first two books in the series were out in the world, followed by the third in 2014. After a period away from the keyboard, the joy of writing called me back in 2025. It's a thrill to once again explore the intricate landscapes and compelling characters of the Tears of Omega, and I'm excited to share the next chapters with readers who love immersive fantasy adventures.

Read more at https://www.facebook.com/solomonwoytowich.

www.ingramcontent.com/pod-product-compliance
Lightning Source LLC
Jackson TN
JSHW021401290825
90146JS00002B/35
* 9 7 8 0 9 8 6 6 2 0 9 9 7 *